MURKY W

HM Stevens

HMSTEVENS

www.hmstevens.co.uk

To Karena

Very Best Wishes

Hm

aka Anthony

X

ISBN – 9798677859670

The fact that this book has made it to publication is due to the efforts of several people, to whom I am very gratefully indebted. My awesome daughter Zoe and girlfriend Kathryn for their support and encouragement together with their valued input reading through my manuscript offering both positive and negative comments, correcting my grammar and spelling. My webpage support and designer Steve Elliot of Thrifty Sites. Finally my old school chum and shipmate Bob Addey using his experience helping me through the intricacies of the Kindle Publishing.

In addition to my fanstatic family there are also the wonderful people I have met throughout my varied career, too numerous to mention here but all of whom have, although not consciously but in many ways, contributed spiritually to my scribings due to the shared comradely experiences we've had together from being schoolchums to shipmates with many an exciting run ashore or to just 'Swinging the Lamp' over a few beers.

Murky Waters

HM Stevens

Synopsis

Take two brothers, useless muppets who having stupidly defrauded HMRC are now facing financial ruin. This is jeopardising their successful small short sea ferry company, Beaumonts and the livelihoods of hundreds of employees. Riding in like the 7th Cavalry to the rescue comes the CEO of BSC a major shipping line. Only this could turn into 'Custer's Last Stand' as his dazzling career could be failing due to his energy sapping philandering causing his wife to seek solace in the arms of a sadistic drugs dealer. Attempting to stab him in the back is his megalomaniac Financial Director, a man hiding years of creative accounting and desperately trying to unseat the CEO to scupper the rescue deal. Whilst lurking in the shadows is a renegade gang of Irish dissidents hell bent on a kidnapping.

Flying high above the waves is an ex Fleet Air Arm pilot turned missionary flyer who crashes into the impenetrable West African jungle leaving behind a distraught golden haired beauty carrying his unborn child. Facing an uncertain future as a single parent, she sails home then just when she thought she could never love again, into her life enters a charming naval officer who sweeps her off her feet.

Aboard the ships there is a secretive group of crew running a tobacco smuggling racket that is the envy of the local crime lords, a ship's purser busy lining his pockets and a kinky sexual predator who has a predilection for bizarre sadistic practices.

Take a look at this maelstrom of 'flotsam and jetsam' and into the 'Murky Waters' beneath.

Army Service Corps as a trainee driver/mechanic or Queen's lorry drivers as they were more commonly known! Following a distinguished and decorated career in the Army, through both war and peace, he eventually rose to the rank of a full Colonel with a DSO and Bar. After retirement, James had become a successful entrepreneur and philanthropist, using his experiences and knowledge he saw an opportunity and made a bid for the old dockyard and buildings. Many, just like his Staff Sergeant during the last war thought he was 'bonkers.' Short-sighted councillors looking for a fast buck had secretly laughed up their sleeves when the contract transferring the ownership from the local council to the old Colonel was finally signed off. The contract immersed in bureaucratic legalise so synonymous of local government and buried in the small print was a time limit stipulating that the buyer was to revitalise the area or face heavy financial penalties. What James had purchased was an eyesore of deserted wasteland and derelict buildings surrounding the penned in *'murky waters'* of an old dock where the lock gates had not opened for many a year, allowing the trapped waters to stagnate instead of being refreshed with the salty seawaters at each high tide. James had seen beyond the horizon of this deprivation and immediately started, on a shoestring, a very basic cross channel ferry service using another redundant product of the war, an ex-military tank landing craft. Thus commenced the first-ever 'roll on roll off' ferry service.

At that time, the UK Government was anxious to rebuild the economy that had been ruined by the expenditure by six long years of war. James, networking with his many military contacts and pulling in favours, won a contract to collect and bring back to the UK some of the hundreds of tons of metal that lay around Europe. These remnants of conflict had been abandoned by both the retreating Axis forces as they laid down their arms and fled to the motherland of Germany and by the Allies as they chased the retreating armies towards Berlin and the final victory, leaving their war-damaged assets behind. All this scrap was vital to the industries of the UK hungry to recycle and rebuild its industrial might. James creatively used the redundant but unique tank landing craft that had seen their glory upon the beaches of Normandy when they'd crashed ashore spewing forth the invading Allied Forces with all their supporting heavy armour, transport and stores. The intelligent management of these constant 'comings and goings' from Europe with his fledging fleet of ex-military ships eventually metamorphosised into a thriving car and lorry ferry service. The managers of the nationalised cross channel ferry operators could only look on in envy at James' advance thinking, as their own traditional vessels were of a design that required vehicles to be laboriously loaded by crane and stowed in the cargo holds. James had been the instigator of a new dawn; he gave transport companies an efficient and economical means to move their lorries between the UK and Europe on what became dubbed a floating bridge. As the forties turned into the fifties, then the so-called 'swinging sixties' the new transport idea was catching on to the fast-expanding, car-loving British public as they realised that this was a way to travel to mainland Europe in their cars and even take their caravan! The wily and cunning old fox James Beaumont had seen the way forward and successfully predicted the future of short sea transportation, which revolutionised the movement of cargoes far beyond even the continent of Europe.

Flushed with the initial financial success transporting scrap metal back from Europe, James Beaumont had soon found more backers wanting to invest in his newfound ferry service. He had set about an ambitious expansion programme building the world's first purpose-built roll on roll off fleet. Building yards had soon chased him for the business, so James spread his work around as he was eager to expand rapidly and stay ahead of the competition as his business model caught on. Not content to wait for a yard to build one a ship at a time, he wanted his ships launched within a short period of each other so he could offer a complete service rather than a 'hotchpotch' of modern ships alongside old ones. Customer satisfaction was the key to his success.

These purpose-built ships with their smart drive through, roll on, roll off features, and comfortable en-suite driver's accommodation were the legacy James Beaumont left to the maritime world. They were entering service during the '70s and '80s with a fanfare of publicity. At the time, their design was advanced thinking with the latest cutting edge technology fitted into their engine rooms and navigation bridges. Now, as time has marched on, it is two generations later with the company having been past down through James's son into the hands of his 'Muppet' grandsons. The once ingenious modern fleet of vessels was, as the end of the '90s approached, coming to the end of their useful days, and the Beaumont fleet desperately needed an injection of modern Ro/Ro vessels so the company could contest the new super jumbo cruise ferries plying the southern cross channel routes. When James had started his business, the channel tunnel was still only an engineering dream, but with this now a reality, only modern monster ferries could hope to compete.

Prologue

Vvvooooo...shooooosh...vroomp, the ground shook as another German 88mm artillery shell screamed overhead and fell onto the Normandy beach.

Diving for cover to avoid the falling debris thrown up by the exploding shell is Colonel James Beaumont, Beach-master for this section of Gold Beach. He finds himself lying next to one of his Staff Sergeants, John Phillips. James rolls over on to his back, spits out sand he's inadvertently inhaled, and looks out from beneath the rim of his helmet to see shells impotently exploding in the sea amongst some of the LSL's, Landing Ship Logistics.

"Their aim is bloody terrible Staff! but they're bound to get lucky as their gun-layers get the range." James cringes as yet more shells fly overhead with nerve-shattering, high pitched screeches.

"Well let's hope in their panic they get it wrong, sir, don't want to lose many of those," John says nodding and pointing as two more LSL's hit the beach with open doors spewing out tanks and men.

During an unexpected lull, both men scramble out of the makeshift sangar and set off down the beach to continue directing the mass of military traffic pouring ashore. James stops, momentarily putting his hand on the arm of Sgt Phillips, "You know, Phillips, I've got a great idea of how to use LSL's after the war."

"Really, Sir, and what would that be?" snaps John, more concerned with just getting through the day alive.

"Look over there, what do you see?" James points to the sea.

"LSL's?"

"No, Sgt, I see the makings of a cross channel ferry service!"

"What?" snaps John, his voice rising by an octave, now more than ever convinced that all officers are bonkers.

"Can we just get through this fucking war first, sir?" doubtful that the Colonel had heard him as James continued to stare out to sea lost in his daydream.

Chapter 1

Along the wild east coast of central Britain sit two small seaside towns, both with similar-sounding names with prefixes denoting opposing points of the compass. Heading south to Suffolk, there is the picturesque town of Southwold while to the north on the Lincolnshire coast and there is the small seaport of Northwold. Their similarities in name and that they are both on the east coast is where any comparison ends. Southwold, a small town at the mouth of the River Blyth, is situated within an area of outstanding natural beauty. Whereas Northwold, surrounded by fertile farmland, is locked in a time warp dating back to Victorian times.

A bird's eye view would show regimental lines of back to back terrace houses, drab flat-faced red-bricked buildings, darkened by time. Dwellings commonly referred to as 'two up, two down' with uniformed square whitened front door steps from pumice stoning, topped off with grey Welsh slate roofs sporting tall chimneys adorned with forests of TV aerials. Narrow streets now made even narrower by the people's love of the motor car jammed together as each household claimed their car parking territory immediately in front of their homes. Single bulb street lighting so insipid as though embarrassed at illuminating too much of the architectural disaster which had seen little development other than the internal modernisation, which in reality means that the toilet is now inside the dwelling and they can be marketed as Town Houses by over-imaginative Estate Agents. It isn't all terraced housing though, there had been some development around the edges of town as modern suburbia of the middle classes stealthily crept in during the '60s.

Behind the port of Northwold lay lush flatlands boasting prime arable fields still dotted with abandoned airbases, these blots on the landscape being the remains of World War II 'Bomber County'. Here, during the summer months, the sun beams down on the vast open fields with a gentle warming breeze, blowing the ripening golden corn in long, undulating, lazy waves like the rolling waters of the nearby North Sea. The hot sun roasts the long abandoned runways heating them until they are like an oven hotplate, causing them to crack and splinter, allowing weeds to push through and flourish. During the winter, this vast open county is laid bare to the wild, easterly winds which race all the way from the Urals across the barren wastes of the storm-tossed seas where white horses ride the huge waves. Winds that chill a person to the bone, winds that incessantly whisper like ghostly airman over the vast, broad, empty runways where huge lumbering bombers once rumbled along.

On the coast, this small port of Northwold is hardly significant, but nonetheless, in its way has played a vital role in the overall picture of the United Kingdom's maritime story. The pre-world war one port had died when the last remnants of the North Sea herring fishing industry went into spiral decline once the abundant hunting grounds were finally fished out. However, during the Second World War, it enjoyed a brief, illustrious renewal when it had become a bustling coastal forces base packed with converted trawlers armed for defending coastal convoys against Nazi attack both above and below the waves. This fleet operated by the Royal Navy's Patrol Service known as Churchill's Pirates, but like many instruments of defence when the 'winds of war' had finally blown out and the calm of peace had pervaded over the land the port had soon become redundant again. It had fallen into decline when the final military occupants had left; it appeared as if they had simply locked up and thrown away the key, leaving the area to the ravages of the hostile, relentless winter environment and time. The windows of the abandoned buildings had soon became inviting targets, irresistible to local vandals; as a consequence, the broken panes allowed the damp, foggy winter atmosphere to invade, slowly eating into the fabric of the buildings causing a steady deterioration and dilapidation.

However, this was not to be Northwold's final breath; luckily for this small port, it had a saviour, a local born and bred lad, one James Beaumont. He had been born in one of the neat little back to back terraced houses built by the herring fleet owners to house their workers. These had long since moved into private ownership but still kept immaculate by the current occupiers keeping alive the traditions of their proud predecessors when the ladies of the houses would religiously 'pome stone' the front doorsteps every morning come rain or shine. Like most young boys, James Beaumont developed a fascination for vehicular transport. Although unlike many of his age who were only interested in the steam train, which was then the fastest, most convenient and modern way to travel, for James it was the lorry that drew his childhood attention. As a youngster, he saved his pocket money to spend on toy lorries made by 'Dinky' and 'Matchbox'. His love of lorries never waned, so it was with little surprise that when the time approached for leaving High School, with a less than exemplary academic achievement, he marched down to the Army Recruiting Office. Here he signed on as an Army Apprentice with the Royal

Army Service Corps as a trainee driver/mechanic or Queen's lorry drivers as they were more commonly known! Following a distinguished and decorated career in the Army, through both war and peace, he eventually rose to the rank of a full Colonel with a DSO and Bar. After retirement, James had become a successful entrepreneur and philanthropist, using his experiences and knowledge he saw an opportunity and made a bid for the old dockyard and buildings. Many, just like his Staff Sergeant during the last war thought he was 'bonkers.' Short-sighted councillors looking for a fast buck had secretly laughed up their sleeves when the contract transferring the ownership from the local council to the old Colonel was finally signed off. The contract immersed in bureaucratic legalise so synonymous of local government and buried in the small print was a time limit stipulating that the buyer was to revitalise the area or face heavy financial penalties. What James had purchased was an eyesore of deserted wasteland and derelict buildings surrounding the penned in *murky waters'* of an old dock where the lock gates had not opened for many a year, allowing the trapped waters to stagnate instead of being refreshed with the salty seawaters at each high tide. James had seen beyond the horizon of this deprivation and immediately started, on a shoestring, a very basic cross channel ferry service using another redundant product of the war, an ex-military tank landing craft. Thus commenced the first-ever 'roll on roll off' ferry service.

At that time, the UK Government was anxious to rebuild the economy that had been ruined by the expenditure by six long years of war. James, networking with his many military contacts and pulling in favours, won a contract to collect and bring back to the UK some of the hundreds of tons of metal that lay around Europe. These remnants of conflict had been abandoned by both the retreating Axis forces as they laid down their arms and fled to the motherland of Germany and by the Allies as they chased the retreating armies towards Berlin and the final victory, leaving their war-damaged assets behind. All this scrap was vital to the industries of the UK hungry to recycle and rebuild its industrial might. James creatively used the redundant but unique tank landing craft that had seen their glory upon the beaches of Normandy when they'd crashed ashore spewing forth the invading Allied Forces with all their supporting heavy armour, transport and stores. The intelligent management of these constant 'comings and goings' from Europe with his fledging fleet of ex-military ships eventually metamorphosised into a thriving car and lorry ferry service. The managers of the nationalised cross channel ferry operators could only look on in envy at James' advance thinking, as their own traditional vessels were of a design that required vehicles to be laboriously loaded by crane and stowed in the cargo holds. James had been the instigator of a new dawn; he gave transport companies an efficient and economical means to move their lorries between the UK and Europe on what became dubbed a floating bridge. As the forties turned into the fifties, then the so-called 'swinging sixties' the new transport idea was catching on to the fast-expanding, car-loving British public as they realised that this was a way to travel to mainland Europe in their cars and even take their caravan! The wily and cunning old fox James Beaumont had seen the way forward and successfully predicted the future of short sea transportation, which revolutionised the movement of cargoes far beyond even the continent of Europe.

Flushed with the initial financial success transporting scrap metal back from Europe, James Beaumont had soon found more backers wanting to invest in his newfound ferry service. He had set about an ambitious expansion programme building the world's first purpose-built roll on roll off fleet. Building yards had soon chased him for the business, so James spread his work around as he was eager to expand rapidly and stay ahead of the competition as his business model caught on. Not content to wait for a yard to build one a ship at a time, he wanted his ships launched within a short period of each other so he could offer a complete service rather than a 'hotchpotch' of modern ships alongside old ones. Customer satisfaction was the key to his success.

These purpose-built ships with their smart drive through, roll on, roll off features, and comfortable en-suite driver's accommodation were the legacy James Beaumont left to the maritime world. They were entering service during the '70s and '80s with a fanfare of publicity. At the time, their design was advanced thinking with the latest cutting edge technology fitted into their engine rooms and navigation bridges. Now, as time has marched on, it is two generations later with the company having been past down through James's son into the hands of his 'Muppet' grandsons. The once ingenious modern fleet of vessels was, as the end of the '90s approached, coming to the end of their useful days, and the Beaumont fleet desperately needed an injection of modern Ro/Ro vessels so the company could contest the new super jumbo cruise ferries plying the southern cross channel routes. When James had started his business, the channel tunnel was still only an engineering dream, but with this now a reality, only modern monster ferries could hope to compete.

The Beaumont Company, having first gone through a period of stagnation in the hands of the Colonel's son Edward, was now past on to the next generation and into the incompetent hands of the deceased Colonel's two grandchildren, brothers Peter and Paul Beaumont. The company now quickly running out of time and money as they face financial ruin. A minor financial 'hic-up' in the brothers' early years tenure of the business, had caused them to seek help and to turn to an investment banking consultancy group in London, this had led the naïve brothers to fall prey to a slick-talking, predatory business tycoon on the make. This temporary benefactor was an Asian businessman, one Amir Chandra, who, before emigrating to England, had survived the brutal regime of Idi Amin in Uganda, where he had been the first generation of Asian immigrants into that country. His life's experiences had turned him into a ruthless, money-grabbing entrepreneur. He had promised to show the brothers the way out of their predicament and how to create vast private wealth as well. Unfortunately, their world had overturned as they and their newfound business partner had produced this wealth through being involved in staggering levels of tax embezzlement. The lust of greed had dragged them into this mire, and thus they found themselves facing huge demands from Her Majesty's Inland Revenue Service as the inspectors uncovered the true extent of the fraud. Peter and Paul, with their erstwhile business partner when the inevitable conviction arrived, would certainly be facing a lot of 'porridge' and would also lose everything their grandfather had worked so hard to create.

These two incumbents of the company had, during their ownership taken delivery of only one new super jumbo ferry to add to their six out-dated vessels from James Beaumont's era. More new tonnage was now needed if the company, at one time far ahead technologically, was not to ironically get left behind by the established Ro/Ro companies which finally have seen the light had surged ahead with ambitious building programmes. Beaumont's urgently needed a huge injection of cash

Chapter 2

Autumnal leaves cover the Suffolk lane, creating a soggy golden blanket. The weak afternoon sun leaks under a thin veil of cloud, casting cold, damp shadows over the winding lanes. The sun's mauve light on the horizon gives the rest of the sky a light grey wash. The landscape looks like a water-colour on canvas. The air is filled with a sweet, heady odour of pine mixed with sour compost from the fallen leaves as they slowly decompose on the damp tarmac road. A hint of smoke drifts from old cottage chimneys in the windless cold day, collectively creating the smell of autumn. A bleak dispiriting time of the year. The memories of the hot, lazy summer days long forgotten giving way to the cold damp water condensed atmosphere by day with dark, freezing night and crisp snow laying outside whilst inside the houses the smell of home-baked mince pies along with chestnuts roasting on open log fires all conjured up the dreams of a magical Christmas to come.

Crows squawk angrily as they are disturbed by the dramatic events unfolding on the lanes directly beneath their treetop perches. Suddenly, they fly en-masse from the tops of the naked wiry trees, soaring high into the sky like a thousand black sci-fi raiders from a distant galaxy. Their ear-piercing, nerve-shattering shrieks replicate the harrowing sounds of a wartime blitzkrieg.

Richard Hartling throws his lightweight sporty BMW expertly along the winding country lanes. He is fully aware of his excessive speed, with just the odd slip from the back tyres as they lose traction on the damp carpet of fallen leaves. Undeterred he focuses on the tight corners, daydreaming of what life would have been like as a racing driver, living a life of speed. He is driving recklessly, not knowing what is around the corner, relying entirely on the modern ABS system. His daydream musings are suddenly disturbed. Looming large, filling his rear-view mirror, he sees a powerful, gas-guzzling, grunting monstrosity of a bright red 4 x 4 pick-up truck. A scourge of the tree-hugging environmentalists but popular with the 'Rednecks' in the sparsely populated American outback where the trails are wide, dusty and straight. Totally out of place along the narrow winding country lanes of Old England, where the road design is barely beyond that required by a horse and cart! The 4 x 4's massive 6 Litre engine roars like a tiger as the driver violently yanks the gear shift, torturing the beautifully engineered gear-box. The engine screams in

brown, beautiful eyes glared around the room, her flawless face was a true picture of beauty, her short auburn hair fell immaculately into place around her face. She looked over her shoulder at her husband – a man she once thought she could never live without, but now feels trapped within a lust-less marriage.

"For goodness sake Richard," she snapped, "This is getting too much; you must do something about it." Her voice showed no concern. If anything, her tone was tinged with an irritancy, but that was from her own nightmare mockingly reminding her of the affair that she had recently been conducting, which had thankfully recently ended but not before reaching a terrifying crescendo of violence. While suspecting Richard might also be having an affair, she would always defend her adulterous actions with the belief that she was driven to it by Richard.

"Sorry I woke you!" he snapped sarcastically, immediately regretting his tone of voice. Richard was equally annoyed at these nightmares that appeared to becoming all too often.

He swung his legs out from under the duvet and felt the expensive soft carpet beneath his feet. He cupped his head in his hands and exhaled deeply as he felt the pounding of his heart start to find its rhythm again. His tall frame slightly bent over, his back looked lean and fit, but this angle hid the sagging stomach he had been obliviously acquiring.

"Just a dream. Just another bad dream," he mumbled.

It may have only been a dream, but the memory of the man in the balaclava was still vivid, this was not just any dream – this was a nightmare, an all too real nightmare. He glanced at the clock on the bedside table. The digital display briefly clicked, it was 2.40 am.

He took a deep breath and swallowed. His mouth was dry and he knew that it would be a hopeless struggle to get back to sleep. Sleep that his body craved, but his brain denied him.

"I'm sick of it Richard!" moaned Caroline as she gently lay back down on the bed exasperation engulfing through her body.

"I'm sorry."

He closed his eyes, rubbing them, trying to erase the image of the man in the balaclava, but it was no good - it was still there, burned on to his retinas. He groaned inwardly as he lifted himself from the bed, trying to get his thoughts together.

"Now, where are you going?" complained Caroline.

"Darling, I'm so sorry, put the light out and try and get back to sleep," his hushed voice emanating momentary tenderness.

"Richard, these disturbed nights of yours are becoming all too frequent. You really should seek some medical help. I'll call the doctor in the morning because you'll never get around to doing it even with that super-efficient secretary of yours."

Caroline used a twinge of sarcasm just enough to sufficiently demonstrate her small amount of jealousy she had about Richard's working relationship with his secretary. Although she knew that if Richard were having an affair, it certainly wouldn't be with Susan. Susan was far too prim and proper for that.

"I will, I'll see him, I'll sort it."

He turned to look down at her, his gaze settled on Caroline's beautifully exposed neck, her flesh giving off the look of honey-dipped in cream, giving him a stirring in his loins.

"Promise?" she whispered, almost seductively.

"I promise," he feebly replied, followed by a sigh, his inner demons tormenting him with the question that, there, laid before him was a beautiful desirable woman, yet he was being unfaithful to her...why they asked...to which he didn't have an answer.

Caroline switched off the light and pulled the duvet protectively around her body and up to her chin. Despite the warmth she shivered involuntarily, recalling the awful place she had just been in the chasms of her mind. She certainly didn't need any help; she knew perfectly well the root cause of her nightmares. She prayed she would not fall back into the same bad dream.

Richard turned towards the bathroom, shaking his head, knowing that he wasn't conducting his life morally as he padded across the cavernous bedroom to the luxurious en-suite bathroom, feeling his erection slapping with his stomach made him realise he must do something about his body! The bathroom with his and her washbasins, large make-up mirrors, huge all-round power shower cubicle, and Jacuzzi was a bathroom of true elegance. He turned on the lights; the brightness made him squint until his eyes adjusted. He breathed a deep sigh and plonked down on the exquisite porcelain toilet bowl and pondered on his current situation;

'What on earth was he doing, playing with fire, trying to hide his infidelity from his wife, his beautiful wife. One day it would probably all blow up in his face, but then, wasn't that all part of the high-pressure gamble he was enjoying? The constant testing of nerves. The game he was playing to stay one step ahead of it all. Cleverly living on the edge, constantly alert. He needed, no, not needed – he wanted the enduring adrenalin rush that

comes with this lifestyle, he liked living on this nervous, dangerous edge, at least that's what he kept telling himself.'

Recently, since the nightmares had started, he felt as though he was losing this 'game'. The sixth sense that had always kept him out of trouble, enabling him to lead a double life, was fading; he was blind to the only one person that would matter in the end - his wife.

He kept telling himself he needed the adrenaline rush; he was scared that if he stopped, then he would have to face everything in front of him. The truth was, he was scared of losing control.

Richard had once gone in search of some medical help, but not in the conventional sense Caroline wanted for him. One of Richard's Boardroom colleagues, Peter Willis, was in his spare time a Surgeon Commander serving with the Royal Navy Reserve. Peter, within the sphere of military medicine, had specialised and written several papers on what was once referred to as 'Shell Shock' or 'Battle Fatigue.' Through ignorance, this had been thought to only affect the weak – the Royal Air Force at one time dubbing it as LMF, 'Lacking in Moral Fibre.' A misguided and ignorant view leftover from the First World War when executions were carried out under this banner. Thankfully, through great strides having been made in the research of the psychological effects of war, it had been recognised as a genuine illness and renamed 'Post Traumatic Stress Disorder'.

Richard recalled the private meeting he'd had with his friend and fellow Board Director.

He pictured Peter standing and looking at him with a serious expression on his face. His very tall, angular frame, which would probably eventually create a bend as Peter aged, but for now, added to his air of confidence. He had chiselled features, clean-shaven looks beneath a thick mop of blonde hair, that at times looked rather unruly, all adding up to make him an archetypical dashing British Naval Officer. His bright blue eyes appeared to twinkle whenever they caught the light and his face sported a permanent smile.

The conversation had not gone as Richard had hoped, the words remained imprinted on his mind;

"Peter, what do you think is the matter with me? These constant nightmares have become intolerable. I've thought of getting some sleeping pills, but I fear that's not the answer, it's something more deep-rooted ... Can you help me? Or at least send me in the direction of someone who can?"

Richard recalled adopting a pleading tone with his friend, hoping by some wave of a magic wand Peter would come up with a cure.

This, unfortunately, had not been the case, Peter had looked at him quizzically, raised an eyebrow, a trait for which he was well known.

"Richard, I've known you now for many years? We're good, close friends, yes?"

"Of course".

"Okay, look, I've never told you this before, but … I do know about Katrina. You may be known as the 'Toff' by a lot of your staff, but I rather think of you as 'Tricky Dickie,' or I'd even go as far as saying you're acting like a cad."

"What!"

"You're a cad! Just look at the way you are leading your life."

"Who told you about Katrina? Who the hell! Surely not my driver, Tim?" Richard remembered his sudden burst of anger, which had quickly subsided, followed by a sense of guilt and panic, *"My God! Do you think Caroline knows?"*

"Thankfully, I very much doubt it Richard, and for the record, no it wasn't Tim, I would say his loyalty to you is beyond reproach, a loyalty I consider you don't deserve, but from an ex-Royal Marine I would expect nothing less, in fact, I am surprised you would even think that of him."

"You're right, sorry, forget I said that, but come on, who told you?"

"Well, you just did. You confirmed it to me anyway, suffice to say London is at times a small village," Peter gave Richard a whimsical look. *"As I was saying, I know! Don't expect any sympathy from me … Caroline is a wonderful woman, and you are cheating on her. As much as you are a good, dear friend, you're a bloody idiot."*

"Well, thank you for the lecture in morals, Doctor! Tell me, have you any actual professional advice you can give me?"

"Yes, you are suffering from PTSD and that, in your case, does not stand for Post Traumatic Stress Disorder … it stands for Post Traumatic Shagging Disorder, in other words, a bloody guilty conscience! So, give up your mistress and spend more time with Caroline before it all goes 'tits-up.' If Caroline finds out and someone steals your rather 'dishy' wife away from you, you will get no sympathy from me or anyone else, so, speaking as one of your best friends – get rid of Katrina before this affair eats you up. Oh, and have a nice day chum," and with that, Peter had turned his back and walked away.

Sat on the toilet bowl, Richard half smirked as he thought about the conversation with Peter. Deep down, he knew Peter was right, but his macho ego had been insulted.

After washing and freshening himself with large amounts of cold water, Richard towelled his body dry, sprayed himself liberally with deodorant, and sighed inwardly wishing he could stop having these violent, frequent dreams. If Peter wouldn't help him, then so be it, he'd learn to live with it. Once dried, he returned to the bedroom to see his wife had rolled over and pulled the duvet tightly around her neck, she had either fallen asleep or was at least pretending to be. Despite their diminished sex life, Richard still slept naked. He slipped back into the comfortable king-size bed in the hope that he could drift off to sleep again. He noticed the bright light from the moon, trying to force its way through the expensive Sarah Sanderson curtains that draped the huge panoramic bay windows. He wished he could block the light out completely. He was tempted to try some over the counter sleeping pills he had recently bought, but knowing that he needed to be up in a few hours, he chose not to as they had always left a nasty after effect when insufficient time wasn't allowed to sleep them off. No, he had to hope that sleep would come naturally. He pulled the duvet back over himself. Despite the size of the bed he could feel the heat of his wife's body as he lay back down and closed his eyes. He hoped the demons wouldn't return for the remainder of the night. He knew he was playing with fire, but it excited him, giving him a recurring tremendous adrenaline rush having his two separate women as well as his high-flying job. It was all like a drug to him, and he was firmly hooked, but every so often, he came back down to earth, only to want more of the rush. He wondered if this was similar to a heroin addict coming off a 'high' already searching for the next hit, again and again, and again, never allowing the drug to be completely out of their system and always needing more no matter what the consequences.

Richard began to drift off to sleep. He pictured his father's mocking face, scolding him as being useless, telling him he would never achieve anything in his life because he had never worked hard enough to be a good scholar. His father, being one of the handful of operational aircrew that had 'crossed the runway' in RAF parlance from aircrew to ground crew, had always made Richard feel as though he was walking in his shadow. His father had joined the Royal Air Force as an apprentice intending to make it a career; later, he was commissioned and transferred to aircrew as a Flight Engineer, getting through the war relatively unscathed apart, from the hidden psychological scars. He recalled his father once briefly speaking of his experiences. It was after a family Christmas when he'd been left alone with his father, everyone else has gone to bed and all the house was still. Sitting together in front of the last dying embers of a log fire, with more than a whisky or two inside them, his father lost in his thoughts started to recalled how on one bombing mission he and the crew had heard the frantic calls come over the radio net from one of the bombers, that having been hit by flak, was spiralling out of control to earth. The words 'Bail Out! Bail Out!' screamed in his leather helmet headphones, indicating that the pilot of the dying aircraft had been gripping the transmit button in his anguish and terror. Another occasion, they had been returning home with their aircraft badly shot up by a German night fighter that had caught them over the North Sea, just when they thought they were home and dry as the Norfolk coast came into view shimmering in the moonlight. The pilot had been hit by ricocheting shells as they tore into the fuselage. He was still alive but suffering badly with pain, loss of blood and on the edge of consciousness. Richard's father helped the young pilot struggle with the controls to land the big damaged bomber to save themselves and the crew. Although down, it had landed heavily, bursting a tyre and careering out of control. Apart from the rear gunner, they had all miraculously escaped but their euphoria at being alive was marred by the death of the rear gunner who had died trapped in his turret. His screams, like the screaming words of the dying bomber, 'Bail Out,' were forever embedded in his subconscious mind. His father had come to dread flying, and as he stepped down from his Lancaster, after his last operational warlike sortie, he'd fallen onto his hands and knees, kissed the ground and involuntarily broken down and burst into tears, mainly with joy knowing that he'd made it through the hell of the bombing offensive alive. There and then, he vowed he'd never fly again. Although somehow, he wanted to stay in the RAF, but despite being a regular he thought the RAF would throw him out when he reported his decision to give up flying. However, to his delight, in consideration of his exemplary record in both war and peace, the RAF enabled him to continue his career with his feet firmly on the ground, retraining into the engineering branch. This quickly led to the rank of Air Commodore (Engineering). At that time, the only Air Commodore (E) with half wings. His final posting was that of a consultant to the Blackburn Aircraft

Corporation at Brough, located on the north bank of the River Humber. It was here where the last 'all British' Bomber was built, which since the Avro Vulcan, was probably the most advanced piece of aviation engineering produced by Britain in the shape of the Blackburn Buccaneer, a low-level strategic bomber. With his mind wandering and thinking of his father, the big factory and Brough, Richard slowly drifted off, dreaming that he was soaring high above the Humber looking down on Brough aerodrome seeing his father looking up at him - his face like thunder.

Thankfully, the demons did not return that night. By the morning, Richard had forgotten about his relationship inadequacies that stalked his nocturnal senses; now he was focussed on the day ahead. A slight sluggish feeling was left over from the disturbed night, but this was soon expunged out of his system by several cups of his favourite strong Columbian coffee. Once again, he was feeling good, his body fuelled by the coffee as it hit his bloodstream, causing an adrenaline boost, his business, and complicated private life - a cocktail mixture of excitement.

He laughed to himself; he'd not done so bad for a once poor scholar who'd left school without a plan. He just hoped his father was up there in heaven, looking down on his son's achievements that he once thought not possible. Richard, with a lack of direction or any career plan, had, after leaving school, joined the staff of a shipping company's office as a junior administration assistant, basically an office boy. At the time, he knew not where the future would take him, but was grateful for the income During this time, something had awoken within him, and he remembered the words he had learned at school from a production. It was a musical play, HMS Pinafore, one of the verses of the song went along the lines of 'it was possible to become ruler of the Queen's Navy, but having never actually gone to sea.' As had one aspiring MP, a Mr Samuel Pepys, who rose to become Chief Secretary to the Admiralty.

He recalled those early days as an office boy and in particular one occasion he will never forget. Whilst sitting at his desk, somewhat in a daydream, he looked across to the office boss man, who also had never gone to sea, sat there in his opaque glass screened luxurious office on the top floor, in charge of a maritime empire, it was at that moment that Richard suddenly realised that was exactly where he wanted to be. So, he had set about learning all there was to know about the shipping business. Richard had started in the agency section of the company, his desk was in a corner, immediately outside the manager's office. From the right angle, and with discretion, Richard could ogle at the manager's secretary, who would sit there every morning taking dictation from the boss. From his desk, he could surreptitiously see right up her beautiful and shapely crossed legs, all the way to her stocking tops. He was sure she knew he was looking, and that she enjoyed knowing he was looking but being a sexually inexperienced youngster of only 18 going on 15 he never had the nerve to do or say anything to her, plus she had a rugby-playing boyfriend, built like the proverbial toilet block and Richard certainly didn't fancy getting on the wrong side of him, so he settled for the odd tantalising glimpse of stocking top and soft milky white thigh.

He'd come a long way since those days, and he was now the boss, not of the Queen's Navy but just as good as. He reigns as the Chairman of a huge commercial shipping conglomerate, housed in a large penthouse office, with huge floor to ceiling toughened glass windows for walls and a panoramic view of London, overlooking old Father Thames.

The difference with Richard was that he had actually been to sea aboard some of the company ships. It had all been part of his grand career plan, and planning was one thing he had become very good at. Once he decided in which direction he wanted his career to go, he had become totally focussed and obsessively driven by a passion for succeeding. His decision in those formative years was to seek employment at sea so he could discover each and every part of the business and how it worked; he had intended to be an expert in everything, working from being a galley boy to standing 'look-out' watches on the navigation bridge and gauge watching in the engine-room. He had learned every part of life aboard an ocean liner, understudying the Captain, Chief Engineer, and the Purser. This had paid off handsomely years later when dealing with trade unions and the negotiating of crewing levels aboard the company vessels.

Suddenly, he was brought back to the present from his musings by hearing the familiar crunch of heavy tyres on the gravel as his chauffeur-driven Range Rover swept into the drive of his six-acre garden. He dashed upstairs to collect his briefcase from his study and to give Caroline the obligatory peck on the cheek, but the bed was empty, she was already in the bathroom.

He went to pop his head around the door to say goodbye, but unusually the door was closed and locked. He shouted goodbye but got no response, maybe she couldn't hear him over the noise of the Jacuzzi.

He grabbed his suitcase from the study before heading back downstairs. He contemplated shouting to Caroline again, to make sure she was okay, but the realisation that her reply would probably be negative and cause an argument, he quietly went back downstairs. He gazed around the immaculate, glistening, showroom-style kitchen. Whenever they entertained at home, which was usually when Richard's business matters needed to be discussed privately away from the office, Caroline always called in caterers, her days of being a domestic goddess had been swallowed up years ago by a lack of enthusiasm. The family now rarely came over. Friends had dispersed over the years, possibly through jealousy. The house and garden had been built to their specification including an indoor swimming pool, he remembered the excitement they had had just ordering the sliding pool room roof and patio doors, their lives ready for the fabulous 'show off' house. As he looked around the spotless kitchen, he couldn't help but wonder why he was working for it all.

He grabbed his jacket and dashed through the front door, his entrance onto the stage of the world in which he thrived as Chief Executive of one of the world's largest shipping empires.

Chapter 3

Caroline had heard Richard shout goodbye, but not wanting him to know she was crying she had chosen to ignore him, pretending she could not hear him over the running water. She listened through the bathroom window, waiting to hear Richard's car to drive away. Once she knew he'd gone, she sighed, tears gently rolled down her soft cheeks. She stepped in to the Jacuzzi, the warm soapy water stung her wounds. Time appeared to stop as she lay engulfed by the soothing bubbles. The jets on the Jacuzzi finished their powerful cycle, the surface foam slowly dispersed leaving clear water. She looked down at the fading bruises on her thighs. Knowing she had to face another day, she got out, wrapped herself in her luxury towelling robe and studied her reflection in the mirror of the beautiful ornate dressing table. She gently combed her wet hair and pondered about how she had come to this. She felt like a victim trapped in her fairy-tale castle.

Caroline was the eldest daughter of a typical middle England family. Her father had been an Insurance salesman from a bygone age when they drove around in Morris 1000 cars and dressed in mohair coats sporting trilby hats to complete their ensemble like some sort of unofficial uniform. They called on their clients to collect premiums in cash – this was long before the banking direct debit system which sent these men in the same way as the dinosaurs. Her father had also been a Methodist Church lay preacher, a strict, non-smoking teetotaller, who ruled his household with a firm hand. It was only later, during Caroline's' late teens whilst at university, that she had discovered the truth; her father was leading a double life. His puritanical image was all a façade; in reality, her father was a fornicating, lecherous, womanising drunkard. This came as a total shock to her when his true life was exposed by a Sunday national newspaper, commonly known as 'The Barmaid's Gazette,' with headlines that screamed:

'The Risqué Insurance Salesman who has everything covered, including your wife!'

The paper had discovered it all. A budding cub reporter, looking to make a name for himself, had been searching for a juicy story befitting of the paper's sensationalising reputation that could make a Vicarage tea party sound like a sex orgy. In truth, Caroline's father was a sexual predator seeking out vulnerable and, at times, willing partners from both his professional life and his church-going flock. The news sent shock waves

reverberating through the church to such an extent it would be felt and talked about for many years. Even that was not enough to make Caroline's long-suffering mother leave her father, with her unshakable naïve loyalty, her mother preferred to bury her head in the sand and not believe what she interpreted as lies being told by the gutter press about her upstanding, devout, church-going husband. Caroline hadn't been adversely affected by the discovery of her father's secret life. She enjoyed the limelight in which she found herself; revelling in the sudden and unexpected notoriety with her peers at university. Her father's exposure demonstrated that he suffered from normal human failings and was not the high and mighty self-righteous disciplinarian he had always portrayed to her. He'd always been a distant, aloof figure who now needed to be understood, turning overnight into a warm-hearted person who craved the love and sympathy of his daughter. It was a strange phenomenon, and at first, Caroline found it difficult dealing with these warm fatherly approaches. He'd been very distant, almost an alien to her, during the years she had grown up through puberty into a young woman. Her father in the past had been so incapable of love and affection towards her that she often wondered if she was the result of a mistake, an unwanted child. Through her teenage years, as her legs grew longer and her skirts grew shorter, the youngsters becoming so much more liberated than previous generations had allowed, Caroline had on occasions caught her father surreptitiously looking at her shapely stocking-clad legs. This had scared her somewhat, causing her to worry that he was in some way frustrated by her good looks. Over the years, her loving and devoted mother had become quite frumpy and matronly whilst Caroline had blossomed vibrantly with youth. These concerns were forgotten when he reached out to her: the huge gulf that had existed between Caroline and her father disappeared, and like long lost soul mates, they developed a warm father/daughter loving relationship.

After this, they remained very close, and it was through a friend of her father's that she met Richard. At first, it was a fairy-tale romance, but over the years, due to his high-powered career and life-style, Caroline and Richard had slowly started to drift apart. Caroline knew she lived what many would term an 'over-indulgent lifestyle,' but she didn't care what others thought. Other people could be envious of Richard's celebrity-like status and his money; Caroline made sure she enjoyed her husband's success. Yes, their marital sex life was on the wane, but that was behind closed doors. In Caroline's eyes, the embellishment of luxury was

materialistic compensation for the lack of love and affection. Caroline had an average sexual appetite, but she yearned for passion and excitement. She missed the thrill of lovemaking with Richard, his tender touch, his eagerness of wanting her. When they first got together, they were inseparable by day and insatiable by night. He used to make her feel adored, idolised even, but those emotions had slowly, without realisation, dispersed. Caroline had attempted to broach the subject with Richard on numerous occasions, but, as always, he was far too busy with work. Deep down, Caroline knew she had become a trophy wife, placed in the limelight at major business events that dominated Richard's commercial life. She held on to the memories of what was once an exciting, active and voracious sex life, when they had made love whenever and wherever; the kitchen, the lounge, the stairs, even in the garage. Car bonnets and driving seats were individually christened by the couple's lust for each other. Caroline would like to daydream about the occasion when on a walking holiday in the Yorkshire Dales while standing beneath a tree during a summer downpour, she had her first multiple orgasm, a mind-blowing experience. Oh, how she longed to return to those carefree days. Now, sex with Richard was just an irregular quick fumble, a push and a shove followed by a moan from Richard leaving Caroline deflated and unfulfilled. It was just 'maintenance sex' as described by the tabloid Agony Aunts. These infrequent occasions left her feeling empty.

When Richard first progressed to his present position, Caroline soon discovered that life is for living, and money is for spending. The new larger house with all the trimmings, her upgraded Mercedes Sports, the expensive holidays overseas, the private cottage in Provencal, the jewellery, the clothes, and the luxury cruises on extravagant yachts. But like her husband, Caroline often found herself questioning what it was all for. Yes, she loved Richard, but that love had changed over the years just like Richard's physique and even more noticeably, over recent months, his mentality. Her once trim husband had slowly grown what was commonly known as a 'corporate girth'. His gym membership was long gone, the caring and the attentive man she had married hardly ever gave her the time of day. His attitude towards her changed. With his prehistoric practical approach to materialist trappings, he believed that as long as she had the limitless credit card, lived in sumptuous surroundings, then she should be content. However, that was so very far from the truth. Caroline's life was plagued with disturbed nights, completely unaware that her husband, too, is having his doubts about his life. It was the lack of

lust and affection that drove her to start an affair five months ago. With her elite members-only fitness retreat personal trainer, Joash, Caroline had taken 'personal' to another level. In her mind, Richard's behaviour had driven her to it. If he had been more attentive, more loving, more energetic, she would never have done it. If she'd been happy and felt loved she would have walked away flattered but not stupid. 'Stupid.' That's what people would say, 'It's your entire fault, Caroline ... you led him on, you stupid girl.' Maybe people would even say that she 'asked for it.'

It had all started so innocently, a bit of flirting, the odd comment, a gentle touch here and there, but within three months, she found herself wanting more from Joash. Sex without commitment, it was all she was searching for. Joash was a Kenyan immigrant brought over to the UK by his mother and father. He boasted a muscular, ebony black body that would glisten beautifully with sweat. The sweet musky smell of sex after they'd made love in the afternoons drove Caroline to heights of sexual arousal that made her go back for more. Deep down, she knew it was just physical satisfaction but she didn't care.

Joash, as well as a personal fitness instructor, was one of the club's masseurs and it was during one of her afternoon massages that Joash had steadily become more probing and amorous to which Caroline had excitedly responded. The pair had childishly, and secretly, been flirting for weeks, and there was little room left for any doubt between them as to where things would go. Eventually, a particular massage session ended up with her on her knees, taking him in her mouth. She had refused Richard this for years, but she revelled in it with Joash as she crouched down on the floor, pushing him back against the massage bed and gagged as he wildly thrusted his huge blood-engorged member into her mouth eventually filling her mouth with volumes of his hot, sticky bodily fluid. Later, he had laid her over the massage bed and taken her stallion-like from behind. After this first explosive, session it was as if the flood gates had opened within her; all the pent-up desires for sex had suddenly burst out of her like the broken banks of a swollen river; she couldn't get enough of him. It was exhilarating to be the centre of attention, to be desired, to get what she wanted sexually, and not just be a dutiful wife. Following each encounter together, she was momentarily overcome with tremendous guilt and vowed to leave him alone. However, like a drug, the carnal cravings for him soon started again. Caroline often wondered if she would ever be able to break free of his magnetism, but the erotic thoughts of feeling him inside her would soon blank out the misgivings. She needed fun, and she craved male attention, and she wasn't getting either from Richard. Caroline thought she could never get enough of Joash, until their last, and what was to be their final get together, took a sudden, strange and sinister direction. The event occurred when, with great stupidity, she went against the very thing she vowed never to do; Caroline allowed Joash to take her back to his flat.

Richard had informed her in the morning, that due to a series of engagements, he wouldn't make it home until the early hours of the following day. Gleefully, Caroline had immediately phoned the health club and booked an appointment for a massage with Joash. That afternoon Caroline found herself in her usual position, laying on her stomach while Joash tended to her back and thighs with a luxurious firm massage that let the tension drain away from her body. As usual, Joash began to tease Caroline with his strong well-oiled fingers, like rods of iron yet soft and gentle, finding their way to places that were professionally out of bounds. He started to slide his hands up and down the delicate soft skin of her upper thighs, running up beneath her draping towel, pulling back just as they gently brushed her erogenous zone, making her pant in anticipation as to what was to come next. Joash had the ability to sensually massage her body to a level of burning desire that removed all inhibitions. Little did she know that Joash had a string of wealthy women club member clients all who were experiencing the same attention to their bodies as Caroline.

"Joash, you are a naughty tease," she gasped with pleasure. "You are such a little treasure … my gorgeous sex slave," she giggled, not realising just how much her upper-class voice infuriated him. Through his eyes, she represented all that he despised of the historical white supremacy of his homeland. Ignoring his desire to give her a bloody good slapping, he replied,

"Yeah Babyee, but don't you know you just looove it."

His hands slowly probed further up her thigh.

"Mmmm … that's so nice," she groaned.

"Hey Babe, your my last client today so let's go back to ma place 'cos we are never really alone here and I wanna do things to ya that will make ya scream with pleasure."

Caroline shivered with delight in anticipation of what was to come later as his fingers strayed into forbidden parts of her anatomy, and Caroline couldn't resist. She admitted to herself that their trysts at the gym were dangerous, and she certainly didn't want the embarrassment of being caught out, suffering the ensuing scandal that would follow. Recklessly, she agreed to go home with him, making a further mistake by travelling there in Joash's car. Her usual practical reasoning was clouded by lust. Once inside his flat, Joash plied her with spiked prosecco. Every time she took a sip, Joash gently tipped the bottom of her glass with his fingers making it overflow down her chin and neck, encouraging her to drink more. She giggled as he lusciously licked the prosecco from her neck. He did not want to knock her unconscious, but he did want to have control over her mind and body while ensuring she knew what was happening to her.

Joash wanted to demonstrate dominance. He needed to show her just who the boss really was. She had the money. He knew he could manipulate her to feed his hunger for wealth and revenge while as an added benefit enjoying having his perverse sexual needs fulfilled. Caroline was just another one of his concubines he was nurturing, by the end of the evening, he would have started the process to ensure she would become dependent on him and hooked on cocaine. Joash was a drug dealer, cultivating a niche market with wealthy women. He never lowered his standards to the 'hangers out' on seedy street corners, he would not deal with desperate men and women who had to sell their bodies or anything else they possessed for their next hit. He already had several very rich women begging him for their regular supply and soon Caroline would be joining this customer base, then he could move on to his next victim. Joash made sure that these 'posh tarts' would have nowhere else to go for their supply; he would have total control over them. He, Joash, the poor immigrant from Kenya, was the chieftain ruling over his harem of wealthy white bitches.

At first, Caroline just felt the usual euphoria of being slightly tipsy as they tore off each other's clothing in the eagerness to get naked. They rolled around on the bed, groping each other in excitement, but Caroline started to feel weak, a foggy drugged state making her lose control. Joash became rough, pulling her hair and rolling her over.

"Wait Joash!" she said, her words slightly slurred. She wanted him to stop, but his laughter and her blurred vision made the realisation dawn on her that she had been drugged.

"Please! Joash ... don't!" She struggled for the words; her breathing became shallow as she slowly sank deeper into a stupor. Before she knew what was happening, Joash had trussed her up in a strange leather harness like a restraint from a bygone era of a lunatic asylum. He made her kneel on her hands and knees. He slapped his huge cock across her face, then bent over her with a large leather whip and set about beating her across her buttocks, the sound of leather on tender flesh vibrating off the walls of the room as Joash administered the savage punishment with glee. He then demanded she bend down further to kiss and lick his feet, Caroline followed his every command, the sickly salt taste caused her to retch. Terrified, she knew she was helpless, under the control of this man who she thought she knew, as he played out his bizarre sex games. Quietly, she held her tears back, praying for the degrading humiliation and pain to be over. After what seemed like hours of torment, Joash finally finished by taking her anally, causing Caroline immense pain. She knew she was injured as she'd felt warm blood trickle down her thighs, after which, he finally released her, with the final insult of throwing her bruised naked body on to the bed. She dipped in and out of consciousness while Joash lay next to her, snoring grotesquely. She felt helpless as the effects of the drug wore off and the pain finally kicked in.

'Oh, dear God, what have I done?' her mind screamed as she lay there. Caroline bit the back of her hand. Terrified, tears ran down her cheeks, she feared of what was to come next if she didn't get away. The pain from her abused body groaned deep within her, seeping into every fibre of her flesh, creaking like an old sailing ship at sea. She felt disgusted, humiliated, and beaten. She had naively walked into a trap all because of her lust for sex with this animal, this beast lying alongside her. She felt sick and swallowed hard to stop the hot bile rising into her throat. Scared for her life, she knew she had to get away from him and fast. Slowly, she slipped out of the bed as quietly as possible, desperately trying to control her breathing for fear of making too much noise and waking Joash, each move slow and careful, terrified that the rustling of the bed sheets would awaken him. The room was so dark, her eyes frantically searching for her clothes, her eyes slowly growing accustomed to the darkness, as soon as she saw them she carefully and painfully, gathered them up. Her limbs trembled as she bent to the floor, each movement causing sharp stabs of pain shooting through her body, most noticeably around her rectum. Quietly, she closed the bedroom door and dressed as quickly as she could, squirming at the pain. Adrenaline surged through her body, the primeval instinct to survive took over. Her heart drummed on her rib cage as though trying to break out of her chest, its echoing thud beat in her ears, and she was terrified he would hear her. Thankfully he didn't even stir, because he too, unbeknown to Caroline, had taken a line of cocaine with a cocktail of alcohol. After so much physical exertion, the cocktail had induced deep, heavy sleep. With most of her clothes on, apart from her trainers and a small handbag, which she held tightly in her right hand, Caroline tiptoed to the front door. Holding her breath daring not to breathe, she had not even thought about keys, what if it was locked, 'Oh my God,' she exhaled. Carefully turning the handle, she stopped, and she held her breath in fear it wouldn't move; fortunately, it was still unlocked, the door creaked slightly as it came open, the sound amplified, she froze. The silence was chilling. Her fingernails dug into the palm of her hand, making her wince as she pulled the door further open and crept out of the grotty flat.

Once outside in the cold night, she gulped down huge volumes of refreshing air amidst sobs of panic. She looked around, unable to recognise anything to indicate as to where she was. She knew she had to run. In her school days, Caroline had been an accomplished runner, and although the years had taken their toll on her knees, she discovered latent energy deep within her. Her naked feet pounded the tarmac, terrified that any attempt to put on her trainers would waste valuable time and slow down her escape. Her blood pumped heavily around her veins straining to take the oxygen to her aching muscles as they worked overtime to keep her legs moving frantically as she ran. The feeling of terror engulfed her as she struggled to put as much space between her and that dreadful flat. Being so foolishly and immaturely engrossed with her sexual desire for Joash, she had not noticed the seedy area in which he had brought her. The desolate run-down industrial estate deepened her fear. The darkness was lit by a few yellowish glowing fluorescent security lights fixed to the surrounding warehouses. The dim lights produced pools of eerie glows. Not fifty yards away, a blazing oil drum illuminated several hobos huddled together in a vain attempt to keep warm the new spring air still cold once the sun had set. The creepy atmosphere created imaginary pools of evil seeping everywhere. Turning each corner was a voyage into the unknown. Her fear forced her to run even harder. She had completely lost her bearings and was petrified she was running in circles as she became disorientated in the broad avenues and alleyways of the estate. She jumped into dark corners every time she heard a car, petrified that it could be Joash searching for her. Terrified, she slipped into an enclosed alleyway to catch her breath. That's when she heard his voice. It had to be him, even though it sounded more like a wild animal howling. The angry scream of someone possessed by the devil reverberated around the industrial buildings winding like tentacles seeking Caroline, ready to drag her back to her tormentor.

Joash slowly woke; the cocaine haze caused his vision to blur. He switched on the bedside light emitting a low red glow creating shadows on the wall which caused him only to see misty shapes.

"Geee man, that was some fuck wasn't it babe?" he mumbled as he stretched out his arm to the now rapidly cooling area of the bed left vacant by the recently departed Caroline.

"Where are you, babe?"

He rolled over and felt down the bed, expecting to find her. When no response came, he leaped out of bed, momentarily dizzy with the sudden loss of blood draining from his cranium. He reached both hands out and leaned against the bedroom wall to gain his balance before frantically searching for the main light switch. Finding it, he flicked the switch and squinted as the light exploded into his retinas. The room now bathed in a blinding white light, which overpowered the glowing red of the bedside lamp.

"Hey babe, where are yooose?" his voice briefly slipped into his Southern African accent. With his balance regained, along with some of his composure, he headed for the bedroom door and hurled it open. His mouth and throat felt as though it was covered in thick fur. He looked back over his shoulder for her clothes, scanning the floor where they had been haphazardly abandoned only a few hours earlier and realised they had all gone. His heart started to beat faster, going into overdrive as it attempted to equalise his blood pressure. Anger exploded at the realisation that Caroline had left, walked out on him, the great Joash. The hurt and rage built, fuelled by the cocaine mixing with adrenaline, causing the seeds of aggression to burst into life. He yelled out in frustration,

"Hey, you fucking white bitch, where are yoouuse? No white bitch of mine walks away from meeee!"

He thrashed around his apartment, going from room to room like a man possessed, the search in vain. He threw on a pair of boxer shorts and ran out of his front door into the deserted road of the industrial estate. His bare feet hardly registered any feeling from the cold, rough asphalt surface.

Joash had been brought up in a small village in the Kenyan bush countryside and had never worn any form of footwear during that period of his life, consequently, the soles of his feet were like leather, a toughness they had not lost.

Filling his lungs with the crisp cold night air, he screamed out,
"Hey you fucking white bitch, I'm coming for you," his voice was loud and guttural, "You won't get far." He followed with a blood-curdling howl, a war cry he'd learned from the tribal elders in his Kenyan village, sounding like a wounded animal as it ripped through the silence. It was such a ghoulish noise that even the homeless tramps, who were huddled around a red hot brazier, shivered at the sound as it engulfed the industrial estate by bouncing and echoing off the huge slab-sided, bleak warehouse walls. Joash focussed on finding Caroline. He guessed that she couldn't have gone far. For him, this patch was his jungle, and he started running. He imagined himself back in the African bush running with a spear held high in his right hand. The adrenaline pumped around his body. He was after his quarry, and the chase was on! Joash was now in his stride and fired up with the intent of catching Caroline to drag her back to his apartment, where he would seek his retribution by beating her into submission. He was going to force Caroline to consume cocaine before the night was out. He'd 'pussy footed' around with her for far too long and now the bitch was going to learn the hard way.

Joash, the dealer, needed to increase his market share, he needed to add to his customer base of what he liked to call his 'wealthy white bitches'. They had the wealth to buy from him; all he had to do was to introduce them to the habit. He preyed on lonely upper-class women who were looking for some excitement in their pampered lives. It was as if he could smell their solitary life from a mile away. The widows, the unloved, the desperate; they were his guaranteed market place. He hadn't got there yet with Caroline. He knew from the start that she was a tough choice, but he was adamant he would eventually break her down so that she would be another one of his posh consumers, totally reliant on him and under his control. He revelled in the feeling of power he had over those already on side. He just needed time with Caroline, then she would soon be joining his client base, but his patience had already started to wane despite the fringe benefits. He was finally done playing games, the bitch was running out on him, and that was the last straw. He'd spent too much time and effort cultivating his relationship with her to let her go now. She was too valuable a commodity, knowing who she was married to.

With those thoughts flashing through his mind. Such was his steely determination that it didn't bother him that he'd just run through some dog faeces. He instinctively knew what it was. As a boy in Kenya, he'd run through elephant droppings thick as mud; dog shit was nothing to him. He also felt stabs of pain coming from running over a piece of broken glass but there was sufficient cocaine still within his body, together with his tough leather-like soles, that it felt like nothing more than a slight scratch. Caroline was sick with fear, the bile flooding her oesophagus. She staggered, grabbing hold of a nearby iron railing and vomited violently, bringing up nothing but white bile. She had not eaten since a light lunch at the health club. Her stomach muscles were in danger of rupturing as she retched. She took a deep breath, gathered what were her last reserves of energy, and ran in the direction of bright light and traffic noise. Eventually, she found herself upon a well-lit but isolated main road. It hummed with late-night traffic speeding through the area like wasps. A streetlamp cast light over a nearby pedestrian crossing. She walked towards the light, hoping it would create a haven of safety for her. As she stepped under the luminous glow, she saw a taxi, and with all of her energy, she desperately waved her hands to get the driver's attention. She tried to scream, but her throat was so sore from the retching that her voice box only let out a whisper.

The taxi was being driven by Bill Richardson. He was taking a short cut passed the industrial estate on his way home from what had been a poor night for cab fares. Seeing the dishevelled state of Caroline as she clutched her trainers and handbag, dressed only in a tracksuit and without a coat, he briefly wondered whether or not he should drive away, call his office on the radio and get the operator to call the police and leave it at that. But Bill was a curious bugger if nothing else. Bill's senses were on high alert for trouble, ready to put his foot down hard to the floor the moment he saw anything untoward; he slowed down, keeping away from the kerb giving him plenty of road room if things went wrong. It was every taxi drivers worst nightmare to be hi-jacked late in the evening when taxis were targeted for easy pickings. He crawled alongside the frantic woman and tried to get a better look at her.

Caroline ran around the front of the taxi to the driver's window; her haste caused a following car to let rip with a long angry blast on the horn as a passing driver swerved to avoid her. Bill, feeling slightly nervous, kept his car slowly crawling forward as Caroline gasped and panted at him through the partially lowered driver's window. It wouldn't be the first time a carjacking had been staged by using the supposed damsel in distress trap. He engaged the safety locks on the car's doors, just in case. It may be a well-lit busy road but it's still an isolated and bleak part of town.

"What's up me luvvie," said Bill, glancing anxiously over to his left, wary of anybody else suddenly appearing from the shadows from where Caroline had emerged.

"Oh, thank you for stopping," she sobbed, "Please can you take me to Leticia Avenue, St. John's Wood?" Caroline gasped as she trotted barefoot, sidestepping to keep up with the slow-moving taxi, panicking that he was going to drive away and leave her.

"Oh, please stop and take me home, please, please, please don't leave me here," she wept, "I can pay you double the fare with cash. Please just get me out of here," she begged, realising that she must look an awful sight as she desperately tried to convince this taxi driver that she was genuine.

"Please take me home. I don't know where on earth I am."

"Alright Missy, just calm down."

"I have money... Please!" She begged, forcing herself not to break down and scream at the driver. Bill quickly realised that with her unselfconscious, distinctive upper class 'plummy' accent, together with her exclusive destination, maybe she was more than likely to be a real damsel in distress. The thought of a double fare to make up for the poor night he'd had so far was worth the risk. He brought the car to a halt and released the door lock, allowing Caroline to scramble onboard. Bill turned to look at Caroline as she clambered into the rear seat, he wondered what had happened for her to get in such a state. Neither Bill nor Caroline had noticed the panting, sweating muscular giant black body of Joash emerge from the shadows. It was the sudden and heavy slam as Joash threw both of his balled fists down on to the bonnet of Bill's cab that got their attention. Later, while cleaning his car, Bill would discover two large dents where Joash had hit his car with such strength that even the paintwork had flaked. Bill jumped at the bang, his bowels breaking wind uncontrollably as Caroline screamed. All Bill Richardson saw was the terrifying sight of a huge naked figure of a wide eyed, wild black man, his body bathed in glistening sweat as it reflected from the bright street floodlighting.

Caroline wailed, "Drive! Drive! Drive! He'll kill me! He'll kill us both!"

For a brief moment, Bill froze in terror. Joash lunged for the passenger door. His right hand grabbed the handle and pulled it open, his long muscular black arm reaching in like an evil tentacle attempting to grab Caroline. She screamed again, curling herself into a ball in the far corner of the seat, trying to make her body shrink out of his reach. Bill, terrified, burst into life and released the clutch with his left foot and slammed his right foot down, pushing the accelerator to the floor. The sudden rush of fuel through the carburettor and into the cylinders caused the engine to misfire and almost stall. Bill momentarily and briefly wet himself. A sudden burst of torque as the engine caught again caused the rear-drive wheels to spin, sending up a cloud of blue smoke from the friction as the rubber strained to grip the road surface. Bill immediately swerved the taxi to the right; this quick reaction caused Joash to lose his balance and fall backwards. The open passenger door slammed shut with the rapid action. Joash quickly regained his balance and sprinted after the taxi. Within seconds his powerful long legs soon had him alongside the car banging his fists on the rear side windows as it steadily began to outpace him. He was screaming in a fury,

"Man, stop the fucking car! If you don't, I'll kill you, man; you fucking bitch come back here!" Those were the last words Caroline heard as the taxi thankfully sped away, leaving an angry Joash bent over, gasping for breath, after his almost superhuman effort to outpace the taxi. Bill didn't need any more encouragement to get away from the area as quickly as possible. He thrashed through the gearbox to increase the speed and get as far away as possible from the crazed mad man. If the police suddenly stopped him for speeding, then he could unburden his pent-up fear onto them about the huge black man with murderous eyes. A sudden feeling of relief swept over Caroline, cocooned in the safety of the cab. Tears rolled down her cheeks, she scrabbled in her bag, put together fifty pounds, and stuffed it through the perspex divide to Bill.

"There, take that, and if you want any more, just say, I can pay," she said tearfully before curling up into the foetal position on the back seat, "Thank you," she whispered.

Thankfully, on that awful night, Richard was still out by the time Caroline arrived home. She'd showered several times, trying to expunge the smell and thought of Joash from her body and soul. She was beaten and sore. Her skin was covered in bruises and scratches that would show for days, maybe even weeks, reminding her of the degrading experience she had endured. It would take months to get over this, if ever. She feared the awful, searing pain in her rectum would be around for some time, reminding her of her stupidity and naivety. She shivered as realisation struck home as to just how little she knew Joash. Yes, he had provided great satisfying sex when she needed it but, at what cost, her imagination ran riot as she considered what would have happened if she had never escaped from that awful flat. She did not realise how comparatively fortunate she was, as, despite the horrifying experience, she had by her actions foiled Joash's attempt to enslave her into drug dependency. Ignorant of the fact that Joash's ultimate goal had been to get her hooked on cocaine, just like all of his other 'personal' clients.

Chapter 4

Caroline came back to the present, involuntarily shedding more tears as the haunting memories filled her conscience. Since that terrible night some weeks ago she had immediately cancelled her membership at the Health Club. Joash's liaison with Caroline had not gone unnoticed by the Health Club's General Manager, Ms Joan Aspinall, who liked to be called 'Jo' by colleagues; she felt this gave an authoritative tone of masculinity toughness in a predominantly male environment. Jo had chosen to turn a blind eye to their possible encounters, selfishly having her eye on her year-end bonus calculated on client spend over and above their membership fees. Caroline was one of the club's Elite Diamond Club members hence a high spender from the club's extra services menu, including Joash; these extra costs more than tripled her basic annual membership fee. When Caroline suddenly cancelled her membership, Jo had her strong suspicions as to why. Despite the customer care team pestering Caroline with numerous telephone calls with offers of incentives to renew her membership, they were unable to ascertain the reason for Caroline's sudden departure. Caroline was adamant though, citing personal medical advice, and secretly vowed never to step back into the club again. She continued to ignore the club's calls and blocked the number on her house phone and mobile.

Joash had never been popular with the club's management; they found him uncooperative, disobedient, and generally abrasive towards their authority. As much as the management loathed him, his saving grace, which he was fully aware of, was his popularity with the wealthy lady clients of the club, Caroline being a typical example. Several male members also spoke highly of him. So while Jo, who was a closet racist, would be delighted to fire Joash, she knew it would be detrimental to the club's income and, more importantly, her annual bonus. When Caroline suddenly left, Jo, suspecting what had been going on between the two of them, felt obliged to investigate the matter with a sense of elation that she may have found the grounds with which to show Joash the proverbial door or at the very least knock him down to size as he was getting too big for his boots. However, the confrontation with Joash came rather un-expectantly and with a perverse conclusion. Joash knew of Caroline's departure, he'd expected it after the events at his flat. He was seething with rage towards her and worked out several scenarios as to how to get hold of her. He knew who she was married to, but other than that, he had no idea where she lived, where she frequented for shopping or socialising. While his anger was like a boiling cauldron, he was savvy enough to know that even if he could track down Caroline, he was too frightened that she would involve the police. This didn't stop him from conjuring up some of way of taking his revenge, first, he needed to find her address, but this was kept secure, filed and locked away in Jo's secretary's office.

Joash, during his employment at the Health Club, picked up the vibes from Jo that she didn't like him. Joash was well aware of just how popular he was with many of the club members, and that was the mantra that made him fireproof. He'd also cunningly befriended Jo's secretary, getting her onside as one of his admirers, although he had no intention of the relationship going any further than just that. This friendship gave him the reason to occasionally drop by the secretary's office for a cheery chat. They were perfect opportunities to pick up the latest gossip and any titbits on new female members, information that he could store away for future use when looking to extend his personal client base for his supply of recreational drugs. His regular visits to the secretary's office had allowed him to 'sus' out how to obtain the key to the filing cabinet where all the club members' details were kept. The secretary had just one key ring on which she carried her car keys, house key, and keys to the club, including the filing cabinets. Joash laughed to himself as to just how easy it would be to get Caroline's information due to the lack of security. He'd have to get the timings right, though. Through keeping a sharp lookout over time, he'd seen the secretary normally keeping the keys in her coat pocket, which she left hung up in her office. Joash just had to bide his time until the bitch of a General Manager was on one of her management junkets.

The perfect opportunity arose one Friday afternoon during one of the secretary's visits to the swimming pool. Jo had been away all week on a leadership training course, letting it be generally known that she wouldn't be back until the following Monday. As far as a Joash was concerned, she couldn't lead her way out of a paper bag. Joash had a brief break between massage clients and took the opportunity to seek out Caroline's personal information. First, he double-checked the secretary was busy in the pool, once he confirmed it with his own eyes, he headed to the management office suite. As he tiptoed into the secretary's office, he couldn't help but laugh at how easy it was going to be to access the members' details. He quickly retrieved the keys from the secretary's coat pocket, throwing them in the air in mock jubilation, then he gained access to the members' filing cabinet. Joash knew Caroline's surname and that she was married to the millionaire, Richard Hartling of the shipping business, but that was the total of his knowledge about her. The drawers of the cabinet were all neatly labelled in alphabetical order. In less than a minute, he had the correct drawer open and found Caroline's file. He lifted the file from the drawer and created a gap to ensure he placed it back in the correct place. He carefully opened the file, laying the documents on top of the open drawer and experienced a sense of excitement as the wrongdoing thrilled him. Joash was so engrossed in reading the file that he didn't hear the outer office door quietly open.

"Just what in fucks name are you doing Joash?" Jo Aspinall stood staring at him, her hands on her wide hips, legs apart, using the physiological power stance as it had become known in the trendy 'physco babble' language of modern-day management teachings. She was known for her rich use of words when annoyed and of getting straight to the point. She had been on several self-assertive courses and studied the modus operandi of powerful women in politics and business. The sudden interruption had made Joash jump and sent Caroline's file flying off the cabinet. Pages fanned out on the floor, including a paper copy of her cancellation email. Hearing Jo's voice initially filled Joash with shock, but he soon regained his composure and put on his tried and tested servile, humble, down-trodden voice that he had mastered when dealing with authority; this incensed Jo.

He bowed his head in submission, "I'm so sorry Memsahib Manager," he mumbled.

Jo walked across to investigate what Joash was looking at.

"Go into my office now, Joash!" stretching out her right arm and hand in the open palm manner that she had learnt to do on another management course she had attended. Joash obediently slinked off, his head low and arms down his side like a naughty schoolboy. Joash knew how to lay it on thick, playing the downtrodden poor colonial black servant which at the same time perversely displayed a certain amount of belligerent arrogance. Meanwhile, Jo busied herself picking up the fallen file of papers; she observed the name on the file, causing her eyebrows to rise, silently acknowledging her suspicions as to what Joash was up to before putting it away and closing the drawer. She followed him into her office and dropped herself down on to the overlarge executive chair that appeared to envelop her. The huge chair was another recent acquisition aimed at projecting her importance to all that visited her office, again another prop purchased since attending a 'high flyer' management training course. She leaned back in her chair and glared up at Joash; his head was bowed in submission.

She leaned forward and held out her right hand, "Keys!" Joash placed the keys on her palm, sullenly avoiding eye contact.

"Look at me Joash, don't just stand there attempting to look humble and embarrassed, I know you're not really, maybe a little embarrassed at getting caught … Tell me what you were doing?"

Joash had already come up with a story for the General Manager, although doubting, it was a convincing one; nevertheless, he went ahead. Changing tactics he looked up, directly into Jo's eyes, trying to outstare her, "I worried about Mrs. Hartling Memsahib manager, why she left so suddenly, I know Memsahib secretary wouldn't tell so I go myself to find out, I'm so sorry and 'ope it wasn't nuffin I did or said to her, I wanted to say sorry if it was anyfin I'd done. I like Mrs. Hartling; she was a good boss lady."

Jo was at the point of exploding, "Look Joash, will you fucking well stop calling me Memsahib, it doesn't wash with me, and you're an insolent black prick. So come on, cards on the table. I knew something was going on between you and Mrs. Hartling. Now is the time to bare your black soul, make a clean break, and don't give me any more of that Memsahib shit. Do you hear me?"

"You can't talk to me like that Mem…I mean Mrs. Asprinol," deliberately mispronouncing her name, hiding his obvious insolence behind his Kenyan accent.

Jo quietly seethed to herself and continued, "Oh yes I can, this is off the record and not an official hearing, that, you can be rest assured, will come later. So right now, I will speak to you however I fucking want to. Feel free to go to the Directors and see if they believe you over me," she stared defiantly at Joash, finally feeling that she had the upper hand. When Joash didn't reply and just shuffled from one foot to another, she continued, "Comprehendi, Kemo Sabe, to use the language you so enjoy," she spat the words at him.

Joash played along and acted suitably contrite. The last thing he wanted was to lose his well-paid job with the fringe benefits of meeting wealthy ladies. He dropped down onto his knees in front of Jo's desk and started bawling like a child. Although they were crocodile tears, he would do anything to avoid losing his job, even if he had to humiliate himself in the process. His sudden reduction to what appeared to be a gibbering emotional wreck took Jo completely by surprise. None of her much-vaunted management training courses had prepared her for this. Rapidly, she turned from being the 'hard-nosed' bitchy management player to an understanding caring Agony Aunt, astonishing herself in the process.

Joash's plan worked, and Jo reneged on her original wish to fire him. She did give Joash a formal warning but allowed him to keep his job, for which he was truly grateful, and in return, he shut the door on the Caroline Hartling episode.

Over the weeks, Caroline had cleverly managed to hide the surface scars from Richard while they healed; at least that's what she thought. The truth of the matter was that Richard himself was far too busy fighting his demons even to notice what was happening in front of him.

It is said that behind every successful man, there is a good woman, but Richard had lost sight of this. He'd become blind, wrongly assuming that he alone was the product of his success, forgetting that he wouldn't have done it without the support of Caroline.

During those weeks following the final tumulus encounter with Joash, Caroline virtually locked herself away from the world as every time she ventured from her home; she felt sure Joash was out there looking for her. Despite knowing that Joash had no idea as to where she lived or shopped, this didn't help; her nerves were constantly on edge. Caroline was always looking over her shoulder, convinced that he was there in every shadow, a fleeting glance of a dark figure, caused flashbacks that were more painful than the physical injuries she had endured. On several occasions, she had nearly shunted into the rear of a car in front, while her eyes were more focussed on the rear-view mirror, looking for his car rather than concentrating on the road ahead. However, as time passed, the fear within her subsided and she began to feel more secure in the knowledge that her whereabouts were unknown to Joash.

Chapter 5

The British Steamship Company, with Richard at the head, had a very diverse operational base. BSC was the last major British shipping company and the largest employer within the now, and thanks to a combination of ship owner incompetence and Government indifference, virtually defunct British Merchant Navy.

Richard's company was originally a traditional liner trade company, consisting of 26 conventional motor cargo-passenger ships, each with an average tonnage of 20,000 gross tons. These ships plied the old colonial trade routes from the UK to exotic sun-drenched places such as South Africa, India, the Far East, South America, and the Antipodes. In addition to the cargo fleet, there were six Panamax tramping bulkers wandering the seven seas collecting 'ad hoc' cargoes as found for them by the chartering department at the company headquarters not far from the Baltic Exchange in London. Penultimately this impressive deep-sea fleet made up of six-passenger liners employed on the main emigrant trades to Australia and New Zealand. Astutely, and as if he could foretell the future, Richard had predicted the end of the conventional cargo and passenger liner ships seeing the future in cargo containerisation or 'Box Boats' as they became known. Richard's company had six new build container ships join the fleet with two more in the planning stage. These vessels alone would carry their equivalent of his old conventional cargo vessels. While the company passenger liners serving the routes to Australasia, New Zealand, and the Pacific fell victim to the new futuristic liners of the sky; the Boeing 747 Jumbo Jets, his passenger ships from the old routes to the Antipodes had now become established cruise vessels sailing out of Gibraltar. From here, they regularly plied the Mediterranean with the new younger breed of party going 'dress down' generation onboard, desired by those who were looking for more excitement than the Balearic Islands offered.

In the 80's, Richard had seized the opportunity to combine the swiftness of air travel and luxury at sea to transport his cruise passengers by charter jets to Gibraltar instead of Southampton. This was a smart move as it prevented the holidaymakers from having to endure the laborious voyage across the Bay of Biscay with the possibility of storms before reaching the sun. It was a marketing coup and had been an instant success for a previously untapped niche market. His company had not only adapted and expanded but it had also diversified when the opportunity had arisen, moving into the North Sea supply boat business, specialist diving boats and continental Ro/Ro ferries. After this, he made one of his most contentious decisions by acquiring two specialist ships and moving into the transportation of dangerous cargoes. Specifically, the movement of nuclear waste, a relatively secretive trade carried out for the UK Government and the Atomic Energy Authority for which he had built two special nuclear waste carrying ships. Despite the secrecy surrounding this trade, it inevitably drew the attention of 'Greenpeace' who had long been campaigning for the UK to stop this type of transportation. While the attention of Greenpeace did cause some minor disruption to their vessel schedules, the bigger worry was the possibility of attracting terrorists. Greenpeace's antics of unsuccessfully trying to board one of these nuclear waste vessels did give them great exposure on the TV news channels for their cause to the delight of the left-wing press, but it did very little in persuading either the UK Government or Richard's company to give up this lucrative trade. Ironically, however, it did demonstrate to the world what a high-value propaganda target these vessels would make for terrorist organisations.

It was following an attempted hijacking on the high seas of one of these vessels that introduced a complete overall of the company's security procedures and a whole range of new security recommendations were implemented. Richard was a high-risk target. Consequently, his package of emoluments included not only a specially adapted top of the range vehicle but also a string of security and protection measures that included Tim Spinks, the chauffeur and bodyguard. Richard's home had so many security measures added that he jokingly now referred to it as the fort. It was rigged with intruder alarm sensors, cameras and panic buttons in all rooms, corridors and staircases. Everything was linked back to the control room of a multi-national security company that could respond immediately 24 hours a day, 365 days a year, as well as alerting the local police to any alarm activation received. The same company also constantly monitored the movements of his specially adapted Range Rover via satellite tracking, probably giving Richard more security surveillance than the Prime Minister or even the Queen. Even his wife's Mercedes sports car was monitored. Conveniently leaving aside his mistress, it was all this extra security that he partly blamed on his failing marriage. He saw Caroline, his wife of 15 years, as an introverted woman who had put on a brave front when necessarily attending all the functions that went with his executive stardom. Since his move up the corporate ladder to this new position as head of the UK's largest shipping company, Caroline appeared to have withdrawn further into a shell or that's what he thought, but then he was blinded and too preoccupied to notice. Richard secretly blamed her and wrongly felt that Caroline would have been much happier if he had remained the simple shipping and forwarding agent he'd once been, living contentedly in their original three-bed, pre-war, semi-detached house in Godalming, Surrey, along with the steady 9 to 5 routine she appeared to enjoy. Caroline's true feelings were quite to the contrary of Richard's view; she enjoyed the regular upgrade of the sporty cars she drove, the magnificent huge house, the fabulous holidays to exotic locations, and 5-star cruises aboard exclusive ships such as the 'Hebridean Spirit'. Caroline felt that these were her just desserts for having stood by her man for so long while he climbed the towering ladder of success. Although the frequency of these trips had slowly declined with Richard claiming his commitments wouldn't allow for such absences from his office, he wrongly assumed that it would satisfy Caroline with promises of more to come in the future. The bread today, jam tomorrow philosophy.

Due to Richard's huge ego, he was too occupied with his ambitions for his shipping empire, which had become a time-consuming monster, together with his insatiable hunger for more power, that he had failed to notice that he was progressively leaving Caroline on the outer limits of his life. When confronted with challenges, he met them head-on focussed on the battle ahead to the detriment of his relationship with his wife.

Richard faced many challenges running his huge shipping empire, one of which was to propel him to national recognition as a somewhat reluctant hero of capitalism. The challenge came in the shape of a rather militant individual by the name of Greg Cooper. Greg, during his school years, was nicknamed 'Gary' by his mates after the legendary film star of the same name and the name had stuck. Gary was a barely qualified Merchant Navy ship's cook - there was some doubt as to his actual qualifications - the certificate was a dubious photocopy - he claimed he'd lost the original! Despite this, he could certainly cook to an acceptable standard, although to be titled a chef would be stretching the imagination. He was an active Union member and also a long-time associate of a certain high profile London city councillor; together, they were both politically far to the left. Rumoured to have both been at one time Communist party members but expelled for their extremist views! Gary was a total convert to the communist ideal, raised in the 'slums' of East London where his father worked on the docks before the National Dock Labour Scheme, the days when jobs came on a favouritism based system. His mother had slaved away as a home cleaner for a less than generous wealthy ship-owning family, causing her to age and pass away long before her time. Leaving school with no qualifications and brought up within the smell of the Thames, he, like so many of his neighbours drifted away to a life at sea. The fact that his mother had worked for a ship-owner just added coals to the anti-capitalist fire that burned within his psyche. These two parental influences on his life had created in Gary a hatred of all things remotely connected to the free market enterprise system, which he, with a deep-seated desire, fervently set out to defeat. Such was Gary's self-induced indoctrination that he had lost sight of the fact that the communist system in many ways was more brutally class conscientious than any western democracy.

Fate played into the hands of Gary and the Union when incompetent managers allowed one of Richard's new completed super ferries to leave the builders yard, but without sufficient crew to sail her for her maiden voyage. In desperation to crew the vessel quickly, the normal company procedure of selection by interview was abandoned to avoid any humiliating delay bringing the new vessel into service. The outcome was a motley crew, a bunch of misfits and rejects that no other shipping company would employ, amongst these men and women were ruthless militants hell-bent on causing trouble. These were the 'wasters' so ideologically corrupted that they only saw life as an urban jungle in which they had to take what they could, with a simple philosophy in life, to get as much as possible for as little as possible. At this particular time, most of these 'wreckers' came from the seaports of the North West. Over the years this area like the North East and other great sea ports had produced many seafaring heroes, especially during the war, when the lifeblood of Britain had depended on the Merchant Navy to bring supplies across the Atlantic. The unsavoury characters that found their way to 'signing-on' to Richard's latest vessel weren't the descendants of once great British maritime heroes but recent immigrants from diverse ethnic backgrounds. It was this situation that provided a great scenario for Gary Cooper to exploit when he gained a place in the crew on the new super ferry. Hardly had the ship entered service, and by using 'Bully Boy' tactics, Gary ensured that some of the more militant members of the new crew got elected on to the local port council. Richard, being a 'people person,' had developed a caring empire, making his organisation the acceptable face of capitalism. He had pioneered the introduction of a local port council with elected representatives from his workforce to meet management regularly; this embodied his consultative style of leadership. When his diary commitments allowed, Richard would attend these meetings.

His ethos had been past down the management chain right through to the officers and crews that ran his ships. Unfortunately, his style of management by consultation wasn't liked by some in the Seaman's Union whose top echelon riddled with men and women who had their own communistic agenda and wanted to see everything run by the incumbent left-wing Labour Government. They wanted nationalisation and to achieve these ends, they needed to show that capitalisation and private companies didn't work. Consequently, they enlisted the militant element led by Gary Cooper. It wasn't long before the port council, now saturated by the militants, started making unrealistic demands. The new super jumbo ferry was an instant success with both the travelling public and hauliers alike, bringing a steady and hefty revenue stream, a success story that was soon exploited by the militants. The success of this new service was so great that the last thing the local management wanted was a stoppage; therefore they constantly gave in to the more outrageous demands of the Port Council. Gary Cooper was one of the puppet masters behind the council members, controlling each move to the ultimate aim, to find a way to manipulate a strike of such gigantic proportions that it would bring down the new service. They held a fervent and misjudged hope that it would put the company in such a mess that a lifeline of nationalisation was the only way out. Nothing could have been further from reality as Ministers had their hands full coping with a struggling fiscal policy and IMF loans to fund an expansive social welfare programme, hence they did not want anything to do with nationalising a shipping company.

Creating mayhem and chaos, the crew of the new vessel continually demanded more pay and reduced working hours; it appeared that they were asking to be paid for turning up and reporting for work, anything else, such as actually working, was to attract even further ludicrous remuneration! To the basic pay was added, speed money, extra duty pay compensation for overtime yet then some overtime was still allowed, Sunday at sea allowance, missed meals allowance, and so on, this list of extras doubled each crew members already very lucrative basic pay. Despite lots of hand wringing and teeth gnashing by Richard's local management, they capitulated as they wanted to keep the service running at all costs. It all came to a head on an occasion just as the vessel was preparing for sea; the Union Convenor stormed onto the navigation bridge delivering an ultimatum to the Captain informing him that the crew was refusing to sail until payment of new recent demand was made. It was the 23:00 hours sailing when this occurred, the ship was full to the brim with cars, coaches and lorries and people looking forward to their annual 'getaway'. Already tired and stressed local managers were dragged from their beds to solve the latest impasse readily caving into these extraordinary demands to allow the vessel to sail that night. It was the last straw as local managers realised that finally, the cat and mouse game to keep the service running at all costs was at an end. Now developing some backbone, it was too little too late, and the militants having tasted the sweetness of success had the upper hand, pushing for more and creating a recipe for a strike.

It is proclaimed, that the person at the top of a large organisation only gets to know five percent of what is going on at the lower levels. One of the main problems running a large empire is keeping an eye on the small detail. Incompetent managers lower down the line can make bad decisions that are not immediately apparent. The result of this management phenomenon had gone unnoticed so the crewing of the new ship, in addition to the shipboard and port councils, were now riddled with diligent militants. When the showdown came, it started on his ferry fleet service, ironically crewed by the highest-paid personnel in Richard's shipping operation. It was a paradox that the personnel onboard the ferries who, along with their already high pay, enjoyed the additional luxury of seeing their families more than those that worked aboard his Foreign Service passenger/cargo fleet. The strike needed to be halted in its tracks before it spread to his other vessels and what could have been devastating for his shipping empire. Thus, Richard took the decision to step in and personally called the bluff of the striking seaman. It was a huge gamble taking the Seaman's Union 'head-on', but accepting their demands was, in his opinion, not an option. It was a gamble he had to take because to give in would have meant he'd lose the battle before it had even started, he would have lost everything, including his company and his standing in the maritime world. Richard did win the costly industrial war and war it was. Thankfully it didn't spread to his deep-sea fleet. Amongst the ferry crews, there were many reasonable seamen with whom he was able to negotiate. The euphoria that surrounded the breaking of the strike prompted Richard's publicist to advocate that he should fly out to the continent, where one of his ferry vessels had been strikebound and sail with her back into Dover, standing proudly on top of the navigation bridge in a manner that was dubbed the 'Nelson Touch'. He posed for National newspaper photographers who were there to witness the service starting up again; they interviewed both the victorious management as well as strikers; both sides claiming victory, this being newsworthy enough to be flashed worldwide.

Since that day, Richard had become a legend in his lifetime, and a darling of the City, ironic as secretly in Richard's heart he was a socialist, but his business brain remained firmly a capitalist.

Chapter 6

Richard's company vehicle was a top specification Range Rover which, in addition to being kept in pristine condition, was also a very special limited edition with bulletproof glass and extra armour plating to the underside. The upper bodywork and roof had been lined with the new lightweight Kevlar, widely used in the manufacture of flak vests for military and police forces. After production, the powerful 6 litre engine Range Rover went to a custom bodywork engineering company in the Midlands to be modified. The company had built up a lucrative business supplying such modified vehicles to a list of impressive clients ranging from film stars to Middle Eastern despots and criminal gang bosses. This extraordinary machine was competently driven by an ex Metropolitan Police officer, Tim Spinks. Tim was totally at ease with its raw power, having passed the arduous Metropolitan Police Advanced driving course. He was also an ex-Special Forces veteran of the Royal Marines and more recently in the secretive and clandestine Special Boat Service.

Back in 1980, Tim was on secondment from the SBS at Chivenor to Pagoda Troop, 'B' Squadron of the 22nd Special Air Service Regiment based at Hereford, when the call came in that terrorists had seized the Iranian Embassy. Tim and his colleagues were soon speeding to London in innocent-looking home removal vans. Once the operation had been accomplished with all but one of the terrorists eliminated, they were sitting, drinking tea in their make-shift forward operating base watching their exploits televised around the world. Never before had the United Kingdom's secret warriors been seen in action in the raw, many didn't even believe they existed; this event unavoidably exposed them to the media. As the dramatic conclusion to the siege unfolded, there was complete astonishment and confusion amongst the many reporters who watched the extraordinary events resulting in them making wild guesses as to who were the black-clad figures making an assault on the building. Many reporters assumed they were some hitherto unknown elite branch of the police. Others acknowledged that the then-fledgling police firearms units were laughingly using WWII bolt action Lee Enfield rifles; highly effective weapons on the battlefields of World War II for open landscape warfare but no match for the close combat fighting in the confines of the Embassy. It was sometime after the siege that the speculation was answered by the Commissioner of the Metropolitan Police, David McNee;

he announced that he had, when all other options had been exhausted and the killing of hostages started, handed jurisdiction over to the British Army and that it was members of the clandestine Special Air Service Regiment who had carried out the operation of storming the Embassy.

Most of the British public thought that the SAS was disbanded at the end of the Second World War. From that moment on, the SAS became more than just a legend; they were heroes of the civilised western world. At the meeting with the troops after the event, they enjoyed a congratulatory cup of tea, a *'brew'* in military language, along with Maggie Thatcher and the Home Secretary Willie Whitelaw at their makeshift forward operating base not far from the Embassy battleground. While the Prime Minister had bathed in their glory and calling them 'her boys,' the Home Secretary had gone around the room shaking everyone's hand with his renown double-clutch, his jowls like a bulldog quivering with excitement and his voice breaking with emotion as he repeatedly had, with a great sense of relief, thanked each soldier individually for doing such a splendid job. The Home Secretary had been very aware of the possible consequences had it all gone wrong, as he was the one who had pushed for the use of the Army. A disastrous outcome would have ended his career and undoubtedly brought about the fall of the Government. Predictably in the aftermath, well after the euphoria of the moment had past, the inevitable human rights left-wing liberals had come crawling out of the woodwork, questioning as to the legality of using the military in this situation. They then demanded a public enquiry as to why the British Military had been so devastatingly and brutally used on civilians, as the terrorists were being called, their murderous role invading the embassy casually overlooked by these zealots. It was as if these 'do-gooders' were, in some perverse way, jealous that the SAS had been seen to be what they are, thoroughly dedicated and professional soldiers displaying that good can overcome evil. However, Britain being a civilised democratic society had procedures and laws. It was the one remaining terrorist who, held on remand, was eventually brought before the courts and charged with terrorism. Here, the events were thoroughly scrutinised in front of all the interested parties which included; police, relatives of those involved, the Army's Legal Services Branch on behalf of the troopers and of course journalists for all the national dailies along with a collection from overseas where the notoriety of the SAS had now spread. The happenings of Princess Gate were aired in open court; the identity of the soldiers involved remained a secret, so they gave their evidence from behind a screen. Once again,

'Guardian' reading metropolitan elite, screamed 'foul', demanding what they termed as 'Government's Assassins should be exposed for the whole world to see'. Thankfully, for the SAS troopers and their families, these protests fell on deaf ears.

So it was Tim, as one of the *'Band of Brothers'*, who was called to give evidence as a prosecution witness in support of the charges against the one remaining terrorist. As trooper 'C' he was asked by the prosecution counsel to give an account of what he had personally done and seen. Tim expertly explained his part as schooled to do by the Regiment's legal team,

"Sir, I, along with Troopers A B & D, was dropped on the roof by helicopter at zero hour. We abseiled down the rear of the building and entered through the windows at level three, as per the brief. Then on to the main landing with access to the rooms holding the hostages. After splitting into two, we started a room clearance operation, again as briefed. Trooper D kicked open the door of room 3."

To avoid being exposed from behind the curtained witness box, Tim used a laser pen to point at a large chart plan of the Embassy, displayed in the courtroom.

"On entering this room, I observed a gunman holding what I clearly identified as an automatic handgun, similar to a British Army issue Browning automatic...He was brandishing it recklessly, and in the general direction of a crowd of civvies sitting huddled on the floor, I believed these to be the hostages. There was a lot of panic, hysteria and crying amongst the group, so I had to shout out, *'I'm British Army, drop your weapon and get down on your knees with your hands on your head.'* By his actions, the man with the gun was clearly highly agitated. He then, in a threatening manner, turned the weapon in my direction, and I feared he was about to shoot, so I had only a split second to decide what my reaction would be. I gave him a double-tap."

Tim continued explaining the technicalities of his involvement in the events and how the hostages were released into the care of the police, and then it was the turn of the Defence Counsel to question him. The Counsel for the defence stood up, clutching the left lapel of his robe, his eyes peering over half-moon glasses as he looked around the courtroom as if to assure he had everyone's attention for his performance that was about to begin. His wig was sitting atop his head, slightly crooked, giving an air of indifference as if worn under protest, making a statement by way of a silent rebuke against an outmoded tradition in an attempt to demonstrate the wearing of such apparel was out of place in a modern courtroom.

He covered his mouth with his hand as he cleared his throat unnecessarily before he started, "Ahem... Trooper C, if you please," again, he looked around the room, ensuring everyone was watching and waiting in anticipation that he was about to expose some shocking anomalies in Tim's evidence. "Double-tap soldier C? Pray, for the less enlightened of us into the 'gun-ho' tactics of the British Army, what exactly does that mean?"

This brought the Counsel for the army leaping to his feet, "My Lord, I object to the accusation and the emotive words used by my learned friend, these young men are highly disciplined, professional soldiers, not some 'gun-ho' renegade cowboy outfit that my learned friend is implying!"

"Yes, yes, yes, quite so," said the Judge agreeing with Counsel for the Army, then from his lofty perch, he turned, squinting over his spectacles, to look down onto the court stenographer.

"Have those words 'gun-ho' removed from the record," then, looking back at the courtroom and the two counsels, the Judge continued, "but, I for one, am not familiar with the expression 'double-tap' and I would like to hear Trooper C's interpretation," he turned to look at Trooper C, "Well young man?"

"Yes, Ma' Lord, it means discharging my weapon twice in quick succession."

The Judge nodded, acknowledging the soldiers reply and then looked across at the counsel before making notes on his legal pad with his stylish Mont Blanc pen and continued, "There you have your simple answer, now pray continue and let's avoid any more emotive words, this is a very serious business we are dealing with."

The defence counsel carried on, "Ahem, mmm...yes quite, thank you for pointing that out, Ma' Lord, indeed this is a very serious matter," he turned to focus on Trooper C, "However, I put it to you, that this is not quite exactly what happened, is it?"

"Yes sir," came the crisp, clipped reply with typical military disciplined authority.

"No, it is not, Soldier C, I put it to you that what in fact happened is that you burst into the room in a frenzy of gun - "

The counsel for the Regiment was on his feet in an instant, but the Judge was having none of it and raised his hand indicating to the counsel for the

Army in a silent acknowledgement that he would deal with the transgression, "Now I've given my ruling that those words are not to be used."

"Yes, of course, Ma'lord, please I beg yours and the court's forgiveness at my stupidity," he mumbled apologetically but with the slight smirk on his hawk-like face, knowing exactly what he was doing and how his words had delivered the effect he wanted them to; those words 'gun ho' would be leaping out of every left-wing national daily within hours, most probably every national newspaper around the world.

"As I was saying, I believe you burst into the room with adrenaline-pumping macho excitement, saw the man with the gun, and said something along the lines of ..."

He paused, referring to his briefing papers on his lectern and again turned to address the courtroom for a dramatic effect before reading aloud, "Yes, along the lines of *'Good night sooty, you're fucking history'* and then proceeded to shoot him quite unnecessarily several times."

The resulting uproar took several moments to be subdued by the banging of the Judge's gavel, followed by a strict rebuke from the Judge to the court in general, threatening to clear the public gallery if there were any more outbursts.

Finally, able to give his answer to a now quietened courtroom, Tim replied, "No, Sir, it was as I said," steadfastly sticking to his story.

Chapter 7

Tim, upon leaving the Royal Marines but still looking for a degree of excitement, joined the Metropolitan Police service. He had the makings of an excellent police officer and should have risen quickly through the ranks, despite being in his thirties. However, this was not the case after a particularly nasty piece of work, claiming to be a member of the human race, had been 'sorted' as military terminology would put it. The individual was one of the new and emerging dangerous breed of the chemical generation, and who, while on a particular nasty ecstasy trip, burgled a small housing association bungalow and had beaten up the little old lady occupant who had disturbed him. Coincidently, this happened to be in the area where Tim was the Community Beat Police Constable. The home of the lady in question was one of Tim's favourite tea stops on his patch; consequently, he had witnessed at first hand the results of the attack; Tim had cried for the first time since his childhood. As a dedicated police officer, Tim had been astonished that many such miscreants were given lenient treatment by the 'wimpish' legal class who appeared to be so prevalent within the British Judicial system. In these days of changing times, offenders were treated like victims rather than criminals – the spineless, privileged metropolitan politically correct elite had seen to that. So, totally out of character, Tim had taken the law into his own hands. However, immediately after carrying out the emotionally charged retribution, his conscience got the better of him, and full of remorse, he tendered his resignation. He felt he had disgraced his uniform and the police service. Fortunately, being the true professional, Tim had covered his tracks well.

The surgically brutal attack had been so unexpected during one of the druggie's ecstasy trips that when he woke in hospital, he couldn't remember a thing. The thug sustained a broken collar bone, broken arm and broken leg. He would never walk again without a limp, in Tim's mind, this equated to social justice as this particular miscreant wouldn't have the agility to break into old folks' houses ever again. However, ironically, the very Social Service that had so failed the young man during his drug-taking years would now swing into action and take care of him to the grave, the zany world of a civilised society.

Not a word of what Tim had done entered either the public or police domain. Tim's peers and colleagues begged him not to resign. Although some did secretly suspect his reasons for going, nothing was ever said, as it was, after all, only rumours. What troubled Tim, was the strength of his emotions, he knew he could have easily gone on beating the boy until his last breath. He was angry that this type of filth was beginning to fill the streets. He was worried that he would not always be able to control his anger. The liberal-minded Government made excuses for these anti-social crimes and through the new style of government spin, endeavoured to make society accept that it was at fault for producing this new breed of criminal.

So once again, Tim had found himself unemployed with only his military pension to live on and no idea what to do next. He had watched a fictional TV series called 'Paras' created by an award-winning author. It was about five friends from the Parachute Regiment who, having been in the Army all their working lives, suddenly found their services dispensed with by the Government who wanted to make massive defence cuts for the Treasury. The big question was, 'could they hack it in civvy street?' Tim found himself wondering if he would end up a criminal like one of the guys in 'Paras' who wasn't able to adapt to life outside the military family. It was only days following this program that he'd spotted an advert in one of the national broadsheets marketing training courses in 'Body Guarding and Lifestyle Management'. Bodyguarding he knew he could do, but lifestyle management sounded rather like babysitting 'posh totty'. His curiosity took over and he found himself going along to the open evening, held in a superior West End London Hotel.

It was a wild, wet and windy night and with his head bowed, and collar pulled up in a vain attempt to keep the rain from finding its way down his neck, Tim dwelled on the fact that the recruitment seminar was being held in one of London's top hotels. The hotel at least gave it some semblance of credibility, but Tim wondered if it was just a front for recruiting mercenaries. If that were the case, he'd have nothing to do with it, mercenaries usually meant, with a few exceptions, all the 'dropouts' and 'dead beats' that couldn't hack it in the real Army. In Tim's view, mercenaries came in various forms, ranging from the 'Psychos' who loved killing and couldn't adjust to 'civvy' street, to the military rejects and finally to wannabe soldiers looking for some highly-paid adventure.

The hotel was lit up; it was Christmas, even outside on Park Lane; a thousand tiny lights twinkled on every tree. Tim entered the warm, cosy atmosphere of the hotel's huge reception hall. His face momentarily flushed from the sudden rise in temperature compared to the bitter cold outside. Not seeing any obvious signs to the seminar, he wandered over to the reception to be greeted by an attractive brunette sporting a very nice cleavage. Her slightly dark complexion, and lovely round moonlike face, was topped with a perfectly groomed trendy bob-cut hairstyle. The dark blue uniform clung seductively to her curvaceous body; the white flowery blouse cut just low enough to expose the top of her perfectly rounded breasts, only just bordering on the acceptable for such a prestigious hotel.

Tim gave her what he described as a 'slow burn,' a tantalising smile he had perfected over time and reserved specifically for when trying to impress the fairer sex.

"Excuse me. I'm looking for a bodyguarding recruitment seminar."

Her face appeared to light up as she smiled at Tim, showing off her beautiful cosmetically enhanced teeth. Tim thought she resembled a porcelain china doll.

"Hello," she beamed, "Name please?"

"Tim. Tim Spinks."

"Thank you Mr Spinks, Yes, it is on the first floor, in the Connaught Conference room. The Colonel running the show, that's how he asked to be addressed," she said rather coyly before continuing, "he didn't want any overt advertising and I can see why, what with the number that appear to have been turned away, I hope you have more luck than some of those," she indicated turning up her nose at two loud young men who were coming down the grand staircase. Tim followed the receptionist's gaze, observing two thuggish looking, tattooed skinheads, sporting some strange facial jewellery, making a loud exit as they staggered across the cavernous entrance hall towards the revolving doors. Even dressed in suits, their attempt at looking presentable had obviously failed; tattoos peered above their collars, all-around their necks. Of the two men, one was skinny but wiry while the other, although thickly built, was stout and slightly taller – the smartly tailored suit couldn't hide the visceral fat of his expanding stomach. Their departure was loud and exhibitionist, obviously intended, looking to make as much noise as possible in an attempt to disturb the surrounding quietness and divinity of the hotel lobby as they staggered passed.

The bigger of the two thugs with the shaved head was Eddie Todd. Eddie was the product of an East End, dysfunctional gangster family, consistently beaten by his father who dished out similar treatment to his mother. Eddie had grown up a 'hard man' and with little respect for the female species. Perhaps it was his father's way of making him tough to face life head-on, but Eddie would never be given a chance to ask him this as his mother had killed his father years ago. She had taken one beating too many and one night, when Eddie's father came home drunk, she took a kitchen carving knife to his father's throat as he lay in bed snoring. Naturally, she went to prison for murder and Eddie was left to fend for himself. East Enders, being of the stock that stood up to Hitler's bombers and the blitz, rallied round and helped Eddie, an only child, unofficially adopting him into the East End extended family. An easy solution for Social Services.

From an early age, Eddie had established himself as a fearsome fighter, taking on all comers in the school playground, even including some girls as in many cases they were harder than the boys. Several girls were attracted to Eddie's apparent raw masculinity, and he soon had quite a following of female friends. However, as Eddie developed through his teenage years, he realised that while most of his peer group were talking about chasing girls and what was known as gaslighting with them, having a fuck up against a wall down a dark alley, he had no interest. The truth finally dawned on Eddie when a new, particularly attractive boy started at his school. Eddie, far from his normal routine of picking a fight with the newcomer to show him who was the 'boss', felt some strange urges completely alien to him and couldn't bring himself to harm the new boy. From that moment, Eddie realised he was a homosexual, known as a *'ponce'* in the East End and ever since then, he had hidden his desires. He despised himself to such an extent that he had started self-harming. The realisation that he was gay created such a maelstrom of emotions that it resulted in the development of nature so violent that no openly gay person whom he came into contact with was safe, and that applied to lesbians as well. He just couldn't come to terms with the fact that he was different.

Eddie left school early, much to the relief of his teachers and Headmaster, without any academic qualifications; hence there was very little work available other than stacking shelves in the local supermarket. He did the shifts and rewarded himself with just enough money to occasionally frequent the seedy, grotty back street clubs where the guys and girls were cheap, but the booze was expensive. One night, luck came into play when Eddie got into a fight with a local gang face. Unbeknown to Eddie, the face had come to this particular club to collect his routine protection wedge. However, this particular enforcer hadn't been doing a very good job of late and the club's owner was 'pissed off' with paying for a protection service he wasn't getting. The club owner had been there that night and witnessed Eddie easily despatch the enforcer; he immediately offered Eddie a job as the new club protector. The job would give Eddie a weekly wage more than he could earn in a month with overtime at the supermarket, plus fringe benefits, such as meals and a pick of the girls, which of course he never accepted.

Overnight, Eddie went from a shelf stacker to a face to be reckoned with as head of security at the club. After a couple of attempts by the previous protection gang to re-establish their authority failed, he found himself indispensable to his new employer. Perhaps it was delusions of grandeur at wearing a suit, and now a person to whom people looked up to, that made him want something more than working in the club. When he saw the advertisement in the London Evening News looking for 'Lifestyle Managers,' Eddie imagined himself in this role, probably driving a flash car and protecting some celebrity, moving him out of the East End seedy club scene. During his time at the club, Eddie had befriended a young down and out lad rather like adopting a stray dog. One evening, Eddie had discovered the lad sleeping rough behind the club waste bins a considerable shelter he had constructed between the bins and the fire escape. Eddie couldn't figure how he hadn't discovered the hideaway sooner, but by then Eddie was a suit and considered ferreting around waste bins beneath him. It was pure chance that he stumbled on the young lad's makeshift home. The young lad, called Lennie, orphaned at a very young age and another product of a failed social system.

Lennie, was what would be described as a delicate person, although not gay in the true sense, but a slightly effeminate male with a boyish face, fair hair, blue eyes, an expressionless face and pasty complexion. Also, sadly, he was a dope head, his empty eyes that were never still, constantly flickered from side to side, fearing everything that was going on around him. Although now in his 20's, he would need to wait three days without shaving to have anything resembling a 5 o'clock shadow. Having been constantly bullied at school, it was ironic that Lennie now found himself under the wing of Eddie Todd - a notorious bully. When Eddie first discovered Lennie, he would have under normal circumstances seen Lennie on his way, but his latent gay tendencies made him decide otherwise. Although Eddie didn't allow his feelings to show, he accepted Lennie like a puppy, and that's exactly what Lennie turned into, Eddie's loyal dog that would do anything to please his master. In return, Lennie gained a warm place to stay, food in his belly and a sort of normality that had evaded him throughout his formative years.

Consequently, Lennie found himself accompanying Eddie on the night he came up against Tim Spinks in this luxurious hotel. Eddie had many flaws in his character, yet despite the world in which he now lived, riddled with drugs and addicts, he had stayed well away from both consumption and dealing. However, he had developed a distinct liking for expensive Napoleon brandy, which he could now easily afford. Not that he would drink at work, he always stayed strictly sober while working his shift, and in return, his boss at the club was more than happy for Eddie to spend his nights off at the bar. It made the club owner feel safe having Eddie around, Eddie would stay because he had nowhere else to go.

On the day of the interviews for potential 'Lifestyle Managers', Eddie, along with Lennie, turned up at the hotel having become tanked-up on brandy at the club beforehand. Of course, the whole idea was doomed to failure from the start. Eddie, in his misguided, naïve mind, had thought that the two Colonels were looking for hard men that lived by their fists. Hard men yes, hard men with a great degree of discipline and restraint, not street hooligans like Eddie, no matter what street cred he'd gained in clubland. Having been politely shown the door by one of the two Colonels, Eddie was enraged. He saw them both as upper class 'posh twits' looking down on him as if he was scum. When told the interview was over before it had even started, Eddie was so furious that he attempted throwing a fist. He completely missed his target, the chin of one of the Colonels, quickly finding himself in a quarter nelson hold, being propelled through the conference room door and flung unceremoniously into the corridor where he was deposited at the feet of Lennie who had been trying to chat up the attractive girl on the adjacent temporary desk. Picking himself up and trying to regain his dented dignity, he staggered off to the staircase, assisted by Lennie.

The young lady at this desk was in the employ of the two Colonels whom Tim was about to meet and she was soon on her feet ready to go to the assistance of the Colonel ejecting Eddie from the room. Although with the looks about her of a model in a cosmetic commercial, this was only skin deep. Beneath this facade, she was as hard as nails ex-Royal Navy Petty Officer Physical Training Instructor and unarmed combat teacher to the Royal Marines. However, on this occasion, her services were not required. Eddie being the type of person he was, realised he was no match for the Colonel who was still standing in the corridor. Eddie just wanted to get away as quickly as possible. Eddie's next target for revenge was to be the Front of House receptionist on the ground floor and where he, unfortunately for him, also met Tim Spinks. Eddie saw the receptionist look across at him with a disgusted expression on her face, he staggered over towards the highly polished, mahogany, craftsman made wooden reception desk, "What the fuck are you looking at daaarlin," he angrily voiced, his crucifix shaped earrings quivered on his ears, his head was so bald that it sparkled like polished wood in the reflection of the overhead lighting, the rear of his skull sporting a huge tattooed swastika. Upon reaching the reception, Eddie rudely brushed past Tim, a big mistake. It was apparent from the alcoholic, hazy, sickly smell surrounding him like a cloud, that logic had flown the nest of this birdbrain. Tim's immediate thought was that if this character's brain was dynamite, then there wouldn't be enough to blow the skin off a rice pudding. Leaning even further over the front desk, Eddie leered at the brunette receptionist, to which she instinctively took a step back, turning up her nose and wafting her hand in front of her face in an attempt to dilute the awful alcoholic odour that emanated from him.

"Well you fuckin' posh slag, what's your problem?" The words had hardly left Eddie's mouth when Tim, with the ease and grace, hit Eddie in a style of unarmed combat termed 'jack slapping'. Tim let fly with a vicious elbow jab to Eddie's throat that completely pole axed him, leaving him writhing on the floor, gagging for breath. Lennie momentarily froze to the spot in terror, having seen his hard case friend and protector so easily and swiftly despatched to the floor. Lennie wasn't quite sure what to do until Tim ordered him, "Get this piece of dog turd out of here fast sonny, you might want to stop off at the hospital pronto before he chokes to death."

Lennie didn't need any more encouragement and was soon helping Eddie up, dragging, stumbling, and gasping for air. They both left the premises but not before the top-hatted doorman and the concierge made a timely entrance from the front doorstep of the hotel, coming to the rescue.

"Where the heck were you two a minute ago?" said Tim calmly, before turning to the astonished, and very grateful, receptionist, "Thank you for directions to the seminar."

The doorman aided Eddie and Lennie out into the cold night air. While the concierge, not wanting Eddie or Lennie anywhere near the hotel, went over and asked the receptionist to call for an ambulance, to get rid of the injured thug pronto rather than have him collapsing outside causing a scene. This was an exclusive hotel after all. The receptionist hardly registered the concierge's request; lost in admiration at Tim's quick but calm attitude, all she could think about was how 'knicker dropping gorgeous' he was. "Now there's a real man I would love to know," she whispered to herself.

Tim ascended the stairs two at a time as if floating, eager to get to the meeting and see what was on offer. He soon found the Connaught rooms on the first floor, again greeted by the young lady sitting behind a desk. Introducing herself, she checked his name off a list, "You're early for your appointment, but as nobody else is waiting, you can go straight in, just knock on the door," she indicated in the direction of the large door marked 'Connaught'. Tim knocked, and after hearing the command from inside, entered. In the room were two men sitting on large comfortable chairs, one, a Colonel John Connolly immediately rose and extended his hand to welcome Tim with a big smile on his face. John Connolly was tall, clean-shaven with a permanent, if somewhat sloping smile, which gave the appearance that he was talking out of the side of his mouth. The other, a broad, stocky man, also stood up, a round but chiselled featured face with the craggy look of a military veteran sporting a close shaved head, belying what would be a full head of grey hair had it been allowed to grow.

"Tim, good to see you again, seeing your name was on the list I was hoping it was you and not some other Tim Spinks," his smile grew, "I reiterate that it's really good to see you again." He pumped Tim's hand enthusiastically.

"So, it is you Colonel, when the receptionist referred to the two Colonels upstairs, I smiled to myself at first, thinking 'yeah right, it's bound to be some squaddie rejects putting on a show,' but your name Sir, well, that has made my expectations rocket."

"Yes Tim, it really is me, and more about that later, but first let me introduce you to my partner in this venture, Bernard Campbell an ex Para."

On cue, Bernard also greeted Tim with the same amount of enthusiasm.

"Hello Tim, welcome," Bernard shook Tim's hand with a vice-like grip, "In my case, though it's only a half Colonel I'm afraid."

"Well a cherry berry," said Tim with a broad grin, "and a Lieutenant Colonel will do fine Sir, at least I now know it is a 'kosher 'outfit, whatever you are running."

"Absolutely Tim, but I usually manage to teach you cabbage hats a thing or two."

The constant friendly rivalry between the two elite units is legendary. The only difference for the uninitiated is the fact that the Parachute Regiment is part of the British Army, but the Royal Marines are sea soldiers and hence come under the auspices of the Admiralty, and they hate being referred to as Army. The Para's are known as 'Cherry berries', because of their uniform red berets, the Royal Marines known as 'Cabbage hats' as their uniform berets are green. These nick names originated from both regiments' service in Northern Ireland.

"Take a seat Tim," the Colonel indicated to one of several comfortable leather chairs situated around the large coffee table in the centre of the room, "Coffee?" he enquired as he strolled to a dining table in the corner of the room laid out with various refreshments.

"Yes, thank you Sir, coffee, white one sugar."

"Let's forget the Sir, shall we?"

The Colonel busied himself pouring coffee for the three of them before speaking, "I heard from my assistant on the desk outside that there was a bit of commotion in the lobby, possibly with the tattooed yard dogs we turned away just before you arrived. Did you, by any chance get involved with them Tim?"

"You could say I helped them on their way...they were mouthing off at the very pretty receptionist. I just reminded one of them about their manners, after which they seemed to be in a rush to leave."

"Well done Tim, beggars belief that it's crap like that, that some of our wonderful master's say we should take into the Army to supposedly sort them out," he chuckled. Returning to the centre of the room and laying coffee down on the table, the Colonel took a seat opposite Tim alongside his partner Bernard Campbell.

"Okay Tim your call; now let's talk business."

The three of them soon agreed that Tim, with his background, would need very little training apart from some areas of the finer points of 'Lifestyle Management'. Tim was a highly marketable resource and both Colonels had already made mental notes as to several very lucrative contracts that would be ideally suited to such a man. They were naturally very pleased when Tim signed up to join their organisation. From that initial meeting, Tim enjoyed working with them both in a training role and mentoring some of the other applicants into the world of close protection duties. Eventually, he had begun work on his first and lucrative assignment as 'Body Guard and Lifestyle Manager' to the successful Richard Hartling, Chairman and Managing Director of the British Steamship Company.

Chapter 8

Sitting in the luxuriously comfortable rear leather seats of the cruising Range Rover, Richard put aside his thoughts about his marriage and mused over the forthcoming buy-out of the Beaumont Company. Although Richard was tall, the rear seating of the Range Rover easily accommodated his once athletic frame.

Tastefully hidden in the walnut facia of the Range Rover sat a special codex UHF radio light and button, which allowed immediate communication with the security company headquarters. Richard noticed the light blink before Tim, the chauffeur and bodyguard, swiftly pressed the button, disabling the light and connecting a call via a small earpiece. Using the latest Bluetooth cordless technology, Tim could privately converse with the Ops room without taking either of his hands off the wheel. Richard's curiosity took over; he leaned forward to acquire Tim's attention, "What is it Tim, is there a problem?"

"No Sir, just the Ops room warning me of some traffic congestion ahead. They have suggested an alternative route for us this morning," he answered confidently.

Richard sat back in his seat, "Very good."

"Sir," came the crisp, polite reply.

The private security company that Tim joined, following his meeting with the two Colonels, enjoyed global reach with a client list of some of the wealthiest people on planet earth. True to its image and promise, it provided 24-hour surveillance for its Principals, as their clients were called. As a consequence of modern technology, an added service provided by the company was to constantly monitor traffic flow throughout the city. The security company could route their clients away from areas of congestion, and more importantly, possible danger.

Such danger could manifest itself anywhere and at any time, thus this morning following Richard's Range Rover, but struggling to maintain a discreet distance in the heavy traffic, was a red saloon MG Rover. Its darkened windows concealed the occupants and their Kalashnikov rifles. The car had been stolen in Hull some weeks ago and stored in a cheap back street lock up. Its identity cloned with a similar car recently damaged beyond economical repair; with the incident still under investigation, the car was yet to be officially written off by the DVLA. Consequently, the MG would pass any casual traffic police roadside check. This group of men in the car were ruthless, out of work Renaissance IRA, or RIRA for short. A few months before, they were nearly caught occupying a similar cloned car during a roadside check one quiet Sunday morning in rural Yorkshire – they had to coldly eliminate a part-time special constable to get out of the situation. This taught them that the next time they used a stolen car they should make doubly sure it would pass any routine police checks. This intricate planning was the type carried out by the IRA, learned through years of fighting a terrorist war against the British establishment. Only now, these tricks of the terrorist trade were being made use of by rogue elements of the IRA, in this case, the Renaissance IRA, a fanatical group that didn't agree with the Good Friday Agreement, they saw it as surrendering to the Colonial power of the Brits. They still considered Britain to be an occupying force in the North of Ireland.

This group, cocooned in the red MG Rover, intended to carry out an audacious, and if necessary violent, kidnap of Richard Hartling. Running short of money to fund their ongoing fight, their plan was to seize him during the early morning rush hour; because of the surprise and swiftness of their attack, they expected to be miles away from the scene before anyone would be alerted. Within 30 minutes, they had planned to have Richard smuggled aboard a small, scrappy, Panamanian registered freighter due to depart from the now disused paper mill wharf just downstream from the Pool of London. The freighter bound for Cork would take a slight detour to a small remote fishing village on the Dingle Peninsular, where Richard would be kept until the ransom had been paid. Despite having planned the operation for weeks, the group's intelligence gathering proved to be amateurish and shoddy as it had not made them aware of the satellite technology that constantly tracked Richard's Range Rover. When the Range Rover suddenly took a different route, the luck of the Irish was not with them.

"Noore Mick that was a right foock up then, why didn't the bleeder go his usual foocking route taday?" said the driver to his front seat passenger Mick Robbins, an ex IRA planner apprehensively cradling his Kalashnikov in his lap.

"Ba Jasus I don't foocking know."

"Weel now faar foocks sake will you just calm down you two," said Stuart Maloney, the man in charge of the set-up, calmly sat in the rear of the vehicle taking a hefty drag on a cigarette, filling the car with blue acrid smoke as he exhaled with a slight cough.

"Tis not to be, but the Good Lord will shine down on us, and it will come another day to be sure. Now will you get us the foock out of 'ere and away to the safe 'ouse."

The three armed men, this time, denied their target as the Range Rover drove away from the pre-planned attack area. It would have been a daring kidnap in broad daylight, the RIRA calling card being audacity and aggression.

Richard smiled to himself at the amount of surveillance his position subjected him to; he was hardly ever alone during the day except when using the bathroom. Who would have thought that this once simple shipping clerk would have arrived into the privileged world that normally only came with celebrity status? He left the thoughts of the day ahead, as his mind took him back over the previous evening. He had attended a rather boring Chamber of Shipping dinner with an awful and disastrous after-dinner speaker. Escaping the evening early, he'd looked for some relief and, against his better judgement, went to the other woman in his life, Katrina Sinclair - his mistress. Though he had only intended to stay for a short while, after an exhausting day and tedious evening, but he ended up staying with her longer than he should have. Katrina's seductive nature and voluptuous body persuaded him to relax and unwind – comparing it to going home to the cold welcome he was expecting to receive from Caroline. Richard was failing to understand that it was his treatment of Caroline that produced the frosty response. At Katrina's house, Richard's favourite single malt was always waiting for him, distilled at Craighouse on the Isle of Jura, one of the many unspoiled remote islands of the Hebrides. Consumption of this had also encouraged him to remain with her longer than expected. During their evening's assignation, Richard's Range Rover and the ever-watchful Tim Spinks sat parked up in the drive of Katrina's house in Roehampton, a rather beautiful house to which she had insisted be part of her divorce settlement.

Since working together, Richard and Tim had built a rapport that made them almost friends more than employer and employee. However, Tim, being the professional he was, would never allow this special relationship to become too familiar. Richard carried a personal attack alarm which, when activated, would immediately be detected by the receiver Tim always carried with him. Tim's receiver, through the use of global positioning satellite technology, had a directional indicator to help him pinpoint Richard. Tim was also a licensed firearms holder and carried a 0.45 thirteen-shot Browning Automatic. He often prayed that he would never have to use it in defence of his employer because, despite that portrayed in the movies, there was no such thing as just giving somebody a leg or arm wound - you shot to kill. The killing didn't particularly worry Tim; he'd taken a life before in the service of Her Majesty. However, killing someone in civilian life, no matter how dangerous the threat, he would be answerable in court where he'd find the very Queen he'd served so loyally charging him with murder. There were only a few things in life Tim feared, and prison was on the top of his list; he therefore always saw the gun as a deterrent only to be used as a last resort. He would always aim to rely on his highly honed, unarmed combat skills. He'd learned close quarters combat known as 'Jack slapping' during his time on Operation Banner in Northern Ireland, where working down back alleys and in small confines didn't leave enough physical room for any fancy martial arts movements used so widely today in films for its entertainment value.

Sitting in the Range Rover outside the private house while the clandestine affair was conducted happened quite a lot, but this mattered not to Tim Spinks. He always received extra payment for these covert nocturnal duties, which he put under the heading of 'Lifestyle Management'. Being an ex-Special Forces man, the slight discomfort of sitting in the Range Rover paled into insignificance compared to some of the jobs that Tim had carried out in the field, ranging from the jungles of Borneo to wet dug outs in the countryside of South Armagh. Confidentiality was another one of the qualities required of a man like Tim Spinks. He hadn't been working for Richard very long before he realised that the nocturnal visits to a smart house in Roehampton fell into the femme fatal category. Tim had seen Katrina Sinclair, and it was obvious what Richard saw in her but, as Caroline was a very glamorous woman, he often wondered what caused a man of Richard's integrity to look outside the sanctity of his marriage. Using the deduction of the typical male, Tim assumed that it was all to do with bedroom performance, believing if it wasn't right there, then no matter how attractive a woman is, men will nearly always look elsewhere for excitement. Perhaps that's what Katrina gave Richard — sex with an addictive adrenaline rush, an escape from reality.

Chapter 9

For Katrina, although her relationship with Richard was not an adrenaline rush, the sexual athletics they experienced together was, at times, mind-blowing. Despite her calm, serene, and outwardly kind nature, Katrina was intrinsically a very bitter woman. Katrina, thought all men were bastards. She had previously been married for 26 years to Steve, her teenage sweetheart. Together, they had worked extremely hard to build up a business, developing it from a small corner shop to a mini-empire with a turnover they could only ever have dreamed of in the early days. Steve's business was renting cash registers and weighing machines to small businesses and market traders. He had cleverly hand-picked all the small corner shopkeepers who were of no interest to the large national suppliers. Steve had bought old equipment previously written off as scrap, he refurbished them himself and supplied these to the market traders on a cash only basis.

Consequently, the cash deals gave him the ability to declare only part of the profits he made. As the empire built, so did the expendable cash flow. This enabled Steve and Katrina to enjoy many luxuries whilst bringing up their lovely daughter in comfortable, homely surroundings in the Sussex countryside. They enjoyed superb holidays overseas, and life was good for the whole family. In the early days, Katrina had worked hard, helping Steve push the business growth at the same time as being a full-time mother. She worked every hour that she could, and week-ends just became extensions of the working week. Once their daughter left home and moved to be with her Australian boyfriend in Sydney, Katrina ensured that she and Steve reaped the rewards of their success. That was, until one day, when her secure and comfortable world fell apart, dropping like a precious porcelain vase, shattering into a thousand pieces.

Like most things in life, no one action or circumstance works entirely alone to change the path one leads; the 'domino effect' was to change her life. The day had started as any other. Steve had left to attend a business meeting when Katrina received an unexpected telephone call from her friend who lived in Northern Ireland. Her lifelong friend, Josie, had caught the overnight ferry back home to visit her parents to tell them of her future plans. Josie and her live-in boyfriend Jerry were bound for a new life to own a sheep farm in the Falkland Islands. Being an extremely close friend to Katrina, she wanted to tell her all about these developments before Katrina heard them from another source. Although Katrina was supposed to be having her monthly cut and blow-dry with Mario, her hairdresser, she rescheduled the appointment for another day. So, the two close friends arranged to meet up at a favourite country garden restaurant, a regular haunt before Josie moved away. Looking forward to seeing her friend, Katrina happily hummed to herself that morning while getting ready, totally unaware of what was about to occur. The first domino to fall was when she agreed to meet Josie. The second was courtesy of a local building contractor brought in to assist the telephone company with the laying of the new broadband cable, taking internet to a local village. A village which had, for some years, been by-passed by the new A road, it was this road, which later that morning, had to close. The third domino was a slip up at the local council office, from where a 'permit to dig' had been issued to the telephone company. This had been issued by mistake by a clerk who was new to the job and who should have sort advice from his supervising county surveyor. The fourth fell, as the contractor having the 'permit to dig' allowed his JCB to commence work and accidentally damaged an underground water pipe, causing localised flooding.

The fifth was Katrina's route which was now diverted from the flooded 'A' road. She'd turned off the main road, following the diversion into the village, slowly approaching the village green overlooked by the 'Green Man' a classic, old fashioned public house, popular with townies wanting to wine and dine at a rural retreat, when the sixth and last domino fell: a black cat suddenly raced out in front of her car. Katrina slammed on her brakes. Breathing a sigh of relief that the cat was unharmed, she watched it slink away towards the pub car park where Steve's car suddenly caught Katrina's eye. Steve enjoyed fast cars, and a symbol of his success was his bright red Volvo convertible. The Volvo was just at the right level of prestige, fast and sporty yet not too ostentatious that it would be difficult to explain considering the modest profits his business declared. Katrina's heart missed a beat, even after 26 years of marriage, she got butterflies whenever she unexpectedly saw him. The blowing horns from the cars behind made her quickly decide to pull in to the pub car park, Steve had mentioned only that morning that he was having a business meeting with some colleagues so she felt it would be rude not to pop in and say 'hello'.

Unaware his wife was currently parking her car just outside, having just finished an excellent lunch and now enjoying coffee, Steve was sitting in the comfortable lounge bar of the 'Green Man' gastropub. He leaned forward to kiss his lovely young lady companion, as his hand tantalisingly brushed against her right breast, her erect nipple fighting for release from the confines of her 38 D cup bra at his soft touch. The turbocharged testosterone racing around his body congregating in his penis looking for a relief valve as he gently whispered into her ear, "You have the most magnificent breasts that I just love to fondle, lick, suck and kiss," he purred like a cat about to get the cream.

She gasped for breath, excited by his desire for her, "Oh Steve, I want you so much," she whispered, "I want to feel you pulsating inside me."

His gentle fleeting butterfly kisses stifled a little giggle from her just at the precise moment that Katrina walked into the lounge bar. Not believing what she was witnessing, Katrina stood there, transfixed with horror, taking in the enormity of the action being played out before her. She momentarily felt as though she was watching a motion picture scene. Astral forces instinctively caused Steve and his attractive companion to turn and see Katrina standing there. Steve's companion had never seen or met Katrina. However, the look on Steve's face told her that she was looking directly into the eyes of Mrs Katrina Sinclair. Katrina wanted the ground to swallow her up. She could not believe what she was witnessing. Quickly, she turned and fled out into the car park, tears streamed down her face, destroying the lovely seductive black mascara she had so patiently prepared earlier. Steve shot up from his chair in hot pursuit like a moon rocket taking off from NASA. Katrina, now by her car, searched to find the keys in her handbag, she wanted to get away as fast as possible, but Steve had caught up with her.

"Katrina! Wait! This is not what it looks like!" he cried.

Finally finding her keys, Katrina turned on him in a fury, "Well, what the hell is it, how could you, you, you," momentarily, she was lost for words then they came like a broadside, "you fucking bastard!" she screamed hysterically. Steve was shocked, as though he had just received a bolt of electricity. He stepped back in horror, temporarily stunned to hear Katrina use such gutter language, never in all their years together had Steve heard Katrina swear. He quickly grabbed her, turning her away from the car as she defensively struggled in an attempt to shake him free.

"Katrina I'm so sorry it's not what it seems," he pleaded. Searching for excuses he continued, "She is a customer that I am desperate to have, she controls a huge trade and can mean a lot to the company and put a great deal of business our way, please, please believe me," he voiced, in obvious desperation to convince her as he tried to salvage the situation but Katrina saw through him, she knew him so well, especially when he was lying.

"Leave me alone!" she yelled as she struggled free from his grip. Opening the car door, she got in as fast as she could. The car door slammed, and she savagely started the engine, yanking the gear lever into reverse. The front wheels spun, causing a shower of loose gravel to be thrown into the air as she viciously stamped on the accelerator. Steve leapt out of the way to avoid being hit before Katrina careered the car around and rapidly left the car park. Angry drivers blasted their horns as she forced her way into the diverted traffic queuing on the road. Steve stood there, dumbstruck. The peering faces from the pub restaurant looked on with morbid curiosity at the drama unfolding before them. Being mid-week, the pub clientele were mainly from the retired, sedate section of society gleefully witnessing a real-life drama worthy of a TV soap opera played out in front of their mature, glazed watery eyes as they mundanely munched through their lunchtime repast.

The queuing traffic suddenly picked up speed, and within seconds, Katrina's car was out of sight. Rubbing his face with his hands, Steve turned towards the pub and saw his lunch companion in the doorway. Her eye contact said it all, she had heard every word he had said, and she quickly turned on him in explosive anger.

"What's all this fucking crap about me being just a customer?" her raised voice, full of venom, as she spat the words out.

Steve walked towards her, "Nothing," he mumbled. He walked straight past her, his head low in both shame and frustration. He wanted to avoid any more confrontation, but for his companion, it had only just begun. Oblivious to the other customers of the pub she quickly followed him, catching him within the double doors of the pub entrance briefly isolated and insulated from the gawping patrons giving the appearance they were actors in a silent movie, "Steve that was obviously the wife who apparently doesn't understand you and who, because of which, you were going to leave to be with me!" she continued with icy sarcasm, "You have just been stringing me along all this time!"

Steve briefly regained his posture with a little of his normal confidence and charm returning. He turned to her with his arms outstretched. He wanted to recover the situation and evade the embarrassment in front of so many people. But it was no use; his girlfriend, who earlier had been looking so adoringly into his eyes, continued like a trapped feline. Her temper rose to boiling point as she came to the realisation that Steve had been using her all along. She looked at him in disgust, "Don't try and deny it, you fucking pig, I was just your fancy piece on the side wasn't I?" her voice rising, "Go on admit it you sod, I'm just a bloody good sideshow shag, aren't I?"

Many of the patrons who could see the arguing couple looked on in anticipation of hearing what was coming next. Interested because true life is always better than fiction, and this was all very real. Many of the onlookers secretly hoped this show would carry on, subconsciously working out what was going to come next. Would it turn nasty? Would the landlord have to summon the police? Would open hands start to fly with faces slapped? Alternatively, other diners turned away to avoid the scene, annoyed that their lunch had been interrupted.

"You are a real bastard, Steve, and you can forget about any business from my company; you can go and fuck yourself... and it won't end there, you pig, I'll make sure all of my business associates know what a low life creep you are!"

"Yeah, yeah," was all Steve could manage as he speedily ran into the bar lounge to retrieve his jacket.

"Yeah, yeah," mimicked his female companion as he returned, passing by her. A huge angry snarl spreading across her face, "I'll screw you, Steve Sinclair, I'm going to screw you right over!" she shouted.

Steve wanted to be out of there as quickly as possible. He avoided any further -exchanges and fled to his car. Her threats lay heavy on his mind. Losing her business wouldn't break the bank, and even if she did attempt to jeopardise his company, most of his clients knew they had too good a deal to risk turning away because of the actions of a bitter scorned woman. Another cloud of stones and dust was thrown into the air as Steve's car roared off, leaving another woman to have tears streaming down her face in both frustration and rage.

The amazed landlord of the gastropub had been, in a perverse way, rather interested to see the situation develop. He was thankful Steve had already paid the lunch bill – he wouldn't want to have to ask the attractive sobbing woman for money. 'Mustn't allow emotions to get in the way of commercialism,' he thought to himself as he carried on serving thirsty customers at the bar. General chatter soon returned, mainly analysing and discussing the impromptu lunchtime debacle. As the landlord looked at his rather stout, shapeless wife helping him behind the bar, he did wonder as to how lucky that young 'fella me lad' was in having two rather gorgeous ladies in his life, albeit not for much longer. 'Oh! But for the chance,' he thought to himself before being brought back down to earth by a customer requesting more drinks. He let out a big sigh and went back to work pulling pints, knowing that with each pint pulled, he was nearer to a cushy retirement!

Steve was confused; he could not comprehend how Katrina came to be at the pub. As a past master at using the dubious practice of half-truths, he'd deliberately avoided telling her where he was having lunch. So how could she have discovered his tryst's location? A question to which he would never discover the answer.

He decided to go home hoping to find Katrina and to be able to reason with her, try to placate her and salvage something from the mess he now found himself in. He was right about one thing, in the emotional fog of the realisation that her hitherto safe, secure world was imploding, Katrina had raced home, all thoughts of her lunchtime meeting with her friend forgotten. Steve, on arrival, found Katrina wildly ripping up some of his best clothes, throwing them out of the bedroom window as she screamed expletives, demented with the grief she was experiencing. Even when Katrina had eventually calmed down, she knew her mind would not be changed by anything Steve had to say. Despite on the one hand hoping it had all been a bad dream, she knew the utter betrayal would bring the marriage to a close. She was a one-man woman, Steve was her life, her past, and had been her future, she could never trust him again. Her whole world now completely shattered. Everything she had worked so hard at: the business, the marriage. She had given Steve everything until there was nothing more to give. Her soul, the very air she breathed, was all for Steve. She felt as though the very lifeblood had been sucked right out of her; there was nothing left. It was the end.

The subsequent inevitable separation and acrimonious divorce left Katrina a bitter, twisted woman; consequently, she had no intention of ever allowing herself to become reliant on a man again. She had had many lovers following the break-up and discovered she enjoyed the new lifestyle she had created for herself. Despite Steve's pleadings to give their marriage another chance, she was consistently adamant that it was the end. Steve had then turned nasty, fighting her every step of the way. He had hidden so much of his earnings from both the VAT and Inland Revenue that Katrina had a hard job of getting him to agree on a reasonable settlement. It all came to a head when Steve offered to buy Katrina a house in an area that was tantamount to a 'slum' council estate, which was known locally as 'Little Beirut' a comparison with the destruction wreaked on that the middle Eastern city due to the civil war. The area here comprised of high rise flats, gaudy featureless townhouses and maisonettes creating a concrete jungle where police officers only patrolled in two's in and only in cars, which were not even safe from being firebombed occasionally. The area, a typical example of a trendy social engineering that had gone so badly and predictably wrong. The house he offered to buy her was in between houses that were both boarded up. The neighbouring house to the left had caught fire after being attacked one night by an angry mob, who were convinced that the house was occupied by a paedophile. The neighbouring house to the right had been empty for several months following a lone man dying there of a drug overdose and not being found for several weeks. The stench of decaying human flesh still enveloped the immediate vicinity hanging around like a cloud of shame over a failing housing experiment.

Steve's offer was the final straw; Katrina wasn't going to take anymore. He had turned into a rat so it had become time for her to fight dirty. She disclosed to her lawyer everything she knew about Steve's business affairs; after all, they had been partners in every sense and shared all. Katrina had managed the bookkeeping and knew of all the unrecorded amounts that Steve had received from the market traders. A word in the right ear at HM Customs and Excise VAT Branch would no doubt be welcomed. When this was communicated through their respective lawyers, Steve realised the folly of his attitude towards her and immediately capitulated. He offered Katrina whatever she wanted as long as she signed a 'gagging' order. Steve didn't want the prying eyes of the HM Revenue inspectors looking too closely at his business books. Ending up in prison was not an option. He should have known better than to treat Katrina badly, but he was a chancer, taking risks had helped make him a successful entrepreneur in the first place.

After it was all over, Katrina enjoyed a comparatively comfortable lifestyle in her lovely home, set in the leafy green avenues of Roehampton. She had a very good job as an area manager for a national company, money in the bank, and a lover who treated her like the lady she was. She had her lovely daughter, who had travelled back to the UK to support her mother through the awful divorce proceedings. After seeing everything unfold, their daughter had cut all ties and become estranged from her father. Much to Steve's disappointment, she wanted nothing to do with him and soon flew back to Australia. Katrina had never wanted what had happened, but she had certainly made the best of a bad situation and had turned her life around. She was happy being single; however, she did have a slight feeling of anxiety that she had developed a relationship with a married man. It was not ideal, not what she wanted, but she enjoyed a clear conscious by repeatedly reminding herself that Richard had been the one to chase her and while she had no intention of taking Richard away from his wife, she felt it was for Richard's conscious to come to terms with their affair, not hers. She intended to play with Richard only as long as she wanted to. She enjoyed the game but always held the ace that at the first sign of trouble, then it would all be over.

Whenever Richard visited her, he always had his bodyguard in the car outside. Katrina enjoyed knowing he was out there on her driveway. It added to the erotic excitement of their relationship and increased her sexual arousal. An armed man sat on guard, ready for any sight of danger, while she and Richard are upstairs 'bonking' in a huge four-poster bed. Her imagination often ran wild – seeing herself as part of a surreal 'James Bond' world. Little did she realise at that point just how close she was to events that would propel her into a world of violence and intrigue. Events that, again, would change her life.

Chapter 10

As Tim progressed along the new route, given to him by the private security firm's Operations room, Richard's mind wandered back to Caroline – she had been asleep, or at least pretended to be, when he had eventually crawled into bed. She hardly ever asked where he'd been these days. Richard suddenly caught sight of the red message alert signal on the codex radio, which brought him back to reality as he spoke to Tim.

"More traffic problems Tim?"

"Afraid so, Sir, but nothing we can't cope with, and we'll soon be at the office," replied Tim as he expertly drove the Range Rover around Marble Arch.

"Excellent," said Richard, confident in Tim's ability. He looked down at the report in his hands and tried to block out his domestic problems, at least for the present. A large sigh shuddered through his frame. The report outlined his proposals to take over a small and ailing shipping company operating from the port of Northwold on the north-east coast.

The first part of the report provided Richard with a historical perspective. He read with interest that the Beaumont Steam Ship Company ran a modest ferry operation that started at the close of the Second World War by Colonel James Beaumont of the Royal Army Service Corps. James had been a career army man. A brilliant logistician and tactician, he had risen quickly through the ranks to become one of the youngest Colonels in the history of the Transport Corps. James had been in charge of one of the sectors on the beaches of Normandy during the D-Day Landings. It was from this experience that the idea was borne in his mind. Starting the ferry service at the end of hostilities had been a good idea. He acquired an old tank landing craft, one of the hundreds redundant at the close of the war, and commenced transporting back from Europe thousands of tons of scrap metal - the remains from the many battlefields that blotted the landscape of Europe. His company fed the hungry industrial might of Britain anxious to start rebuilding and exporting again to repay the massive debts created by the war. James had seen his company flourish to the point that he was able to commence designing and building his own style of vessels, these soon hailed as the way forward - the future was 'Ro/Ro'. After reading the background on James Beaumont Richard felt a tinge of regret that he'd not met this remarkable man.

James had long since passed away and left his company in the hands of his son, Edward. He was nicknamed 'Steady Eddie' in the maritime circles. Eddie had held the fort following his father's passing but lacked the dynamic approach. Eddie took the first opportunity he could for retirement aiming to expand his repertoire for painting, the real great love of his life, and to live like a recluse buried in the Derbyshire Dales.

Eddie past the company down to his two sons, Paul and Peter Beaumont. Having inherited their grandfather's entrepreneurial skills, they had initially successfully continued their legacy for a few years before things started to go wrong. They'd fallen prey to a fast-talking whizz kid, who had been recommended to them ironically by their bankers. The man, one Amir Chandra, was introduced first as a consultant and then put on to the payroll. He was, without doubt, a very shrewd businessman and helped the brothers enormously, but Amir Chandra was greedy and saw a way of making extra money by tax evasion. Peter and Paul, convinced of Amir Chandra business credentials, were swept along with the tide and failed to see what he was really up to within the company. Amir Chandra, having long since departed to pastures new, had started his own enterprise only to fall foul of the tax authorities. It was during these investigations into Amir Chandra business dealings that he had unwittingly drawn in Peter and Paul. Now faced with an investigation themselves and the resulting possibility of an enormous demand for unpaid tax, not to mention the possible jail sentences, the brothers had approached Richard Hartling for help. The only financial solution they could envisage that would get them out of their predicament was to sell out. Grandfather James would have turned in his grave if he could have seen what was happening to his beloved company.

Richard's company already had a small fleet of fast, modern Ro/Ro ferries but had almost reached saturation point on the short-haul routes they operated. With the foreseeable end of the duty-free perks, on which they made so much extra money, Richard needed to either merge his Ro/Ro ships with another company or sell off the Ro/Ro interests and concentrate on his deep-sea routes. Richard had, for some time, been weighing up possible options for the Beaumont brothers. He concluded that a take-over was the right move, but it wasn't without its snags: apart from one new vessel, the ships of the Beaumont fleet were worn out and desperately in need of replacement.

Scrutinising the business synopsis again, he looked up from the papers and out through the Range Rover window to the pressure of the London morning rush hour - he was a worried man. His domestic life was messy and now he must take a huge gamble and persuade his board to pay, what some city experts were saying was a greatly over-inflated price, for the Beaumont Company and all who sailed with her.

As the Range Rover pulled up in front of the British Steam Company office, Bert Thompson, retired army sergeant-major and now a member of the Corps of Commissionaires, an organisation which recruited from the military to provide highly visible uniformed security services for large companies and public buildings throughout London and the home counties, was busy unlocking the large plate glass doors at the entrance. Originally built as a hotel, Richard had acquired it for his company's headquarters. The cleaning lady was putting the finishing touches to the mirror-like shine on the marble floor entrance of the main foyer, "Morning Bert," she said, allowing some cigarette ash to fall from the end of her roll-up cigarette. She tutted to herself as it crashed into millions of specks of dust spreading over the floor, "I see the Toff has just pulled in to the car park along with that foooking big bloke that's always with him these days," she said with the cigarette stuck like glue to her bottom lip.

'The Toff' was their affectionate term for Richard, one which had stuck over the years thanks to his smooth and stylish manner. He knew of it and was secretly rather proud of it; he felt it added to his image. Although he didn't realise it, Richard was one of those men who turned women's heads whenever he walked into a room, despite his recent slight increase in his girth. Currently, the rather overbearing, well-nourished, dominant local Chairwoman of the Towns Women's Guild in Esther was chasing him. She was always asking Richard to go along to one of their numerous dining evenings and deliver a speech on his career and experiences. It had reached a point where it was becoming embarrassing to have this woman constantly writing and calling him and he did wonder whether he ought to make an effort and go along - if only to get the awful woman out of his hair, but running a multi-million-pound international organisation, a home and not to mention a mistress, took up most of his time.

"Now then Gertie you know that big bloke is the Toff's bodyguard, he has to go everywhere with him, that's his job to protect him," explained Bert.

"But why Bert? I don't see the point me'self," challenged Gertie as she rinsed out a floor mop and started to clear away the cigarette ash.

"We've been through this Gertie a dozen times," replied Bert patiently as though he was talking to a child.

Gertie didn't understand the dangers of the world, and although she did watch the news, terrorist action and other atrocities around the world were what happened to other people - not in her little world in the East End of London where she had lived all her years, only ever venturing to Southend for her annual summer holidays.

"Good morning Sir," said Bert Thompson coming crisply to attention and giving Richard a smart parade ground salute while opening the large glass door for him.

"Good morning to you Bert," replied Richard, "I've been meaning to have a word with you ... how's your wife these days, it's Pat isn't it?"

"That's right, Sir, but not too good to be honest. Rheumatics play'er up rather badly. Don't complain mind, always 'as a smile for everyone. Keeps things to 'erself, see."

Richard nodded in sympathy, "Yes I remember meeting her at the staff summer party, a lovely lady and I'm sorry to hear that, I'm in rather a rush this morning Bert but I'll find sometime later this week to talk to you and see if we can do anything to help."

"That's very kind of you, Sir, but I think it is just old age, you know," replied Bert, grateful for Toff's concern.

"Maybe, but I would like to talk to you all the same. I was speaking to Commander Willis only the other day and he was telling me of a new treatment just coming out of China using bee sting, we'll see what we can do."

"Thank you, Sir, much appreciate it."

Richard made a mental note to call the Personnel Manager, all BSC staff and their spouses were in a private medical scheme and he felt sure that Bert hadn't even thought about using this to see if there was anything that could be done for his wife. Even if the bee sting was not an option, there were some marvellous drugs on the market these days that could ease the pain.

Richard was a product of Henley College for Leadership Training in Commerce and Industry, and he put the skills learned to good use. He also had a good memory for names and faces. He made personal notes on his laptop of all his management and staff, consistently updating the information when changes occurred within their personal circumstances and immediate families. He ensured that the personnel department always kept him updated with staff details. He always refreshed his memory from this database before meeting staff he'd not seen for some time, it was one his many ways of motivating his staff, and it had proved very successful in his time at the company.

"Oh, and by the way, Bert?" said Richard as he paused before carrying on with his journey.

"Yes, Sir," replied Bert, almost coming to attention.

"Bert I have had an idea regarding your flying experiences; you are still an active pilot I believe?"

"Yes, indeed, I am sir," replied Bert, curious as to what was about to come.

"Well Bert, with this proposed take-over of Beaumont's and if it's successful I will need to be spending a bit more time up in Lincolnshire and I noticed the other day when looking at some maps of the area that there is an old wartime airfield almost next door to Northwold, called North Croft. Susan, my secretary, did some research for me and apparently it is an activate light aircraft airfield. Now, if the company were to finance the purchase of a light aircraft, you could fly me up there whenever I needed to go, save the long car journey.. What do you think?" asked Richard.

Bert was gobsmacked! "I'd be delighted to Sir, it will be just like old times when I flew Monty around."

"Good, do some research for me regarding aircraft and let Susan know to arrange a meeting with me!"

"Yes, I certainly will sir," replied Bert with a half salute and a slightly opened mouth as he still couldn't quite believe what he'd just heard Richard say. Before he could say anymore, Richard had gone.

As Richard crossed the foyer to the lift that takes him to his suite of offices on the top floor of the building, Bert Thompson smiled and muttered to himself, "A company airplane with me as the pilot and then bee stings for the wife, cor blimey whatever next," he could picture his wife's reaction if he told her that the Toff had offered to get her treated with bee stings as she was bloody terrified of bees.

Bert had noticed how drawn and pale Richard was looking lately. He compared Richard with some of the senior officers he served under in his army days. He wouldn't have had their job for all the tea in China. Bert had trained with the Army Air Corps qualifying as a pilot flying a high winged Auster, before moving on to Miles Messengers flying around the 'Top Brass'. During the war, Bert had lied about his age to get into uniform and by looking older than his years he'd pulled it off! Also being an avid reader of the 'Biggles' books which had lead him on to reading books on how to fly an aeroplane, he knew the theory. It was desperate days and Bert had been able to 'blag' his way onto a pilot training programme. Being in the army, he didn't need to have an officer's commission to fly. At only 16 years of age but looking 20, he had been the personal pilot to General Montgomery and, even on one occasion, flown the King on an inspection tour. He always likened Richard to Monty, all that responsibility in your hands – something Bert didn't like the idea of, no, flying airplanes was what he loved, up flying high was where Bert was in his element. Even now, with his advancing years, Bert was in excellent health and able to satisfy the CAA Doctor by passing his annual medical. According to his records, he was still younger than he really was, even his wife didn't know his true age. These days, he was a part time instructor, probably currently the oldest on record if the truth be known, and he enjoyed nothing more than flying his ex-Military Auster and passing on his flying skills to the next generation of 'young eagles' as he called them. A telephone burst into life on Bert's desk, in the corner of the main foyer. Daydreaming pushed to one side; he walked quickly across to answer it. Another day had begun.

Chapter 11

Richard sat behind his immense, highly polished ebony desk. The room's rich dark mahogany panelled walls created an environment similar to a ship's cabin. Richard's office was full of stylish furniture he had accumulated over the years; all brought back from the Far East aboard some of the company ships by obliging sea Captains. He enjoyed being surrounded by these pseudo trophies from distant shores. Each piece, in their own way, represented his success. He somehow had always known that this was to be his destiny, in charge of this vast fleet of ships sailing the sea lanes like tentacles, stretching into every corner of the world, lifelines from the old world to the new, pumping the lifeblood of trade throughout the world. He felt immensely proud of his achievements. There came a light tap at the door and Susan Windsor entered his office with a tray of freshly brewed coffee, her high-heeled 'killer' stilettos for which she had become well known, clicked loudly on the brief space of parquet flooring before being silenced by the thick Persian carpet, "Good morning," she beamed unconsciously alluringly. Susan Windsor, had one of those natural seductive personalities, plus the figure to go with it.

Her flawless, perfectly rounded face, with only the trace of make-up, seemed to exude sunlight whenever she entered a room. Her slightly turned-up nose, on which rested heavy black-rimmed glasses, gave her a look of sexy authority. Her naturally bouncing golden locks fell perfectly into place after any movement of her head. She was the perfect model for any hair shampoo manufacturer. Blonde but certainly not a 'bimbo,' hailing from the north with the just the occasional hint of her Yorkshire origins when she spoke expressing 'oh' as 'eer' and no as 'neer'. Susan was a highly proficient Personal Assistant as well as secretary to Richard. She was loyal and totally devoted to him, a career woman with an eye on her own future development, and fully aware that Richard would be the key to her future advancement. Susan had never had any maternal feelings to have a family and be 'the little lady at home,' well, not yet at least; this would change in the future but for now, Susan was focused on her career. In return for her hard work, Susan was paid handsomely by Richard, so much so that it had once been brought up at board level but, as it was highlighted, she was virtually on call 24/7 for Richard, consequently the subject was dropped. Susan was so good at her job that many of the board members wished they could clone her. Richard was a considerate person and he never abused her dedication. Susan always carried her laptop and mobile so that Richard could contact her anytime, any day. On the odd occasion this did intrude annoyingly into her social life, she always took consolation in her monthly pay cheque. Richard enjoyed his working relationship with Susan, and although his natural primate urges secretly wished it would be good to find out what Susan would be like between the sheets, he knew that in the old adage *'you mustn't screw the crew'* was a rule he should stick to. Just the thought of sexual liaisons with Susan made him smile. He watched her carefully place the coffee on to his desk, his eyes briefly wandered to her breasts, before he composed himself, quickly looking the other way and letting out a little cough.

"Everything okay Richard?" she sympathetically asked.

Richard's thoughts momentarily embarrassed him, creating a slight flush to his face, he soon regained his composure.

"Oh, nothing Susan, just laughing inside at the after-dinner speaker last night at the Chamber dinner, it was funny one way, but embarrassing and disastrous in another."

Susan just smiled demurely and instinctively knew Richard was making excuses. Susan's intuition told her that Richard secretly fancied her. She was flattered, as she too had regular thoughts of them together – one thought, in particular, included the beautifully polished desk, but they were only fantasies. They had worked closely together for eight years, and Susan would never jeopardise her position at BSC; anyway, she now had her own amour.

Chapter 12

Besides admiring, and sometimes fantasising, about her boss, Susan Windsor, also appreciated the strong loyalty of Richard's Bodyguard, Tim Spinks. Like her, he had a lot of respect for Richard and his safety was paramount. Susan, totally devoted to her boss and always being professional, secretly found Tim intimidating; dangerous yet sexy.

Keeping her life outside of work totally private, nobody knew Susan's heart remained with an old boyfriend from Junior High school; despite losing touch as their schooling had taken them down different avenues due to the aspirations of their parents.

This childhood boyfriend was one Charles Barrington-Smythe who soon learned to stick up for himself because of the constant jokes and 'mickey-taking' he had to endure from his peers about his aristocratic surname. In reality, the landed gentry to which the name implied was as far removed from Charles' family as the moon is from the earth. Although Charles was certainly a very clever scholar, as time would readily tell, he was unfortunately rather weedy in build. His slight stature and rather goofy, thick, black-rimmed jamjar bottom spectacles gave him a 'geeky' persona. His appearance, along with his name, made him a natural target for bullies. This was eventually rectified thanks to an old friend of his father. Charles had turned to his ex-army father, imploring him to somehow help toughen him up and enable him to face his tormentors.

The friend in question was an old army chum, one Brian Edwards.

Brian, upon leaving the army, had turned his passion for boxing in to a business and after achieving reasonable success, in both notoriety and financially, he'd decided to get out of the ring while the going was good and opened his own gymnasium. Charles' father had invested in Brian's business idea, gambling his army pension and savings, much to the chagrin of Charles' mother who worried that they would end up penniless if the gym business didn't pay. However, the gym had become so successful that Brian's brand was eventually bought out by a national company. Before all this occurred, and in answer to the pleading of Charles, his father handed him over to Brian who took him under his wing, built him up, and taught him the finer points of the Queensbury Rules. These new-found skills not only sorted his tormenters but had brought him to the rescue of a young Susan Windsor, who found herself in a similar situation with which Charles had readily identified. In Charles' case, it was his posh sounding surname that had constantly got him into trouble, whereas with Susan, it was her pretty looks, she was destined to become a very glamorous young lady.

Following the altercation from which Charles had rescued Susan, they developed a short-term friendship that, unbeknown to them, would be rekindled later in life when their paths crossed again.

In the odd quiet moments of her business life, working for the dynamic Richard Hartling, Susan would occasionally daydream about Charles, her childhood hero. She was often wondering what had become of him. Wrongly assuming that he would have followed some sort of 'macho' career like joining the military, imagining him resplendent in uniform, however, nothing could be further from the truth.

From an early age, Charles realised that he was a true 'home-bird', enjoying the home comforts provided by his doting mother. Charles was an only child. Despite his upper-class double-barrelled name, Charles' parents came from humble stock. On leaving the army, Charles' father went into horticulture, a business not renowned for paying film star wages. His mother returned to her original career in nursing. It was Charles' father who hit the jackpot when Brian's gymnasium business was bought out, his initial investment immeasurably multiplied, and overnight he became a very wealthy man. As a result, they moved home to a semi-rural location on the fringes of London, buying a house with several acres of land and turning it into a small Garden Centre and Nursery. Charles' mother gave up her nursing career to look after their new and much larger mansion-like home. Charles settled easily into these idyllic, comfortable surroundings, got his wish for having a dog and just enjoyed the lifestyle his parents had created. So the very thought of leaving his comfortable home and surroundings was an absolute anathema to him.

It was during his attendance at a Christmas pantomime, while still only ten years old that Charles discovered that he could work out very quickly what the magician was doing to perform his tricks. When he tried to explain this to his parents, they naturally humoured him, believing it to be just childhood fantasy and imagination as they hadn't a clue what he was trying to explain. They did, however, acknowledge his other skills. As Charles grew up, he would help his father at the week-ends selling nursery plants and other gardening wares through his shop at the Garden Centre. Charles discovered that not only could he identify and memorise the price of all the plants and seedlings for sale but he also could tot up the sales of large orders within seconds. His father, astonished at Charles' gift, tested him on several occasions; while he used a pocket calculator, Charles would always beat him being a hundred percent correct every time while his father would make the odd error as he entered the numbers into the calculator too quickly in an attempt to beat his son. With his amazing memory and mental arithmetic abilities, Charles became a master at card games and was soon fleecing his school friends out of their pocket money during school playtimes. This resulted in Charles' parents being summoned to see the headmaster following complaints from other parents claiming that Charles was cheating their children. This accusation of cheating was soon laid to rest when Charles was called in to see the head and, in front of his parents, demonstrated his amazing powers to the astonished adults. Regardless of his honesty, his card games had to cease.

On the recommendation of the headmaster to his parents that Charles' outstanding abilities should be harnessed, he sat the entrance examinations for a local Grammar School, St. Egberts; not unsurprisingly passing the entrance examination with flying colours while others in his peer group were still a year away from sitting the 11 Plus National Examinations. From St. Egberts he went to university to take business studies and accountancy specialising in what had become known as forensic accountancy, the study of false accounting or in other words *'cooking the books'*. Charles' amazing brain relished the challenge of unscrambling and solving the mysteries of fraudulent accounting. Charles' name and accomplishments preceded him, and no sooner having graduated with a First with Honours he was head hunted by several leading City accountancy firms. Charles was also invited to be a guest lecturer at the Adult Education Centre, ironically the very same Centre that Susan Windsor attended.

Before their chance meeting occurred, Susan was in her office one day sorting through the daily newspapers for placing on Richard's desk, these included the Financial Times, The Times and, strangely, The Mirror; Richard liked to get an all-round view of national life! There was also the magazine "Accountancy Daily", the front cover of which caught Susan's eye.

'Charles Barrington-Smythe - is this young man the new Einstein of Accountancy?'

There, under the heading in black and white, was a photograph of a slightly geeky but very attractive man she recognised.

Susan's heart did several summersaults at seeing the face of her childhood sweetheart and hero. Looking at the photograph and the unusual name, she knew it was him. She could see it in his eyes, the boy she once knew.

She mused herself with the idea of contacting him through the magazine, but then she realised that he'd probably met a beautiful lady, maybe even engaged or already married. At that precise moment, Richard came into her office to witness Susan's discomfort,

"What is it, Susan? You seem distracted and flustered, is everything alright"? He enquired in a fatherly fashion.

"Yes, yes, of course, it's just that I've seen the picture of someone from my schooldays, it brought back some happy memories, that's all," answered Susan rather demurely. Putting the magazine to one side, beneath the other papers, her curiosity made a mental note to read the article later that day, there was no harm in doing a little research she thought.

Momentarily forgetting about Charles, she turned her attention to the needs of her boss, "Nothing of importance," she smiled.

"Oh, okay," replied Richard in a rather dismissive off-hand tone, indicating that he was keen to discuss more pressing matters with his PA. Some of these matters included details of a Time Management course that he wanted Susan to attend.

Sadly, once Richard had taken the papers, it was the last Susan was to see of that magazine; despite an exhausting search, it ended up as they all did, doing the rounds of the various offices before disappearing. The end of her fruitless search, after most of the offices had emptied for the day, left Susan back in her office with tears streaming down her beautiful, flawless face.

Being a homely sort of guy, Charles loved nothing more than the simple things in life, such as taking his Golden Labrador for long country walks around his home's locality and the delicious meals his mother prepared using lots of produce from his father's market garden. Consequently, he wasn't interested in the partying and clubbing that most of his generation enjoyed. In fact, both his parents had voiced private concerns about their son's sexuality. Their concerns were squashed when his heterosexual preference was confirmed by meeting his childhood sweetheart again, after nearly 15 years apart.

Susan had, through Richard's prompting, signed up for the night school course in Time Management for PA's, one of the latest management '*wheezes*' from over the pond currently sweeping through the business world. Other PA's and secretaries within the BSC headquarters were to attend and despite Richard's scepticism at such modern management training, what he termed '*gobbledegook*', he felt obliged, as the company CEO, to be seen supporting the training department's new initiative, and he'd thus persuaded Susan to attend the taster evening for the course. It was on the same evening that Charles was presenting to a group of accountancy students in an adjacent classroom. Their chance meeting couldn't have been more perfectly timed than if it had been stage-managed. Their individual bladders were also playing a major role as they literally bumped into each other as their paths crossed coming out of the respective bathroom facilities. At first, the chance encounter was a fumble with mumbled apologies as they each sidestepped, initially not recognising each other. It's often prophesised that our lives are subject to a higher power than here on earth. As they moved out of each other's way, in opposite directions, a fleeting glance as they passed gave them both a sudden light bulb moment; Charles turned and spoke first,

"Susan!" he exclaimed, clicking his fingers loudly as he realised it was indeed Susan Windsor.

"Yes?" She turned and instantly recognised him from the magazine cover, "Yes, is that you... Charles?" she queried, not entirely convinced but becoming more so with each passing moment.

They walked towards each other, their faces projecting beaming smiles.

"I don't believe it," she almost screamed.

"Neither do I, let me look at you," he replied, as he gently placed his hands on her shoulders. Within seconds, they were both hugging each other before parting to drink in each other's appearance. Susan enjoying the feeling of butterflies in her stomach followed by a genuine rush as endorphins surged around her body... she hadn't felt this way since having a teenage crush on a guy some years ago. Susan had a little 'giggle' to herself as the euphoria she was feeling morphed in to 'I want to have this man's babies!'

Charles too, was feeling a manly stirring in his loins! He had similar lustful thoughts, thinking along the lines of 'I want to impregnate this woman'!

Since that moment, Susan and Charles dated regularly, progressing rapidly to arranging to meet their respective parents where talk had soon turned to that of wedding bells. This eventually led to Susan introducing Charles to Richard at one of the staff '*meet and greet, get to know you*' social functions that Richard was so keen on having at regular intervals as an aid to improving team building and communication within the company. The two men warmed to each other immediately as Richard could see something of himself in Charles. Charles, on the other hand, could see himself one day rising to the exalted high office of a company Chief Executive. By the end of one particular staff function, to Susan's great delight she learned that Richard had offered Charles a position within the company. With the takeover of the Beaumont Company, Richard would need an injection of suitably qualified people, Charles fitted the bill perfectly.

Charles' appointment wasn't to everyone's liking and before long, just after the official announcement, the BSC Financial Director, Bob Somers, was beating a hasty path to Richard's office to vent his anger, complaining bitterly,

"What's the meaning of this, I should have been consulted before making such a senior appointment?" Richard, although initially taken aback by the venom of Bob's verbal attack, did understand where Bob was coming from. Richard was very much aware that one of his failings was making decisions on the 'hoof' when he felt that an immediate decision was needed. Whereas on other occasions he consulted when he felt the situation warranted a joint input in the decision making process. However, on the appointment of Charles, Richard had no doubt whatsoever that he would be a great asset to the company and needed to be caught quickly and brought onboard.

Consequently, he was mystified by Bob's aggressive, belligerent and rude behaviour. How Bob had reacted to Richard's quick decision without consulting had left him in a quandary as to why, what were his motives, surely not just a matter of having his nose put out by not being asked? Charles joining the company would hardly affect Bob's position; he shouldn't have felt any threat from Charles. Bob was at the pinnacle of his career being the Chief Finance Officer of a company such as BSC. This alone was an accolade of the highest honour and his position was virtually unassailable. In a nutshell, Bob had it made in life both socially and financially. Surely he couldn't be feeling that his nose had been put out just because Richard hadn't consulted him over the appointment of Charles? This extraordinary reaction by Bob was to play on Richard's mind for some time, before he finally decided how to bat the ball Bob had bowled to him.

Chapter 13

As the black digital clock on Richard's desk blinked 9.13 am, two hundred miles to the north, Peter and Paul Beaumont were sitting together in the comfortable, but humble, surroundings of their offices in the old military administration buildings. The offices, made of rendered breeze block with old metal-framed windows, overlooked the windswept quayside of Northwold. It was a bleak autumnal morning. The cold wind from Central Europe blustered and squalled across the North Sea, picking up the chill of the slate grey sombre mass of the water covered with dancing white horses. Despite the busy activity, the small dockyard looked drab and miserable as the easterly gale buffeted the rain against the office windows, wind and rain from a frontal system that hadn't quite progressed as far south as Richard's plush office in the city of London.

The Beaumont's recent and only new super ferry, m.v.'Lincolnshire', had just sailed for the continent as the brothers watched her start to pitch and roll. She cleared the harbour entrance, meeting the teeth of the wind and sea in the strong force eight gale. Unfortunately, she had departed only half full: rumours had been circulating for some time that the Beaumont Company was in trouble after the court case brought by HMRC at Hull Crown Court involving their one-time Asian business associate Amir Chandra. This had prompted transport companies to transfer some of their cargoes to a new service running from Hull, some 40 miles to the north. As the m.v. 'Lincolnshire' headed for the open sea and a bumpy crossing to the continent, the inbound overnight ferry, s.s.'Beamish', slowly pushed her way into the harbour, each ship giving a 'toot' of recognition on their foghorns as they passed just outside the harbour entrance. The s.s.'Beamish' deftly handled by its Captain using the vessel's twin propellers and bow thrusters. Although a reasonably modern innovation, when the bow thrusters were retro-fitted to the s.s.'Beamish' a mistake was made in the power calculations which meant they weren't as effective as had been hoped and were thus nicknamed the 'bubble blowers' by the crew due to its lack of power. Despite this handicap, the ship manoeuvred beautifully onto the roll-on roll-off berth and was soon secured, her stern door lowered in readiness to spew out her cargo.

Standing alone on the exposed port side of the navigation bridge was Captain Arthur Sanderson, a tall but portly man, who, if he'd had grown a beard, would be a contender for the now-famous TV Commercial featuring Captain Birdseye. His thick, navy blue, greatcoat collar was turned up against the biting wind, and his captain's hat was pulled down tightly on his head. The brass on the peak of his cap, commonly called scrambled egg had long since gone dull by continuous use in the hostile environment of the North Sea. Sadly, for this 45 years of sea service veteran, it was with a great feeling of nostalgia that he rang *'finished with engines'* on the big old bright brass engine-room telegraph, as it was for the last time, Captain Sanderson, like the engines on this voyage, had finally finished his career. He was retiring from his years at sea; this journey was the completion of his last continental trip in command. As he stood alone, Arthur pondered with melancholy thoughts that he'd not been ready for this momentous event. The Chief Officer, after a quick handshake and a few words, had rushed off below to supervise the discharge of the cargo. The Second Officer had also offered his hand mumbling something inaudible then disappeared below. Both young men were far too pre-occupied with their years of service ahead of them to make this old sea dog's last day at sea memorable.

'Some event,' Arthur thought as he stood alone on the bridge, with nothing but the whistling of the wind and the lashing of the rain against his face together with the tune of the rattling signal halyards above the bridge. The *s.s. 'Beamish'* had been his first command in the company, brand new she had been then, so it felt fitting that he onboard for his final voyage. He'd been offered the new super ferry, *m.v. 'Lincolnshire'* with all the 'state of the art' equipment; modern, powerful bow thrusters, electronic chart navigation systems, global positioning systems, satellite telephones, computers ... the list was endless. While he had easily, and readily, adapted to the new ways, he was much happier to be on this old tub for his last voyage. Thinking of all the modern equipment now available, he thought back to the days when radar had first been fitted to ships. He had started his shipping career as an apprentice with 'Athel Line', a specialist product tanker company that moved cargoes of molasses around the world. During the Second World War, Athel Line had the 'new-fangled' radar system fitted onto their ships. When the equipment had first been installed, a rumour went around the fleet that standing too long near the cathode-ray tube receiver on the bridge caused men to become impotent. Also, in those days, as a junior second officer, Arthur would only have been able to switch on the radar system with the Captain's permission, how times had changed! Now the officer on the bridge of a modern ship sat in a large, comfortable chair in front of a console with constantly running multiple radar screens and electronic chart plotters, which resembled the flight deck of a commercial airliner. So, Arthur was rather pleased that this old ferry should see him into his retirement. He doubted that the old girl would see much more service. Ever since the disastrous, and tragic, sinking of a ferry in the English Channel, legislation was being slowly introduced that would eventually require all roll-on roll-off ships to have transverse bulkheads fitted into their cavernous cargo decks. While this new thinking was easily constructed into new designs, it was not economically feasible to fit into old ships such as the *s.s. 'Beamish'*. Like himself, the ship was growing old, and while he still had many years of active life left in him, he doubted that the old *'Beamish'* did. As Arthur wandered into the bridge wheelhouse to get out of the wind and rain, he looked ahead through the bridge windows; towards the bow. Momentarily he imagined he was back deep sea, with the bows of the ship rising to meet imaginary large Atlantic rollers. Suddenly, his thoughts were interrupted as the Quartermaster, Tommy Smith, popped his head around the door.

"Dreaming of days to come Arthur?" Tommy said with a cheery smile.

Tommy was an ageing seaman quartermaster who had known the Captain for years, for he had made his first voyage as a deck boy when Arthur was a first trip apprentice aboard a then brand new molasses tanker *m.v 'Athelknight'*. Consequently, Tommy could be familiar with the old captain – but only when out of earshot of other crew members. Arthur turned to meet the friendly countenance and smiled back, "More of the days gone by Tommy. I've loved this old tub more than I realised. A few months ago I looked forward to retirement, but now, I don't know... this ship and I have gone through quite a lot in our time," he laughed.

Tommy started to hand-roll a cigarette from the contents of a battered leather pouch, "Aye, you two have had some good years Arthur."

"Ah well, we all have to go sooner or later. Reckon me and this old girl are going about the same time – she won't be seeing much more service. At least I have many happy years of retirement to look forward to, whereas she has only the scrap yard and cutters torch," he exclaimed.

"Well, I only wish the best for you Arthur and hope we can stay in touch. We'll all see you at the company bash to send you off properly."

"That'll probably be cancelled if this takeover goes ahead," said Arthur stifling a short laugh.

"Ooooh, I doubt that Arthur, I've heard nowt but good things about the BSC and how they do look after their staff."

"You're probably right, Tommy, after all, it's the last British shipping company, the only one left in British hands at least. Whatever happened to our proud Merchant Navy eh?"

"Sadly all gone," Tommy replied before licking his cigarette paper, "and what's left is now in American hands, look at Cunard and P&O, still flying the red dusters though."

"Yes, but for how much longer?"

"Well, as long as our mate, John Prescott, keeps the government's eye focused on the plight of the Merchant Navy."

"Well, it needs all the help it can get when you look back to our first days at sea, then you could guarantee to see the red ensign in just about every port in the world."

"Aye, glorious days those, when you could go down to the Shipping Federation Offices, there you could have your pick and choose your ship or company, depending on where in the world you wanted t'go. Companies like Brocklebanks, Buries Marks, Port Line, Blue Funnel, Ben Line, Shaw Savill & Albion, Clan Line, aye the list is endless, happy days, eh, but sadly all gone now."

Both men momentarily became lost in their thoughts of the romantic golden era of the Merchant Navy during the 1950's and 60's, imagining the barmy breeze, the white foaming phosphorous wake of a British Merchant ship steaming through the twilight of the southern oceans, the skies above covered with stars twinkling like diamonds. Then with a nod, a smile, and a shake of hands, Tommy happily went below for a cup of tea. Tommy realised that, in fact, he was literally in the same boat as Arthur, with retirement beckoning.

Chapter 14

Arthur leaned over the bridge wing, the top of which curved outwards; designed to deflect the incoming wind away from the eyes of whoever was standing watch in the harsh environment at sea. To someone ashore, it would be like looking out of the office window only with an ever-changing picture. He smiled to himself remembering an occasion at school when a teacher, catching him daydreaming looking out of the classroom window across the wide-open expanse of the playing fields, gained his attention by remarking rather harshly, *"Sanderson! Pay attention! Do you think someone is going to pay you to look out of the window all day when you grow up?"*

Arthur laughed inwardly, if only that teacher could have seen the life he'd led, spending hours on the bridge of a ship, keeping a lookout, starring at the vast open sea!

With one last look down towards the bows of his old ship, he observed one of his sailors, known as AB's or Able-Bodied seamen. This particular AB was Dave Dundas, a rather arrogant individual who did just enough to get by – the bane of the Chief Officer's life. The Chief Officer, being head of the deck department aboard ship and Dave's shipboard line manager who then reported to the ultimate Boss on-board, the Captain. In years gone by, the Captain or Master of a merchant vessel was often referred to as the Master before God, such was his power and influence over all on-board. Although in modern enlightened times, this has been watered down somewhat but the Captain still has a pretty powerful authority aboard any ship. Dave wasn't a tall man, standing only around 5 foot 8 inches in his stocking feet. Barrel chested, his midriff ran down into a thick waist and hips, creating a shape likened to a Rugby player. He hardly had any neck, and with his blonde hair and round face, he could have been termed a 'baby face' but a terrible bout of acne during his teenage years had left him with a pocked marked, scarred face. He was by no means a handsome man, but as he grew older, the remnants of the acne on his face developed into a battle-scarred, weather-beaten look. His scars gave him the air of a man who was raw, tough, confident and worldly-wise, giving off an aura that he knew what he wanted from life – with an air of determination to get it. This made him immensely attractive to women. Dave Dundas wasn't a deep-sea sailor; he'd come from the former fishing fleet that had once sailed out of Hull on the River Humber. He'd first been a Galley Boy, then a Deck Boy, eventually becoming a Deck Hand.

Unqualified, he earned plenty of money in the heyday of the fishing fleet when fish stocks were plentiful, and trawler owners paid huge bonuses. These fishing voyages were usually around three weeks duration, followed by a break in port of three days. With a pocket full of money, these trawler men became known as three-day millionaires. Making the most of their time ashore, away from the harsh environment of the northern fishing waters, they'd spend three days partying with their girlfriends, money no object, before returning to sea. When all that had come to an end, Dave Dundas had developed a lifestyle that needed some serious financing.

Dave had married the daughter of a wealthy local builder, Harry Needham. It was no secret that Harry was not enamoured with his daughter's choice of man. Marrying a trawler seaman did not go down well, but Dave Dundas was a slick operator, if somewhat rough around the edges. Used to living on his wits, Dave won the heart, not only of his future wife, but also his mother-in-law to be, consequently Harry knew when he was beaten and dropped his barrier against Dave. Harry was a self-made man who had come from nothing. He hoped that Dave was motivated like him to make something more of himself than a seaman. Unfortunately, Dave, despite his harsh upbringing in the world of trawler fishing in some of the remotest and harshest environments of the world's seas, he was just plain lazy and wanted to take the easy way to riches. He was one of life's social-economic gamblers who had discovered tobacco smuggling, producing hitherto unrivalled cash dividends beyond his wildest dreams. Dave's wife, Samantha, had grown up with the good things in life. It was Dave's raw, rough sexuality and carefree reckless attitude that had first attracted Samantha to him. Sam, although she didn't realise it, was a spoilt rich-bitch who needed taming, and Dave knew he was just the man to do it. However, he soon realised that it would take more than his raw charm and sexual prowess to keep Samantha firmly in his bed, an Able Seaman's wage just wouldn't cut it.

Luck, if it could be called that, played a part in helping Dave come up in the world financially. It was a chance conversation with the landlord of his local pub that formulated the 'get rich scheme' in Dave's mind. As a merchant seaman, HM Government granted what was known as a 'Landing Allowance', comprising a mixture of duty-free spirits and tobacco that each seaman was allowed to bring ashore upon leaving their vessel. This was strictly monitored and controlled by HM Customs & Excise Officers at each port, known collectively as the Waterguard. Anybody caught by the Waterguard exceeding this allowance was dealt with by way of confiscation of the duty-free goods, followed by an appearance in the local magistrate's courts resulting in a hefty fine. However, this threat didn't deter Dave from taking the risk of bringing an amount slightly over his legal customs allowance of tobacco and cigarettes ashore – starting with the odd extra packet or two of cigarette tobacco for his Dad, long retired and living on a meagre pension. It didn't take long before this developed into an ever-increasing amount for friends of his Dad, and a problem for Dave. He didn't mind being caught with the odd packet or so over his allowance, but he was feeling all the more uncomfortable as he ran the gauntlet, passing through the Customs Check-Point when leaving the ship for his rest days. He knew most of the Custom Officers personally, and they just waved him through, but more and more younger Customs men, straight from Training School, were now being drafted into the ever increasingly busy port, and it was some of these keen young types who had started picking crew members at random and searching their kit bags as they went home on leave. His problem was how to smuggle in large quantities of tobacco to make it worthwhile running the risk of being caught. As with most things in Dave's life, an answer to his problem came completely unexpectedly while he was working on the ship's car deck. During another casual 'off the cuff' conversation with the foreman Loading Master, Dave brought up the subject of cigarettes and the recent case of a crew member being fined by Customs for taking more than the allowance ashore.

"Not a problem, if you know the right people and places to stash it," said the Loadmaster.

Dave was curious and further enquired.

"Weeell now, that would be telling, wouldn't it mate, and what would you be wanting with that information anyways?"

"Oh, nothing really, other than I just wanna bring a little extra for me old man, you know."

"Fuck me, 'ardly worth the fucking bother me telling ya then. It would only be worth knowing if you intended to bring some serious stash back," replied the foreman. Dave didn't want to push it any further, not knowing if the Loading Master was trustworthy. So that was that, Dave forgot about the conversation, that was, until he found himself on leave, sat at the bar of his local hostelry in Northwold, having a few beers. The landlord mentioned how the brewery was squeezing him and that his profits weren't what they used to be. It was then that Dave's 'get rich' quick idea flashed into his head.

"Well, what if I was to bring you some fags and tobacco for you to re-sell?"

"What dodgy foreign fags? Nah, more than me jobs worth bud," replied the landlord.

"Nah, none o' that rat piss shit, the real deal mate, not nicked either, it's just that 'Her Maj' would be missing her cut, that's all," Dave said encouragingly.

"Mmmm ... Dunno, sounds dodgy to me like, this is the only life I know, wouldn't want to lose this job as me and the Mrs would be without an 'ome."

"Nah feckin' way," said Dave again, "I work on ships don't I, I'll get it for ya, over from Belgium or from the ship's bond, you's sell it at the normal price then me and you pocket what would have gone to Her Good Old Majesty Inland Revenue scuffers. We just have to be careful who we sell it on to, that's all."

Eventually the landlord agreed and could see, albeit risky, a way of earning a few extra quid. Dave couldn't wait to get back on-board the ferry and strike up another conversation with his newfound friend – the Loading Master. What neither of them realised then was that the trickle of a few extra quid would soon turn into a flood and they would both be so preoccupied with the amount of money they were making that they'd never give a second thought about that original conversation.

Despite initially keeping their operation small, it was that natural human failing of greed which allowed them to increase their illegitimate business to such an extent that it became a money-making monster beyond their wildest dreams. It all developed as Dave soon realised that he couldn't work entirely alone if he were to make some real money. The quantities he was purchasing, legally exported from the continent, were not enough. By the time he had slipped the Loading Master a cut, and the landlord had taken his share, it was, in reality, little more than 'peanuts'. The Loading Master was becoming frustrated with Dave and threatened to pull the plug unless the quantities and cash increased dramatically. So, Dave approached the on-board storekeeper of the vessel and put a proposal to him. If Dave could use some of the vast areas within the storerooms on-board to load the tobacco, he would then pay rent to the Storekeeper, who, in return, would turn a blind eye. All well and good in theory, but it soon turned out that the Storekeeper wanted an even bigger slice of the action.

Dave's empire grew, but so did the demands of palms to cross with silver, which in turn, required a larger payload to be smuggled to feed this hungry monster he had created. The rewards for him personally were now growing so large; there was no turning back. Samantha knew of Dave's tobacco moving, but he had lied to her about the quantities and she never asked any awkward questions. However, when her father, curious about Dave's newfound wealth, asked the question, Dave informed him that a distant relative had left him a windfall, and that seemed to be all that was needed to be said. As originally planned, this new wealth helped keep Sam in his bed.

The operation was simplicity – the ferries consumed huge amounts of stores to keep the galleys and shops well-stocked. Consequently, these vessels took onboard stores from both the UK and continent via local ship's chandlers. Dave, in association with the Storekeeper, purchased large quantities of cigarettes and tobacco legally from the local warehouses on the continent. These cargoes were simply loaded on-board along with other ship stores, all with the appropriate and legitimate paperwork, not that these stores ever found their way into the ship's books. With the help of the Loadmaster and precise planning, the cargoes were offloaded using a few selected men driving the tug masters. They hauled the large cargo trailers from the vessel before taking them to a massive compound where they were met by lorries for their onward journey. Tug master drivers were used that could be trusted to keep their mouths shut, for suitable recompense, of course! These little tugs ran back and forth like angry monsters, spewing diesel fumes as they raced to load and unload the ships' cargoes. Time limitations drove the turnaround of unloading and loading the vessels, speed was the essence and the tugs raced back and forth with impunity, under the very eyes of HM Customs & Excises officers, who would hesitate without very good reason to ever interfere in this slick commercial operation. The illicit cargoes which the tugs carried in their driver cabs just disappeared as if by magic, along with a little help from the Loadmaster. Once clear of the ship, the next member of the chain was the driver of the ship's chandler lorry, who picked up the contraband from one of the cavernous warehouses and took them away from the docks. These lorries were such a regular sight, in and around the dockyard, that they were never given a second thought by HM Customs or the dockyard security staff. Another political cost-cutting exercise had also played into Dave's hands, and that was the demise of the British Transport Police Officers from the docks. In a rush for short term savings, the dock management had gone along with the modern craze of privatising everything. The old-fashioned dock coppers had been notorious for their crime-fighting prowess, an august body of men and woman who had been protecting and keeping a grip on crime around the dock estates since the late 1800's but now the protection of these vast vulnerable dockland areas had been reduced, handed over to private security firms which proved to be nothing more than watchmen in uniform. By the time the Dock's Board realised they were losing more financially in criminal activity than they had saved in disbanding the BTP Docks branch, it was too late.

On the odd occasion that a security guard on the dock gate did look in the back of the wagon, he would be looking for anything that might have been stolen from the docks not from ship's stores, what could be more natural than a ship chandler's lorry returning unwanted stores that had been over-ordered? The enquiring mind of a trained professional BTP officer might not have been so easily 'hoodwinked', but thankfully for Dave, those days had gone. The driver always had forged documents on hand, so nothing would be found missing from the ship's inventory, even if an investigation could have been mounted, now unlikely as there was no one to carry out this task. However, a trained docks police detective would have looked deeper to untangle the illicit paper trail covering up the smuggling racket. Another thing in Dave's favour was that around the same time as the last dock copper hung up his helmet, truncheon and handcuffs, locked up the police station door and left, another very efficient law enforcement agency, the HM Customs Water Guard, was also being disbanded. Yet another front line of defence was gone, leaving a great big gap through which the Dave Dundas' of this world could exploit. So, it was Dave who became known as 'Mr Big' in what was one of Europe's biggest black economies. Dave knew that the days of Duty-Free were numbered and intended to make a killing while the going was good. Dave enjoyed his newfound status and had difficulty hiding his pleasure, so it wasn't surprising that he made enemies.

For the time being, Dave was, as he would describe, 'King of the Heap', and as Captain Sanderson looked down on him from the bridge, Dave hadn't a care in the world. Arthur Sanderson had heard the rumours and was well aware that whatever Dave Dundas was up to, it would be of no good, but it was, after all, just rumours. Alone with his memories of yester-year and thoughts of the morrow, Sanderson pulled his battered cap further down on his forehead and turned his collar up. He walked out on to the bridge wing to gaze up at his Commodore's pennant, pulling hard on its halyard in the strong wind. With a heavy heart, he climbed on to the Monkey Island and hauled it down: he would keep it as a memento to hang on the wall of his study at home. The company's new Commodore would soon be flying his own flag probably from Beaumont's only new super ferry, not this old battered steamer, or so he thought.

Back on the bridge wing, glancing down to the quay, Arthur saw the Marine Superintendent striding up the gangway followed by Arthur's wife, Muriel. Arthur was pleased that she had come down to welcome him. He had not asked her to, but sometimes it was if they could read each other's minds. Over their forced separation during his years of seafaring sailing the seven seas they had developed between them a sixth sense, instinctively knowing how the other was feeling. For Arthur, going forward, life was to be a future of gardening and forecasting the weather from his home on the Lincolnshire coast, pleased to have had these forty minutes on the bridge to himself, walking around what was often termed his office, absorbed in the nostalgia of his 45 years at sea. Of course, his sea days were not completely over. With retirement in mind, a few years ago, he'd bought a small semi converted coastal cruiser as a DIY project. She was an ex Scottish North Sea trawler, and with months of work during his off duty spells, he had completed the conversion, turning her into a 'well found' comfortable cabin cruiser. Maybe she would take him and Muriel around the world – if they so chose, but for him, he would be content with day trips just to feel the movement of a deck beneath his feet. Leaving the bridge behind him, he turned, gave it a fond final salute and went down to his cabin to join his wife and the Marine Superintendent.

Down in the crew mess, Dave Dundas had just poured himself a big steaming mug of tea. He sat at the table and pondered on how he could get ashore for a few hours without being missed. He needed to collect some monies from one of his customers and he also quite fancied the idea of popping home for a quick shag with Sam – this brought a broad smile to his face. Sitting alone, at the other end of the long mess room, was the Quartermaster, Tommy. Tommy didn't like the Dave Dundas's of this world, young 'whippersnappers' he called them, always trying to buck the system, doing less for more. 'No respect, these youngsters of today,' thought Tommy. He preferred the old ways where you knew where you stood, disciplined and regimented, not quite military discipline but rules and regulations that kept everything in order. The likes of Dundas and his mates questioned authority. Little could they see that it was their type that had helped ruin the British Merchant Navy, making owners look at foreign crews and foreign flags to avoid the constant disruption that the new breed of so-called union sailor was always causing. Tommy knew exactly what Dundas was up to with his tobacco smuggling. It was only old fashioned shipmate loyalty but in this case, misguided loyalty that stopped him from shopping Dave Dundas.

Despite Dave Dundas outward appearance of confidence, he was in reality far from it. His tobacco smuggling business had grown so much that, at times, he felt as if he was losing control. Especially now that there was a rumour that the smuggling had come to the attention of the Triesus brothers. The Triesus brothers were a product of a large Northwold council estate who modelled themselves on the legendary Kray twins of London's East End. Like the Kray twins, the Triesus brothers suffered from dysfunctional psychological defects in the makeup of their characters. The Triesus brothers controlled a large empire of brothels, street girls, protection rackets and a couple of seedy dockside cafés. They had heard of the Dave Dundas tobacco empire, and while they tolerated it, what really annoyed them was when they discovered that their two cafés were selling Dundas smuggled tobacco.

Managing the two cafés for the Triesus brothers was an unfortunate soul called Les Green. Les was small in stature, probably brought about by his mother's constant drinking and drug use while she was pregnant. She'd died a few years after giving birth, resulting in Les being in and out of care all his life. He had no idea who his father was but heard rumours about his mother's over liberal sex life. He'd avoided education whenever possible, playing truant to such an extent that teachers had given up on him along with the string of social workers appointed to his case. He was bullied throughout his teenage years. Miraculously, and despite his wayward upbringing, Les managed to stay away from drink and drugs, and when he wasn't stealing, he spent a lot of time at the local gym working out, trying to make himself tougher. It was here that a kind, old amateur boxing trainer took Les under his wing, and for once, Les had a purpose in life; he was determined to learn how to box sufficiently well to outsmart his tormentors. However, Les never did get around to taking his revenge, as his amateur trainer soon realised that Les was a natural when it came to fast movement and coordination of hands, arms, legs and feet. It wasn't long before Les hit the big time as a Bantamweight professional boxer and would probably have gone on to more stardom had an evil witch, in the form of Jessica Hunt, not walked into his life. Jessica was as hard as nails, and according to rumours had had more 'pricks than a dartboard'. Jessica was no lady, all-woman certainly, but no lady. With a coarse, guttural, heavy smoker's laugh that would send shivers of fear down the spine of many a man, but not Les, and more tattoo-covered than bare skin, she was an alpha female attracting the nickname Jess Cunt. Due to his lack of education, Les was backward in many areas, including the ways of the world. He had only experienced sex once, if it could have been called that, with a young neighbourhood girlfriend before meeting Jessica. Until meeting her, sex had never been of much interest to Les, he couldn't see what all the fuss was about, but Jessica took Les in-hand and introduced him to sexual enjoyment that most men would never experience. He became totally and utterly devoted to her; she knew how to play a man. Les was literally blown away, that being one of Jessica's specialties! Les was totally under her control. It wasn't long before Jess and Les were married, giving her access to the money Les was earning as a Bantamweight professional boxer; she lived the 'high life'.

Suddenly, just as his career was taking off, he suffered his first defeat. Les, instead of withdrawing from a fight that was not going his way either on points or practically, unwisely and against his old trainer's advice, fought on. Sitting in the ringside was Jessica. She was out-screaming most of the men around her, screaming at Les to carry on, which he did until he suffered a deadly knockout blow, falling to the canvas and into a coma. Although the brain, floating in a protective coating of serum, can withstand some tremendous shock, there comes the point when the serum can no longer protect the brain, and consequently, Les suffered brain damage. When Les eventually came out of the coma in the hospital, it took him some time to figure out where he was and what had happened to him. When he spoke, it felt like he'd been to the dentist for an extraction with one side of his mouth completely numb, useless and lopsided, he couldn't control it when he attempted to speak.

Once Jessica discovered that Les' boxing career was over, she took what she could and disappeared, leaving Les with divorce papers. The good times were over; she didn't want to be around in case Les needed a full-time nurse. Jessica drew the line at having to give any man, even her man, a bed-bath plus all the other associated ablutions that she feared would be necessary if, as it appeared, Les was not going to be the same man.

The damage to his brain had left him with almost total amnesia, although the doctors said that with time his memory would return. When he eventually arrived home from the hospital, he returned to a beautiful big house he could hardly remember. He found it hard to believe he could ever have afforded such a luxurious home. He found he was being sued for divorce by a woman he couldn't even recall being married to. Les was looked after by his old trainer, who was more like an uncle, he took care of all financial and legal matters and Les, unlike Jessica's worst fears, didn't require the full-time nursing care, but just needed to be guided and told what to do each day, just like a child. The regular home visits from the physiotherapist and voice therapist aided Les on the road to partial recovery from his terrible injury. If Jessica had displayed some loyalty to Les and stayed around long enough, she would have discovered that her life could have been a utopia, but she wouldn't realise this until many years later when she learned the invaluable lesson of life *'you reap what you sow'*.

When the Triesus brothers went to visit Les, it pained them to see him in his child-like state. The Triesus brothers had followed his career and regularly backed him to win, which had resulted in lucrative earnings for them. The brothers felt an abstract loyalty to Les as, like them, he had come from humble beginnings and made something of himself. The brothers had built a vast empire of wealth, and Les could have produced even more himself if he'd not fought on during that fateful night. Despite their own poor upbringing and the violent way they had made it to be kings of the local criminal heap, the Triesus' didn't like Jessica. To them, she was a 'slag' who belonged in the gutter. Their world was full of women like Jessica, 'financial whores' looking for a good meal ticket.

Les was left with a slight speech impediment, similar to that of a stroke victim. One thing was for sure, he would never enter the ring again. On medical advice, he retired from boxing; the risk was too great, suffering another blow to his head, could have devastating consequences, including death. Les had no financial worries; even with Jessica taking what she could, his earnings from boxing had made him secure for the rest of his life, but being retired from the boxing ring, he needed a new purpose in life. When the brothers heard about Les' demise, they took pity on him and recruited him to take charge of their dockside café empire. These apparent seedy cafes, were, in fact, nice little earners for the Triesus brothers and gave them a legitimate business to launder their ill-gotten gains from their criminal activities.

Dave Dundas had been at school with Les but they lost touch with each other as they started out on the journey of adulthood, having taken different roads. It had been Les's brief exposure under the spotlight whilst boxing that Dave Dundas recognised his old school chum. When Dave heard that Les had taken over the running a couple of dockside cafes, it was an opportunity Dave could not resist. Renewing their acquaintance, it didn't take Dave long to persuade Les to sell some of his imported rolling tobacco, a popular brand amongst the hand rolling cigarette smokers on the docks. Dave Dundas didn't know the Triesus brothers owned these cafes; otherwise, he would have given them a wide berth, as it didn't pay to cross the Triesus crime family. When the Triesus brothers did discover that their cafés were selling Dave's illegally imported cigarettes and tobacco products, well, that was, in their eyes, taking the piss to the extreme!

Chapter 15

Several decks below the bridge deck, Captain Arthur Sanderson was in the main passenger lounge, next to the Purser's Bureau. A beehive of activity as the Immigration Officers, Special Branch, and various other port officials dealt with the business of checking passengers into the United Kingdom. The *s.s.'Beamish'* had accommodation for 100 passengers, including lorry drivers and business people taking their cars across to Europe; it provided a 'Club Class' way to travel, offering comfort and service that echoed a bygone era, an alternative to the mass transit 'pack 'em in on the cheap' aboard the larger ferries on the south coast. When travelling with Beaumont's, the passengers would be requested to leave their cars at the bottom of a gangway and board the vessel on foot. They would then be greeted by smartly dressed, courteous cabin stewards and shown to a cabin. While they then enjoyed the amenities the vessel had to offer, their cars would be driven on to the car deck. The passengers would not see their vehicles again until the following morning when they disembarked in Rotterdam, here their cars would be waiting for their owners at the foot of the gangway. This lavish style of short sea travel gave the passengers time to experience the full service of the vessel, including minibars in the cabin, full cabin service if they preferred, although most enjoyed going along to the first class lounge to mix with other like-minded travellers before enjoying an 'a la carte' menu in the main dining room, for which, most evenings they would be joined by the Captain or at least a Senior Officer. The lorry drivers had their own club room and were as equally well looked after by the attentive staff, enjoying a well-earned break in their long trans-continental journeys. During the daylight crossings in the summer, both passengers and lorry drivers could enjoy a relaxing afternoon on the spacious decks with chairs, loungers and full bar service. As such, this had been the dream of James Beaumont, to take people across the North Sea in style.

In one corner of the lounge, oblivious to the hustle and bustle going on around them, stood two people; one was the ship's Purser, Guy Hollins, tall, athletic, fair-haired and blue-eyed with finely chiselled facial features, cutting a dashing figure in his Merchant Navy uniform with its three gold rings inlaid with white around the cuffs of his jacket. The other, a young woman, Alexandra Evans, standing just five feet three inches tall, but perfect in every detail from her petite but lithe figure to the silky blond hair which cascaded down her back. She truly was a golden girl, with a beautiful complexion that goes with youth, the kind of girl that men tend to fall in love with at first sight. A truly modern girl, she had been intent upon seeing some of the world before settling down to family life. She now found herself on the last leg of her journey of adventures; after this, her path would take her to her parents' home.

Alexandra, much to her parents' dismay, on leaving college made a career choice that would not keep her local to the family home. She had written to the Crown Agents, and following a successful interview and medical had flown off to her first posting at a British Embassy compound on the Gold Coast of West Africa. This, being one of the many countries which had once been part of the cumbersome Great British Empire but following its independence had then struggled with economic problems, going from one political coup to another, now mired in endless corruption. Alexandra had stayed there for four exciting, and at times frightening, years. She had seen happiness, famine and bloodshed. Taking to her job with relish and the enthusiasm of youth, she had involved herself within the community, working far beyond her official responsibilities. She could have chosen to work and live within the protection of the British Embassy, with its constant social life of cocktail parties and extravagance as the representatives of HM Government paid court to the subsequent governments as they came to power, but she was not content to just settle for that; Alexandra was hungry to experience the real Third World life.

It was while she was carrying out this extra curricula voluntary work that she met and fell in love with an Air Ambulance pilot who flew for the Charitable Christian Air Brigade in Africa, known as 'CAB' for short. As with most things in life it had been one of those chance encounters, a day off for Alexandra and she had chosen to go down to the beach to laze in the hot West African sun, work on her tan and swim in the huge blue Atlantic rollers as they came in from thousands of miles away, crashing spectacularly on to a vast sweeping, golden, deserted beach. Thanks to the discovery of oil, together with the local warring tribal factions, package holiday companies had yet to find this beautiful part of Africa. Laying in the baking African sun, soaking up the rays, Alexandra had started to drift off, thinking to herself that she must be careful not to fall asleep and burn in the scorching heat, even the Factor 45 which she had liberally applied before stretching out wouldn't protect for too long against the strong equatorial sun's rays. As she daydreamed, she heard her housekeeper, Enuna, calling as she ran down the beach towards her.

"Missy, Missy Alex, please come quick," she called as she struggled to run in the soft, thick sand.

Alexandra jumped up with a sense of alarm, "What is it Enuna?"

"Dis Oranje, my friend's daughter, she with bambino and somting very wrong Missy," gabbled Enuna excitedly in her West African pidgin English. Alexandra was so revered among the local compound that they would often come to her for help. Grabbing her clothes and beach bag containing her brick like mobile phone, Alexandra was soon running up the beach towards the compound's nearby native fishing quarter. Quickly covering herself with her kaftan and slipping on her sandals she carried on with Enuna into the village and eventually to a basic little stone and plaster house. Inside was Oranje, it was obvious she was in pain, something was terribly wrong and she clearly needed medical attention very quickly.

The British compound enjoyed the facilities of a clinic, which was capable of providing most routine medical care for the Consular staff and servants, but the more critical cases would need the facilities of a large hospital. Such hospitals were rare in this part of Africa and the acute cases had to be medevacked by helicopters operated by local Defence Force, although their helicopters were often grounded for technical reasons, basically lack of spare parts thanks to the endemic Government corruption. The alternative was the Christian Charitable Air Brigade, operating small aircraft, world-wide in some of the most inhospitable and remote places on the planet.

Thinking quickly, Alexandra realised that there was no time to spare – Oranje needed urgent hospitalisation. She ran like a gazelle back to the main office, grabbed the keys to the Landrover Discovery, one of the Embassy pool cars, then returned to collect Oranje and Enuna. She was driving as quickly as she could along the rough tracks that would eventually lead to the small local airfield used by the oil companies for moving men and equipment as well as for the air ambulances. On the way she began to become sick with worry. Numerous questions raced through her thoughts. Had she been too hasty? What would she do at the airfield? How would she get hold of an Air Ambulance? Maybe it wouldn't be there if already deployed on a mission? Perhaps she should have tried to find the British compound doctor and let him decide, had she bitten off more than she could chew in her haste to help? Would she be criticised again by her superiors for getting too involved in matters with the locals that were none of her business?

Alexandra was looked upon as being a feisty, headstrong, renegade that didn't quite gel with the Foreign and Commonwealth office management style. However, she in turn, saw her bosses as being chinless wonders, Colonel Blimp types, and descendants of the old upper class, interbred aristocracy still living in the glory days of the Empire, who treated the locals as nothing more than servants. Within less than half an hour, she was driving through the entrance to the small airfield, which was little more than a collection of rough huts, looking completely out of place next to a tall watchtower that was more akin to that of a regional UK airport. Telling Enuna to stay with the groaning Oranje, she leapt up the tower's stairs and, despite her fit body, she was soon feeling her lungs near to bursting, gasping for air as oxygenated blood pumped furiously through her body. Finally, at the top, she entered without knocking, surprising the controller, a chap she vaguely knew from one of the Embassy cocktail parties.

"Please, you've got to help me," she gasped. Momentarily startled, the duty Flight Information Officer, Mike Parker, soon recovered and smiled slowly at Alexandra, taking in her lithe, suntanned body scantily clothed in a wrap-around kaftan.

"Good day, Alex isn't it?" came the reply, in an antipodeans' drawl of a Queenslander, clicking his fingers as if in celebration at remembering a name.

"Alexandra... yes," she panted in reply, slightly confused at being addressed as Alex, she didn't like her name shortened and always discouraged it.

"I need to contact the air ambulance service or the army, one of my native workers is pregnant and could be having a miscarriage, she might die if I don't get her to hospital," she stuttered like a machine gun between gasps for breath. Still grinning, Mike had difficulty in taking his eyes of Alexandra's beautifully rising and falling breasts as her lungs sucked in volumes of air. "Well, you are in luck, Alex, one of the CAB aircraft, has just called up and is on his way. I'll give him another call and see what he can do for you, in the meantime, you better get back to your girl and try and keep her calm while you wait."

"It's ok, another one of my girls is with her, please hurry, call the air ambulance," she gasped again as her breathing began to recover, fighting the sickening butterflies in her stomach as she realised the enormity of her actions in bringing the poorly woman to the airfield in the hope of getting her flown away to hospital. What if Enuna's friend lost the baby, what if the mother too died? Had her actions endangered the lives of two people? Would her actions not be looked upon so much as an Angel of Mercy but that of a headstrong, impudent young woman who'd made decisions and acted way above her pay grade. Would she be sent home in disgrace?

She wasn't in the best place with her immediate boss, one Tristan Cardington-Fowler, whom she saw as just an arrogant twerp who had tried more than once to get into Alexandra's knickers, unsuccessfully, and thus was now trying to seek revenge by conjuring up ways to have her removed back to the UK. Tristan came from the long line of a Shropshire land owning family who'd packed off their totally useless son into the Foreign Office where they'd hoped that he would make a name for himself, but so far failing spectacularly with only his family connections keeping his head above water! He was as useless as a diplomat as he was at being a gentleman farmer! Tristan, due to his privileged upbringing, together with his landed gentry family background, had developed an overbearing, full of his own self-importance superior attitude to life, wrongly assuming that his family name would propel him along with a minimum of effort on his part. What would his hero Grandfather, decorated with the VC at Passendale, have made of him? Tristan had yet to understand the error of his ways if he ever would! On more than one occasion, Alexandra had saved Tristan from creating some absolute diplomatic howlers, which would have certainly brought about his downfall. However, such was his blind belief in himself, together with an idiosyncratic approach to his duties and being a total pratt; he just didn't see it that way! These characteristics, together with the failed sexual conquest of Alexandra, all added up to seeing her as an interfering busy body he could well do without on his team.

Consequently, he had developed a deep-seated loathing for her, looking for any excuse to end her career in this part of Africa. Despite this fact, Alexander considered contacting Tristan, but realising that even if she did get hold of him, which was doubtful as he was like the proverbial Scarlet Pimpernel and never around when needed the most, he'd no doubt order her back immediately to see the base Doctor. No, she reprimanded herself, she had made the decision so, right or wrong, she must stick with it, although Tristan's image hung like the '*Sword of Damocles*' over her, as she continued to vacillate on her hasty decision.

"Ok, ok, slow down, it won't get here any quicker," replied Mike before pointing towards the west.

"Look there she is now," he directed Alexandra's eyes to a small dot in the distant sky that was slowly becoming larger. He picked up a hand microphone from the desk in front of him and called in a concise Aussie drawl, "Kawas Tower to November three, two, seven, delta bravo."

"November, three, two, seven, delta bravo, joining overhead for a downwind left for runway 29," came the calm reply of ex-Royal Naval pilot, Steve Gaunt, as he manoeuvred the new large Cessna Caravan 208, to join the circuit and land at the airfield.

"Goodday mate and hiyah Steve," replied Mike with the familiarity that had developed between the controllers and the 'CAB' pilots who regularly flew mercy missions into this jungle airfield.

"I've gotta beautiful little lady down here with an urgent case for transporting to Banju hospital, can you do it mate?" questioned Mike, knowing that it would be most unlikely that Steve would turn down such a request, although he'd have to call his Ops Base in Banju to clear it with them.

Controllers normally wear headsets while communicating with aircraft, but in haste, Mike had picked up the alternative handset, and consequently, the conversation between Mike and the air ambulance pilot echoed out of a large wall-mounted loudspeaker.

"Yeah, no problem, providing she's got nice big tits," came the affable, relaxed reply from the pilot, Steve Gaunt.

"Well, I'll leave you to make that decision, Steve," smirked Mike as he turned and winked at the slightly horrified Alexandra, the redness of a blush creeping up her neck as she turned to leave to get her patient ready, but not before stopping at the door. She turned to Mike, "You can tell your male, chauvinistic pig of a pilot that I have great tits..." she shook her head in disbelief that she had used the word 'tits' and continued, "I mean breasts....oh and thank you." she said, a feeling of relief now sweeping over her, knowing that help was on its way.

Leaving the control tower and ascending the steps, all she could hear was Mike's voracious laughter as he explained over the air to Steve that Alexandra had heard his comment.

"Oh bollocks, me and my big mouth," Steve muttered to himself

"Yep, you and your big mouth," laughed Simba, Steve's passenger, a Doctor who was working with CCAB as part of a joint co-operation project. Steve shook his head in embarrassment. "Right, c'mon baby, lets land," said Steve as he started running through his final pre-landing checks.

"Brakes off, undercarriage down, fuel on and sufficient for a go-around, flaps lowered."

He turned the Cessna from the base leg and on to its final approach to the landing strip.

After making a textbook landing and roll-out, Steve taxied the powerful single-engine aircraft and parked in front of the control tower. Opening the large cargo/passenger door, he jumped out of the aircraft with the agility of a much younger man, closely followed by Simba and they headed for the tower. Mike and Alexandra stood outside, waiting to greet them. Mike grabbed Steve's hand, at the same time giving him a great big bear hug in the genuine warmth of old friends and with a large grin almost bursting into laughter as he turned and introduced Alexandra.

"Hey, this is the little lady with nice tits, Alex Evans."

"It's Alexandra, not Alex," she snapped in annoyance. She ignored Steve's outstretched hand as at the same time he introduced Dr. Simba Abioye.

"This is Simba who is a local doctor working with me and he'll look after your casualty." Steve tried to sound reassuring, hoping to cover up his previous faux pas but realising he had failed spectacularly. Alexandra gave Simba a her beaming heart warming smile, expressing her gratitude as she shook his hand, but immediately changed her look to anger as she turned to Steve.

"And I haven't got time to waste on sexist morons," she said sternly. "I need to get a young girl to hospital as quickly as possible, and you're the only way of achieving that!" Her impatience was obvious. Feeling duly rebuked despite being the pilot of life-saving transport, Steve was left standing feeling slightly gormless as Dr Simba followed Alexandra as she hurried across to the waiting Landrover to collect Oranje and Enuna, swiftly followed by Mike. Steve, still extremely embarrassed, swung into action, ran back to his plane and opened the large cargo doors in preparation to accept the casualty and passengers. Dr Simba supervised the boarding of his passengers into the rear and Steve encouraged Alexandra into the front co-pilot position. Steve secured the large side doors and climbed back into his front left-hand seat. After a quick safety briefing to Alexandra, leaving Simba to settle in Enuna and the casualty Oranje in the rear, he commenced the start-up drills. Steve soon had the Cessna lined up and ready for take-off. Once given the clearance to depart by Mike, Steve pushed the throttle fully forward, put in some left rudder and aileron to counter the crosswind and headed straight down the centre line of the grass and dirt jungle runway into the hot African air.

Within minutes, the aircraft and its passengers were soaring high into the hot blue sky. Levelling out at cruising altitude of 8,000 feet, they sat just above the scattered cumulus cloud, where they would be free from the turbulent thermals. Steve dialled up the data for Banju airport into the Garmin GPS on the centre console of the well-equipped Cessna. He should have done this while on the ground but with the atmosphere of urgency he just wanted to get everyone airborne and on their way. Within seconds, the direct track came upon the moving map display as Steve turned the aircraft to intercept the track line, putting the beautiful large aircraft on course for Banju. Once Steve had signed off over the radio with Mike back at Kawas, he set up the auto-pilot and started to relax for the thirty-minute flight to Banju, he intended to break the ice and to redeem himself in Alexandra's eyes. Alexandra, Steve and Dr Simba were wearing communication headsets, but the two women in the rear of the plane were only wearing ear protectors, and before Steve had the chance to strike up a conversation with Alexandra, she asked if it was ok to leave the seat next to him to go and see how her patient was coping.

"Of course, no problem," he said slightly rejected. He so wanted to get on to good terms with Alexandra after the earlier faux pas. He was really rather taken with Alexandra, whom he considered to be an absolute stunner, her close proximity causing his heartbeat to increase. Fortunately, after being reassured by Dr.Simba, Alexandra was soon climbing back into the front right-hand seat, brushing gently against Steve in the confines of the cockpit. Her subtle fragrant, feminine scent mixed with the aroma of the beach and sea enveloped Steve, sending tantalising shivers down his spine. Her light flowing kaftan hid very little of her magnificent tanned body. She carefully placed her headset back over her ears and gave a slight chaste smile to Steve.

He smiled back, "Can you hear me loud and clear?" he enquired.

"Yes," came her slightly husky voice through the intercom system.

"All okay with our passengers back there?"

"Your Doctor has given her an injection which has eased the pain, thank goodness he was with you," she replied, a feeling relief sweeping over her knowing that having Dr. Simba onboard giving professional medical attention to Oranje would boost her confidence at the decision she had taken, helping her enormously when the eventual confrontation would come her Boss, Tristan Cardington-Fowler, who would without doubt be demanding a full explanation and more than likely use this as another attempt at discrediting her.

"Look ... I'm dreadfully sorry about earlier," Steve babbled, feeling like a love-struck teenager, "it was only meant to be innocent boyish chat between mates," he said embarrassed.

Dr. Simba, although watching over and monitoring Oranje's condition, gave a huge smile as he listened in through his communications head set as Steve attempted to reconcile himself with Alexandra.

"Yes, it was rather infantile," she teased, putting on a stern, matriarchal like voice followed with a little giggle. Secretly she thought Steve, for a slightly older man, was still 'knicker dropping gorgeous'. Hearing the amusement in her voice, Steve kept the conversation flowing, desperate to redeem himself and wanting to know more about her. With one eye on the GPS, watching the miles count down towards Banju, Steve soon realised that he was going to have to call the approach controller at Banju and the serious side of flying would have to take over from their intermittent light-hearted chatter. Although quite a busy airport, Banju Air Traffic Control didn't have any approach radar, so all approaches had to be done by the 'Mark 1 Eyeball.' With his relatively small aircraft having to mix it with large 747 cargo planes, local domestic aircraft, and some international airliners, Steve would need all his wits about him to slot into the circuit pattern to land safely. He briefly explained this to Alexandra, asking her and Dr. Simba to look out for other aircraft. Steve soon had the Cessna lined up for the final approach and landed. Following a short taxi onto the apron, he spotted the land ambulance waiting for them, a battered ex delivery van that had seen better days. All too soon, Alexandra, Enuna and Oranje were in the ambulance ready to leave, accompanied by Dr. Simba who had volunteered to go along and brief his colleagues at the hospital. Steve, not wanting Alexandra to leave, tried not to sound too desperate.

"How on earth are you going to get back to Kawas?" His mind raced to work out a way to stay in contact with her in an attempt to establish their relationship; he wasn't going to let this foxy lady slip through his fingers that easily.

"Right at this moment in time, I don't care, all I want to do is get Oranje to hospital, so we must go now," she said, raising her voice towards the driver.

"Ok, ok, of course, I understand, stay with Simba he'll look after you and bring you back here and in the meantime I'll get clearance from my Ops to fly you back to Kawas.

The doctor at the hospital decided it would be best to keep Oranje in for a few days in an attempt to save the baby. Simba, Alexandra and Enuna came back to the airport by taxi where Simba parted company for the day. Steve quickly offered to fly Alexandra and Enuna home and they gratefully accepted. Once back, much to his delight, Alexandra invited Steve back to her compound house for dinner and to stay over; in the guest bedroom, she had emphasised. After enjoying a lovely dinner, prepared and served by Enuna, the stress and exhaustion from the day's events soon became apparent as their bodies craved sleep and rest. Too soon, they chastely said goodnight to each other and went to their separate rooms, both feeling the magic in the air between them. In the morning, Alexandra took Steve back to the airfield. Before he climbed aboard and under the large wing of the Cessna, he took Alexandra in his arms and gently kissed her beautiful lips – Alexandra returned his kiss with a passion that left no doubt in his mind how she felt about him.

He flew off into the bright blue sky, feeling like a man walking on air. After this encounter, they dated regularly whenever Steve could fly across to see her, and it wasn't long before Steve proposed. It was in a perfect setting; they sat on the beach, drinking champagne, taking in the starlit night, listening to and watching the moonlit fluorescence of the huge Atlantic surf crashing on to the bleached white beach.

Chapter 16

Steve thoroughly enjoyed his job. Flying around West Africa, high above the steaming jungle. In many ways, it was a carefree life and relatively easy after the stress of flying fast jets for the Royal Navy. His Navy instructors had always rated him as an average pilot, but average was enough to make the grade on Buccaneers, which were then the backbone of the Fleet Air Arm. His score of 'average' was in all probability because Steve had transferred to naval flying older than the normal entry age.

Consequently, he had the experience of age but slower reaction times than his younger counterparts. Steve, having trained at a 6th form Naval College, had applied for entry into the Navy as a pilot at 18, but an incompetent civil servant failed him on his eyesight test, saying he was slightly colour blind – automatically precluding him from flying duties. Steve had then elected to train as a Supply Officer, and some years later, as Lieutenant Commander (S) Steve Gaunt, he found himself on a temporary exchange transfer to the Royal New Zealand Navy aboard the frigate *HMNZS Dunedin* on passage from Wellington to the Falkland Islands via Cape Horn. It was to be a long passage of several weeks at an economical steaming speed, to save taxpayers money.

A long time to spend working in an office at sea, deep in the bowels of a ship, even on an active warship with all its daily military activities and drills designed to help pass some of the time. In the evenings, after dinner in the wardroom, Steve would wander up to the bridge and talk with an RNZN Lieutenant Commander he'd befriended, Stathis Santakidies, a New Zealand born, second-generation Greek immigrant, whose father had been a sea captain. Stathis followed in his father's footsteps and answered the call to join up while studying classics at the University of Waikato, near Auckland on the North Island. Stathis was not how most imagined an archetypical dashing naval officer, being rather short and rotund. He had a dark olive, Eastern Mediterranean complexion with a thick mop of jet black curly hair. His very round hirsute chubby face created a 5 o'clock shadow long before the end of the day. Despite his cuddly physic, women were easily lured by his glib tongue, wild wit and his penetrating eyes. Stathis' eyes were dark ebony and always appeared to be laughing, eyes that could almost mesmerise a woman rather like a rabbit caught in the headlights of an oncoming car. His secret weapon, as he liked to call it, was being hung like the proverbial donkey, but then the women didn't know this at first; they soon found out either to their pleasure or in some cases horror! Stathis, after a couple of beers, used to regale the story of one woman who, on seeing his erect penis, ran to the bathroom, locking herself in shrieking, "Don't come near me with that thing." The story, whether true or not, had certainly earned him a few free beers over the years.

Steve and Stathis would talk away the evening watch, discussing anything and everything. The topic of conversation would often turn to girls, sex and the variety of conquests they'd encountered in the various ports of call around the world.

"The thing is Stathis, me old mucker, how does a chap like you pull the popsies, I mean with all due respect you're short, and a tad over weight," Steve said, laughing in a way that only very close friends could laugh and take the mickey out of each other.

"Ahh, but that's my secret Steve, me boy," replied Stathis, who thanks to his time in the RNZN and his officer training at the Britannia Royal Naval College, Dartmouth, England, had lost his Greek accent which only returned occasionally after enjoying several glasses of beer with 'Ouzo' chasers.

"You see, this large belly of mine works as a rocking a horse when I'm riding the ladies."

"What ladies you Greek plonker, you mean old tarts," chuckled Steve.

Stathis squinted at Steve, then continued, "As I was saying, me young English mucker, while riding a lady, I use this rather large midriff to start a rocking horse motion like this." Stathis motioned his rocking horse mimic, his broad smile showing off a flash of bright white teeth. "So, you see, it is a kiss fuck, kiss fuck, kiss fuck motion, drives them crazy," exclaimed Stathis lustfully with a burst of raucous, infectious laughter, causing Steve also to burst out laughing.

As their laughter subsided, Stathis looked out of the bridge window and saw a ship in the distance. He grabbed one of the handsets from a bank of phones in front of him.

"Radar plot, what have got bearing green 060?" snapped Stathis.

"Target, Sir … small craft on that bearing."

"Well damn it, man, why didn't you call it? That's sloppy," he reprimanded the seaman in the operations room.

"Sorry Sir, lost it in the clutter; it is only a small target."

"Very well, start the plot and keep me advised."

"Aye aye Sir," came the smart reply.

Down in the operations room, all was quiet after a hectic day. Most of the watch had been stood down, which left just Leading Radar Technician, Dave Watkins. Dave was known as *'Dodgy'* to his mates because he was always dodging the PTI work-outs on the flight deck. His 'oppo' at the adjoining communications panel was Leading Communications Technician John *'Buster'* Crabb; he was like the famous Royal Navy Commander Crabb a diver as well as a communications technician.

Dave didn't like that Stathis had called him 'sloppy.'

He turned to John, "Fucking officers! What's Greeko getting all upset about, he's got a fucking repeater up there, didn't he see the ship, why is he giving me a hard time … we're all fucking tired after today's drill."

John laughed, "He's not a bad bloke, old Johnny Greek, better than that snotty-nosed Sub I've got as a divisional officer, straight out of training and thinks he's Admiral fucking Horatio bleeding Nelson."

They both ended up having a good laugh as Dave turned his attention to the plot chart, tracking the small vessel.

Steve sauntered towards Stathis, "You are a pratt at times Stathis, there was no need for that."

Stathis wagged his finger at Steve, "Keeps them on their toes, dear boy." He reached for a pair of binoculars to look for the ship.

"Well, be that as it may, what do you want those things for? The ship is right over there, I can see its lights without binos," exclaimed Steve.

"Oh really," replied Stathis rather sarcastically, positioning the binoculars to his eyes.

"Yes, I certainly can, can't you?"

"Of course I can see dear boy, it's just that I'm slightly older than you and need a little help these days."

"Yes, but I'm talking colours, I can see the red, green and the white mast headlights, so she is coming towards us from the southeast, so how far away do you reckon she is Stath?" Steve had a hint of excitement in his voice.

Lowering his binoculars, Stathis turned to Steve and grinned, "You are right, my boy, so what? You've spotted her navigation lights!"

Steve, almost whooping with joy, could hardly contain his excitement. He slapped Stathis on his back, "Well, don't you know what this means," he momentarily stopped mid-sentence before carrying on, "No, of course, you don't, look I'll explain. When I joined the Navy I didn't intend to be a Supply Officer, I wanted to be a flyer, but when I attended for the medical, I passed on all counts but for my colour vision. The medics said it wasn't bad, but it wasn't good enough for flying duties, they said I couldn't distinguish green and white at a long distance, something to do with weak whatchamacallits," then snapping his fingers, "well they're commonly known as rods and cones in the back of my eyes. All of which was fucking galling when I passed the same eyesight test to get into the Naval College!" Steve almost shrieked as he felt his temper rising as he travelled back in time to that dreadful day when he failed the eyesight test.

"Well, Stevo, it looks as though they were wrong!"

"Too damn right they were," Steve's voice hardening, "I always knew they were, said so at the time but nobody would listen to me, couldn't believe it when the little prick gave me a fail, I was heartbroken. He wasn't even a bloody medic just some pen-pushing bloody civil servant, if I met the bugger now I'd give him more than a piece of my mind."

"Now, now, calm down, otherwise you'll be giving yourself a coronary me young English bucko, well come to think of it, you're not that young anymore!" said Stathis with a smirk on his face, but Steve wasn't listening, he was too excited.

"Calm down? I can hardly contain myself, I can see the lights clearly on that ship out there and that's all that counts. I'm gonna pop to the wardroom later and see our good old Doc, me old Greek mucker," giggled Steve.

"In fact, I'm going to see him right now," and with that, Steve dashed from the bridge and headed down to the wardroom like a man possessed. The New Zealand Surgeon Commander carried out some checks using Ishara Plates and confirmed that he could see nothing wrong with Steve's eyes. Once his deployment was over with the Royal New Zealand Navy, Steve flew back home to his base at Portsmouth and immediately set about pestering the Navy Higher Command along with the Naval Personnel and Appointments office. He even put in a request to meet the Admiral, who was Head of Naval Flying. Eventually, due to his persistence and probably because he was making a nuisance of himself, he was finally granted the opportunity to join a new intake of 'wannabes' to commence training and become a naval pilot. Being slightly older than the usual applicants, the Board was a little reluctant at first to accept him, mainly due to costs, but as he had already been in the navy for some years, they bent the rules slightly.

So, Steve had arrived at Linton-on-Ouse in Yorkshire to commence his basic flying training with RNAS 802 squadron Operational Conversion Unit.

At first, he learned the very basics of flying on light Bulldogs and motor gliders before moving to RAF Valley for conversion on to Jet Provosts. He graduated with his wings and went on to further training at the OCU based at RNAS Lossiemouth on the Firth of Forth flying Buccaneers. The Lossiemouth runway had a section marked out to simulate the deck area of a carrier fitted with arrester wires. It was on this section of the runway that pilots like Steve constantly trained for weeks, day and night, to get used to landing on an aircraft carrier. However, landing on a small area of a huge, long, concrete runway with space to carry on if it all goes wrong was one thing, spot landing on a carrier was another; that was where the real danger and precision came in. On his first outing, to join the aircraft carrier HMS Ark Royal in the English Channel, it took him three attempts to land safely. The Flying Control Officer, Flyco, aboard Ark Royal, was about to order Steve to return to Culdrose before his fuel state went beyond critical, having a multi-million-pound jet aircraft either crash on the flight deck or ditching into the sea from where it would have no chance of recovery was not an option.

At the first missed approach, Steve felt the disappointment in the pit of his stomach, but he wasn't the only one that had made a missed approach. The other pilot calling a missed approach had been with Steve on his conversion course and was a real hotshot, coming top in every part of the course. Consequently, he didn't feel so bad but when he failed on the second occasion, and the hotshot made a perfect landing, Steve started to sweat with the stress. His adrenalin levels increased when he realised he had the responsibility of his rear seat navigator/weapons officer to worry about as well. After his second attempt, his rear seat partner came over the intercom,

"For fuck's sake, Steve, we don't have the fuel for this, you've got to land on the next time around, or we're out of here."

Steve felt the pressure increase; bile started to rise in the back of his throat. Thankfully, the next landing was textbook and, according to 'Flyco', the best deck landing that day; the only flaw being that he had two practice attempts before nailing it!

Although Steve enjoyed flying, he didn't like the constant pressure of flying to a rigid system that the military standards insisted. Steve was always nervous every time he 'strapped on an aircraft', navy parlance for climbing into an aeroplane. The instructors would tell their students that 'the day they didn't feel nervous before climbing into the cockpit to go flying was the day they started becoming complacent, and you cannot afford to be complacent in the air, like the sea, the air is a hostile environment with very little room for mistakes.'

Steve knew he wasn't becoming complacent, but too rigid to be a natural reactionary pilot like some of his younger colleagues.

In addition to this, every time he flew, he felt like he was flying against the ghost of his dead father, also a naval pilot who went on to become a highly acclaimed test pilot. These two reasons combined helped shape his decision to leave the Navy early, and to search for his dream job, he found it flying an air ambulance in Africa.

Chapter 17

The western part of Africa is so close to the equator that the moist air rises quickly, sucking it in from the vast, empty, tropical maritime area of the South Atlantic. This air mass then flows into the upper atmosphere, where the prevailing westerly winds drive the tropical weather front towards the bulge of West Africa. Here, it meets the rising hot air created by the steaming jungle after being exposed to the cruel, blistering sun, rather like a boiling pan of water under a grill. When these two masses collide, a huge force builds, and like a pressure cooker, it has to find some form of release. When this occurs suddenly, often without sufficient warning, it creates a tremendous tropical monsoon storm. The monsoon brings thousands of gallons of water and when released it forms huge raindrops, the size of golf balls, accompanied by down draughts of such velocity that any aircraft entering one of these storms cells would have little chance of survival. Even the large commercial airliners avoid these ferocious storm cells, which at times reach 30,000 feet.

Steve was once more flying into Banju. The day was like any other working day, never knowing what flight schedule the day would bring, so, just as he always did, he had kissed Alexandra goodbye with the words, "I will see you later, darling, I love you." While self-briefing at his previous stop, he had gained some sketchy information about the impending storm front moving in. Technology still had a long way to go in this part of Africa, up to the minute information on the weather was something for the future, pilots were lucky if weather reports were only a couple of days old. Tele-printers, long ago confined to the scrap heap of history in the west, were still in abundant use out in the bush of Africa for passing pre-flight information such as NOTAM's and weather reports to the outlying aerodromes where pilots would self-brief from this information.

Consequently, these weather reports were only ever the 'actuals' as to what each aerodrome or station was experiencing at the time. The limited forecast broadcast came from information gained by met forecasters, who relied mainly on listening to the BBC World Service, which was only able to give a brief overview of the weather to be expected on this huge continent. Had the forecasters at Banju been bothered to step outside their air-conditioned offices and look to the west, then they would have seen the storm gathering. What is known as the invisible disease of complacency had crept in, Steve's fate sealed by the men he'd never even met but who held his life in their hands. Steve had very little warning of the maelstrom into which he was about to fly his light aircraft.

As he flew towards Banju, he could see the gathering storm clouds on the horizon. He switched on his storm scope radar. Although the airports of Africa sadly lacked in many of the basic navigation aids, CCAB had made certain that their aircraft carried the very latest technology available, which included storm scopes. The scope linked to his moving map GPS and, at a glance, he could see his position relative to that of the gathering storm cell, an area showing bright red on the screen. Smiling to himself, he felt reassured that, with God's will and a following wind, he would be safe on the ground, having a cold beer in the airport bar before the storm crossed Banju aerodrome. As he drew nearer to his destination, he saw bright flashes of fork lightning briefly illuminating the sky, momentarily sending his instruments 'hay-wire' from the huge amount of kinetic energy being released by each flash as the static electricity earthed itself on the ground. He frowned in concentration as he watched each flash of light, convinced they were getting nearer. He could only just make out the lights of Banju in the gloom.

Though it was the middle of the day, the advancing thunderstorm had cast a dark shadow over the city, causing lights on the ground to be switched on in buildings and vehicles. The controllers had not only Steve's Cessna inbound to them but also a large DHL Boeing 747 cargo plane, the pilot of which was acknowledging instructions to join the circuit to land. The circuit pattern is an imaginary circuit in the sky that resembles an oval race track with the landing runway running down one side. The landing runway is parallel with what is known as the downwind side to the landing run, at the end of which the aircraft then steadily turns in the shape of a giant U to line up with the runway and make its final approach. From the direction of Steve's approach to the main runway at Banju, he was in a position to make a direct straight-in approach. The large DHL 747 was flying in the opposite direction and Steve could see its huge powerful landing lights on the leading edge of the main wings as they penetrated the dark murk as the 747 flew the downwind leg of the approach pattern. Steve had already slowed down at the request of the controllers as both he and the 747 would arrive at the same time to start their landing approach. Steve wondered if it was the luck of the draw that he was requested to give way to the giant cargo plane, but it was more likely the influence of big business and costs as just one of the huge engines on a 747 burns 4 litres per second, multiplied by four that's an awful lot of fuel burn for such an aircraft to be kept holding giving way to a small single-engine Cessna Caravan to land. Steve knew that, from his approach direction, he could have been given a direct in approach to the runway. Whatever the reason, as he advanced nearer to the aerodrome, the turbulence increased as it spread out further from the eye of the storm.

Everything had begun to feel like it was in slow motion as he watched the lumbering giant of the 747 slowly turn to line up with the runway. He willed it to go faster so he too could get safely on the ground. As the 747 turned, Steve briefly lost sight of its bright landing lights; the only light left in the sky was the aircraft's stern light which was hardly visible in the ever-darkening sky. The huge, bulbous, Mammatus black clouds were hanging from the heavens like grotesque haemorrhoids, black as coal, and coming lower with every passing minute. It wouldn't be long before the clouds would envelope the airfield, through which, even the high-intensity runway lights would be unable to penetrate. Steve realised that he was fast closing on the 747 and the only way to fit in behind it comfortably was to make a complete 360-degree turn. The turn would allow enough time for the 747 to complete its final approach and land, permitting sufficient space for Steve to avoid the huge wake of turbulence caused by the four mighty Pratt & Witney engines and massive wings span of the 747 design. Steve's little craft was suffering enough turbulence from the storm cell to risk taking anymore from the 747 wake turbulence. As the 747 lined up for its final approach, he overheard the confident American drawl of the pilot reporting to the controller as if enjoying the experience.

"Gee Banju, this is like riding the rodeo, yeee hah!"

However, seconds later the pilot's tone of voice changed drastically as the aircraft hit an immense downdraft, "Jesus H, Christ! This is going to be fucking heavy landing, let's have some more power," he called out to the co-pilot, not realising that he still had his thumb on the transmit button as he pulled back on the yoke in an attempt to round out the aircraft for landing.

Jet engines take longer to spool up and it was with little doubt that the additional power may have come too late to stop the sudden sink being suffered by the landing 747. The sink occurred just before the wheels touched the ground, as a huge, yellow, jagged line of lighting struck the aircraft. The bolt gave the plane such a tremendous blow that control was lost as several tyres burst, collapsing part of the port undercarriage. The pilot desperately tried to regain some control and bring the monster to a stop as the collapsed undercarriage legs dragged along the concrete runway, burning white-hot flames from the friction caused a trail of sparks. The controller had already hit the fire emergency button and the airport fire crew were on their way to the stricken 747. Amazingly, as the pilot struggled to fight with the crippled airliner, his thoughts momentarily turned to the pilot of the small Cessna Caravan he had heard call up to follow him in. With the weather the way it was, he wanted to give the Cessna sufficient room to land. His selfless thought came from being an experienced flying veteran, understanding that the Cessna needed to land as soon as possible. Fighting with the controls, the pilot of the 747 swerved the aircraft to one side of the runway, the damaged metal landing gear dragged across the runway surface together with almost empty fuel tanks creating a potential bomb. The friction raised the temperature igniting the inert gases, causing a fire to start. As the first explosion ripped through one of the wings, the pilot and co-pilot quickly released themselves from their seats and evacuated via the cockpit emergency exit, just below the cockpit deck. Thankfully, they were free and running away as the second explosion erupted and consumed the cockpit. The detonation shock wave caused them to both be blown off their feet and into the air, fortunately landing on grass. Realising they had suffered nothing more than scratches and bruises, they both sat up and looked back in disbelief at the burning aircraft as they subconsciously thanked God they were alive.

As the fire crews arrived on the scene and started to fight the blaze, the 747 pilots thoughts turned to the Cessna Caravan that had been attempting an approach behind them. The darkness that had engulfed the runway was now lit up by the 747's flames, the burning heap blocking part of the runway. Was there enough room behind the huge conflagration in which the little Cessna could land safely? They simultaneously looked into the darkened sky searching for the Cessna, but neither of them could see anything. Huge raindrops came racing from the sky and reduced their vision even more.

Steve watched the horror unfold beneath him, his problems increasing as the storm's cell moved across the centre of the airfield and slowly obliterated it from view. He decided that a tactical retreat from the storm was the best option. He wrestled and fought to get away from the violent grip of the storm. The old saying echoed in his mind, *'There are old pilots, and there are bold pilots, but there are no old bold pilots,'* and he definitely wanted to be an 'old' pilot. He pushed the throttle fully forward, the big turbofan engine showing maximum torque on the indicator, just nudging the dials red sector as the plane fought to get away from the storm cell. All around him, the sky was a brilliant red, dotted with pockets of black and bright flashes of yellow forked lightning. 'If there is a hell, then this is indeed what it must be like,' thought Steve as he continued his struggle against the huge forces hitting his small craft. His eager plane was screaming along at its maximum possible airspeed, but the storm encased it all too quickly. Steve had no time to react; one minute, his craft was being pushed to the heavens, and then the next; it was dropping like a stone. The altimeter failed to make any sense, Steve knew that despite the strength built into this particular design of aircraft, specifically constructed for airlines operating in tough hostile and remote environments, it suddenly felt far too fragile to sustain the battering it was currently suffering. Steve realised that he hadn't a clue as to where he was. He had lost all radio contact with Banju approach controllers and his GPS had long ago ceased to function as the high voltage static electric content of the storm blocked out all satellite signals. The moving map display had frozen and he was feeling very disorientated. He attempted to keep the plane in a steady flight, but it was being tossed around like a feather. Once again, he worried as to how long the airframe could take this punishment as the strength of the swirling storm flung the fragile craft miles off his original course. He felt every second as the plane was thrown through the air at speeds that would only have been capable had it been jet-propelled.

Unknown to Steve, he was now over some of the most desolate and isolated jungle in western Africa. The fact that his aircraft hadn't already broken up in mid-air was indeed a testament to the designers at Cessna. 10,000ft above the stricken and struggling Cessna, two forces of the kinetic energy of such magnitude gathered momentum and collided. They created an explosive force of such power that it was equivalent to a massive bomb. The streak of lightning that bolted to earth contained enough electricity to power a small town for a week. Unfortunately, as the lightning bolt searched to connect with the earth, the starboard wing of Steve's Cessna was in its way. The force of the impact ripped off the starboard aileron and caused the control yoke to flex with such a kick that Steve lost his grip, and the aircraft started a long, slow spiralling descent to the ground.

Steve knew there was no escape; all he could do was attempt to lessen the impact as much as possible. There was no denying he was going down in a violent but fortunately steady motion. He raised the nose of the craft to reduce the air speed; this cut the screaming engine, stopped the propeller, and caused a drag, which, if miscalculated, would cause the aircraft to go into an unrecoverable spin. With his nerves in tatters, he desperately tried to stop himself from screaming out in fear at the realisation that he had only seconds to live. If he could only slow the aircraft to the point that would reduce the impact, he might just survive. He screamed, "Alexandra", petrified that his life was about to end and that he would never see the love of his life ever again. The miracle he silently prayed for, came in the shape of a swollen jungle river which, thanks to the very same storm that was bringing down Steve's aircraft, had filled the rivers beneath its path to overflowing. It was into this deep, swollen river that Steve and his Cessna were heading. The Cessna eventually hit the water just as it had turned in the same direction of the raging river. The sudden positioning with the river flow reduced the impact on the airframe, but the power of the collision resulted in Steve's head connecting directly with the side window stanchion of the plane, knocking him unconscious. The water gripped the Cessna as the swollen torrents pushed it like a boat along the strong path which would eventually lead to the open huge Atlantic Ocean.

Chapter 18

The news that Steve was missing, presumed dead, had been delivered to Alexandra by the local church minister, Reverend Arnold Kimboshasa. Arnold, was a soft-spoken gentleman with a deep, gravelly voice, the sort of rich, throaty voice that could be mistaken for a heavy smoker, which he certainly was not. In fact, in another life, he could have been a wonderful singer, likened to the famous American singer Paul Robeson.

So, it came to pass that Rev Arnold Kimboshasa appeared in the compound early one morning two days after the dreadful storm. Alexandra was used to not hearing from Steve for several days at a time, due to the nature of communications in some of the remote areas where he operated. Steve would always telephone at the first available opportunity and Alexandra understood. Although preoccupied with her work, Steve was never far from her thoughts with hardly an hour going by before she would wonder where he was and what sort of vital mission he was flying. She never let on to Steve that, apart from being so irrevocably in love with him, she completely hero-worshiped him. He was unlike any other man she had ever met, kind and gentle; a strong, silent type, and yet on other occasions he had a sort of vulnerability about him which made her want to protect him. Steve was her knight in shining armour, and as her mother would describe, *'Still waters run deep.'* Alexandra never really believed that it was possible to love somebody like this, but she was living the thrill of a real-life *'Mills and Boon'* love story. Her love for Steve had taken over her whole body; it was planted deep within her soul.

Reverend Arnold Kimboshasa, had become a personal friend of Alexandra's both socially and through Steve's work with CCAB, both Alexandra and Steve became members of Reverend Arnold's congregation at the local Anglican Church. They had discussed with Arnold Kimboshasa about the possibility of officiating at their planned wedding. Having a strong conviction to God was one of the prerequisites for a pilot with CCAB and although Alexandra was undecided and a sceptical member of the Christian society into which she had been born, she soon became a strong believer after meeting Steve. She felt that only a force as powerful as the Lord could have brought her and Steve together.

Alexandra's employment position dictated that she had her own office, which was like a large glass box, an office within an office, and on this fateful morning, she wasn't aware of the Reverend Arnold's presence as he approached. By a sixth sense, she looked up and saw him coming towards her. She began to smile and stand in greeting; those actions, however, slowed in motion as the look on his face was enough to transmit that the message would be bad news. She stood up from her desk, waiting for Reverend Arnold to reach her.

"Oh my God ... it's Steve, isn't it?"

Reverend Arnold quickened his step, dashing through the open inner office door, his arms outstretched,

"My dear Alexandra," his voice was soft, "I'm so dreadfully sorry, but Steve's plane has gone down, and I'm afraid he is missing ... but there is always hope; please keep your hope."

"Tell me it's not my Steve," she wailed before screaming, "No, no, no, no, tell me! Tell me, no!" Her voice was at such a pitch that it sent reverberations throughout the office walls, momentarily causing colleagues to jump, for some, it made their blood run cold. Every negative thought ran through her mind; her body felt numb. She raised her limp hand to her mouth in fear, and accidentally sent her third cup of coffee of the day flying across the desk onto the floor. The coffee mug smashed into tiny pieces. She looked down at the spilled liquid dotted with pieces of china before suddenly feeling extremely faint. Rushing towards her, Reverend Arnold caught Alexandra as she collapsed into his arms and started to sob.

By now, many colleagues had rushed towards Alexandra's office. They gazed through the glass partition; it was obvious that something was terribly wrong, and some even started to cry involuntarily in sympathy. Reverend Arnold sat Alexandra down on the adjacent small sofa and ushered everyone away, requesting privacy. Her tears continued to fall uncontrollably. The Reverend Arnold gently sat next to her and placed a comforting arm around her shoulders, "We mustn't give up hope; God will look after him."

On this occasion, even the Reverend wasn't sure whether he meant in this world or the next. He had delivered bad news before to members of his congregation, but this was the first time he had to be the messenger for someone he held so dear. He loved both Steve and Alexandra so much that he found himself having to hold back his own tears. As he expected, Alexandra was inconsolable. Steve's disappearance consumed her with grief. Reverend Arnold had come prepared for this, and while Alexandra cried her heart out, he quietly slipped away into the outer office. He filled a glass of water from the fountain and discreetly emptied the powdery contents from a small sachet into the glass and mixed it thoroughly, ensuring it had dissolved completely. It was a secret potion which had been given to him years ago by a wise old lady, passed down from generations of local tribeswomen who had used this as a form of anaesthetic long before modern medicines had arrived in this part of Africa. Avoiding the questions from Alexandra's colleagues and friends who wanted to know what on earth had happened, he slipped quickly and quietly back into Alexandra's office and offered her the drink. He coaxed her into taking small sips of the water. He had used the potion on numerous occasions when dealing with grieving members of his flock. The secret potion was tasteless and after a few more sips, the elixir eventually kicked in, making her feel calm and sleepy. While Alexandra remained in this state, Reverend Arnold was able to explain to her friends and colleagues what most of them had already figured out for themselves. Although a very independent girl, Alexandra had many friends and so there was no shortage of offers to help take her back to the compound and to be with her through the next few hours or days.

Upon hearing the news, Alexandra's parents were naturally extremely concerned for her welfare and wanted her to go home to England. Her father offered to fly out and be with her until she was ready to leave, but Alexandra was reluctant. She hated the idea of leaving the part of Africa that held all of her memories of Steve. She felt his presence whenever she looked up into a starlit tropical sky or heard another one of the CCAB planes coming into the local strip. Her heart would jump, wishing and praying it was Steve.

After three weeks, she had a change of heart and decided she did need to leave Africa. What had been keeping her there was now pushing her away. She couldn't cope with facing all of the memories alone. She knew she needed the love and support of a close family. On leaving the Embassy, one of her last jobs was to act as a courier; she was to travel home via the British Embassy in Amsterdam. From there, she would proceed overland and take the overnight ferry from Schevenigen to Northwold to visit Steve's parents who lived in North Yorkshire. She wanted to see them personally to tell them that she was carrying Steve's baby. Having never met them before, she had no idea to how they would react.

Alexandra often sensed that Steve was looking down upon her, her guardian angel! The unborn child was all that kept her going; the baby was going to be his legacy. It was as though her heart had been ripped out, and the blood pumping around her body was cold, polluted with grief. She knew that it was not better to have loved and lost, as she now realised that anybody who said otherwise, had never truly been in that position. Having once thought that there truly was a God, who had delivered Steve to her, she now found it difficult to believe; her faith shattered.

Alexandra felt like a non-person. The only thing that mattered to her was the baby growing inside her and she would face the cruel world and live on for that reason only.

Chapter 19

Sometime later, at the official Air Accident Board enquiry, the controllers would say that they had made a mistake and should have let Steve's much smaller plane take priority over the much larger 747, easy to conclude in hindsight. In fairness to the controllers, Steve's fate was sealed by events earlier that day when the meteorological forecasters had failed to notice the forming localised storm cell that had been fast approaching the Banju aerodrome, along with an event in the morning at a remote jungle airstrip. Steve's departure had been delayed as he had to wait for petrol from an old fuel truck that suffered a broken axle and should have been withdrawn from service years ago. Once again a chain of events had occurred which would lead to tragedy. If only the chain had a recognisable weak link which could be broken then many accidents may never occur. In Steve's case, the chain had already formed ... there were no weak links and luck was not on his side. The enquiry concluded that although mistakes had occurred, they would have had little effect on the ultimate outcome of the day, it was a tragic accident and despite an extensive and exhaustive search of the area Steve Gaunt was missing presumed dead.

Chapter 20

Boarding the overnight ferry to England, the first person Alexandra met at the top of the gangway was the purser of *s.s Beamish*, debonair, womaniser, Guy Hollins. For a brief moment, as he collected her ticket, her heart missed a beat, thinking it was Steve. As he turned his face fully towards her, she realised it was just a trick of the imagination, and there was actually no resemblance at all. On many occasions, since Steve's death, she had met men who had often taken on a fleeting likeness to Steve, resulting from the ache in her heart, unable to accept that he was dead.

Guy, a tall handsome figure with blonde Nordic looks, tended to be somewhat self-centred and assured of himself. Very much a playboy, with so many affairs under his belt, he would have put Don Juan to shame. He knew that he had the looks to turn girls' heads; he made the pursuit of women his number one hobby, and the opposite sex had been his only interest. However, Guy had become tired of his playboy lifestyle, with longings to settle down with a lovely wife and have a family. To prepare for his dream future, Guy had purchased an old cow barn on the outskirts of Northwold. He had spent a great deal of time and money on the dwelling, turning it into a luxurious abode. Keeping its original name, 'Tithe Barn' had become notorious in the neighbourhood, attracting a great deal of local publicity and gossip, all for the wrong reasons. Despite this, many single women, even some married, had still crossed the threshold of his love nest.

Each one, a potential Mrs. Hollins, but all just became another ephemeral amour.

So, as Alexandra approached the gangway, Guy's heart skipped a beat, he was taken aback by her beautiful face which held such sad eyes, and he wondered if Miss Right had just walked straight into his life.

Guy liked to position himself just outside the Purser's office and greet the passengers individually as they boarded from the gangway into the large embarkation area, commonly known as the Purser's Square. It was rather like the reception area of an up market hotel. The floor was covered with a thick, soft carpet. Settees carefully placed, interspersed with real pot plants. To the left was the Purser's Bureau, which resembled a bank counter, this was the information centre for all passenger dealings. Guy always checked the tickets for names, this was so he could address them personally before handing the ticket across the bureau desk to his

Assistant Purser, a personal touch Guy liked to implement. Taking Alexandra's ticket, he said the briefest of professional greetings, "Hello Miss Evans, welcome aboard."

"Hi," was all Alexandra said after being momentarily thrown by the fleeting resemblance Guy had to her beloved Steve. There was a brief silence between them as they stared into each other's eyes, long enough to make the next passenger give a discreet cough, breaking the spell that had appeared to have enveloped Guy and Alexandra. With the spell suddenly broken, Guy apologised and passed Alexandra on to one of the stewards who was lurking just behind him. The steward enticed Alexandra forwards, "This way, Miss, I'll show you to your cabin."

Slightly ruffled, Guy focussed his mind back to his duties and dealt with the remaining passengers. As if in a trance, he went into auto mode as he took tickets, greeting them in a sotto voice, before passing them along to the stewards. His mind was totally occupied with Alexandra Evans. Had he imagined it? Had he really felt something magical upon looking into those beautiful, saucer-shaped eyes, a pool of love into which he wanted to dive and be totally immersed?

Once his boarding duties were finished, he telephoned the Captain to advise him that all passengers on the list had safely boarded the vessel. The Captain could now, once he had heard from the deck officer that all the cargo was on board and safely stowed, make his own brief 'welcome onboard announcement' over the tannoy system, and put the ship to sea for the crossing over to the UK. Guy left his assistant to complete the administrative duties and set off in earnest to find Alexandra. The ship began to vibrate as the engines powered in preparation for sailing. Guy tried to look casual as he searched for her. He headed straight for the bar lounge, but she wasn't there. Next, he checked the library room, checking all quiet corners, but she wasn't there either. He wandered the alleyways aimlessly in the hope he would accidentally bump into her, but it felt like every passenger on the ship wanted to stop and talk to him, everyone apart from Alexandra. As his assistant announced over the tannoy system, dinner was to be served, he headed straight for the dining room; she was bound to arrive there at some point. He waited for half an hour, his eyes darted everywhere as he scanned the room, but still no sign of her. He spoke to the Head Waiter, reserving a table for two, describing Alexandra. He requested to be informed the moment she came to the dining room, ever hopeful that he could entice her to join him for dinner. The Head Waiter made a mental note of Guy's request, just the hint of a sly grin forming on his face, he knew his boss of old having served with him for several years. Taking the bit between his teeth, Guy went to her cabin and tapped lightly on the door. No reply. Once again, he set off to search for her.

Guy was an intellectual, confident young man who, at the age of sixteen, soon matured in the real world of seafaring. Signing on with a large, ocean-going passenger shipping company, he quickly worked his way up the ladder, gaining officer status into the Purser's office. He had loved the life of endless cocktail parties, dinners and balls as he sailed on the traditional passenger ship routes to Australia and New Zealand. The long sea voyages supplied an endless string of willing young ladies traversing between the old and new worlds in search of adventure and excitement. For Guy, those testosterone charged days were now but wonderful memories to lock away, only to be rekindled in moments of melancholy. He momentarily recalled an old adage that a man knows when it is time to settle down when he gets fed up with getting up at 3 o'clock in the morning to go home to his own bed! He felt that time had arrived. Now, he wanted nothing more than to settle down to a married life of domesticity. Although to achieve this would not be easy, Guy harboured a secret that would need the love and understanding of a very special woman. His senses was telling him that Alexandra Evans was a strong contender for this role.

As the ship steamed through the calm but chilly, moonlit, North Sea night, Guy hoped Alexandra hadn't retired early as he continued to roam the decks in search of her. Pure chance, or was it fate, maybe the hand of a guardian angel guiding him, whatever it was, an extra-terrestrial force took him on to the open weather deck where he spied her beneath a lifeboat. She appeared to be totally lost in her thoughts as she leaned on the rail and looked out on to the darkening sea, watching the twinkling lights of Holland sink slowly beneath the horizon. Guy, thankful he had finally found her, wasted no time in introducing himself, "Good evening again," he said softly, but she had not heard him over the splashing gurgling sea as it ran down the side of the ship.

He spoke a little louder, "Good evening Miss Evans."

This time she heard him. She slowly turned to face him, her eyes sad and red with two huge tears rolling down her cheeks.

"Oh hi, again," she replied with a sniff as she tried to hide that she had been crying. She wiped away the tears with both hands, "Sorry", she gently whispered. Seeing the tears glisten with the reflection from the deck lights, Guy was momentarily embarrassed that he had caught her at a vulnerable time, lost in private thoughts, now it was his turn to apologise, "Oh, I'm so very sorry for interrupting you … please, I'll leave you to your thoughts," he stepped back, ready to turn and quickly depart.

"No, please, don't go, it's just me being silly about a missing …" she briefly lost her words, realising she was talking to a complete stranger. "I'm sorry, I'm just emotional," she said, chastising herself. Since Steve's disappearance, Alexandra, refusing to believe Steve has actually gone, has only ever used the word 'missing' when talking about him. In a way, this helped her get through each day because she was incredulous that she lived in a world where he didn't exist. Her tears started to well up again momentarily embarrassing Guy, but he soon took control of the situation and moved his body closer to her, she felt his tall frame shadowing yet comforting. Alex quickly became aware that Guy was chivalrously hiding her and her grief from other passengers as they walked by. Composing herself, she smiled at Guy.

"Thank you," she sniffed.

"For what?" replied Guy.

Again, she smiled, "For just being there and hiding me from prying eyes, it's very kind of you."

"Oh that," replied Guy with a smile, turning on the charm.

"It just felt like a natural thing to do … I can see you are very upset; perhaps you would prefer me to go?"

"No, please, there's no need, most people run a mile when they see me cry," sniffed Alexandra.

Like a magician, Guy quickly produced a clean, starched handkerchief doused in Calvin Klein Eau de Toilette and gently handed it to her.

"Thank you," she said, wiping her tears.

"Now," he said confidently, wasting no time, "Would you care to join me for dinner?" he offered her his crooked arm, "Or would you think that's terribly forward of me?"

Alexandra suppressed a little giggle for the first time in months and happily hooked her arm through Guy's. She felt light-hearted at Guy's touch and was more than happy for Guy to guide her towards the entrance doors and inside the ship to the dining room. As Alexandra sat opposite this handsome, fair-haired young officer, she started to feel incredibly relaxed. It was a feeling she welcomed and had almost forgotten. Over dinner, she soon poured out the story of her lost love in Africa. Guy, being a good listener as well as a smooth talker, listened intently to her tale without interruption, saddened and appalled that she had undergone such a tragedy. Dinner was soon followed by brandy for Guy but mineral water for Alexandra. They sipped their drinks, both eager to learn more about the other. So absorbed in each other that when the dining room's background music stopped, they were drawn back to reality upon discovering the dining room empty. The other tables, now laid ready for breakfast, made them both realise just how late it was. The Head Waiter and stewards were standing in a line, discretely at the back in the dining room, watching their boss and his beautiful young lady companion, quietly estimating the amount of overtime pay they would be getting as the dining room was long past it's official closing time. After hurriedly leaving and bidding each other good-night, Alexandra and Guy went their separate ways to their cabins, both having enjoyed a wonderful and memorable evening.

The next morning s.s. 'Beamish' had pummelled her way into harbour against the gale that had blown up during the night. Guy was desperate to see Alexandra again, but his busy morning routine meant that he couldn't get away from his office. His only chance was to find her as the passengers disembarked. Thankfully he found her just as she was about the leave the ship. Guy placed his hands on her shoulders, looked into her eyes, and asked if he could see her again. His work rota meant that he had a scheduled leave starting the following day. Hesitantly she agreed and they arranged to meet in London in three days. She then walked carefully down the gangway and through the Passenger Arrivals Hall, she was filled with a mixture of grief and joy. She felt she had met someone with compassion and understanding, and although she had told Guy so much about herself, she kept just one fundamental secret from him.

Chapter 21

As Guy watched Alexandra disappear down the gangway and into the passenger hall, his mind wandered back to his many past encounters. A colourful past that supported his urge to settle down into a stable and permanent relationship.

He recalled the time he had encountered the gorgeous, if somewhat volatile, Tina Souter, a clerk in his then shipping company employer's offices in Southampton. Tina lived with her parents and after several dates, she insisted on him accompanying her home to meet the family, and, against his better judgement, he went along with her wishes. Previously, Guy had always avoided this type of family encounter as it appeared to make a relationship more permanent if endorsed by a girlfriend's immediate family. Hence, the best way in Guy's eyes was always to avoid these meetings. Similarly, as a young man, Guy's philosophy on safe sex was not letting on where he was living! Tina's mother, Barbara, large in both size and personality, was a domineering, overbearing woman and immediately saw Guy as a perfect son-in-law. For years she had been endeavouring to get Tina, the youngest of her three daughters, married off so that she and her husband, Tom, could sell-up the large family home and downsize into comfortable, early retirement. As much as she loved Tina dearly, Barbara was beginning to be annoyed that she hadn't found a suitor, after all, her daughter was certainly glamorous enough.

At that time, Guy too, was still living with his parents. His family home in Hampshire was only about an hour's drive away from Southampton. He was becoming increasingly dissatisfied with leaving Tina and having to drive back home every night; consequently, Barbara, like a spider, commenced weaving a web into which she planned to trap Guy into marrying Tina. The initial strands of this web started by persuading Guy to spend the rest of his leave living in with them, after all, they had plenty of room in the house with the other two daughters having already flown the nest. Guy offered to pay his way, but Barbara was having none of it, declaring he was part of the family now. Slowly, Guy was unwittingly drawn into the Souter family as Barbara plotted and schemed to have him marry Tina as soon as possible.

Tina was a bubbly, vivacious, little sexpot, of whom Guy couldn't get enough. For him, this new arrangement of spending the rest of his leave in their house had the added advantage that Tina's parents, Barbara and

Tom, enjoyed a very active social life, leaving Guy and Tina alone most evenings to fulfil their sexual desires. The thought of marriage had not entered Guy's head at any stage of their extremely physical relationship; for one thing, Guy soon realised that Tina had a rather violent temper that was likely to unexpectedly flare up at any time, for the slightest of reasons. Once, Tina had even thrown a carving knife at Guy during a trifling argument. Luckily, her aim was weak, but the threat behind it was serious. Eagerly aware of what was going on beneath her roof, Barbara hoped for the mention of engagement. It galled her to know that her daughter was giving herself regularly to Guy, but in return, apart from his material generosity, Tina was not getting any promises for the long term. In Barbara's eyes, Guy was certainly having his cake and eating it. She carefully watched the pair together. It annoyed her that Guy made no future plans, he was living each day as it came, and he was starting to get under her skin. Despite her thoughts about Guy's lack of commitment, she still thought there was a good person deep down, and he just needed a good woman to control him.

Barbara was an extroverted woman who tended to flirt with most good-looking men openly, including Guy. Barbara enjoyed the flirting, which she told herself was just a bit of harmless fun. For sex, she had her husband Tom subserviently, and obediently, under her spell. After several weeks, Barbara decided it was time to take matters into her own hands, by fair means or foul, she swore to herself that she would see her daughter walk down the aisle alongside Guy Hollins. However, the more time Barbara spent with Guy, the more she experienced latent sexual desires for him; her feelings soon turned into a schoolgirl crush that gave her a tingling sensation whenever in his company. Barbara struggled to suppress these feelings and often wondered if Guy suspected ... woman's intuition had convinced her that he felt the same. She knew full well that Guy was at an age where he was overloaded and fully turbocharged with testosterone, not rocket science, just a well-known fact. She intended to put this mixture into the cauldron and spring a trap, which unfortunately for Guy, he unsuspecting and obligingly walked into like a lamb to slaughter.

Often, when staying over at Tina's, Guy would lay in bed while Tina and her father went off to work. Tina, first having sneaked into Guy's bedroom for a quick cuddle and fumble. It had become routine for Guy to go down to the kitchen to make tea for himself and Barbara. As Barbara always seemed to sleep-in late, he would take the tea upstairs, knock on the master bedroom door and leave it on a tray outside. Following Barbara's customary 'thank you' acknowledgement, he would then take his time to shower and dress, later joining Barbara for a late breakfast. However, one particular morning she stayed in bed to await her room service, which she planned would be more than tea, if Guy was willing. Guy dutifully laid the tray, and following his usual knock on the door, Barbara unexpectedly called for him to enter. Unusual as it seemed, curiosity got t he better of him. He hitched up his loose-fitting pyjama trousers, and rather sheepishly entered. His heart beat rising wondering what to expect on the otherside of the door. Barbara always slept naked, and today was no different. Guy's eyes immediately came to rest on her bare shoulders. Barbara, who at forty-one years young, looked after herself and apart from being very slightly overweight, was a magnificent woman in all respects. Barbara lifted her left arm, placed her hand behind her head, and smiled, creating a sensuous pose. From her shoulders, Guy's eyes moved to the glorious mounds made by her ample breasts beneath the sheets. His heart began to beat faster, the blood coursed through his veins and reached his groin where Barbara's gaze unashamedly lingered, watching the bulge slowly form in his slightly loose pyjama bottoms. Barbara knew exactly what she was doing. As Guy placed the tray of tea on the bedside table, she threw back the bedclothes to reveal flawless white flesh and nestling between her porcelain-like thighs, the biggest mountain of black pubic hair Guy had ever seen. With a broad, warm, inviting smile, Barbara growled, "Come here, big boy, you know you've wanted some of me for ages ... well, now you can have me."

"Bloody hell," was all he could manage to mumble before jumping on the bed and into her arms. His engorged penis burst from his pyjamas like a spring. Her soft, warm body excited him; the smell of her made him feel he would explode before entering her. He calmed himself down to savour the moment as he removed his incumbent pyjamas. He gazed down at her, taking in and memorising all her luscious curves.

"Whoa there, easy boy slow down, we don't want to climax too quickly, either of us," she panted deeply. "Oh, how I've longed for this moment, and I'm sure you have too, don't think I haven't noticed the way you look at me," she breathed huskily.

"Yes, yes, of course, I've wanted you from the moment we first met," he lied. He'd often wondered how she would look naked, but never actually desired to find out, but here she was, curvaceous and sexy and he wasn't going to turn down the opportunity laid to him on a plate.

"Here put this on," said Barbara holding up what looked like a rubber tube.

"What's this?" he replied.

"A french letter you fool," she snapped impatiently.

"I haven't been through the change yet, so I don't want any nasty surprises at my age," purred Barbara like a large predatory jungle cat.

"Yes, I can see that, but it's so thick it's like a marigold glove," he exclaimed.

"Well, it's a re-useable one, and not only that, it will reduce the sensation for you, slow you down and avoid you coming too quickly, my darling. Tom uses one, and he thinks they're super, but don't worry this is a new one," she answered, smiling demurely.

"Oh, great thanks. I don't think we should be talking about your husband at the moment like this," he replied, frowning.

"Look, either you want me or not? I rule the roost in my house, and if you really want me then I'm for the taking, but this is your only chance, so go for it Tiger, or it will be the last opportunity you get. I want you inside me now!" she demanded. Guy didn't need any more encouragement; he was bursting at the seams with adrenaline and testosterone. So he quickly slid on the rubber and straddled Barbara with a knee down each side of her ample stomach. Looking at her mountainous body, he felt sure that she must have had a 'boob' job at some time as her breasts stayed amazingly upright and didn't droop to either side of her chest. He didn't care; they were magnificent, and he couldn't wait to get his hands on them and his mouth around the large pert nipples. Guy thought he was dreaming, he couldn't believe his luck. Barbara closed her eyes. Her red lips slightly parted as she breathed in short gasps of anticipation. Her nipples were the largest Guy had ever seen on a woman, and he immediately took one in his mouth causing her to cry out in ecstasy, he inwardly groaned and fought an internal battle not to climax too soon. He couldn't wait any longer and eagerly mounted her, slipping easily into her moist vagina, his athletic body starting to plunge into the mound of flesh beneath him as she continued to heave and pant. It was akin to surfing a huge wave of pleasure and passion. He smiled inwardly to himself as he heard the bed start to creak in unison to his thrusts. The same sound he'd sometimes heard at night from his adjacent bedroom when he assumed Barbara had allowed Tom to copulate with her. With his every nerve tingling with pleasure, to heights he had not experienced before, he matched the sighs and groans of his uninhibited partner. His mind in a crazy whirl at the bizarre situation into which he now found himself, fucking both mother and daughter. Not unsurprisingly, Guy soon found himself drifting into the chasm of lust from which there was no return until completely spent. Suddenly, a movement from the direction of the balcony doors distracted him; something wasn't as it should be.

A flash followed by a resounding 'pop' of bright white light momentarily lit up the room, startled, he quickly withdrew, the French letter flew from his ramrod penis like a Christmas party rocket balloon and he ejaculated all over Barbara's thighs. Then, another flash and 'pop'. Barbara reached out and tried to hold him, "No don't stop" she screamed. She felt like a volcano about to explode. Guy was having none it. Slightly disorientated, he leapt up and stumbled before he fell all his length on the bedroom floor, his legs tangled in bed clothing. He struggled free, jumped up and quickly made his way across to the balcony, unashamedly naked. A ladder was purposefully leaning against the balcony. Guy checked the area beneath him before looking further afield and caught sight of a chubby man attempting to run across the large lawn. Guy watched in disbelief as the man fell over the garden wall in a clumsy and undignified manner, reminiscent of a scene from a 'Carry On' film. The portly man picked himself up, grabbed hold of a large camera that was swinging around his neck, and fumbled with a bunch of keys as he waddled further away towards an old Ford saloon.

"Hey!" shouted Guy impotently, as if that alone would somehow stop the fleeing cameraman.

Blessed with good eyesight, Guy just had a chance to make a mental note of the number plate before the driver gunned the engine and raced away from the curb side with a backfire of smoke and squealing of tyres, leaving a small trail of rubber on the road. Guy was dumb-struck. Shaking his head, he could make no sense of what just happened. He wandered back into the now-empty bedroom and heard Barbara in the en-suite bathroom. He sat down on the dishevelled bed linen, his head in his hands, his mind was in turmoil as he tried to make some sense of what had just occurred. Who could have known? Had Tom Souter suspected something and employed a 'snoop' to watch him? But on what grounds? It had been a spontaneous thing. The questions kept coming, spinning around his head.

Barbara came from the bathroom, dressed in her smart kimono bathrobe, she appeared too cool and calm under the circumstances; in fact, she almost had a slight trace of a smile. Before Guy could question her, she breezed past him and went downstairs. Grabbing his discarded pyjamas from the tangled heap of bedclothes, he went through into his room where, foregoing a shower, he quickly dressed and then followed her downstairs, desperately inquisitive about Barbara's sedate mood.

He interrogated her, demanding answers, he wanted to know why she was being so laid back. Someone had been spying on them for goodness sake. Despite being caught in a sexual encounter, this was a police matter. Guy anxiously questioned her, over and over, but Barbara remained calm about the whole matter. The final straw was when he accused her of setting it all up as some sort of 'kinky' side show with him as the star. This accusation annoyed Barbara. She remained tight lipped and refused to listen to any more questions. Walking away from Guy, she returned to her bedroom, dressed, and left the house. Guy didn't see her for the remainder of that day and tried to act casual when Tina came home.

With her parents out for the evening, Tina took advantage of her time alone with Guy and enticed him to make love to her, but it was no use; the morning's antics lay heavily on his mind, completely affecting his libido. Tina felt rejected, instantly assuming it was something that she had done to upset him. When she attempted to stimulate him with a blowjob, he pushed her away. His brain was in overload, still deep in thought about the morning events. It all seemed far too odd that Barbara hadn't been in the slightest way perturbed that a man had gained access to her bedroom via a set of ladders and taken photographs. He just didn't get it, none of it made any sense. Something obviously wasn't right; surely this was all some sort of cruel joke or a bloody nightmare? After a sleepless night, he intended to question Barbara again, as soon as Tom and Tina had left for work the following morning. The minute he heard the front door slam, he knew the coast was clear and marched straight to Barbara's bedroom. He rapped hard on the door, but her voice came from downstairs, "Down here!"

He cautiously stepped down the stairs, anxious as to what may unfold. He walked into the kitchen; there stood Barbara, arms folded, composed and ready for confrontation. Without saying a word, she presented Guy with a large brown envelope. She smiled at him, but he was blatantly confused by the whole situation, the motive hadn't even registered, Barbara sighed at his dumb-stricken expression.

"Darling boy, if you think you can screw my daughter and me without consequences, well you've got another thing coming, it's payback time sweetheart. I do not wish to have you as a lover … but as a son-in-law, and the sooner, the better I say, so we can both put this episode behind us."

Guy looked at the envelope as though it contained a bomb, under the circumstances, it may as well have done.

"What's this?" he nervously asked as he opened the top of the envelope.

"What does it look like my darling … some wonderful pictures of us fornicating, you look a sight, I think it's caught you with just the right amount of surprise and shock… don't you?" she had a hint of a giggle. From the angle the photograph had been taken, Barbara's identity wasn't discernible but that fact had yet to registered with Guy.

"But what's the meaning of this?" Guy's temper began to rise as the realisation dawned on him what Barbara intended to do with the pictures.

"It's very simple sweetie, you request my daughter's hand in marriage immediately and announce it to the family. I've booked the church for six months time, I'm afraid that was the earliest date I could get from the local vicar," said Barbara, smiling like a cat who had just got the cream.

Guy let out a sarcastic laugh "I beg your pardon! I have absolutely no intention of marrying anybody, and especially not your crazy-ass daughter!"

"Well, in that case, copies of these delightful photos will go to your employer and, of course, your mother and father," said Barbara firmly.

Guy was in no doubt that she meant every word. It's the only time in his life that his placid nature almost snapped. He was so filled with rage, that he clenched his fist intending to lash out towards Barbara, luckily, his common sense got the better of him, and he held back, controlling his anger to avoid contact. Noticing his body language Barbara had instinctively backed away out of arms' reach.

"Now, now Guy, as my future son-in-law, I urge you not to do anything stupid, lay one finger on me or harm a single hair on my head, and you'll wish you'd never met me," said Barbara sternly.

"I already do!" snapped Guy.

"Let's get something straight my lad! I do the fucking in this house! You thought you could screw me, and there wouldn't be a price to pay? Well, that just shows how naive you are. Even Tom has to pay for sex with me, maybe not in monetary terms, but, as I said, I'm the only one that fucks people in this house, and it would do you good to remember that … You may think that you've been having your cake and eating it with my daughter, but she has got a lot to learn and I'll be the one to teach her. So, Mr. Hollins, welcome to the Souter family," announced a defiant and all-conquering Barbara. She stepped forward, gently lifted her right hand, and patted the side of Guy's face, "So just enjoy it, lay back and think of England – I believe that is the saying." Before Guy realised, Barbara, with the speed of a striking snake, had retracted her hand and landed a fierce slap on his face, the crack of which was just as painful to his ears as it was to his cheek, causing a deep burning sensation as well as leaving the perfect red outline of Barbara's hand. The slap caught Guy completely off guard. He staggered back, totally stunned by her sudden burst of aggression. The pain was so intense for a moment he thought she'd broken his jaw!

"That will teach you a lesson for even daring to attempt to strike me, and don't think you could ever overpower me, lad, I was a fierce, dirty fighter at school and I haven't lost it, I've taken down and overpowered far bigger men than you, some that lived to regret it bitterly! Now, sit down over there!" She ordered, pointing to one of the easy chairs in the adjacent open plan dining room.

A very subdued Guy, tried to work out what had actually just happened. Obediently, and somewhat sheepishly, he sat down in the armchair. His mind in a whirl as to how he was going to get out of this predicament. He had to think logically and sensibly but was struggling to comprehend the situation. Barbara sat herself on another easy chair opposite him. Guy was in a daze but noticed that as Barbara sat down, she did so in such a way that she provocatively showed a great deal of her white upper thigh, contrasting with a black stocking top. Not that the totally confused Guy actually registered what he was looking at!

Barbara noticed him looking at her thighs, "Have a good look and make the most of it lover boy because that's the last you'll see of that I can assure you! From now on, Tina is the only one you'll be getting intimate with, and I've also decided that I will talk to Tina about this, well not what has happened between us of course, but in true traditional Christian style, there'll be no screwing with Tina until after the wedding," she announced triumphantly, aiming to rub salt into sore wounds. "Do you hear me? You and Tina are going to be abstinent until the wedding night. Tina will see it from my point of view, and I'm sure she'll obey, I know exactly which buttons to press with her."

Guy looked blank, his face still stinging.

"Do you hear me, captain? No sex for six months," Barbara grinned with an obvious hint of sarcasm in her voice euphemistically using the naval rank.

"Yes," mumbled Guy humbly and dejectedly.

Guy was too stunned, he was metaphorically pinching himself. How the hell had this situation blown up so quickly?

"Excellent," said Barbara, "Now we've got that straight, I'll reiterate my demands to ensure that these photographs don't end up in the wrong hands."

Guy started to take in the initial shock of the sudden turn of events and began to feel his confidence seeping back; he was determined not to let this demented woman ruin his life.

"So, what if these pictures go to my employer and father ... I've done nothing wrong, these photos are just a single man sowing his wild oats, nothing more," he said with a slight grin.

"Are they now, well I wonder. You see, first of all, you've told me often enough about how self-righteous your immediate boss is. With him being a lay preacher at his local Catholic Church and with a Northern Ireland ancestry to boot, well, we all know just how tyrannical a man with that sort of background can be. Maybe you won't get fired, but I reckon he'll give you a hard time. After all, as a purser with one of the top British passenger liner companies, this sort of thing would never do. I may consider selling the story to a newspaper as some recent high profile articles about the shenanigans aboard cruise liners have shown that there is a thirst for anything like this. I doubt your boss or your company would take kindly to one of their officers exposed as a sexual predator," answered Barbara, her voice heavy with sarcasm.

Guy quickly retorted, "So what? That will just be between him and me," he snapped angrily, not wanting Barbara to get the better of him.

"Well my luuuvver," emphasising the word, giving it a West Country twang, "that's where you are very wrong, a very good friend of mine is a freelance newspaper tout, she is always on the look-out for some nice juicy, smutty stories to sell and I do believe that these photos are right up her street. She'll make sure that these photos end up on the desk of the right editor who will publish it in the type of newspaper that can write a story such as this in a way that it will make even the smuttiest of men's magazines read like a docile romance novel." Barbara allowed herself to laugh, wanting to ensure that Guy did not doubt that she had thoroughly thought this through.

"Then there's your father, a prominent Tory MP; I wonder what he would make of it all? His wonderful son's sex life splattered all over national newspapers?"

Guy quickly concluded he was a beaten man.

Barbara stood up, stepped over to where Guy was sitting, dangling the photos in front of Guy's face to rub his nose in it, literally.

He snatched them and quickly tore them up in frustration, disgust and anger, finally throwing them over Barbara like confetti.

"Petulant boy," she laughed, "there are plenty more copies. I expect a proposal of marriage to Tina as soon as possible. Today is only Tuesday so no rush, I will give you until the weekend. It can go into next week's local newspaper on their Saturday engagements page," she stated, and with that, she turned and left the room but not before giving one last parting shot, "Oh, and you can clear up that mess" she said sternly, like a mother telling off her errant child, pointing to the torn remnants of the photographs and envelope. Then, she was gone, leaving Guy fuming and to contemplate his future.

Guy, in a black mood, was left thinking through his predicament. While sending the photos to his employers would probably be nothing more than an embarrassment that he felt he could probably live with, but Barbara did have a point about his immediate boss. The Purser Superintendent was a puritanical bastard at the best of times, and he wasn't on good terms with him, often voicing his opinion about his boss's bullying management style. Such a self-righteous pratt and he would undoubtedly give Guy a hard time if those pictures became public via the newspapers. But would it be of interest to anyone? It's just pornographic photos of a single bachelor enjoying some carnal pleasures while home on leave. Mind you, according to his Bible punching authoritarian boss, there was no such thing as carnal pleasure. No, a hard time at work he could deal with just so long as he wasn't sacked.

A copy to his parents would be a different matter altogether. His father was both a devout Christian, being a frequent churchgoer, as well as the local Tory MP. He was very high profile, an outspoken critic of ethics and behaviour in politics and public service. On top of that, he had recently been appointed chairman of the MP Standards and Ethics Committee. If Barbara were true to her word, then some of the left-wing press would certainly take great delight in tarnishing his father's reputation through his perceived play boy son.

Guy shuddered to think of the consequences, not only for the relationship with his father, but it would certainly have enormous ramifications for his father's position. Guy knew he was beaten, trapped, well and truly 'goosed'. He was beside himself with rage at his stupid indiscretion. He had allowed his *'bollocks'* to rule his brain. He couldn't see a way out of his predicament and there was no way he was going to attempt to call Barbara's bluff; she had made an eerie transition from a promiscuous, titillating flirt to an evil fiend. He just couldn't risk the problems it would cause for his parents. His mother would be broken-hearted, and as for his father, well, that didn't bear thinking about. Therefore, reluctantly, he duly proposed to Tina, who was surprised at his sudden decision. She, of course, excitedly agreed, immediately asking when they could go shopping for the engagement ring. Totally overwhelmed with excitement, she failed to register the lack of passion or commitment in Guy's demeanour when he proposed. Tina was getting what she had wanted, having seen her two sisters walk down the aisle, marriage at last.

An ecstatic Tom, completely ignorant of the events that had led up to the sudden change of heart by Guy, went about arranging the biggest and best wedding reception he could. Even Barbara, the conniving bitch, cleverly feigned surprise and delight. The church booked, the reception arranged, and even the honeymoon destination decided without any input from Guy. The days and weeks that followed were confusing for Guy. All decisions concerning the wedding were taken out of his hands, and Barbara added insult to injury by deliberately not consulting him on any matter. Never had he felt so helpless, events were spiralling out of his control.

Meanwhile, his hatred for Barbara, his soon to be mother-in-law, intensified with each passing day. The way she always gave him a triumphant smile and offered her cheek for a quick, chaste *phmaw* kiss whenever they met, something she'd never done previously, was her way of demonstrating to him her strength and matriarchal domination over him. Guy's parents were somewhat surprised when he announced his intention to marry Tina, they had met her only fleetingly, but sufficiently to make a sound judgement. Neither of his parents saw Tina as a suitable partner for Guy, or as their daughter-in-law for that matter. Following the marriage announcement, the obligatory meeting of future in-laws for dinner was organised at a swanky restaurant. While Guy's father, Geoffrey, hit it off with Tom. Guy's Mother, June, soon realised that she couldn't stand Barbara. June's dislike for Barbara grew throughout the evening as she watched Barbara sip one too many cocktails, then pour the expensive French wine down her neck as though it was going out of fashion.

Each alcoholic mixture made Barbara louder and more obnoxious than when she was sober. Barbara was celebrating big time. Not only was she getting the last of her daughters married off, but she was impressed with Guy's family pedigree, as a social climber it was as though all her Christmases had come at once. She saw this as the start of a new life for her, the financial freedom that would come with downsizing their home now that Tina would be leaving and a retirement latching on to the social circles of her new relatives-in-law. Barbara had already earwigged Geoffrey mentioning different mixed functions to Tom, the Hunt Ball, cocktail parties, garden parties and other socialite soirees she could invite herself to. Being a 'hen-pecked' husband, Tom didn't dare say anything about his wife's excessive drinking. Even when they were alone later in bed, Barbara commented on how well she felt the evening had gone; he never mentioned the issue.

Barbara was all about social climbing. In her twilight world, as she drifted off, snoring grotesquely, were visions of her becoming involved with Guy's mother, accompanying her to the many social functions June would attend as a wife of a prominent Tory MP. Barbara felt certain she now had her feet on the ladder of status. June, on the other hand, thought Barbara was a frightful woman and had no intention of allowing the relationship to go any further than that of an arms-length in-law. She had already chastised Geoffrey for mentioning to Tom possible invitations to various functions. June had found Barbara to be a common, overbearing, bossy, obnoxious woman and was terribly worried on her son's behalf. She could see that Barbara was the driving force behind her daughter and obviously had a controlling involvement in the forthcoming marriage and probably beyond. Despite her worries, June remained outside of the situation. She didn't want to upset her son and accepted that times change with each generation. Reluctantly, she went along with the arrangements in the hope that her son was making the right decision. Little did she realise the real torment that Guy was going through. As the news spread, Guy received many messages of congratulations along with sarcastic comments from those of his friends to whom he use to claim that he would never marry.

Unexpectedly, an answer to his predicament manifested itself in the shape of an old school pal, Anton LeStrange. Anton, came from a mixed marriage of an English father and a beautiful French, Algerian, Arabic mother. Anton and Guy both attended the same pseudo-military-style school, where they became good friends. Following school, Anton joined the Royal Marines. Although achieving a high enough pass in his academic studies, Anton had failed to get on the selection course for direct entry as an officer and joined up as what was unkindly known as a 'grunt'. Anton took to the life of a Royal Marine well, soon impressing his senior officers. He progressed rapidly from basic training to obtaining the coveted Green Beret, followed by two hostile tours overseas, after which Anton was recommended for a commission. Upon passing out successfully from the officer training course, he became Captain Anton LeStrange, serving with the Royal Marines Mountain and Arctic Warfare Cadre. From a 'grunt' to a 'Rupert', as Anton put it.

All guests had, at this point, received their 'save the date' card, and Tina was pressurising Guy to pick a Best Man. Tina's suggestion that 'if he didn't have a best friend, then Mummy would organise someone,' filled Guy with even more horror than he was currently experiencing, this galvanised him into action. While Guy had made many friends over the years, he knew that Anton would be the best man for the job, in more ways than one, but explaining the situation would be the tricky part. Guy knew he had to bare his soul to Anton and hoped that his old friend was still the non-judgmental, loyal mate he had been over the years, despite the lack of recent contact.

Hearing Anton's voice over the phone gave Guy a warm, comfortable feeling; it felt as if they hadn't spoken for just a matter of days, not months.

"Now then me old seafaring chum," chortled Anton, "Always knew the old one-eyed snake would get you into trouble. Shotgun wedding I take it?"

"No, no, it isn't actually Ant," replied a somewhat sullen Guy.

"Jesus Guy, for someone who is getting married, you don't exactly sound excited."

Guy sarcastically laughed, "No, not excited at all. Ant … mate, it's a long story, but I've got myself into a rather tight spot and, to be perfectly honest, I don't want this marriage to go ahead."

"Good grief, what's going on? If it's not a shotgun jobby why on earth did you ask her to marry you?" Anton tried to keep his voice calm, but it was obvious he was both shocked and troubled by Guy's words. Anton thought of Guy as family; he was like a brother.

"I don't really know where to start."

"Look, tell you what, don't try to explain over the phone, I'm due some leave, how about we get together for a couple of days? We could go through the arrangements and your obvious doubts over a few beers and a curry. You can sort anything out with a good vindaloo and pint, what say you?" offered Anton eagerly.

"Sounds great Anton, it will be good to see you and explain."

"I'll sort you out mate, it's just a feeling of cold feet, only to be expected from the guy who normally has a girl in every port, city, town, and village. Can't wait to meet the lucky lady," enthused Anton.

Guy could feel Anton's grin coming down the phone line and knew he really was 'the best man for the job.'

Chapter 22

The following weekend, Anton had kept his promise and checked in at a pub local to Barbara and Tom's house. Guy went straight over to see him, and before Anton had time to down his pint, Guy poured out his tale of woe.

"Blimey, me old son, what have you got yourself into?" enquired a puzzled Anton, "We can't have this, we've got to get our hands on the originals, what do you know about the man that took the photos?"

"Nothing but the fact that he was overweight," Guy paused for a while, then remembered, "Wait, I've also got his car registration, but unless you know a copper, what use is that?"

"Well, my lad, it's your bloody lucky day! Leave it to me, I've a mate, ex Royal, broke his wrist and had to leave, he's now in the police, and he owes me a big favour, a very big favour as I saved his lanky ass life on a 'Black Ops' job we did together," exclaimed Anton proudly.

With Anton's help, Guy found the name and address of the man who'd taken the photographs, Frank Smith, a private enquiry agent working from an old run-down office in a seedy part of Southampton. Guy made an appointment to see him on the pretext of wanting some photographs taken of an errant wife. On meeting the man, Guy saw him for what he was, 'pond life' who immediately clammed up when he realised Guy's identity. Guy courteously enquired as to what could be done to take the photos out of circulation. Frank Smith had none of it, a client was a client, and there was nothing he could do, even bribery didn't make Frank budge. Guy had seen enough and soon realised that there was only one way he was going to get those photos back. He would be breaking the law, but he saw no other way out. He quickly discussed his plan with Anton, who readily agreed and offered his help. Guy declined, he didn't want anything going wrong that could jeopardise Anton's military career.

"Think nothing of it old son," was Anton's reply, "Who dares wins, I'm sure there is some outfit that uses that as their motto," he grinned.

Guy's intuition was right, he had definitely picked the 'best man' to help him.

Guy had been very observant on his visit to Frank Smith's office, noting that there wasn't a burglar alarm. The only form of security in Smith's office appeared to be a large, old metal filing cabinet, which Guy felt sure would contain the evidence. Everything to do with Smith was cheap; an old cheap car, old cheap offices and old cheap clothes, probably from a charity shop. Guy took a reasonable bet that the horrid little runt of a man didn't have anything better to keep his work in than the old metal filing cabinet. So, late one night, with Anton's help and experience in picking locks, a skill taught to him by a fellow marine who, with a mild criminal past, had been given an ultimatum when appearing before a Stipendiary Magistrate to either join the army or face a short spell in prison. He'd chosen the army and then later transferred to the Royal Marines. Once Anton had dealt with the lock, Guy entered into Smith's office, leaving Anton to stand as look-out. Smith was far from security-conscious and ignorantly left his keys to his cabinet in the drawer of his desk. Guy found the photos and negatives he was looking for along with several others. Never had he done such a risky thing before; he was terrified, but it was nothing when compared to being held in the grip of the Souter family. With a thumping heart, that felt it was going to burst out of his chest, he took away the evidence and destroyed it.

Confident that Barbara could no longer blackmail him, he walked out of the Souter family for good. Naturally, he experienced several weeks of worry that there could have been other copies that would mysteriously turn up and reduce his frightening night's work to nothing. He did receive persistent and abusive phone calls from a very irate Barbara, but when she discovered that the photos had gone missing, she realised there was nothing she could do to blackmail him anymore. She involved the police by making a complaint. The police, following up the complaint from Barbara Souter, sent a young DC to visit Frank Smith who, acting furtive and cagey, aroused the DC's suspicions, but he came up against a wall of silence, a very adamant Frank Smith denied all knowledge of any break-in or stolen photographs. Frank didn't want the police poking their noses into his business dealings as it would be extremely bad for business if the loss of the photos became public knowledge; he just wanted the whole thing covered up and forgotten. He simply claimed that Barbara Souter was just a dissatisfied client, and as far as he was concerned, it was a commercial matter that shouldn't involve the police at all. The DC reported back the outcome of his interview with Frank Smith to his supervising officer who was keen to meet crime statistic targets, he wrote off the complaint as 'no crime.'

After having been paid by Barbara Souter, Frank gave her back the money for his fee to show no hard feelings and to calm her anger. This gesture eased his conscience and made him feel totally detached from the whole affair. The only effect the whole incident had on him was that he had to go against his miserly nature and buy a second hand safe.

Eventually, the pleading from a distraught Tina faded, and the Souter family passed out of Guy's life for good. Able to resume his career and feel like a man as free as the sea on which he sailed, Guy did, from time to time, shudder at the thought of how narrowly he had escaped what could have been an unbearable marriage. He was also very thankful that Frank Smith was 'old-school' and never bought or used modern digital technology.

Sometime later, Guy did hear down the grapevine that Tina Souter had been detained under the Mental Health Act. The story was that one evening she attacked her new fiancé with a knife, causing serious actual bodily harm and hospitalisation. For Guy, how true the story was didn't bear thinking of. Guy was only too aware of just how close he had been to be on the wrong end of a knife in the hands of a Souter woman. Even now, years later, he winced at the thought of Tina and Barbara Souter and prayed that he never has to cross the same path as them ever again.

Chapter 23

The tension in the Boardroom was electric with excitement as Richard made his final address to his co-directors, "I feel the price is right gentlemen and the location is ideal for enabling us to move from the south coast into new areas."

To Richard's right, sat Gordon Pool, a very young Deputy Chairman. He was a wiry man, tall, very slim with a hawk-like face and sporting a pair of pince-nez spectacles on the end of his nose, a peculiar choice for one so young. Gordon, with his crew cut and strange glasses, was an oddity if ever there was one, but, as regards to work, he was like a human dynamo whose output could be that of two men. At times, Gordon's secretary had to enlist the help of the admin assistants within the office to keep on top of the workload. Gordon had a very shrewd approach to problems and an uncanny instinct for knowing when something wasn't right. He was also a very clever and formidable negotiator with the seaman's union who, in turn, held him in high respect. It was no secret that Gordon's qualities had put him where he was – sitting alongside the most powerful man in British shipping. He was a hundred percent behind Richard's decision; this was not only self-interest, because he thought that he might be chosen to take over the running of the potential new subsidiary, but because as one who knew the shipping business well, he understood that this take over made sound commercial sense. BSC needed to keep moving forward if it was to survive against some of the US and European conglomerates who were swallowing up all the major shipping companies.

Next to Gordon, with his eyebrows joined in what appeared to be painful concentration, sat Mark Chappel, the Operations Director. Mark didn't share Gordon's appetite or love of work, despite eating, drinking and sleeping the company to the point where he neglected his wife and home, he didn't have aptitude or ability. Mark was once described as a square peg in a round hole. His role is to shoulder the everyday operational problems of the company, having the third-highest pay of the Board following Richard and Gordon and rightly so for the amount of responsibility he had to handle. Mark had attained his high office by being in the wrong place at the wrong time; some might say he inherited his position by default. It could never be said that he wasn't, to the core, a company man; however, he operated far beyond his capacity, something Richard had observed and intended to put right with a re-shuffle, following his planned acquisition of the Beaumont Company.

Unfortunately for Mark, every decision that loomed in front of him was a major crisis; whenever a decision deadline drew near, he would reach for his coat pocket and pull out a bottle of pills that would help ease his developing duodenal ulcer.

Across the table, doodling on his blotter as he listened to Richard, sat Bob Somers. Bob was the company's Financial Director. A rotund, little man, bald except for a thin line of grey hair at the sides. He had a round face with flabby jowls and on his nose rested a pair of black, thick-rimmed glasses with such a magnification they gave his eyes a bulbous look, enhanced by the rolls of fat on his face. He was often referred to by the many who didn't like him as 'The Toad'. Bob made up for his lack of stature by being the most ardent critic of Richard's Chairmanship. Bob felt that it was his work that really ran the company. However, Bob being typical of many bean counters, had no commercial flare, no feeling for situations, lacked foresight and, most importantly, the talent necessary for being a good entrepreneur. Bob Somers was dead against the take-over of the Beaumont Company, declaring that it was throwing good money after bad. Their British Shipping Company was making handsome profits, and although they might have reached saturation point on their present routes, in his opinion, this was no reason for the buyout of Beaumont's. At the back of his mind, Bob had formulated an idea to get him nearer the Chairman's position; if the vote went for the take-over, then he would discreetly stir up opposition to have a shareholders' emergency meeting, tabling a vote of no confidence in Richard Hartling.

As Richard continued, Bob Somers' mind was miles away. He was planning the new plant beds in a two-acre part of his garden at home just outside Sevenoaks. Yet to decide what to do with the other six acres of his eight acre land that he had inherited with the house. Local builders would jump at the chance to build on the secluded section, but Bob knew that the only access would be through his beautiful garden, and he would refuse to have his magnificent views interrupted by greedy builders. Unlike Chappel, who was wiping his sweating palms with a handkerchief, Somers would not neglect his beloved wife and home. He often mused to himself that once he is comfortably in Richard's chair, he will run things to his advantage. In his blinkered eyes, he'd soon have the whole operation running as smoothly as his Accounts Department.

In contrast, John Cook, the Sales & Marketing Director, was a debonair bachelor who gave encouraging grunts as Richard spoke. Flamboyant and good at his job, John was the type of man who could sell a refrigerator to the Eskimos or sand to the Arabs. Average height and build, he sported a dark drooping moustache, bearing an uncanny resemblance to the film star idol Omar Sharif. Though not gay, John did not particularly care for the close company of women, and he enjoyed living a very single life. At cocktail and dinner parties, he was the perfect host, a witty and charming sycophant. Many women ate out of his hand, but that was as far as they got. No woman could compete with the two joys in his life; his stylish Lamborghini sports car and his golden Labrador, Charlie. John was a superb salesman who had started his career with a carpet manufacturing company at eighteen years old. He wholeheartedly agreed when Richard announced, "We will be buying into our own dockyard, which with good marketing, will enable us to attract other ship owners to this vital link to the heart of the industrial Midlands." Though hailed as a marketing genius, who could have made his fortune in the city, John loved anything to do with ships and was more than happy with his position at BSC. In total, eleven men held the power of this great shipping conglomerate.

The twelfth and final member and the singular woman, a situation Richard aimed to change after the takeover when the Board would increase, was Janet Houchell, a high flyer. Richard had ironically 'head hunted' her from the executive management recruitment agency he'd often used. Janet had two great specialisations with her main thrust being PR in addition to her HR skills. Capitalising these two incredible strengths, he'd brought her in as Head of PR and HR. She was proving to be an outstanding success, Janet was in every sense a powerful woman. She exuded power, she looked powerful, she spoke powerfully and always gained everyone's undivided attention when she spoke to an audience. Janet had taken power dressing to a new level, having a penchant for leather. More often than not, wearing leather trousers, a new idea which some frowned upon, and was only just beginning to gain acceptance in a male-dominated business world where suits were the norm, but despite this, Janet was a pure through and through feminist. Tall with thick black hair pulled back in a stylish, perfectly made bun. When God had given out good looks, Janet had obviously been at the front of the queue. A flawless complexion requiring very little make up other than a daily moisturiser; she didn't need makeup. Her high cheekbones lead to oval-shaped eyes that gave the slight hint of the orient in her blood line and required only the hint of mascara topped off with perfectly shaped eyebrows. Her favoured shoes were usually patent leather red to match her red painted finger and toenails. Her smile was what could only be described as smouldering, an archetypical James Bond poster girl: she would certainly pooh pooh this idea. Janet described herself as a liberal feminist. Her aura of power frightened many men, resulting in the typical male defence mechanism of criticism and antagonism. Some describing her as Dracula's daughter as she could be heard approaching due to flapping of her leather coat making a sound like the fluttering of bat wings. Some even went as far as to describe her as a dyke, firmly convinced that she was a lesbian. Actually, when the mood took her, she could swing both ways and had any of her critics had the balls to find out, they would have discovered that she had the ability to take sexual pleasure to totally new heights. Two of her main dislikes were uncouth, chauvinistic men, and weak, fawning females. Janet was secretly in love with Richard, but that would forever stay just a figment of her fantasies.

The six others, being part-time directors, who also sat on the Boards of other companies were: Lord Timothy Morgan-Boast, Sir Peter Rayner QC, the company legal adviser, Rear Admiral Roy Clarke; Surgeon Commander Peter Willis; David Kirton and finally, James Walker, Managing Director of the engineering consultants used by BSC. James, despite being an accomplished and successful engineer, unfortunately, displayed all that Janet Houchell hated in men. James was a politically incorrect male chauvinist of the first order. James smoked a foul-smelling pipe, the size of a bucket, permanently clamped between his tobacco-stained teeth. A trademark more than a habit, tolerated on the rare occasions he visited the BSC head office. It was with little surprise that James turned out the way he was, he cut his engineering teeth as an engineering apprentice in the engine rooms of vessels owned by a Hartlepool tramp shipping company, sailing the seven seas for months on end in an all-male ship's environment. Voyages of such a length, that James completed his apprenticeship of three years in only two trips at sea! He had developed a sarcastic sense of humour and called a spade a spade. His sense of humour, based on gutter comedy, was usually at the expense of women, referring to them as 'tarts' which his chauvinistic persona thought was a term of endearment. Probably, this was why James had been married three times and was currently divorced and single again. James was left-handed and whilst writing in his large notebook, if his right hand wasn't caressing his pipe with his right hand then it was nearly always beneath the desktop giving the impression he was permanently scratching his nether regions, which he often was! Janet disliked James intensively and would have made moves to have him dismissed if that had been possible.

Janet had, on more than one occasion, voiced her disgust face to face on overhearing him make some disparaging remarks about one or more female employees at BSC. On one occasion, far from feeling admonished, James had merely acknowledged her disapproval, and then as she'd walked away he'd past some remark within earshot along the lines of 'she must be having a red rag week.' When Janet had frozen in her footsteps and turned to confront him, he totally denied it and made no apologies claiming she must have misheard him saying 'she must be having a bad week.' Unfortunately for Janet, there was little she could do, James was co-opted onto the Board of BSC, as the company he owned outright had virtually an in perpetuity contract to oversee the maintenance and repair of BSC vessels. The best Janet was able to do was to inform Richard, who promised he'd deal with James' improprieties.

Richard looked around the assembled power group, "I am now more convinced than ever that the take-over is a good thing for us and that we will not have a similar chance for many a year if ever." Some heads nodded in agreement, and others looked studiously into thin air. Bob Somers had been staring blankly at the glass case containing a model of one of the company's early traditional steamships, his heavy jowls seeming to ball out like an angry puffer fish. Hardly waiting for Richard to finish, Bob slammed his hand down on the blotter in front of him with a sharp slap, making several of the board jump. When he knew he had everyone's attention, he began, "I'm not happy with it, Richard, not one little bit! We would be tying up too much of our reserve capital, apart from Beaumont's one new jumbo ferry, the other ships in their fleet are worn out. Their recent accounts are dismal, and in my book, the whole thing will be a liability to us … a gigantic risk. Believe me, gentlemen, this spells out disaster."

"Bob," Richard declared, "that's my whole point, we are getting the Beaumont's at a bargain-basement price, this is a chance we can't miss otherwise they'll be picked off by the US or some Far Eastern interest."

Ever since Richard had proposed the purchase of Beaumont's, Bob Somers had made it known that he was against it. Whenever the opportunity arose, Bob had surreptitiously attempted to plant doubts in the minds of the BSC powerbrokers. This did not go unnoticed by Richard, he was good at working out who his enemies were and astute enough to know that Somers' opposition was based on personal greed rather than sound financial argument.

Gordon Pool quickly offered his support to Richard, "Bob, I see where you are coming from, but we must take the long term view and anticipate possible moves by our competitors. We have competition in Hull and they could easily try and grab the most of the lucrative overnight freight market from the North and Scotland if we don't move quickly. Look around the UK coast, where can you see any other possibilities for expansion into new routes, we can't hesitate, we have to go for this now."

The suave, debonair Surgeon, Commander Peter Wills, added his support, "I whole-heartedly agree with Gordon and Richard, it was the buccaneering spirit that put the 'great' in Great Britain, and that's what we need to apply to this situation, as someone once said, *'Screw it, let's do it'.*"

This last comment raised a few smiles around the table as most knew who could be attributed to uttering those words. Richard also displayed a slight grin but quickly composed himself as he was on the point of bringing in Janet for her input on PR and HR. Part of his school boyish, immature mind had an internal giggle at the word 'screw' as he recalled some recent bedroom athletics with his mistress Katrina. Turning to look at Janet and despite his inner thoughts keeping his face impassive.

"Jan, you've been up to Northwold and spoken to their head of HR, what are your views on the set-up and then secondly we'll need to formulate a plan to deal with the local action group that are against any development at the port. I believe they go under the banner of PANE?"

"Yes, they do," replied Janet as she continued, "For those of you who don't know of that acronym, it stands for 'People Against Northwold Expansion'. Some local wag came up with this slogan after being interviewed on local radio, saying that our proposed take-over and expansion plans were a pain." Janet paused as a few heads around the table nodded with grins, acknowledging the clever adaptation of the word and the banner headlines which had even reached the national daily newspapers.

Richard took up that point.

"Well Jan," Richard had started calling her Jan shortly after she joined the company and as she had never objected he continued using this shortened version of her name. He hoped this would, in a small way, demonstrate a relaxing but business like closeness and to demonstrate how much he valued her as an inner member of the top team. She had taken this as a compliment where Richard was concerned as Janet only allowed him to use this abbreviation. When any of the others in the company had attempted to address her as such, they were soon asked to desist as she pointed out that she preferred to have her name used in full.

"Once, and if, the take-over is successfully agreed then shortly after your presence is going to be vital up there to work your PR skills and counter this local opposition."

"Yes, Richard I couldn't agree more, but first let me tell you about the HR operation."

"Of course" he replied, although Janet's comments sounded a little like a rebuke they were not meant so. Richard had always shown nothing but professional courtesy towards Janet. He'd be totally surprised and flattered if he knew that, as she was looking at him during the conversation, she was thinking to herself 'God I'd so love to go to bed with this man!' As she continued.

"I recently spent two days up there talking to various heads of departments and spent some time with Roy Brooks, their head of personnel and I must say, credit where credit is due, I was impressed with the way things are being run. That's not to say I don't see ways for improvement, I do. Roy shoulders responsibility for both the shoreside personnel and the marine personnel operation. I believe these two functions need to be split with Roy at the head."

Richard nodded in approval at what Janet was explaining but could see that this meeting could soon become bogged down with the intricacies of what Janet had in mind and this wasn't the place or the time, so he interrupted her before she went any further.

"Excellent Jan, I can see you've already got your finger firmly on the pulse up there and if the outcome of today is successful then we can schedule a series of meetings together and plan a way forward."

Janet smiled demurely at Richard, momentarily basking in the praise from his last comment.

"Of course Richard, thank you."

At this junction, the morning coffee arrived and a cacophony of conversation broke out amongst the Board. Richard sipped his coffee, feeling slightly detached from the others. His thoughts drifted off to the previous night's encounter when he had been making love to his mistress. A slow grin crossed his face as he recalled their sexual athletics. Katrina had dressed up in her favourite bedroom attire, consisting of a beautiful lace pink Basque that accentuated her seductive, voluptuous body. Her sexy black stockings...

"Mr. Hartling!" Susan was almost shouting as she tried to attract his attention. She always used a formal address when in the company of others.

Richard, still picturing the stockings, was suddenly brought back to reality as Susan touched his shoulder. He placed his coffee cup on the table and quickly regained his composure. Looking at Richard, Bob Somers had misinterpreted Richard's slight smile as being aimed specifically at him; such was the depth of his megalomania. James Walker, sitting at the far end of the table, uncharacteristically removed his smouldering pipe from his mouth with his left hand and raised it to catch Richard's eye, his right hand still hidden beneath the tabletop.

"Yes James what would you like to add?"

"Coming back to Bob's point, I would just like to add that I don't see the condition of the vessels as a major stumbling block, there are several yards that will be falling over themselves for business; naturally, any work would go out for competitive tendering, but I would hope that our British yards would sharpen their pencils. There's Welton Ship repairers at Hull, then Cammell Laird at Birkenhead, all itching do a deal with us. That's all I wanted to add and hopefully alleviate Bob's fears."

"Yes, quite right, good, thank you, James … Right, gentlemen no more time for discussion, let's have a break, finish our coffee and reconvene in an hour to take a vote," with that, Richard rose from the table and returned to his office, annexed to the Board room, to speak with Susan.

Later, as Richard expected, the Board decided to follow his lead and approved the purchase of the Beaumont Steamship company. With that, the power people of the BSC Company filed away into the Directors' dining room, all but one being happy with the outcome. Bob Somers was seething with resentment that his concerns had been dismissed 'out of hand', quietly admitting to himself that his concerns were based not on sound commercial judgement, but personal greed.

During this decision making in the Board room, Peter and Paul Beaumont were seated aboard the Scotland to London mainline express as it raced its way south, both unsure as to whether they were going to have made a wasted journey. Despite Richard's confidence during their previous conversations, it had not been a foregone conclusion that the Board of BSC would approve the price or the purchase of their now ailing company. Throughout the journey, they kept nervously glancing at their mobile phones, hoping that Richard would call or text with the news. On arrival at King's Cross, a smartly dressed driver met them and escorted them to a company limousine which quickly whisked them away to the main office of BSC. Over afternoon tea, the brothers learned with a great deal of relief, that the Board of BSC had decided almost unanimously to the take-over. After the formal meeting and preliminary signing, the deal had yet to be finally approved by the shareholders, but although they had the power to stop the deal, it would be an astounding decision for them to go against Richard's plans as they had all become very wealthy people from their investments in BSC. With Richard at the helm, his track record was legendary. After the signing, Richard and several of the Board took the brothers out for dinner where they got gloriously drunk, happy in the relief that the deal was going through, confident that they had enough money to pay the taxman and hopefully, with a good Brief, keep themselves out of prison.

On the other hand, Bob Somers had left the brothers in no doubt as to how he felt about the situation, and although reluctantly attending the celebration dinner, he spent most of the evening in sulky silence. Not that any of the Board members gave Bob's demeanour a second thought as he was notorious for having many and differing mood swings. Following dinner, Bob caught the train to his local railway station before driving home in a fury. He was so incensed with rage and not paying enough attention to his driving, that he carelessly put a small dent in his beloved old Bentley as he caught the nearside fender on the gate post at the entrance to the lane where his house lay.

Chapter 24

Bob's family house was large and detached, surrounded by its sprawling grounds. Should it ever be put up for sale, then Estate Agents would describe it as *'an imposing residence suitable for the country gentleman and his family.'* It had been built at the turn of the century and modernised several times since, boasting three floors, the top floor originally being servants accommodation. Beneath ground, there was a huge cellar which housed Bob's beloved, and almost priceless, wine collection. Although he very rarely imbibed in alcohol, the wine was just an investment commodity to him. There were five bedrooms, all en-suite, it was really far too big for the almost hermit lifestyle he and his wife, Rachel, lived. The house cried out to be the centre of an active social calendar or a large, boisterous family to fill its cavernous rooms. Bob had inherited it from his parents, and as it was free of any incumbencies, he saw no point in downsizing, plus he loved the huge garden and adjacent paddocks where he had played as a youngster; he loved the memories it held.

Fortunately, the gatepost Bob hit on his drive home was very old, probably older than the house, and likely to have been from days when it had just been a gate into a farmer's field. Taking the brunt of the impact, the gatepost soon splintering from the glancing blow, causing minor superficial damage to the Bentley. But damage was damage, and as he had spent years lovingly restoring his beloved car, at the cost of thousands of pounds, this mishap put more coal on the fire of anger that was burning within him. Automatically putting the car away in the spacious detached garage, and in the heat of the moment, he uncharacteristically didn't even inspect the damage. Anger still writhing around his head, he charged straight upstairs and stormed into the bedroom. Rachel quickly rose from beneath the duvet, reached out an arm for the bedside light switch, "What on earth is the matter Bob?" failing to hide her momentary anger at being disturbed.

At the sight of his wife, Bob regained some composure, "Oh, sorry petal," he replied, suddenly realising the rage he'd worked himself into, never intending to take it out on his beloved Rachel. As always, he addressed her by his pet name, which she secretly couldn't abide but was too timid to say anything. The years of living with him had knocked the stuffing out of her, she felt like a rag doll abandoned in a large empty toy house. To Bob, it was a term of endearment comparing her to the flowers that he also loved and cared for. Rachel sat up in bed, now fully awake she yawned, rubbing the sleep from her eyes.

"Something must be very wrong for you to be in such a temper. Is it about this take-over business?" she tried to sound concerned, but she wasn't really bothered, just annoyed that Bob had disturbed her slumber. Bob was totally devoted to his wife, but she, however, was living a lie. Marriage to Bob was one of sufferance she had come to accept it as her lot in life. Bob walked around the bed to Rachel, bent forward, and kissed her on the forehead before gently taking her hand and sitting on the edge of the bed.

"Forgive me, petal," he said softly, "It's that damned fool, Hartling. At one stage, I felt as though I had the Board behind me, but his smooth as silk talk won them round. They're fools; they can't see what a millstone it will be around our necks! Mark my words, they'll rue this day!" he shrieked as his blood pressure started to rise again.

"What an exasperating day for you, my dear," Rachel tried to sound sympathetic, annoyed with herself for allowing Bob to see she was now wide awake. Bob had an insatiable appetite for sex, and he expected it at least once every night, Rachel had begrudgingly accepted it as her wifely duty. She saw from the look in his eyes that she wasn't going to get out of it tonight. Rachel enjoyed the few nights when business took Bob was away from home or resulted in him returning very late, then she could snuggle up in bed, relax with a good book and not have to put up with Bob puffing and panting over her. Bob smiled at her lovingly, giving Rachel a telepathic signal indicating that she should understand what he expected of her. The thought of making love with Rachel gave him a degree of momentary relief,

"I need a coffee, and there are just a couple of things I need to do in my study."

He needed some downtime for the coffee and Viagra to work, as well as thinking over some plans in an attempt to bring down Richard.

He quickly undressed down to his comically large, baggy boxer shorts and socks, held up by suspenders on his calves, which he insisted on wearing. In Rachel's opinion they looked ludicrous. But her opinion didn't count. Although she did, to a certain extent, find some amusement in the sight which she compared to the rotund, older gentleman depicted on the saucy cartoon picture postcards sold on the promenades of popular sea-side holiday resorts. Having made some coffee, Bob swallowed the little, blue, triangular pill and placed a cup of tea for his wife on the bedside table. He went back downstairs and into his study, sat in his large leather chair, and began to devise a plan to not only politically attack Richard but to have the deal cancelled by the shareholders.

Bob had one underlying motive for trying to derail the take-over, it had little to do with the company. He desperately needed to avoid personal disaster. Over the years, he had milked off small amounts of money from BSC and hid them away in an overseas Swiss bank account. These amounts, tiny in themselves, had amassed into a small fortune. The operation had stopped a few years back, when the company accounts went computerised, but what frightened Bob was that with the take-over, there would be an expansion of his department and a new eye might just spot the small discrepancies that would lead to questions that Bob wouldn't be able to answer. Bob mused to himself at the vision of taking over control from Richard, he was already aware that Barrington-Smythe was a particular threat to his world and he'd be the first to go. After an hour, Bob felt confident that he had a workable plan for scuppering the whole deal, it would mean calling in a lot of favours, but this should not prove to be a problem. He finished his cold coffee, thoughts of Rachel in the bedroom stirring his loins as the Viagra started to take effect. He turned out the study light and returned upstairs expectantly, looking forward to snuggling down beneath the duvet with his wife. Upon entering the bedroom, a soft, gentle snore greeted him. Rachel lay there, her mouth open and the cup of tea untouched. With an inward sigh, he looked down at his burgeoning penis as it attempted to break free from his boxer shorts and considered whether or not to disturb his wife. Reluctantly deciding the bathroom and one of his hidden away adult magazines beckoned.

Chapter 25

For some time, Richard had been the subject of covert observations, and it was to the great frustration of those watching him that he was a man with very few regular habits. This irregularity made planning very difficult for what they had in mind. So much so, they began to question whether or not to give up and turn their attention to other sources of criminality. However, when they discovered that Richard's visits to the large secluded house in the quiet leafy suburbs of Roehampton, were not entirely proper, it gave them a break they needed, offering the very opportunity they had been seeking. Their haphazard monitoring of Richard's habits and movements had identified that he employed a driver, but failed to discover the real extent of his responsibilities, putting him down to be just another inconsequential body to incapacitate.

As Tim Spinks skilfully handled the Range Rover through the wet streets, the lights of London town played tricks with the reflections on the surrounding infrastructure, pavements and roads, so much so that Richard's tired eyes strained as he looked out at the display of colours. Richard was yet again grateful that he had a bodyguard to take the strain of driving, especially after such a long day in the office. He began to enjoy a feeling of a warming glow, knowing that at the journey's end, the warm embrace of Katrina, along with his favourite single malt, would be waiting for him.

The houses of Roehampton were of a design from an era when the land wasn't at a premium, sitting in large plots, far back from the road and sporting long gravel driveways, reminiscent of Hollywood movies, together with huge garages the size of a small bungalow. Tim pulled off the road and up to a set of electronic gates. He keyed a code into a handheld unit and waited for the huge gates to silently open, sliding away on either side. Just a few hundred yards from the house, he'd noticed a parked, blacked-out, MG Rover saloon. The position of this vehicle, unobserved by Richard, was of immediate interest to Tim. His training, during the Body Guarding Course, had taught him to question the unusual and never accept anything as it might at first appear. It is called the 'ABC of life; Assume nothing, Believe no-one and Check everything.' Making a mental note to check it out once Richard was safe in the house, he manoeuvred the Range Rover into the drive, the gates closing quietly behind them. Katrina's house was lit up as normal. Richard left the vehicle after a quick word with Tim, stating he'd only be about an hour or so. From previous experience, Tim realised that Richard's hour usually meant three at least, but this did not bother him as he was paid handsomely for his services, which more than countered the inconvenience he sometimes suffered. As far as Tim was concerned, it was all money in the bank going towards the day when he would take early retirement and head for a place in the sun. All that was missing from this plan was someone to share it with; he hoped that she would materialise sooner rather than later.

Waiting until Richard had let himself into the house with his key, Tim quietly slipped from the vehicle, deftly tiptoed across the gravel drive and on to the grass, hidden by the mature undergrowth. He intended to scale the wall and sneak up on the parked Rover. His instincts told him it shouldn't be there. Years of serving in Northern Ireland had honed Tim's skills of a sixth sense, fine-tuned from working in the shadows of back alleyways. As he approached the garden wall, his senses rang extrasensory perception alarm bells, signalling that he wasn't alone amongst the undergrowth. Adrenaline suddenly burst into his bloodstream as he realised that he was now the hunted. All thoughts of checking out the Rover MG faded. His survival instinct kicked in, ready to turn into the direction of the attack he felt was about to happen. Despite his stealth, he soon felt the cold steel of what later turned out to be a Kalashnikov assault rifle prodded into the back of his neck and heard the chilling, rough broad Irish accent of Pete McAvoy, ex-IRA enforcer and cold-blooded killer.

"Ba Jasus, to be sure noore, what 'ave I got here, tis that yoouself noore?" said the hissing, broad, rasping Irish accent, with a significant tell-tale hint of a heavy smoker. Pete McAvoy, one of the three members of the renegade RIRA gang that had previously attempted a daring, if foolhardy, broad daylight kidnapping of Richard, only to be unwittingly foiled by Tim with his sophisticated satellite command and control system that on that day had routed him away from danger. The RIRA now back for a second bite at the cherry had selected Pete McAvoy to take care of Richard's driver, incapacitate him, killing him if necessary.

"There now, that'll be a piece of piss," McAvoy had proudly boasted to the others.

Due to their incompetence that had seen them thrown out of the regular IRA, they had failed to fully understand what they would be dealing with when it came to Tim Spinks.

Unaware of the drama unfolding outside, Richard had let himself into Katrina's house, as he called her name, "Hi K!" he announced loudly using only the initial letter of her name, wondering if she was waiting for him upstairs. Occasionally, Katrina would greet him dressed only in a flimsy light chiffon robe which tantalisingly covered a pink and black lace Basque, black stockings and suspenders; at other times, she would lie in the bath surrounded by scented candles, seductively waiting for him.

In a strained voice, she replied, "Here, in the snug."

Richard, with his mind on a glass of warming malt followed by a jolly good fuck, failed to notice the unusual tone of Katrina's voice. Removing his overcoat, he threw it casually over the large banister post, then, as taking off his suit jacket and loosening his tie, he entered the snug and stopped short. He gasped, shocked at the scene before him.

Katrina was strapped to an upright chair, terribly dishevelled, her chiffon robe ripped back, exposing her glamorous body, clad in only her usual Basque; her stockings ripped and laddered caused during the brief, vain struggle she had put up when she had unwittingly opened the front door. Her normally beautiful and immaculately coiffured hair, hung loosely over her face, her bruised swollen cheeks smudged with black mascara, and one eye appeared half-closed, all the result of being subdued during her short but valiant attempt to defend herself. So assured by her security of a high wall surrounding the property and electronic gates to the road, she had assumed the knock at the door had been Richard wanting some role play, rather than letting himself in with his key. The RIRA team had easily scaled the wall and crept upon the house. Luck had played into their hands with Katrina expecting Richard. Their original plan to use Katrina to lure Richard to her home proved unnecessary as he had obligingly walked into their trap. She raised her head and looked to Richard through locks of loose hair as she sobbed,

"I'm so sorry, Richard," she choked, releasing yet more tears; her body gave an involuntary shudder causing her to wince as the binds that held her dug deep into her tender flesh.

Catching his breath in a spasm of shock, Richard dropped his jacket, failing to grasp the reality of the scene. He attempted to run across to her but was brought to a sudden halt by a menacing looking Kalashnikov rifle pointing at him. A voice angrily yelled, accompanied by a shower of spittle, "Get down, get down on tha chaar," Mick Rielly shouted and viciously gesticulated with the barrel of the gun to the large easy chair opposite to where Katrina was so roughly trussed.

"And keep thaself quiet, sit down on your hands, don't dare move," he barked, "And naarbody gets hurt."

In a flashback, Richard replayed his nightmare; he was having difficulty perceiving what the reality was. Events appeared to be happening in slow motion, just like in his dream, but when realisation suddenly kicked in, his initial thought screamed that they were about to die. He was violently pushed back into the chair with the butt of the gun being thumped into his stomach, winding him, causing him to let out a deep grunt and making him feel like vomiting as the hot bile rose in his throat; this action took away any immediate thoughts of bravado and retaliation. Richard had never before had to activate his personal attack alarm, the trigger for which was discreetly hidden as a small button on his wristwatch, pressing it as he bent double from the pain of the blow, then sitting down on his hands hoping that Tim would respond.

Several minutes passed, to Richard and Katrina it felt like several hours. Knowing he had to do something, Richard looked up, "Please," he began to plead. The Irishman moved so quickly that Richard didn't see the second blow coming. This time it was a fist, a fist with so much power that Richard was once again winded. Mick stepped back, pleased with his punch, "No talking! Right! Noore, all we've gotta' do is just wait here for our Pat while he takes care of your bleeding driver, tha foocker, and then we'll be on our way with you, Mr. Richard high and bloody mighty Hartling, you are going to be a nice little earner for us, now sit back on ya fooking hands, de ya 'ear me."

Richard, still hadn't taken in what was happening. Still reeling from the shock and pain, slowly it dawned on him that he was being taken hostage for ransom and consequently, at least for the time being, his life was not at risk, he then tried to work out what they would do with Katrina. His anger welled, looking at her, taking in the sight of her semi nakedness, wearing the erotic clothes that were meant for his eyes only, not for these rough Irish monsters. He felt powerless and weak. The other man, who had yet to say anything, kept a gun levelled at Richard's slumped body. Richard desperately wanted to regain some dignity and control of the situation, so used to giving orders and making decisions, he was finding the situation completely alien. He kept his head bowed, calculating what to do next, he knew he mustn't antagonise his capturers, at least they hadn't bound him and he wanted it to stay that way, knowing that trussed up like Katrina he would be useless to the both of them. He might just as well have been bound, being forced to sit on his hands. He knew he didn't have the agility or speed to attempt anything before he'd be incapacitated with another hefty body blow. He guessed that his removal was imminent after they had dealt with Tim, and what of Tim ... perhaps he was also overpowered or even dead?

His imagination ran wild as he tried to formulate a plan. He struggled to fight the pain of the vicious blow to his stomach, concentrating on getting his breathing under control and bring his blood pressure down to regain his composure. At the same time, he started to pray that they would leave Katrina alone, if necessary he would beg them to save her life, but first, as his breathing started to return to normal, he risked slightly raising his head to survey the scene. At a glance, it appeared hopeless, both men were standing back and out of immediate range, if he tried anything they would surely shoot. He looked towards one of his attackers; it was as if he was reading Richard's mind, his smile broadened as he slightly raised the Kalashnikov, the barrel of the gun now pointed directly at Katrina's head. The Irishman's look said it all, one movement and Katrina would die. Richard retched and again fought to keep down the hot bitter bile that was rising in his throat. It was just at this point that Tim burst into the room and Katrina let out a blood curdling, hysterical scream.

Chapter 26

Having seen no reason to take his weapon to creep up and spy on a parked car. Tim, both hands free, momentarily froze, having only nanoseconds to turn the tables on his enemy before the RIRA man would further dominate the situation, he instantly spun around. He brought up his right arm with as much force as he could muster, pushing the muzzle of the gun skywards, his left hand striking the lower open palm under his opponents jaw with such ferocity he heard something crack, one thing was for sure, the recipient of the blow started to collapse ground like a sack of potatoes. Years of close quarter unarmed combat situations had ensured that Tim could successfully overpower his target. As the Kalashnikov dropped to the ground, landing silently on to the mushy undergrowth, Tim found the chin and top of the assailant's head, with his military instinct for survival and expert precision, he broke the man's neck in one swift movement creating a deadly crunch. He gently lowered the now lifeless body to the ground.

Only then, realising how hard he was breathing and sweating, did he understand how severe the situation was. Richard must be a target as nobody, not even the Irish, would carry Kalashnikovs to burgle a large house in Roehampton. Richard had to be the reason. Quickly making his way back to the Range Rover to retrieve his gun, he silently opened the passenger side door to gain access to his Browning .45 automatic, stowed in the strongbox between the two the front seats. Momentarily fumbling with the keys from his pocket to release the lock of the heavy box, he noticed the flashing alarm light on the instrument panel indicating that Richard's panic button on his wristwatch had been activated. This confirmed Tim's worst fears.

All he had to do now was to hit the large red alarm button on the car's instrument panel which would inform his private security company's control room that he was in trouble and needing immediate assistance. They'd inform the police and, from the GPS information, find the exact location for sending in the cavalry. Tim shuddered at that thought; there was already one dead body that he would have to explain, and he couldn't see the local constabulary turning a blind eye to that! However, he felt sure he knew somebody who would overlook the situation, if he could just rescue Richard first. So taking the biggest gamble of his life, reneging from raising the alarm, he cancelled the button on the Range Rover's dashboard and decided to attempt the rescue alone.

He removed his jacket to allow more freedom, tucked the .45 between his belt and the small of his back and started to creep towards the house. His adrenaline was increasing with every heartbeat but he was in his element, once more a Special Forces soldier, as he rapidly but quietly entered the house through the open front door. From the rear room, he heard the unmistaken broag of an Irish accent informing Richard, and whom he assumed to be a sobbing Katrina, that nobody was going to get hurt. Words Tim had heard before, he knew he had to act quickly. He literally glided through the hall as though on-air, manoeuvring himself towards the half-open door of the snug. Tim was unsure of how many he was up against and worked on a maximum of four, as their MG saloon car wouldn't take anymore with Richard, maybe it could only be three if they had decided on taking the woman as well but for the time being, Tim would have to work on 'one down three to go.' As he moved towards the room he clocked the large wall mirror, from which his position in the hall gave him a partial view of the interior. He could see the top of Richard's head, obviously seated, and at least two attackers were standing with weapons at the ready. One took a blow at Richard before informing him that as soon as his driver had been taken care of, they would all be on their way, reiterating that if everybody played along, nobody was going to get hurt. It was clear that the captors believed Tim posed no threat to their plans.

"Well, I'm still here, you bastard," muttered Tim to himself, frantically trying to formulate a plan as to what to do next. He couldn't see whether Richard was bound or restrained, so he had to consider Richard wouldn't be of any help to him in overpowering the thugs. Quickly deciding that he had no time for finesse, it would have to be a 'do or die' attempt. Tim had heard countless times about how time supposedly appears to stand still in moments of extreme violence; seconds can drag so that you can clearly see everything. Tim's view was that in reality, that was a total load of bullshit. He momentarily recalled the firefight during the Iranian Embassy siege when the time appeared to speed up, and that was what was happening now. Slowly retrieving the gun from his belt and silently cocking the top slide, putting a bullet into the chamber, an action he could do with one hand. He took a deep breath, tensed his muscles, ready to release like a coiled spring. Lunging at the door, he dived through on to the floor. Spinning around, shooting a double tap at the target doing all the talking. Katrina screamed, Richard saw his chance and leapt up, throwing himself at the remaining thug, both of them crashing to the floor: the Irishman fired several shots causing quite a crescendo in the room as the bullets found their way into the ceiling, sending down a shower of plaster like wedding confetti. Richard's heroic move allowed Tim time to compose himself; he spun around crouched on the floor, gun outstretch at the ready, looking for the next target to eliminate, the possible fourth man who thankfully didn't appear. Tim leapt up and helped Richard tackle the third man, between them they quickly had him overpowered as he spat and swore in a broad Irish accent.

"Ya fucking bastards you'll fucking die for this," but that was all he got to say before Tim knocked him unconscious with a vicious crushing blow with the base of the grip of his gun, causing a huge split in the flesh that went down to the bleach white bone, immediately oozing forth a river of rich red blood down his unshaven face. When Tim finally took stock of the situation, he realised that Katrina was tied up in a high backed chair, hysterically sobbing uncontrollably at the carnage that had suddenly burst in on her hitherto comfortable world. Tim quickly confirmed with Richard that there were only the three Irishmen, turning, he knelt down to the other Irishman laying spread eagle in the centre of the room. The body was slowly pumping rich, dark red, foaming blood onto a beautiful beige carpet, it jerked in the final movements of death, the mouth-foaming as the last remnants of air expelled from the dying body. Tim, feeling in vain for a pulse in the neck, realised that he now had a body count of two to explain to the authorities. Of course, this couldn't happen.

Richard released Katrina from her bonds, taking her away from the scene into an adjoining room and attempted to console her while she cried hysterically. Tim, meanwhile focussed on the matter in hand, realising that in the eyes of the law he had just murdered two men, possibly even three judging by the state of the third man whom he had pistol-whipped. Leaving Richard to his attempt to calm down the totally distraught Katrina, Tim dashed outside to the Range Rover and used the car phone to put a call into a number in Northern Ireland. A number he had memorised from his time over there, never thinking he would ever use it again. Through his contacts he aimed to call in a favour hoping he'd have the bodies, dead and alive spirited away speedily and quietly. Despite having an Irish ancestry, albeit several generations back, he maintained a total indifference to the rights and wrongs of the various religious warring factions. He had dubious connections across the water developed from ties with a certain notorious family, links that he had lost contact with, never believing he would ever again renew them, but that was until this night's events had dictated otherwise.

It was during the mad wild, often glamorised, days of the IRA's campaign of armed struggle produced for Tim a life-changing encounter that inadvertently put him right at the heart of a branch of the IRA high command. During his service throughout the troubles, he never imagined that his allegiance to the Crown would be so severely tested. Perversely, it was as a result of his experiences there that he could now call in a debt would that would hopefully keep him out of prison!

Chapter 27

Despite being Navy, Royal Marines were still British Army in the eyes of the Irish locals. Mostly hated after the debacle of 'Bloody Sunday', when the 'Paras' had opened fire on allegedly unarmed civilians. The Para's claimed they had been fired upon by paramilitaries, hidden in the rioting mob, and had returned fire. Highly trained military units react swiftly and decisively in combat zones. Crowd control of a rioting mob is not combat. The question thus remains as to whether elite forces, who through their training and conditioning for war, should ever be placed in this situation by their political masters. Whatever really happened on that day, it was a propaganda coup for the IRA. The aftermath would rumble on for decades, keeping many lawyers lucratively employed.

For patrol commander, Royal Marine Lieutenant Tim Spinks, it had been just another average day, patrolling the roads of Belfast. On a mission, called a *'swoop'*, this consisted of a patrol with three military land rovers roaming an area of Belfast and its suburbs, waiting for the patrol leader to initialise the operation. The military has a unique language of words that, through mnemonics, expand into plain language, consequently, *'swoop'* translates as *'Select, Watch, Obstruct, Operate, Pullout.'* In other words, an impromptu stop and search vehicle roadblock. These tactics had proved to be very successful, an element of surprise to both the IRA and Loyalist paramilitaries who had no idea as to where and when these patrols would suddenly appear. The roadblock, then removed just as quickly, keeping both groups of paramilitaries constantly on their toes. It was such an operation that took Tim unexpectedly, and frighteningly, straight to the centre of the IRA.

Tim was sitting in the passenger seat of the lead Land Rover. The recent downpour of rain, followed by sunshine, created a fresh, clean atmosphere on the lush land. He had allowed the patrol to meander out into the suburbs of Belfast and was momentarily enjoying the scenery when his thoughts were interrupted by the Corporal Driver.

"Sir - ," said the young Geordie voice, eagerly waiting for a reply.

"Yes," Tim snapped, rather uncharacteristically. "Boss, we've been driving around for nearly an hour, and you haven't given any orders?"

"Yes of course," he said, his voice calmer, "let's stop along this road and see what turns up, traffic seems light," he turned to the signal Trooper sat in the rear of the car, "Radio the others, tell them we will stop on my signal and set-up."

"Roger Boss," replied the Signal Trooper, who immediately contacted the other two vehicles. The patrol pulled over alongside Loop River, normally a quiet waterway which flows into Conns water and eventually Belfast Lough, but on this day the water was dramatically higher than normal, swollen by the recent heavy downpours. Tim observed the fast-flowing torrent that had risen powerfully up the slight grassy incline adjacent to the road. Tim's Troop Sergeant, Colour Sergeant Damon Brown, ironic really as he was a second-generation Jamaican, his father being a Major in the Jamaican Defence Force before migrating to the UK. Damon was in the rear Land Rover; a second Corporal was in the other vehicle.

The roadblock was soon set-up, and despite the quiet area, a long line of cars quickly developed as Tim's Royal Marines stopped and searched vehicles as they came to the 'check-point'. Tim, kept a watchful eye, looking for signs of an attack. This could occur at any time, by gunmen of either side who wanted the chance of *'slotting'* a Brit. Both sides had sadly spawned a breed of youngsters, brought up in the troubles, eager to prove themselves by earning their spurs with their relevant Godfather by taking out a couple of Brits, especially Royal Marines. All appeared to be going well, but Tim felt that a cautionary word to those on the look-out on the opposite side of the road wouldn't go amiss. He left his Colour Sergeant supervising the traffic check, walked across the road, and briefly spoke to the two marines monitoring the offside of the road. Everything appeared to be under control, as he headed back to the checkpoint he noted the strange lack of bollards or guard rails on the roadside to prevent a car from accidentally leaving the road, rolling down the embankment and entering the water. Normally only a babbling brook, but now transformed into a raging torrent, surging with the huge extra volume of water from the recent storms, deepening the watercourse by several feet.

One of the cars in the line of traffic, a blue VW Golf, contained a young couple, Sean O'Connor and Teresa O'Donaghue. Teresa had always suspected her father had connections in the upper levels of the IRA, but she had never sought evidence, girls were discouraged from becoming involved. Her father, Ryan O'Donahue, a very successful scrap metal dealer, could look back through his family history and trace connections with the movement back to its birth. Little did Teresa know, that in fact, her father was one of the Godfathers sitting on the Army Council, the ultimate IRA supreme echelon that wielded vast powers over the organisation, making decisions that could mean life or death. However, her expensive private education, a finishing school in Switzerland, had made sure that for the most part, she was well out of the way, not touched at all by the IRA operations that her father commanded. It was a different life for her two brothers, though; they were firmly entrenched into the IRA family, having been blooded on operations against the British. Having his boys involved was more than enough for Ryan.

Teresa was the apple of his eye; he wanted to keep her as far away from the culture of killing, bombing and all the other hallmarks of the struggle for a United Ireland. Teresa, being the highly intelligent girl she was, had a completely neutral outlook on the so-called armed struggle and its aims. Her hard-line brothers accused her of lacking commitment to the cause, they expected her to have a sympathetic view of their beliefs and behaviour. However, the teaching and discussion groups at finishing school fostered her indifference to the cause. Her Political Science lecturer had posed several hypotheses as case studies asking what exactly an amalgamated Ireland would mean in real terms. After a great deal of informed soul searching, Teresa concluded that the war was completely futile, a tragic waste of human life, totally unnecessary and pointless as it had destroyed families on both sides of the religious divide. Although Ryan disagreed with his daughter, he respected her viewpoint, as after all, it probably came about because of his choice to give her an expensive education. Ryan had seen what had happened to other young women and how they had become radicalised by the movement — determined that his daughter was not going to become one them. When Teresa's brothers once complained about their sister's lack of support for the cause, Ryan put them in their place; for fear of facing his wrath, it was a subject they were never to raise again.

Teresa, apart from being a bright, intelligent young lady, was also extremely attractive with an hourglass figure. Her round, almost angelic face had a perfect symmetry, with deep-set, smouldering green Irish eyes that always appeared to be smiling. This, coupled with the family's position, ensured that there was no shortage of young men anxious, not only to win the heart of this girl, but also to gain a foothold in to the ranks of the cause by impressing her father. Such was the glamorous romantic myth created about the organisation going right back to its founder Michael Collins. Being the headstrong, very independent girl she was, it would take more than some glory-seeking naïve Irish lad to tame her, not that this stopped Teresa from enjoying the attention and adoration of these 'pups' because of the notoriety of her family name. It would have delighted her mother and father to know that she was true to her Catholic faith as even now in her mid-twenties, Teresa was still a virgin.

It came to be that as Tim had set up a roadblock with his patrol, Teresa found herself as a front-seat passenger in a car driven by her latest boyfriend, Sean O'Connor. Keen to make his mark with the IRA, he had been entrusted with his first job, that of delivering some Semtex and accessories smuggled ashore the previous night from a yacht into Belfast Lough. Young single men moving about alone were automatic targets for the RUC and Army patrols; hence Sean deviously chose to take along his latest girlfriend on his first mission for the cause. Teresa had no idea what Sean's car carried, the inventory of which listed 20lbs of Semtex; 65' safet fuse wire; one box of fulminate mercury detonators; electric detonators; a carton of slow burning fuse; various timers and finally, a book on how to make a super bomb from garden fertilisers.

When Sean had collected Teresa from her parent's home, he was full of bravado, keen to impress. He knew who Teresa's father was and his position within the IRA. Fortunately for Sean, and despite his eagerness to impress Teresa's father, he didn't give a hint of what he was carrying in his car, wrongly assuming that Teresa's father would know anyway. He was too naive to understand how the IRA worked; they kept apart in small cells, totally independent of one another at street level. The style of operating in individual cells was for their protection if caught and interrogated by the RUC or Army. Ignorance of other IRA cell operations being bliss. It was left to others, way up in the high command, to co-ordinate everything. Movement of cargoes, just like the contents of Sean's car, had been arranged by a local IRA unit's quartermaster and wouldn't have reached the notice of Teresa's father. If he'd known that his beautiful daughter was being put in harm's way, travelling in a car with such a secret and lethal cargo, then young Sean O'Connor, far from being an up and coming star, would probably have suffered a disciplinary 'kneecapping' for his audacity.

Sean had been briefed on the route to take that day, which was a route far from the Army's patrol area. Sean soon realised, to his horror, that the cause of the queuing traffic could only mean one thing; there was an impromptu Army check-point. He was told his route was safe, and this shouldn't happen. He had no idea what to do. His earlier brash Irish bravado and quick lip with which he had been trying to impress Teresa started to break down. He had to think fast. His breathing deepened as fear started to rise. Teresa had no idea of the serious, tenuous, and potentially lethal, position she had unwittingly placed herself in when she had agreed to go for a drive with Sean. Sat in the slow-moving traffic, Teresa soon sensed the change in Sean's demeanour.

"What's the matter, Sean?" she questioned, in her rather plummy, posh girl's school voice, still with its slight trace of a soft Irish lilt.

"Will ya stop worrying me girl," he snapped, his nerves getting the better of him. Sweat beads appeared on his brow, slowly, they trickled down his face, making it fairly obvious that all was not well.

"Well, look at the state of you, it is only a stupid Army checkpoint, and it's obvious that you've gone from being absolutely fine to panicking, so what's going on?" She tried to hide the anger in her voice, annoyed at his hostility towards her, as she watched him become more and more agitated, it dawned on her why he'd suddenly changed his attitude.

"If you are mixed up in anything, you just tell me right here, and now, this minute, do you hear me?" He looked straight at her, his eyes full of anger, "Yeah I hear you girl!" he spat back before slamming the car's gears into reverse, pushing his foot hard on the accelerator, making the wheels spin under the amount of torque they were receiving from the engine in an attempt to turn the car through 90 degrees and leave the line of traffic. Teresa screamed, "Sean, what are you doing?"

"Shoot the fook up," he shouted, whilst wildly struggling to change gear and wrestle with the steering wheel. He shunted the car back and forth, trying not to hit either the car in front or behind. The driver of the car behind him slammed on his horn in protest at the crazy manoeuvring, worried his car would get bashed. This commotion soon got the attention of Tim's patrol, and several SLR rifles were now pointing in the direction of the car with the gunning engine and blasting horn. Tim went automatically into the standard kneeling, crouch position to reduce his target profile, his rifle pointing directly at the perceived threat. Upon signalling to two of his Marines to follow him at the trot, they then ran up the slight incline towards the offending car, rifles at the shoulder, ready for action. Speaking urgently via his throat mic, he ordered Sergeant Brown to hold all the traffic and stop any cars coming in either direction. Anxious faces peered out from the queuing cars, watching as Tim and his men doubled up, desperate to get to the problem car before the other motorists started panicking, fearful that they might be about to get caught in a crossfire between the army and paramilitaries.

Sean struggled with the car; he only had one more manoeuvre before he was free from the traffic and able to make the high-speed escape he needed to outrun any military Landrover that attempted to follow. Teresa, realising this, leaned over and grabbed the steering wheel; her attempt to stop him earned her a resounding elbow in her face, splitting her lower lip, making it bleed profusely and momentarily stunning Teresa into releasing her grip on the wheel. Noticing the blood and alarmed at what his sudden violent action had caused, Sean's panic increased. With concentration lost, he inadvertently put the car into reverse and floored the accelerator, the car shot backward, mounting the kerb and hitting the soggy grass. He slammed on the brakes, but it was too late, the brakes couldn't hold against the sudden inertia, coupled with gravity and wet grass, the car quickly slithered down the embankment and into the fast-flowing river. Tim and his men watched in horror; they could hear the occupants scream as the car tipped sideways and then over onto its roof just before entering the water. The raging torrent grabbed the car like a boat and started pulling it on a journey downstream. People got out of their cars, witnessing for themselves the disaster that was unfolding before their eyes, forgetting their earlier fears of a possible gun battle. Tim, commanded over their communications net "Sergeant, release the checkpoint and get the cars moving away from here," he turned to his radioman who'd accompanied him with the mains radio back-pack, "Wilson, call this in to ops and get the police and medics here fast!"

"Yes Boss," came the quick, firm acknowledgement.

Tim could see what was going to happen; there was a culvert only a short distance down the stream, this would hopefully stop the car in its mad adventure like a park ride along the waterway. He called to *Taffy* and *Badger*, two others in the troop, "Get the cars on their way, keep everyone away from here. *Rogers* and *Stevo*, follow me." Tim yomped down and across the bank, half skating as he slid on the wet grass. His two Marines in pursuit, following him to where the car came to a violent halt. A sickening crunch echoed, as metal hit the unyielding concrete that covered two large hollow pipes, through which the water was surging, increasing in speed due to the venturi effect. Arriving at the scene, they discovered the car, still upside down and slowly being pulled down at the rear. It was immediately obvious that the rear passenger compartment of the car was fast filling up with water. Tim's eyes searched the car for movement, but he could only see one lifeless body being held inverted by a safety belt in the front passenger seat.

Unobserved, the driver had miraculously been able to get out of the car and was nowhere to be seen. Unbeknown to Tim, Sean had escaped the car, ducked down and swum like a water rat through one of the culvert pipes, before disappearing across the adjacent fields.

Tim's immediate concern was for the body trapped inside the car. He waded into the water, holding his rifle above him, he fought the water which had thankfully lessened in pressure as it hit the covert. He reached the car, struggling in an attempt to break the rear window, first with the butt of his FN rifle, then with his police-issue baton, both to no avail. Without a moment to think, he took up his rifle and discharged one shot, completely shattering the window. Throwing off his helmet and releasing himself from his waistcoat webbing, handing his rifle back to one of his men, close behind, he then dove into the rear compartment of the car, now submerged with the wild *murky water*. He could just make out the imprisoned body. Knowing he needed more air, he swam back out, searched for his bayonet, took a deep breath, and dived back into the vehicle. He frantically searched for the safety harness. Just as he felt as though his lungs would burst, he was able to cut the harness and drag the lifeless body from the car. The two marines who had waded in to help him, were joined by two more of the patrol, taking up defensive positions. Tim with the help of his men, dragged the young girl out of the water and to the safety. With adrenaline circling his body and his lungs demanding air, he managed to lay her down. Kneeling alongside her, he cleared her airway to commence mouth to mouth. Soon, he was aided by the patrol paramedics who took over the administration of CPR. He stepped back, giving them space. Miraculously, the girl started coughing, and spluttering, water and vomit erupted from her mouth — sirens of the approaching emergency service vehicles resounding through the air. Tim, who had now caught his breath, looked down at the girl he had just saved, his heartbeat raised as he took in her natural beauty, her symmetrical face and her wet, auburn hair straggled across her forehead. Her eyes opened and immediately met his, he felt a surge of pleasure, unsure if it was because she was alive or her sheer beauty.

The emergency service vehicles attended, followed by Tim's immediate superior, Major David Plange. David had heard of the developments over the radio net back in the ops room and, being the natural leader he was, he had immediately called for his land rover and driver to proceed to the scene and assist Tim's patrol.

Leaving his beautiful victim with the paramedics, Tim felt like the proverbial drowned rat. He reported to his senior officer and briefed his 'Boss', the Major. One of the paramedics came across and advised Tim that they were ready to transport the young woman to the trauma unit at Queen's Hospital in Belfast. Tim requested permission from his Boss to go in the ambulance, a natural reaction that often occurs as the stress of the rescue sweeps over the rescuer, a strange phenomenon of a bond that develops on these occasions. David was concerned for Tim's welfare and granted his wish, ordering him to get checked over by the doctor upon arrival at the hospital. David informed his driver to follow the ambulance so he could keep a watchful eye on Tim.

Upon arrival at the hospital, Tim felt very much out of it due to his bedraggled state. He tried to follow the events as the trauma team set to work on Teresa, but a nurse insisted on checking him over and leaving the doctors to monitor Teresa. Thankfully, he needn't have worried; the medical staff later informed him it was thanks to his quick reactions at the accident scene that had certainly saved Teresa's life. It wasn't long before Teresa's family arrived to see her. Tim attempted to slip quietly away, intending to return later after the family had gone, but he was soon tracked down by Ryan O'Donoghue, Teresa's father. Ryan had heard of his daughter's plight and wanted to thank the man who had saved her life. Tim was a reluctant hero, and humbly accepted the outstretched hand of a very grateful father. The thanks were somewhat marred by the open hostility he felt emanating from the two other men with Ryan, Teresa's brothers. Tim was used to this as it went with the job serving in Northern Ireland.

Teresa, as well as nearly drowning, had suffered internal injuries and a broken arm. Consequently, she was kept in hospital under observation to ensure that there was no permanent damage. Tim visited her on several occasions when his duties allowed. During these visits, Tim and Teresa became very close, Tim was charming, attentive, entertaining and his old English charm won Teresa's heart. Tim, in turn, was smitten by Teresa's natural beauty and her soft, gentle Irish lilt that even expensive elocution hadn't quite eradicated. They discovered just how relaxed they were in each other's company, the conversation came easy, and in Teresa's eyes, Tim was her real-life hero, her knight in shining armour. It soon became obvious to both of them that, once discharged from the hospital, they would want their relationship to develop further.

Teresa's cowardly, escape-artist boyfriend was not to have the future he'd hoped for. Unbeknown to Tim, the RUC had discovered the body of Sean O'Connor, several days later, having suffered a single gunshot to the head. On occasions, while visiting Teresa, Tim had again met her father, Ryan, along with Teresa's mother. Teresa's mother made a big fuss of Tim and soon sensed the magnetism and attraction between the two. Although staunchly an Irish nationalist, she wouldn't be against her daughter's liaison with Tim. On the other hand, Teresa's father, since the initial enthusiastic meeting with Tim, had become distant and cold. Tim didn't pick up on this at first he was somewhat swept along with both his feelings for Teresa and the obvious enthusiasm from Teresa's mother. The devastating reality that this relationship couldn't go on was brought home to Tim when he was summoned to see his Lieutenant Colonel. In the meeting, the Lt.Col showed him photographic evidence as to who Teresa's father really was. Torn between his duty to the Corps of Royal Marines and his love for a girl, his Colonel put it to him bluntly, it wasn't negotiable, he had to give up Teresa as her father was the enemy. The Colonel felt for Tim, he could see in Tim's eyes that it was more than just a fling with a local girl. The Colonel, had before, sat in judgement on several occasions when service members had found themselves in similar situations. It was a problem that went with the job. Tim offered to resign his commission, but that was not an immediate option, if that were the route he would choose, then he would still have to face finishing his current tour as part of his contract to Queen and country. During that time, if the liaison continued, then he could be arrested and Court Martialled under some obscure paragraph in Queen's Regulations.

He spoke to Teresa's father about his dilemma, but although Ryan was sympathetic towards Tim for having saved his beautiful daughter's life, for which he acknowledged he'd forever be in Tim's debt, he felt their lifestyles and beliefs were poles apart, and the relationship was bound to end in disaster. Tim knew he was beaten and had no choice but to break off the friendship. It took pure will and heartache, along with a lot of tears on both sides, but he knew he had to walk away, leaving Teresa wrecked and distraught. He knew he could never look back. Unbeknown to Tim, after he'd walked out of her life, Teresa confronted her father. Being the perceptive young lady she was, she knew there was more to the situation than either man had explained. She intuitively felt her father was behind the sudden decision. He tried to console her with explanations, saying it was better to break the tie now, rather than later. He avoided using his

IRA commitments as the reason that his and Tim's paths could easily cross with disastrous consequences.

Naturally, Teresa couldn't see it from her father's viewpoint, and she didn't speak to him for several years. She had never known what it was like to be in love until Tim had come into her life. The days that followed Tim's departure were the worst she had ever endured in her short, privileged life. For once, she had lost something she wanted; she felt as though her heart had been ripped from her body. She dragged herself through each day, longing for the evening to close so she could go to bed and try to hide in her darkened bedroom. Sadly, the demons were still there in the dark, taunting her with the face of Tim, his infectious laughter, his warm smile that melted her heart, and his wonderful, soft kiss. She took to keeping the light on before eventually falling into an exhaustive sleep. Her rapid weight loss worried her mother, while her father seemed totally oblivious to what was happening to his daughter.

The death of Sean O'Connor only added to her feelings of despair. It had still not been explained to her why Sean had panicked the way he did and put her life in danger, although now in light of what she had learned, she could guess. She read about the finding of Sean's body in the local newspaper, and when she asked questions as to the way he died, she met a wall of silence from her father and brothers, whom she now understood were with the IRA. She'd briefly been interviewed by the police who accepted that she was an innocent passenger in the car and ignorant to the fact that it had been carrying explosives. There after diverting their attention to focussing on the murder of Sean O'Connor. Teresa remained loyal to her Catholic principles of celibacy and vowed she would never allow herself to fall in love again. Using her excellent educational qualifications, she went into teaching at a multi-faith school specialising in religious studies, vowing to teach reconciliation and understanding between different religious persuasions in the fervent hope that she could make a difference and avoid a repeat of the terrible war of attrition that had blighted the Emerald Isle for the last 30 years. The official ending of hostilities by the IRA and the Good Friday peace agreement brought about many changes for the O'Donaghue family. Perversely, one being the use of one of Ryan O'Donaghue's scrap yards, which was inspected by the Canadian General Chastelain, and deemed as a suitable safe place for entombing some of the IRA arsenal of weapons to place them beyond use. A political way for one side to say the other had given up the weapons only for the opposite side to say that they hadn't surrendered.

Then, suddenly, one day Ryan O'Donaghue answered his house phone.

"Hello" greeted the gruff, deep voice of Ryan O'Donaghue.

"Sir, it's Tim from across the water," replied Tim formally, and somewhat hesitantly. Maybe Ryan had completely forgotten about him? Despite their differing ideologies, Tim had always treated Ryan O'Donaghue with the greatest respect from when he first met him at Teresa's hospital bedside. He knew that would be the only way to be if he was to stand any chance of gaining mutual respect. Of course, at the time they first met, he had no idea just how entrenched Ryan was in the ranks of the IRA. His original hopes were that both he and Teresa could rise above the conflict to keep their love alive. A love he knew had never died within him and often wondered how Teresa felt.

"I know exactly who it is...no one else addresses me like that" he chortled with a smile spreading across his face...." how are you me olde son?" asked Ryan, the obvious warmth projected down the telephone line towards Tim. It was a call Ryan never thought would ever happen and he was now inquisitive as to why. Tim felt relieved that the greeting from Ryan was obviously expressing some friendliness, so he went ahead and gave a brief outline of his predicament. Ryan cut him short, asked him for the number he was calling from, and then curtly said he would call back before cutting the connection dead. In the short time it took Ryan to call back, Tim surmised that despite the peace process, he did not doubt that the intelligence services would still be monitoring the telephone lines of people like Ryan O'Donaghue. True to his word, the return call came back to Tim from a pay as you go mobile phone.

Tim explained the situation, his mind immediately put to rest as Ryan told him not to worry, he'd organise a clean-up operation. As Tim thanked him and was about to close the call, Ryan's mind had been in overdrive realising that this contact with Tim may have a chance of breaking the icy relationship he endured with his daughter and, even to a certain extent, his wife. "Tim before you go, and while I make arrangements, would you like to speak to Teresa...I'm sure she would like to speak to you?"

Tim's heart missed several beats as he never in a million years expected the conversation to take this path. "Of course," he croaked, his mouth and throat drying up, suddenly lost for words, wondering what he was going to say to Teresa. Ryan called out for his daughter, who was in another part of their home. Teresa, upon hearing Tim's name, initially froze, staring at Ryan as if in a trance. Then suddenly she rushed forward, grabbing the phone, screaming Tim's name as tears poured down her cheeks. Their dormant fire of love for each other bursting back into life. Tim, had urgent matters to deal with and reluctantly had to cut short the call, promising to call back and arrange to travel to Ireland to see her. Ryan had made a discreet withdrawal from his study after handing the phone to Teresa and was standing outside facing her as she left the room. No words were spoken but before he knew it, Ryan was being hugged by his tearful daughter. The Good Friday Agreement had changed everything. Ryan knew he could now allow the relationship between Teresa and Tim to flourish. Ryan had become tired of all the killing and unnecessary bloodshed his life involved, and much to the surprise of his hard-line sons, he'd embraced with enthusiasm the peace agreement. For Teresa, the day she dreamed of had finally arrived.

Chapter 28

Whilst Tim was busy making a phone call to Ryan O'Donaghue in Ireland, Richard tried to comfort Katrina. He couldn't leave her; she was burbling incoherently, interspaced with the occasional burst of hysterical laughter. Richard called Caroline and made excuses that he wouldn't be home that night, claiming he had an unexpected meeting to attend in the north the following day, and Tim would drive him there that evening. Richard always had an overnight bag with him packed with all the essentials he needed; such was the nature of his business lifestyle. It amazed him how easily he could lie to Caroline; little did he know that she had become tired of his excuses, her woman's intuition suspecting his 'unanticipated overnight trips' were to be with a mistress he had hidden away somewhere.

Tim's duty was clear; he had to stay for the clean-up and ensure Richard's safety. During the call through to Ireland, Ryan had assured Tim that he knew of the team in question and confirmed there were only three men in the gang. Although officially disbanded, the IRA still had a very effective intelligence network. IRA intelligence had expected the renegade gang to try and rob a bank or Building Society, but they had never expected a hair-brained scheme such as kidnapping the CEO of a large British company. They had chosen not just any company, but one with offices in Ireland on both sides of the border, employing many brothers and sisters. The IRA never contemplated that these three 'eejits', as the three-person renegade ex IRA team were disgustingly referred to, would have been so stupid as to try and pull off such a crazy stunt. With great relief, Tim was re-assured that the situation would be dealt with, if he could keep the location secure for the following couple of hours, phone calls would be made to contact local sympathisers from the large Irish community in London who would be summoned to assist. Such was the power of the Good Friday Agreement that the genuine members of the old IRA Guard didn't want renegade RIRA units upsetting the peace process. Senior IRA politicians had been emphatic about this and woe betide anyone that disobeyed. They had re-invented themselves as acceptable public figures, elder statesmen, one had even recently been introduced the Queen. Nothing was going to be allowed to upset their newfound power they'd gained through the ballot box. The days of Mao Tse Tung's teachings that political power came from the barrel of a gun were confined to history, just so long as the delicate balance of peace between the Provos and the Loyalists held.

Consoling Katrina was proving very difficult; she was beside herself. She appeared totally oblivious of the fact that Tim had just saved her from a terrible fate, and after several large brandies, her mind in turmoil, she targeted both Tim and Richard with her anger.

She screamed at them, demanding, "Call the police now! And why the fucking hell is Tim carrying a gun? What the fuck have you involved me in? This just isn't real, not in my life," she wailed.

Richard took her in his arms to console her, wrapping her tightly in a blanket he had found to cover up her semi-nakedness. She mumbled between sobs,

"What kind of man have I got myself involved with?" She slurred her words as the brandy took effect, and the tears kept coming, "Who has a chauffeur who shoots people?" Her questions, that would forever remain unanswered, just kept coming. Richard was sure she was on the road to becoming completely deranged but knew somehow he had to calm her down,

"Tim is more than a driver Kat; he's a bodyguard as well," Richard tried to explain, his nerves stretched to near breaking point, taut as the strings on a guitar, causing him to accidently shortening her name

"But this, this just isn't real!" she wailed again before wriggling free from both Richard's arms and the blanket, her half-naked body suddenly exposed as the blanket fell away, her eyes blazing, she looked directly at Richard and hissed like a wild cat, "Don't call me Kat you bastard!" Richard momentarily recoiled at the venom in her voice; he'd never seen her so wild-eyed and aggressive. He knew he couldn't react. He had to dismiss it, putting it down to a toxic mixture of the traumatic events and liberal quantities of 5 star Napoleon brandy. Ignoring her spat, he reached out his arms to console her, and in her vulnerable state, she fell back into his arms. He was slightly embarrassed at Katrina's state of undress and sent Tim to find a robe from upstairs.

Placing her into the robe, Richard cuddled her, gently stroking her hair. It appeared to be working; she was starting to relax a little. Normally, Katrina felt safe in Richard's strong arms but not tonight. He had brought this evil into her home; he had destroyed her once safe haven. An aversion to him was starting to seep into her psyche. She carefully untangled herself from his arms, poured another large glass of brandy, and moved into the lounge. She curled up on a single small chair and wrapped the robe tightly around her body, as if to form a protective shield, keeping out the grotesque goings-on around her.

Her comfort was short-lived. As her sobbing subsided, she heard a shuffling noise followed by Richard's voice. Her instincts told her to stay, but an abstract force beyond which she appeared to have no control made her look. Hesitantly, she tiptoed to the hallway where she saw Tim and Richard dragging in another lifeless body. She screamed before collapsing into a tight foetal position, tears rolling down her cheeks. Tim ignored Katrina; she was Richard's problem, he suspected that she would need professional attention and soon, it was obvious that she was suffering extreme emotional stress. He also knew that time was of the essence. He rifled through the clothing of the dead Irishmen, eventually finding the keys to the MG Rover, "Open the gates," he demanded of Richard as he dashed outside. In only a matter of minutes, Tim drove the MG into the driveway and parked it behind the large garage, hidden from view. The dirty old car would be suspicious in the smart, residential estate, and he didn't want some local patrolling bobby checking out the stolen vehicle and scuppering his plans to make the evening's violent happenings disappear.

Several times, Tim and Richard had to restrain Katrina from going to the phone to call the police. Unbeknown to them, a neighbouring householder, who had heard what they believed to be gunshots, had already placed a 999 call. When Katrina got as far as dialling the first '9', Richard momentarily forgot himself in the stress of the moment, grabbed the handset from her, together with a brutal slap across the face, something he immediately regretted.

"You fucking bastard," she hissed at him as the colour of her face changed slightly, displaying the shape of his hand in red welts across her cheek. Richard was also having trouble remaining calm, and in coming to terms with what had happened, but his energy needed conserving to control her, he was fearful she would do something stupid that might put all three of them in conflict with the law. Tim, on the other hand, displayed remarkable coolness as he dealt with the aftermath, as though it was an everyday task. A true professional ex-marine. Richard watched Tim, in awe, realising what an outstanding, loyal bodyguard Tim had proved to be. Richard owed Tim his life. To Tim, a Northern Ireland veteran, this was just another kind of soldiering; it was just another day's work.

The 999 call placed by a neighbour of Katrina's came into the Metropolitan Police main control room at New Scotland Yard, the caller was very anxious, explaining that she'd heard what she believed to be gunshots nearby. The Ops Room Duty Chief Inspector authorised an Armed Response Vehicle to attend, the unmarked high powered blue BMW 4x4 car, containing two qualified Firearm Trained Police Officers of Scotland Yard's SO19 branch was soon speeding to the reported location. The Duty control room Chief Inspector requested they only use the blue beacon lights and not sirens so as not to give an early warning of the impending arrival on scene. The duty controller at Roehampton police station was also alerted who passed this on to one of the local area beat cars with the information that an Armed Response Unit was attending.

Meanwhile, in the office of the serious crime squad at the Westend Central police station, Detective Superintendent Brendan O'Malley was sitting at his desk in semi-darkness, his desk lamp throwing an eerie pool of light over the pile of paperwork. He was coming to the end of what had been a successful day in court where he and his team had just put away a notorious criminal gangland lord. An evil man who thought he was untouchable, but hours and months of dogged police work had finally caught up with him. He was now in custody awaiting sentencing, which would probably see him being 'banged up' for the rest of his natural life. It was the tedious paperwork tidying up operation that Brendan was busy working on while the rest of his team were celebrating at the pub just around the corner. The rest of the office was in total darkness, giving Brendan's form a ghost-like appearance as he hunched over his desk. His mobile phone, currently set on silent, lit up; the vibrations gently reverberated, causing it to dance slowly across the desk top. This startled him; such was the depth of his concentration. Sighing gently to himself, he reached out to pick up the phone, believing it to be his doting wife of twenty-five years, wondering why he was still working. Opening the message, it appeared not to make any sense, but as he looked again, it did; it was in code, a message that he hoped he would never ever receive. He shivered, as if someone had just walked over his grave, with the realisation of knowing what he now had to do. It could only mean one thing; there will be trouble ahead which he didn't want to contemplate, knowing he had no choice.

Exhaling a deep sigh, he proceeded to tidy up the paperwork on his desk by carefully filing it away in the correct box files on an adjacent desk, he stacked these all together and placed them into a nearby secure store cupboard, grabbed his coat, car keys, switched off the desk lamp and made his way down to the underground staff car-park. Leaving the lift, he activated the remote locking to his sturdy Range Rover, the headlights and indicators momentarily flashing together as if to say 'here I am.' He approached the rear of the vehicle, lifting the top half of the rear and dropping down the tailgate. Looking around to make sure he was alone and checking that he was not in the arc of any of the surveillance cameras. He lifted the floor covering of the boot area, which exposed a small metal lidded box moulded into the bodywork of the car with only the combination lock showing. Entering numbers to a specific code he could recall from memory, the lid slowly opened on its gas-filled hydraulic hinges. The box contained a mobile phone on a 'pay as you go' network, a Beretta PX4 storm 19 round magazine, short barrel and long grip handgun together with a slimline black silencer.

Picking up the mobile phone, he had no sooner switched it on when it started ringing, the display lit up and gave the message 'number withheld'. He knew this could only mean one thing, big fucking trouble. Cautiously answering the call with a discreet 'yes,' he heard a voice he'd not heard in many a year say, "Tis that yourself now Brendan?" which continued before he could reply, "Now listen carefully I have a little clean-up job for you." The sound of the caller addressing Brendan by name relieved some of the anxiety and stress he was suffering. In the past, for security reasons, first names were never used during phone conversations, so whatever he was wanted for, it couldn't be that bad...or so he thought. Brendan was not a corrupt police officer in the financial sense of being in the pocket of criminals but, he had a dark secret that not even his wife knew of. He was an IRA mole, buried deep within the police establishment. A mole that had never been activated; tonight was going change that.

In his youth, Brendan had been a staunch Catholic who had joined the RUC from leaving school — becoming caught up in the troubles, he'd witnessed some of the atrocities carried out on the Catholic community by the notorious Ulster 'B' Specials before they were disbanded. Their sectarianism drove him to the cause of the IRA, who welcomed him with open arms. It was when he was inside the IRA that he discovered they were just as bad as the B's, with punishment beatings as well as robbery and other criminal activities to keep the coffers of the cause topped up for the supply of arms. Regretting his decision, he'd soon found out that leaving the cause was not an option so he could do nothing except pray every day that he would never be activated. When the troubles were over, the hostilities supposedly ceased, and the RUC reconstituted as the

Police Service of Northern Ireland, he applied to and transferred to the Metropolitan Police. Despite this, his handler, one Ryan O'Donaghue whom he'd never met, made it clear that one day his services may be required. It would appear that day had arrived.

Brendan listened intently to his instructions to meet a group of brothers and sisters, loyal to the cause, and go with them to an address in Roehampton where they were to clean up a mess created by some dissident IRA gang. After cutting the call, Brendan pocketed the mobile phone and placed the Beretta that came complete with a clip-on leather holster onto his trouser belt where it fitted snugly in the small of his back and slipped the silencer into his trouser pocket. He then set off to the location given, where he would team up with the others before going on to Roehampton.

Chapter 29

The Armed Response Unit car allocated to answer the call was driven by John Baxter, *'Banjo'* to his police mates, although how he'd attracted that nickname was a mystery. John's partner took the call, acknowledged that they were responding, and switched on the car's light bar. They made their way at high speed, reaching 80 miles per hour through the partially deserted streets. John Baxter, a twenty-year service police officer, had a problem with guns. As he drove, beads of sweat began to appear on his forehead. Earlier in his service, with the specialist team, John had shot a man dead. The man was threatening both John and his partner with a sawn-off shotgun at a bank robbery that had gone horribly wrong. He'd never gotten over this incident, after which he'd nearly quit the Firearms Team. Ironically, not because he had been upset at the taking of a life, quite the opposite, the frightening truth was that he had enjoyed pulling the trigger and seeing the man go down. Of course, he could never admit this to anyone, not even his wife. Even after having attended the mandatory counselling, he was still, several years later, having intermittent dreams about gleefully shooting people. He thought of seeking specialist treatment, but evaded the idea, aware it could open more doors which would raise more questions about what might be lurking in his psyche.

Having arrived in the vicinity of the 999 call and liaising with local officers, they made house to house calls but soon drew a blank to their inquiries; no one had any information for them on which to act. After several patrols throughout the area, officers were beginning to be reluctant to knock on more doors as it was becoming obvious that some residents were annoyed at being woken for what appeared to be no reason. However, John Baxter thought he'd try one more, he walked up to Katrina's gate and pressed the bell. Ignoring the chimes, Tim and Richard were monitoring a CCTV camera that clearly showed an armed police officer observing the property. As well as the MG, Tim had wisely also moved the Range Rover into one of the large garages, so along with the house lights doused and the drive empty of vehicles, to a casual caller it gave the impression that the house was unoccupied.

Conscious of time and money, and other incidents coming into the operations room, the duty Chief Inspector had ordered 'stand-down' and resume duties. John reluctantly returned to his vehicle. The Ops room Occurrence Sheet was marked as *'Unconfirmed discharged of a firearm area searched by the local beat officer and officers from SO19, nothing discovered, all appeared in order, no further action.'*

Following the stand-down command, John Baxter was his usual sarcastic self when he and his colleague stood alongside their vehicles, talking to the one remaining local neighbourhood beat officer tasked to attend this incident. John was a big copper in every sense of the word, standing a 'tad' over six feet tall with a matching girth, he was starting to resemble the original laughing policeman so often seen encased in a glass cabinet at seaside amusement arcades. His rotund figure was exaggerated by the tailor-made stab vest he wore. His round, chubby face made his aquiline nose look out of place. John would say his size was inherited from both his mother and father, who he described as 'big-boned' rather than admit that it could be associated with his passion for alcohol. John had a love of real ale, the copious consumption of which he had turned into a hobby, a daily ritual when he would drink at least three pints of the delicious brew after finishing his shift. The only shift he would finish without ending up in the pub was coming off a night shift at seven o'clock in the morning. By contrast, his partner SO19 officer was lean and mean, his physique obviously from the outcome of spending a lot of time in the gym. Despite John's rotund figure, they both looked scary in their all-black, soldier style combat kit.

As the three of them stood talking, John showed off his weapon to the local officer displaying and describing his admiration for the gun; to him, it was a meticulously engineered thing of beauty, rather than a tool that killed. John lifted it up to his shoulder, looked down through the sights, and held the grip with his right hand, the barrel grip resting perfectly into his left hand. The lighting from the street lamp enabled him to see every contour of the gun, producing an illuminating glint that bounced off the smooth surface of the breach. His apparent fascination for the tool of his trade made the local beat officer raise his eyebrows; to him, John appeared to be in love with his lethal weapon. Lowering the weapon to his side, John interrupted the officer's worrying thoughts that John might be slightly unhinged; he considered if he should report his worries to someone higher up the chain of command.

Casually waving his weapon skywards, John said aloud, "This lot, round here, don't know they're born, all this wealth could wipe out the Third World Debt." The two other officers nodded in unison, not saying anything, as they scanned the area. The wide roads lined by mature trees and the houses hidden from view by tall hedges; it was hard to realise that this was prime real estate in Greater London, it looked more like a rural community in the Cotswolds.

"No wonder their bums twitch every time a car backfires," said John, "not that I'm jealous. It's just that I'd love a bit of it," he said with a roaring laugh.

As they were about to part company and climb into their respective police cars, they noticed the lights from another vehicle slowly approaching. As it drew closer, John recognised the outline of a Range Rover. Nothing strange about that around here he thought, this place was full of what some would call 'Chelsea tractors,' where the only 'off-roading' they ever did was driving over a gravel drive to the front door or garage. The Range Rover cruised slowly towards them, causing all three men to immediately become alert; ever ready for the unexpected, John approached the car with caution. The driver's door opened and out stepped Detective Superintendent Brendan O'Malley, who immediately introduced himself and flashed his warrant card, John visibly relaxed.

"Evening Sir, what brings you out to this?" enquired John, his two police colleagues standing back while John spoke with Brendan. John knew of Brendan, but until tonight had never met him.

"Well I was in the area and I heard the call over the radio and thought to meself now what can that be, so decided to amble past on me way home and see if there was anything in it for me," explained Brendan, in his slight Irish lilt that he'd never lost.

John briefly explained what had happened or what had not happened, and with that, Brendan appeared satisfied, bade John goodnight, climbed back into his Range Rover, executed a smart U-turn and quietly drove away.

John walked backed to his colleagues.

"What was that all about?" asked one.

"A Super from the serious crime squad...said he'd heard the call on the radio and came for a look."

"As if he hasn't got enough to do," quipped one.

"Mmm..." mused John, "Bit odd don't you think?" questioning to no one in particular.

"Fucked if I know," replied his fellow firearms colleague, "senior officers move in fucking mysterious ways."

"Yep, guess so," said the local beat officer, "well, I'll be on my way, need to call in on the complainant and close this job off so see you guys around." With that, he walked back to his police car, jumped in, and drove away with a brief toot on the horn.

John and his colleague picked up another call on their radio earpieces and they too soon left the area.

Brendan, after leaving the immediate area, had surreptitiously turned down an adjacent side road just around the corner and was now sitting and waiting. Here, he met up with the rest of the Irish contingent whom had also been lurking in the shadows. They were in a large Peugeot Boxer van immediately behind Brendan, this was the clean-up mob allocated by Ryan O'Donaghue. The rear of the van was becoming thick with acrid smoke as several of the group puffed away on cigarettes to help ease the nervous tension of being so close to armed police officers. Once Brendan had seen the two remaining police cars leave the area, and on hearing the call over the force radio in his car to the two SO19 officers, he felt confident that he'd not be seeing them again as they were required some miles away to attend an armed 'car-jacking'.

Brendan signalled to the van driver to follow him and they proceeded to Katrina's house. Tim electronically opened the huge iron gates, allowing both vehicles to quietly enter and park on the large driveway immediately in front of the house. Due to the huge curvature of the drive, the vehicles were partially hidden from view.

With the police officers long gone and the lateness of the hour, Brendan was confident they wouldn't be disturbed and the team went about their 'clean up' operation.

Chapter 30

The 999 call that John and his colleague had rushed off to had been a domestic argument that ended with a son-in-law threatening his father-in-law with a pistol, but as this had turned out to be a plastic replica, the Firearms Team were not required and stood down.

The remainder of their shift had been quiet, sufficiently quiet for John to reflect and ruminate on their earlier call to Roehampton and the unexpected appearance of a senior Serious Crimes Investigating officer arriving on the scene. In John's view, it didn't add up; O'Malley's arrival had all the hallmarks of being planned. Detective Superintendents don't just casually turn-up at potential crime scenes, which is all it was at that stage. O'Malley was doing what was referred to as 'ambulance chasing' and men of his rank just didn't do that. John knew enough about Brendan O'Malley to know that he worked on high profile cases, such as major heists and gangland murders. So he began to wonder if there was more to their Roehampton call out, his inquisitive mind signalled that he might be missing something. He knew that serious villains made lots of money from their crimes, and many lived in luxurious places such as those found in the tranquil backwaters of Roehampton.

On the other hand, it was an area which painted a picture of respectable middle England, the genteel world of 'ladies who lunch' and men that 'did something in the city'; evenings being one round of cocktail parties and sumptuous dinners where the biggest risk people could possibly experience, apart from a hangover, was indigestion. However, something wasn't quite right; John decided that, after his shift, he was going to go back to the scene for another look. Maybe he wouldn't discover anything, but his curiosity had got the better of him, suspecting and hoping he may discover something that would be of interest and get him noticed by Senior Officers.

John's love of guns started like most boys; while playing cowboys and Indians with pretend six-shooters and replica Winchester rifles. This desire fuelled when visiting local summer fairs and having a go on the air rifle ranges, shooting at metal ducks and rabbits. It developed further when John, upon leaving school, joined the army. Looking for excitement, he joined the Pioneer Corps as the regiment had an exciting name; it sounded Special Forces, like the U.S. Rangers. It was only after joining this unique regiment that he discovered they certainly were very specialised, but not in the way he'd imagined. They were unfairly referred to as 'latrines and gravediggers'. Although infantry soldiers, they were in fact a light engineering group with many varying and dangerous tasks, hence their nick name; one being the clearing of battlefields littered with light ordnance and discarded weapons.

During his service, some years after the Falklands war, John found himself with a Pioneer Company down in the islands, engaged in the never ending task of clearing some of the old battlefields still littered with buried ordnance which was causing major problems for the farmers. Here, he came across what he would describe as a magnificent Colt 45 semi-automatic handgun, beautifully engraved, not only with the crest of the Argentinean Army but also, with the name of the Argentinean army officer to whom it had been issued, who he later discovered had died during the battle. Despite some corrosion, it was still in perfect working order. To the victors, the spoils of war, he secreted the gun in a stores container buried under an assorted collection of military kit destined for the UK. Later retrieving it on his return to the UK, John achieved his childhood ambition of owning a real gun. He was already a member of a local gun club and had, when home on leave, been content to use the club's stock of firearms, but now he could use his fully restored pride and joy. He was naturally very protective of the gun's true identity, knowing it wouldn't take much for someone to put two and two together knowing his occupation and service history. So when John eventually left the army and joined the police service, where better to keep it than in his personal locker at the police station.

John was working a half night shift that day finishing at 0100hrs. Back at the Firearms HQ, and after waiting for the initial activity to fade away as other officers working half nights changed and went off duty, John entered the now deserted locker room where he took his gun from the steel box within his locker and slipped it into the holster on his stab vest, which would normally hold his taser gun. Over this, he donned a lightweight raincoat to cover his uniform and went out to his car. He drove out of the Firearms Branch discreet headquarters car park, but instead of going straight home to an empty house, his wife and two children were away visiting in-laws, he decided to take a detour and drive to the scene of the earlier call in Roehampton. Suddenly with doubts as to what he was doing, he pulled over to consider his options. Minutes later, overcome with anxiety at the possibility of some excitement, his gut instinct convinced him that some major criminality had gone on and that he could probably make a name for himself discovering what it was. Such was his determination to carry through; he completely overlooked the possibility that whatever he uncovered could result in his unauthorised firearm coming to light and that it would be a game-changer for his police career. This was the furthest thing from his mind as he drove through the empty streets towards Roehampton. Arriving near to Katrina's home, he slowed down to drive past the large metal gates. This time, the gates were wide open and parked on the drive he could just make out a Range Rover next to a large van.

"I fucking knew it, I fucking kneeew it!" he exclaimed before excitedly slamming the palm of his hand on the steering wheel. "I've caught a you, you fucking senior officer, obviously up to no good, this is my lucky day," he happily mumbled to himself. "This place has got to be the home of some big time criminal, this fucker is in his pocket and up to something. But why the van?" he queried, trying to think of any recent major heists similar to the London Heathrow Brinks Matt gold bullion job.

Continuing passed Katrina's house, John looked for somewhere to park and hide his car, it had to be close enough by in case he needed to leave in a hurry. He was in luck, just a few doors from Katrina's house; there was a property undergoing renovation, obviously unoccupied as the building was without windows and the front-drive was littered with builders materials and equipment. Slowly guiding his car onto the driveway, he was able to secrete his car behind a workman's portokabin, from where he deftly crept back to Katrina's house, keeping himself hidden in the shadows created by the huge oak trees that lined the Avenue. Fortunately for him, the wall surrounding Katrina's home was interspaced with railings which enabled him to peer through into the garden, and by moving to the right angle, he could just see through the bushes to the driveway beyond and the two vehicles parked there. It wasn't long before he could see several men and two women, moving about between the van and the front door of the house. "Hmmm... Curious, they look like cleaners," John muttered to himself before the penny dropped and realisation dawned on him that this was exactly what they were; cleaning up a crime scene. There could be no other explanation, and it involved a corrupt senior copper. While pondering as to what his next move would be, John was aghast to see them carrying what appeared to be a body wrapped in polythene — stunned at what he was witnessing when they dumped the body into the van with a quite a thump. They then went back into the house and returned with a similar wrapped package and again threw the baggage unceremoniously into the back of the van.

"Christ what have I stumbled on? This is a fucking multiple murder scene," John thought, "more to the point what the fuck do I do....I need to get help here and fast."

However, fate decided what John's next move was to be, as looking again at the scene, he saw a man being dragged out of the house squirming and wrestling with his captors, immediately followed by Brendan O'Malley. John couldn't believe what he saw as Brendan O'Malley withdrew a gun and, from another pocket, pulled out a tube, which was obviously a silencer. Brendan screwed this onto the end of the gun as the struggling man was forced down onto his knees. John was terrified, realising what was about to happen.

The driveway was so big and curved that the gang was confident that they were well and truly hidden from prying eyes by the high walls and what appeared dense shrubbery. John, fuelled by adrenaline and a superior force, drew his pistol in one hand and then pulled out his warrant card with the other. Making the short sprint through the open gates, John saw Brendan O'Malley lowering his pistol towards the back of the man's neck as he frantically struggled in an attempt to get free. Taking a deep breath as he came into the view of the assembled group John shouted,

"Armed police officer stay where you are, don't move, put down your weapon."

Inside the house, Tim was walking past the open front door in the darkened hallway when he heard John call out. From his vantage point, he could see the scene before him and momentarily froze. Fortunately, Richard was upstairs with Katrina and had planned to stay there with her while the Irish team cleaned up the snug. Tim cautiously slipped into the depths of the house and out through the back door, creeping silently around to the front-drive, where he came upon a side view of John Baxter holding out his gun and warrant card. John, intent on keeping those in front of him in plain view, was not focussed on his peripheral vision, nor did he sense Tim's presence. With his gun drawn, Tim crept upon John. Tim had surmised that this wasn't a kosher police raid; they didn't operate like this, particularly as the gun was definitely not a police issue, although the warrant card appeared genuine as he could just make out a silver badge catching the light. Too many questions Tim was thinking, but he knew he needed to quickly regain control of the whole scenario, which was fast deteriorating into a 'cluster fuck'.

Addressing John, he said quietly but firmly and politely, "Put down the gun officer."

John slowly turned his head but kept his gun covering Brendan and the others. When John and Tim's eyes locked they were both startled, Tim spoke first, "John?"

"Tim!" John exclaimed, suddenly recognising each other, having previously served together in the police.

Tim was bemused, "Shit John! what the fuck is going down?"

John frowned, "That's my fucking question! Tim, what the fuck are you mixed up in?"

"It's domestic John and nothing to involve the police," Tim answered.

"Oh really, then what's he doing here?" asked John nodding towards Brendan.

Tim replied, "Look, never mind that, there's a simple explanation, but for now we appear to have a Mexican stand-off, so what's next?"

"Some fucking explanation with a senior cop about to top someone," exclaimed John, a note of incredulity in his voice.

Brendan intervened, "If you two fuckers know each other, then can we all lower our guns nice and slow before this turns into the fucking gunfight at the OK Corral?"

Feeling reprieved of assassination, the bound and gagged man visibly sagged. The two Irishmen restraining him had remained quiet and transfixed throughout, the rest of the gang were too busy cleaning up inside the house to notice.

The three armed men, each pondering as to what their next moves would be, Brendan spoke first,

"Well, as you two know each other and I gather you," nodding his head at John, "you're working alone, can we go into the house and sort this fucking mess out?" His obvious anger being tinged with fear as what had at first appeared to have been a quick clean up job was fast turning into a fiasco, which could be his undoing. After years of keeping below the radar, his IRA connections could be about to be blown, ruining all his plans to retire into obscurity.

Tim was also fearful for his position and that of his boss, Richard. He needed to get into the house and quickly explain what was going on. Tim hoped that Richard was keeping a discrete distance and keeping a tight rein on the traumatised Katrina.

They all had some serious life-changing choices to make before the night was out.

There followed a moment between the three main players; the rest of the Irish contingent not being interested, they just wanted to get the job done then disappear back into the London Irish community. Brendan had his orders, distasteful as they were, they weren't optional, he had to terminate the remaining RIRA man. The three of them found themselves in a ludicrous stand-off situation, each holding an ACE card against the other, knowing they all possessed unauthorised firearms which could incriminate them consigning each to a considerable time behind bars. A solution had to be found and quick. If there was to be a positive outcome all three acknowledged that they would have to take their next actions with them secretly to the grave.

"Well what now?" questioned Brendan gruffly.

"What now indeed," replied John, still holding his gun in his outstretched arm, rigid and ramrod straight.

Tim had also adopted the same stance but slightly crouched in military gun drill fashion, his weapon aimed at John.

No one spoke, all considering their options. John didn't want to shoot a fellow police officer, and Tim didn't want to shoot John.

The two members of the clean-up gang were looking bewildered; this wasn't part of the plan. They were still holding tightly on to their captive who had momentarily stopped struggling but was still sweating profusely while silently praying to the Holy Mary Mother to be spared. He'd already urinated and now feared he would lose control of his bowels. An ex-IRA hard man enforcer himself, he wished he could break free, grab a weapon, and kill all these bastards. It was a total humiliation for him, gagged and on his knees, subservient to these three men. He'd show them - given half a chance. His emotions were a mixture of fear and belligerence, wanting to avenge his friends who he knew had died at the hands of that bloody chauffeur.

'What sort of fucking chauffeur was he to carry a gun,' he thought.

Tim had no intention of shooting John, but the unknown factor was the obvious leader of the clean-up gang. Brendan was about to assassinate the remaining RIRA man and it would appear, from the way he'd overhead John addressing him, that this man was a police officer, and a senior one at that. Despite his outward appearance of being in control, Tim now seriously doubted he was going to get out of this situation unscathed. Having at first a feeling of relief, given by Ryan Donoghue's assurances that all would be taken care of, the intervention of his old police mate had thrown a large spanner in the works. The only saving grace was that John appeared to be working alone, so at least Tim didn't expect to be suddenly surrounded by armed police.

It was Brendan who broke the tension. "Now, why don't we all relax and let the chauffeur go inside, then you and I can work this out?" he said, looking at John but nodding in the direction of Tim.

Slowly the tension relaxed, and they all simultaneously lowered their weapons.

"Suits me," said Tim as he carefully backed out of sight but still keeping his gun ready just in case one of the other two, thinking more than likely Brendan, pulled a fast one. Tim's experience, during the troubles in Northern Ireland, had taught him just how ruthless the IRA could be. He didn't want a bullet in the back.

Once Tim had disappeared, both John and Brendan relaxed a little.

Brendan turned to the two men holding the RIRA gang member. "Don't you let go of this bastard." He pointed down to the kneeling man, one Stuart Maloney, leader of the RIRA gang that had attempted to kidnap Richard.

Then he turned to John who was stood there wondering what on earth to do next.

"Come over here John and let me introduce you to the scum that's kneeling here; he is the worst of the old IRA," he said, bending and looking into the eyes of Stuart Maloney.

It was at that moment when Stuart Maloney saw into the eyes of Brendan and knew his reprieve had only been temporary. He realised that whoever was pulling this man's strings was top IRA and his assignation preordained. John stood alongside Brendan as he continued looking down into the eyes of the kneeling Stuart Maloney.

"This is the true face of the old guard; this man has been responsible for more murders, kneecapping and punishment beatings than you'd care to remember. Well, my loyal IRA fiend, your past record won't help you now." Brendan moved behind Stuart, aiming at the back of his head as the captive struggled uselessly in the vain hope he could shake off his captors and escape. Just at that moment, John, his heart beating rapidly with excitement, felt he was becoming sexually aroused. He needed this.

He swiftly put his hand on Brendan's gun. "As we are all in this together, let me be the one to pull the trigger?"

By now, the RIRA man, despite wanting to scream, had stopped struggling and decided to meet his maker with some dignity, knowing his fate, he wasn't going to let these bastards see him squirm.

John took the gun that Brendan willingly relinquished, as although he'd been prepared to carry out his master's orders; until now Brendan had never actually killed anyone. Although in the eyes of the law, he was an accessory to the murder, he would be able to carry on in the knowledge that he'd not pulled the trigger. Brendan promised himself that once this was over, he would bring to an end his service to the IRA, he was going to ditch the Beretta and the 'pay as you go' mobile, change his mobile phone number and hopefully forever sever all links with his past.

John took the pistol; it was all over with a slight 'phut.' As the bullet was a dum dum it didn't make the mess an ordinary bullet would from such close range; a normal round would have blown the man's head wide open like a ripe melon. John, thoroughly wiping the gun clean, handed it back to Brendan. "This never happened, right?"

"This never happened," replied Brendan.

With that, John slunk away down the drive, dodging in the shadows as he went back to his car. There, sitting in his car with the door open, he composed himself letting out a long sigh as though he'd been holding his breath for a long time, then taking in a lung full of fresh air, he wasn't surprised that apart from his heavy breathing he was remarkably calm. As tears ran down his cheeks, he knew that for the sake of his sanity, he needed help; he did not want to be the cold-blooded killer he realised he obviously was. Taking a handkerchief, he wiped away the tears, closed the door, started the engine and reversed out of his hiding place, driving off into the night and home to thankfully an empty house. His wife always enquired as to what had happened during his tour of duty and he couldn't have explained tonight. He could never tell her what had occurred or the fact that he realised, almost animal-like, that he had a taste for killing others.

As John departed, Brendan turned to the others in the clean-up gang. "Right, let's be having you and get this mess cleaned up for fuck's sake, before anything else happens, or we'll all end up in the fucking shit."

The clean-up was soon accomplished; the detritus from the night's carnage all cleared away as though nothing had ever happened. Like the three Musketeers, *'all for one and one for all'* Brendan, John, and Tim had parted company, vowing to take each other's secret to the grave.

Throughout the entire gory goings-on downstairs and in the drive, Katrina was kept in total ignorance upstairs with Richard as she drowned her sorrows in brandy. Initially, she'd seen several scruffy and rough-looking men with heavy, broad Irish accents, a couple smelling of whiskey and chain-smoking, set to work removing the evidence of the night's carnage, cleaning up with the thoroughness and professionalism of a contract cleaning company. As she drifted in and out of her alcoholic induced haze, she was partially aware of things going on downstairs but was too weak and distraught to attempt to get away from Richard, who had kept her safely corralled in her bedroom — having laid beside her, cuddling and attempting to soothe her as if she was a distressed child.

Some hours later, after the gang had left, Katrina wanted to discover what had been going on in her beautiful home. Feigning sleep, Richard had left her, she seized the opportunity and staggered downstairs but it was as if nothing had occurred.

Too much for Katrina to comprehend, once again, she was reduced to uncontrollable, hysterical tears. The disruption of her comfortable, privileged lifestyle made her both furious and miserable, all she could think about was that events like this should not happen to her; for that, she blamed Richard. He was the reason for this whole hideous affair.

Now that the 'clean up' gang had left, Richard relaxed somewhat. When Katrina came downstairs and started to cry again, Richard left her to her own devices. He needed to consult Tim on what to do next, he was totally in Tim's hands and needed to be guided by him. Left alone, Katrina continued a tirade of crying and intermittent yelling of abuse out aloud as she went from room to room looking for evidence of the night's terrifying events, eventually finding another bottle of brandy that she began to drink in an attempt to blot out the nightmare. She was beginning to think she was losing her mind and had dreamt the whole thing, causing her to become even more hysterical. Now, with some relief that one major hurdle had been crossed, the tirade from Katrina was starting to adversely affect both Tim and Richard. With the evening's events, which had been so quickly and expertly dealt with, it appeared Katrina was going to be a much bigger problem. Thus, Tim suggested calling Richard's close friend and Board member, Surgeon Commander Peter Willis, as he was becoming increasingly concerned that Katrina might do something rash that would expose them to the Authorities. Although thankfully, with the bodies removed, the clean-up so meticulously carried out, even carpets removed, there was very little chance of any microscopic forensic evidence to be discovered should the police become involved.

When finally, it looked as though Katrina had drunk herself into a stupor and collapsed into an easy chair, Richard was able to take a respite from her ravings and put in a call to Peter Willis. The last time Peter and

Richard had spoken socially, Peter had been very blunt about his thoughts on Katrina, but now was not a time for Richard's ego to get in the way. Richard had forgotten the lateness of the hour as the phone rang for some considerable time giving the impression that Peter wasn't at home, just as he was about to replace the receiver Peter answered, half asleep.

"Hello?" Peter cleared his throat, aware he sounded groggy.

"Peter, it's Richard."

Peter, stifling a yawn and looking at his bedside clock was suddenly concerned at the hour of the call. "Richard, what can I do for you at this time of night?"

Richard let out a sigh before replying wearily. "Peter, if ever I needed you, my dear friend, it's now." Suddenly, Peter's persona went from a laconic, half asleep state to fully alert, wondering what on earth had happened and what was coming next. "Richard, fire away, you know I would do anything to help you... " he paused, "That is of course if I can," he added like a vague 'Get out of Jail' card.

Richard sighed again. "It might mean breaking the law."

"Good grief, really!" he said incredulously, suddenly sitting up in bed, now fully awake.

There was a slight silence before Richard continued. "It might mean you would be an accessory to murder."

"My god Richard, hell's teeth, whatever you have done, you must call the police."

"Peter! No! I can't, and it's not like that, I've not murdered anybody ... but my driver, Tim, has, all in self-defence though, it was a kidnap attempt on me! Oh, Peter, it is so complicated. I don't know where to start... You know all about Katrina, she was involved, and she needs medical attention, you're the only one I can turn to," he pleaded.

"Medical?" gasped Peter.

"Well, maybe more psychological or psychosomatic, I don't know, but I do know I need your help."

"Richard, this is one hell of a request, but as a good friend, one of the best, I will help you where I can, but as to how far that goes depends on the circumstances, you must be truthful, tell me everything, don't hold anything back. I will then decide how far I can help and how involved I'm prepared to be."

"Peter, I wouldn't expect anything more of you, I promise that I won't put you into any compromising positions. I can get Tim to collect you and bring you over to Katrina's. I will explain everything, and then you can choose to help or just walk away. I will go along with whatever you decide."

"Okay Richard, I accept those terms."

"I will send Tim right away."

"Okay, but - " he paused, as thoughts rushed around his head, "wait, Richard, you say Tim?"

"No!" interjected Richard, knowing what Peter was thinking. "Trust me, Tim has saved mine and Katrina's lives, he is not a murderer. Yes, he's killed someone in self-defence but, without him, I believe we both, that's Katrina and myself, would have at best been kidnapped or at worst murdered."

"Good grief! Okay, I'll wait for Tim to collect me."

"Thank you, Peter. Just so you come prepared, the main reason I am calling is for Katrina. She was involved, saw everything and understandably she is in a terrible state; she needs your medical expertise. Right now, she's drunk herself almost senseless, but I'm not sure how to handle her when she wakes up. I think in all probability, she will need some psychiatric help."

"Okay, Richard, I have a few things here that might help, sounds to me that Tim should get me over there pretty damn quick."

Tim collected Peter Willis, explaining everything that had occurred as they returned to Katrina's, everything except for the events when they had been disturbed by John Baxter and the killing of the third gang member, only the Three Musketeers would ever be a party to that.

When Peter arrived, Richard also went over the night's events as he knew it, giving a blow by blow account, again leaving out some of the unsavoury aspects. Fortunately for Richard, Peter didn't hesitate to become involved. Upon entering the snug, Peter glanced around where the carnage had occurred; it seemed hard to believe that the events Richard related had actually taken place in the meticulously clean and tidy room. Peter went upstairs and administered sedation into Katrina's arm while she slept. Moving in the type of medical circles he did, with the rich and famous as well as a smattering of Middle Eastern clients, he was able to conjure up a private ambulance to have Katrina whisked away to a private hospital on the outskirts of London. Peter accompanied her in the ambulance to be on hand and to fully brief the duty night medical staff, all of whom he knew personally. Before the ambulance left, Richard wanted to assure Peter that whatever the cost of Katrina's medical care, he would, without question, cover it. Not that Katrina couldn't afford private healthcare, she could, but Richard's guilt would not allow him to do otherwise. He gently stopped Peter as he climbed into the back of the ambulance, "Just tell me the cost, I don't want any paperwork or invoices, just the figures as and when, okay?"

Peter, trying to inject a bit of humour into the terrible events, replied, "Dicky, I don't talk about money; it's so vulgar, don't you know." With that, the door closed and the ambulance quietly pulled out of the drive with no sirens or lights for fear of attracting attention. It just sedately glided away.

Chapter 31

Since the abortive kidnap attempt of Richard and the spell she'd spent in the private hospital under the care of Peter Willis, Katrina appeared to be getting over the shock and trauma of what she had endured. Peter acknowledged that she wasn't, in his opinion, fully recovered, but he decided that she had recovered enough to be released from the hospital, with the intention that she would remain under his care for the foreseeable future. Katrina left the clinic a much calmer person than the night she had been admitted. Peter and the drugs he prescribed had worked their charm; she had come to accept, with the aid of some couselling by the psychiatric team, that far from being a cold-blooded murderer, Tim Spinks had saved her life. However, after only one restless night in her home, she knew she couldn't stay there alone and contacted her ageing Uncle and Aunty, Claude and Maude. She gave them a yarn that her house had been broken into, and they didn't hesitate in inviting her to stay with them for a while. As Katrina drove up their long, sweeping shingled driveway leading from the main road, the fresh country air filled her car and she knew this was exactly what she needed. The country house was well hidden from the road, its driveway, almost a quarter of a mile long, opened out to a large circular parking area centred with a beautiful fountain. On either side of the long drive lay open green fields where horses roamed and grazed on the lush pastures. Scenes that were lovingly recreated on canvas by the many artists, amateur and professional, that would be seen in the spring and summer months sitting inspired at their easels.

Maude and Claude lived in the beautiful Cotswolds. Their delightfully spacious home, built around the turn of the century, had once been the home of an American 1950's female film star. When the film-star passed away at an amazing 105 years old, the house was left empty and started to decay. Although the film-star had living relatives, they resided in the US, never venturing out of the country, choosing instead to live a monastic Amish lifestyle. The relatives had virtually forgotten about the house in England, probably by choice, as they had shunned their film-star relative, believing her hedonistic, extravagant lifestyle to be totally at odds with their biblical learning.

Maude and Claude discovered the abandoned house in the early 1980s, who, as soon as they set eyes upon it, fell in love. They were only able to purchase it due to Claude's audacious determination; he flew out to the

US to meet the star's heirs face to face and thus successfully negotiated the purchase price way below the market price, not that it bothered the sellers, money to them was of very little consequence, they were just glad to be shot of the burden. Since then, it had been lovingly restored by local craftsmen under the guidance and watchful eye of Claude.

Stepping from her car and pulling out her suitcase, Katrina greeted her Aunty Maude and Uncle Claude, who were standing arm in arm on their broad, semi-circular doorstep. They were thrilled to see her, but Maude, being a very perceptive lady, knew straight away that something was not quite right. Katrina's eyes revealed an underlying sadness. Maude's extrasensory perception picked up that all was not well with Katrina as she walked across the gravel drive and into the embracing arms of Maude and Claude, where, just for a moment, letting down her guard, she released a slight whimper.

Maude was the quintessential favourite aunty type, sister to Katrina's dear mother, who was long since departed, having been one of life's cancer statistics. Maude had done her best to keep in contact with Katrina, having promised her dying sister that she would care for her like she was her own. Sadly, Katrina had not reciprocated, although Maude had attempted to keep her part of the bargain with regular phone calls, she got a distinct impression that Katrina thought she was just being a fussy, interfering, old busy body. Although Katrina had felt this way in the past, right now, in her time of moral and emotional need, she'd come to realise just how cruel she had been to the last living relatives from her mother's bloodline.

Claude and Maude's marriage had been blessed with one girl, Isabelle, who had grown up into a very caring young woman. Claude, although an Army Royal Engineer by trade, had fulfilled a lifelong ambition to fly, and the obliging British Army had trained him as a helicopter pilot. Isabelle, his daughter, had followed in his footsteps after her first flight at 16, and she had become hooked, so much so, she eventually gained her wings as a professional commercial pilot. Isabelle was now flying mercy missions in far-flung corners of the world for a Christian Aid Charity. Claude and Maude were very proud of Isabelle, and almost every Sunday, they went to church praying for her safe return. Hopefully, that day was fast approaching, as Isabelle had recently met a British doctor working for the same organisation. In one of her recent telephone calls home, marriage and returning to the UK had been briefly mentioned.

Maude, just turning seventy, was a very fit, active lady. She led a fulfilling, busy life, and, despite her age, sported a full figure, completely free from any artificial support. She kept herself very trim with regular keep fit classes which took place in the local Village Hall. Her auburn hair, with just the slight hint of grey, was still full-bodied and kept in perfect shape by the local hairdresser. The only grey thing about Maude was her eyes; they were a sparkling metallic hue. Some people said they gave her the appearance of a clairvoyant, little did anyone know how close they were to the truth. Only Claude and Maude were to know the extent of Maude's perceptive ability.

Maude, through her life, had treated her body as if it was a temple, careful not to be exposed to too much sun, despite her and Claude's many foreign travels. She had used the same gentle, moisturising face cream since her teenage years. This regular use now bore fruit as only close up could her laughter lines and crow feet around her eyes be distinguished.

Consequently, Maude was much younger looking than her true age and, as a result, attracted many younger admirers with an eye for older women. A great sense of amusement to both Maude and Claude; she would often joke with Claude that he had to keep on his toes, otherwise, she would run off with one of her 'Toy Boy' admirers. Not that there would ever be the slightest possibility of that, Claude was Maude's rock, as well as her soul mate, they had been happily married for 40 years and were just as much in love today as they were when they walked down the aisle. They had been through thick and thin together. Claude had served his Queen and country with the Royal Engineers, retiring with the substantive rank of Colonel. Although, unlike many ex-military, he dropped the title on retirement and very rarely referred to his career, often just saying that he had been in engineering all his life. Not that he was in any way ashamed of what he had been, quite the contrary, but he had seen and done more than most could do in several lifetimes. Seeing action, as well as heartache, from the Balkans to the Falklands then the Middle East, losing many dear friends along the way but still keeping in touch with those left, attending various nostalgic reunions and remembrance parades. Claude, like many quiet heroes, preferred not to talk about it. Only on entering his study would his past come to life with the memorabilia and artifacts he had collected during his action man life. The walls adorned with many photos of men in uniform, just some of his many 'Brothers in Arms'. Some photos, with faces blackened out, the only hint of his time with Special Forces. Claude still had the distinguished bearing of a military man, he, like Maude, took good care of his health, still able to run for 10 miles without appearing to lose his breath. Only, unlike Maude, his hair was completely silver, it had been like that since his formative years, and it had earned him the nickname within the Army as the 'Silver Fox'. The only clue to his former dark hair colour being his bushy, almost black, eyebrows. Maude and Claude still made love at least twice a week.

Maude was delighted that Katrina had finally made an effort to come to stay with her and Claude, despite the circumstances of the supposed burglary surrounding the event, she was nevertheless overjoyed, finally able to fulfil her sister's dying wish that she would look out for Katrina. After greeting Katrina on the doorstep and ushering her ahead into the house, Maude had surreptitiously turned her eyes skyward as if in a signal to her long-dead sister that she was here at last.

Maude showed Katrina to a guest bedroom, "You can stay as long as you like dear," she said, smiling lovingly, "Now, why don't you get settled, then come downstairs for some tea."

Katrina carefully emptied her suitcase, finding drawers and hangers for her clothes, placing her belongings in the elegant room. She felt relieved to be away from her home and relaxed a little at the thought of being with family. Once unpacked, she headed downstairs to the lounge.

Both Claude and Maude had a good eye for quality, and it showed throughout their house. Katrina entered the luxuriously furnished lounge, she sat down and admired the room; its bookshelf lined walls, large house plants with glossy leaves, the highly polished array of wooden furniture and large comfortable, easy chairs with matching settee, much larger than those normally seen for sale in the average furniture shop. Standing next to a beautifully crafted mahogany cocktail cabinet, hand-built by Claude who had trained as a shipwright before joining the army, was a ticking Grandfather clock, giving off an air of tranquillity. The open French veranda window let in a light breeze, gently lifting the long chintz curtains hanging on either side. Sitting in the large inglenook fireplace was a huge wood-burning stove, ready for the coming winter with its stacks of freshly cut birch, slowly drying, releasing a rich aroma. Which, together with the pungent smell of furniture polish, gave the room an aura of the 1940s. Looking through the veranda windows, it wouldn't have seemed out of place to see a wartime Spitfire come flying across the landscape.

Claude was busying himself in his workshop; he enjoyed putting his practical engineering talents towards making wooden toys; these he donated to a children's charity, of which Maude was an active volunteer and committee member.

Maude had made afternoon tea with homemade fruit cake, some scones with rich, locally churned cream along with homemade blackberry jam. She was the equivalent of Delia Smith in her kitchen and obtained as much enjoyment from home cooking and baking as Claude did from turning wood on his lathe.

Maude poured some dark rich Ceylon tea, its aromatic blend, along with the smell of birch fire logs, filled the room with a heady scent, an aroma which could transpose the mind to where the tea plants originated, on a glorious sunshine hillside in Sri-Lanka. It was the ideal refreshment to accompany her bakery delights.

Maude served the tea but was saddened when Katrina refused the offer of either her fruit cake or scones. No wonder Katrina is looking so pale and drawn, she thought; the burglary had certainly deeply scarred her, or was it something else? Maude had a distinct feeling that Katrina wasn't telling her the full story. As they both sipped their tea, Maude turned to Katrina, "Now my dear, would you like to talk about the burglary? How frightful it must have been for you, goodness knows how I would feel if my home had been broken into."

Katrina was lost in her thoughts and only heard part of the sentence, she gazed out through the French windows, her mind far away over the distant hills. The double glazed doors, carefully constructed by Claude, perfectly matched the décor and the style of the house which Claude and Maude had created. Katrina, refusing the cake and scone, had hardly touched her tea. Since that terrible night, she had hardly eaten, the nurses at the hospital had tried to encourage her to eat more, but to no avail. As each day went by, the pain only got worse not better. Every time she heard or saw a police car, she shuddered, thinking that they were looking for her. The guilt that she was carrying, knowing that she has been party to a murder, no two murders, and then those gruff Irish hard men, they were terrifying too; it was a recurring nightmare.

In many ways, she willed the knock at the door to be the police so she could unburden herself. After all, she was the innocent party in all this; it was her private space and sanctum that had been violated. She hadn't done anything wrong, yet Richard had made it quite clear that if she went to the police or even breathed a word of it, the Irish men who cleaned up her house would soon be back, and in his words 'clean her up.'

Suddenly her Aunt's voice cut into her thoughts.

"Katrina, my dear," Maude leaned over to catch Katrina's attention, "You're a million miles away, I know you have suffered a terrible trauma, but you know you can stay here as long as you need."

"Oh, I'm so sorry, Aunty," replied Katrina, coming back to the present, "Yes, the burglary," suddenly, she burst out crying.

Maude put down her tea to comfort Katrina, sitting next to her on the chair arm, relieving Katrina of her tea cup and saucer and placed her comforting arms around her. Katrina slumped into Maude's embrace, crying like a baby and shuddering uncontrollably.

"There, there, my dear, let it all out," cooed Maude, gently rocking Katrina back and forth as though cradling a delicate child. Just at that moment, Claude, who was in search of some afternoon tea with Maude's wonderful baked delights, quietly opened the large wooden door, but seeing the sight before him, he caught Maude's eye, put his finger straight up to his lips, winked at her and made a tactical withdrawal, deciding to leave the girls to themselves and find his afternoon refreshments in the kitchen.

"Oh Aunty, I'm so frightened, most nights I just can't sleep knowing what happened in that house," more sobs came as Katrina took in great gulps of air as she tried to control her breathing, "What if they come back?" she wailed.

"I understand, my dear, it must be awful for you ... what did the police say? Do they have any idea, they usually know or suspect who can be behind these awful things?"

"Oh yes, the police, I suppose they are doing their best," she said, rapidly realising that she had nearly blurted out the truth between bouts of self-pity.

Despite living in leafy suburbia and leading a relatively sheltered life, Katrina had read all about the troubles that had occurred in Ireland: the disappeared, the maiming, the kneecapping, and the harsh, rough street justice handed out by the various warring factions of Irish society, justice that didn't distinguish between the sexes. She certainly didn't want to end up in a shallow unmarked grave ... Richard had not said as much, but his threat certainly had sinister overtones. These thoughts made her feel even more miserable and even more sobs welled up from deep within. She felt helpless in the situation she found herself and just wanted to be out of it.

Aunty Maude clutched her all the more tightly, as though trying to squeeze all the bad feelings out of Katrina, with soothing words, "Katrina my dear, the pain will pass given time. Maybe you should seriously consider selling that property, after all, it was always far too big for you."

How could Katrina explain that the house was not the root of the problem?

That evening, despite Aunty Maude's pleadings, Katrina only picked at her dinner, consuming just a small amount. However, she readily accepted her uncle's offer of a large Napoleon brandy, his favourite, after they moved to the drawing-room. Against the wishes of Maude and having ignored her glaring frowns, Claude repeatedly offered Katrina 'one last tipple'. Later, having consumed one too many, Katrina eventually dragged herself out of the armchair, kissed both Claude and Maude goodnight, tearfully thanking them for allowing her to stay over, before heading off to bed with a slight stagger in her gait, and fumes of brandy in her wake. She felt the alcohol had helped to reduce her anxiety, the light headiness brought on by the excellent brandy together with the comforting homeliness of Claude and Maude's house. After climbing the sweeping staircase, that curved around the large atrium hallway, Katrina soon found herself in the lovely guest bedroom, literally flinging her clothes off her body before throwing herself on to the sumptuous double bed. Once enveloped in the beautiful soft linen, she fell into a long-overdue deep sleep of oblivion.

Maude, slipping out into the hallway to look up to landing area, could see that Katrina had closed the guest bedroom door, returning to the drawing-room she admonished Claude for feeding Katrina so much brandy.

"It will do her good and help her to sleep," replied Claude nonchalantly.

Maude tutted her obvious disagreement, announcing that she was going to encourage Katrina to make an appointment to see their family doctor first thing in the morning.

"Katrina needs professional help, not brandy," she chided Claude.

A few days passed with Maude growing more suspicious; she had, inadvertently, overheard a telephone conversation between Katrina and someone she had addressed as Richard. Maude knew very little about Katrina's social life but soon realised that this man was more than just a friend. Since coming to stay, the mysterious 'Richard' had called several times. Maude had caught snippets of the conversations and concluded he was a married man. The whispered, sometimes angry, exchanges that she'd overheard caused her to worry even more, she had only picked up a small part of the discussion but she'd heard enough to make her realise that her intuition was right, it wasn't just a matter of a straight forward burglary at Katrina's house. Something truly awful had occurred, no wonder Katrina was fraught with worry.

Maude was frustrated; she wanted to help and understand but didn't want Katrina to think that she was interfering. Maude was experienced and wily enough to be able to broach the subject in a motherly fashion, without hurting Katrina's feelings. However, even when Maude thought that she had Katrina relaxed enough to talk about her social life, any mention of a man made Katrina tense. She knew Maude was fishing for information, so to give Maude something rather than nothing, she admitted that she has been silly enough to get involved with a married man, who she was now trying to forget. Maude was convinced that Katrina was only telling her part of the story. Understanding the precarious state of Katrina's mind, she didn't want to push it any further, not just yet.

Maude did eventually persuade Katrina to go and see the family doctor, who, along with his wife, were personal friends of Claude and Maude. After an initial consultation, he was not happy at all with Katrina's state of mind and decided he wasn't going to meddle and make matters worse. In his opinion, she needed professional psychiatric help. When put to her, Katrina readily accepted the doctor's advice, she would accept anything that would rid her of the demons that constantly taunted her. She also knew that what she said would be in medical confidence and enable her to unburden her soul without the fear of reprisal.

Katrina had thought of going back to see Richard's friend, Peter Willis, she liked him; she felt that that he had a calming influence over her. Peter, however, was not an option, he was far too close to Richard and she made the decision to completely sever all her links with Richard and close that chapter of her life, avoiding his friends and associates.

Two more weeks passed, Katrina finally felt able to commit to plans and agreed with her Aunty and Uncle to move in with them on a semi-permanent basis. She put her house on the market, with the possible idea of, once it sells, buying her future home nearby her Aunty and Uncle

During a visit to Katrina's house, to collect needed belongings, inquisitive Maude went along to help with the intention of secretly trying to investigate what had actually happened in the house. So, while Katrina busied herself upstairs in her bedroom, Maude sauntered casually throughout the house, coming eventually to the snug at the rear of the property. Upon entering the room, she was overwhelmed with a feeling of malevolence.

Maude had a spiritual gift that enabled her to sense abstract feelings from her surroundings, much the same way a medium would sense a connection between the present and the past. She'd had a slight psychic ability from an early age, but for many years she was too scared to embrace it and tried her best to block it out. However, her first precognition experience made her so thankful, that she would often open up her mind and allow the images to be released in the hope that the outcome would be of benefit to others. Her first memorable vision involved Claude who had been injured while on Active Service, and although the circumstances surrounding the event were horrific, she had felt a warm aura of peace, telling her that he was safe. When her foresight had been confirmed by visiting officers, only a few hours later, she had begun to realise that her 'visions' were of a positive and useful part of her psyche and she was willing to accept more. Confirmation of these extraordinary powers came into play when out walking with Claude, where she had been able to save a young child from death. Having the premonition images and acting rapidly, Maude managed to stop a young boy from running into the road where, seconds later, a speeding car would have claimed the little boy's life. Claude was the only person Maude felt would understand her mysterious gift and they vowed never to tell anyone else, unless the outcome might be a matter of life or death.

Finding herself looking around the room, she realised there was nothing that gave any idea that a burglary had taken place, yet a feeling of threat crept over her. She felt a sudden drop in temperature and, momentarily, it appeared as if the room was spinning, followed by a sense of weightlessness. She carefully knelt down, touched the carpet and closed her eyes, allowing her senses to take over, opening the door into her psyche, hoping she could visualise what happened. She waited patiently, but nothing arose. She let out a sigh as she opened her eyes and scanned the room. Standing up, she had an unexpected head rush. She quickly held out her hand to find the wall, giving her back her balance. She closed her eyes and took a deep breath; she could feel her heart beating; its rhythm thumping inside her. A dark, evil sensation engulfed her, its malevolence frightening, snapshots of distant muffled voices spoke to her. With her eyes still closed, she concentrated on the voices, trying to make sense of them, hoping they'd become louder and clearer. She felt a cold breeze against her neck, then the sounds of someone breathing, it was so close she could have sworn someone was standing right next to her. Out of nowhere, a loud, hysterical scream. Maude jumped backwards, quickly opening her eyes, she saw shadows in her peripheral vision. The shadows danced out of view, making it difficult for her to focus on a particular shape, but they seemed to be everywhere. Suddenly, they disappeared, but the cold, dark feeling had manifested itself within her. The room was trying to tell her something. She walked into the middle of the room.

"What happened?" She whispered.

She thought what she heard were foreign voices, then, no, she recognised the accent as Irish.

'Bang! Bang! Bang!'

The gunshots, coming from behind, threw her completely off balance, causing her to fall to the floor. Maude screamed in both fear and at the pain inflicted on her eardrums. Her knees cracked under the rapid fall. She scanned the room, expecting to see a gun pointing at her head, but nobody was there.

Katrina ran into the room, "Oh gosh! Aunty, are you okay?"

Maude realised the room was at peace again, but the experience had left her badly shaken and perspiring profusely. It was as if the room didn't want her to leave until it had given up its secrets. Her body felt cold and she started to shiver.

Katrina helped Maude to her feet.

"Aunty, are you feeling alright, I heard a bump, and then you yelled out. Are you okay?"

"It was nothing Katrina, I just came over a little faint and dizzy, it's nothing, probably my blood sugar level, that's all," she lied, it was all she could think of saying.

"Are you sure you're ok?"

Maude smiled, "Honestly, my love, I'm fine; let's get some lunch on the way home."

"Good idea, let's get out of this horrible house."

Maude was now certain that something awful had happened in that room, far more than a simple burglary, but she didn't wish to push Katrina any further and hoped that Katrina would, in time, reveal all. She did briefly consider sharing her perceptions with Katrina, but felt that she might look upon her as a silly, ageing aunty who was losing her marbles. She would, however, share her feelings with Claude, then they would both pray at church the following Sunday. They would pray that Katrina did not continue to be placed in harm's way, asking God to keep her safe. As for the rest, well, that would be kept just between her and Claude.

Katina's house soon sold, and her belongings went into storage. She enjoyed living with her Aunty and Uncle; they made her feel warm, calm, safe and valued. It was the start of a new chapter in her life. She instinctively knew that a new book would open for her once she was free of the demons from that dreadful night and free of Richard as well. He was the link in the chain which she must break.

It wasn't very long before Katrina had her appointment to see the psychiatrist. The lady psychiatrist in question was also engaged in a lot of work for the Ministry of Defence medical branch, treating servicemen and women who were suffering from post-traumatic stress disorders.

Katrina believed it would be difficult to discuss what had happened to a stranger, but, in actual fact, she found it incredibly easy. When she first sat in the huge comfortable couch in front of Dr. Lucas, Katrina held up her guard. She only answered questions with short sentences, never giving too much away. They discussed her childhood, her choice of boyfriends, jobs, marriage and the divorce, family, friends and eventually, the burglary. Katrina had told the story so many times that even she started to believe it. But, by session three, Katrina let everything out. She told Dr.Lucas exactly what happened on that awful night.

When Katrina left the psychiatrist's office, she felt free. Free from the burden of the truth that had buried itself so deep in her mind. She had finally said the words out loud to someone and, as she almost skipped to her car, she had no idea Dr. Lucas was left troubled.

Dr. Lucas had heard many horror stories in her time, but for some reason she couldn't shake Katrina's out of her mind. A triple murder, a cover-up by a group of men with Irish accents in the leafy suburbs of Roehampton, you couldn't make this up. The location was what worried the doctor, particularly as her parents lived in a neighbouring Avenue. Believing Katrina was of no harm to herself or others, it was the bodyguard that worried Dr. Lucas. Her career was important to her, but not as important as her loving parents. She needed to investigate.

She made some discreet 'back door' enquiries with a colleague who worked as a criminal profiler for the Metropolitan police who, in turn, was able to speak off the record to the Serious Crime Commander with whom she worked. After some digging, they found a mysterious incident that matched Katrina's details. The incident recorded as a *'No further action'* with some brief notes stating apparent gun shots reported, no evidence found, assumed car back firing. Her enquiries resulted in a referral to a Regional Crime Commanders meeting. The meetings convened bi-monthly were to discuss unsolved crimes and decide whether to direct the ever-diminishing investigative resources towards them or not. The room of senior commanders gave the subject of the supposed happenings in Roehampton a mixed response. It wasn't a reported crime that could be claimed unsolved; this caused a heated discussion about wasting resources.

The chairman, being an Assistant Chief Constable for Special Projects, considered that as the information had come from what was a reliable source, then it should be given a run to see what turned up, if anything. He requested further enquiries to be made, then one way or another, the matter could be either laid to rest or become a live enquiry. The house that Katrina had owned, the scene of the supposed crime, had new occupiers who were more than happy with their very expensive new home and mystified as to the police enquiry. The two police officers who called round to see them were somewhat embarrassed at asking awkward questions; how they found their home on moving in? Were there signs of blood or gunshot damaged to the structure? These questions, unsurprisingly, unnerved the new owners which resulted in them lodging a complaint. Discussed at the next Commander's meeting, the report concluding that the police couldn't unearth as much as one small piece of evidence of any wrongdoing; as such, the file was closed. Despite that portrayed by TV crime sleuths, modern-day policing doesn't work on hunches. There were far more crimes with lots of factual evidence to chase up rather than chasing 'cold case' shadows. Also because of the clandestine way in which the information had come to light, Katrina herself couldn't be approached for an interview.

It was to be some years later when strange things started happening in the snug room of Katrina's old home that the couple remembered the night two police officers called making, what was to them at the time, strange enquiries about the possibility of a crime having been committed. Once again, there was a 'For Sale' sign in the garden of the house in Roehampton.

Chapter 32

Richard had seen nothing of Katrina since that night, only keeping in contact by phone. During the first few weeks after she left the hospital it was evident their relationship was over. Richard was relieved. He knew the distance between them would create the divide he felt he needed. He'd started to feel that the stress of leading a double life was beginning to take a toll on his health. With the events of that fateful night, like it or not, he was now implicated in a criminal offence. He felt he had no choice other than to go along with Tim's plan. He had to protect both himself and his loyal bodyguard. Had it not been for Tim's quick and decisive actions that night, he would most certainly have been kidnapped and possibly killed. It was a wake-up call making him suddenly realise what really mattered in his life. What was precious to him and what was not!

As for Katrina, following the quick sale of her house, she made a clean break and out of Richard's life. She started with a make-over that included changing her name. She was very secure financially, she took the advice of her kind Aunt and Uncle and booked a special singles round the world cruise. The day she stepped on to the cruise liner at Southampton, she felt her old life slip away, being refreshed and happy as Miss Melissa Rosenfelt. It later transpired that Miss Rosenfelt met and fell in love with the ship's Staff Captain, a lady by the name of Patricia. Melissa, with her new life and new partner, went to live in a beautiful house on a remote Scottish Hebridean Island, the Isle of Coll.

Chapter 33

Despite believing he was astute, Richard had been so engrossed in his mistress and that awful night that he had completely lost sight of what was of real importance in his life. With Katrina having now moved house and living with her relatives in the Cotswolds, this gave him a modicum of relief, finally closing that chapter of his life. Richard came to realise his true lack of affection for Katrina and that he was unmotivated to offer her any emotional support. He soon realised that it was all about the excitement of clandestine copulation. His friend, Peter, had been right, he was suffering from what Peter had laughingly called *'Post Traumatic Shagging Disorder'*. When he unwittingly recalled the night's events, he always felt a pang of annoyance at Katrina's hysterical reaction in the aftermath.

Thoughts of Katrina became a burden to him, a burden he could now do without. Slowly, he acknowledged that his feelings towards her had been driven purely by the fire of lust. With the embers now doused, there was nothing left in it for him. Their relationship had passed its 'sell-by' date.

He tried so hard to concentrate on moving forward with his life; he felt powerless.

As the weeks passed and the dust settled, he started to realise just how much he had neglected Caroline, to the extent that they were leading separate lives. In his mind's eye, he had always pictured Caroline as the 'stay at home, loyal wife' who was immersed in her own little world of retail therapy, keeping fit and lunching with friends. The truth was the complete opposite. Caroline had changed dramatically, and Richard had been far too occupied to see that the young women he had married had slowly and eventually metamorphosed from a caterpillar into a beautiful, serene butterfly. Caroline had become a vibrant, hot-blooded woman. She wanted more out of life than just being Richard's trophy wife as and when it suited him.

Little did Richard know that a new perspective was going to give him the clarity to reclaim ownership of the situation that had been weighing him down. This stark awakening came via a private letter.

Susan would always sort through her boss' mail, opening the majority, acknowledging and dealing with routine matters and diarising forthcoming events. Very rarely did she need to consult Richard as he trusted her judgment explicitly. Email was fast catching but many letters still came via Royal Mail. Some marked 'Private & Confidential', which, more often than not, was a ruse to get by the eagle eye of personal assistants and secretaries. Susan could usually identify these and opened them accordingly, leaving Richard with only those written by hand, marked strictly private and confidential. The recent events had somewhat clouded Richard's thoughts so he'd put any private mail to one side. The take-over of Beaumont's was complete and Richard now had some time to catch-up with this so called private mail. These where usually some form of begging letter, be it for sponsorship of one shape or another whilst others were an incessant round of invitations to attend a multitude of social functions.

He sat in his oversized chair and sighed at the mound of envelopes. He contemplated asking Susan to go through them but, as he fanned them across his desk, his attention was drawn to a heavy white manila envelope with a distinct blue border, obviously expensive personal stationery. It was marked *'Strictly for Mr. Hartling'*. The handwriting was impeccable, obviously written by someone with a well-educated 'good hand'. He was intrigued by the lack of postage stamp or address. He carefully slid his letter knife into the envelope, slicing it open. He was always extremely careful at opening post following an incident earlier in his successful career when a grudge against his newfound wealth came in the form of a razor blade hidden underneath an envelope's fold. On that occasion, he had absentmindedly opened the letter with his finger, giving him a very nasty cut, from which had poured red blood like red wine split from a bottle. Ever since that day, Richard always used an envelope knife.

After gingerly opening the envelope, he pulled out the contents. It was a small piece of blue bordered paper matching the envelope with the same impeccable, almost artistic, handwriting, addressed personally, did he know this person? Obviously written by a lady as he could only see a lady using such stationery and probably religious to, by the tone of the message.

'Dearest Richard, Joash is more than your wife's personal trainer, the truth is right under your nose. Proverbs 30:20!!!
A friend.'

Richard suddenly stood up in shock. He threw the piece of paper on to his desk as though it was contaminated, infected by some unseen virus, and stared at it in disbelief. He was nervous to touch it, as though it was something grotesque and vile, he starred at it where it lay, reading it over and over again. He went over to the large bookcase, along one inner wall of his office, and retrieved a leather-bound copy of the Holy Bible and returned to his desk. Still standing, he opened the large, heavy book. Turning to the Proverbs 30:20 he read:-

This is the way of an adulterous woman: She eats and wipes her mouth, And says, "I have done no wrong."

He exhaled and sat back down. Blood rushed from his head. Never, in a million years, had it crossed his mind that Caroline would even contemplate risking her lifestyle by being unfaithful to him! No, he couldn't believe it, wouldn't believe it, not Caroline. The Neanderthal inner man rising to the surface – how could she? She wouldn't do this to me? She loved him … didn't she? Had he neglected her to the point that he'd driven her into another man's arms? Suddenly he felt out of control, his wife having an affair? His emotions, mixed, confused, hurt, anger, frustration all whirling around in a maelstrom. Momentarily oblivious to his own transgressions with Katrina.

Words uttered by his grandmother many years ago came back to haunt him, *'What's good for the goose is good enough for the gander!'*

He reluctantly picked up the piece of paper, collected the envelope, keeping it at arm's length, and marched to Susan's office.

"Susan," he accidentally rudely snapped. "Sorry, I, er, this letter," he held up the envelope, keeping the letter tightly hidden in his other hand, "who delivered it?"

Susan gently took the envelope from Richard and examined it, "I'm sorry, Richard, but I haven't seen it before." She passed it back to him.

"But it must have been hand-delivered, look! There is no postage or address on it, just my name."

"Yes, it may well have been hand-delivered but only as far as reception downstairs. Mikey, the post-boy, he brings everything to me late morning," she replied softly.

Richard's immediate thought was that he could check the CCTV, maybe spot the culprit red-handed, but then that wouldn't work as hundreds come in and out of the main reception area, it would take hours trolling through the tapes.

"When was it delivered?"

"I'm sorry Richard, I can't say, I'm afraid your private mail has been building for the past few weeks." Susan was polite but firm in pointing out that Richard had not been his usual organised self. "If it's marked *'strictly private & confidential'* and handwritten, you know I don't give it a second thought and pass it to you," Susan tried to study his expression, "Is everything okay Richard?"

He let out a vocal, deep sigh, "Yes, sorry to have bothered you." He strained a smile, "It's nothing really, just some begging letter," he lied. "Nutters and cranks most of them," he muttered, returning to his office. Susan wasn't convinced with his explanation but didn't pry.

Richard would often receive letters pleading for money, but he never followed them up. He was an extremely generous man when it came to his chosen charity organisations, but not random people who believed they should have a share of his success.

Back in his office, he scrutinised the letter. The idea that "*his*" Caroline had been having secret liaisons with someone else appalled him, it made him sick with despair. Had Caroline discovered his affair and wanted to get back at him? Who the hell is Joash? Of course, it crossed his mind that this letter could just be some sick joke, but the reality of how separate their lives had become made Richard's gut instinct tell him this letter held some truth.

The letter had actually come from a bitter, jealous, gym member, a so-called friend of Caroline's. The lady in question, a wealthy widow, had her own desires towards Joash. However, after seeing Joash and Caroline together one dark evening in the car park, she hadn't taken the rejection lightly. She had all but thrown herself at Joash, making it perfectly clear that she was his for the taking, and he would want for nothing. However, Joash preferred to pick his clients on his own instincts, and this particular widow was not to his liking. She had the funds, being an extremely wealthy widow, but she didn't match his requirements; he saw her as an old worn-out hag. If he was going to sleep with wealthy, white trash they had to have some sex appeal at least. When this particular lady saw Caroline and Joash together, she was both humiliated and angry. She firmly believed that she should be the one enjoying the pleasures of Joash, not the Mrs *bloody* Hartling who had everything! She'd hand-delivered the letter, which had sat unopened on Richard's desk for weeks. As each day passed, the widow believed she had ruined Caroline's picture-perfect life, totally unaware that Richard and Caroline's lives had taken dramatic new twists of their own.

The recent events, together with the anonymous letter from a so-called 'friend,' were making Richard finally realise what a hash he was making of his private life. Searching the depths of his memory, he vaguely remembered someone called Joash from one of the rare occasions he'd accompanied Caroline to the Health Spa recalling he was one of the instructors and masseurs. Going to the gym together was supposed to have been a relaxing period of quality time spent together. This initial enthusiasm had soon passed as he'd attempted to juggle all his other work and clandestine commitments! It was all too easy to let the gym time slip. Now, it looked as though his timid little wife, well in his eyes at least, had probably been experiencing a 'right royal rogering' by one of the muscular keep fit instructors.

Richard didn't care about the source of the letter, just the contents. He knew he had to be rational about how he dealt with the situation. He needed time to think and absorb exactly what was happening. He requested Susan to stop all incoming calls and clear his diary for the rest of the day.

He hypocritically ignored his own indiscretions with Katrina and focused on the belief that Caroline had been intimate with another man. He couldn't help but picture another man's hands-on Caroline's body, kissing her, caressing her, stroking her, entering her. He was furious, yet at the same time, heartbroken. His emotions were in turmoil as he mulled over the history of their marriage. With the aid of a brandy, from the small entertainment cocktail cabinet in his office for special occasions and important visitors, his anger turned in to remorse.

Another piece of the jigsaw puzzle that played on his mind was that Caroline had mentioned she had given up her membership of the local gym. When Richard queried this, she stated that she preferred to work out at home by herself — suggesting to Richard that they convert one of the downstairs rooms into a home gym — adding sarcastically that the house was big enough. At the time, Richard thought nothing of it, but now that information seemed relevant. Had she given up the membership or was she lying? Had she broken off the supposed affair? Did this confirm that she had indeed been in a liaison with one of the gym instructors? So many unanswered questions.

How had two people, who were once so in love, become almost strangers to each other?

He looked out of the huge office window as the night sky grew darker over the Thames. The indoor lighting created a mirror image of the office. He studied his reflection, astounded at the face looking back at him. Did he even recognise himself anymore? Losing his appetite, since that awful night, which had resulted in rapid weight loss. It was not just the weight loss he noticed, his face was drawn. His sunken eyes were dull and lifeless. He felt that he was looking at a shadow of his former self and he knew he had to pull himself out of this dark hole.

Despite his own philandering, the fact that Caroline was conducting an affair bit deeper than he expected. Richard experienced a crisis of conscience like he'd never experienced before. He started to realise just how selfish he had been and was truly disgusted with himself. He needed some form of salvation and redemption.

Richard knew in his heart that he did not want his marriage to collapse. What a fool he'd been, displaying a type of weakness he would have criticised in other men. He had become so vain where Katrina was concerned, so self-conceited that finally, the realisation dawned on him that he had been carrying his brain between his legs.

The events of that fateful night, and the discovery of Caroline's affair, brought him crashing down. He was in a dark place he didn't want to be. He'd never been so miserable before.

Although hardly a practising Christian, he had, as a youngster, taken Confirmation classes eventually being confirmed by the Archbishop of Winchester. This, at least gave him a certain amount of affinity with the church and the Christian teachings of the Bible. Not that he had been living by Christian standards. The depth of selfishness and depravity he'd sunken to really started to hurt him emotionally and he was beginning to have difficulty in reconciling these facts. Perhaps Caroline's affair had come about as a way of punishing him for his own infidelity, together with the lack of appreciation for his wife? All these thoughts and emotions swirled around constantly; he was sinking into the mire of blame and guilt.

It was Friday night, and Caroline had arranged to go away with some girlfriends for a weekend at a health spa up north in Rutland. He contemplated following her, so he did just that.

After secretly following Caroline to the Health Spa, witnessing with his own eyes that at the start of the journey she collected two female friends from their homes, he spent the rest of the weekend with his favourite brandy and the relief that Caroline was not spending the weekend in another man's arms. That Sunday morning, while walking to the local village shop for a newspaper, he found himself lingering outside St. Stephens – the local village church. He was taken aback by the sheer volume of cars; many doubled parked due to the size of the now burgeoning congregation.

Richard later discovered the reason for the sudden and amazing revival of Christian faith amongst his fellow villagers. It was due to the recent and new appointment of a vicar who originated from the West African

Country of Ghana. He had studied theology at Cambridge before eventually becoming a naturalised British citizen and a member of the Anglican Church ministry staff.

The vicar introduced his service and sermons with his deep, rich, booming voice, coupled with an extraordinary, if somewhat slightly cheeky and risqué, sense of humour. The light-hearted approach to biblical teachings had widened the church's appeal and obviously halted the dwindling attendances. The vicar's name quickly travelled far and wide. Couples young and old alike were queuing up to have the new vicar perform their nuptials, christenings and blessings.

That Sunday morning, Richard stood outside the church and listened to the hymn singing as it reached a huge crescendo. The singing emitted from the church seemed to call to Richard. On impulse, he entered the church and slipped into the only vacant pew at the rear. An eager Church Warden offered him a hymnbook, and Richard soon joined in. The service had only just started, during which, and when appropriate, Richard prayed as he'd never prayed before. Once the service had come to a close, Richard was overcome with a feeling of well-being. While his troubles were far from over, he did feel that he had at least been able to share his troubles. He couldn't quite understand the feeling, but in some way, he felt that some of his burden had been lifted. Upon leaving, the vicar's warm, firm handshake, beaming smile and *'Please come again'* comment, strangely made Richard feel calmer, a magic wand waved over him. With this new sensation, he knew that while not going as far as to be "born again," he would definitely be visiting St. Stephens again, very soon. So with a light spring in his step, a feeling he'd not experienced for quite some time, he went cheerily on his way home for what he hoped would be a relaxing Sunday reading the paper and with a determination that he was going to put things right in his marriage.

Despite his indiscretions, he arrogantly felt the cuckold husband wanting to know more about the man with whom Caroline had an affair. He had a violent desire to destroy the man's reputation, even to the point of causing him some form of physical harm. It was at the very heart of his soul. Nothing was going to take away the pain without some form of retribution or revenge, but as he ruminated on this he suddenly felt angry, questioning himself, wasn't he now looking to God and the Christian faith for salvation? Christian teachings didn't countenance revenge. Revenge would only make him bitter, wouldn't it? But he still felt the need for information on this man, finding out who he was may help ease his distress. He wanted to know his adversary; like the hunter hunting his prey and when achieved, he could decide what action to take next.

Caroline arrived home late on that Sunday evening. Richard thought she looked even more beautiful and radiant than ever before. Perhaps that's how she always looked, but he had been too blind to see it. He realised that he would have to confront her and pick up the pieces of his fragmented marriage, but for now, he decided to keep the contents of the 'well-wisher' letter to himself.

The following Monday, he pondered over the problem and as to what his strategy might be. He decided that it called for the confidential services of a private investigator. He'd never needed to use such services and wasn't sure where to start looking for a reputable company or individual. He didn't want to involve Susan and was on the point of looking through Google or Yellow Pages when it suddenly dawned on him; there was only one person whom he trusted to collect the information discreetly. He picked up the phone and dialled Tim's mobile number.

Tim was working out at the gym when Richard called. He never let his mobile out of sight; this included keeping it on an upper armband while he trained. Tim's mornings generally had a similar routine – as soon as he had safely delivered his boss Richard to the office for the day, if there wasn't any need for his services until the evening, then Tim was a pretty much a free agent and spent some of his spare time keeping fit. Tim's preferred gym was not only handy for the office, in case he was suddenly called by Richard, but it was owned and run by an old mate from his military days.

The guy, rather like Tim, had found himself at a loss once outside the Corps. As a 'keep fit fanatic,' he decided to put his passion for fitness into a business and opened a gym, teaching everything from dietary control to boxing.

Tim knew from the pre-programmed ringtone that it was Richard calling. Although slightly out of breath from the rowing machine, Tim immediately took the call.

"Sir?"

"Tim, I wonder if you could help me out with, well, let's say a delicate matter?"

"Of course, Sir."

"Would you mind coming to the office?"

"I'll be there in twenty minutes, Sir."

It surprised Richard how loyal Tim was. Nothing appeared to be too much trouble, and Richard often found himself thinking that if they had met through different circumstances, they would be good friends.

Tim's profession had become his life; he only ever returned home to sleep and relax when his boss did. When time permitted, he'd date occasionally, but he'd yet to meet another girl like his lost love, Teresa. He still mourned having to leave her, but the recent turn of events had helped spark a candle of hope that their love story would be rekindled. After having heard her voice again with its beautiful Irish lilt, which had made his heart pound, he resolved to find a way to see her again. Unbeknown to him, Ryan O'O'Donaghue had secretly also been trying to find a way to engineer a meeting between Tim and his daughter. He didn't say so to Tim, but he was getting old and he wanted to make amends for quashing their fledgling romance. Ryan was tired of the animosity which existed between him and Teresa; despite all his best efforts to make amends, nothing had satisfied her. Now, maybe something good was about to happen despite coming out of the events of that disastrous night in Roehampton. He'd never felt happier. He knew both he and Tim desired to make Teresa's dreams come true.

The Beaumont Shipping Company employed many attractive women, including Richard's Personal Assistant, Susan. Once, a rather pugnacious female union representative visiting the Beaumont's offices for a meeting had made a disparaging remark saying, 'Aren't there any ugly woman employed here?' hinting that Beaumont's practised a clandestine discriminatory employment policy when selecting potential female recruits to the organisation.

Susan was the only employee Tim would communicate with in-depth. He would politely acknowledge all personnel, most of whom knew who Tim was, but other than pleasantries, Tim preferred to keep everyone at arm's length. Susan, like Tim, was devoted to Richard and this gave them a mutual interest. They enjoyed each other's company and often found time for a chat. Tim found Susan highly attractive, and would often sneak a glimpse of her slender tanned legs gorgeously displayed by her short skirts, her long, perfectly shaped calves accentuated by the high killer heels she always wore. Tim's loyalties lay strictly with Richard and he knew to keep things on a professional level. While Susan was not too sure of Tim, she did find him very attractive. Her ego, deflated that Tim had never made a pass at her, made her wonder why that was? Through women's intuition, she knew he wasn't gay, thus reasoning that maybe he'd been badly hurt in the past, causing him to be wary of any new relationship. Although she would never admit it, Tim slightly frightened her, which only added to the magnetism she felt when in his company. Of course, she knew that Tim was more than just a chauffeur to Richard, but also his Bodyguard, perhaps that was the way they acted, not getting involved with the staff. Her only encounter of knowing a 'Bodyguard' was seeing the film of the same name starring Kevin Costner, and while it was only a film, she'd surmised that it must be a very difficult job having to be constantly alert to potential dangers, assuming a bodyguard could never relax when in the company of their employer. Susan had been in on the security meetings, taking notes of the discussions resulting in the decision that Richard and his wife needed strong-arm protection, after which Tim came onto the payroll.

Tim, quickly showering and changing, arrived at the office and was ushered by Susan straight into Richard's palatial office. Richard directed Tim to be seated in one of the large, red leather-bound, chesterfield easy chairs that faced his huge mahogany desk. The unique desk had been specially made for Richard in Burma then transported to London aboard one of the company vessels, which were the remnants of the once vibrant trade route between the UK and the Far East. The smell of the leather chairs, together with that coming from the highly polished desk, produced an aroma of expensive coffee.

For Richard to offer Tim a seat was a sign that something very unusual was happening 'Although what could be more unusual than recent events?' Tim thought to himself.

Tim rarely entered Richard's office; there was never any need. Usually, Tim would be sitting in the Range Rover either outside the front door or down in the basement car park, waiting. He'd seen the office; of course, when he first started working for Richard his training made him demand to know the outline plan of the offices, stairs, elevators and washrooms. It was essential, as a bodyguard, to have a memorised map of the layout of the area in which Richard worked; this knowledge could be a lifesaver.

Richard paced in front of the huge floor-length window, gathering his thoughts and choosing his words carefully.

Tim sat and watched Richard stride back and forth. It was clear to him that his boss had not been handling things too well since the murders. Even Susan had mentioned, confidentially, that she was worried about Richard's appearance. Tim respectfully put her mind at ease with a few carefully selected lies. Richard slowed his pacing until he was standing still, his hands behind his back as he looked out through the window across the London skyline and Thames, obviously lost in his own thoughts. Tim's eyes followed, waiting for Richard to address him. Tim was a good people reader, and the tension in the room did not go unnoticed. Richard slowly turned to face Tim.

"Tim, I owe you my life. I will never forget that."

"Sir – "

For a fleeting moment, Tim thought he was about to be dismissed, surmising that Richard wanted to close out the dramatic happenings of that night in Roehampton, seeing Tim as a link he wanted to break.

Richard raised his hand to interject him as he walked towards his desk "I know you'll say you were only doing your job, nevertheless, I will always be in your debt. Please, do be honest with me and tell me if you would rather not take on the request I am about to ask of you," Richard sat down, waiting for a reply from Tim.

Tim shifted in his seat, "Of course, it shouldn't be a problem, Sir, although naturally, I can't say until I've heard your request, but I'm always delighted to help you out. I must say, I'm intrigued as to what the request is."

Richard appeared to relax his shoulders. Tim took this as a sign that he was relieved he'd agreed to be of assistance.

"Good ... Excellent," Richard leaned forward, hunching over his desk towards Tim, in a conspiratorial pose, not wanting the conversation overheard, not that anyone would be able to, his office had good soundproofing, even the large panoramic windows were designed to avoid noise listening devices penetrating the room. Richard's stance caused Tim to automatically lean forward too. Richard explained his predicament about the anonymous letter.

Tim both admired and respected Caroline, and while he was very surprised at the information Richard gave him, he kept his personal opinion completely hidden, not even allowing his facial expressions to show signs of judgement.

It had always astounded Tim that Richard played away with Katrina. In Tim's eyes, Caroline was the perfect wife, but he was well aware that not everything on the outside was the true story.

The following day, armed with the name 'Joash' and Caroline's gym address, Tim duly set about his task. With a few discreet enquiries he'd soon identified who Joash was and, over the following weeks, Tim shadowed Joash as much as he could when his other duties allowed. Tim was no stranger to covert work, having experienced many hours, if not days, tracking terrorists in Northern Island. Terrorists who were streetwise, hard individuals so used to being followed that they adopted all manner of evasion techniques to throw trackers off their trails. Stalking Joash, who had no idea he was under surveillance, was easy by comparison. Tim soon built up a broad picture of the lifestyle Joash led. It appeared that Joash certainly had no end of admiring 'posh' female company; for a single man, he very rarely slept alone. Tailing Joash took Tim into some very dark and run down seedy areas of the city, and it soon became apparent that many of these areas were the centre of the narcotics trade. Tim watched Joash conduct meetings in a couple of dubious public houses, brief meetings which evidently were for the purchase of drugs.

Slipping in and out of the shadows, Tim soon picked up that he was not the only one watching Joash's movements. He wasn't sure who they were, but they were obviously working as a team, changing tactics and faces. Tim guessed they were law enforcement, watching and noting Joash's meetings. Judging by the number of encounters that Joash made there was no doubt in Tim's mind that he was a drugs dealer.

It wasn't long before Tim pieced together the puzzle of Joash's existence. Just like Caroline, the other female encounters of Joash all came from the classy up-market set. He was clearly supplying the ladies with more than just personal training; he was their main source of the up-market recreational drug cocaine. Evidence which he was not looking forward to passing on to his boss. The thought troubled him that Caroline could be involved with Joash for supplying her with narcotics. With Richard's mind focussed on the fact that his wife was sleeping with someone else, this new information could destroy his marriage and Tim believed, despite Richard's philandering, he didn't deserve this.

Driven by a desire to give Richard a thorough report on the man supplying his wife with favours, Tim wanted to discover where Joash lived. Every time he had picked up the tail on Joash from the gym, it led to downtown pubs, clubs and addresses of the ladies he was servicing. On those occasions, Joash had ended up either staying the night or so late that Tim had always called it a day. After all, he still had his day job of guarding and chauffeuring Richard around. He did consider calling in for some help from ex-police colleagues, but for now, he wanted to keep his discoveries to himself. Although Richard tried to question Tim as to his findings, Tim remained tight-lipped and claimed that there was still more work to be done. Richard, although impatient, knew that he had no right to push Tim further. He would just have to wait until Tim had all the facts to lay before him. Richard found it difficult to be patient. In his position of power and authority, he wasn't use to being kept waiting but he was astute enough to know that this was a different situation. Tim, with his military and police background training, was like the events in Roehampton; definitely in the driving seat.

Tim struck lucky a few nights later when he saw Joash leave the gym and make his way to the staff car park where he kept his outdated Ford Capri. Tim was sitting in the Range Rover over to the far side of the gym car park. He had positioned himself under the dark shadow of some large trees; this gave him a full view of both the client car park and the rear of the gym building. The car park, almost empty, had just a scattering of a few cars from the late-night fanatical keep fitters or those of shift workers. The security lights were strong, lighting up the car park for staff and clientele's safety. Joash, vacated the gym from the staff exit at the rear of the building and headed towards his car, soon to be followed by a woman who appeared from the main entrance.

Tim watched through his superb pair of powerful battery powered night vision binoculars, courtesy of HM, his only guilty conscience souvenir from his Special Forces days that had stayed in the bottom of his kit bag when he'd finally walked out through the gates at Chivenor; property now officially listed as missing by MoD 'Bean Counters'! He saw the woman almost jog to the staff car park where she and Joash hid from the security light and became shadows in the darkness. Tim could see, almost as clear as day, the scene taking on a greenish, ghoulish tinge so synonymous with night vision lens, viewing as Joash and his lady friend fell into each other's devouring embrace. Joash suddenly grabbed his acquaintance and threw her against the wall, taking control of the situation. Looking as though Joash was about to assault the woman, Tim was ready to dash to the woman's rescue, but then her response clearly showed she was enjoying herself.

The woman slid seductively, like an erotic dancer, out of Joash's grip and slowly slipped down to his groin. Tim felt uncomfortable, like a 'peeping tom,' but as quickly as the woman went down Joash pulled her back up. They appeared to have a rather heated discussion before the woman broke away from Joash and dashed out of the shadows into the main car park.

As Joash climbed into his old battered car, the women jumped into a Mercedes AMG S 63 class coupe, her actions hasty. The Mercedes fired in to life, Tim let out an involuntary whistle, he knew that the on-road price of such a machine weighed in at around a hundred and thirty thousand pounds. With screeching tyres, the Mercedes swung out of the parking bay and headed towards the staff car park before coming to a halt at the entrance, flooding the area with light from its powerful halogen headlights on full beam. Joash, in his beaten up car, backed out of his space and turned his car to face the Mercedes. The two cars faced each other, like two snorting wild animals. The wisps of exhaust fumes enveloping them in the cold autumnal air. After a brief exchange of flashing headlights, the Mercedes reversed to allow Joash's car to move off towards the main exit, the Mercedes swung around and closely followed.

Tim started up the Range Rover and moved out of the car park on to the main road, in close pursuit of the two cars. He was sure that they were taking their meeting to a more private, secluded place, he just hoped they were leading him to Joash's residence. The cars led Tim to a completely new area; somewhere he had not encountered with his previous tailings of Joash. Guessing correctly, they appeared to be going to Joash's home. He did begin to wonder though, when the meandering took him on to a dingy industrial estate, that it was the sort place where drug dealers might hang out. The two cars pulled off into a small drive beside a building of business units. Tim, not wanting to be spotted, drove past, following the road to the right and around the next corner. The location led him to a spot almost diagonally opposite where his quarry had pulled off. He parked up out of sight and quickly killed the lights and engine. He stealthily alighted from the Range Rover with the grace and speed of a cat, binoculars in hand.

Some years previously, an attempt at turning the particular industrial estate into something green and pleasant had resulted in a line of heavy bushes and trees planted along one side of the road, opposite and facing the unit where Joash and the mystery woman had disappeared inside. This attempt at cultivation had, through lack of attention, grown into an urban jungle giving Tim the feeling of déjà vu from his military days, back in the jungles of Borneo. Tim used these bushes to his benefit, creating an excellent vantage point.

The building was on two floors, appearing almost like a row of terraced houses.

Tim's attention was taken straight to the corner unit, where some internal lights were coming on. Tim wondered why they would both come to such a dark and grotty industrial estate. It was understandable someone like Joash would be found in such an unpleasant area. It appeared a perfect place for a drug dealer to keep a low profile, just like the scrappy, battered old Ford Capri he drove, all aimed at keeping below the radar of the law enforcement agencies. Joash did not lead the flashy, expensive celebrity type lifestyle portrayed in Hollywood movies. What was unclear was, why the woman would go with him.

Lights came on in the building, meaning Tim no longer needed the night vision facility on his binoculars. However, his field of vision wasn't very good from where he was secreted. He knew he couldn't go across the road as he would be totally exposed. There was only one thing for it; he had to shin up one of the mature trees standing amongst the bushes. This new position gave Tim an almost bird's eye view of the unit. He was surprised to see that the ground floor unit was, in fact, someone's living accommodation. He could work out a dining room, a kitchen, plus a small lounge. Tim was shocked that anyone would live in such squalor. Another light flicked on, clearly showing a rather seedy bedroom. He felt confident, as he watched Joash move around the rooms, that this place was Joash's home.

It didn't take long for Joash to strip down to his underwear, his already burgeoning crotch region clearly indicating that Joash was expecting a night of lust. He went to his female companion who lay in wait for him on the sofa, glass of wine in one hand while her other hand beckoned him to sit next to her. It was clear by her mannerisms that this was not her first visit. Joash retrieves a small box which he placed on the glass coffee table in front of the sofa. He sat down, opened the small tin skilfully and carefully scooped out two small piles of white powder. The woman was laughing and joking as she stroked Joash's back and muscular shoulders. Joash shrugged her off as he concentrated on turning the piles of white powder into lines using a credit card. He picked up a packet of straws and offered one to his female companion. She didn't hesitate in taking the straw and snorting one of the powder lines, Joash quickly followed suit. Tim used the inbuilt camera on his binoculars to snap the evidence he needed to place before Richard.

Tim correctly imagined that Joash's game was cultivating the wealthy women from the gym club into becoming dependent drug users. They were obviously perfect clients for what would be a profitable market.

Despite the industrialised, rough setting in which Joash had chosen to make his home turf, this wasn't some sleazy back street drug trading frequented by sad individuals who would sell anything to pay for their habit. Clearly, the top end of society, women who had more money than sense and therefore able to fund their habit. Yes, the predatory, white-hating, Joash had developed a very lucrative market place for himself. All of Tim's late-night prowling to investigate Joash finally revealed all he needed; the puzzle was complete, his work done.

The following morning, a very dejected Richard sat at his desk and stared down at the array of photographs Tim had put before him, downloaded from his special binoculars, then printed off in black and white. Tim gave Richard a rundown on what he had discovered. Richard was silent and pensive, his emotions in turmoil at what he was hearing and seeing.

He looked bleakly at Tim, "Tell me, Tim, have you ever come across a user in your line of work?"

"Several, Sir."

"And it's obvious, yes? That they are, how do you say it … *high*?"

"Yes, Sir."

"And Caroline," he paused, deep in thought about his wife's emotional state, "Did you personally see her take drugs from this man?"

"No, Sir, I never encountered her on any of my surveillances."

Richard sat back in his chair and took a deep breath, "Not even at the gym?"

"Not once, Sir."

"Very well, thank you for your time and hard work Tim, you will be rewarded in next month's pay."

"Thank you, Sir," and with that, Tim, sensing the meeting was at an end, withdrew tactfully, leaving Richard alone with his thoughts.

Part of Richard was relieved. He had prepared himself to witness pornographic photos of his wife. Instead, he had found no hard evidence of her doing anything wrong. It even appeared that she was telling the truth about no longer frequenting the gym where the drug dealer worked. He tried to make sense of the information; she wasn't having an affair, Tim never caught her with the drug pusher and although he hadn't taken much notice of her recently, he couldn't pin-point any drug using evidence in her everyday demeanour which, despite his lack of attentiveness towards her, surely he would have noticed any change in her characteristics. He decided that the note was a malicious attempt to hurt him; despite this, he knew in his heart, he had to salvage his marriage.

Richard felt the tears build. He stood up behind his desk, took a large white handkerchief and loudly blew his nose to clear his sinuses of the mucus brought about by his tears. Putting away the handkerchief, he inhaled, bent down, and with one flying sweep, cleared his desk with his left hand and arm, crying out, "No! No! No!" Papers, together with desktop executive toys, flew on to the floor with a crash. This caused Susan to burst into the office in surprise, wondering what on earth was happening.

"Oh my goodness," she exclaimed as she dashed across the room to help clean up the items from the floor. Richard stood, forlornly blank, as he looked at the mess he had just created. His actions were so out of character, he had even surprised himself. Susan had never known Richard lose his temper before and started fussing around him, collecting the items and placing them back on the desk.

"Oh, Mr. Hartling, what's the matter?" Susan asked, both concerned and worried, referring to Richard formally feeling that the situation warranted it rather than their usual intimate use of his Christian name.

Suddenly, Richard seemed to snap out of his trance, "Susan ... I'm so sorry. It was a momentary lapse and bad manners. I've just received some bad news, please, let me finish tidying."

To Susan, it sounded like a plea, so she quickly placed the papers on his desk and turned to leave. She caught a brief glimpse of some of the photographs, but their significance was lost on her.

"Susan ... please don't worry; it was nothing, I have some private matters that are giving me some grief. I will soon settle them. What you've witnessed was just a moment of stupidity on my part, please forgive me?"

"Of course, Richard,' she replied softly, falling back so easily into addressing him by his first name 'but if there is anything you want to discuss, you know I'm always willing to listen and I'm a soul of discretion."

"Of course, Susan, I trust you implicitly, you are very kind-hearted, and if I feel the need, I shall certainly talk to you about it, but for the moment, let us just leave it be?"

"Yes, of course," she smiled before leaving the room and gently closing the door behind her.

Richard sat down in his large executive chair, leaned back, and let the tears fall. Misery engulfed him; he had created this situation through his selfishness and stupidity, a multitude of questions reeled around his mind as to what had happened to Caroline. Was she now drug dependent? Had that bastard, Joash, introduced her to cocaine for the sole purpose of getting her hooked? How was he going to broach this with her? What if this got out to the wider society that he, the most powerful man in British shipping today, had a wife who snorted cocaine? The worst situation he'd ever faced in his life; everything else paled into insignificance. He realised just how much he needed faith in God, more now than ever before. He decided that there was only one way forward; he had to bare his soul and confront Caroline. He had to deal with the situation sooner rather than later. So, with a heavy heart, he buzzed through to Susan and asked her to get hold of Tim take him home and he would be un-contactable for the remainder of the day.

Chapter 34

I t had become far from usual for Richard to be home before midnight. Recently, his late nights had been down to work and the buyout of Beaumont's, but a few weeks ago his late nights would have been because of his regular visits to his mistress. However, today, Richard's attention had been focussed on Caroline. His mind had been in turmoil, going over the recent events and revelations. He was nervous about how he was going to deal with the situation in which he found himself. He needed to confront Caroline if he was to save his marriage; to do nothing wasn't an option; otherwise, the suspicion that existed between them would slowly eat away and ultimately destroy their marriage.

Richard had not seen Katrina since she went into the care of Peter Willis. His attempt at respectfully keeping in touch with her by phone always ended in an argument. He finally realised that their relationship was weak; it had no substance, broken down, it was purely sex without intimacy or commitment. It had become clear to them both that the affair was well and truly over; they both wanted rid of any reminders of that awful night, and that included each other. It had been an easy break-up for both parties.

With Richard's busy career, he had never had a routine when it came to work, making it extremely easy for him to have a mistress. With Katrina out of his mind, and no longer requiring attention, he had been using his evenings to concentrate on the managing the take-over. He had purposefully avoided Caroline as he had anxiously waited for Tim to collate information on her recent indiscretions. Although he avoided her, it didn't stop him from thinking about her day and night. His emotions were like a boiling cauldron, but he had been determined to keep a lid on them and not to lose control. He had become sick with worry; it was gut-wrenching with his mind wandering to vivid scenes of seeing his wife cavorting in drug-fuelled sexual antics with another man. His inner conscience tormented him by reminding him what he had got up to with Katrina. Richard wanted his wife back; he wanted the life they used to have. Whatever she had got herself in to, he was damn sure he was going to pull her back out. He owed it to her and their marriage. The guilt of his affair was starting to eat him up, and he was determined to get himself back on track. How had he, the great Richard Hartling doyen of British Shipping, let everything get so messy and out of control?

Over the past few weeks, their lives had been like two ships passing in the night, they purposefully avoided each other, wrapped up in their own emotions. While Richard avoided Caroline until he knew what she had been up to, Caroline avoided Richard as she dealt with the haunting of what Joash had done to her. Her bruises had started to fade, but she felt a part of her had faded with them. The awful abuse she had suffered at the hands of Joash was still in her head. Hopefully, the images would fade with time, but for now, the feelings were still raw. Caroline was a shadow of her former confident self. Slowly, she had slipped into a lonely world. She had so desperately wanted to talk through her feelings with Richard, hoping he would scoop her up and tell her everything would be okay, but she was petrified that he would reject her. She felt like a little girl in a man's world. Caroline had always believed that Richard was her soul mate, but over the years, it was as if they'd lost sight of this and didn't know each other anymore.

The confrontation with Caroline came about that same day when, uncharacteristically, he'd arrived home very early — driven by Tim. Richard, as usual, sat in the rear of the Range Rover, but unusually not on his laptop, he was lost in his thoughts, staring at the bouquet lying on the seat beside him. As he tried to work through how he was going to conduct the talk with Caroline, he looked at the beautiful flowers and couldn't help wondering when he had last, personally, bought her something with affection, knowing full well it would have been a job he delegated to his PA, Susan Windsor. The Range Rover turned into a small gravelled approach drive, just off the minor country lane; here, Tim remotely activated the huge wooden gates to the property. The gates parted effortlessly, sliding away and disappearing behind the massive brick wall that surrounds the house like a Wild West fortress. The Range Rover drove onto the huge expanse of gravel frontage to Richard's home, the tyres gently crunched before coming to a well guided stop just outside the front door.

Richard slowly stepped out of the car, as if he was a condemned man about to meet his maker. Richard, throughout his career, had made himself into a renowned architect of expertly directing meetings at all levels, whether unions, the management or Government ministers. However, this was to be one meeting where he knew he was struggling to gain his normal self-confident approach. He already had that old adage of feeling butterflies in his stomach, along with acidic bile now rising to produce a bitter hot taste in the back of his mouth. He held his briefcase and flowers as if they were some sort of life's crutch. Tim skilfully turned the car around on the large gravelled drive and returned through the open gates back on to the road. The gates, once again, silently shut behind the retreating Range Rover. Richard stood there momentarily, unsure of what to do next. He took a deep breath, hesitantly stepped forward and approached the stately front doors centrally situated between two large neo-gothic pillars which supported the balcony above. The doors quietly clicked open, as if by some unseen hand, the security mechanism having been activated by the electronic key card hidden in Richard's jacket pocket.

He entered the hallway and called her name, his heart sank momentarily as having hyped himself up to meet her, he couldn't bear the thought that she might not be at home. He didn't get a reply.

Without a sound, Caroline appeared at the top of the staircase. The sweeping, circular steps spiralled around the atrium-style grand entrance hall of their multi-million pound home. She remained at the top of the landing, astonished. She didn't know what was more surprising – the fact that Richard had flowers or that he had actually called her name.

"You're home early?" questioned Caroline, momentarily unsure what else to say whilst taking in the massive bouquet that included her favourite Asiatic lily. The colours were so beautiful, they made her heart miss a beat, reminding her of the excitement she had enjoyed when Richard had been a loving, attentive husband.

"You hardly notice me these days, so why the flowers!?" resentment in her voice.

Richard cringed inwardly at the barbed remark, knowing he deserved all the shit he felt Caroline was going to throw at him when the discussion about their marriage eventually started.

He looked up at her, still standing at the top of the stairs. He placed his briefcase and coat on the large ebony hall table, another trophy from the Far East, courtesy of one of his ships' captains.

Standing in the centre of the atrium, he took on the image of a condemned man standing in the Lion's Den of ancient Rome, waiting for the beasts to come charging out and maul him. He clutched the bouquet and held it out as a peace offering.

"Darling, can we talk?" the desperation in his voice could not be masked.

"Darling is it?" replied Caroline as she descended the stairs towards him, "It's been a long time since you've addressed me like that Richard," her voice had softened slightly. She wanted to be angry with Richard, but the sight of him with the flowers had somewhat taken the wind out of her sails. What she wanted to do was to run down to him and be taken in his arms and kissed longingly and passionately. Her fluttering heart signalled that this might be the old Richard who had just walked in the door. The old Richard she had so desperately been wanting back.

Caroline was dressed very casually in a pink all in one soft comfortable suit. It clung to her shapely body, as though a second skin, accentuating her beautiful curvaceous outlines. Richard gawped at her, realising just how sensual she was. He must have been blind not to see his childhood sweetheart develop into this magnificent woman.

"Home early, wanting to talk, and bearing flowers, should I feel very privileged, Richard?" She asked, continuing her slow descent of the stairs. It was agonising for Richard watching her as she appeared to provocatively step down to meet him, he was only just realising how naturally glamorous his wife was. An inner accusing voice screamed at him, 'How could you have been unfaithful to this beautiful woman?' It was a question Richard could not answer, but he suddenly realised what a complete pratt he had been.

She took the bouquet from Richard's outstretched arms and held them to her bosom before offering Richard her left cheek. He dutifully kissed her, but what he really wanted to do was to take her into his arms, cry out and beg for forgiveness, not because of Katrina, he hoped that would be forever a dark secret but forgiveness for ignoring her.

Turning, she headed off through the door beneath the atrium stairs and into the cavernous lounge. She didn't want Richard to see the tears flowing freely down her cheeks. These, she quickly and casually wiped away with the soft fleece encasing her right arm, in a motion she hoped wouldn't be seen by Richard.

Richard followed her.

The room's huge plate glass windows took up an entire wall revealing an opulent marble indoor swimming pool with a sliding roof, beyond that lay the beautiful English country of the South Downs. The décor and every piece of furniture yelled grandeur. The central part of the room contained an enormous square-shaped settee which could seat, at a squeeze, fifteen people, although it rarely did these days — the central area filled with a beautiful glass-topped coffee table that could easily hold a banquet of food. The top of the table was supported by eight wooden carved elephants, yet another purchase from the Far East brought home aboard one of the company vessels. Caroline placed the flowers on to the coffee table before looking over at Richard.

"Does our talk call for some wine?" She said, trying desperately to stop her voice from breaking as it was swallowed up by the vastness of the lounge. She was yearning for the calming influence of some alcohol to settle the butterflies flying around her stomach like a barnstorming air show.

Richard momentarily hesitated in the lounge doorway, unsure of how he was going to broach the subject of Joash and the drugs business. He rightly suspected Caroline was trying to hide her tears as she walked through to the kitchen. He followed her, like a lamb to the slaughter, waiting for the trigger to be pulled. He knew this was the hardest thing he had ever faced in his life, but he was damn sure he was going to fix it that evening.

Caroline opened the huge refrigerator door, "Well, I fancy a drink," she announced reaching for a bottle of Don Cayetone vintage Chardonnay. She felt lost for words, other than describing the wine out loud as if she was addressing her choice to a group of wine connoisseurs.

She extracted the bottle from the internal wine rack before turning and skilfully kicking the refrigerator door shut with her right foot in a smooth, gentle swish.

Caroline busied herself, opening the bottle on the vast, central, marble-topped work surface. Although she now felt she had control over the tears, she was unsure if she could control her emotions. Richard stood on the other side of the work surface, looking at her with a pathetic, pained expression on his face.

"Caroline … We need to talk about us."

Caroline appeared to ignore Richard's plea as she busied herself taking the cork from the bottle using an electronic corkscrew, one of the many labour saving devices that came complete with such an expensive, designer kitchen as theirs. The cork came away from the bottleneck without the slightest hint of a pop, then, opening a large drawer beneath the worktop she extracted two large wine glasses, gently nudging the drawer shut with her hip. The drawer slid to a close, slowly and quietly.

Richard hated the silence, "Caroline? Please."

Caroline finally met Richard's eyes, "You're damn right we need to talk about us, because at this moment in our lives, there is no us," she spat, "and what happened to the darling?"

Before giving Richard time to answer, she collected the bottle and glasses and tiptoed across the soft Persian carpet, another import courtesy of one Richard's company vessels, and back through to the lounge. Richard duly followed. She placed the bottle and wine glasses on the huge coffee table and poured two large measures. She held one out for Richard to take; the chilled wine glistened with dewdrops of condensation forming on the side of the glass. Again, she met his gaze, "So, tell me, to what do I owe the pleasure of your company? I've forgotten when we last did anything together, oh except when you wheel me out on special occasions like a Hollywood Trophy wife!" She took a sip of wine, her eyes still burning into his, "As for the lovemaking or rather lack of it, well, I won't even go there."

The conversation was not going the way Richard had planned and all he could muster was a feeble response in his defence, "Don't you think I realise that!"

Caroline took another sip of the wine, the cool liquid danced in her mouth and fuelled her confidence to finally speak her thoughts, "Don't tell me that you haven't been having an affair, Richard! Your absences are not all down to work!" Caroline felt relieved she had eventually said it out loud and to his face, although it was the only suspicion in her mind she felt like there was no time like the present to release her inner doubts. She had removed the lid off all her bottled up emotions, and she wasn't sure if she could stop, "and before you even think about lying to me, I should point out that women have an instinct that knows when their man has strayed. It has been written all over you for months!" She took another sip of wine as if a reward for the way she had attacked him.

"Let's sit down," was all Richard could offer in reply, he was unsure how to answer Caroline's accusation. Not wanting to admit to the affair with Katrina, he tried desperately to think of some way to avoid the truth without having to tell downright lies. It was at this moment that Richard realised he hadn't planned his attempt at reconciliation very well at all. He had the distinct feeling he was blundering along and started to regret his stupidity in believing that he could fix it all so easily.

Caroline did as Richard suggested and they sat down opposite each other looking across the large coffee table. They glared at each other like heavyweight boxers sizing each other up. Richard felt very uncomfortable and averted his eyes. All he could think of doing was removing his jacket and loosening his tie, playing for time while he worked out how he was going to answer her.

"Well, I'm waiting?" demanded Caroline, breaking the silence, "Are you going to deny having an affair?"

Richard was experiencing an inner turmoil; he was searching for the chance of reconciliation. He wanted to avoid a slanging match and knew that was where it would head if he retaliated with the knowledge of Caroline's infidelity with the drug pusher, Joash. Richard tried to dominate the conversation, "Ok, Caroline. Cards on the table. I'm not going to lie to you, I could but I don't want to. Yes, I've been indiscrete, which I bitterly regret. Everything we have; all the money and success, I would willingly give away to turn the clock back," Richard placed his untouched wine on the table.

Caroline remained silent. She looked away, her fears confirmed. She clutched her glass in both hands and softly placed it on her bottom lip. Her tongue gently licked the top of the glass, deep in thought.

Richard starred back, waiting for a response. He watched her closely; his groin came to life as he saw how adorably sexy she was. He wanted to jump up, grab her and taste the wine on her lips and make love to her there and then, but he knew he had to stay in control.

Caroline allowed the silence while she confronted her own demons. She contemplated showing outrage at what Richard had just told her, but knowing she was far from innocent herself, she recalled the famous Biblical words, 'Let he who hath no sin cast the first stone!' so she kept quiet.

The truth was, she loved Richard and if he was going to be contrite then so be it, she so desperately wanted her normal life back; she wanted the life they had together. On the other hand, she definitely wasn't going to let him off lightly. The air needed clearing; she wanted Richard back on her terms. She blamed Richard for her disastrous liaison with Joash. Yes, the sex with Joash had been good, but the way he treated her, tormented her and assaulted her body on that horrible night at his dingy apartment, disgusted her. Caroline inwardly shuddered at the thought as to how that night could have turned out! God, how she so wanted to get back at Joash, cause him pain and grief for what he had done to her. Have him humiliated as he had done to her. It was that humiliation that reminded her that Richard would never ever do such a cruel thing. So lost in her thoughts over the hatred she felt towards Joash that she missed what Richard said, only hearing the name that haunted her: 'Joash.'

"What?" she exclaimed, unsure if she had heard him right.

"I said … I know about Joash," Richard repeated. There it was, out for better or worse. He waited anxiously for Caroline's reaction.

The words felt like a stab right into Caroline's heart, momentarily taking her breath away. Her hands started to shake; she quickly placed the wine glass on to the table to stop the obvious trembling. She was stunned into silence and just stared at Richard, unsure how to answer this startling revelation. Her mind raced. Her first reaction was to deny even knowing Joash, but then Caroline was nobody's fool, and she knew it would be futile to deny it, pointless to attempt to bluff out. If Richard knew this much, he undoubtedly knew more than Caroline could imagine. Her only retort was to attack.

"Well, what did you expect?!" she exclaimed.

Richard was taken aback at the ferocity of her reaction, but he had no time to reply as Caroline raised her voice, "You didn't bother with me! You didn't care about me or what I was up to. You just thought, in your typical male way, that so long as I had a credit card, I would be happy: well fuck you Richard!"

Richard was stunned at her words, but he was not going to let her have an argument. He tried to keep calm, "I know, I know, I've been an utter fool darling."

"Stop calling me darling, you don't mean it," she shot back, her voice cold as ice.

"Yes, I do, I do mean it!, from the very bottom of my heart," he pleaded.

Once again, Richard found himself on the back foot but relieved that Caroline hadn't denied knowing Joash. He felt like he was halfway to tackling the question of the drug dealing Joash. He just hoped to god that Caroline hadn't become mixed up in Joash's sleazy drug world. How could he, the great Richard Hartling, the luminary of the Conservative Party and hailed by the city's financial institutions, have his wife associated with the lowlife gutter snakes such as Joash? If this got out, it would ruin his reputation. He remembered his friend, Peter Willis, warning him he was playing with fire. He never thought it would be like this, though, his beautiful wife associated with a drug dealer. What if the police had Joash under surveillance? Maybe they'd observed Joash with Caroline? Maybe they already had photographs on record? Could he expect a knock at the door, the flash of the warrant card, then the ignominy of his wife's arrest? He felt sick with fear of where this could go. He had to gain control somehow. He took a sip of wine before looking at her, "Yes, I do know about Joash, and I've only myself to blame, I get that," he said resignedly.

Caroline didn't let his calmness influence her, she was still angry, "So what do you know about Joash?" She snapped.

Richard hesitated before continuing. "Well ... I do know that he is a drug dealer."

"What!" exclaimed Caroline, her voice rising several octaves.

"I know he deals in drugs."

"How do you know?" she frowned.

"That doesn't matter."

"So, you've had some spy following him? Oh god, I bet you sent someone to follow me, didn't you?" Caroline said accusingly.

"It doesn't matter how I know, let's just say, I know."

"So what? It has nothing to do with me," she said indignantly.

"Please tell me you didn't take drugs from him, Caroline."

"How offensive! You don't know me at all!" She retaliated and sighed heavily, followed by a large gulp of wine, "Yes, I knew he took drugs, but I had nothing to do with it. Surely you know that drugs disgust me, as does that obnoxious cretin who I haven't seen for weeks now. I haven't even been to the health club. Anyway, I guess you know all this as you appear to believe you have all the facts. I suppose your spies have told you where I've been and who I've seen! You have no idea what I've been through."

"So, you promise you never touched any kind of drug?"

"No!" pausing and taking another hit from the glass ... It was more, how did you put it? Ah, yes, he was my indiscretion!" She sarcastically replied.

"Touché!" replied Richard.

"So now what now? ... DARLING!" Caroline countered, but her eyes were softening. Richard judged that if he worked hard enough, he would be able to remind her how it used to be. Show her how much he wanted her back. "We have each other, our years together," he pleaded, gazing into her eyes, "Isn't that enough for starters? We have a solid foundation that we can build on. I love you, and love can conquer all, can't it?" He asked, rather naively. Caroline's body language became relaxed; it was as though a weight had visibly lifted and that's exactly how she felt.

Richard stood, walked around the coffee table and over to her and gently took her hands, knelt in front of her, "I won't disappoint you again, I give you my word," he stated with a clarity that came from his heart.

They talked late into the night and eventually fell into bed, both exhausted and emotionally drained. They had reached an understanding with each other, deciding to try to start again, taking each day at a time. They made a promise that they would work hard to rebuild their relationship. There was no lovemaking that night; instead, they fell asleep in each other's arms, all emotion completely drained and spent from their bodies. They agreed to put their experiences behind them, move forward together, putting into practice that old adage that couples should never go to bed before resolving an argument.

Although Richard did have one niggling worry that played on his latent prejudices. His working career, as he climbed the corporate ladder, had led him to meet and work with many nationalities as he tramped around the world aboard company ships, learning how the company ticked. So despite considering himself a non-racist, he did wonder about his convictions in this respect when considering that Joash was both a Kenyan immigrant and drug trafficker as well as a womaniser with many sexual relationships, could he be carrying an STD or worse: was Caroline infected? For the moment, he decided to let sleeping dogs lie, despite the horrifying thought. He needed to have a clear conscience without the worry eating away at him. He was terrified at the mere thought of the consequences should his fears ever be realised.

He knew he had a lot of ground to make up with Caroline. He needed a plan, and as he knew himself to be a successful organiser he decided upon old fashioned courting. He would make a fuss of her and show her just how devoted he was. He acknowledged that it would be no good showering her with materialistic goodies, no, he knew this was about demonstrating how he felt. He had to show her that he was loyal. He would ensure that they spent quality time together, something they hadn't experienced in a long time. He needed to show commitment. He wanted to treat Caroline as though she was the only woman on the planet.

Some nights later, Richard was, again, working late, but he had been thoughtful enough to phone and apologise in advance to Caroline, who had been both flattered and comforted by his consideration. When he finally arrived home, the house was in darkness; Caroline was obviously in bed. He placed another beautiful bunch of flowers, which he had personally purchased that morning, in the middle of the kitchen island. Along with the flowers, he placed a note neatly leaning beside them. Ordering a lavish bouquet had been easy, writing the note to show his love had proved incredibly difficult. In the end, he wrote three simple words, 'I Love You,' making him realise that, in the early years, he used to tell her daily because he did, indeed, love her dearly.

Richard climbed the impressive staircase and carefully opened the bedroom door. Caroline stirred and turned over, facing away from him. The soft linen was draped around her waist and revealed her silk nightgown. The bedroom curtains were slightly open, allowing the moonlight to cast a glow that accentuated her beautiful, curvaceous silhouette.

Richard stood and stared, realising how sensual Caroline was. He felt the urge of anticipation, something he hadn't felt for years, mixed with a yearning to take her in his arms and protect her. How had he let this precious gem risk her life, part of his life? He should have been looking after her, keeping her safe. Guilt riddled his body, making him shudder.

He quietly undressed and slipped into the super-sized king bed. He studied Caroline's soft skin, then leaned over and softly touched her bare shoulder. She jolted at his touch before slowly rolling over to face him. Their eyes met, but neither of them said a word.

Richard gently stroked her cheek, his soft touch slowly moved down to her neck; her eyes still fixed on his.

Caroline felt enormous relief at her husband's touch and the feeling of safety that came with it, she knew all too well what the opposite of this felt like, it had terrified her.

His gentle caresses made her body tingle, reminding her how much she used to love his strong hands touching and caressing her. His fingers brushed across her nightgown, lightly touching her nipple; her breathing quickened with excitement. The designer nightgown she wore parted at the front and fell away, exposing her body.

Richard leaned down and tenderly kissed her lips, she responded, letting out a small groan before wrapping her arms around him. They explored each other's bodies as if they had never seen or felt one other's nakedness before, both enjoying the sexual arousal and eager to please one another.

Afterward, Richard held Caroline in his arms and whispered into her ear, "My darling, I've missed you so much."

Caroline smiled, a tear rolled down her cheek. Female intuition told her that if Richard had been having an affair, it was now well and truly over. Of course, it would always be in the back of her mind as an unanswered question, but she suddenly felt closure on her "indiscretion." She knew that if they worked together, they could rebuild the cracks that had slowly appeared in their marriage. For the first time in a long time, she felt thankful she had Richard. That night, neither of them had nightmares.

During their reconciliation period, Richard and Caroline discussed having children. They both agreed, hoping that their renewed intimacy would enable them to start a family. However, following a few months with no luck, they jointly decided that Caroline should visit Richard's fellow board member and long-time friend, Peter Willis.

Chapter 35

Caroline arrived at the surgery of Surgeon Commander Peter Willis RNR, located just around the corner from Harley Street. First, through the voice controlled electronically operated doors, Caroline then entered the inner beautiful engraved plate glass doors, sporting the medic sign of a six-pointed star featuring the Rod of Asclepius in the centre, known internationally as the Star of Life. The office oozed money, distinguishing it from a National Health GP's surgery, the room was more like a five-star hotel reception area. Caroline was the only patient waiting to see Peter, no doubt his next patient would be at least a good half an hour or so behind her. Under NHS guidelines, it would be 7 minutes per patient 'in and out' but not under Peter's private care, here every patient was made to feel like the only patient.

Caroline approached the reception desk with a young lady seated behind who greeted her softly and after introductions took down details, entering her particulars into a classically embossed folder which would eventually contain her medical history.

The receptionist, Michelle, looked demurely at Caroline before stating in a whisper, "Please take a seat, Mrs.Hartling, Mr. Willis won't keep you long," indicating, with a nod of her head, in the general direction of the sumptuous seating area. Caroline took note of the 'Mr.' Willis title, although Peter was definitely a doctor, holding a Ph.D. in medicine as well as a Naval Commander, choosing to be addressed by the preferred title of 'Mr.'

Caroline mused that she hadn't seen Michelle move from her seat, nor did she rise to greet her when she had first arrived, followed by the way she had just nodded indicating the general direction of the seating area. Why she should find this strange she didn't know, perhaps she was just being snobbish as all the comfort of surroundings and gentleness made Michelle's rather off hand actions seem out of place, discourteous and a little rude. Michelle's chair looked far too comfortable, no wonder she didn't want to get up! Although mentally labelling the receptionist as the Blonde Goddess, Caroline was conscious that her face appeared almost too flawless, mask like even. Too much make up she pondered. With a murmur of thanks, as Caroline turned to go to the seating area her eye just caught sight of what looked like a model of human hand down on Michelle's desk behind the counter. Strange she thought but then this was a doctor's surgery so no doubt there would be things like that, this was confirmed when she noticed in the corner of the room a full sized replica human skeleton with labels identifying the various parts of the bone structure. She negotiated her way between two towering Yucca plants and eased herself into a large comfortable armchair that almost swallowed her, sinking into its sumptuously padded leather upholstery. Looking around she observed on one of the walls large charts showing from various angles colourful cut away of the human skull. All this amused Caroline concluding it was a way doctor's can subtly demonstrate their intelligence, showing just how complicated the human brain is.

Recalling from memory, what was it Peter once jokingly said to her, *'What is the difference between God and a Doctor?...* She, nor any of the group she was with, knew the answer and Peter replied *'Well, God knows he's not a Doctor.'* Remembering this made her smile. Sitting in the tranquil reception area Caroline recalled another one of Peter's antidotes from a dinner party some time ago. He had held the entire dinner table spellbound with tales of his younger days, not only as a junior medic but also as a dashing British Reserve Naval Officer. Some of his stories about the old Naval Base at Gibraltar and its Naval Hospital, along with its complement of QARNN's, were simply outrageously funny. After the laughter had died down following one of his stories, a question was aimed at Peter by a young female guest. She had inquisitively asked him the reason behind Doctors of Medicine being addressed as 'Doctors' yet surgeons addressed as 'Mister'. Peter told the amusing story of two Scottish brothers living in the 18th Century; both involved in medicine, one went down the academic route to gain the then equivalent of a Ph.D. and hence to be known as a Dr. He moved in high society where he had gained notoriety as a lady's man rather than for his medical skills. His brother, on the other hand, with no medical qualifications, was self-taught in the art of surgery through experimentation, he became known for his advanced thinking and carrying out some of the very first recorded minor transplants. He had also spurned the high society life in which his brother so enjoyed being immersed. Without any formal qualifications, he was but a mere Mr, a tradition that modern surgeons carry on with to this day. However, in Peter's case, he wasn't a general surgeon; despite the naval title, he just liked the title of Mr. The whole table had sat and listened spellbound to his answer. Peter on the other hand had turned his attention, with a twinkle in his eye, towards the young lady who had voiced the question. Caroline remembered noting that Peter was adept at making someone feel like they were the only person in the room, later the lady maybe became another one of his conquests. Peter had, so many times, gossiped about overt 'flings' that Caroline once suspected that he might be gay; she later discovered that nothing could be further from the truth. Despite his many apparent 'bedding' of ladies, very few made it to his bedroom, or he into theirs. Languishing in the glow of his sexual notoriety, Peter was searching for 'the one', as yet to find her. It was going to take a very, very special woman indeed to walk down the aisle to Peter Willis.

Caroline became aware of Peter's receptionist approaching, breaking her thoughts with the sudden realisation of why the receptionist didn't get out of her chair to greet her... she was in a motorised wheelchair! The sudden sight of her made Caroline gasp being both slightly embarrassed and annoyed with herself for her rash and narrow minded assumptions.

Michelle on hearing Caroline's exclamation,

"Is everything alright Mrs Hartling" she enquired politely.

"Oh yes, just... I'm mean... I didn't," replied a rather flustered Caroline, not knowing what to say next, before Michelle came to her rescue.

"Please don't worry Mrs.Hartling most people seemed surprised and some a little embarrassed when they see me in a wheelchair in these surroundings, I'm used to it."

"Oh I'm so sorry for sounding surprised how awful of me... it makes me sound prejudiced and that I am certainly not," then in an attempt to redeem herself and genuinely sorry, she continued, "you fit into these surroundings perfectly."

It was just then that Caroline noticed the stump at the end of one of Michelle's arms controlling the power lever on the chair. This again caused Caroline another sharp intake of breath. This time and seeing Caroline's gaze caused Michelle to apologise as she was now the one to be embarrassed.

"Oh, Mrs Hartling, my turn to apologise, please forgive me for a momentary lapse I should have put my false hand back on, I'm only just getting used to it and leave it off now and then when my stump as I call it becomes a little sore. I shouldn't, Mr.Willis will chide me." With that, using her stump and the little joystick on the arm of the chair, Michelle caused the wheelchair to turn on itself silently as she returned behind her desk and retrieved the false hand then quickly fitting it in place on the stump at the end of her arm as she returned to the somewhat startled Caroline.

"There we are, that looks more presentable. So, Mrs. Hartling, Mr. Willis is now ready for you, if you would like to follow me, I'll escort you to his consulting room," she said. Michelle had such an air of authority that Caroline momentarily felt like a child being escorted to the headmaster's office. As she negotiated the corridors passing what appeared to be other consulting rooms, it was obvious that despite first appearances, Peter Willis shared the building or this floor at least with other prominent medical professionals.

Caroline walked quietly beside her not quite sure what to say when Michelle broke the silence, "I know you must be wondering about me, just to quickly explain, I was a Navy medic and picked up these injuries in Afghanistan. I'm one of Mr Willis's pioneers as we call ourselves, others would say guinea pigs in the group of injured military personnel he oversees in recovery." There wasn't time for anymore conversation as they had arrived outside Peter's consulting room where the Michelle quietly and efficiently ushered Caroline in to the room after pressing a large stainless steel button an obvious aid for Michelle's use.

Peter wasn't anywhere to be seen. Caroline scanned the room, which appeared to be equipped with every device known in the medical world. There were rows of glass showcases, brightly lit and filled with stainless steel instruments and bottles, strange lights and gadgets hanging from the ceiling and a collection of electrical equipment including computers with screens surrounded by buttons and switches looking more like an aircraft flight deck than a medical surgery. The large traditional oak desk, so synonymously portrayed in TV drama doctor's surgeries, was missing.

Michelle guided Caroline to yet another large well-padded designer chair, fitting like a glove as it seemingly wrapped itself around every contour of Caroline's body as she manoeuvred herself into it. Definitely not NHS, Caroline inwardly giggled to herself as Michelle gave Caroline an nice but slightly lop sided smile, showing off a mouthful of perfectly aligned teeth framed by glossed red lips, before turning to leave the room and closing the door by again pressing the button outside in the corridor. Just as she disappeared, it dawned on Caroline that the injuries Michelle had suffered must include nerve damage to her lovely face. Caroline experienced a sudden feeling of humility and admiration for Michelle. She would like to get to know Michelle but, her thoughts were suddenly broken when she heard the sound of running water coming from behind a screen. Peter soon appeared drying his hands on a fluffy white towel.

"Hello there," he said cheerfully, "I must say you're looking positively radiant."

Peter dropped the towel in a waste bin and crossed the room, "No please don't get up, just make yourself comfortable," he said in response to Caroline's movement to leave the chair. He leaned towards Caroline and gave her a peck on each cheek before sitting down in a large, executive style chair, its wheels hidden under highly polished chrome legs.

"Right, now tell me what has prompted you to come and see me ... when Richard called, he did mention that you weren't all that happy with your own GP, so how can I help?"

"Richard and I have been trying for a baby, but without any luck, and when I went to see Dr. Clark, he was somewhat dismissive, told me not to worry and that it would happen in good time ... he said that with the lifestyle Richard and I live, it would be a miracle anyway," her voice rising slightly, letting her feelings demonstrate what she thought to that comment!

It was music to Peter's ears; Caroline had just confirmed what Peter had hoped for, that Richard and Caroline had obviously had a reconciliation. Peter had kept his distance from Richard since the night he helped Katrina. Peter's mind briefly drifted as he rose and busied himself assembling some tools of his trade on a stainless steel trolley then wheeling it alongside the reclined Caroline. Peter often wondered if he would come to regret helping Richard on that fateful night while knowing in his heart he had been right to help a friend, a small part of him continued to suppress the fear that one day there would be a knock at the door from the police asking searching questions. He hoped that day would never come, as being an accessory after the fact would ruin his brilliant career and have him ignominiously dismissed from the Navy too. Thankfully, so far, all appeared to have been buried.

Peter dragged his mind back to the present and the job in hand, telling himself that he was a medical practitioner, not James Bond, although he sometimes fancied himself in the role as they did have the same naval rank in common.

Caroline went on to explain how she had not taken her contraceptive pill for some time, hoping for a baby, but nature had not taken its course. Her usual GP had planted doubts in her mind of ever being able to have a baby. "Well, first of all, Caroline, let's check you over, vital signs, and all that, then I'll need to do a physical examination. Would you like my medical receptionist to come in and act as a chaperone?"

"Peter, don't be ridiculous," laughed Caroline, "If I can't trust the great Peter Willis, well then, who can I trust?"

"Ok, but please, you're embarrassing me, the great Peter Willis indeed, I am but a minor Harley Street practitioner," he retorted.

Peter checked Caroline over while listening to her talk about Richard and their future. He was genuinely pleased that it sounded as if Richard had finally given up Katrina and was focussing on Caroline.

"Well, from what I can see, Caroline, you are in fine fettle. I think the next thing would be some further tests such as blood and then a scan to see what is happening with your fallopian tubes and other reproductive organs for want of better words."

Peter pushed himself back on his wheel assisted chair at the same time turning around towards a small desk in the corner of his surgery to make some notes.

"We also need to have your records from Dr. Clark, my receptionist will get you to sign a release form before you leave, and in the meantime, I am going to have you admitted to the Spire Hospital in Richmond for some tests. It will only be as a day patient, and while some of the tests that will be carried out by a gynaecologist colleague of mine will be a little uncomfortable, they are nothing to worry about," he said with a smile.

"Oh thank you, Peter, I hope there's nothing wrong, Richard and I so want a baby."

"I'm delighted to hear it, Caroline, you two will make fabulous parents."

Peter stood to open the door for Caroline, "Now, any questions before you leave?"

"Well, only that you mentioned fallopian tubes, it's just, my friend, she couldn't have a baby because hers were blocked," Caroline looked down at the floor, "Would that mean I would not be able, if mine are blocked?"

"Now Caroline, that's just a possibility and trust me, it's not a problem these days; usually it's a simple procedure of passing some compressed air through them and in nine times out of ten cases it works a treat, and I'm informed it is not an uncomfortable procedure."

"And if it's something else?"

"We will deal with that if it happens."

With that, Peter courteously guided Caroline towards the door to see her out.

"I'm surprised that Richard didn't want to come along with you," enquired Peter.

"Oh, but he did Peter; in fact, he tried to insist, but I wanted to do this on my own."

Within days, Caroline was admitted for her examination. Just as Peter had suspected, it was a small lesion that was soon sorted out by a non-intrusive keyhole surgical operation.

Several weeks later, Caroline once again found herself lying in the large examination chair in Peter's surgery.

"Well, last time I saw you, you looked radiant now you're positively blooming Caroline," Peter said excitedly.

"I feel wonderful, Peter. I don't know how, but I have resisted taking a home pregnancy test. I guess I'm scared it will be negative. Oh Peter, what if it didn't work? I mean, I think I'm pregnant, it sounds silly but it's like I can feel I am, you know?"

"Well, let's not get carried away," said Peter studiously, "while not wanting to put a dampener on your high spirits, we need to do some tests."

"I just feel that a baby is growing inside me."

"Certainly a good sign Caroline, I'm a great believer in listening to your own body and knowing what it's telling you, but let me do a scan. Please just lay back and relax while I set things up."

Caroline tried to relax, but the anticipation had been building for days. She lay back, lifted her blouse to expose her midriff while Peter busied himself, setting up the ultrasound machine. He smeared her midriff with gel and gently ran the handheld scanner back and forth across her tummy.

"Do you want a boy or a girl?" asked Peter as he earnestly starred at the computer screen.

"Surely, you can't tell this early?"

"No, I just wondered if you had a preference?" he said as he stared at the computer screen. Caroline stared up at the ceiling; silence filled the room. Suddenly, she heard a rhythmic underwater gurgling noise and turned to face Peter.

"Is that what I think it is?" she asked in suspense.

"It's more than that," replied Peter with a huge grin breaking across his face.

"What is it, Peter? Tell me!"

"I'm extremely pleased to tell you, Caroline, you are expecting twins," he exclaimed.

Caroline shrieked, "Oh my God!" Before she burst out crying with tears of joy.

Chapter 36

Dave Dundas felt 'on top of the heap' as he would put it, having dragged himself up from what he saw as his humble background. He was married to the gorgeous daughter of a wealthy local property developer, and they lived in a beautiful bungalow in the so-called 'stockbroker belt' to the west of Northwold, an area called Kirkstella. The bungalow was a wedding present from his wife's father who, although initially against the marriage to Dave Dundas, had warmed to him over a period of time, having recognised some of himself in the hard, streetwise *'Jack the Lad.'*

Dave had wanted to take out a mortgage and take ownership for himself and Samantha, but there was no way he could have legally afforded a house in Kirkstella. Samantha's father only wanted the best for his daughter, insisting on buying a house for them in the 'right area', so, in the end, Dave didn't argue. The neighbourhood was purely for the wealthy, full of solicitors, accountants, doctors and business owners. Not bad for a boy born on the wrong side of the tracks in a humble terrace house with an outside toilet, near the old fish docks, in Hull.

Before meeting Samantha, Dave considered himself a 'man's man,' usually getting what he wanted with the deft use of his fists and quick-witted attitude. Not that he was a trained boxer, strictly a savvy street fighter. In his early twenties, with his newfound social status, he'd more or less disowned his parents; his mother had been a cleaner and his father a school caretaker. The nearest Dave had come to showing any acknowledgement of his parents was the tobacco he brought in for his father and a few of his friends. Always meeting his father in his local pub, virtually avoiding his mother despite his father pleading with Dave to go and see her.

Although he'd recently renewed their acquaintance at the insistence of Samantha, who, despite having been brought up in a privileged and luxurious life-style, was no snob, she could see the way Dave was going, and so she took control of the situation. Dave liked to think he wore the trousers in their relationship but it was Samantha that efficiently managed their life to maintain this illusion.

Dave had lost sight of the fact that, having left school with no academic qualifications other than the ability to read and write, his first and very well paid job had come courtesy of his mother, who was house cleaner to a wealthy, fishing trawler owning family. The Barr Family of nearby

Grimsby had been in the fishing business since the days of sail, originally accumulating their wealth in the east coast herring business then increasing this wealth when they built specialist trawlers and moved into Boxing Fleets in the North Sea before World War I. Here, their fleets fished the plentiful fishing grounds supplying the famous Billingsgate Market to feed the masses. The money passed down through the generations where it helped turn the business from sail fishing smacks to steam-driven trawlers then modern deep sea, stern trawling, freezer ships. Thanks to Dave's Mum, he had been taken on by the Barr family as a trainee deckhand aboard one of their modern trawlers. He was no slouch and soon learnt the ways of becoming a competent seaman. He only left Barr's thanks to the EEC Common Fisheries policy which orchestrated the demise of the once great and proud British fishing industry. However, the astute Barr's being a resilient family had weathered the storm and engineered a future for their fleet. Undeterred when many of the trawler owners sold their ships for scrap metal value, the Barr's converted their newer vessels into survey and oceanic research ships and successfully took them worldwide.

The change in direction meant that the three-week trips to the fishing grounds around Iceland, Bear Island, and the Norwegian coast became four to five-month voyages to the other side of the world. That was not the life for Dave Dundas, so with his crisp new seaman's ticket and radio operator's certificate, all courtesy of paid training by the Barr fleet, he joined the Beaumont fleet, enjoying the rostered two weeks on-duty followed by two weeks off.

Dave's new job had given him the opportunity to set up a nice little extra earner in tobacco smuggling, which was quickly followed by meeting his future wife, Samantha.

Dave had met Samantha at the local Locarno Ballroom in Northwold. Samantha loved to dance. Every Monday evening, Samantha and her friends would be found dancing the night away at the iconic ballroom, bedrock of the Mecca organisation. Samantha enjoyed dancing so much she would even go on her own if her friends were otherwise engaged. Alone, she would join the crowd on the dance floor and lose herself in the beat of the music, dancing away to her heart's content, lost in her little island of tranquillity, almost trance-like. Her body was swaying and spinning, pulsating in time to the sounds of the rhythm and beat. It was on this dance floor where Dave first laid eyes on her. He was in the upper concourse balcony bar, looking down on the seething, gyrating masses, which resembled the motion of a field of corn in the wind as they danced in harmony. He was peering through the protective glass partition when he saw her, dancing alone, mesmerised as she moved perfectly in time to the music. The erotic scene went into slow motion as he watched her. Her long, glossy hair bounced in unison with her body. Her eyes closed, lost in her own private world of rhythmic movement. Her skirt flared out like a spinning top revealing her bare, beautifully sun-kissed legs.

Most of this beauty tantalisingly hidden from Dave in his lofty position but, he instantly knew that he wanted this girl more than he'd ever wanted anything in his life. Leaving his drink unfinished, he was determined to meet her. With his heartbeat rising, he moved away from the balcony and headed towards the stairs. He wound his way through the multitude of tables and chairs occupied by revellers taking a break from their energetic cavorting on the dance floor. Each set of tables and chairs were like a barrier on a military obstacle course, slowing him down physically but speeding up his eagerness to get to the stairs and the ground level before the girl disappeared forever. If the tables and chairs weren't enough, once down the stairs and on to the ground floor, the crowded mass of bodies moving around made Dave feel like a salmon swimming against the current to reach the spawning grounds. The whole mass appearing to be going in the opposite direction to him. Dave, standing slightly less than the average height for a man, couldn't see over the horde of people in front of him. He anxiously strained, stretching to his full height in an attempt to see over the multitude of heads and shoulders in a vain effort to try and spot this golden girl.

He used his broad shoulders to force his way through the crowd as his eyes darted everywhere, searching for her. Oblivious to the odd curse of 'Hey, watch it mate' Dave finally made it to the edge of the dance floor and quickly broke through the ring of young men eyeing up the single dancing girls.

Seeing Samantha still dancing alone, Dave quickly moved on to the floor. Encouraged by the loud beat of the music, he started to dance around her as she spun and twirled her body. He desperately tried to make eye contact with her, but she was too engulfed by the music to notice him.

Close up; he thought she was even more beautiful than he originally thought. Aware of someone so close, she suddenly opened her eyes and smiled, not breaking her rhythm once.

"Hi," she said as she spun a 360-degree twirl.

"Hello," he replied as he danced closer to her, watching her movements in awe.

Dave, the master of cool, or so he thought, didn't attempt to break the movement but to go with the flow. When she next twirled, he caught her hand, and with the momentum of her motion, she was suddenly in his arms for a brief moment before continuing as she turned away. He gripped her hand as they both leaned out and turned in a classic jive motion. It all happened so naturally it couldn't have been choreographed more perfectly. And so, they danced until they were both out of breath with the passion of their movements. Finally, they staggered from the dance floor arm in arm, giggling in exhaustion. Samantha was giddy with the elation she was experiencing. Amused at the cheek of Dave moving in on her like that but secretly admiring him for his sheer audacity. His confident bravado, quick wit and sharp tongue were extremely attractive to her. She had never met anyone like him, and although she knew her parents wouldn't approve, she didn't care. Samantha was used to getting her own way.

When they first started dating, he used to plead with her not to go out dancing. He would tell her, 'It's not you I don't trust, it's all those men out there,' but the truth was, it was himself he didn't trust. Dave was a realist and knew Samantha could have almost any guy she wanted; he lacked the confidence that he could keep such a beautiful woman happy and prevent her from being tempted away by sexier, wealthier men. He didn't grasp that she only had eyes for him. Dave's insecurity was made worse by her father letting Dave know of the line of bachelors driving Ferrari's, Porches and Aston Martin's that would often roll up to her parent's house with the owners keen to date the gorgeous Samantha. So Dave had quickly requested her hand in marriage and it wasn't long before they became husband and wife and he set about settling down.

Luckily for Dave, his work rota meant he was only on duty for two weeks at a time, and the ship was in Northwold every other day, making it easy for him to wrangle a couple of hours off to get home and make sure his presence was felt and known to all. Nobody was going to get into his nest! During their courtship and into marriage, Dave's little tobacco empire, as he liked to describe it, was slowly making him extremely wealthy. He did, however, keep his money and goods safely hidden; after all, he was a man who apparently lived on a basic seaman's wage. He had told Samantha of his lucrative business, but he had massively played it down. He told her he received the odd box of cigarettes that he sold on to his father and father's friends. Samantha, not knowing the full story, let it slide, after all, what was the big deal? It was just a few boxes of cigarettes for those hooked on a habit she found as distasteful as drug taking.

Chapter 37

Everything was running smoothly for Dave, until one fine spring morning when trouble appeared. Trouble that had all the hallmarks of spoiling Dave Dundas' lucrative little world, it came in the form of the dysfunctional and notorious criminal crime Lords, the Triesus Brothers.

That morning, Dave was at home on leave. He had been making himself busy in the garden, keeping on top of the weeds that were now springing into life and threatening the beautifully laid out garden. Dave was a hard man, but marriage to Samantha had softened him. He loved nothing more than pleasing his wife, and if she wanted manicured lawns, surrounded by lush bright, colourful flower beds, that's exactly what she got. When Dave was away at sea, a local gardener would come by and tend to the bushes and lawns, never touching the flowers; they were Dave's precious beds which Samantha loved and enjoyed seeing the pride and joy that he took over their care and maintenance.

He realised how lucky he was to have a girl of Samantha's class. He had to keep reminding himself that it wasn't a dream, and he really had married one of the most eligible, beautiful women in the area. Samantha felt the same about Dave, and she adored his charming masculine but boyish magnetism.

Dave had the morning to himself while Samantha was on one of her many shopping trips with her mother. He was totally engrossed in his garden. He felt that in another time, or with a different background and education, he could have been a botanist. He laughed inwardly to himself, if a few years ago he'd been told by any of his mates that he would become a devoted gardener he would probably have whacked them one, yet here he was becoming a gardening anorak almost to the point of being, and what some behind his back described as anal. He could, with ease, quote the horticultural names of many the plants he was now tending and his bedtime reading these days was Gardeners Weekly.

Just as he was bending down to collect a bunch of pulled weeds to place in the wheelbarrow, he heard the noise of an approaching vehicle. Looking up, he caught a glimpse of sunlight flash off the bright alloy wheels as the car swept into his large wide driveway. It was a huge Bentley Continental.

The driveway was laid out in an 'L' shape, the hammerhead finishing right in front of his home. He slowly straightened and felt his back twinge slightly from being bent over for too long.

'Who the fuck is this?' muttered Dave to himself, annoyed at having his quality gardening time disturbed by uninvited guests. Fancy cars were not strangers to Dave's driveway. Samantha's friends were, like her, from a world of money. Dave didn't really like any of Sam's acquaintances; the feeling for them was mutual. Many with money and status were highly surprised that Samantha had fallen for Dave, a common seaman. Many of her lifelong friends, both male, and female, visited to check up on how the newlyweds were coping. At the wedding, bets had secretly been taken amongst some of the young male guests as to just how long the marriage would last. Dave, to them, was a novelty, a sideshow, what did Dave have to offer compared to their materialistic world of wealth and privilege? Some hoped it wouldn't last, expecting Samantha to wake up and 'smell the coffee.' Many were frustrated when they could see just how loved up Samantha and Dave were.

The car came to a halt, and Dave watched curiously. This car was different; observing it was chauffeur driven. Dave continued to frown at the interruption to his quiet life and stood rigid as if protecting his land, but as the rear doors of the car opened, he unexpectedly felt his stomach muscles tighten with fear. Dave didn't recognise them initially and assumed they had the wrong property. As he walked over towards them, realisation smacked him flat in the face; he knew exactly who the two men were.

The two Triesus brothers were twins; both had round faces with baby like features. Their peculiarly large flat noses and dark skin gave their faces a slight Asian appearance. Rumours abounded that their biological father was a sailor of Far Eastern origin and they were conceived while their named father, a notorious but not very good criminal who could link his ancestry back to France, hence their surname of Triesus, was serving one of several short prison sentences he'd attracted throughout his illustrious criminal career. One unwitting soul, after a few drinks too many, had referred to this, rather indiscriminately, in a pub owned by them. Naturally, anything said in a Triesus owned venue went straight back to them. The unfortunate soul was never to be seen again. It was conjecture that he was further north in one of the concrete supports holding up the M62 spanning the River Ouse near Goole. Since that day, the Triesus brothers' ancestry would never be questioned again, at least, not publicly.

Neither of the brothers were tall, standing at about 5'4," with broad shoulders and narrow waists. Their lack of height never gave them a problem attracting women, as their persona produced an aura of animal magnetism. Their reputation always preceded them. Despite being the 'hard men', the Triesus brothers were generous to their friends and family alike. If you were in with the Triesus brothers, then you would want for nothing. In return, this bought a tremendous amount of loyalty and alibis when they were most needed. The North East Lincolnshire Constabulary had for years been trying to put them both away, without any success.

Dave approached them. He was guarded, but tried to sound friendly, "Hello gentlemen, should I know you?" Dave kicked himself for the way he'd phrased his greeting realising that his dumb question had rather given the game away. There was only one reason these two would visit Dave, and he knew exactly what they wanted. He felt his mouth go dry; he had to swallow hard to produce some saliva to lubricate his vocal cords. He did not want to show the two men that he was frightened by their presence. It had concerned Dave for some time that his smuggling enterprise was becoming too big, bringing with it greater risks, not least competitive, jealous villains. The danger now appeared to be manifesting in the shape of these two 'goons.'

The Triesus Brothers opened up with a very friendly greeting, as they moved forward towards Dave. He walked off the lawn and on to the tarmac where the car was parked. The brothers again stepped forward in unison, both offering their hands, like a double act joined at the hip; Dave didn't know which hand to take first. Momentarily recalling a local saying about the brothers, "check your fingers after shaking hands with the Triesus brothers to make sure you still have all of them!"

Both brothers spoke with a slight lisp, "I think you know who we are, Dave, if I may call you Dave!" It wasn't a question. "Well in case you don't recognise us, I am Gordon Triesus, and this is my brother Gary."

Before Steve introduced himself, Gordon Triesus continued, "Friends call me Gort, but for now, you can call me Gordon, until we become friends that is." There was no disguising the slightly if somewhat comical sinister and menacing undertones in Gordon Triesus' voice.

Gary stepped forward, his hand still outstretched in a friendly gesture.

"Please to meet you, Dave," Gary smiled.

Dave Dundas nervously shook both hands in turn. He knew the Triesus brother's reputation, feeling very uncomfortable that they had invaded his personal space by coming to his home.

"Yeah, call me Dave, no problem," muttered Dave in an attempt to sound in control. "So ... what can I do for you?" trying to show genuine wonder, but the crack in his voice made it obvious he knew only too well what the Triesus brothers wanted.

Standing in the driveway like chess pieces waiting for the next move, Gordon Triesus broke the brief silence, "Can we go inside Dave, if you don't mind that is." Dave fully understood he shouldn't refuse.

He knew a confrontation with these two was not an option to be considered, knowing better than to antagonise, he played dumb, "I'm sorry gentleman, but I don't see why you're here?"

Gordon smiled, "We would like to discuss a business proposition with you, Dave, wouldn't we, Gary?"

"Yeah, that's right," Gary added with a slightly threatening edge to his voice.

"Please come this way," replied Dave obligingly and indicating with his outstretched arm as he walked around the Bentley. Dave noticed the large driver sat motionlessly, his stony expression looking as though his face had been hacked from granite, it sent a shiver down Dave's spine, making him unsure of who he was more frightened of, the Triesus brothers or their menacing looking driver. Dave took off his Rigger boots. He used them for gardening, they were shipping company issue but being so comfortable to wear he'd casually worn a pair to come home one day having a few hours off and returned to the ship in a pair of his own shoes then drawn another set from the storekeeper on board his ship. Just like the proverbial wheelbarrow thief who walked past company security every day with a different but empty wheelbarrow! Dave was a born thief; he couldn't help himself.

He opened the door allowing the Triesus brothers to follow him inside. The brothers looked around at the spacious entrance hall covered in a deep pile, beige carpet.

"Shall we take off our shoes?" asked Gordon with a hint of sarcasm that presumed they wouldn't be asked to do so. All part of their psychological weaponry designed to intimidate Dave.

"No, that's not necessary, gentlemen, this way," Dave directed.

Dave always requested people to remove their shoes before entering the expensive hallway carpet, but he didn't want the men slowed down on their departure. A departure, Dave hoped, that would happen very soon.

The brothers followed Dave through an open archway and into another spacious room sectioned off from the main lounge, this room was what

Dave and Samantha called their 'Garden Room'. It sported panoramic windows overlooking their magnificence garden. The room had several sumptuously cushioned wicker chairs, and Dave offered these to the brothers.

"Thank you," the brothers said in unison, both pulling up their trousers slightly; the old fashioned habit adopted by gentlemen that avoided trousers becoming stretched and baggy at the knees. The brothers every move synchronised.

Dave remained standing, he felt sitting would make him vulnerable, "Would you like some tea?"

"Tea?" said Gordon over-enthusiastically, "how very civilised."

"Yes, very civilised," smiled Gary.

The double act was beginning to unnerve Dave, and he couldn't stand the suspense, "Look, just tell me, what do you want with me?"

The two brothers looked at each other with the slight hint of a smirk passing between them and raised their eyebrows.

"That's good, Dave. Let's get straight to the point. We've come to discuss your import business Dave." Dave felt crestfallen on the one hand and relieved in the other. He knew there was no point in denying his tobacco scheme as things could only get nasty, and that's not what he wanted. He was a survivor with too much to lose and had no wish to be a victim.

Gordon spoke in a mild tone, "Dave, we don't want to take anything away from you. We admire you and what you have achieved right under the noses of those "Customs scuffers.""

"We like your style," interjected Gary.

Gordon smiled at Gary's comment but never took his eyes off Dave, "You see, Dave, you've been carrying on your business on our patch, and yet we cannot remember you asking us, now that's taking liberties, isn't it Gary?"

"Liberties!" Gary repeated.

Dave swallowed hard, hoping the brothers didn't sense how uncomfortable he really felt. He had no intention of questioning their authority as to 'their patch'. Assuming the moral high ground about it being a free country, blah, blah, wouldn't work with these two. They were the undisputed lords of the Manor, overseeing all the organised crime in the Northwold area. Dave had often wondered what it would feel like if he ever did come up against the likes of the Triesus brothers, now he knew. Despite keeping his smuggling racket low key, he had always feared that one day he might come up against the big players. He was surprised it had taken this long. Dave was terrified that, despite their outward friendliness towards him, they might easily arrange for Dave to be given a 'spanking' just to prove a point and show who was in charge. The Brothers' modus operandi in the urban jungle where they operated was to be judge, jury and executioner. As Dave had taken 'liberties', in their eyes, he was expecting retribution.

Dave's mind was in overdrive as he tried to calculate his next move, a game of chess where the checkmate would not be his. The only way he could see out of his predicament was to offer them a monetary cut, 'buy them off' as it were. The main worry for him was whether he could meet their financial expectations. Would they expect him to negotiate or roll over and cough up whatever they demanded? Resisting wasn't an option where these two heavies were concerned. Paying them off would mean increasing his smuggling activity. Until now, the key to his success was that he and his cohorts hadn't been greedy, just making enough for a comfortable living but not big enough to attract attention from HM Customs & Excise.

Gordon Triesus studied Dave's face and could see that he was squirming internally in anticipation as to what they were going to say.

"Dave, I can read the concerns on your face, but don't worry we don't want to spoil your business... do we, Gary."

"No," Gary chirped, "tobacco is not our game."

The relief that flooded through Dave was somewhat premature.

"Shall I tell him Gary, or do you want to?"

"No, Gort, you tell him," answered Gary, a smile broadening across his face.

"You see, Dave, all we want to do is use your network and work alongside you with, well, how can I put this, shall we say the commodities we import."

Dave frowned before the penny dropped, "Wait... You mean drugs?"

The Triesus brothers starred at Dave impassively.

"Please, let's not be vulgar, we'll stick to the description of a commodity," a slight hint of a smile from Gordon as he continued, "or we can say pharmaceuticals for a discerning clientele?"

"You mean cocaine?" said Dave, shocked, "I don't want to be involved with drugs... I don't do drugs... I don't want to be killing kids with drugs." Dave tried to sound assertive but not too aggressive. He knew aggression wouldn't wash with these two; they were past masters at maintaining gangland discipline amongst their cohorts by taking violent aggression to a new level only exceeded by the likes of the IRA.

Gordon soon answered Dave back, feigning a polite manner with a tinge of menace, "Well, may I suggest you have a moral dilemma then Dave, as doesn't tobacco take lives? Getting kids hooked on cancer sticks!" sniggered Gordon. Gary sat with a half-smile as if in admiration at Gordon's powers of negotiation.

"Anyway, if it will salve your conscience Dave, you don't need to know what will be in the piggy backed packages."

Dave took some small consolation in the fact that the brothers didn't want to muscle in and take over his tobacco smuggling business, but drugs scared the living daylights out of him. He didn't want anything to do with illegal narcotics and didn't find Gordon's argument convincing, but he had no choice. He would just bury his head in the sand and ignore, working on the principle that ignorance is bliss. After all, it could be currency, gold, although he doubted this argument would stand up in court should he ever get his collar felt. His internal voice wasn't convinced and he shuddered with fear knowing that there was very little he could do, he didn't have the muscle or balls to go up against the Triesus brothers. He knew he was in a jam and had to go along with what they wanted or else. The 'or else' wouldn't be his elimination, he was sure of that, but it would be a good beating with broken bones or even threatening Samantha with something unspeakable, the thought made him shudder again. He'd be jelly in their hands if they threatened to harm a hair on his beloved Samantha's beautiful head. He tried not to come across as being frightened by their offer, attempting to show bravado when agreeing their proposal, although he doubted it would fool them.

Dave didn't get around to making tea, much to his relief as he wanted to be rid of the brothers as quickly as possible before Samantha came home. He couldn't see himself convincing Samantha that these two were a couple of 'chums' who had popped in to socialise over tea and biscuits. Negotiations concluded, not that Dave had much to negotiate. The brothers wanted in, and that was that, no discussion, just a talk about the technicalities. Dave and the brothers shook hands on an understanding. Now he had to sell it to the others in his group, not that they would disagree under the circumstances. They were all making a lot of tax-free money, the racket was too lucrative to give up just yet, and they would all know of the Triesus brothers' reputation, and like Dave, they would want to avoid conflict. So the collaboration deal was in principle 'signed and sealed' now it just had to be delivered.

The Triesus brothers, satisfied with the outcome of their visit, left. Dave watched from the front door as they simultaneously opened the car rear doors and slid effortlessly on to the thick, luxurious leather seats. The robot-like chauffeur remained motionless in the driving seat. Both rear doors closed with a comfortable, almost inaudible solid click, synonymous with a quality built car. Crime had certainly paid handsomely where the two Brothers were concerned. As he stood there in a slight trance assimilating what had occurred, Dave realised that crime had been good to him too, but he involuntarily shivered at the knowledge that he had just entered into the premier league. The Triesus brothers were underground royalty and, as such, owned a collection of cars that they kept in the vast garage at their home, not far away from where Dave was now standing. In addition to the Bentley, they also had an Aston Martin DB6 of James Bond fame, a Ford Mustang and a Range Rover. The Range Rover built like a tank with bulletproof windows; goodness knows what for. The Triesus Brothers didn't have enemies, well apart from certain sections of the police force, but they would hardly need that sort of protection from the local CID. Others, including the criminal fraternity, all wanted to be friends with the Triesus brothers.

On cue, the Bentley's engine purred quietly into life and reversed sedately out of the drive, executing a perfect 90-degree reversing turn backward towards Dave's double garage, where he housed a very modest Landrover Defender; the sinister driver never looking over his shoulder to carry out the manoeuvre. Dave guessed the car had an instrument panel reversing camera, only to be expected in a car of such quality, either that or the driver had eyes in the back of his head. The Bentley faced down the drive towards the road and smoothly sailed toward the open gates, its powerful engine giving away a mere whisper of the power lurking beneath the bonnet.

As the Bentley moved out of the drive, across the footpath and grassed verge to the road, it suddenly came face to face with Samantha's bright yellow Mini Cooper convertible.

Samantha, deftly handling her car, quickly manoeuvred her Mini up on to the grass verge where it screeched to a halt, allowing the Bentley access out to the road. Samantha was not amused as she cursed the Bentley driver under her breath. The day had a hint of spring, so she had taken down the roof to enjoy the sunshine. Not wanting to sound crude in her neighbourhood, she merely mouthed the word 'arsehole' at the stony-faced driver of the Bentley as it slid past her. Her anger switched to shock and surprise when she saw through the open rear window, the two brothers grinning at her like two Cheshire cats.

As the scene had unfolded, Dave held his breath for one brief moment, expecting the two cars to collide. Samantha raced her car up the driveway as though she was driving off the grid in a Formula One race, the tyres squealing as she came to a halt. Dave stepped down to meet her, going around the front of the car, opening the driver's door with a huge grin on his face. His visit from the Triesus Brothers momentarily forgotten.

"Hello, darling," he smiled.

Without getting out of her car, she looked at Dave and then nodded towards the road, "What did those two 'tossers' want?" she demanded with no attempt to hide the venom in her voice.

Without saying a word, Dave stood to one side and held out his hand to help Samantha out of the car. Her hair, so long, hung down between her shoulder blades, short at the front, layered and feather at the sides, fanning out like a cloak as she swung her head to one side. Samantha had a face of considerable beauty. Her vivid green eyes and high cheekbones gave her a Nordic look. Her mouth wide, with luscious lips, full and red, that mesmerised men. These attributes, along with her 5'5" perfect, some would say hourglass, figure made men desire her. Dave was still thrilled by the vision; he stared at her round, symmetrically braless breasts strained slightly to break free from her beige cotton top, and her shapely legs revealed as she exited from the car. Her flawless, suntanned legs exposed just a hint of white underwear. Dave jarred back into reality as she grabbed him by the shoulders, looked piercingly into his eyes, and said.

"So?"

Dave ignored the tone of her voice and attempted to brush off the meeting with a casual remark, "Oh, just some friends of mine," he replied, turning away from Samantha's penetrating green eyes in an attempt to bring the conversation to a close.

"Don't lie to me, David Dundas!" Samantha always addressed Dave by his full name when she was annoyed with him or having a 'tiff,' not that this occurred very often, but like all lovers, they could get irritated with each other at times.

Samantha first embraced Dave, giving him a chaste peck on the cheek as they hugged tightly. Both became enveloped in colliding clouds of Sam's expensive Gucci perfume and Dave's Aqua Marine cologne. Then, bending over to collect her belongings from the rear seat, Sam filled her arms with bags, clearly advertising well-known boutiques from the morning's retail therapy

She headed towards the front door while speaking over her shoulder, "They were the Triesus brothers. What were they doing in here contaminating my house with their presence?" She emphasised 'my house' which slightly irked Dave; he didn't need the subtle hint that it was her father who had paid for their home. As she wandered into the house, Dave knew she would not let this one lie. He followed her, trying to think up an excuse for the Brother's visit.

"I really do hope those slimeballs are not friends of yours; otherwise, I really don't know you at all."

She placed her bags on the floor and turned to Dave. She stood and looked at him, her hands on her hips, "So, tell me … what, exactly, were the Triesus Brothers doing here?"

Dave was shocked that she knew who they were, and he now knew that he couldn't lie. There was a brief silence between them as they stood facing each other in the spacious entrance hall with its parquet flooring, the space seems to amplify the silence between them. Dave, normally used to thinking on his feet and known for his mastery of slick answers, struggled to think clearly with Samantha's large gorgeous green eyes boring into him; he was without a diversionary comeback line.

Samantha knew a little about Dave's tobacco dealings, but he had only told her part of the story. He claimed he only brought in small amounts for his Dad and his mates. It was the only point on which he'd not been totally honest with her. Now he feared that the truth would have to come out as he could see no other way of explaining the visit of the Brothers. He was scared of what Samantha's reaction would be. He'd not lied to her over his tobacco dealings, but he had been very economical with the truth.

He took a deep breath and started explaining, "Ok, it was the Triesus Brothers," he admitted, "come through, and I'll explain."

They went through to the garden room, now warm from the early spring sunshine.

They sat down on a sofa. Dave took her hand, faced her, and gave his account. Dave was still reticent with the truth, claiming that the Triesus Brothers had got the wrong end of the stick, thinking that he had a vast empire of tobacco smuggling, again reiterating that he was only small time. He looked into her eyes as he spoke. It worried him deceiving Samantha like this, so much so that he suddenly relented and poured out his heart, telling her the real truth of his involvement. Samantha was stunned at first, completely overlooking the fact that Dave had lied to her. She was more concerned that what he was doing was not only criminal but that he was going to get involved with the Triesus brothers and drugs. She could only see disastrous consequences. How would she survive if Dave was inside?

"So there you have it, sweetheart, that's why they were here."

Again there was a silence between them, Dave expected a rumpus, even fearing the end of their short marriage? He just had no idea as to how she would react. He feared the worse and felt physically sick, seeing all he'd worked for about to come crashing down. Her reaction surprised him when she jumped up and looked down at him, his head bowed, looking at the floor, not daring to see Samantha's face or her reaction to his revelations. Dave leaned forward with his elbows on his knees looking miserably at the floor, fearing what was about to come. Samantha paced up and down in front of him.

"Right, I'm going to talk to Daddy, he'll know what to do … you see that's how I knew who those two were, Daddy knows them."

Dave interrupted her before she could go any further, "Hang on Sam, I don't want you to bring your father into this, even if he does know the Brothers. Believe me, those two are dangerous. I really don't want your father to know. This is my problem and I want to sort it out for us on my own."

"Oh yes, Dave, I know they're dangerous, but so is Daddy," Samantha raised her voice to emphasise and drive home the point.

"You are getting in too deep with those two creeps, this needs sorting out and Daddy can do it, I'm sure."

"Sweetheart, your Da-" he stopped himself and tried again, "Your father is not in the same league as those two. Please don't be foolish!"

"Me? Foolish?" She yelled, throwing the words back at him, but then smiled and looked Dave in the eyes, "You are the naive one, David Dundas! You can't deal with the Triesus Brothers; they are pure evil. They're threatening you, and that means they're threatening me as well … Daddy's not going to like this."

Dave's mind was now in overdrive. He'd often wondered how his father-in-law had created his building empire; he knew that Harry Needham had come from a similar humble background as he had.

"Tell me how your father knows the dynamic duo," he asked with a hint of sarcasm, his old confidence growing back with the thought that just maybe Harry Needham could get him out of a jam with the two gangsters who, although not admitting it, had frightened the living daylights out of him.

Samantha looked at him. She was not about to divulge everything she knew but knowing Dave wouldn't let it go; she gave him half of the story, the rest she would keep to herself.

I'll tell you, but you swear, you don't ask any questions and you never repeat a word!"

"Of course," he said intrigued.

"Well, I don't know the full story," she lied, "but in a nutshell, it was something that happened some years ago on one of Daddy's building sites. It was a derelict site he had bought, and he discovered some human remains. It was during the days when Daddy was more hands-on. He'd bought the land complete with derelict buildings that had once been part of an old wartime aerodrome. It was one Sunday, and Daddy was doing some surveying work along with Uncle Jake. They discovered the grisly remains and, naturally, were going to report them to the police. Somehow, and I don't know-how, the Triesus Brothers got to hear of their discovery and approached Daddy offering to clear up the remains providing it was all kept quiet. Daddy, being the clever chess player, was several steps ahead of them. He knew the Triesus Brothers rep for sticking their noses into everything and trying to muscle in on any business that took their fancy. Daddy saw an opportunity of ensuring this never happened with his fledgling building business. Obviously, the Triesus Brothers must have had a vested interest in the discovery not wanting it to come to the attention of the police. Unbeknown to the Brothers, Daddy and Jake took photographs using daily papers to confirm the date of the find and then secured them away in a bank deposit box. The brothers then took care of everything and were forever, and still are, in Daddy's debt."

Samantha disclosed all this information in such a matter of fact way. It was as though she was reciting a fictitious detective story. She appeared completely unaffected by the horrors of what her father and uncle had discovered. She continued, appearing deep in thought, trying to recall the incident from her memory while looking out into the garden, "Apparently, Daddy and Uncle Jake even photographed the Triesus Brothers using telephoto lens cameras as they removed the remains." She finished abruptly and appeared lost in her own thoughts.

Dave was gobsmacked at the revelations he was hearing. He knew not to ask more questions, but one burrowed into his brain, 'How the hell do you know all this?' but he knew better than to ask, instead, he kept his questions to himself and thanked the Lord for his wife.

He shivered momentarily, he always thought of himself as a 'hard case,' but this was a totally different game, it made his tobacco smuggling pale into insignificance. Realising that Samantha's father was involved in the cover-up of a murder.

When they met up with Harry to explain their predicament, Harry listened quietly to their story. Samantha did all the talking, despite Dave trying to be assertive and put his view forward; Dave meekly allowed her to carry on. Harry studied the situation much as he would study his hand in a game of poker. He asked very little about Dave's tobacco business, preferring to know as little as possible. However, Dave got a clear message when Harry looked at him. Harry's eyes said it all.

His feelings about Dave's tobacco business were made abundantly clear when Samantha had gone through into the kitchen to speak to her mother. Harry's house was palatial, as only to be expected being the home of a successful builder. They were seated in the study that was more of a lounge, being some way from the kitchen, Harry could have easily raised his voice to demonstrate the anger he felt towards Dave without being heard. Instead, Harry's voice was hard, low and guttural, sending a shiver down Dave's spine, acknowledging that that Harry Needham and the Triesus Brothers had something in common – they knew how to frighten him. Harry told Dave exactly what he thought of the smuggling racket and stated in no uncertain terms, that it was to be brought to a close, as his daughter was not going to have a con for a husband. Harry admitted it wasn't all sweetness and the like in his world; in a small way, he admired Dave for his audaciousness in hoodwinking the Customs, but where his daughters were concerned, he would do whatever necessary to keep them safe and secure from the world of criminality. Not having the courage to stand up to his father-in-law, Dave reluctantly took it on-board meekly agreeing that his racketeering must come to an end. However, pleading with sincerity to Harry he convinced him that he needed time. His connections and organisation was such that he just couldn't close it down overnight, it would have be to be done gradually and surely Harry as a businessman could see that. Although

Dave felt that he was probably in too deep with the Brothers to get out now, it was worth a try. The last thing he wanted was a 'head to head' with Harry because, despite what he had discovered, he knew he would be the loser in any confrontation.

Not long after the meeting with Harry, Dave heard from the Triesus Brothers, they had decided it was not in their best interests to go into business with him, claiming they had other import arrangements to honour. Dave appeared to be genuinely surprised by the Brothers' change of plans but avoided questioning their decision. The Brothers' wished Dave good luck and offered their help, should he ever find that he needed it to resolve problems that couldn't be sorted by conventional means. Dave's relief was tangible, knowing that despite what he had agreed with Samantha's father, he was free to continue running his empire a little longer. He realised that eventually, he would have to honour his word to her father, but he wasn't ready to give it all up, not just yet. He'd grown used to the 'wheeler dealings,' to such an extent, he couldn't imagine life without it. He had a passionate need to be more than just a seaman aboard one of the Beaumont Ferries.

Chapter 38

For the cogs of the Dave Dundas tobacco smuggling racket to run smoothly, he needed to have several people on side, or in his pocket to be more precise. One such person would be the area salesman for the British & European Tobacco Company in the region of Northwold who, with the right sort of financial incentive, would keep their Head Office in the dark. That man was Douglas Munro, the Lincolnshire and East Anglia Sales Representative for the British & European Tobacco Company. His business card described him as a manager, which sounded rather grander than it was, but, as head office pointed out, he was managing his own area, hence the appropriate title.

Douglas, or Dougie to his family & friends, was a contented man as he neared retirement from a lifetime with the tobacco company. Before coming to the Northwold area, Dougie had worked as a desk salesman in the company's Scottish office. Following his success in this capacity, the company bosses offered him an 'on the road' position; he had jumped at the offer to join the outside sales force as this was tantamount to promotion. Consequently, not only having a top of the range Jaguar estate car but by far, the biggest benefit was the freedom of getting away from the rigid 9 to 5 routine of the office. True to form, Dougie didn't disappoint those who had selected him for this new position, and he excelled in the role steadily increasing the company's market share. That was, except for one small enclave of his area, the port of Northwold, where he had failed to increase sales turnover. His poor performance there initially plagued him until one day, the answer to this problem manifested itself. It transpired that Dougie had taken over this patch just about the same time as Dave Dundas was building his empire of illegally imported tobacco. Dave had been several steps ahead of Dougie and had recruited several lucrative outlets, including corner shops, owner/landlords of small pubs, railway kiosks, a small family-run chain of mini supermarkets and the two cafes owned by the Triesus brothers. When Dougie had first come to the area, he had come across Dave Dundas by accident, or so it appeared, although it had been Dave that had engineered the meeting with the help of a friendly co-conspirator pub landlord.

It came about after what had been a long day for Dougie. He had been on his last call of the day to a small pub that he had on his customer database list. With his wife away visiting relatives in Scotland, Dougie rather hoped that the pub would be offering meals so that he could both relax and catch up on some of his admin work, while at the same time miss the evening rush hour that otherwise he would have to drive into on his way home.

Dougie found the small pub with the very traditional name of 'Coach & Horses' hidden away, squeezed in between two large modern office buildings, conspicuously built a couple of centuries earlier. Catching his eye was a much-worn set of stone steps just in front of the pub on the cobbled street, originally placed there to make it easier to enter horse-drawn cabs. Dougie was later to discover that the pub had a preservation order attached to it, gained when some local history anoraks had fought its corner when it was threatened with demolition. Despite its tired furnishings, it had become a favoured 'office workers' watering hole for lunchtimes and early evenings.

The front of the pub sported a white facade with black timbers on its five floors. As Dougie entered, it was like walking back in time. The dark interior was lit by gas lamps, adding to the authenticity of a bygone age. The open fire, in the centre of the main bar, emanated heat in all directions as the flames and smoke went up its huge stone chimney, which seemed magically suspended over the hearth. The fumes were reminiscent of his grandparents' parlour. The atmosphere wrapped comfortably around him like a warm blanket. The sign outside had advertised food until 9 at night. It was early evening, and only a few patrons occupied the bar area. Two men wearing suits, probably discussing office politics, burst into spontaneous laughter. He could overhear them sharing a sexist joke at the expense of a female work colleague. A lone bearded man sat nursing a pint of a dark brew whilst reading 'The Times,' his dark blue NATO-style sweater gave him the look of a retired seafaring type. The very nature of Dougie's job brought him into contact with all sorts of characters, and as a consequence, he felt that over the years he had developed an ability to be able to identify people's lives and occupations just by their look and the clothes they wore. Unbeknown to him so far, he was spot on with the three people already in the bar. Dougie didn't see the other person tucked in a corner at the end of the bar, to whom the man behind the bar was talking. The barman broke off his conversation with the patron, moved down the back of the bar and greeted Dougie cheerily between the two office suits and the naval type.

"Good evening sor, what can I get you?" The barman pronounced 'sir' with a slight West Country lilt.

Eying the ice-cold Guinness pump, Dougie was sorely tempted to order a pint, after all it was Friday night but reminding himself he was driving, he thought better of it.

"Good evening," replied Dougie, his eyes scanning the back of the bar registering the cigarettes and pipe tobacco on display, mostly manufactured by his company. His eyes wandered down to the rows of glass-fronted fridges sporting a whole host of bottled beers and soft drinks. Spotting his favourite soft drink, he elected for that.

"A bottle of your best Dandelion and Burdock please," said Dougie with a grin, "and something to eat, do you have a menu?" he enquired.

"We certainly do sor," he replied. Picking up a menu card from the neatly stacked pile next to the till, he then bent down to take the bottle from the chiller unit at the rear of the bar. The bar's top had the obligatory mirrored wall festooned with a vast array of optics and shelves of wine. The barman busied himself preparing Dougie's drink; ceremoniously he held up a sparkling clean glass checking that it was spotless and then expertly decanted the Dandelion & Burdock gurgling and fizzing into the glass. The landlord laid Dougie's fizzing drink on the bar counter.

"Everything on the menu is available this evening, including the specials on the board over the bar," he said whilst indicating with his head and eyes to the large blackboard above the bar, which only had one special listed, "We 'ave a very nice Steak and Guinness Ale pie, freshly made today by the wife, can thoroughly recommend it, comes with lovely creamy, mustard mashed potatoes or our 'and cut 'omemade twice cooked chips, so popular the wife can't make enough of 'em," he proudly announced with an obvious speech impediment.

Dougie was salivating as the barman gave his graphic description of the pie, and at least he'd get a small taste of Guinness too, thought Dougie to himself with a little smile.

"Och, aye, that sounds delicious tha noo, that will do nicely indeed," responded Dougie, who despite living in England for some years occasionally lapsed into Scottish phrases and words.

As the barman busied himself with Dougie's order, Dougie went into his inside pocket, bringing out his business card, which he handed to the barman when he'd finished writing out his order.

"Grateful if you would let the landlord know I'm here," stated Dougie, to which the barman replied, "Well that'll be me then guvnor, Brent King at your service, owner and landlord along with tha Mrs of course, mustn't forget 'er, this place would be not'ing wit'out 'er excellent cooking."

Not wanting to let a sales opportunity pass, Dougie engaged the landlord in a conversation and enquired about why the pub seemed locked in a time warp.

"Nice to meet you Brent. You've got a little gem of a place tucked away here," said Dougie.

"Indeed I have sor, me and the wife 'ave been 'ere for twenty years, not long to go before retirement," replied the landlord affably.

"I see from the set of steps outside that it was a coaching inn?"

"Oh indeed, ya see, the name is not just a coincidence, it was an old coaching 'ouse on the road from the north to London. I tell ya, these 'ere walls could tell a tale or two I reckon, rumoured that even Dick Turpin 'imself stayed 'ere, in disguise of course," said the landlord with a laugh as he excused himself to take Dougie's order through to the kitchen.

With so many hostelries claiming to have been visited by Dick Turpin, if only half the stories were true, then he would have been too drunk most of the time to have ever become the most notorious Highwayman of his time. Dougie laughed to himself, realising that these stories made good public relations for attracting trade.

Dougie took a long pull from his Dandelion and Burdock, quietly smacking his lips, the taste momentarily taking him back to his childhood days. He remembered how the Lemonade man would call on households, just like the milkman, and his mother would buy two bottles a week. He recalled how he was only allowed 'pop' on special occasions, high days and holidays.

The naval type didn't glance up from his 'Times' and the two men at the bar continued their secretive talk, interjected with the occasional laughter. The landlord returned and took up the conversation again.

"As I was saying, sor, the pub 'as quite an 'istory attached to it," Dougie interrupted Brent before he was subjected to the chapter and verse history of the 'Coach & Horses.'

"Can I buy you a drink?" enquired Dougie affably, intending to get the conversation around to tobacco sales.

"Well, thank you, I don't mind if I do, I'll 'ave an 'alf for later and just add it to your bill," replied Brent cheerily, as he made a note on the pad on which he had previously written Dougie's meal order. Brent had no intention of pulling the half-pint later, for him and his wife were often offered drinks but, even though they took the money, nothing was ever poured our pulled. These all added up to a nice bit of weekly pocket money. Money they could easily hide from the taxman and put towards their burgeoning pension pot.

As Brent looked up from his order pad, Dougie again attempted to swing the conversation around to tobacco sales talk, "As you can see from my card I'm the area representative for the British and European Tobacco Company, can we talk about tobacco sales for a moment?"

Brent gave a sharp intake of breath, sounding more like a sigh, "We can Dougie, if I may call you Dougie," the business card having provided this information.

"Of course, please do,'" replied Dougie.

"Well Dougie, I don't sell a lot of tobacco these days, you know 'ow it is with all the government 'ealth warnings, just no call for it. So what little I do sell to some of my regulars I buy from the local wholesaler, just not worth putting in orders directly with the minimum quantities they require, I'm sure you know what I mean Dougie," he said with a smile shouldering the blame on to the tobacco companies for their terms of sales minimum quantities. With that, he closed the conversation to serve a group of four ladies who had just entered and were making their way over to the bar.

Carrying his glass of Dandelion and Burdock Dougie wandered over to the fire and turned his back against the comforting flames, deep in thought, taking an occasional sip of his drink. It had been a frustrating day for him, his large rural and coastal patch was on the whole very lucrative for him in respect of tobacco sales, but here in and around Northwold, he had come up against negativity not experienced elsewhere. Some prospective clients had even been bordering on hostility when he had introduced himself. Dougie mused that the sales of cigarette rolling tobacco in this area should buck the national trend of statistics for what was a popular product with the predominately large blue-collar working class. With his posterior warmed he turned to face the fire, as he did so his eyes wandered around the large lounge bar area. Taking in some of the old paintings hanging on the rough grey stone walls, darkened over the years by the pollutants given off by the gas lamps and huge central fire, which according to the framed poster hanging above on the chimney stack had never been allowed to go out for more than 200 years! Hanging adjacent to this proclamation were several framed newspaper articles spanning the years, all stories about the pub's fire and the whys and wherefores as to why it had never been left to burn out, even the two World Wars had failed to extinguish the flames. Turning around, he went to find a cosy little corner of the pub lounge in which to enjoy his meal when it arrived.

Walking over to a far corner to claim the inviting looking vacant nook seat, his eyes caught an oil painting hanging on the wall just above. It was a dramatic night scene of a beach in a secluded cove, a full moon illuminating a glassy, calm sea as it lapped on to the smooth, sandy beach mirroring the full moon and bathing the scene in a ghostly bright light. The centrepiece, a sailing ship riding at anchor in the bay; in the foreground a longboat aground on the beach and several men looking like ruffians as they all did from that era. The men were busy unloading bales and barrels, obviously smugglers landing illicit spirits and tobacco. Above the scene, on the clifftop, were two men with telescopes, the lookouts keenly sweeping the sea and lonely countryside, no doubt looking for signs of the Revenue men that could either arrive overland on horse or by cutter from seaward. The artist had captured the moment perfectly, producing an illusionary vision where the figures appeared to be moving while portraying the beauty of the night and capturing the urgency of the smugglers to get the contraband away from the beach and hidden away before the Revenue men appeared. As Dougie admired the artist's work depicting the scene of criminality, he pondered whether it still went on today. After all tobacco and alcohol products were still cheaper on the continent, were they being smuggled into this port he mused? That sort of thing didn't go on today, surely not? Just at that moment, his thoughts were interrupted by the landlord's wife as she came across with a tray holding the 'Steak and Ale' pie and condiments, including a side of crusty bread.

"Hello luvvie, was it you who ordered the pie?" she asked cheerily.

"Certainly was, smells delicious, can't wait to taste it," replied Dougie enthusiastically, taking his seat in the snug corner as the landlady laid out his meal before him with cutlery and serviette.

"There you go luvvie, there's mustard, horseradish and a small boat of extra gravy along with some bread all homemade, as well as the pie, my gravy and fresh baked bread are also specialties of the house, now is there anything else I can get for you?" she beamed with pride at her culinary creation she had just laid before him.

"No thank you very much," replied Dougie, eager to dig into the golden topped pie.

"Enjoy luvvie," said the landlady as she turned away and headed back to her kitchen behind the bar, the cheeks of her large posterior beneath her white cook's overcoat moving in perfect harmony giving the impression that she certainly enjoyed her home cooking.

Dougie neatly laid out the serviette across his lap, and taking the knife and fork attacked the golden crusty pie topping, which caused a head of steam to escape loaded with the wonderful aroma of the rich ingredients. Dougie, realising that the contents would be too hot to attempt to eat at that moment, allowed himself to indulge in the wonderful smell, briefly closing his eyes as he inhaled. As his eyes opened, he was aware of someone approaching him with the appearance of striking up a conversation. It could only be that, as he was tucked away in a cosy corner which wouldn't allow for any passing traffic, exactly why Dougie had picked the spot. He groaned inwardly, that's the last thing he wanted, some talkative local spoiling the pleasure of devouring the excellent pie which he intended to do slowly, taking time with every mouth-watering mouthful. As he looked up, the approaching figure seemed to have a change of mind, or realised there was no access past where Dougie was sitting and so turned around and crossed over to the other side of the fireplace disappearing from Dougie's view. Thankful, Dougie went back to fantasising over his pie, thinking the other person must have possibly been looking for the toilet. Dougie thought no more of it, lifting the glass of Dandelion and Burdock to his lips and took another sip while he waited for the heat to escape from the pie. The pie was obviously a dish to be savoured, no way was he going to attempt to eat it so hot that it would be spoilt by having to suck in large quantities of air to cool each mouthful, rather like a gigantic 'puffer' fish. So, taking some papers from his briefcase, he looked through the day's programme, once again pondering why this area was so poor for tobacco sales. His Head Office had never queried the analysis of his sales figures, probably because on the whole they were so good. Putting the papers down with a sigh, he decided the pie would have cooled enough to start devouring it. As expected, it was everything he could have wished for, a culinary experience par excellence. The pastry was crisp on the outside yet soft and buttery inside, the cube cuts of steak infused with the taste of Guinness just melted in his mouth, all coated in a thick, rich gravy, almost as black as Guinness itself. Never before had Dougie tasted such a magnificent pie. This pie could be the winner of cookery awards.

Dougie had lovingly swallowed the last mouthful and placed his knife and fork on the plate beside the now empty pie dish, the remnants of the creamy mustard mashed potato having been scrupulously cleaned from the plate with the last chunk of homemade crusty bread. As if on cue, the landlady appeared ready to clear away the empty plates from the beaming Dougie, he looked up at her and before she could ask if he'd enjoyed the pie, he expressed his appreciation, "That, I have to say, was the most delicious steak and ale pie I ever had the privilege of eating... it should have a culinarian stamp of approval."

"Why thank you, luvvie, actually it has won a few awards, local ones in the main, although it did take a first at the Lincolnshire Show, now is there anything else I can get you?" she enquired with a lovely, cheerful, matronly smile.

"Thank you, but no," replied Dougie, "I must be on my way, if I sit here any longer after that wonderful dinner, I'll fall asleep."

"In that case, I'll get you the bill luvvie, and while I do that, there's someone here who would like to meet you," then as she stood aside, the frame of the man Dougie had observed previously approaching his table appeared, as if by magic. The man held out his hand for Dougie to take, which he did, politely standing up at the same time as he grasped the outstretched hand.

"Hello, my name is Dave Dundas."

Chapter 39

The mystery of the poor sales in the Northwold area had been revealed to Dougie. Since meeting Dave Dundas, Dougie had been happily accepting backhanders. The British & European Tobacco Company never enquired about the reason for the poor sales in the Northwold area and Dougie never enlightened them.

Dougie, now nearing retirement, was showing his patch to the next generation of salesman, one Alastair Henderson, also of Scottish ancestry, but unlike Dougie, Alastair was a born and bred an Englishman. They'd been working together for nearly a month with one more to go before Alastair finally took over the reins. Perversely, for two tobacco salesmen, neither of them were smokers. During their time working alongside each other, they'd called on all forms of retail outlets, from corner shops, supermarkets, pubs to specialist tobacco shops and the Head Office of a well-established local supermarket chain. However, Alastair was curious as to how little business Dougie had in the town of Northwold. When he questioned Dougie about this, Dougie replied that despite several attempts at trying to sell direct to the pubs and shops in Northwold, he discovered that they preferred to deal with a local wholesaler who ran his business from a large converted Methodist church. Being in the pay of Dave Dundas, Dougie had no idea how, if ever, he was going to explain the situation to Alastair.

Dougie suspected that once Alastair took over the area he would waste no time in repeating Dougie's original efforts of trying to gain a foothold in the local market and would probably, in time, find out why he couldn't make any headway. However, he saw this as a problem for Dave Dundas. Dougie had already passed on the information regarding his forthcoming retirement, after that, it was between Alastair and Dave. His 'gravy train' had come to the buffers, and now Dougie wanted nothing more than to rest quietly in retirement. The money he had taken from Dave Dundas was all secretly squirreled away in an overseas bank account in the Cayman Islands, where he and his wife intended to retire to. He knew others may raise their eyebrows as to how he could afford it, but then he did not care; people could make any assumptions they liked. Dougie didn't see himself as a criminal; he had just avoided certain outlets on his patch, leaving them free to buy from Dave. He salved his conscience by reminding himself that all he was doing was depriving his company of legitimate domestic home trade tobacco sales. The product Dave Dundas was supplying to local outlets was still from his company but coming via a roundabout route and thus merely depriving HM Revenue of their tax. Sales, which would have indeed earned him a commission, were nothing compared to what Dave Dundas was paying him to turn a blind eye. Maybe Dave would attempt to secure the same deal with Alastair. Dougie was right though, Alastair fully intended to work on increasing sales in the area Dougie claimed was unworkable. Alastair was a career-minded individual and intended to rise to the higher echelons of the tobacco company; being a successful area representative was one of the ways he intended to prove his credentials.

Chapter 40

Guy was in a smoke-filled room, flames licked and danced under the door. The smouldering clouds were thick and acrid; it grabbed at his throat, making him wretch. The more he wretched, the more he would suffocate. He needed to breathe in clean air. His lungs burned with the pain as he inhaled the dirty smoke. Suddenly, with a loud 'whooosh,' he was faced with a wall of fire. He threw his arms up to block out the powerful brightness that was blinding his vision. The flames came closer, and the heat increased. He turned to run away, but the flames were now behind him too. Trapped in the maelstrom of blinding white heat. There was no way out. He was going to die, burned beyond recognition. The searing heat scorched his body. He tried to scream, but the huge flames sucked the last ounce of oxygen from the atmosphere.

Guy Hollins awoke, terrified. His body covered in sweat. He gasped for breath, taking in huge, deep gulps of clean air. His heart raced, his head pounded, and his chest ached from the feeling that his lungs were on fire. Slowly, his heart rate returned to normal and his breathing became steady. It was always like this, the nightmare which recurred every now and then. He struggled to understand the meaning of it.

Disturbed by Guy's sudden movement, Alexandra stirred at his side. She gently opened her eyes and stretched. She immediately realised something was wrong. She lifted herself up on to one elbow and softly rubbed her expectant tummy, a reassuring touch she automatically did whenever she woke. A soft light reflected from the full moon that penetrated through the glass balcony doors. The night sky was still light as the late summer receded into winter, with the longer nights yet to come. The curtains had been left undrawn, Alexandra found it comforting to fall asleep with the night sky visible. Sometimes, the moonlight would cascade into the room and cast ghostly shadows on the walls, something Guy disliked, but he never said anything. The bedroom was built in the former galleried deck of the upper loft of the original barn. At one end were glass doors that allowed access on to a balcony offering spectacular views over the Lincolnshire countryside. The wall at the other end of the room held a beautiful, coloured stained glass window that Guy had discovered in a reclamation yard, it created a kaleidoscope of colour when caught by the sun or moon.

Guy turned to Alexandra, "I'm sorry sweetheart, I didn't mean to wake you."

Alexandra laid back down, "It's okay," she smiled, did you have another bad dream? Can I get you anything?"

"No … thank you, you go back to sleep."

Alexandra gently twisted on to her side to face him, "I think it's a bit late for that," she grinned, "you've woken us both up."

Guy instinctively placed his hand on her tummy to feel the baby wriggle around, "Are you restless little one," he whispered lovingly.

"Tell me about your dream, my love."

Guy shuddered, "It's odd, really. I find myself struggling through this thick smoke, it starts to choke me as I become surrounded by fire, and then I wake up."

Alexandra snuggled up to Guy, "It's only a dream," she said softly.

"But it's a dream I keep having. What if it's like … a premonition?"

Alexandra lifted her head slightly, she looked startled, "You don't believe in premonitions?"

"Too right, I do! And ghosts."

"Really? Wow, I didn't think you would."

"Why not?"

"I don't know really; I guess I just didn't think you were the 'type' to believe."

"Oh, trust me," Guy lifted his arm to allow Alexandra to snuggle up closer to him. He protectively placed his arm around her and gave her a soft, loving squeeze, "When you've seen what I've seen … you believe," his words hung in the air.

They lay in silence. Alexandra contemplated her next question. Just beyond the balcony doors, the tall conifers swayed back and forth. Guy watched the moonbeams as they gently danced around the bedroom. The night was breezy but mild. They listened to an owl hoot followed by a fox's strident piecing cry in the distant woods.

"Okay," whispered Alexandra, "tell me."

"Ha! No, you need to get back to sleep."

"I told you," she said as she gently touched her unborn baby, "we're both wide awake now."

"Okay, so I have often dreamt things, small things, and then they have come true."

"Like what?"

"Erm, let me think of a good example," Guy paused wondering which story to tell her, "Okay, I once dreamt that my girlfriend's Mum was going to hit on me," Guy quickly looked at Alexandra, "Maybe that's not a good example."

Alexandra laughed, "Are you sure it wasn't wishful thinking?" she smiled, seeing the funny side.

"Hmmm, maybe," he joked.

"Oi," she gave him a playful nudge, "pick another story."

"Okay, so, I had just done my first voyage, and I was on my way home to my parents for leave. I had this awful feeling in my gut that there was something wrong with Barney, my dog.

"Is this going to make me cry?"

"No, it's a sad but nice story."

"Was Barney old?"

"He was, he must have been about fourteen. Anyway, I just knew something was wrong. I had a weird feeling in my gut on the whole drive home, and when I finally got there, Mum opened the front door and burst into tears."

"Oh no, was he already gone?"

"No," Guy smiled, "that's the funny thing, it was like he was waiting for me ... to say goodbye. I ran into the house, he looked at me, wagged his tail and then he fell asleep. Forever."

"Oh Guy," Alexandra wiped a tear as it rolled down her cheek, "that's a beautiful story."

"It was so weird, but so, I don't know how to put it ... calm and peaceful," Guy smiled at the memory.

Alexandra smiled at how compassionate Guy was, "Okay, so you're trying to tell me that you are a bit freaky?" she laughed to lighten the atmosphere.

Guy gave her a tight, quick squeeze, "Oi you! That's not fair," he giggled.

"When you said, 'when you've seen what I've seen' I thought you were going to tell me a ghost story."

"Oh," chuckled Guy, "I have plenty of those too."

"Really?"

"Absolutely. One in particular still feels like it was only yesterday."

"Oh, do tell me Guy ... as long as it won't scare me?"

Guy softly kissed her head, "That depends, do you get scared by ghosts?"

"No, I don't think so," she frowned, "as long as they are nice ghosts."

"They were okay," he laughed, "so, this particular time was when I was still living at home with my parents. Our little village in Hampshire had seen a sudden expansion of new housing as more people moved further away from London. These new houses were all built alongside the village church."

Guy sat up slightly and, with his forefinger, drew imaginary lines in the starched sheet.

"My home was here," he pointed, "the village pub there, and before these houses were built I would walk through here to get to the pub. But here was the church graveyard boundary. Here, there was an old railway line, long since gone, that had become a country lane and a track to stroll along to the pub there. Then, along came a developer, and due to a 'cock-up' within the planning department, the old railway line track was covered in houses. This shouldn't have occurred as the track was meant to be left as a bridleway. The argument as to whose fault it was rumbled on for ages and eventually just got forgotten about, I guess. This meant that the only way of getting to the pub was by meandering through the housing estate which was quite a distance."

Alexandra pulled the duvet closer to her neck, "I know what you're going to say ... the new shortcut to get to the pub, from your parent's house, was through the graveyard?"

"Exactly!"

"So, did you? I don't think I would. I would go the long way round," she shuddered.

"Yes, but after a few pints and a nice meal, I couldn't be bothered, I just wanted to get home."

"Oh yes, and who were you having dinner with?" teased Alexandra.

"Nobody," Guy gave her a gentle squeeze of reassurance, "my mother and father were often away, and rather than cooking, I would enjoy the home-cooked meals at the pub. I tell you what," Guy momentarily reminisced, "the landlady was a fabulous cook, she made a blinding Beef Madras, full of spice and flavour just like when ashore in India, I've never had one as good since."

"Oh, so my cooking doesn't compare," Alexandra giggled.

"You are an amazing cook, my love; I've just never had a curry that tasted like hers."

"C'mon then, back to your story. I'm guessing you are on your own, walking through a graveyard and suddenly ..."

"Hang on, I need to paint you the full picture," smiled Guy, "okay, so, it was a dark, cold, wintery night."

"Was it?" she interrupted, sarcastically.

"Yes!" laughed Guy, "it was getting late, and the rain was really coming down. I finished my second pint and decided to take the shortcut."

"I bet it was dead quiet," giggled Alexandra.

"Hey! I was going to use that joke. Anyway, the path was a straight line from one end of the graveyard to the other. There was a lamp post at each end, not the brightest, but they gave off sufficient light to see the full length, apart from a very small patch of darkness right in the centre of the path. When it rained, the wet path would reflect the light, giving off a glistening sheen."

Alexandra yawned.

"Is my story boring you?" he smiled.

"Sorry honey, please go on, I'm listening."

"The gate at the pub end of the graveyard was one of those old, creaky iron ones, coated in thick black paint. There was an iron arch over which had an old oil-burning lantern hanging in the middle that it gave off an eerie glow."

"An oil-burning lantern? How old are you?" laughed Alexandra.

"Oi! Not that old," smiled Guy, "it was something to do with the gate being paid for by relatives in memory of a local World War One hero who died at the Battle of the Somme. As a mark of respect, the local vicar made sure it was lit every night at dusk by one of the churchwardens. Anyway, I digress. The strong wind made the tree branches sway, which produced moving shadows on the path. The few lights high up on the side of the church did give off a very weak light down the church walls, but to be honest, they were scarier because they made the graveyard look really gloomy and appearing if things were hiding in the darkness."

Alexandra twisted closer to Guy's warm body, "this sounds awfully creepy."

"It was ... I left the pub and headed down to the gate. The wind was blowing, and the rain was really coming down. Shadows weaved all over the path, creating even more shadows and a very eerie atmosphere. At this stage, I was tempted to run the full length, but the beef curry and two pints were sitting heavily in my stomach so I decided against it. I was nearly halfway when I saw something in the corner of my eye. It appeared to be an outline of a hooded figure moving across some graves to my left. I froze, unsure whether to turn or keep going. I was about to carry on walking when I suddenly saw another figure, but this one was clearer. At first, I'd only seen two, but then I realised there were others following him. They were all dressed in hooded cloaks, well habits I guess. I was already freaked, but then it dawned on me that they weren't actually walking. They were floating, passing effortlessly over gravestones. They came from the left, from behind several big old oak trees to the side of the churchyard where the new houses had been built, then crossed about fifty yards ahead of me. It was so weird; I didn't know what to do. I was rooted to the spot. Before I realised what I was doing, I was shouting loudly."

"What did you say?"

"Well, it seems daft now, but I just said, 'Excuse me'."

Alexandra giggled nervously, "Oh my hero!"

Guy frowned, "Yeah, okay, I agree it was a little odd but, due to fright, I couldn't think of anything else at the time."

"Then what happened?"

"Nothing really, apart from the one leading turned to look at me briefly, he didn't stop, he just turned to look at me. I couldn't see his face, just blackness inside the hood. I then saw the church door open and the light inside spilled out, they all quickly filed into the church, and the door closed."

"What happened next, did you turn around?" asked Alexandra, eager to know.

"No, I carried on. The thing is, as I got closer to the church, I realised that there weren't any lights on inside, it was pitch black. I was suddenly feeling quite brave, probably due to the four pints I had just – "

"Hey, you said you had two?"

"Oh, did I?" Guy sniggered, "anyway, I went up to the church door, twisted the handle and pushed, the door was well and truly locked. It just would not budge."

"Maybe the seven beers made you weak."

"Ha!" laughed Guy, "I promise it was only four. Anyway, as the door was locked, I carried on my way down the side of the church. That's when I heard it, the singing. Well, it was more like a rhythmic chanting than singing, and it was, without a doubt, coming from inside the church.

"And it was definitely coming from inside the church?"

"I promise, hand on heart, I promise. It made the hairs on the back of my neck rise."

"So, what did you do?"

"I made a sharp exit. I hurried towards the main church entrance, one of those small wooden gates with a roof. I turned to close the gate and looked back at the church. Now this is the scary bit, one of them was just stood there, as if he was looking and pointing at me but all I could see was the same darkness where a face should be."

"Then what happened?"

"Nothing. Suddenly, a van drove by, splashing through a large puddle. It made me jump, and when I looked back, the figure was gone … he'd just vanished."

"You promise this is all true; you're not winding me up are you?"

"Darling, absolutely not, everything I've just told you is the truth. I never went near that church again."

"I bet you still went to the pub, though?" smiled Alexandra.

"Of course, I just went the long way round."

"So, did you ever find out who they were?"

"Well, I did some research about the village. I found out that there was a small monastery near the church. It was demolished just before the First World War. The route the monks took to walk to the church for morning and evening prayers was exactly where I had seen them."

"So it was them? Wow! Did you tell anyone about what you had seen?"

"No way! I kept the whole episode to myself. I surmised that no one would believe me."

"Maybe you should have spoken to the local vicar or the churchwardens, even a local Parish Councillor."

"They would have thought I was just attention seeking … or drunk."

"For all you know, someone else may have seen monks?"

"Funny you should say that. It was a few years later, I took my parents out for dinner at the pub, oh! Guess what the pub is called?"

"Oh, crickey … something to do with monks, maybe?"

"Yep! The Hooded Monk! Weird eh? Anyway, we were in the main bar area when I overheard a conversation between some locals. One had lived in the village for some years, but the other had moved into one of the new houses that backed on to the church. The newcomer was saying he had seen a hooded monk walk across his garden one moonlit night."

"Did people believe him?"

"Ha, no, they said he was drunk."

"But you did? You believed him?"

"Absolutely!" Guy snuggled down into the bed covers, "I'll take you there one day, show you the pub and church."

"Maybe not at night, though," shivered Alexandra, suddenly feeling cold. They both lay in silence for a few minutes, enjoying each other's warm embrace.

Alexandra lifted her head slightly, "I understand you believe, but I don't think you need to worry about your dreams being premonitions or anything."

Guy smiled; he loved how he could tell her anything, "I'm sure you're right, it just gets to me sometimes, you know?"

"I do … but you've got me now and this little, gorgeous baby on the way. Nothing is going to happen to you; I won't let it," she said.

Guy turned to face Alexandra. He looked into her beautiful, big eyes and pulled her close. They kissed long and passionately.

Chapter 41

While Alexandra gently drifted off to sleep, Guy laid back on the pillow and reminisced about when they met on the ship. He smiled, remembering how fragile and vulnerable Alexandra had appeared. They'd shared so much within the few hours of meeting each other, he had known instantly that he wanted to spend the rest of his life with her.

Their second meeting had been just as intense. Having pre-arranged to meet at The George and Dragon pub, situated in the Earl's Court area of London. When in London, it was a favourite haunt of Guy's for a lunchtime meal and drink. Built on three levels, on the top floor, there was a cosy bar and restaurant where the music was soft, the lighting subdued, and the meals delicious. He often visited there for a nostalgic walk down memory lane. The area brought back many poignant memories, mainly of a previous relationship. A relationship that was never more than an affair of the heart, although their feelings towards each other were strong, they both knew it was doomed to failure. It had all started when he was seconded ashore by the Ministry of Defence in the nearby Empress State Building. Guy being a supply officer, although at that time albeit junior in rank, he was an ideal candidate to be appointed as the 'gofer' to a special projects team involved with the design of some planned new naval store ships. There, he met and fell in love with a young civilian lady working in the same offices. She claimed to have felt the same way towards Guy, the only problem being she was only just recently married. Guy remembered thinking that she was his one true love, only now did he realise that his love for Alexandra burned so intensely that all his previous encounters with the opposite sex were just immature infatuations.

Guy, despite the character building lessons of his encounter with the Souter family and his near miss with the lady who claimed he had made her pregnant, Guy was single and reckless and was more than happy to take part in the affair. Working in the same office made it very easy for them to meet up at lunchtime for a 'social office drink.' One thing led to another, and they soon started secretly meeting regularly. *'If only we'd met a couple of years earlier,'* they would say to each other during their lunchtime trysts, cuddled up in the corner of the top floor bar, stealing illicit kisses when no one was looking. Their romantic talk often planned the possibilities of eloping, childish talk that they both knew was in vain.

Eventually, the time came for Guy to complete his shore deployment and return to his base in Portsmouth, causing a painful lunchtime parting. Guy left in a taxi for Waterloo station to catch a train to Portsmouth Harbour, and she headed back to her life before she met him, her life of work, marriage and routine. Where ever Guy went in the world, those lunch meetings were forever etched in his romantic heart. Neither of them ever knew that their lunchtime meetings had not gone unnoticed. They were often the topic of conversation by the staff and quite a few regular lunchtime visitors who'd come to recognise the couple sitting in the same cosy corner nearly every lunchtime. They had been labelled the 'The Lovers.' Guy, when on leave, would often return to the Inn in the hope of seeing her again, but he never did. He heard that the office where they'd met had closed down and now housed a branch of the Metropolitan Police Authority.

Guy didn't really think about it when he chose that particular pub for him and Alexandra to meet, it was just a place he knew she would like, but looking back, he wondered if it was his subconscious laying to rest the ghosts of his past love.

His attraction to Alexandra had been so deep, intense and romantic. There was something about her that made him want to crawl inside her brain to see the world through her beautiful eyes. He hadn't understood it when they first met, but it was 'love at first sight.'

A part of Guy had panicked that Alexandra would cancel their second meeting. He was a positive and confident man, but it didn't stop him worrying that she might slip through his fingers before he had a chance to show her love and affection. Guy, on this occasion, was unusually late arriving at the Inn. Although he'd left in plenty of time, the traffic was incredibly heavy, and then he encountered problems parking his car. The usual places he'd used for parking in the past had long since gone. He finally found an underground car-park which left him with a brisk walk. Consequently, Alexandra was already at the venue, nursing an orange juice anxiously questioning if Guy was actually going to stand her up. Part of her wondered if she should have cancelled the date, she presumed he would run a mile once he knew her secret, but her feelings were so strong for him after just one encounter that she told herself it was worth finding out rather than guessing.

As she sat waiting, contemplating how much longer she should give him before she gave up, Guy bounced up the stairs and frantically searched for her. When their eyes eventually met, they both felt an enormous surge of passion and relief. Guy couldn't get to her quick enough, Alexandra stood waiting for the embrace. She inhaled his lovely aftershave, felt his strong arms around her, his warm chest against hers and thrilled that she was feeling a mixture of anxiety and adoration.

"I'm so sorry I'm late, my love," he whispered. He could smell coconut in her hair; he didn't want to let go. Guy suddenly realised that Alexandra had occupied the exact same seat as his past love.

As they sat and talked over lunch he revealed to her the story of when and why he frequented this pub. Was it fate that Alexandra had chosen to sit in the very same spot? To Guy, it was a good omen, but he felt that Alexandra wasn't in agreement, her restraint in sharing his enthusiasm would come clear to Guy much later.

During the afternoon, they decided to visit HMS Belfast; something Guy had wanted to do for some time. Alexandra readily agreed, although one ship looked very much like another to her she was just happy to be with Guy observing his passion for the old vessel. As they explored the warship, she was captivated by his knowledge of the ship and the way he explained every compartment, the different equipment, radars, plotters, gun laying and what had gone on when the ship had been fully operational during World War II, all a foreign language to her but second nature to Guy.

Alexandra became so engrossed in her attraction to Guy that every time she thought of her baby, her heart sank. Although now about 4 months she was still not showing, her baby was the only part of Steve that she had left, and she wasn't going to let that go. She knew she had to tell Guy before the day was through. She would understand if he didn't want to be with her but she prayed he would. Mourning the loss of a man she adored was something she already knew, it didn't make it easier, but she knew it was possible to finally lay the ghost of Steve to rest now that Guy had come into her life.

She prolonged the inevitable, enjoying her time with Guy as it blocked out the pain.

As the afternoon progressed into early evening, Alexandra grew more and more withdrawn. She had no idea that Guy was feeling the same anxieties, hiding a secret that could push her away forever.

"Alexandra, are you ok?" he asked as they sat for dinner.

Guy had chosen a restaurant recommended by a friend. It was one of the few remaining venues that actually served English cooked cuisine but it's astounding feature was the spectacular night views over London. When

Guy called to reserve, he asked for a quiet, secluded table in the far corner of the restaurant.

Alexandra was about to answer when the waiter approached them, "Sir, Madam, are you ready to order?"

"Just give us ten minutes, please," Guy stated politely.

"Of course," said the waiter, dressed traditionally in a white shirt, bow tie, waistcoat and long white apron. He was a middle-aged man with the air of an experienced professional, pale-faced from a life of working indoors, his complexion accentuated by thick black hair that was Brylcreemed flat and straight back in the style of the 1950's. Beneath his broad nose, he sported a large black moustache; tall but with a slight stoop, resulting from the years of bending over tables taking diners orders. He was polite and efficient with a slight air of forced humbleness that was the hallmark of a service professional. He quickly retreated, sensing an air of tension.

Alexandra looked at Guy, "I'm sorry," she said as she tried to hide her emotions.

Guy knew he had to tell her now. He took a deep breath and prayed that she wouldn't run out on him.

"I need to tell you something," he said softly, "I'm falling in love with you, but – "

"Don't," she said as the tears began to fall, "Please Guy … "

Guy quickly moved to sit next to her, "Please don't cry, my love."

"I'm falling in love with you too Guy; it's just – "

"No," Guy said tenderly, "I need to tell you something, and if you decide to walk out of this restaurant and never see me again, I will understand," he lowered his eyes.

Alexandra wiped her tears and took his hands, what could Guy possibly say to make her walk away from him. She was the one that had something which would make him leave her.

She momentarily forgot her burden as she looked at Guy, he appeared vulnerable, helpless, and worried.

He gazed into her eyes, and she could see the glaze of tears forming.

"Tell me," she whispered.

"I want you to know that I have never felt about anyone the way I feel about you," he wanted to smile, but he couldn't, "but I need you to know that I will not blame you if you choose to walk away."

"Guy, please, you're scaring me."

Guy looked around the restaurant; he felt like everybody was looking at him. The waiter had been ready to go back to their table but soon redirected his steps once he saw the two in a deep, tense conversation.

"Okay," he took a deep breath, "I cannot." He struggled for the right words, "I cannot give you something you may want."

Alexandra looked bewildered.

"A child." His voice was full of sadness.

"Oh, Guy," she gasped, relieved, "I didn't know what you were going to say." She gently touched his cheek and smiled; her emotions bouncing between relief and anxiety were all over the place. "Guy this must be very difficult for you, but please do not be downhearted."

Guy hurriedly continued, "I have learned to live with it, but I understand if you cannot. I need to say though, having thought about it over the years, it's not the be-all and end-all. I mean, there are things like adoption and fostering or even IVF."

Alexandra could see Guy's determination to convince her that their relationship could work; however she needed to interrupt him.

"My turn," she said, unintentionally blunt.

Guy narrowed his eyes; her reaction was so far from what he had expected. He had played it out in his head many times with a variety of outcomes, but this was not one.

She looked down and placed a hand on her tummy. She hadn't started to show yet, but she knew her body, and she could just tell that a bump was forming. Suddenly, she couldn't hold back the tears and let them flow freely, "I am pregnant. It's Steve Gaunt's."

Guy's eyes widened, and a smile spread across his face, "May I?" he asked, looking at her tummy.

"Of course," she lifted her hand on to his and pressed against the small bump, "he moves around a lot."

"A boy?"

"I don't know," she half-laughed through the tears, "I will find out next week, it's just become a habit that I say 'him'."

"Wow," smiled Guy.

Alexandra collected her thoughts. Guy's reaction had been better then she could ever have expected, but they still had a lot to talk about.

"Guy?" she looked at him adoringly, "you don't have to."

"Don't you see? It's perfect. You are perfect."

"Are you sure? Don't you want some time to think about it?"

"I knew, from the second I saw you that I wanted to be with you no matter what. If you let me, I would be honoured to help you raise your baby. Everything you told me about Steve sounds like he was one amazing guy," he squeezed her hands.

Alexandra struggled to hold back more tears as she pictured Steve and recalled the promise she'd made to herself that she would tell their child all about him; she would honour his memory.

"Are you okay?" Guy could tell she was deep in thought.

"I am now," she beamed.

They gazed into each other's eyes; they couldn't stop smiling.

The waiter, sensing the lighter mood, quickly returned to their table, "Sir, Madam, are you ready to order now?"

"Two more minutes," requested Guy, not taking his eyes off Alexandra.

"Of course, sir," replied the waiter as he politely backed away, he figured it was going to be more than just a few minutes. He attempted to figure out the situation between the two diners, a mind game he often played, his vivid imagination conjuring up endless stories to the scenarios he'd witnessed over the years. He often thought that one day he should write a book, as he and the restaurant bore witness to numerous intriguing conversations that went right back to between the two world wars, when first established. The restaurant had played host and voyeur to celebrities, Government Ministers, foreign dignitaries and ordinary folk engaged in lover's trysts; yes, its walls were keepers of secrets, like the famous wartime warning 'Walls have ears.' Fortunately, walls have no voice; if they had, then what they might tell could have made an international bestseller, maybe have brought down the odd government or two or even the odd murder occasioned by a jealous lover. As he thought about the book, he probably would never write, he turned away to concentrate on some of his other customers who actually required his services. He would go back to Guy and Alexandra later.

"Sorry to keep asking, but I'm looking for reassurance... you still want to be with me? Even with my baby?" she asked, hesitantly.

"I want you, and the fact that you are pregnant is just a bonus. I promise to be as involved as you want. You're the boss," he chuckled.

"If you want to, then I want you involved in everything. But ... "

"Tell me, please."

"I do want to keep Steve's memory alive for the baby. I want this child to know the biological father. I owe it to Steve."

"I understand, I think it's amazing that you're doing that. You are so thoughtful and loving."

Alexandra threw her arms around Guy.

The waiter appeared from nowhere, "Are you now ready to order?"

"She's pregnant," shouted Guy with glee. Applause came from the other diners making Alexandra laugh.

"Congratulations," smiled the waiter.

It didn't take them long to select a couple of dishes, both feeling slightly embarrassed at both the outburst and having kept the waiter waiting so long for their order.

Over coffee, Guy asked Alexandra to go north with him to his home in Lincolnshire.

"I've nothing with me for an overnight stay, I've left everything at a girlfriend's where I was going to stay tonight."

"Don't worry about that; we can sort out the logistics tomorrow."

"I would love to," she beamed, "I want to be with you all the time. Now, tell me more about this old barn you call your little home."

Guy laughed, "No, wait until you see it for yourself."

The drive through the night to Lincolnshire was wonderfully romantic for Guy. He sped northwards in his sky blue, recently rebuilt, classic blue Reliant Scimitar. Alexandra by his side, her eyes closed, her long blonde hair laying provocatively around her sun-tanned face. Out in the countryside, the clear night sky covered in a shower of sparkling starlight. Soft, beguiling music trickled from the stereo radio, tuned to a popular 'Night Owls' radio station. The DJ's soft, seductive voice seeped out of the quadraphonic speakers Guy had installed while rebuilding the car. He felt totally relaxed and at ease with the world as he guided the powerful car along the deserted country roads. The car headlights penetrated the inky blackness, creating dancing, ghostly shadows in the passing hedgerows. Guy could want for nothing now. He'd met the most wonderful girl in the world, and he was going to have a ready-made family. He was over the moon.

When they finally arrived at Tithe Barn, Alexandra was happily surprised.

"Hardly a 'little' house," she said in admiration.

"It's smaller than a ship," he joked, "A quick tour?" he offered her.

Alexandra wandered from room to room with a huge smile on her face.

"It needs a woman's touch," she said as she noted the blank walls and minimalistic furniture.

"This room," said Guy as he opened the door to an empty room at the back, "I didn't know what to do with, but on the drive home, I had a little thought."

"Go on," queried Alexandra.

"I was thinking … it would make a perfect nursery?"

Alexandra put her arms around Guy, resting her head on his chest. "It's perfect," she said, "and you're sure this is what you want?"

"I've never wanted anything more," he grinned.

The following morning as they both lay naked alongside one another, Guy woke with a smile on his face. Alexandra was still fast asleep. He laid there starring at her, watching her breathing, finding it difficult to believe that she'd come into his life. He quietly leaned over to his bedside table, opened the drawer, and removed a small box. He slowly opened it, just as he had so many times over the previous days. He knew he would ask Alexandra to marry him, he hadn't realised it would be so soon, but the timing seemed perfect. He smiled to himself, 'she will love it,' he thought.

He quietly got out of bed, the box and ring hidden in his hand, and tiptoed to the kitchen.

When he walked back into the bedroom, carrying a tray of breakfast, Alexandra slowly stirred. She looked at him and smiled.

"Good morning, my love," he said, smiling back at her.

She sat up in bed and welcomed the tray on her lap.

"I didn't know what you two would like, so I've made toast, boiled egg, peppermint tea, and coffee."

She smiled, "Thank you, it all looks so lovely, the bump, and I are very grateful."

Guy had chosen a pink flower from the garden and placed it on the tray. Alexandra picked it up, smelt its sweet aroma, and thought about how lucky she was. She looked at him; his smile was so big she thought he was about to start laughing.

"What?" she asked, also smiling.

His eyes directed her to the tray; her gaze followed his. She gasped as soon as she saw the box.

"Open it," he said eagerly.

She slowly picked up the box. Her grin was so big; her cheeks felt like they would pop. She pulled the lid up and the ring gleamed. Its sparkle reflected in her beautiful eyes.

"Oh, Guy, it's stunning."

Guy knelt down on one knee next to the bed and took her hand, "Alexandra, please do me the honour of becoming my wife."

Alexandra didn't hesitate, "I would love to," she beamed.

Guy gently placed the ring on her finger, "Oh, it's a little loose," he said, disappointed.

"Can we have it altered?"

"Absolutely, anything for my fiancée."

"Fiancée," she couldn't control her huge smile. "Fiancée," she said over and over again. She couldn't believe how happy she was. She studied the ring, "It's a beautiful ring, Guy, it must have cost you a fortune?"

"It's actually a family heirloom, so it didn't cost me a penny; it was my grandmother's engagement ring which was past to my mother when she died. Mum was the custodian while she was alive, and then it passed to me, to me it's priceless. I knew that one day I would meet someone very special to give it to," he looked deep into her eyes, "I knew, Alexandra, the second I saw you I just knew I would be giving it to you."

"I love it. I love you."

"If you would prefer a new ring..."

"No," she said quickly, "it's perfect. You are perfect; it's all perfect" She gazed at the ring as if mesmerised by the four glittering diamonds, "Darling, I shall treasure it as long as I live."

"And me you," he said as he leaned towards her and gently kissed her, then removing the breakfast tray to one side he pulled her into his arms, gazing into her eyes, and tenderly stroking her face. Alexandra let out a moan of pleasure as she wrapped her arms around Guy's toned torso. Feeling the hardness of his muscles she became distinctively wet between her thighs as her love juices started to flow, she spread her legs, inviting him in. Guy, now hard as a rock, moved on top of her and in one swift move, his penis penetrated Alexandra's vagina with ease, and she let out a loud gasp of delight. With Guy deep inside her, they made love, exploring and appreciating each other's body. Alexandra felt complete, nothing else in the world mattered.

Chapter 42

When Guy had found out that he couldn't father children, it was to blight his otherwise happy and successful life. He'd only discovered he had a problem after maturing into manhood. The bizarre circumstances surrounding his entanglement with the dysfunctional Souter family had left him somewhat wary. He was extremely careful not to get too involved with the opposite sex, keeping his relationships on a purely platonic basis. That was until one particular, sexy young lady walked into his life. He pushed aside his cautious mind and allowed the relationship to grow. Guy, always the gentleman, ensured he took the lead in contraception; he'd heard too many stories of male friends becoming entrapped after being careless. He was always very careful to use a condom when sexual athletics appeared to be in order, so it was a bitter pill to swallow for Guy when the lady announced she was pregnant with his baby. When Guy protested his innocence, that it wasn't possible because they always used condoms, she became extremely aggressive.

She argued, "Well, one must have split, burst, or something. You obviously weren't as careful as you thought!" and angrily demanded that he do the honest thing by her and arrange for them to marry before the baby was born. Guy experienced 'déjà vu,' upon recalling the Souter family escapade.

Suspiciously, the announcement that she was pregnant coincided with rumours reaching Guy's ears that she was seeing someone else. At first, Guy didn't believe it, their sex life had been exhilarating, and he didn't believe she would need to go elsewhere. She obviously wanted Guy and the security of marriage, so he didn't understand why she would jeopardise things.

While Guy was prepared to do the honourable thing, he had no intention of rushing into an ill-conceived marriage. However, he promised to support the mother and child financially and morally. Despite the protestations from the woman's family, Guy was adamant there would be no 'shotgun wedding,' his offer was the best they were going to get. Times were changing, and unmarried girls were not treated as the society pariahs they had once been. Weeks turned into months, and Guy was true to his word. Whatever the mother and unborn child required, Guy supplied.

One evening, following another day of 'nursery shopping,' this time for a pram, which cost the equivalent to one month's wage, as Guy washed the day away with an evening shower, he became aware of a large red spot on his scrotum. Guy, as part of his training in the Navy, had attended a medical course. The course included studying the dangers of STD's, as was the modern idiom for describing the seedier side of human social interaction of the noblest professions when sailors found themselves ashore in foreign lands. This particular part of the course was so vivid and descriptive that it could damper the ardour of the hottest blooded men. For Guy, armed with the knowledge gained from the course, seeing the red spot sent alarm bells ringing. At the first available opportunity, he booked himself an appointment at the local clinic. He was relieved when the doctor he had an appointment with was not an attractive, young lady, but an older, battle-axe of a doctor who had the looks of a matron from an old peoples' rest home or a crusty old Sergeant type running a 'Boot Camp.' A fierce-looking woman, with greying auburn hair, pulled tightly back into a bun. She had hawk-like features, sporting no makeup, her face crowned with a pair of heavy black-rimmed, featureless glasses. There was an iciness in her voice, demonstrating her disapproval that, in her eyes, Guy obviously had a cavalier attitude to sexual relations. Guy had attempted to make light of his presence, but she explained sternly, her expression completely blank, that VD was no laughing matter as it could lead to brain damage and even death. Syphilis, being the most virulent disease, displayed large red spots as its initial symptoms. Having described the spot on his scrotum, which had recently disappeared, the doctor explained it was doubtful to be VD. However, as he was there and, in her opinion, appeared to be living a very hedonistic lifestyle, they may as well do some tests. It was obvious that the doctor didn't approve of his liberal, so-called enlightened approach to sexual relations. Guy, by this point, was beginning to regret his attendance at the clinic. If he'd known then about the rather degrading examination he was going to have to go through, he would have got up and left. This was never part of the course he recalled as he was examined unceremoniously. He went ahead, suffering the ignominy of the examination with large rough fingers inserted in him, pushing against the grain to offer samples of both his blood and semen. Guy, grunting at another bodily intrusion, convinced that the battle axe of a doctor had a sadistic streak and was enjoying her job a little too much.

A week later, he was summonsed back to the clinic sending him into a mild panic. He assumed the tests had proved positive, and he was being called back to start treatment. Otherwise, surely the clinic would have just sent a letter explaining that he was in the clear.

Arriving at the clinic, he was told the doctor would see him shortly. He expected to be called to the same room as before with the battle-axe doctor. Guy was astonished and embarrassed to be called through by the most beautiful doctor he had ever seen. She resembled a movie star more than a medical professional. She had beautiful, large blue eyes and short, light blonde, naturally curly hair. Sitting demurely with a beguiling smile, he noted her facial skin was flawless. Unlike the battle-axe who had worn a traditional white coat, this doctor was wearing a figure-hugging, green two-piece trouser suit. She reminded Guy of a medical TV show, looking like she was about to enter the operating theatre. The only thing the two doctors had in common, were the plain black-rimmed spectacles she was wearing, but even these just enhanced her attractiveness and sexuality. Her green top accentuated her large breasts, the short sleeves exposed muscular biceps and broad shoulders. It was obvious that this doctor was a gym fanatic.

Within minutes, Guy was feeling very inferior to the beauty in front of him. He felt himself start to blush, something that he'd not experienced in a long time, and agonisingly he hoped she hadn't noticed. She had noticed, it was something she was used to. She looked down at the paperwork on her desk and spoke in a low, comforting voice that could melt a man's heart.

"Well, Mr. Hollins," she smiled, "the good news is that your tests are negative, there is not a trace of any sexually transmitted disease in your blood."

Guy smiled inwardly, hiding a sigh of relief, which was short-lived as the Doctor continued, "Then there is the not so good news."

Guy momentarily caught his breath, wondering what on earth was coming.

"I'm afraid we have discovered an anatomical hormone imbalance."

"Okay?" questioned Guy, unsure what the doctor was inferring.

"Do you understand what that means Mr. Hollins?"

"I don't think I do Doc, is there something wrong with me?"

The doctor gave him her Hollywood smile, "Mr. Hollins – "

"Please, call me Guy."

"Very well. Guy, I'm afraid fertility is influenced by many factors, including genetics, anatomy and hormones."

"Hang on; you're saying I am infertile?"

"Basically, I'm afraid so Mr. Hollins. I can offer you some information regarding counselling and – "

"Guy, I said call me Guy."

"My apologies. Guy. We can offer – "

"So, you're telling me that there is no way that I can father a child, right? One hundred percent no chance?"

"Yes, Mr. oh, sorry, Guy, that is what I am telling you."

"Wow!" Guy was momentarily speechless. How could he have been so stupid to fall into the trap?

"And the spots?"

"Not linked Mr. Hollins. I don't think they were anything to worry about."

Guy felt the blood drain from his face and wipe away the previous hot flush of embarrassment.

"Please do not think of infertility as being an insurmountable issue. A great deal of research is being made in this area; Cambridge University is making great strides with IVF treatment. There are numerous ways to father a child if you would wish to."

Had this drastic information been imparted to him by anyone other than this gorgeous medical professional, he would have felt dejected and miserable, but she had broken this news in such a way that it almost made the problem sound like a 'blessing in disguise.' In a perverse way it had, it proved that he could not possibly be the father of his girlfriend's forthcoming baby.

When he later questioned the parentage of her pregnancy, the infuriated young woman threw an angry tantrum, insisting that Guy was the father. When he explained his recent revelations, she lashed out, claiming that it must be a mistake. Guy threw down the gauntlet and offered to undergo further tests. Of course, he had no intention of bothering, the results from the clinic were sufficient for him. Guy was not surprised when the lady quickly disappeared from his life. He later heard that the baby produced some months later was of mixed parentage!

Guy soon got over the initial disappointment. It didn't make him feel any less of a man. He had a positive attitude to life; he accepted that in life, as in playing cards, 'you play the hand you are dealt' and get on with it. He felt that one day he would meet a partner who would accept the situation, and if they both so desired, they would then look for alternative ways to have a family. All this had changed when he met Alexandra. He'd agonised over how to tell her. Convinced that if she felt about him the same way he did her, then it wouldn't matter. To his utter astonishment, the tables had turned when Alexandra announced she was to have the baby of a dead man. This revelation turned to joyous pleasure; it was, in his eyes, as if they were destined to be with each other. Guy felt as though he had come to know Steve Gaunt, having listened to the way Alexandra talked about him. He instinctively knew that if they had ever met then they would have become firm friends. Guy, in a way, felt humbled to become the surrogate father of the late Steve's child.

...coming back to the present... Having made love they'd both fallen asleep again with Alexandra's untouched breakfast now stone cold. Guy gently slipped out of bed, taking the breakfast tray, and went downstairs to make some fresh tea.

Guy and Alexandra had one more hurdle to cross... informing all parents. Alexandra's parents knew all about Steve and their romance down in Africa, everything except the fact that she was pregnant with his child. She felt sure that they would be both shocked and happy at the same time, but now she was worried as to how they would feel about Guy. Would Guy's parents accept her and her unborn baby the way Guy had? Would they think she was looking for a meal ticket? So many questions ran around her head. Guy wasn't worried at all, he knew his parents would be over the moon and feel like both Alexandra and her baby will be part of their family. The people Alexandra was most anxious about telling was Steve's parents and as to how they would react. Despite Steve's death, this didn't alter the fact that his parents were soon to be grandparents too.

Chapter 43

After the takeover of 'Beaumont's' by Richard's British Steamship Company, the port of Northwold saw rapid expansion with the accompanying influx of new staff, both ashore and afloat. One of the newcomers was one Roger Holt. On the day Richard Hartling had discussed the future dockyard plans with Paul Craig, Roger had said goodbye to his wife and children before setting off on his way to Northwold for an interview with the company's Head of Shipboard Hotel and Catering, James Porter. James, disparagingly called 'Kitchen Porter' behind his back, did not try to make friends. He saw friendship as a sign of weakness; he was a bull of the first order and known to manage by fear. Few people, and that included some senior managers, had the necessary anatomy to confront him, most withering under his verbal broadsides. Many in the company hoped that one day James Porter would get to hear of his nick-name and be suitably contrite, but, unbeknown to them, Porter knew full well about the alias and revelled in this notoriety. To James, those who called him names behind his back were simply spineless morons.

Roger Holt, had spent many years as a purser for a deep-sea, cargo liner company. He had, for some months, been knocking on the door of the Beaumont company trying to get into the home coast trade. He had become fed up with leaving his home and family for months on end and yearned for more home life but without losing the connection with the sea. The ferry companies offered employment that would create a good work/life balance. To the casual observer looking at Roger's lifestyle, it was easy to understand his point of view of not wanting to be away for long periods. Roger, with his doting attractive wife and children, lived in an impressive house set in several acres of Norfolk's picturesque countryside. Roger realised he had reached a stage in his life when it was right to indulge himself with his family in the splendid homely and comfortable surroundings he had created.

On his way to Northwold, for the much-anticipated interview with the Beaumont Company, Roger had become lost amongst the many winding lanes of the Norfolk to Lincolnshire border countryside.

Roger pursed his lips as he neared Northwold, even after allowing himself what had appeared to have been more than enough time, he was going to be late for his two o'clock interview.

"Damn," he cursed out loud, slamming the palms of his hands against the steering wheel in frustration, "if only I had one of those mobile phones."

The invitation to attend Northwold had come as a surprise to Roger. For some time, he had been badgering the Personnel Manager but kept being dangled on a hook by the man with the same reply each time, "We do intend to employ more purser's, but they'll have to be interviewed by our Catering Boss Man, and he's very busy since the takeover by BSC, please phone back in a week or so."

It sounded like the old saying, 'Don't call us, we'll call you,' but Roger's eagerness had not gone unnoticed.

Taking a big chance, Roger had resigned from the deep sea cargo company to be readily available to attend an interview that would hopefully come his way. He'd lost the opportunity once before with the large P&O ferry fleet sailing from Hull. They'd called his home to attend for an interview, but he'd already left and was on a train going to Liverpool to join his ship and had therefore missed the opportunity of a super job with their ferry fleet. He didn't want that to happen again, and with enticing possibilities with the Beaumont Fleet, along with a few other companies he had applied to, he took a huge gamble and handed in his letter of resignation. Roger knew his finances wouldn't last forever, and even though he had other financial resources, he didn't dare touch that just yet.

Shortly before the surprise call from Roy Brooks, Personnel Manager of the Beaumont Company, one of the other companies Roger had applied to, a shipping company operating both deep-sea ships and ferries, had offered him employment. Unfortunately, the company had been unwilling to guarantee that Roger would be assigned to a plum job on the ferries, he was told it is a matter of 'Dead Men's Shoes.' Roger had no wish to take the chance of, once again, ending up on a deep-sea vessel being away from home for months on end and asked for a little time to think about it, stalling in the hope of something cropping up from the Beaumont Company. At the eleventh hour, the phone call had come from Beaumont's inviting him for an interview. Roger had immediately drafted a letter to the other company, politely telling them he was not interested. He'd left the letter in the safe hands of his wife with instructions, 'Post-it when you've heard from me.' If successful at the interview, he'd call his wife and tell her to post it, first class. On the other hand, if the interview did not go according to plan, then the letter was to be ripped up and replaced with another he'd written accepting the position. Now it looked as though he was going to screw the whole thing up with Beaumont's by being late for the interview appointment.

While driving around, lost, all he could think was, 'Oh, why hadn't I left even earlier.' The time for the interview was fast approaching, and he had a heavy feeling in the pit of his stomach that by being late, he was really going to be on the back foot, miss out on this job, and have to accept the other job offer as a consolation prize.

As he mentally beat himself up, a beacon of hope in the form of a red telephone box loomed in the distance. In the middle of nowhere, as if it had risen from the ground like a mushroom. Roger did a double take, he couldn't believe what he was seeing, his stressed out mind was in such a whirl he thought it was mirage! Why would there be a telephone box in such an isolated area? It mattered not, he was both thankful and relieved. He pulled the car over, praying that his joy wasn't premature and that it had not suffered from being vandalised. Eureka! It was in full working order. He rang through to the Beaumont company's offices and asked to speak to Mr. Porter's secretary. Turning on the charm, he introduced himself and she immediately knew all about Roger, having seen his C.V. when arranging the interview for Roger with her boss. Roger lied and played the sympathy card claiming he'd experienced a puncture, an excuse that was as old as the hills, but thanks to his smooth-talking he persuaded Porter's secretary of his misfortune. She told him not to worry as Mr. Porter was also running late with a lunchtime appointment. She kindly told Roger not to rush and risk an accident and that she would explain everything to Porter and re-arrange his afternoon diary to allow the interview to go ahead.

Beyond relieved, Roger jumped back into his car, searched for his large paper map, and started again down the road to Northwold, glad of the breathing space. He could take his time to find out exactly where he was and re-route the remainder of the journey, rather than rushing and arrive at the offices flustered.

Finally arriving at Northwold, he found his way to the dockyard. The docks were no more than a small, sleepy, seaside backwater community, an area not known as a holiday spot despite some very nice beaches. Thinking the docks looked neglected, dilapidated and in desperate need of repair, Roger's heart sank. To him, this looked like a place on its way down, not up. If it hadn't been for his wife reading him reports in the paper about the Beaumont Company, along with the dockyard having been taken over by the powerful and successful British Steamship

Company, then he would have turned around there and then. The reports claimed that the Chairman, Richard Hartling, was going to pour money into the dockyard and turn it into a thriving international passenger and freight hub, thus providing stiff competition for the nearby port of Hull. It was this statement that had started a campaign from the local residents who objected to the plans, wanting their quiet life in this rural, coastal backwater to remain just that, quiet. A protest group had started under the banner of PANE, People Against Northwold Expansion. Apart from a few diehards, they were beaten before they had really started. Richard's slick PR team headed up by Janet Houchell had moved into the area with the promise of lucrative jobs along with a major investment programme boosting the local economy which for years had stagnated with only agriculture to rely on as the major source of employment.

Having parked his car, Roger straightened his tie, retrieved his immaculately pressed jacket, which matched his knife edge trouser creases, and made his way over to the main office entrance. The receptionist led him along a corridor to an office where he met Porter's secretary. Once again, he thanked her for allowing the interview to be delayed and showed his appreciation with a winning smile. She reassured him not to worry as Porter was still running late.

"Oh don't worry Mr Holt, Mr Porter is still running very late, anyway I haven't had to mention about putting your interview back so he'll think you arrived on time," she giggled childishly. Roger was a handsome chap, and she had become somewhat flustered when he made such a fuss of her, being older, married and slightly on the 'frumpy' side, she wasn't used to younger men showing such an interest in her. Roger made her feel like a teenager again.

Roger had to wait for just over half an hour for James Porter to arrive. Roger was yet to discover that Porter had a reputation of being arrogant, overbearing and intentionally rude to everyone, in fact, an all-round nasty bastard.

When Porter finally entered the room, it felt like an explosion coming through the door. Porter was a man full of his own self-importance with a build to match. Not only was Porter the Head of Catering, he was also the company's Purchasing Manager, giving him immense power and influence over suppliers, this added fuel to his already over inflated ego. Leaving aside his less than amicable personality, he was extremely efficient at his job, having saved the Beaumont Company tens of thousands of pounds over the years. He was known to every company representative, from those working in the supply chain business to the merchant shipping industry, such as cigarette manufacturers through to victualling companies that included deck paintbrush makers, chart makers, engine spares, and so on. Just about everything needed for the Beaumont ships were purchased through Porter's office. Roger jumped as Porter erupted into the office. His large frame was overpowering and his shiny bald head made his face appear abnormally round. Roger thought Porter's surly expression was of a man who had just bitten on a piece of lemon or suffering from a perpetual toothache. Instinctively Roger stood and offered his hand. Without waiting to be introduced, Porter took Roger's extended hand and gave it a vigorous shake in a vice like grip causing Roger to wince. Compared to Roger's slender hands, Porter's were like shovel heads. Roger felt elated by what appeared to be a friendly greeting from such a weighty man, however, his feeling of euphoria was soon destroyed as Porter turned to his secretary and said, "Who is this, I didn't know I had any appointments this afternoon?"

Roger, feeling demoralised, kept a brave face as Porter's secretary quickly interjected, "This is Mr. Roger Holt, Mr. Porter, he's here for you to interview him for the purser's position." Her voice was calm yet assertive. Over the years, working with Porter, his secretary knew exactly how to handle him. Porter, in turn, relied on her enormously. He knew he'd be lost without such an efficient secretary come personal assistant. She was one of the few staff to whom he showed any semblance of courtesy.

Porter frowned, "Purser? I didn't know we were hiring any just now?"

Roger's stomach did a series of somersaults as he felt a mix of dread and nervousness.

Porter was a 'Bull in a China Shop' and often needed to be directed by his secretary as he multi-tasked. His methods looked confusing to an outsider, but he could and would move mountains, essential for the takeover by BSC.

His secretary replied politely, in a quiet but firm manner, gently reminding Porter of his current schedule of events, "You had a meeting last week with the Personnel Manager, Roy Brooks, when he pointed out that the company will be short of Purser's due to the planned new tonnage."

"Oh, yes, yes," snapped Porter, annoyed at himself for forgetting such an important fact. Although, it was probably more to do with the several large gin and tonics he had enjoyed over lunch in the Director's Dining Room while hearing all about the future under the umbrella of Richard Hartling's Company, rather than his memory failing him. Much to Roger's relief, Porter turned to him and said, "Yes, of course, Mr. Holt, do forgive me, I've rather a lot on my plate at the moment," Offering his hand again to Roger, "Do come through into my office, and we'll discuss where we are." Roger was to later learn, when he joined the company, that this was the nearest he would ever come to getting a polite response from Porter. Porter ushered Roger into his large office, closed the door, and walked behind his large pine desk.

"Well, anyway again, good day to you," said Porter in his distinguishable gruff voice, "take a seat."

"Thank you, sir," replied Roger meekly as he waited for Porter to be seated before settling himself in the chair opposite the huge desk.

Porter was reading through some papers on his desk; Roger could see that one was his C.V. He sat in silence waiting for Porter to finish, there was nothing he could say or do but just wait.

Porter carefully inspected the certificates of qualifications and eventually looked up through screwed-up eyes and a furrowed brow.

Porter questioned Roger at length, giving Roger the impression that all the questioning was just a delaying tactic to justify the interview. Roger had a bad feeling that he was going to be given the usual 'Don't call us, we'll call you bums rush' as it was proverbially known.

"Mmm... should we decide to take you on, Mr. Holt, I trust you won't emulate one of our previous pursers?"

"Sorry sir, I don't follow, I don't know anyone in this company, purser or otherwise."

Porter grunted and continued, "We have a system here whereby the purser draws the money he needs from the bank by cheque written out in the wages office for the crew wages each week. He then hires a taxi, goes to the bank to draw out the money. We did this on the advice of our security consultants. It's less predictable to the criminal fraternity than if one of our Accounts staff goes."

'Yes, and keeps them out of harm's way,' thought Roger, better a common seaman getting attacked than some posh bird in Accounts. He recalled the robbery on London docks some years ago when a lone clerk was accosted and clobbered for a ship's crew wages.

Porter continued in his gruff, almost angry voice, probably due to an increase in his blood pressure as he recalled the story he was about to relate.

"Well, one particular purser drew the money from the bank as required, then went straight around the corner to a Bookies and placed the whole lot on a horse," Porter's voice reaching a crescendo.

"The bloody horse won, and he pocketed a small fortune!" he added, his face becoming flushed as he remembered the sheer audacity of the event.

"You're joking, sir," Roger said, laughing, highly amused at the act of mischievousness.

Porter did not join in with the laughter; instead, he looked blank at Roger, "I'm not in the habit of joking about such a matter!"

Roger's smile quickly faded.

"To continue, Mr. Holt, as I said, fortunately for him, the horse romped home."

Roger tried to appear contrite, "Blimey, what a cheek! I wonder what he would have done if he'd lost the lot?"

Porter looked bitter, "Oh, he'd thought that through alright, working on the principle that we wouldn't have fired him or had him charged as it wouldn't have been in the company's best interest, not wanting the bad publicity. Furthermore, assuming we would make him pay back the money in instalments from his salary. Anyway, thankfully and very lucky for him, it goes without saying that we have changed our internal accounting procedures to avoid that ever happening again."

Then as if drawing a line under the event he continued, "Anyway he doesn't work for us anymore," followed by mumbling incoherently to himself what sounded like to Roger, "the bastard could afford to take early retirement on the money he'd won."

Unbeknown to Roger, what really annoyed Porter more than anything about the incident was that the purser in question had won so much money he didn't need to work anymore and told Porter so one day quite publicly in front of a large audience of staff members and guests, at a social function onboard one the vessels. More people turned up for the function that had been anticipated coupled with the fact that Porter had arrived late, making a grand entrance in front of the assembled group. Porter predictably did this so as to make an impression. However, due to the unanticipated increase in guests, canapés were in short supply, although chefs in the galley were feverishly attempting to catch up producing more. The lack of canapés incensed Porter, causing him to throw a tantrum openly admonishing the purser who had been in charge of the event. The very same purser who had won the windfall using company cash. He turned on Porter saying,

'Porter you can stick this ship up your arse sideways' and then walked off leaving Porter astounded and lost for words, as well being totally embarrassed in front of so many others.

Roger, answered Porter said, "I can assure you, sir, that it would be beyond my imaginings to carry out anything so audacious and foolish."

Roger, throughout his career, had often been referred to as the 'Artful Dodger', and had made illicit financial gains for himself but nothing was ever proven, so until found guilty, he swore by his innocence. Porter then surprised Roger with a complete change of posture, "Well, Mr. Holt, there's nothing else I need to know at this stage. I've seen your qualifications on paper but, as to what style of man you are in the job will only be revealed during your probationary period. So, if you'd like to wait outside in my secretary's office, she'll get you a cup of tea. Meanwhile, I'll make a few phone calls, check out your references, and if all is in order we can take things a stage further."

"Right sir, excellent, thank you sir," Roger smiled at the speed of the change in circumstances and quickly went through to the secretary's office. He closed the door and let out a huge sigh of relief.

She was smiling sweetly, "How did it go then?"

"He told me to come out here and have a cup of tea while he makes some calls to check out my references," said Roger smiling.

"Oh, I can tell you that is a good sign, Mr. Porter usually tells people he has no intention of employing right now and that he'll write to them in a day or two, so I'll go and get you a cup of tea then tonight you can have something stronger to celebrate," she said with another little giggle. Secretly she was captivated by Roger, wishing she was so much younger.

Once Roger was settled with a cup of tea, the secretary resumed working on her computer, a recently installed innovation courtesy of the BSC take-over. Roger sat quietly, cradling his tea with a smile. He looked out through the office window to watch the busy scene down on the dockyard as big tug master units ferried containers back and forth like worker ants. Suddenly, he was startled from his musings when Porter flung open the door with such force it created a small pressure wave causing Roger to spill some tea in the saucer.

"Mr. Holt, would you?" gesturing for him to go back into his office.

Standing up and putting down his tea Roger duly followed Porter in to his office.

After closing the door, Porter spun around and offered his hand to Roger, "Welcome to the company, Mr. Holt. I'd like you to join your first ship the day after tomorrow. Will that suit?"

"Err, yes. Yes, of course," Roger was somewhat taken aback.

"You don't sound too sure?" frowned Porter.

"Oh, sorry, I just, yes, I am sure I wasn't expecting an appointment so soon. It's a little short notice to get things sorted."

Roger suddenly regretted uttering those words of hesitation as it produced a look of thunder on Porter's face as he replied with a tinge of anger in his tone.

"You must get used to that, Mr. Holt, you now work for a modern ferry service. In days long gone you received three weeks' notice before joining a ship. Here it is a matter of hours," snapped Porter, not attempting to hide his annoyance with Roger.

"Yes, of course, sir, no problem, I'll be there," Roger blurted out, flustered, in an attempt to remedy his *faux paux*.

"Good I'll see you onboard soon," snapped Porter, again offering his hand and pointing to the door indicating rudely that the interview was concluded.

Having suffered Porter's iron grip once more, Roger made a swift getaway, not wanting to prolong being within the vicinity of this cold, austere, megalomaniac a moment longer than necessary. With a quick smile at the secretary, who mouthed *'well done,'* he was through the outer office door and gone.

Once in his car, he raced off to find the nearest telephone box and break the news to his wife, at the same time promising to buy himself one of the new *'fan-dangle'* mobile phones as a celebration present. He told her to post the letter he'd left with her, all being well, it would be on the other company's Personnel Manager's desk the next morning, declining their offer of employment.

Chapter 44

Roger duly joined his first Beaumont ship and soon settled into his new environment. As hoped, he worked a routine of three weeks onboard followed by three weeks home leave. This new rota gave him plenty of time to enjoy the company of his young wife, Siobhan. He also enjoyed more time with his children than he ever did when working in the 'deep-sea sector,' as the British Merchant Navy was known. He was quick to discover flaws in the company accounting system, flaws which he could easily exploit. Roger was a born fiddler; he couldn't help himself; it was like a drug to him. He prided himself on being able to spot 'loopholes,' which he could exploit for his financial gain. He always had Porter's interview story at the back of his mind, but as he said to himself on the day of the interview, 'He wouldn't be so foolish,' that is, he wouldn't be foolish enough to get caught. It had once been said of Roger that he was so crooked that if he swallowed a nail, then he would 'shit out a corkscrew!' Throughout his career in the Merchant Navy, he had fraudulently, plus a lucky gamble paying off, made himself so much money that he had to open a bank account in Liechtenstein to hide his ill gotten gains. Roger was very careful about how he spent this money, the last thing he wanted was to attract the attention of the HM Tax Inspector's office. He even kept it a secret from his wife, just in case, God forbid, he ever ended up in the divorce courts. He didn't want his private income to become the matter of a vicious argument that would expose everything to the tax authorities. Yes, he was one shrewd bugger. Whenever possible, he attended the races with his wife as she enjoyed the social occasion. Roger never bothered with betting, he left that to Siobhan who would bet the odd small amounts, Roger just needed his presence to be noted should he ever be investigated by HM Revenue'. It was a stock answer, 'Won it at the races guvnor.' Using an old ploy that a friend had told him about in order to avoid paying unearned income tax.

Roger had not always been so careful with his illegitimately acquired money and had learned some valuable lessons along the way. Before marriage to Siobhan, Roger lived with his parents in their Suffolk farmhouse, with its seven acres of land and gardens. Although a few acres were landscaped, the rest was made up of rough grass and trees. Once there had been an orchard, but over the years, neglect had taken its toll and left the orchard as a dense undergrowth of bracken. This overgrown area helped to seclude the farmhouse from the track road, a popular byway for ramblers and ensured a degree of privacy. The trees blended in nicely with the surrounding countryside and became a border to the little village church adjacent to the farmhouse. In this wooded area, Roger had buried some of his ill-gotten gains in a waterproof, fibreglass suitcase.

After one particularly lengthy sea voyage to the southern oceans of Australasia, Roger had arrived in Liverpool to learn, via a letter waiting for him, that his parents had moved to another village a few miles away. With his father's forthcoming retirement, they had felt that their current property and grounds were becoming too much for them and so they had snapped up the chance of a modern bungalow with a small garden, slightly nearer to the sea and in a location they both loved.

The letter, from his mother, dated over two months prior, had not, for some reason, been forwarded to him. It explained that the house and orchard were sold to the Diocese of the adjacent church and the remaining land sold through auction. Roger's panic in reading this was exacerbated by the speed in which the sale had gone through, anxiously he dropped everything and rushed back to the old family home. His hopes of finding the property empty were squashed as soon as he drove up the driveway. It was clear that not only had the vicar moved into the house but he had also started on his plans for the orchard. Roger's heart sank when he saw the JCB digging exactly in the position of his 'financial grave.' The whole area was dotted with workmen, all busy getting on with the job while the foreman stood discussing the land and plans with the Vicar. Interrupted by Roger's arrival, the Vicar lifted an arm in acknowledgment, "Why, hello, my boy," he had called cheerfully with a pleasant familiarity; the Vicar being a good friend to his parents who took part in the church social activities. Roger approached him, distraught and astonished at what he was witnessing around him.

The Vicar was somewhat worried by Roger's appearance, misreading his expression, "I knew you were away at sea when your parents made the sudden decision to move, but they assured me that they would write and tell you..."

"Er, no," lied Roger, before quickly remembering that the truth always came out in small villages, "I mean, yes, they did, I just er ..." His voice trailed off as he took in the new layout of the orchard.

"What was that, my boy?" prompted the Vicar.

"Yes, sorry, well, I knew they were moving, but not aware it was to be quite so soon," said Roger as he stared at his former private bank vault,

"You've torn it all down!" he accused. If the vicar noted the hysteria in Roger's voice, he dismissed it.

"Yes," replied the Vicar calmly, and with a beaming smile, "the Bishop and I had yearned for years to buy this property. As you can see, my boy, we are clearing and flattening the old orchard so turf can be laid to extend the church grounds. It will allow folks a pleasant place for a Sunday stroll in the summer, even in the winter, for that matter. It will also enable us to hold the church fetes here too. I'm afraid the old graveyard is getting rather full, leaving little room for a recreational area."

The Vicar droned on about future plans for the area, but Roger was not listening, distracted, he continued to stare at the mounds of rubble and turf. His only thoughts concerned as to how on earth he was going to recover his treasure. All the landmarks had disappeared, he was now no longer sure of its exact location. His guts were somersaulting with the task that lay before him. *'Jesus. H. Fucking. Christ,'* he thought, *'How the fuck am I going to get my money now?'*

He was jerked out of his depressing thoughts as he heard 'suitcase' followed by a chuckle.

"What was that?" Roger snapped, "a suitcase?"

"Yes, my boy. Just a few days ago Mr. Ingram here and his men were clearing that area over there," the Vicar indicated to the approximate area which was all now neatly flattened, "They were busy levelling off, clearing the ground in readiness for the topsoil before the turf could go down when the digger unearthed a large suitcase. It turned out to be full of used banknotes. None of us could believe it," exclaimed the Vicar looking skywards with open hands coming together in mock prayer, as though it was a present from God.

"S'right Gov," confirmed the foreman, still standing next to the Vicar. The foreman had an unshaved, grey, flaccid face, weather-beaten from years of working outdoors, and a noticeably large stomach from years of sinking too many pints in his local pub. "I tell ya," he said as he slowly and methodically made a roll-up cigarette as though it was some sort of art form, "couldn't believe me eyes when I sees it."

Roger's stomach contracted into a tight knot at this revelation; for a moment, he felt as though he was going to vomit. He knew he had to contain himself in front of everyone.

"What, er... What exactly did you do with it?" he breathed through clenched teeth, hardly believing what he was hearing. Roger noticed the Vicar's almost wicked smile. "Well, firstly, I contacted your parents, but they knew nothing about it, so I took it to the local police station. There's no indication as to how long it has been there, but the police were ever so helpful and explained that the banknote numbers could be traced to a particular period by the Bank of England. At first, the police thought it might have been part of the money from the Ipswich bank raid some years ago. Did you know they caught one of the fellows in the old railway cottages just over the meadow behind the church? Anyway, the numbers didn't correspond to their records so it certainly doesn't appear to have been stolen."

"Oh," Roger exhaled, "what happens now?" He tried to control the hysteria in his voice.

"The police need to make a few more enquiries, but I've been told that if it is unclaimed within six months, then there is no reason why I cannot keep it. If that is the case, then naturally, I shan't personally gain by this find, It will go into the church funds."

The foreman gave a loud cough to remind the Vicar that he was still there.

"After rewarding Mr. Ingram and his men appropriately, of course," added the Vicar with a beaming toothy smile.

"Sounds like you've hit the jackpot," Roger tried to hide the venom in his voice.

"Well, it was thanks to Mr. Ingram and his team here," said the Vicar, "the money could have been here for years," the Vicar's eyes focused on Roger giving him the feeling they were trying to bore into his brain looking for answers, "even before your family moved in."

Roger was furious at the Vicar's last remark, but kept calm as the Vicar again looked up to the sky and continued, "Of course, I believe God moves in mysterious ways and it was he who brought this nest egg to our church's door."

He gently rubbed his hands together, still looking to the heavens with a beaming smile.

Mr. Ingram smiled, placed the cigarette in his mouth, and lit it. The cigarette stuck to his bottom lip, a common failing with roll-up paper, he allowed the cigarette to rest in his lips as he breathed the smoke in and out. His fingers entwined his braces which were keeping up his baggy, corduroy trousers and he happily grinned as he rocked back and forth on his heels, no doubt looking forward to the little windfall that the kindly Vicar was going to bestow on him and his men. *'Act of God my arse'* he thought to himself.

Unable to speak further, lest he lost his temper and said something he shouldn't, Roger turned away in stunned silence, walked back to his car, climbed in, and drove off without so much of a backward glance.

"What a strange boy," pondered the Vicar, "not to say goodbye."

"Pe'raps 'e's jealous Vicar. T'was found on 'is old land, after all, yep, I bet he wished it were him that got it."

"You may well be right there Mr. Ingram," the Vicar turned, ready to change the subject, "Well, how would you and your men like some tea?" he enquired in his fatherly, ecclesiastical way.

"Yep, gov'nor, that should do the trick."

It took Roger several years to replace the lost cash. However, he was to make even more illicit money in his new position with the Beaumont Company. During the first few months of his employment, he kept his nose clean, his 'fingers out of the till' and settled into his new job. He intended to watch and learn the accounting ways of his new company, looking for the loopholes that his fertile mind could exploit.

Not long after joining his first ship, he discovered that BSC, the company that'd recently acquired Beaumont Ferries, announced that if it all went to plan, they would put two of their newest vessels on the Northwold to Europe service. Roger thought the future looked rosy, and he set his heart on being appointed to one of the new super jumbo ferries. In the meantime, he sought from colleagues information that would indicate the existence of an established scheme in which he might participate. His discreet enquiries proved fruitless; he was greeted with a wall of cold, obstinate silence. This silence convinced him that something lucrative was going on, but that being the newcomer, he wasn't going to be allowed in on it. Nothing could have been further from the truth. Despite what he convinced himself to believe, there really was nothing going on.

One of his purser colleagues became so exasperated with Roger and his constant niggling, "Look Roger, for fuck's sake, stop looking for something that isn't there. You know as well as I do that, yes, it used to go on, even the companies knew it went on, starting at the top and working its way through. It's well known the substandard meat that came on-board was paid for as prime best, with the difference in cost getting split between the chandler and the purser, even Masters. Things are different here, we are all well paid, some shore-side say 'too well paid,' so just forget it before you draw attention to yourself as a 'bad penny.' With a bugger like Kitchen Porter, you won't last five fucking minutes, although it's no doubt he was probably the biggest, robbing bastard that ever sailed the seven seas!" As he continued, "But that was yesteryear, we live in a different world now."

Roger, suitably admonished, took the hint conceding that indeed this was a good berth, as it is said in maritime circles. He had waited long enough for this sort of job to turn up and thought no more of it. That was until events took an advantageous turn when an opportunity quite unexpectedly came his way.

Chapter 45

n his position as purser, Roger came into contact with many of the office staff. It was purely by accident that he picked up on a gem of information as to how the company accounted for passengers, the commercial drivers and the number of meals consumed. He discovered that providing what was known as the 'feeding rate per head per day' was within the budgeted figure, then the company finance managers accepted that all was in order with very little, if any, checking done. Management used the 'old adage', 'If it ain't broke, don't fix it.' In fact, the way the system worked was very hard for retrospective checking to be carried out effectively. Roger realised that he had discovered the loophole he could exploit. After very carefully doing his homework, he was convinced that he alone had discovered the flaw. He soon managed to confirm what he thought; the Freight Department worked independently from the Passenger Department. The ferry had separated accommodation for commercial drivers from the car passengers, and while the car passengers were ticketed and allocated cabins on a cabin manifest, the commercial drivers were not. Sometimes, vehicles would board as a tractor unit and trailer with the driver taking a cabin, but often the trailer was just dropped on board, and the tractor unit returned ashore, leaving the trailer to be hooked up to a tractor unit on the other side of the crossing.

Consequently, when this happened, not all the commercial cabins were occupied. The number of trailers on the vessel matched the number of cabins available, but in reality, many cabins were left vacant. Roger then showed these cabins as occupied which when calculated into the daily victualling rate produced an on paper cash surplus. However, if he submitted the victualling accounts in this way, someone in the accountant's office would question the surplus. So, Roger just needed some false invoices to balance the books, have these false invoices paid, and then somehow launder the money.

The key to this was, of course, a crooked supplier. A supplier who would submit the invoices and collect the money for distribution to those involved with the fraud. The final piece of the jigsaw fell into place in the form of local chandler, Freddie Naylor, a Beaumont supplier with whom Roger had cultivated a friendship along with Freddie's wife, Tatiana. They had become good friends and often went out to dinner, along with Roger's wife, Siobhan. As their friendship developed, it included going to stay at Freddie's large detached villa on the Portuguese, southern

Atlantic, Algarve coast. It was while staying there, following a long lazy lunch down by the beach in their favourite fish restaurant, that the opportunity arose for discussion. Siobhan and Tatiana had taken themselves off for retail therapy, leaving Roger and Freddie to enjoy a few brandies in the relaxing atmosphere. They moved out of the air-conditioned restaurant to occupy comfortable, well-upholstered chairs in the shaded patio area. The smell of the ocean gently lingered in the warm sea breeze, the aroma fresh and clean. The sun's reflection, sparkling and glinting as it danced off the inshore wavelets surrounding the many moored pleasure boat toys of the rich, mixing in with the hard worked fishing smacks having returned from the morning's expedition.

The conversation soon turned to reminiscing about days gone. In particular, when Purser, Chief Steward, and Captain would regularly receive an envelope from the ship's chandler containing an appropriate offering of thanks for the store's order to replenish the vessel's stock of food, oil or ropes and shackles. Of course, the reality was that the invoices had been padded to cover this 'backhander.' Thus, this so-called gift was, in reality, being paid for by the ship owners.

"Aah yes, those were the days," sighed Freddie, "but with computers, the times have changed."

"Not necessarily," said Roger eyeing Freddie over the rim of his brandy balloon as he took a sip of the smooth, golden nectar trying to judge Freddie's reaction before revealing more, gambling, not wanting to spoil their friendship with what he was about to say.

Freddie raised an eyebrow, "Go on... how?"

"Never mind how, but if it doesn't bother your conscience Freddie, would you be prepared to submit invoices for stuff I haven't actually received on-board?"

Freddie was intrigued, "Why do you need my invoices?"

"To make us both some extra money, that's why. So, what do you think?"

"I like it, but I'm not sure I understand," Freddie was slightly puzzled as to why Roger should want invoices for foodstuffs he wasn't actually going to receive; it was not innocence that was slowing his thought process, but the haze of brandy. After all, he thought to himself, his beautiful property, here in the sun, was a paid for product of the long-gone 'Good Old Days.'

Roger stared at Freddie for a few moments with a slight hint of a grin. Suddenly, the penny dropped with Freddie and with a snap of his finger and thumb, causing the distant waiter to look in their direction anticipating that they required some service, "By Jove, I see where you are coming from old boy," he leaned forward with excitement, "do you think it can be done, I mean, seriously?"

"You bet it can; otherwise, we wouldn't be having this conversation Freddie," Roger smiled. "All you need to do is present me with the invoices, I'll tell you what I want to be listed and the total amounts, I'll sign them as received, and then you present them for payment in the normal way at the end of each month." Roger enjoyed a sip of his brandy before carrying on, "After payment from Beaumont's, you keep forty percent of the total, the remaining sixty percent comes to moi, couldn't be simpler."

Freddie was silent for a few minutes; this briefly worried Roger that he'd gone too far, suspecting Freddie didn't want anything to do with his proposal.

"Are you sure it can be done?" queried Freddie, still unsure of what he was getting himself into.

"Positive," smiled Roger.

Another silence followed as the two men regarded each other, both wondering if their friendship could stand this sort of skulduggery.

Freddie looked down in thought, "Isn't the cut a trifle uneven?"

"No, not when you consider I'm taking all the risks, having to lose those invoices through the ship's books."

Freddie cleared his throat as he thought it through, "Ok, I understand and I'm not going to ask how you'll do it."

"I wouldn't tell you anyway," interjected Roger, "trust me... best if you don't know."

"Yes, I agree. Who else would be in on it? You're not on the ship all of the time, what about your opposite number, what if he found out and blew the whistle, I'm too old to end up doing a stretch, 'cos that's what we'd get Rog."

"Nobody else would need to be involved, just you and me. As for my running partner, I've already taken care of that. I have agreed with him that I'll manage the victualling account, leaving him to do the bar and cash accounts. The victualling account is always a pain, stock-taking the freezers and dry storerooms, so he's more than happy with the workload split. When I'm on leave, and the accounts are due to be closed, I'll just come back to close them; he will do the same for me with the bar and cash accounts. Anyway, we can only do it for the first part of each quarter, the latter part being far too easy for anyone in the accounts office to check up on."

"Are you sure we can't get caught out?" There was obvious worry in Freddie's voice.

"Absolutely Freddie, what I've discovered is fool proof, trust me, I wouldn't do it if I thought there was a chance we would get caught."

"You've obviously given this a great deal of consideration."

"Indeed. You could say I was a past master at this sort of thing," Roger smiled, "the only way this will get discovered is if you or I mention it to anyone, but that is not going to happen, is it?"

"Certainly not," declared Freddie before he slapped his knee and declared, "Right, count me in! When do we start with invoices?"

"When we get home, after this holiday, when I re-join for my next tour."

"Fine by me, but remember Beaumont's aren't very prompt payers so I can't promise when I'll be able to settle with you," Freddie said hesitantly.

"Not to worry, any time will do. I trust you Freddie."

"This calls for a celebration, shall we have a bottle of champagne?"

"No I think not," replied Roger sternly, "we don't want to attract attention by living the high life, that's something you mustn't do, this will be our rainy day fund for later in our lives."

"Yes, quite right, sorry. Okay, two more brandies it is then," said Freddie, lifting his arm indicating for the waiter to come over.

A shake of hands and another brandy each sealed the deal.

"You two look very happy," said Tatiana as she and Siobhan sat down, both surrounded by bags of shopping, "in fact, you look as though you are the cats that have got the cream."

Roger and Freddie just looked at each other with a knowing grin.

And so it began, Roger and Freddie started their little, well actually a large scam, filling their coffers at the expense of the Beaumont Company.

Chapter 46

Not only was Roger Holt a born thief, not that he would ever go to the lengths of robbing a bank as he thought of himself as a strictly white-collar criminal, but another side to his character was that of a philanderer, he just couldn't help himself despite being married to a very attractive, sexy lady. Roger was basically like a tom cat seeking his prey; while he loved his wife Siobhan dearly, he just couldn't resist the excitement of the chase to conquer the women who took his fancy sexually. The fun of the hunt was all it was to Roger. He would never dream of leaving Siobhan for another woman. He loved the gameplay, sex with no emotional entanglement. His boyish looks and glib tongue were the only tools in his armoury but it was enough to get him what he wanted. As a predatory male, Roger was very particular when choosing his conquests, always focusing on women who had just as much to lose as he did; this being a form of insurance policy. His sixth sense enabled him to pick out women who were sexually bored but not stupid enough to risk losing what they had through the divorce courts.

They were always married women, ladies who were well provided for by their husbands but who wanted or needed a little something on the side with no strings attached. Roger was the tonic they were looking for.

It wasn't long before Roger received the *'come on'* from several of the young women who worked in the company shore offices at Northwold, but much to their annoyance, he gave them all a wide berth. It was not his intention to become involved with some young 'filly,' as he called them, looking for marriage, security, kids and the like. The fact that Roger was married was a mere obstacle to overcome in the eyes of some. After all, divorces were happening all around, it was par for the course in the stakes of love and marriage, but Roger did everything he could to ensure he would never be facing a divorce settlement, what would be a costly price to pay for a casual 'shag.'

Since joining Beaumont's, Roger felt he had found a suitable target for some extra-marital fun. He had cultivated a friendly relationship with a lady called Ann Clark, who also worked for the company. Ann was apparently an estranged lady, ten years his senior, brunette with a luscious full figure and the gift of looking much younger than her years. To look at, many wouldn't believe Ann had a teenage daughter. Ann worked for the Beaumont Company's Engineering Superintendent's department, which looked after general shipboard maintenance repairs, her role included visiting the vessels of the Beaumont fleet regularly. Encountering Roger, on one such visit, she had been flattered by his charm and attentiveness. She was a woman who had several male conquests in her life, and it didn't take her long to realise that she wanted Roger as much as he wanted her.

It all started one Sunday afternoon when Roger's ship was in port at Northwold on lay-over. Lunch was over, and most of the crew had disappeared for the remainder of the day. He was in his cabin, immediately behind the Purser's Bureau, lounging on his day-bed and browsing through a recent issue of *'Sea Breezes'* magazine when he heard a knock on the outer office door.

"Yes, come through," he called lazily, slightly annoyed at being disturbed. Probably one of the crew, he thought, no doubt after an advance on their wages, there was always someone who had run out of money at the weekend, despite having just been paid on the Friday.

"Hello there," said Ann's soft voice as she delicately pulled back the curtain hanging over the inner doorway from the office to Roger's cabin. Aware she was suddenly encroaching on Roger's private living space, she hesitated, unsure if she was welcome. Roger threw down the magazine and jumped up off his bunk, "Well, hello there yourself, what a delightful surprise Ann, come in. To what do I owe the pleasure?"

Ann instantly felt at ease and meandered further into Roger's small private cabin, "Oh, it is such a beautiful day, I was with my daughter, Karen, down on the beach but some of her friends came along, and I felt somewhat out of it as I listened to their girlie chatter. Anyway, I noticed your ship was in port, so I made my excuses, and here I am."

"Very nice too, if I may say so, it's always a pleasure to see you," said Roger cheerfully laying on his charm. He eyed her more closely; she was wearing a light, see-through kaftan over her two-piece bathing costume.

Roger grinned, "I must say, that's a lovely dress, the sun coming through that porthole behind you catches you beautifully."

Realising what Roger was referring to, Ann gave a mischievous grin, "Cheeky Boy! I'd better sit down then."

Ann Clark was no pushover and she was always in the driving seat in her relationships with men. However, a recent encounter with a woman that she had initiated as purely an experiment and whilst enjoyable at the time, she regretted it when it started to develop beyond the experimental stage. It had ended badly with the lady in question claiming she had fallen in love with Ann; not wanting the relationship to end. Following the acrimonious conclusion to the fling, as that is all it was as far as Ann was concerned. Her casual female partner had then taken to overtly stalking Ann and bombarding her with tearful telephone calls. It reached a crescendo when a final confrontation had taken place with Ann threatening to go to the police – that had drawn a line under the matter and the stalking ceased or so it appeared.

Ann liked the flattery dished out by Roger, but she could get that anywhere. Ann was a temptress; she knew she had the looks, charm and personality to bowl over most men. She was a *'femme fatale,'* and the only person she cared about in her life, apart from her daughter, was herself. Ann was definitely sexually attracted to Roger, and she had already 'sussed' out that Roger fancied his chances with her, yet she was still unsure how far to let things run with him. That's why she had come down to the ship to see him. She knew full well that Roger's ship would be in port that weekend and had planned accordingly having casually checked the crew rostering board displayed in the open plan personnel office. Ann had indeed been on the beach relaxing but not with her daughter Karen, she was away for the weekend in London, staying with Ann's sister.

Ann, depending on the company she was in at the time, portrayed differing stories of her marital status, in the main explaining that her husband worked overseas on a lucrative but single posting contract and she only worked to keep herself occupied. In truth, there had been an acrimonious separation which had left her financially weak. Ann had laid such a web of secrecy; no one, daughter included, really knew the truth. She had to work but her intention was not to; she just needed the right man to come along. Roger wasn't the right man, he was married, and Ann had no intention of becoming involved in someone else's messy divorce scandal, which would probably leave him potless anyway. In the meantime, however, she thought that she might just have some fun. She was no fool; she knew full well, that's exactly what Roger wanted. She'd seen Roger's wife drop him off at the company office several times on his way to join a vessel and had noted the warm embraces with long kisses that occurred between the two of them, even though he was only leaving for three weeks at a time. Then there was the photographs of the happy couple, along with one of two youngsters clearly their son and daughter, spread around his cabin. Roger wasn't a man who was going to jeopardise his marriage. Ann was astute enough to realise he needed adrenalin-fuelled encounters rather than affection based lovemaking. Whether she wanted to play that game, Ann had yet to decide.

Roger watched Ann as she sat down and gently crossed her legs, showing her beautiful, smooth, tanned thighs, He smiled at the view, "Would you like some tea, or perhaps a cold drink?" he enquired, "although cabin drinking is not actually allowed by the company, I always keep a bottle of gin along with some tonic in the fridge for when the Boss comes down, he likes a 'tipple' in private."

"Oh lovely, yes, a G & T would be fabulous."

"Excellent. I was thinking of having one myself, but they say it's not good to drink alone. Now you're here I have an excuse. I'll nip up to the lounge bar for some ice out of the machine. Oh, there's a thought, would you like to come up for a drink with some of the lads? There's probably a few still on board." Sly as a fox, Roger challenged Ann's intentions. How she replied was music to his ears.

"No, your company will be perfect for me, thanks. Now run along and get that ice, there's a good boy. I'm dying of thirst, and if it's not slaked soon I'll have to go somewhere else, won't I?" she grinned. Roger may have had the cunning of a fox but, on the other hand, Ann was an angler, playing Roger as a fish hooked on the line.

"I'll give you 'good boy,'" taunted Roger, "just wait until I get back!"

"I'll be here," replied Ann with a sultry smile.

Roger couldn't get to the bar quick enough. The bar was not just a lounge bar for passengers; it doubled as an officer's bar, which the ship's officers were privileged to use. With it being a Sunday, there were no passengers on board, allowing the officers to relax and to enjoy some downtime. The lounge was forward of Roger's accommodation, on the next deck up, with panoramic views to the front so that passengers could sit during a crossing to the continent looking out over the bows of the ship. In his eagerness, Roger tripped, almost falling into the lounge, as he pushed against the huge glass, exquisitely engraved, lounge door, making his entrance not go unnoticed by some of his shipmates who were sitting there watching the TV.

"What's this then?" enquired one, following on with a sarcastic comment, "Wardrobe drinking Roger?" The common term used for those that hid their alcohol consumption from shipmates.

"Get stuffed!" was all Roger could think of saying in his haste to get some ice and leave.

"Charming, I'm sure, on the Lord's day too! Bet you've got some popsicle down there." Roger was known amongst his shipmates as a ladies' man, although it was all supposition as he'd never given anyone any tangible evidence.

Roger's mind was racing; he needed to say something quickly to deter any unwanted company, although unlikely, but one or two of them might decide to try to cramp his style by calling down to his cabin just for 'fits and giggles.' In a flash of inspiration, as he dived behind the bar and shovelled some ice into a pint pot, he quickly remarked, "It's just my bloody boss, probably kicked out of the house by his wife, with nothing better to do he thinks he'll come down and give me a hard time. So unless you want to get involved with him..."

"No bloody fear, the man's a management bastard of the first order, keep him to yourself, you deserve each other," came the anticipated reply.

Having filled the pint glass with ice, Roger turned to leave the lounge bar with a great big smirk on his face, believing he had discouraged any unwanted intrusion. He eagerly headed off back down to his accommodation to join the luscious Ann.

Roger gingerly descended the internal ladder from the upper forward deck lounge into the cross-ship alley, and as he turned the corner into the alleyway leading to his cabin, his nose twitched at a distinctively sweet, sickly smell permeating the alley which became stronger as he neared his cabin.

Upon entering, he was immediately greeted by a thick, thuggy atmosphere. Ann had been smoking a 'spliff.' He smiled, greeting Ann with his prize offering of ice to go with the gin and tonic she so readily wanted.

"Here we are, that didn't take too long, did it?"

"Long enough, I'm gasping." Roger hoped these words from Ann meant gasping for more than just a drink!

Not seeing any evidence of a cigarette, or whatever Ann had been smoking, he asked,

"I didn't realise you smoked?"

"Only when I'm nervous, I smoke the occasional weed, you should try it sometime," she chided, "it's very relaxing."

"No, not for me," he laughed wafting his hands about trying to clear the air, feeling slightly nervous of the smell pervading further into the ship. He opened up the internal vents to maximum capacity hoping to quickly clear away the smell.

"Look, Ann, please don't smoke on board, it could cause me all sorts of problems, and you wouldn't want that, would you?" he asked rather sternly.

"Ok," replied Ann somewhat belligerently, "point taken, now where's my G & T."

In the interim, Ann had changed her seat; she was now perched on the bunk in such a position that Roger couldn't help but notice her legs and thighs. Ann was provocatively revealing more than was strictly necessary.

He quickly prepared two gin and tonics, trying hard not to spill the liquids in his haste, all thoughts of the marijuana soon forgotten as all he could think about was turning around and pouring the gin on Ann's body then licking it off. 'Whoa there lad,' he thought to himself, 'calm down, this is a little too close to home.' He finished pouring the drinks then, with an unsteady hand, passed Ann's across to her, the glass already frosting invitingly with condensation.

"Cheers," she smiled.

They clinked their glasses together, he took a sip and sat down in the only chair in his cabin, directly opposite to where Ann was sitting, not realising that was exactly what Ann hoped he would do. During his absence, she had spent the time considering where to sit to ensure maximum effect. Ann swallowed almost half her drink in the time Roger had merely taken a sip. He couldn't stop his eyes wandering to Ann's thighs, which were at his eye level. As his mind wandered, driven by his groin. She watched him intently, causing him to blush slightly. She said nothing, but looked at him with a knowing smile of encouragement. He thought, 'if I haven't scored here, then I'm a monkey's uncle,' his confidence and manhood swelling with each passing minute.

"Drink OK?" he asked casually. He contemplated if Ann was playing with him, she could just be a good old fashioned *'prick teaser'* and he wasn't sure how to find out.

"Lovely, thanks." Ann finished her drink off with one final gulp followed by an appreciative lick of her lips, emphasising just how much she had enjoyed it.

"May I have another?" she asked, holding out the empty glass.

"Of course, you're very welcome," replied Roger. He stood up and stepped over to the small coffee table holding the bottle of gin, tonic, and ice. As he set about refilling their glasses he became aware that Ann had slid off the bunk, feeling her presence close at hand. He finished topping up the glasses with tonic and carefully turned, hoping she was behind him, waiting and wanting him. He was right. She was stood so close, all he could do was look into her eyes. He carefully lowered the drinks onto the table, not once taking his eyes off hers. Ann bit her top lip; this, Roger couldn't resist. His left hand grabbed her waist, pulling her against him, he felt her breathing quicken, with his right hand, he gently ran his fingers through her hair before leaning in and kissing her. Her reaction was exactly what he wanted. Her hands wrapped around him, her nails dug into his back through his shirt, making him wince slightly. Her eagerness excited him.

"Mmmmmm," she gasped sensually, shuddering intently before pulling back, "I've waited a long time for this moment," she lied, but she knew that's what Roger's ego would want to hear.

Roger's hands held on to her, not ready to let go, "Steady on with the nails, you'll ruin my shirt," he mocked. Later, he'd discover small spots of blood on the back of his shirt.

"Give me half the chance to," she whispered huskily. Her voice coming from deep within her throat, as though from a different person. Her breath came in short pants, her cheeks were flushed, and her eyes appeared to have changed colour with her pupils dilated; they looked as black as night. It was almost frightening, as though her persona was changing in front of him. Their bodies parted, Roger feeling anxious, shook his head as if he was trying to come out of an exotic, surreal dream. He was yet to realise the significance of Ann's remark.

'Christ,' he thought, 'she really is worked up.'

Suddenly and again, before he could catch his breath, her lips locked on to his, low moans came from her restricted throat, her fingers carefully ran down his shirt buttons, each one popped free to expose his bare, lightly haired chest. It was only a matter of seconds before she was whipping down the zip on his trousers, ecstatically groping for what lay beneath the material and lowering to her knees. 'Geeze,' thought Roger, 'I'd have more chance if I was grappling with a Bengal Tiger.'

He scooped Ann up in his arms and pushed her on to the bunk before collapsing on top of her. Her kaftan had loosened, exposing her tanned body. To Roger's surprise, she had nothing on under the soft material; she was as naked as a Jaybird. Ann had removed her bikini while Roger had been to collect the ice, she was one scheming bitch.

Roger's breathing shortened to sharp gasps in anticipation. His sap was rising to boiling point.

Suddenly, in an instant, Ann, like a snake, slid lithely from beneath him, stood up and repositioned her kaftan, "NO! Not here," she said, straightening the material so as not to look so bedraggled, "come to my place tonight, there we can have a great time."

Roger sat up and quickly slid down from the bunk. He realised the stupidity of what he had been about to do, even though he had shut the outer office door he had not locked it. Someone could have easily wandered in, even his boss, who was known for just turning up unexpectedly like a mushroom in the early morning dew! The anticipation of what could have happened excited him; the abrupt stop tantalised him; he wanted to find out what this woman was all about, what she was made of, what made her 'tick.'

"What time?" he asked eagerly.

"How about coming for dinner?" said Ann as she ferreted in her beach bag for a comb to gently run through her tousled hair. Roger stared lustily at her. She picked up her glass and finished her gin and tonic with one gulp.

Roger came back to reality, "Tonight? Yours? Oh, I've let my number two go home, so I must be here for when the crew report back and 'turn to' for duty at six. I shan't be able to get away until seven at the earliest."

"Ok," Ann nodded, "that'll be fine; we'll have a late dinner."

She picked up a pen and a scrap of paper lying on the desk and scribbled down her address, "Here's my address."

Roger looked at it briefly then stuffed it into his trouser pocket, "What about your daughter? Karen, isn't it?"

Ann walked towards him, stood on her tiptoes and gave him a quick butterfly kiss on the lips, "Don't worry, Kaz goes to a disco with her friends on a Sunday night, so she won't be home until late, plenty of time left before you have to leave!"

"Oh," said Roger, feeling rejected, first an invite but then putting him firmly in his place squashing any thoughts he might have had to stay the night.

Ann smirked as she quickly picked up the other glass of G&T, taking down a large gulp then replacing the now half empty glass back onto the table.

"Now come and see me off at the gangway," she instructed, subtly putting it across that she would be in the driving seat of any developments.

Standing at the top of the gangway, Roger watched Ann safely down and onto the quayside, returning her brief wave as she turned to look at him before disappearing into the passenger terminal building. He glanced down at the gurgling water between the ship's side and the stonewall quay, it looked black and ominous which made him wonder if it was an omen signalling that he might be entering waters that would prove too murky to see beyond sexual desire to screw Ann Clark!

On returning into the accommodation, Roger saw the duty steward and asked him what he was doing.

"Just taking this tray of tea to the officers in the lounge," came the reply.

"After that, please bring a tray of tea to my cabin, will you?"

"Yes, Chief," replied the steward as he scurried away.

His tea soon arrived, and Roger took some time, looking out of his cabin porthole at the dockyard. His mind mulled over the afternoon's events; he could still smell Ann's perfume lingering in the air, mixed with the odour from her smoke of weed, still taste the lips that recently clung to his own.

If Roger had taken a little more time before allowing this relationship to develop to the level it did, he would have discovered some worrying facts about the sultry Ann Clark and no doubt would have put the brakes on. Unfortunately for him, he was so eager to get his leg over that he forgotten to engage his brain.

For Roger, he was looking forward to embarking on an exciting and tantalising game. Little did he know, Ann was called the 'Black Widow' in the offices of Beaumont's and Roger had already unwittingly been drawn into her 'spider's web.'

Chapter 47s

Despite what she claimed, in reality, Ann wasn't a widow or divorced but separated, at least that fact was the only truth in her marital status, however, a certain member of the local constabulary had a different, but unproven, view. Unbeknown to Ann, she had been nicknamed the 'Black Widow,' an assumed myth created by office gossip.

Her husband had gone missing. Nick, was an ex Warrant Officer 2 who had served in the Army Air Corps as a helicopter pilot. Upon leaving the army, he went to work for the Electricity Board, where he piloted one of their inspection helicopters. He flew up and down the countryside, overflying the miles of hanging electric cabling and pylons that covered the landscape; the National Grid distributing the nation's power. Despite previously being an Army wife, accustomed to Nick leaving her regularly, it was said by some that his continued absence from home, albeit for only short periods, had led to Ann leading a separate life that included seeking solace in the arms of another man or in her case, men.

However, one day her husband just simply vanished. Well, that's what she claimed, and initially, she appeared fraught with worry, apparently blaming herself. Contact with his employers produced nothing; they were equally as concerned as it was so out of character for Nick. Years in the military instilled discipline as well as dependability, and Nick was as dependable as they came. Ann claimed it was down to their deteriorating relationship, telling family and friends that she'd felt for some time that Nick wrongly thought that she had the odd fling here and there. In fact, he accused her of such. They'd had a blazing row where fists and hands had flown, and faces slapped, mostly Nick's.

Ann had grown up with two brothers; thus, she learned at a young age to fight her corner and knew how to handle herself. This stubborn fighting streak stayed with her and into their marriage, Nick had soon learnt to defend himself, but he still usually came off the worse for wear. The chivalrous part of him holding back from actually raising a fist towards Ann other than in self-defence. One particular argument, which had come from nowhere, Nick was suspicious of philandering on Ann's part, consequently, Ann had gone into battle. The noise from the row, which turned out to be their final row, caused the neighbours to call the police. Never had they heard such an intense argument from Nick and Ann's house. By the time the police arrived, the situation had calmed down. Ann and Nick were able to convince the policewoman that called on them that everything was ok and it was just a quarrel that had got out of hand. This was all recorded accordingly in the police logs. When Nick hadn't shown up for two days and calls to relatives drew a blank, Ann went to the local police station where Detective Sergeant Peter Marsh eventually saw her.

During the initial statement, Ann portrayed herself as having a loving relationship with Nick, declaring how distraught she was and how in love they were, she just wanted him back home. She stated that he was a loving husband and a great father to their daughter, Karen, who was also beside herself with grief that her daddy had disappeared. In Karen's case, she was genuinely distressed by her dad's sudden disappearance, whereas Ann was putting on a show worthy of an Oscar. Ann asserted that something terrible must have happened to Nick. He was ex-army and made of strong stuff, he wouldn't just 'up-sticks' and leave without a word. Definitely not without saying something to his daughter, Karen, whom he adored. Peter Marsh was very sympathetic towards Ann, picking up on the fact he was ex forces asking if he'd ever suffered from PTSD. Veterans that had been diagnosed with this affliction were known to just disappear.   This comment played into Ann's hands, allowing her to express more grief. Undeterred by Ann's outpouring of grief, Peter Marsh went on to explain that the police had limited resources and couldn't spend a great deal of time or manpower looking for every missing person unless they had concerns for Nick's well-being. Naturally, despite Ann giving the appearance of great concern, something didn't quite gel with Peter. He sensed that something wasn't quite 'kosher' with the story Ann was spinning him.

Peter worked with Detective Inspector Harry Joseph, a streetwise, old school copper who always worked on gut instinct. Harry was a third-generation Jamaican, his grandfather having come to England as part of the s.s.'Windrush' immigrants. Harry was one of the first black police officers to join the Metropolitan Police. He had initially endured a great deal of racism; a lesser man would probably have resigned rather than put up with the 'shit' that was doled out to him by his so-called colleagues. However, he'd stuck with it, eventually making a name for himself when he'd answered a call for help from another officer being attacked by an axe wielding, drug-crazed youth who was vainly attempting to rob a bank. Despite being some distance away and on foot patrol, Harry had raced to the officer's assistance, arriving on the scene even before others in a patrol car. Harry had talked to and disarmed the youth, persuading him to give up the lethal-looking machete. Without a doubt, he had saved the young, badly injured officer's life. Despite this, whilst at the scene he had to endure racists comments from one of the patrol car officers who made derogatory remarks about Harry's ethnic background with his long legs being use to running through the bush. Harry ignored the comment but a by-stander witness didn't, and quickly reported the officer for this racial abuse. At the subsequent hearing, Harry saved the officer's job by claiming he hadn't heard the comment. This soon got around and colleagues that had previously been abrasive towards Harry suddenly changed their tune. Following this event, Harry discovered he had more friends than he could shake a stick at! Hailed as a hero, one senior officer saw the opportunity to make good use of Harry's origins and persuaded him to transfer to CID, where he was appointed to a special squad dealing with the Jamaican gangs. Successfully working amongst the 'Yardy' culture of East London, he solved many crimes that others found impossible as they were greeted with a 'wall of silence.' Harry went on to pass the necessary exams and was promoted by a police force that was becoming more politically aware. With the increase in immigration from the former British Colonies, and long before the Brixton riots, some astute senior officers realised that they needed to recruit more 'Harry Joseph's' so that force would be more representative of the society they policed. Harry soon became a recruitment poster boy.

While planning a summer holiday for his family, Harry had selected their destination by using a pin and a map of England. He hit upon the county of Lincolnshire, a locality they'd enjoyed so much that, in agreement with his family, he transferred to the local police force. He was the first black, rural policeman, initially in uniform, but due to his record in London, he was quickly moved into the CID branch stationed in Northwold. Promotion to Detective Sergeant then Inspector soon followed along with Peter Marsh as his DS. Harry's old school investigative style of coppering had rubbed off on to Peter, one of the new breed of university-educated coppers, already fast-tracked to the rank of Sergeant after barely two years on the beat. They made an odd couple once being dubbed 'the Dynamic Duo.' However, some clown soon metamorphosed this into 'Blackman and Robin!' Peter, although a bit of a whizz kid because of his education, had learnt a lot from Harry, a case in point being never to ignore a 'nagging doubt.' Hence Peter questioned that all was not as it seemed with Ann Clark, if asked to describe her, he would call her a 'Sinister Ice Maiden.'

After the interview, Peter escorted Ann down from his office to the reception area of the police station to politely see her off the premises with the promise that he would be looking into her husband's disappearance.

Ann descended the wide circular steps leading down from the main entrance to the car park level, ascending the stairs into the main office was a uniformed police officer, PC Lyndsey Smith, the same young policewoman who had attended the disturbance at Ann and Nick's home. Although Ann didn't remember or recognise her, Lyndsey, one of the Forces breed of natural 'super recognisers,' immediately recognised Ann Clark and greeted her with a cheery smile and 'hello.' Ann did not acknowledge her, instead she kept her head low and sped off down the steps into the car park towards her car. Lyndsey shrugged off the apparent rebuff and continued up the steps towards Peter Marsh who was watching Ann depart. Without taking his eyes off Ann he called to Lyndsey, "You know that one Lyndsey?"

"Yes Sarge," she replied as she reached the same step. Lyndsey stopped and turned to follow Peter's eyes, "she obviously doesn't remember me though."

"Doesn't remember you from where?"

"I was called to a domestic at her home a few weeks back. According to the neighbours she and husband were having a right ding dong."

"Really?" replied Peter, studiously chewing his lower lip.

Lyndsey frowned, "Go on then... what's she doing here?"

"Reporting her husband as missing, replied Peter, his mind beginning to add more misgivings to his already suspicious thoughts, "tell me about the circumstances?"

"Well, there's not a lot to go on really, it was a three nines call from a neighbour saying that there was an almighty row going on, screaming and yelling. The sound of glass or pottery breaking caused them to call us in. Apparently, it was very out of character for the pair to make such a racket. When I got there everything appeared to be in order, apart from the husband that is. Both went to great lengths to convince me that they had made up and all was ok."

"Apart from the husband?" queried Peter.

"Yeah, in most cases of domestic disputes it's obvious what's happened, macho man beats up wife. This time I was rather surprised to find the husband looking worse for wear."

"Worse for wear?"

"Well, his shirt was torn and he had nasty wound across his face, it looked to me as though it could only have been made with some sort of whip. Also, a patch of blood was forming on his shirt from a hidden wound but he was most insistent that it was nothing, declining my offer to call for a paramedic. To me, he looked embarrassed."

"Interesting. Your thoughts on it Lyndsey?" asked Peter curiously.

"Wife got a bit heavy handed and let loose on the husband. Another domestic disturbance. That's about it really. Neither would say a bad word about the other once I was there. No arguing, no finger pointing, both just wanted me gone."

"And then what?"

"And nothing, neither party admitted that anything was wrong, they even got the daughter to come down from her bedroom to confirm everything was ok. She acted furtive but as her parents had just had a huge row, she had probably been keeping well out of the way. I guess that was only natural, so I left it at that and went to see the neighbour who made the initial call to explain all was in order. I added the comments to my notebook and occurrence sheet, and that was that."

"Interesting," said Peter.

Lyndsey turned to walk up the final steps but suddenly stopped, "Oh," she said, remembering extra information, "I also sent a report through to social services as well, just to be on the safe side."

"Ah yes, the daughter. What state was of mind would you say she was in?"

"She looked shaken but other than that ok. Why... what you thinking?"

Peter took a deep breath and smiled, "I'm not thinking anything, I'm smelling a large rat, there's something not quite right about all this."

"Ok. Well, if you need to see my pocket book, just say, I've made quite a detailed entry."

"Yes, that would be useful, let me have a photocopy of the relevant pages and send it to me in the internal mail. Thanks."

With that, Peter turned and gave Lyndsey a big smile. Lyndsey just briefly acknowledge his smile, she knew of Peter's reputation as a ladies' man, she was having none of it and didn't give him any encouragement. They both headed towards the security door into the main building before going their separate ways.

Peter Marsh caught up with his supervisor, Detective Inspector Harry Joseph, and talked through the situation involving Ann Clark. Harry sat there listening intently, sitting behind his desk with his hands in his pockets, he laid back in his chair as it reclined allowing him to stretch out his long legs. Harry had a bald, shiny black ebony crown with thick hair on the sides of his head, almost hiding both ears; he looked more like a University Professor than a copper. He was forever sniffling due to a continuing sinus trouble which he'd never bothered to see a doctor about. Even when he was standing, Harry's hands would be dug deep within his pockets. He was a copper of the old school, firmly believing in following hunches. After listening to Peter, he told him just that, "Follow your nose and make some enquiries to see where it leads."

Peter did speak to the neighbours who confirmed what they had said to PC Lyndsey Smith. However, it was a different scenario when Peter started talking to Nick Clark's work colleagues. He was unable to meet up with Nick's fellow helicopter crewman John Charles as he was on holiday but, he was able to speak with his line manager Andrew Cooper. Andrew had occasionally flown with Nick covering for John as the observer aboard one of the inspection helicopters. What Andrew imparted to Peter certainly raised more questions than his eyebrows. Questions that needed some urgent answers. Andrew recalled that on the last occasion he had flown with Nick they had finished up at Nottingham Tollerton airport. They left the helicopter for the night before going off to a local hotel. It was over a few beers that he recalled Nick spilling information about his marriage. Andrew got the feeling that Nick needed to air his marital problems and kindly sat and listened while Nick off-loaded. Andrew remembered him saying that he was genuinely frightened of his wife as she had a violent temper. He proceeded to tell of one such occasion where Ann said she would be glad to see the back of him and in a fit of piqué she threatened to do away with him. Nick told Andrew that his wife's character had changed dramatically over the years of marriage.

Andrew recited how Nick had in an attempt at black humour jokingly said, "Well if I turn up dead, you'll know where to look!"

When Peter questioned Andrew Cooper further, he was quick to voice his opinion, "Nick was a hard bastard in many ways, he'd been awarded the Military Medal in the Army, he was no push over but believe me he was genuinely scared of that dragon of a wife."

Peter Marsh got it all down in the form of a signed witness statement. However just as the interview concluded the final closing comment by Andrew Cooper didn't register with him, although the significance was to later come back and haunt Peter.

"You know, maybe it's a strange coincidence but John Charles suddenly went on unannounced leave just before the enquiries about Nick's disappearance began."

Peter with his mind firmly focussed on Ann Clark's possible involvement in her husband's disappearance just acknowledged Andrew's comment as just that, coincidence.

Following the interview with Andrew Cooper Peter put in a request to see Nick Clark's Army Service record.

When this eventually came through, it made very interesting reading, making Peter concur with Andrew Cooper that Nick was indeed no push over. He was rated as one of the Army's top pilots and would have, had he stayed in the Army, been selected to train on the new Apache gunship helicopter just recently announced by the Ministry of Defence to be purchased from the United States. His records confirmed that he had been awarded the Military Medal for some covert work in the first Gulf War, working with Special Forces. That bit was restricted information which would require further authority to access the circumstances. Peter also noted that Nick had been a member of the Army's Judo team. What he'd read was more than sufficient for Peter's instincts to be confirmed.

Nick Clark's Army file was hardly back in the courier's sealed delivery bag when another part of the jigsaw fell into place. A call from the front desk informed him that a relative of Nick Clark was at reception wanting to speak to somebody about his disappearance. The plot slowly thickened. Peter Marsh felt excited realising that he could be on to something big, over what had first appeared to have been a simple 'missing person' enquiry.

Peter left his desk in the CID office and took the courier parcel down to the front office reception. He handed the parcel to the duty receptionist, a civilian employee. Not having police working on reception was all part of the cut backs in an attempt to get more police officers out of the police stations and on the beat. Many of the admin positions such as manning the front desk had been handed over to private contractors, but this coincided with a reduction in front line police officers, so in actual fact the exercise didn't put any extra police officers on the beat. Having civilians on reception had its own problems, especially when members of the public came in with strange enquiries that needed a police officer to deal with. After speaking briefly with the admin assistant, regarding contacting the courier company for returning the file to the Army, Peter was directed by her to a little, old lady sitting quietly in the reception area. It wasn't so long ago that police station reception areas were pretty spartan places, with the only furniture for sitting on being rough wooden benches anchored down to stop the less desirable members of society picking them up to use as a weapon.

Before the introduction of armoured glass, wooden furniture seats made an ideal battering ram for throwing through the glass counter screen by miscreants of society expressing their dissatisfaction at the police and life in general. Now that had all changed, the reception area was designed to take on the appearance of a hotel with comfortable seats covered in mock leather, there were even pot plants, imitation of course. It was all about image and an attempt at making the police appear more friendly and approachable for the general public.

Peter unlocked the door at the side of the reception area and went to introduce himself to the lady. As he approached her, she attempted to rise but showed difficulty. Peter quickly indicated for her to remain seated as he plonked himself down on the settee alongside her, sinking into the thick cushion seat.

He offered his hand to introduce himself, "Hello I'm Detective Sergeant Marsh, I believe you have come in because you have some information about a missing man by the name of Nick Clark. Is that right, Mrs… ?"

"McBride, Mrs. Annie McBride," said the old lady looking at Peter. Despite her obvious age Peter noticed how her eyes sparkled.

"Well Mrs McBride, how can you help us?"

She leaned back into the soft upholstery and nervously clasped her hands together as she looked out of the window opposite. The view overlooked the police car pound and beyond the perimeter wall to the distant Lincolnshire Wolds.

"I told him not to marry her, I said she was evil," Annie appeared to be lost in thought. Peter interrupted her before she rambled on too far.

"Mrs McBride, can we start by you telling me what your connection or relationship is to Nick Clark."

"I'm his grandmother, didn't you know, on his mother's side?" she said almost accusingly.

"Mrs McBride, no I didn't until just now. So, what information you can give me to help me find Mr Clark?"

"Oh, I'm so sorry Mr - "

"Please, call me Peter."

"Yes, Peter, well you see I'm his grandmother and until the police rang the other day I had no idea anything was wrong. Was it you? Did you call me?"

"No, that would be one of our researchers following up with phone calls and general enquiries."

"Ahh yes," she said with a warm smile, "now I recall, it was a young woman who called me."

Peter warmed to this lady, she reminded him of his own grandmother.

"Mrs McBride, what about his mother, did we try and contact her?"

"His mother is sadly dead, didn't your young lady tell you that?"

Peter was momentarily embarrassed that he hadn't read up the notes the researcher had given him following the telephone calls to Nick's relatives.

Before Peter could apologise, she continued, "His poor mother died far too early from the dreaded cancer, it's not often parents outlive their children, is it? And now it looks as though I've outlived my grandchild too! I'm 88 you know."

Peter thought she was about to cry, but bravely she held back any emotion she was feeling.

"Mrs McBride do you have any information about the whereabouts of your grandson?"

"No, I don't, but I need to tell you things, things you may not know about that 'floosie' he married."

"I can see you obviously don't like Ann Clark but this will hardly help me find him."

"You probably won't 'cos I bet she's done away with him!"

"Mrs Mcbride, just tell me your thoughts, then I'll decide where we go from here, let me take a few notes." Peter took out his police regulation pocket book from his inside jacket pocket and made some preliminary notes.

"When he first brought her to see me, all those years ago, I instinctively knew she was a little hussy, a gold digger. Call it woman's intuition: I tried to put him off but he wouldn't see it my way, probably thinking I was a ranting old woman. I saw it in her eyes, she is no good, she's evil."

Peter just nodded making notes. He felt that he should hear her out but doubted he would learn anything of help other than circumstantial evidence which would support his view that had been formulating in his mind that Ann Clark may have murdered her husband Nick Clark.

Mrs McBride continued, "Well he came to see me he did, not so long ago and said 'Gran you were right I've married a wrong un.'" Mrs McBride stopped in mid-sentence as if she was trying to recall the events. "That was the last time I saw him you know. He confided in me that he was afraid of her but he didn't know what to do about it. I told him he must leave her and take Karen with him."

"What did he say to that suggestion Mrs McBride?" enquired Peter as he scribbled furiously in this pocket book.

"Said he couldn't but he'd think about it, he said the problem would be trying to convince Karen. He knew, only too well, that woman was very clever at manipulating Karen. Apparently, during a row she baited him about Karen, said that she knew exactly which buttons to press when it came to their daughter. It was if she had guessed that he might try and leave her, and take Karen with him. That woman is the devil incarnate… mark my words Peter, when you get to the bottom of this you'll find she's behind it. I know she is."

Mrs McBride started to become tearful so Peter suggested she stopped there and let him get her a cup of tea.

"No," she said holding back the tears, "I've said my bit, it's up to you, the police, to find out what she's done to him. My beautiful soldier grandson. I'm so proud of him. He's a hero, they gave him the Military Medal you know," the tears flowed freely. "Oh, I'm sorry Peter, you must think I'm a silly old woman."

Peter put down his notebook and pen, instinctively taking Mrs. McBride's right hand in both of his, not sure what to do next, "Now then Mrs. McBride, let's look on the positive side, we'll get to the bottom of this."

"Thank you, Peter; you're very kind. It's just… I'm scared she'd done something unforgiving. I have no doubt in my mind that she's more than capable of… of murder!" Mrs. McBride withdrew her hand from Peter's and rifled through her handbag. She took out a handkerchief to blow her nose and then placed the spoiled handkerchief in her coat pocket. Using the aid of her walking stick, she slowly raised herself of the chair to stand and Peter joined her.

"If you ask me, Peter, it's her, that awful woman he married."

There was a brief silence between the two of them, then Mrs. McBride said, "Can I go now, I've told you all I know, I just had to come and speak to someone to get things off my chest."

"Yes, of course, you can go, Mrs. McBride," said Peter as he placed a reassuring hand on her shoulder, "if there is anything else I can think of asking you, then I'll make an appointment to come see you, the researcher has your address?"

"Yes, she does, there'll always be the kettle on, but I think I've told you all I know, really."

"Ok, Mrs. McBride, I promise I'll be in touch as soon as I hear anything."

He guided Mrs. McBride to the door and waved her farewell. As she left the police station, Peter Marsh experienced a feeling of déjà vu, once again he found himself standing at the top of the steps, only this time it was watching Mrs. McBride as she departed.

He returned upstairs to his office to ponder the case. He certainly had a lot of circumstantial evidence against Ann Clark but no hard evidence, no body for starters. Always preferable to have a body to start a murder investigation, but then it wouldn't be the first time that someone had been found guilty of murder without a body.

Peter decided to follow his nose by inviting Ann Clark into the police station for an interview under caution. He said that she could bring a solicitor along to which she retorted, 'No need as I've done nothing wrong.' Ann was immediately defensive and did not question why she needed to be interviewed. All this stoked the fire of Peter's suspicions.

The interview proved inconclusive, although he was able to needle Ann Clark a couple of times, hoping her mind was so overburdened with guilt that she might give something away, all it did was cause Ann to lose her temper. She was ready to change her mind about having a solicitor with her and demanded to be allowed to leave. She wasn't under arrest, stating her case that she believed she could leave if she wanted to. Peter conceded that she was indeed free to go at any time as that was her right; she was there purely on an invitation basis, although a statement was being taken under caution purely to meet the rules. Peter charmed her into staying; he knew he was skating on thin ice following a hunch; he didn't want to formally arrest her and cause more complications as he didn't have sufficient evidence and it would just be a waste of time and resources. He explained to Ann some of the queries and questions he had that required clarification about the mysterious disappearance of her husband. He also outlined the circumstantial evidence he had come across.

Ann retaliated by accusing Mrs. McBride of being a 'batty old cow' who had never liked her and tried everything to stop her marrying Nick, she doted on her only grandson. No woman would ever be good enough for him. Ann did become annoyed when Peter questioned if their marriage was at breaking point. Ann painted a rosy image, strenuously denying anything was wrong and claiming that all couples go through bad patches, she stated that when a nosey neighbour had called the police, it was simply a rough patch that had turned into a blazing row.

Peter didn't believe a word of it but he had been unable to get through Ann Clark's defences. She was hiding something, but he knew that without any firm evidence, he couldn't get any further. So, the file on the missing Nick Clark, although not closed, was filed under 'unsolved pending further investigation.'

Some weeks later, Peter was out on a job when he received a radio message to return to the station as Mrs. Ann Clark wanted to see him. Rather than make an appointment for her to call back, Peter was able to break away from investigating the stealing of lead flashing from some local churches and made his way back to the police station where he met Ann again. He guided her into one of the small interview offices off the main reception area. Once inside the room, with a dramatic flourish of indignation, Ann produced a letter from her husband, Nick.

"There, read that Mr. Marsh. Then perhaps you'll believe me, I know you think that I murdered my husband! This is a letter from him."

Her very words, '*I know you think that I murdered my husband*' struck a chord with Peter as he had never as much as given her any indication to his thinking along those lines, so why would she make such a statement? Once more, alarm bells rang within his subconsciousness.

Ann Clark handed Peter an opened single flimsy sheet of blue paper, originally folded along predetermined lines into the shape of a normal letter. It was commonly known as a 'Bluey,' a favourite of the British Forces overseas, it was the cheapest way of sending a letter because of its light weight meant only the minimum of postage charges.

Peter gently took the folded airmail letter as though handling a delicate historical document that could easily disintegrate into shreds and carefully laid it on the table.

"Before I open and read this letter, Mrs. Clark, who else apart from you, and of course the post office of several countries, have handled it?"

Looking at Peter Marsh as though he was stupid, she said with a note of resentment, "No one. After opening it today, I came straight here to see you. I haven't even told my daughter."

The tension in the room was heavy.

"Mrs. Clark, you understand that I'll need you to leave this with me as there may be forensics that we can lift from it."

"Why don't you just bloody well read it, it will explain where he is and that he is alive. What do you want forensics for?" Ann didn't attempt to hide her frustration.

"Well, it may not be all it seems."

"Oh for god's sake! What are you accusing me of now? You think I've killed him, well this letter will prove you wrong, read it," she demanded.

"Nothing, it's just procedure, Mrs. Clark. I can put it in a see-through evidence bag to protect it; then I can read it and take it from there."

"Oh very well, but once you've read it you'll see that my husband is far from dead, and I'll be expecting a written apology from the Chief Constable after what you've put me through!"

"Of course," replied Peter keeping calm, not knowing what was in the letter he still had his doubts about her. In his eyes, she was a cold, calculating bitch.

Ann Clark left the police station in a huff. She threw a comment over her shoulder about Peter hearing from her solicitor. Peter had nothing to reproach himself for, his actions had been fully justified under the circumstances. If the Chief wanted to apologise for political correctness and appearances' sake, then so be it. Peter still believed that Nick Clark could be dead, and if so, Ann Clark had something to do with it.

The letter was checked by forensics who were able to lift several good prints from the writing paper; these were compared with Nick Clark's army record prints. None were Nick's. The typed letter did appear to be from him; in it, he explained that he felt their marriage was over. The letter went on to say that he had been recruited by a London Company after replying to an advert in the magazine, 'Soldier.' He had accepted employment as a helicopter pilot to fly for Government Security Forces in the Congo, where they were fighting a war of attrition against communist insurgents who wanted to overthrow the so-called democratically elected government. He said he was sorry to have left so suddenly, sent apologies to Karen and that he would write to her soon. He promised that on his return he would visit her, but in the meantime, he wanted Ann to start divorce proceedings, saying he accepted full responsibility for the breakdown in their marriage. He would sign anything she wanted. She could have the house, the car; he wanted nothing from the marriage other than to stay in contact with his daughter. On the face of it, Nick Clark was alive in South Africa. Peter Marsh wasn't convinced; what about the rosy marriage that Ann had described? Why had he suddenly left, not saying anything to the daughter he supposedly adored? There were too many loose ends, thought Peter. As a detective, he knew he had to shelve the investigation as they had no evidence or even clues as to what had really happened. The case of Nick Clark was closed. The Chief Constable never did hear from Ann Clark or her solicitor demanding an apology. Peter Marsh went back to chasing the lead flashing thieves, his hope of making a name for himself cracking a murder case unfulfilled.

Little did he know that he would, in the not too distant future, come up against Mrs. Ann Clark in the most bizarre of circumstances that he could never have envisaged in his wildest dreams.

Chapter 48

I t was into this cauldron of evil that Roger Holt, through his own stupidity and immature sexual needs, was going to be drawn with devastating life-changing consequences, not only for him but for his dear wife Siobhan, Ann Clark and her daughter Karen. The fall out would reverberate throughout Beaumont's and Northwold.

Roger found Ann's home without trouble. It was the last house in a cul-de-sac with exceptional views across open countryside to the sea. Views that would make estate agents break out into ecstatic, colourful descriptions without the fear of being guilty of misrepresentation. The properties, built between the wars, had well established secluded gardens. There were big, thick trees and shrubs in Ann's front garden, inside them a curved pathway leading to the front door. The greenery gave the impression of walking through a small wood that concealed the front door from the road and the immediate neighbours. To the left of the property was a small drive with open wooden gates, Roger took this as an invitation and drove straight in. He didn't want, however unlikely, for his easily identifiable car to be recognised by someone he knew. He was very proud of his special edition Dagenham's finest and would rather hide it away from prying eyes. With the car nicely parked in Ann's secluded drive, Roger was stepping out of the vehicle as Ann opened her front door.

"Hello there," she welcomed him cheerily, "bang on time, too, I am impressed."

"That's me," quipped Roger, "I don't like to keep a lady waiting."

Roger was more interested in gaining brownie points with Ann, rather than any chivalrous intentions to impress her. He didn't want any indiscretion, such as arriving late, to spoil his ultimate goal of bedding Ann and showing her who was the boss.

As Ann walked towards the car, Roger couldn't help but notice that she was wearing an attractive kaftan robe which parted slightly as she moved, giving him a flash of beautiful tanned legs setting his heart racing.

"Nice wheels," she smiled trying to sound cool, "what sort of car is it?"

"You're not a car fanatic, then?" smiled Roger.

"No, is it obvious?" What's that funny wing thing on the rear?" Ann was clever; she knew men well enough to know how to play them into her hands. She didn't care about the car, but she could tell Roger did.

Roger closed the car door, "This wonderful piece of machinery is a completely re-built, with my own fair hands I might add, Ford Escort RX

2000, winner of several saloon car championships included the Monte Carlo Rally," he paused, "or was it the Paris Dakar rally?" he paused again while he pondered, "never mind, just accept it as a thing of beauty and the wing thing, as you so politely put it, is an aileron which is designed to keep the tail of the car steady at high speed."

"Why is it fast?" she asked sceptically. Roger was too wrapped up in talking about his car to realise Ann was rather patronisingly enjoying herself as she played with him.

"Is it fast?!" he replied as if emphasising that he was after all dealing with a woman, what did they know about men and their toys, unable to believe that Ann had really asked that question. "This car was made to fly, it should have been fitted with wings."

Ann moved closer to Roger, "Ooooh," she purred seductively, "I just love fast cars, would you take me for a spin?"

"Sure thing, hop in."

"No, not now silly, another time. Come inside and have a drink; it's becoming quite chilly."

Ann deliberately brushed lightly past Roger allowing the fragrance of her perfume to linger around him. Roger followed her into the house in what he felt was hot pursuit. However, through Ann's eyes, he was a little puppy following his mistress.

Once in the hallway, Ann showed Roger through to the large lounge with bay windows. The lounge was modern, tastefully decorated with gold-embossed wallpaper of enormous chrysanthemums. In the centre of the room sat a chocolate brown velvet suite, appealingly comfortable to the eye. In one corner of the room, there was a craftsman built-in bar and cocktail cabinet, in another was a Bang and Olsen music centre, everything conveyed the fact that Ann liked to enjoy the good things in life, this did not escape Roger's attention. He had a good idea as to what Ann's earning potential was at Beaumont's; he doubted that it could support this lifestyle, he, therefore, assumed that her overseas high-income husband was the benefactor, probably an unwilling one at that. Roger had heard the many and varied rumours amongst the crew about Ann's mysteriously absent husband, which he chose to ignore, preferring Ann's explanation. 'Husband,' the thought flashed into his mind, 'I'm a husband, what am I doing?' Despite the feeling of guilt sweeping over him, he quickly silenced the voices in his head; "countering them with this is a no strings attached fling."

"Pour yourself a drink," said Ann indicating towards the bar, "there's bound to be something to tempt you, take your pick. I'll have a gin and tonic; mix it for me, would you. I'll just get some ice from the freezer." Ann left the lounge and called over her shoulder, "Bombay gin, please, not the Gordon's."

Roger went behind the bar and busied himself, searching in the small cupboards looking for all the various accoutrements to mix Ann her gin and tonic and a Horse's Neck for himself. Opening one of the small cupboards, a collection of X rated magazines caught his eye; they were of the more erotic nature called 'Reader's Wives' and some about the pleasure of ropes! He'd seen the 'Reader's Wives' publication before, knowing little about it other than it was pornographic, probably to do with wife swapping. As for the others it was obviously not a seaman's guide book of knots and splices but bondage for Christ's sake! He quickly shut the door, not wanting to be caught when Ann came back into the room. Roger guessed the magazines were hidden away for a reason; maybe Ann had hidden them from her daughter. In one corner of the room was a showcase cabinet displaying several silver trophies. On closer inspection Roger saw that they had been awarded to Ann for winning various local 'kick boxing' competitions, one was even a national award. Tough cookie indeed thought Roger starting to realise that there was a lot more to Ann than he'd initially thought. By the time Ann returned, Roger had moved to the other side of the bar with their drinks ready to have the ice dropped into them. Ann approached, placed the ice bucket next to the drinks, but before she could attempt to put ice into their waiting glasses, Roger caught hold of her arms, turned to face her and nuzzled her neck, the blood pumped around his veins in the excitement of what he expected to come.

"Hey, just you be patient," she playfully squealed as she pushed him away, "or I'll drop some ice down your trousers to cool you off. Anyway, we've got to have dinner before we move on to dessert, I've not been slaving over a hot stove all afternoon for my creation to go to waste."

"Of course," said Roger winking at her with a large grin across his face. He took a sip of his drink and licked his lips, "so what's for dinner then?"

"You'll have to wait and see," she said as she dropped ice into her gin and tonic.

Roger couldn't make up his mind about Ann. He had the distinct feeling that she was playing with him. She came on to him in his office, invited him round but now stalling as she wanted to sit and eat dinner. Maybe she was untouchable. He couldn't work out the game she was playing. Roger had noticed that she had changed her clothes. Ann was now wearing a sexy two-piece joined in the middle with decorative brass rings around her stomach. Roger couldn't decide if the dress was elegant or slutty, but he liked the combination and couldn't help but look her up and down.

"If you've finished mentally undressing me, come and sit down," Ann moved to the large settee, sat down, and patted the area next to her. Roger obeyed and sank into the sumptuousness of the soft upholstery. He started to tremble in anticipation; he wanted to grab her and rip her dress off. Before he even had a chance to make a move, Ann stood up and went back to the bar area. She topped up her glass with more ice and sat down opposite Roger in a single, matching chair. She crossed her legs; her short skirt was pushed even higher, giving Roger a full view.

They sat in silence, sipping their drinks. Roger wondered how to make his next move; he desperately wanted to get Ann into bed. He was beginning to wonder if she was teasing him. She appeared to be running hot and cold. There was only one reason Roger had gone to Ann's house, and it wasn't for dinner.

An alarm broke his train of thought, and Ann stood up.

"That's the oven, dinner will ready in five minutes," she said as she departed, "come through to the dining room and choose a bottle of wine from the rack unless you prefer to stick with your whisky? You can talk to me as I serve up our meal."

Roger followed Ann as instructed, "I'll stick with what I've got thanks, don't want to mix my drinks, as I'm driving," he said enquiringly, hoping for Ann to reply with the offer of a bed for the night. Much to his annoyance, she didn't.

"Oh yes, of course, can't be too careful the cops around here seem quite keen on catching drunk drivers," said Ann speaking over her shoulder as she went into the kitchen.

Suitably rebuffed, Roger was beginning to get annoyed. He quickly decided that Ann was playing a game with him, 'Two can play that game,' he thought to himself, 'a nice dinner and I will shoot off.' He wandered around the dining room, sipping his drink.

"Dinner won't be long," called Ann from the kitchen.

"Excellent," replied Roger. He was admiring the dining room, which was joined on to the kitchen but separated by a long purpose built-in breakfast bar from where dishes could be easily be past through to the waiting diners. It gave the kitchen a showcase effect so that the host could talk freely to those in the dining room while preparing culinary delights. Roger saw a substantial wine rack in the corner and busied himself choosing a wine, although he didn't intend to have a glass himself, hoping that if Ann had some wine, then she may loosen up. In the centre of the room, a large table suitable for at least six had been neatly laid out just for the two of them. Roger took note that the place settings had been laid side by side rather than opposite each other. To Roger, this displayed an anticipated intimacy which cheered his inner man; he wondered if he was on a promise after all. He was confused; Ann was proving to be a rather complex character.

"You hungry?" asked Ann.

"I'm famished, haven't eaten since breakfast," he said as he chose a wine, "will this do?"

Ann didn't even look; she was too busy preparing the food, "Yes, whatever you've chosen will be fine with me. There are glasses on the table."

"Have you got –"

"Here," she passed him a fancy bottle opener, "I'm sure you can figure it out," she said, grinning.

Roger opened the bottle of wine, "So tell me about yourself."

"There's nothing much to tell. I'm married with one daughter, and as I've told you hubby works away, we lead separate lives, what more is there to know?" The tone of her voice indicated that she didn't wish to give away any personal information.

Roger ignored the obvious rebuff and continued, "Do you still see your husband? I mean, surely he keeps in contact with you and Karen?" Roger was digging to ensure there were no hidden surprises that were going to leap out and compromise his position. He kept reminding himself he was a married man too, despite his philandering nature, he did not want to engage in anything that would upset the status quo.

Ann sighed, stopped her chores, turned and eyeballed Roger; she did not attempt to hide her annoyance at the constant questioning, "Look! He's not even in the country, he flies helicopters in the Congo for their military, he's ex British Army. I haven't seen him for some time. He writes to Karen and no doubt he'll come to see her when he comes back, but for now, he doesn't exist in my life, ok? So can we now stop talking about him?"

Roger let it drop, knowing that her husband, apparently in name only, was out in Africa, giving him some comfort that he wouldn't be walking in the front door any time soon.

He wasn't disappointed in Ann's culinary skills. She obviously had been busy, they feasted on an Avocado and Crab salad, followed by a filet mignon baked Beef Wellington style, cooked to perfection with an exquisite green salad tossed in balsamic vinegar with a hint of basil. For dessert, she had prepared Crème Brulee and a cheese course with Roger's favourite cheese, Stinking Bishop.

Over dinner, they engaged in small talk, Ann divulging office gossip, and associated politics. Roger found this interesting as it provided information that would help him understand how Beaumont's ticked. After they had exhausted that, they lingered over the coffee, both being lost in their own thoughts, both probably planning what, if anything was coming next.

Roger sighed inwardly, fed up with being rebuffed several times and bored with the small talk, thinking to himself it was best to call it a night. Breaking the silence that hung between them, "Here let me help you clear away and make a start on the washing up, then," he briefly looked at his watch, "I must be making a move back to the ship and leave you in peace."

"Ok, but don't worry about the washing up; that can be left until the morning or I might make a start on it when you've gone."

This remark didn't come as a surprise or disappointment to Roger as he had become convinced that he wasn't going to get anywhere with her, well not tonight at least.

They stood up together, and Roger made his way through to the hallway, thankful that he hadn't had any more to drink or mixed his drink with wine. By the front door, they turned to face each other. Roger knew full well that he had wasted his time. He questioned what had happened to the confident, sexy woman who had come on to him in his shipboard office earlier that day. Accepting the fact that nothing would happen between him and Ann, he leaned forward, gave her a chaste kiss on the cheek and said, "Thank you very much for a superb dinner and what I can only describe as a very interesting afternoon and evening."

Suddenly, catching Roger completely off guard, Ann grabbed him and pulled him towards her. Reaching up, instinctively found his lips, which he greedily accepted, and she rammed her tongue into his mouth. Then, as quickly as it had occurred, Ann pulled herself free, speaking in a voice which sounded hard and almost threatening, yet unmistakably husky and full of sexuality, "Not here Roger. Give me ten minutes then come upstairs to the back bedroom. I'll be waiting."

"OK," he murmured meekly, slightly confused by the sudden turn of events. Judging from what he had previously experienced, he had not expected her to submit so eagerly, let alone take charge of the situation.

"What about your daughter?" he called as Ann trotted up the stairs.

"She's not here, won't be back until tomorrow night," she said before she disappeared into the back bedroom.

Smiling to himself, Roger crossed the hallway into the lounge, where he helped himself to a large brandy. He might have an interesting night, after all, guessing he wouldn't be driving again tonight, or so he sincerely hoped.

The minutes ticked by, and he couldn't wait any longer. He swallowed the last of the brandy and headed up the stairs. He felt his blood pumping fast through his veins; his hands were slightly clammy with sweat in anticipation of what awaited him. He opened the door to what he presumed to be the back bedroom, slipped in, and closed it behind him. The room initially appeared empty. His eyes rested upon a large padded stool similar to a vaulting horse found in school gymnasiums. Immediately, he thought he had come into the wrong room; then he caught sight of the clothes she had been wearing strewn carelessly across the room. 'Wow, she had been in a rush,' he thought momentarily. There was a movement behind a curtain in the corner of the room. Roger glanced at his watch, had he come too soon? He was about to call her name when suddenly there was a 'swish' of fabric being drawn aside to reveal a sight that struck Roger dumb as Ann stood before him.

She looked at him and said, "Well, well! Who's been a naughty boy then... Get over here and take your punishment!" Her voice was deep, guttural, and frightening.

Roger stepped back in horror, then froze. Ann stood before him, feet apart, left hand on her ample hip, in her right hand a lethal-looking, long whip that he had only ever seen before in the Indiana Jones films. Ann, from her toes to the tops of her thighs, was clad in neatly laced black leather boots with her upper body squeezed into a black lace corset which nipped her in the middle, accentuating the flair of her fleshy hips and pushing her breasts up so high that they threatened to overflow and pop out like champagne corks. Her arms were covered in elbow-length gloves and her face was covered in a matching black PVC mask, only her mouth and eyes were revealed.

Her left hand suddenly rose snapping back, then forwards, making the lethal-looking whip snake through the air, creating an almighty crack before landing on the floor next to Roger.

Roger was momentarily gripped with the 'flight or fight' syndrome, but his pulsating manhood was ready for action. Not only was Ann dressed as an evil-looking Dominatrix, but on the wall previously hidden by the curtain hung leather straps, handcuffs, riding crops, chains, and other assorted macabre objects of torture. Now he realised, only too well, the purpose of the vaulting horse and the instructional magazines downstairs in the lounge.

"Come along... come to your mistress, you naughty, naughty boy. I'm going to thrash you," growled Ann. Roger found it hard to believe that it really was her; it was as if she had metamorphosed into an alien. Again, she lashed the whip, but this time she aimed it clearly for Roger's head, causing him to duck instinctively in fear. His inner thoughts screamed at him to make a hasty retreat. He turned, reached for the door handle, but before he could grab it, the whip cut through the air again. The leather bit viciously into his hand, causing him to cry out in pain as the blood ran freely.

"That's right," came Ann's voice, "over here! Get down on your knees!"

Roger just looked at her in horror, "What the fu- "

But before he could finish the sentence, the dominatrix growled again.

"Don't even think about leaving this room. The door closes on an automatic lock; you're going to have to beg to be let out, you naughty, naughty boy."

Her frightening laughter rang out, like a vampire in a horror movie. It was obvious how much she was enjoying herself at Roger's expense. Again, he reached for the doorknob jerking his hand away just in time as the menacing whip lashed out with a loud crack.

"Good God, you're a sadistic bitch; let me out," he cried.

"Don't go," she mocked, "this can be fun, come on; let's have a game."

The increase in adrenaline gave him an unexpected determination to make the most of the situation, "All right," he snarled, "I'll play it your way, you bitch... I'll show you. You're right it could be fun," he said as he advanced on her, ready to dodge any lashes of the whip she aimed at him. Ann's laughter was ghoulish as it reverberated around the room, echoing and bouncing off the walls.

Roger wasn't one for role play, but if Ann wanted to play, then he would join in and give it all he'd got. He'd try anything at least once.

After a night of ferocious shagging, as that's what it was, no passion or lovemaking involved just basic animal rutting. Roger staggered back on board his ship in the early hours of Monday morning. The previous evening felt like a dream or was it a nightmare? He'd read about such sexual acts in various 'smutty' men's magazines but he'd always passed them off as figments of the writer's imagination. The funny thing was, although he didn't want to admit it to himself, he had enjoyed it. It was different, exciting. At first, he had been a little terrified of the woman, thinking that she had perverted sexual needs. After Roger had joined in with her games, he had become a willing partner.

The morning after conscience was getting the better of him. It wasn't the first time he had been unfaithful to Siobhan, but his other conquests had been casual affairs that suited both parties, *'it didn't mean anything'* sex, nothing more. This was different; the night's events made him feel like Ann owned him, perhaps that was her intention; it frightened him. He regretted his indiscretion, told himself it would be the first and last time. However, that thought didn't last long, and he was soon thinking about going back for more. There were things in that room yet to be experienced, he thought, *'I could, maybe, just go back one more time, if she was up for it.'* As much as he loved Siobhan, sexual relations between them seemed boring almost mechanical when compared to the night he had just experienced.

Roger, completely exhausted, climbed into his bunk at 3 a.m. As his head hit the pillow, he drifted off to sleep, his limbs ached, and the soreness kicked in. Feeling the aches, he smiled, *'Who needs a gym with a girlfriend like Ann Clark!'*

Chapter 49

The following morning, after struggling to get out of his bunk at 06:00hrs, Roger was busy with passengers as they boarded at 08:00. He felt totally washed out, his body ached, still stinging from where Ann had caught him with that damn whip of hers. It had even drawn blood in some places. He had physically fought Ann for the whip and discovered that for a woman, she was extremely strong. 'Oh hell,' he thought with a sudden jolt, 'How on earth do I explain the lacerations to Siobhan,' his skin crawled, sending a shiver down his spine. The problem gnawed at him all day as he tried to think of excuses. He considered volunteering to do some extra duty so that the marks could have time to heal. His saving grace came the following day, quite unexpectedly, when the ship arrived back in Northwold from the overnight Continental trip. Roy Brooks, the Marine Personnel Manager was first up the gangway when they arrived in the dock, Roy was even boarding ahead of the port customs officials and while the passengers were still enjoying their sumptuous, full English breakfast.

Roy was a taciturn individual who would never answer a question with a clear, decisive or concise answer. He would have made a good politician. Many people complained that after a meeting with Roy Brooks, they left his presence wondering what on earth the meeting had been about, the conversation appearing to be pointless. Perhaps this characteristic was the result of his constant dealings with the various Unions. Whenever there was a personnel problem, it was to his door that a local seaman's union representative beat a path. Roy was always at the forefront of these meetings, the local general manager would sometimes attend, but all the other managers hid behind Roy when it came to dealing with union bosses. He'd been a seaman and union representative himself for several years before 'swallowing the anchor,' as going ashore was known, because of this, the seagoing staff thought that he would have more sympathy towards them, but he didn't. He'd gone over to the other side, a poacher turned gamekeeper; to many he was known as 'Mr. Shifty.' Roy had the air of a teacher; he even wore jackets with the leather elbow patches, synonymous with male professors. He had a sharp face with chiselled features and a pale complexion. When Roy spoke, his voice sounded nasal, giving the impression he had a cleft palate, which he didn't. From a young age, he had been a heavy smoker. Aware that he struggled to be without a nicotine rush for more than half an hour, Roy had taken to using a cigarette holder with an extra filter tip in an attempt to reduce his nicotine intake.

As Roy entered the main embarkation area, he could see through the glass-covered counter where Roger was working at his desk.

"Morning Holt," called Roy as he went around and entered the Purser's office.

Roger groaned inwardly; he really didn't want Roy Brooks getting in his face this early in the morning. Apart from his immediate task of having to deal with the port authorities and seeing the passengers safely ashore, Roger had too much on his mind following his encounter with the luscious, kinky and slightly frightening, Ann Clark.

"Morning," replied Roger as he stood up and held out his hand. Roy looked at it suspiciously as if unsure what to do before he accepted it in an offhand manner. Before Roger had a chance to enquire what Roy wanted, as coming on board at this early hour with the ship hardly tied up was unusual, Roy quickly asked, "Any chance of some tea and toast, I've had an early start this morning."

"Certainly," replied Roger. He pressed the button on his desk, which rang a bell in the steward's pantry, summonsing a steward, then carried on with his paperwork in the hope that Roy would leave him in peace. The steward arrived, took the order and scurried away.

Brooks spoke again to make polite conversation, "Fine old ship this, you know. First Roll-on, Roll-off ship in the Merchant Navy."

"Yes," said Roger, keeping his head down, "I am aware of that," he tried not to sound too exasperated with Roy as he wondered what he was doing aboard so early.

"No crew problems then?" asked Roy suspiciously.

"No, everyone on-board is fine, thank you."

"Good. Don't like problems, you know, I prefer the quiet life."

"That's a strange remark from a man working in personnel," replied Roger.

"I suppose so," said Roy absently, "can we speak in private?"

"Of course," Roger was surprised at the request and a little annoyed, "I just, ...erm, let me get hold of my assistant so he can take over the desk and deal with the clearance. The passengers will be disembarking shortly."

"Sure," said Roy. Then, without waiting to be invited, he went through from the office into Roger's private quarters.

Roger used an internal phone to summons his assistant purser to the office and quickly followed Roy.

Before Roger had a chance to sit down, Roy turned to him and asked, "Right. So then. How are you enjoying your new surroundings?"

"Very much, I only wish I had made the move sooner."

There was a knock on the door, and the steward entered with a tray bearing a pot of steaming hot tea together with a rack of fresh toast, butter and Old English Oxford marmalade, "There you go, sir, just nicely brewed and the toast straight from the grill, enjoy."

"Thank you," mumbled Roy as the steward left, closing the door behind him.

Roy hungrily attacked the toast. He spread the butter thick with a great dollop of Oxford marmalade on top before devouring it in big bites.

"Mmm... excellent," he said through mouthfuls as he shovelled in another slice.

Roger busied himself, pouring tea for the both of them. He had no liking for management breathing down his neck, which is what Roy Brooks appeared to be doing. Roger couldn't help but feel anxious. Management arrivals on-board were nearly always close to lunchtime, when there were a few quiet hours before the boarding started again, this had the added advantage of joining the officers for an excellent onboard lunch. Maybe it was Roger's guilty conscience playing tricks on him, maybe it was just the presence of Roy annoying him, but either way, Roger decided to take the bull by the horns.

"I don't wish to appear rude Roy, but as I'm sure you'll appreciate I'm a busy man at this time in the morning, is this a social call which could have waited until later or is there something wrong?"

Brooks eyed Roger as he crunched on his toast and marmalade, swallowing a mouthful before attempting to talk, "Don't go on the defensive just because I pay you an early morning call. Don't worry; you're doing fine, the company is very pleased with you."

Roger smiled in relief. A wave of smugness passed over him in the knowledge that he was screwing the company and nobody knew.

Brooks continued, going into his welfare enquiry mode, "Anyway, how's the wife and family? I'm sure they are pleased that you get home more often."

Roger sighed inwardly. The events of the night before reminded him of the guilt that had plagued him all the previous day. Roger looked down into his cup of tea, "They're fine, thank you; naturally they enjoy me being home regularly, being away deep sea was putting a strain on my marriage, although Siobhan knew what she was taking on when we tied the knot."

"Hmm, I see. Well," said Roy sheepishly, "how would your wife regard you if you did some extra work for us? It would be mean taking you away from home for a little longer than a normal tour of duty."

"Oh," said Roger looking up from his cup of tea in surprise, "it would rather depend on the circumstances, of course, and for how long."

"I see," replied Brooks in a very non-committal tone which was beginning to annoy Roger.

Roger thought about it for a few minutes before continuing, laying it on thick to show willing, "Naturally, I'd try to do what my employers ask out of loyalty. I'm sure Siobhan will be excited for me as she knows how happy I am working for Beaumont's, so any extra work will not be a problem." Roger was surprised at his loyalty speech, almost believing it himself.

Roy coughed again, but this time it was a deep, grisly cough. He cleared his throat and carried on, "Well, we want to appoint to you to one of our new vessels currently being built on the Clyde," he said, still trying to release the frog in his throat, "If you should accept the appointment then it would mean standing-by up there until the vessel's completion, followed by bringing her into service, say about two months all in. One month while she is completed followed by the sea trials, then, if they are successful, handover will be accepted by the company, and she'll come straight down here to Northwold, store up, start-up on the cross channel run then you'll be relieved. Of course, while you're up in Scotland, you can get home for weekends so it's not as though you'll be leaving your family for the whole two months."

"I feel very honoured," smiled Roger, a feeling of euphoria creeping over him.

"Good, good. There is one more thing that is a bit of a sting in the tail, it means you going up there tomorrow. How's that?" asked Brooks hesitantly, expecting some protest from Roger.

Roger's mind was doing somersaults, he tried to hide his excitement as well as relief. Unbeknown to Roy Brooks, he had just thrown Roger a lifeline. Half an hour ago Roger was struggling to get started with his day's work as he was trying to figure out how to handle his current predicament. After his violent sexual and athletic encounter with Ann Clark, all he could think about was the possible consequences after having to explain his battered and bruised body to Siobhan. Roy had just given him a perfect way out of his somewhat awkward situation.

"Of course, I'll go. Siobhan won't mind at all; she'll be very pleased for me, I'm sure."

Brooks stifled a sigh of relief.

"I'll need some time to nip home for some more kit if I'm to be away for a month or two."

"Naturally. Well, I'll be off. There'll be a letter on board later today to confirm our conversation along with details concerning your hotel plus an introduction for the new vessel's building Superintendent who's in charge up there. I presume you'll want to go by car?"

"Yes," Roger nodded, smiling at the chance to give his beloved Ford Escort RS200 a blast up the A1.

"No problem, claim your expenses in the normal way," Roy stood ready to leave, "I'll arrange for your relief to join here tomorrow, goodbye for now."

"Cheerio Mr. Brooks."

Roger's eyes gleamed as he watched Brooks leave. He would be able to make some excuse to Siobhan for not getting home for the first couple of weekends in order to allow some of the lacerations he bore to heal up. He would have to contact Freddie Naylor and close the victualling account to avoid scrutiny by his relief. Best of all, he could start again aboard the new, much bigger ship, which would mean a bigger 'rake-off' for him and Freddie.

"Oh yes, the future was beginning to look very rosy indeed," he mused.

Chapter 50

Roger duly travelled up to Glasgow to 'stand-by' the new ship. He soon made a name for himself, gaining the admiration of the new vessel's building Superintendent. Roger had an eye for detail and plenty of experience from previous positions standing by the building of several luxury cruise liners. As the interior of the ship slowly developed, Roger's task was to sign acceptance as the ship owner's representative, a responsibility handed to him by the new building Superintendent. At first, the new building Superintendent had Roger down as just another glory seeker whom he would have to handhold, increasing the already immense pressure and stress he was under, chivvying the building yard to ensure the vessel came out on time ready for the already advertised sailing schedule. After seeing Roger in action, dealing with the shipyard managers completing the interior of the ship, he knew that Roger was unknowingly relieving him of a huge load on his overburden shoulders.

Against his better judgment, Roger did not break off his relationship with Ann Clark. Roger, still working on the new ship in Glasgow, had the ideal excuse to give to Siobhan for not getting home for the odd weekend. He and Ann made the most of his weekend flexibility, which coincided with Karen's absences allowing Roger to stay overnight. It was all too easy for Roger to give his wife wrong information about his work rosters. So inevitably, he became more embroiled with Ann's kinky sexual performances, which at times turned quite violent with most of the sadism aimed at Roger. This should have sent warning signals to him, but Roger never ducked away from a challenge; he was determined to eventually dominate Ann. One scary encounter with Ann had culminated in a row during which Ann had actually attacked Roger with a knife. Not any old knife either, this was a vicious razor-sharp gutting knife normally used by fish merchants. Even this did not deter Roger, who never questioned as to why on earth Ann owned such a dangerous combat style knife which, if carried outside on the streets, would be classed as a dangerous weapon with the risk of arrest. Roger was too besotted with Ann's sexual predilections to register just how serious a web of evil he was being drawn into. Making light of the knife attack ended up in Ann kicking him out so he had to book into a local hotel that night, but she was soon back on the telephone, whispering sweet nothings, luring him back into her macabre lifestyle. If Roger had been tuned in to the Beaumont office rumour machine surrounding the disappearance of her husband, then perhaps Roger would have made a hasty retreat back to the loving, docile arms of his wife.

The affair was a closely guarded secret, this suited both of them. Ann's daughter, Karen, had accepted that the marriage between her mother and father was over. She believed her father was flying helicopters in the Congo from the infrequent letters she received from him. Karen appreciated the letters, but she missed him dearly. She adored her father, as a soldier he had been her hero as she grew up, he still was. Her bedroom was adorned with several photographs of him in uniform from smart parades to full battle dress camouflage, then more of him at the controls of a helicopter. One of the best days of her life when she went with him to Buckingham Palace to collect his Military Medal from the Queen, Karen had been so proud. Although only very young at the time, she felt really grown up with a new dress and hat bought by her father especially for the occasion. She loved to boast to her friends that her father was a decorated war hero. Now she felt like he had deserted her, despite the explanations given by her mother that it was a once in a lifetime job. The letters she received from him, promised he'd return to see her. Karen had written replies to her father's letters but was very frustrated that he never directly answered her many questions. She felt that he was ignoring her. A request to visit him was firmly put down with the explanation that the Congo was by far too much of a dangerous place. Karen accepted this, much to her mother's apparent relief. Detective Sergeant Peter Marsh, had he known about the situation, would have come to a much different conclusion had he been able to read the letters Karen received. Karen often wondered why her mother, a very attractive mature lady, didn't attract admirers. She guessed her father was far from replaceable but, she often wondered why she didn't appear to date anybody at all.

Deep down, Karen enjoyed the set-up with just her and her mother; they respected each other's lives and privacy. There were only two house rules her mother had; tidy up your own mess and never attempt to enter the back bedroom. Ann told her daughter that the room was her sanctum. As a young lady, Karen had become very involved with her aunty, Ann's sister. Her aunty and uncle lived in the south, so she would often spend weekends at their house. Ann had always encouraged this relationship. Although not that close to her sister, Ann knew that her sister, being married to a London businessman and with no children could offer a far more interesting lifestyle for Karen than she ever could stuck up in the deserted wilds of Northwold.

The truth was, Ann was desperate to find a man to provide both for her financial and personal needs. She was becoming bored with the brief encounters with Roger. Although their sexual activities were always mind-blowing, Roger was a married man and likely to stay that way. On more than one occasion, he'd hinted to Ann that this was just 'fun,' discouraging thoughts that there could be anything more than brief encounters for sex. The time was approaching when she was going to ditch Roger to enable her to move on to find her 'meal ticket.' Roger was a very generous man, often arriving with gifts of jewellery and perfume, they were payment for her 'services' but would not provide for her future. Ann decided she needed to end the fling. She was confident Roger wouldn't offer any resistance; they had both agreed it wouldn't last forever. Ann cooked them another excellent meal, a 'last supper' in Ann's eyes. 'Have a fun night and call it quits,' thought Ann as she prepared the meal. Later, as they lay entwined in bed, exhausted after their sexual athletics, enjoying a bottle of Bollinger champagne, several in fact, that Roger had brought. The old adage that alcohol loosens tongues was one lesson that Roger was going to wish he had taken heed of.

"Oh darling," said Ann, fondling Roger's genitals as she nuzzled his neck, "However, do you get your hands on this lovely champagne? You don't have sticky fingers at work, do you?"

"Ha," laughed Roger at the irony of her remark.

"Doesn't your wife ever ask what you spend your money on? She must notice, or are you one of those prehistoric men who keep their earnings a secret?" Roger lifted himself on to one elbow and stretched to the bedside table to pour himself another glass of bubbly, "Siobhan knows exactly what I earn, we have a joint account, in fact, she holds the purse strings, handles all the family finances. I earn it; she spends it," he laughed. Ann became concerned, "If she watches the finances, then surely she questions your spending when you're away? And what about the gifts you give me?"

"Let's just say I have a little private income."

These words struck a chord with Ann, "A private income?" she said as she twisted some of his pubic hairs.

"Ouch," squealed Roger.

"Have you got a rich father then, or some wealthy relative that's left you an endowment trust fund? Talking of endowment, I think you are rising to the occasion again?" she giggled as Roger felt himself stiffen.

"My Dad's a retired school teacher, the rest of my family are just simple sailors like me, married to ordinary middle-class ladies with typical average families. You could say though that I'd won the football pools." As soon as the words had left Roger's mouth, he knew he had already said too much.

"Oh, come on, seriously... have you won the pools?" she squeezed Roger's testicles. Ann didn't want to appear too eager, but she was intrigued at Roger's worth, maybe she and Roger could have a future after all. Ann wasn't averse to becoming the other woman. It could suit her down to the ground, fitting in very nicely with the lifestyle she craved. She often wondered if perhaps she should become a high-class escort, or as some called it, a high society hooker. The excitement got to her, and she squeezed just a little too hard.

"Ow, fuck that hurt," he said sternly, "what are playing at?"

"Oh, did Mumsie Wumsie hurt you?" she chided, the pretence of actually caring was excruciating to Ann. She had been so clear in her head that she was going to call it a day on their relationship at the end of tonight, but now she appeared to have inadvertently stumbled on something that could be very interesting indeed.

"Here, let me kiss it better," Ann snaked beneath the bed sheet and took Roger's penis in her mouth. He quickly reacted, becoming rock hard to the point of bursting as his testosterone went into turbo drive.

Between mouthfuls of Roger's penis, Ann asked, "Have you really won the pools?"

"No," he managed to stifle a gasp as the heady mixture of champagne and sex got the better of him. Ann sucked Roger to the point of orgasm then drew back, keeping Roger on the knife-edge of ecstasy. He was putty in her hands.

"Do tell me, darling," she begged, "You know your secrets will be safe with me, I'm the pillar of discretion over our little affair. You know I'm not an evil scheming woman trying to make you give up Siobhan for me, you know I won't, so please tell me."

"Yes, alright," panted Roger, "just don't keep me like this, please finish what you started," he groaned.

Ann had begun to do what she knew would break down his defences, she marvelled at how easily she could twist him round her little finger, he was so vulnerable when she had him like this.

"Come on, baby, tell me about it," she whispered as her head came up from beneath the sheets, then she was down again, slowly building him back up to a climax. His body tingled with passion; he felt like he was flying in the stratosphere. In the aftermath of a climax, Roger told Ann everything. The whole story of his fiddles throughout the years, of monies stashed away in overseas bank accounts and of the property in the Antipodes. In this weak moment, he even confessed to his current arrangement with Freddie Naylor.

That night, Ann never said a word about ending the relationship; instead, she gave him the best night of his life, sexually. The following day, after Roger had left to return to Glasgow, Ann sat down to ponder on her discovery. She found it hard to believe, surely Roger was spinning her a tall story. Undoubtedly, the jewellery which he had bestowed on her had cost a pretty penny; she felt that he couldn't have done that on his wages. Beaumont's were good payers, giving their staff more than comparable companies, but not that good. Ann decided to check for herself just to see if there was any truth in the yarn he'd spun. It took Ann three weeks to collect the information without causing any suspicion. She had to fend off a couple of searching questions from some of the staff she approached for information. Thankfully, she had been able to 'blag' her way out of awkward questions, especially where men were concerned. Ann was very clever, knowing exactly how to get what she wanted with sexual innuendos. 'Men are such gullible Neanderthals,' she thought to herself. She eventually discovered some vague loose ends but nothing of any substance. The figures did not appear to amount to very much when she knew that the money was split between Roger and the Ship's Chandler, but when she extrapolated the figures on an annual basis, she was staggered. However, it was still all very vague and she couldn't actually prove any wrong doing other than believing what Roger had told her. Ann now believed that Roger could, actually, be her passport to the lifestyle she craved. Although he didn't know it yet, he was going to provide a lot more than just some expensive trinket jewellery and champagne. He was to become her key to a comfortable life, a very comfortable life indeed. This was 'Big Bucksville,' she thought, recalling a quote from an American movie she'd once watched.

Chapter 51

Bringing his department of the new super ferry into readiness for service, kept Roger very busy. James Porter, Roger's boss, was constantly on Roger's back about one thing or another; the man was never satisfied. Roger was convinced there was a sadistic streak in him, coupled with being a first-class belligerent bully. Porter had such an abrasive attitude that he had been banned from senior management meetings with the seaman's unions as several meetings had broken up in disarray thanks to Porter's belligerence. Those instructions had come down from the local Managing Director, appointed by Richard. Of course, the 'spin' that Porter put on it when telling others painted a very different picture, that was Porter through and through. Conforming to the characteristics of the megalomaniac he was, he had complete and unshakeable belief in himself. Some would say 'he's a legend in his own mind!'

Due to unforeseen circumstances, Ann's daughter stayed at home for a long period during the summer holidays, which, together with the pressure of work on Roger meant he was unable to get to see Ann. Not that it mattered that much to Roger, he was considering bringing the relationship to an end anyway. He felt the guilt was becoming a burden he no longer wanted. His previous indiscretions with ladies had all just been flings; as soon as they had started, they were over, but the involvement with Ann was becoming too psychologically consuming and energy sapping, adding to the strain he was already suffering. However, he did hear some enlightening news down the grapevine that Ann had apparently started seeing a middle-aged bachelor who owned a wholesale warehouse and general grocer's shop in Northwold, one of the dying breed of corner shops epitomised in the TV series *'Open All Hours.'* It later transpired that the owner sold tobacco on the side for Dave Dundas.

Another worrying aspect for Roger, as he became more involved with Ann, was the true state of her marriage. Roger wasn't convinced that Ann had given him an accurate explanation. Although she and her husband supposedly lived separate lives, there was always the distinct possibility that divorce proceedings would loom into sight. Such proceedings could see him named as a co-respondent. That was a situation he wanted to avoid at all costs and definitely another equally good reason to get out of the relationship he now felt to be sordid. So Ann's recently rumoured 'hook up' with the 'jolly grocer,' as Roger thought of him, would mean he could pass that particular baton to another. This pleased Roger immensely; it relieved the strain and pressure of possibly being found out for the womanising philanderer he was, which could eventually lead to the destruction of his cosy marriage and lifestyle.

Early one morning, Roger's ship; the brand new, gleaming, leviathan ferry *m.v.'Northshire,'* arrived on schedule from the continent after its recent maiden voyage. It was 'hand-over' day, and Roger was certainly looking forward to going home for some well-earned rest and relaxation. His affair with Ann was playing on his mind, taking the edge off the normal elation he felt when about to go on leave. He knew he had to get a grip of the situation and break all ties with Ann. If there was truth in the rumours he'd heard about her dating someone else, he assumed this would make the process of ending the relationship all the easier.

Having seen the last of the passengers ashore, Roger was busy with the process of handing over the reins to his relief, Mike, when the shore telephone burst into life, causing him to jump.

Instinctively grabbing the handset, Roger answered in his formal professional voice.

"Hello there, Purser's Office *m.v.'Northshire,'* Chief Purser speaking."

"Roger, darling, it's me. Are you alone?" asked Ann.

"Oh, hi, sweetheart, you're up early. Couldn't you sleep?"

Roger groaned inwardly, turning to Mike, "It's my wife."

How he wished it really was Siobhan, Ann was the last person he wanted to talk to.

Mike smiled and nodded.

Ann understood Roger was not alone, "Ok, I get the message, how about coming over today? I checked the roster with the crewing department and knew you'd be coming off today, so I have taken a day owed to me. Karen went off to France yesterday, so I'm home alone, my luuuvvver."

Roger felt hollow in the pit of his stomach, he didn't really need this, but on the other hand, he needed to see Ann to bring everything to a close.

"Ok, can do," he said cheerily, "I'll be leaving at around eleven o'clock. See you later."

No sooner had he hung up the phone, and being on tenterhooks anxious about the forthcoming confrontation with Ann, he nearly wet himself to hear the gruff voice of James Porter walking into the Purser's Office.

"Good morning gentleman, ahh, I see you are handing over, right then, have you finished?" Roger thought it sounded more like a demand than a question.

Porter thought of himself as royalty and believed everything should stop for him. Roger raised his eyebrows at his relief purser, showing his annoyance of Porter's brash entrance and interference.

"Well, don't let me disturb you as I'm sure you're busy, but could one of you invite me to breakfast, I just fancy one of our renowned shipboard English breakfasts." Porter appeared to be in very high spirits as he rubbed his hands together in anticipation, knowing full well he wouldn't be refused.

"Of course sir, follow me," said Mike as he stood, "Roger's just got some loose ends to tie up, then the 'hand-over' is complete."

Roger smiled at Mike, silently acknowledging his thanks. Porter quickly walked out of the office, heading off in the direction of the ship's main dining room.

"Thanks, Mike, although I suppose I'll have to come along too, if I don't Porter will only take umbrage."

"Too right he will, plus if you don't join us, I'll never forgive you, trying to eat breakfast alone with him will only give me indigestion," said Mike as he gave Roger a gentle punch on the arm.

"Yeah ok, I'll just throw the last few items in my case and get changed; I'll join you asap."

"See you in ten," said Mike as he left the office.

Roger took the opportunity to ring his home in Kettlestone. He told Siobhan that due to various meetings he had to attend in the company office, she was not to worry but he wouldn't be home until much later that evening. He could sense the annoyance in her tone and did his best to soothe her. He promised to make it up to her with dinner the following night at their favourite country restaurant, owned and managed by an award-winning Michelin Star chef, then selfishly asking her to book the table. As always, Roger's charm worked and Siobhan soon accepted her husband's promises. Roger nipped up to his cabin, changed out of his uniform and then went down to join his colleagues for breakfast. He had very mixed emotions, the euphoria of going home on leave after such a long spell onboard were tinged with the anxiety, knowing that he had to face Ann later and bring to an end, the ill-conceived relationship. Consumed with these thoughts and looking forward to enjoying a sumptuous breakfast after being up since five o'clock that morning, Roger failed to tune into the frosty atmosphere surrounding Mike and James Porter as he sat down and joined them. Before Roger had arrived, James had just remonstrated with the dining room steward who, on approaching to take his order for breakfast, had casually asked him if he would like the 'Full House' as the full English breakfast was so commonly referred to. The steward had to face being berated by James Porter, pointing out that he should have referred to the breakfast offering as the grilled breakfast menu option as against the light continental offer!

No sooner had Roger taken his seat when the same chastened steward approached him with a menu card, and before he had chance to offer it to Roger, he cheerily said to the steward, "No need for the menu, just bring me the 'Full House' please." With that, James Porter exploded like a latent volcano, much to the amazement of the other breakfast diners. The day wasn't auguring well.

As Roger drove to Ann's house, he felt nervous. He wasn't sure how to broach the subject of telling her that their relationship had run its course. He pondered on her response, would she be sad, angry, or relieved. He had no idea. Perhaps he would have to stay overnight and comfort her? He soon changed his mind thinking, no certainly not, out of the question, how could he clear that with Siobhan? Maybe it was best to face the subject as soon as he arrived, get it over and done with, and speed off home to give Siobhan a nice surprise by being home earlier than expected.

As usual, Roger parked his very recognisable car off the road, well-hidden on the drive which runs at the front and side of Ann's house. Within seconds of getting out of his car, Ann had appeared at the door. They greeted each other with a chase peck on the cheek and went through into the kitchen.

Ann busied herself, making coffee using a coffee machine that ground the whole coffee beans before brewing, another expensive present from Roger. As they sat in the kitchen, sipping their coffees, both recognised the tricky atmosphere, and the silence that persisted was deafening. As Roger sat thinking about how to open the conversation, Ann interrupted his thoughts.

"Roger. The time has come, my darling, for you to pay for past pleasures." Roger was startled, "Oh? Okay. Why, what do you want? More jewellery, perhaps something for the house?" He knew his response was wrong; he stupidly thought he had to keep her sweet before breaking her heart. He still hadn't learned that Ann didn't have a heart to break! He smiled at her, but not for long. Ann's intense stare sent a shiver down his back.

"Jewellery doesn't pay the bills, Roger. I've decided that you're going to keep me in the style I deserve so I can reduce my hours at Beaumont's.

£500 per month should do nicely. This house will be mine once I divorce, and the bills aren't that big but of course, I shall review this amount occasionally, inflation, you know."

Roger was stunned; he couldn't quite comprehend what Ann had just said, "I'm not sure what you are getting at Ann; you want me to finance you as though I am a sort of surrogate husband?"

"If you have to put a label on it, then yes."

"On your bike Ann!" he replied with guffaw and bravado. "I enjoyed buying you gifts now and then, but that's as far as it goes."

Ann stared at him, contemplating her next move. Roger was furtive, glancing quickly away from the menace he saw in her eyes.

Roger stood, ready to make a hasty retreat, the look he'd seen in her eyes gave him a warning that Ann was on the point of turning nasty. He'd already had a taste of what she could dole out when crossed. He recalled the vicious knife, once was enough for Roger. Although he was reasonably confident he could fight his corner with her, Ann wasn't to be messed with. He had worked out that she was a tough cookie, having learned kickboxing in the past. He recalled the trophies she'd won, prominently displayed in the lounge glass cabinet.

Clearing his throat, he shivered, then declared, "Actually Ann, I want to bring our relationship to a close, although this is not how I wanted it to end. We've both had fun, but the time has come to move on. I've heard you are seeing someone else and I'm actually really pleased for you. It would be better for all involved if I back out and leave you free to pursue your new relationship." Roger avoided making any remark about the absent husband.

Ann remained seated, not threatened in the least by the standing figure of Roger.

Ann's voice took on the deep huskiness he'd first heard on the night she introduced him to her 'sex room.' It was a voice that frightened him; it was the precursor to a total change in her temperament; it signalled her Mr. Hyde personality. Since the start of their brief encounter, Roger had come to the conclusion that she had the traits of a psychopath. All too late, he realised he should have left her well alone.

"Roger, sit down," it was an order, not a request. Something in Roger made him obey. He didn't want to rile her, wanting to get out of the house in one piece. He could see he was going to have to work harder to make her see that bringing the relationship to an end was the best for both of them.

Ann was in no mood for negotiating; she had a fire in her belly, Roger was going to do as she demanded or she would let him know that there would be consequences he wouldn't want to contemplate.

"Now listen here, boy," her husky voice growled with menace and intimidation, "you are going to pay me what I want, make no mistake about it. You know very well you can afford it. Remember you told me all about your scheme with your mate at the chandlery? Well, you could say that I am asking you to pay for my silence. I don't want a lion's share, just... well, shall we say a retainer. I have a good idea of what you are making out of Beaumont's as I've done some digging." There was a hint of a smile on her lips as she saw the realisation dawning on Roger as to exactly what she was demanding. He attempted to show some bravado in a vain attempt to regain some control.

"So what? Who will believe you? People will think it's some fanciful tale. I've made sure all the accounts are correct, why should anyone believe you?"

"Oh, Roger, you think you're a clever boy!" Ann's voice was loaded with sarcasm, "Is it a risk you want to take? You know that I could convince the powers that be that something untoward has been going on and if I told them it had cost the company tens of thousands, don't you think they would want to investigate?" Ann smiled, "I mean, it didn't exactly take me that long to figure it out, so..."

Roger stayed silent, in shock.

"If you are found out, then you know you'll more than likely go to prison, do you really want that?"

An icy feeling of fear crept through Roger's body.

Roger finally snapped, "You... you dirty whore!" He was red with rage.

Instantaneously, Ann leaned over the table and slapped Roger's face, "No need to be abusive, Roger! If I'm a whore, then you're a bloody criminal, a dirty, scum bag thief!" she yelled.

Swift to retaliate, Roger was up in a flash and, without thinking, threw his right hand up, striking Ann a blow to the lower jaw. The force was so hard that he sent Ann sprawling out of her chair and across the floor. Roger gasped at his action as he watched Ann slowly sit up. Her eyes met his; they were full of fury. She grabbed the sink edge and hauled herself up. Once she caught her breath, she tore a piece of kitchen paper from the nearby dispenser and dabbed her mouth, tasting the warm, salty blood where one of her teeth had cut into her mouth.

"Bastard!" she spat.

Roger's mind was still processing the fact that he had hit a woman; never before had he even contemplated it let alone do it. It was as if some superior force was in control of his body.

"That was very foolish of you, that little outburst of manliness will raise the price."

Roger flopped back into his chair, his sudden bout of aggression quickly draining from him, "Blackmail," he muttered.

"Call it that if you like. I prefer to refer to it as an allowance, let's say for services rendered."

He starred at the floor, his thoughts all over the place. He had to try a different tactic. He looked up and outstretched his arms submissively, "Look, Ann, I'm really sorry, please forgive me, please, I don't know what came over me," he pleaded, "there's no need for us to fight. Okay, so you want me to give you a piece of the action," He kept his voice light, "that's ok by me, it could be good for both of us. In fact, with your position in the office, you could be useful."

Roger had no idea how she would help, as her position in the company was far divorced from any of the accounting functions, but he was desperate. He stood up, attempting to put his arms around her in the act of reconciliation, but sneering, she pushed him away.

"Don't you understand Roger, I want no part of your sordid crime, what's more, as you so readily wanted our relationship to end then so be it, it ends today, right now. I never want to see you again. Post the money to me in cash on the last day of each month, and your secret will be safe with me. Try to double-cross me, and I'll make sure you and your mate go to prison."

In response, Roger lunged at Ann, rage clouding his vision, his hands ready to grab her throat, but she quickly sidestepped him, moving like a gazelle, the terrifying knife he'd feared came from nowhere as its sharp point pierced Roger's shirt and skin causing blood to flow and soak into his shirt. He rapidly stepped back in horror, aware of how close its razor-sharp edge was to causing him even more harm.

"Come one step closer, and this knife will be inside you as I scream the house down. I'll claim that you were trying to rape me," she growled, "Now, get out of my house you fucking bastard."

Roger, totally terrified, did as he was told. He backed away, carefully retreating to the front door mat, not taking his eyes off the huge knife. Suddenly, she raised the knife above her head; it was glinting as it caught the weak, late afternoon sunlight streaming in through the hallway windows, then she let out a nerve-jangling, piercing scream as she charged towards him. He put up his hands in a futile gesture of protection as the knife now came slashing down towards him, cutting through the light linen shirt sleeves and slicing into his forearms. Blood splattered and was soaking into his shirt as he tried to grab her arm. She was now screaming dementedly, all self-control vanished.

Roger tripped and fell backward against the staircase, convinced that his end had come and that he was going to die. Strangely, as he was about to accept the inevitable, his thoughts momentarily wondered what Siobhan would make of it when she heard that her husband had been murdered in the hallway of this woman's home! He seemed to be completely removed from the vicious attack he was undergoing and had, as if by some magical force, transcended above the scene and was looking down on what was happening to him, as if he was but a spectator. Unexpectedly, as quickly as the attack had started, it was over. Ann stood back from his cowering body. She stood panting over his blood-covered upper body, taking in great gulps of air. She looked lost in a trance, totally unmoved at what she had just done. Roger, fearful that her next move would be to lunge downwards, driving the knife deep into his body, he took his chance of escape by scrambling up from his prone position and ran towards the front door. He cried out in frustration as his bloody hands slipped at his attempts to open it as he focused on looking over his shoulder, expecting to see her lunge towards him and bury the knife into his back. As if by a miracle, the door opened, and he staggered out in the driveway. Ann slammed the front door firmly shut, still screaming expletives at him. Roger could hear the deadbolts slamming across, together with the safety chain.

Crying in panic, his blood-soaked hands fumbled for his keys, desperately trying to get away as soon as possible. Once inside his car and totally oblivious that everything he touched was becoming covered in blood, he somehow managed to start the car, engage the gears, and quickly reverse out of the driveway. A shocked and utterly miserable Roger drove away a broken man.

He drove to the outskirts of Northwold, pulling into the first lay-by he saw. Once stopped and still holding the steering wheel, his head slumped forward onto his bloody arms, he sobbed in frustration and anger, as the enormity what had just happened to him kicked in. After what seemed like ages, he looked at his forearms where the blood was now beginning to congeal. Feeling weak and faint, he knew he must seek medical attention. On autopilot, he drove to the small injuries unit at the Northwold hospital. Having given no thought as to how he would explain his injuries, he walked into the small, casualty reception area where a nurse rushed over to guide him to an empty cubicle. She directed him to lay down on the bed, at the same time calling for a colleague, as she swung into action and busied herself, removing his blood-soaked shirt.

"My name is Angela, I'm the Charge Nurse," another nurse quickly arrived, "and this is my colleague Staff Nurse, Brenda. Now what has happened to you, young man?" she enquired as she efficiently inspected Roger's injuries while her colleague prepared cleaning solution and dressings to deal with his wounds.

Laying back with the two nurses attending to him, Roger felt relief wash over him, making him lightheaded, feeling as though he was going to pass out. Despite this, he tried hard to conjure up a story in reply. He knew he couldn't say he'd been mugged; it would only bring in the police, that's the last thing he wanted. Irrationally, he concluded he'd say he'd had a domestic dispute with his wife that had got out of hand when she'd lost her temper.

"I had a fight with my wife," he groaned with a sob, followed by genuine tears running down his cheeks as he relived the recent events.

"Oh dear," replied Angela without batting an eyelid but looking at her colleague and raising her eyebrows. Angela had seen everything in her 17 years working as a nurse. Domestic disputes, incurring such injuries as Roger's, were not uncommon.

"My wife has quite a bad temper and in a fit of rage went for a kitchen knife which I tried to wrestle from her," he explained, and as an afterthought, "It's nothing, just a stupid argument that went too far."

"And how is your wife?" Angela enquired, her mind racing to wonder if there could be a woman lying somewhere severely injured or maybe even worse.

"No, she's ok. I took the brunt; she's no doubt at home full of remorse," Roger sighed, trying to sound convincing.

The two nurses soon had Roger nicely cleaned up and tidily bandaged.

"There we are, that looks a lot better," said Angela standing back admiring her work, then turning to her colleague,

"Pop along to the nurses' station and get this gentleman a nice cup of tea while I get some details from him".

"What details?" asked Roger, suddenly aware of what he might have to reveal.

"Oh, just the usual sir; name, address, how you came to get these injuries, etc."

"I've told you," snapped Roger it was a fight with my wife that got out of hand, "No harm done."

"Well, that may be the case, but I still need some more information from you for the records. It's just routine; we can't treat anybody here without some form filling I'm afraid."

Roger was now beginning to panic and wondering what to say next. His mind in a whirl, trying to think through what he was going to say to cover the circumstances of his situation.

The nurse, Brenda, had disappeared from the cubicle to make Roger some tea as Angela finished tidying up the first aid injuries trolley alongside the bed.

"You just lay back and wait for Brenda to bring you some tea while I nip out to collect some forms to complete. Try to relax, you've lost quite a bit of blood," she said, patting him gently on the shoulder.

"Don't worry, once the duty doctor has looked you over, I'm sure you'll be able to go home."

Angela slipped through the closed cubicle curtains and went to collect some forms from her office, from where, she intended to call the police. She wasn't happy at all with Roger's explanation and was worried that something horrible might have occurred to his wife. If his story was true, then his wife may just be at home nursing her pride, but on the other hand, the alternative didn't bear thinking about. This situation needed police attention.

Nurse Angela had hardly left the cubicle when Roger's mind and hormones went into 'fight or flight' overdrive. This was definitely a flight scenario as far as Roger was concerned. It dawned on him that as soon as he gave his home address as Kettlestone in Norfolk, the question that would immediately arise as to why he was attending this minor injuries clinic here in Northwold. He couldn't think of another address to give to cover this, certainly not Ann Clark's! The very thought of her and that house made him let out an involuntary sob. He had to getaway. Easing himself from the bed, he looked around for something to cover himself with, but there was nothing, not even a dressing gown. The nurses between them had cut away his shirt and T-shirt beneath; the bloody remains still in the corner on a chair. He was naked from the waist up, the situation was desperate, but thankfully he could feel his car keys in his trouser pocket.

Listening intently against the curtain, he could only hear some distant voices. It was early evening, and the unit was quiet as it would soon be closing down for the night. Cautiously putting his head out between the curtains, he could see that the waiting area was almost empty with just three people waiting for attention. Two were reading magazines, and the third was leaning forward grimacing, rubbing his back, obviously in pain, and oblivious to Roger's head appearing. Across to one side was the reception office, containing a young lady sitting behind the closed glass panels with her head down working. Turning the other way, Roger could see two nurses who were down the other end of a long corridor; they appeared to be the two that had attended to him a few minutes ago. Stealthily, he slipped out of the cubicle and across the waiting area, one of the two men who had been reading a magazine looked up, an expression of curiosity across his face at seeing a half-naked, freshly bandaged man half running through the waiting area. Roger passed through the double doors, which opened automatically with a low hiss, fleetingly slipping out into the night like a shadow, he shivered involuntarily as the cold, early evening air enveloped his naked torso. He had a change of clothing in the car, but this would have to wait, he needed to put as much distance between himself and the hospital. Roger was soon gunning the engine of his car, tyres squealed on the road as he sped out of the hospital car park, just as an astonished Charge Nurse, Angela, came dashing through the doors, staring incredulously at the departing bright red car. She stopped in her tracks and squinted her eyes in an attempt to read the registration number plate but to no avail. Later she gave a detailed description of the car to the police who correctly identified it as a Ford Escort RS2000.

Driving like the wind, through the country lanes of Lincolnshire to put as much distance between himself and Northwold, Roger prayed not to be caught by the police. Later, when feeling he was sufficiently far enough away, he came across a small 'lay-by.' Pulling over and stopping the car, his hand still clutching the steering wheel, his head bowed forward and tears of anger and frustration poured from him. After what seemed like an age, and his tears had finally subsided, he suddenly felt very cold. Darkness had enveloped the countryside and there would be a frost before morning. Feeling completely drained as the enormity of the situation he was in began to kick in. Looking at his bandaged arms and midriff, he tried to put some semblance of order in his mind as to what on earth was he going to tell Siobhan. Just when he thought he was completely drained of emotion, yet more tears came and he started sobbing again. Eventually, he regained some composure, sufficiently enough to think through an explanation for his injuries. In a light bulb moment, he recalled an incident, some years ago, with a ship's crew member who'd had a mental break down. When another member of the crew, not understanding what the man was suffering, inadvertently made some sarcastic remark, and caused the man to lose all sense of reasoning, using a knife in retaliation. On that occasion, Roger had been a witness, not physically injured. He'd never related the incident to Siobhan, and so, he had the beginnings of a plausible story. Sighing with relief, he retrieved a fresh shirt from his kit bag on the back seat, dressed, then started the car and resumed his journey home at a stately pace, running through the story he was going to tell Siobhan, knowing he would have to put on an award winning performance worthy of an Oscar!

He had also concluded that it was inevitable he was going to have to succumb to the demands of Ann. All he could do for now, was to hope that, in time, he would find a way out of that predicament.

Chapter 52

Roger was not prepared to call Ann's bluff, he did as she demanded, and each month he sent an envelope containing five hundred pounds in used fifty and twenty-pound notes. As risky as this was, Roger didn't want to go down the avenue of bank transfers or cheques, because they were easily traceable. He had a computer that could print envelopes, but he knew computers could auto store and leave an information trail, so he acquired an old portable typewriter, long since consigned to museums and this avoided him having to handwrite the envelopes.

Accumulating this sum of money from his various sources without drawing attention to himself put a considerable strain on his mental wellbeing. His mind played tricks on him; he started seeing things that weren't there, imaginary people followed him from the bank. Shadows lurked behind corners. He believed he was receiving suspicious looks from the bank clerk when he drew out the money. He even started going to different branches. On one occasion, he became quite angry with a bank clerk who had cheerily queried as to why Roger didn't go to his local branch as that would be more convenient for him as he was putting request transfers for money from an international bank. The bank clerk was clearly upset by his outburst, even summonsing the supervisor, which caused an even bigger scene, resulting in Roger running from the bank like a frightened rabbit. He was so scared, he left without his withdrawal. Later, chastising himself for being such a bloody fool, he turned to whisky for relaxation. Roger had never been a big drinker, however, what at first started as purely relaxation soon became consumption for relief. Roger's paranoia made him concerned about postmarks on the envelopes. Having watched too many fictitious TV detective stories, he convinced himself he could be traced that way. Nothing could have been further from the truth, but such was the depth of his paranoia, he was ready to believe anything.

So, he turned to friendly lorry drivers on the ferry asking them to post the monthly envelope; that way, they'd always arrive at Ann's house from different destinations, convincing Roger that they would be impossible to trace back to him. It cost him the odd bottle of liquor or carton of cigarettes, but that was a small price to pay for his assumed anonymity.

On one occasion, an envelope did not arrive at the expected time. Thinking that Roger had stopped the payments, Ann was soon on the phone to him. Thanks to her network of gullible, besotted, male office colleagues, including one who worked in personnel rostering, she had the opportunity to keep a track on Roger's whereabouts, ensuring she could chase him at work and never have to contact him when on leave. She was cunning and clever enough to know she was on to a very good thing, and upsetting the balance would not benefit her in the slightest.

On the occasion of the perceived late payment, she called Roger and gave him hell. She made all sorts of threats which she couldn't possibly keep, but Roger's state of mind believed that Ann was capable of anything right now. He pleaded with her to be patient, promising the money was on its way, and if it had not arrived within a couple of days, then he would send more. This appeased her, but before ending the call, she commented that she had noticed the different postmarks and asked why. Roger told her to mind her own damn business, asking why she would worry as long as the money kept arriving. Before she could answer, he slammed the receiver down.

A few mornings later, Roger's ship was docked in Northwold. It was eight-thirty in the morning, and the disembarking passengers, car drivers and HGV's had long since departed the vessel. With everything quiet, Roger left his assistant, David Tutty, in the office and slipped away for some early morning amber liquid sustenance.

David was busy organising paperwork when the shoreline telephone rang, "Hello, Purser's Office, Northshire —"

Before David could introduce himself, on the other end of the line, Ann Clark mistook David's voice for that of Roger and spoke over him, "Darling, how nice to hear your dulcet tones."

David was polite, "I'm very sorry, madam, I think you may have the wrong number?"

Ann immediately realised her mistake and continued with charm, "Oh dear, please do accept my sincere apologies. Can I please speak with Roger Holt, I believe he is on-board? Your voice sounded just like his, how silly of me, again, I'm ever so sorry," said Ann oozing smooch and charm down the telephone line.

"Oh yes of course madam, just bear with me while I get hold of him for you, he's not in the office at the moment, but he can't be far away," said David reassuringly, thinking the lady was a bit over the top with apologies for a simple mistake of identity.

David laid down the receiver, turned in his swivel chair, and picked up the internal telephone to call Roger's cabin. On the new vessel, unlike the older Beaumont ships where the purser lived in accommodation immediately behind the purser's office, Roger's private quarters were tucked away behind the navigation bridge along with the other officer cabins, well away from the passenger decks. Roger liked this set-up; he could sit up in his cabin away from the hustle and bustle of the passenger life, drinking in privacy. David informed him that a lady was on the phone, wishing to speak to him. Thinking it was Siobhan, Roger did not hurry down. Things between him and Siobhan had been far from amicable lately, due entirely to his personal demons and stress. When Roger eventually meandered down and reached the office, he picked up the handset giving a sullen, "Hello," He was already on his third drink of the day, but it had little effect at lifting Roger's dark mood.

Her taunting voice sent a shiver down Roger's spine.

"You should be careful darling, who you let answer your phone."

A sudden flourish of anger rose within him, "What's it got to do with you who answers this phone, it's the fucking purser's office. Anyway, what the fuck do you want?"

"Tut tut, no need to get offensive I just wanted to give you friendly thank you and to let you know that my allowance arrived," said Ann in a cheery voice, "Albeit six days late."

Before she could say more, Roger spat out furiously, "Bloodsucking bitch," before slamming down the phone with such a force it made David Tutty jump.

Roger was eager to get out of the office, anxious to get back to his cabin for another drink. David attempted to speak to him, but Roger just waved his hand in the air, "Not now," he said before slamming the office door behind him. David, slightly irked at Roger's tone of voice, reflected on the lady's voice he'd heard as it sounded familiar. He just couldn't quite place it. He pictured some of the female crew but drew a blank. Later in the day, it suddenly came to him that it could have been the luscious Ann Clark, who he had met on several occasions when she'd come aboard the vessel. Her voice was very unique, 'velvet-like,' he thought to himself as he pictured her attractive features and a sexy body. As quickly as he believed he had put the correct person to the voice, he soon dismissed the possibility. 'Why on earth would Roger be speaking to Ann in that tone? No, I must be wrong,' he thought, 'it must have been Roger's wife.'

A few weeks later, Roger discovered the reason for the delayed delivery of Ann's envelope. The HGV driver, with whom he had entrusted with the envelope, had been involved in a road traffic accident causing damage to his cab resulting in it being towed back to the nearby haulage company's yard for repairs. In the ensuing aftermath of the usual inconvenience following such an occurrence, the driver had momentarily forgotten all about the letter he'd promised to post. It had been left in the driver's small locker in the sleeping section of his cab from where he had retrieved it some days later and then posted.

The following Sunday morning, at around ten-thirty, Roger was carrying out his weekly main safe cash check as demanded by the company accountants. The accountants expected a report from each of the company vessels to be on the senior finance manager's desk first thing every Monday morning. All discrepancies had to be reported, not that there ever was any. Anything less than a one hundred percent correct return would cause eruptions of gigantic proportions in the steady, predictable life of the finance department. Despite the early hour, Roger had already consumed a couple of glasses of malt. His weekly bar mess bill had been causing some concern for the ship's Captain, who asked Roger about his habitual consumption. Roger had expected it was knowing his mess bill was slightly excessive, that the ship's master viewed the officer's and crew's onboard purchases account every Sunday, around about the time Roger was checking his safe.

Through an alcoholic induced laissez-faire attitude, Roger hadn't been particularly bothered, that was until he'd been called up by the Captain to explain his excessive alcohol intake. The Captain warned that he wanted to see a considerable reduction; otherwise, he would be forced to send a written report to the shore management. This brought Roger up with a jolt, and he promised faithfully to reduce his alcohol intake to avoid this course of action being taken and James Porter finding out.

As a result, he had chosen instead to smuggle alcohol aboard the ship, thus reducing his on-board mess bill but not his whisky consumption. The last thing he wanted was for James Porter to find out.

Roger had started stacking all the bundles of paper cash on top of the safe before transferring to his desk for counting. Just as he was about to move the last bundle of some five hundred pounds, he was disturbed by the assistant purser, David Tutty, who came into the office to informing Roger that the chef would need to make a change to the menu due to a non-delivery of stores. David quickly grabbed some paperwork from his desk before turning and saying, "I'll sort it mate, back in a bit." Roger never even looked up, his alcoholic haze kicked in as he stared at the notes of money on his desk. "Choors meet," Roger slurred as David left.

Roger tried to focus on the money, knowing he had to count it slowly and carefully to not make a mistake. He was about halfway through counting it when he realised that he'd left a bundle on top of the safe. Turning in his chair to grab it, he felt a little tipsy as his eyes didn't see what his brain told him should be there. In his drink-fuelled mind, which appeared to be getting worse, he concluded that David Tutty had taken the bundle of notes as a practical joke. Roger and David had been sailing together for some time now, since the inception of the new ship, they had become good friends, often going for a run ashore for a beer when the opportunity arose. With the friendship, came good banter and criac, often resulting in the odd practical joke being played on one another. However, that friendship had diminished slightly over the past few months. David had seen the progressive change in Roger's persona; he'd made sure he distanced himself from Roger outside of work and Roger was too caught up in his personal life even to notice or care. Unbeknown to Roger, and due to his change in his attitude, David had asked the crewing department if he could be either moved to another company vessel or change his work roster. When asked why, he made up a story that it was due to his roster clashing with the shift patterns of his new girlfriend, a member of the recently formed Dockyard Police.

Thinking that David had taken the money as a practical joke, Roger picked up the tannoy handset, flicked a switch, and spoke in a somewhat slurred voice that reverberated throughout the ship, "Attention. Plase... Would the Assischant Purser come to da purser's... burooo."

On hearing the announcement, David headed straight for the ship's office, but not before overhearing one of the crew comment, "Sounds like the Chief Purser's pissed again," which was immediately followed by guffawing from several of the crew nearby. Contrary to Roger's belief that he was hiding his drinking habit well, this was not the case.

Annoyed by this, David hurried to the bureau, wishing his transfer would hurry up before Roger's deteriorating reputation rubbed off on him. David had grand designs for himself, looking for his career to progress by moving up the next rung of the promotion ladder. As soon as he walked into the office, Roger, still slightly slurring his words and looking a little worse for wear, shouted, "Alreeeght, you clever sod. Juke fucking ovvver. Gimme it back. C'mon, let's have it, I'm in no mood for procticol yokes today."

"Sorry Rog, I don't know what you mean," David could smell the fumes of alcohol pervading from Roger's breath, even though he was standing a few feet away.

"Cum on, Dave, as I said, I'm in no moo.. fur jukes. I'm toking about the muney, the fove hundred poond bundle of ten pund notes th'was on top of the safe when you came with the chef's menu problem," demanded Roger struggling to form his words coherently.

David shrugged his shoulders, "Honestly Rog, I haven't taken any money; I wouldn't do such a thing, not even as a practical joke. I draw the line at taking money."

David, like Roger, sported boyish good looks, although, in David's case, he always gave the appearance as having a smile on his lips as though he was about to burst out laughing at any minute. Those that met David for the first time warmed to him immediately. He could easily put anybody at ease, a very useful side to his personality that came in handy when dealing with complaints or stressful issues. However, on this occasion, David's natural hint of a smile on his face backfired spectacularly. Roger's alcohol befuddled mind took exception to what he thought was David smirking at him. It was too much for Roger, who was on a very short fuse, his temper snapped. Standing up unsteadily, he knocked over his chair. A couple of strides took him around the desk, where he grabbed David by the lapels of his uniform jacket. Roger's face was beetroot red, contorted with anger, "You dirty liar!" screamed Roger as he tried to shake David.

"The money's fucking gune, and yooose the only one who's bin in 'ere this morning, so give up!" spat Roger.

Suddenly, another voice booming several decibels higher interrupted their confrontation,

"Good God in heavens above, what in heaven's name is going on here?" the voiced demanded with authority.

David struggled free from Roger's grip.

Roger turned to see, towering in the doorway to the office, his Nemesis, James Porter.

Roger was stricken with embarrassment. His boss catching him like this made the bile rise into the back of his throat, he swallowed hard to avoid vomiting as he started to gibber apologetically. David quickly moved to one side, breathing deeply, looking visibly shaken at the sudden assault from Roger.

"My God!" exclaimed Porter, astonished at what he had just witnessed.

"Word's fail me, Holt! I make a social welfare visit to one of the company vessels on a Sunday morning to discover this. The main safe wide open, money laying all over the place and two pursers fighting. Never in all my working life have I seen such disgusting and appalling behaviour. I want explanations now!"

Roger, shocked at his own behaviour, bent down to right the overturned chair.

"Sorry, Sir," were the only words he could find to mumble as he started to feel on the brink of bursting into tears.

"It's... it's him sir," blurted out David, pointing an accusing finger at the stooping figure of Roger with his head hanging in shame, "He's gone mental, accusing me of stealing money. I wouldn't do such a thing, sir."

"All right, Mr. Tutty, calm down," Porter injecting a calming tone to his voice, "I shall be making a full investigation into this abhorrent spectacle."

There was a moment of silence amongst the three of them, Porter glared at Roger with looks that could kill. Roger, avoiding Porter's eyes, retrieved his chair and fell back into it with an audible sigh.

Porter turned to David, "Mr. Tutty, I suggest you leave us, go off and have a cup of tea to calm down, I'll seek you out later for your version of what has gone on this morning, meanwhile, I'll be speaking to this man," he pointed menacingly at Roger.

"Yes sir," mumbled David as he left the office as quickly as he could, closing the door behind him.

Porter turned to Roger, who was now looking totally lost as he fiddled aimlessly with some loose change on his desk. His expression gave the impression he wasn't quite sure where he was. He had the air of a person who couldn't quite comprehend what had just occurred.

Porter continued in his gruff, gravelly voice, "As for you, Mr. Roger Holt," his voice emphasised just how disgusted he was at the scene that had been enacted before him, "Well, I trust you are thoroughly ashamed of yourself, because I certainly am, make no bones about that."

Porter stood in front of Roger's desk, looking down at him like a judge looking down on a condemned man, which is exactly how Roger was now beginning to feel as the realisation kicked in as to what he had just done.

Smelling weak fumes of alcohol, Porter picked up the empty whisky tumbler from Roger's desk, lifted it to his nose and inhaled deeply to sniff the remains, causing him to scowl.

"Whisky? At this time in the morning? You know very well the company's alcohol policy. This is very serious Holt. Leave everything as it is, lock up this office, go to your cabin and wait for me there while I go and see the Master."

Roger, keeping his head bowed, stepped outside of the office. Porter followed, holding out his hands in anticipation of the keys. Roger locked the door and handed the keys over, still avoiding eye contact. Before he could turn to walk away, Porter raised his voice, "Since there is an allegation of stolen money, I'll be calling one of your colleagues to come down and take a full inventory of the safe. In the meantime, I am taking up this matter with the Master, Captain Ernest."

Thankfully, the Sunday lay-over meant the main purser's entrance area was devoid of passengers. However, behind the large glass doors, entrance to the nearby dining room, several figures of the crew could be seen hovering, obviously attracted by the commotion, nothing quite like a bit of juicy gossip to spread around the ship.

Roger shuffled off to his cabin in a daze. It was like a ghastly nightmare, could this really be happening? Once back in the privacy of his cabin, he stupidly poured himself another whisky to steady his nerves. He gulped a mouthful; the liquid fire entered his stomach, spreading a warm feeling throughout his body, easing the tight knot he felt there. The whisky gave him only a fleeting feeling of relief before he was dashing to his bathroom, where he spewed into the toilet bowl, the whisky and bile stung his mouth and throat.

Meanwhile, Porter had stalked off in search of Captain Ernest. He discussed the whole episode with the Master, who listened intently, taking in what Porter was telling him. Ernest didn't like Porter, he saw him for what he was, an overgrown 'Bully Boy' displaying characteristics of a management style that, in Ernest's view, went out with the days of sail along with cat o' nine tails. However, as Porter was a senior manager in the company, Ernest reluctantly tolerated him, and taking in what Porter was saying, he found it very difficult to speak in Roger's defence. Although Ernest had previously found him to be an exemplary member of the shipboard team, recent discussions about his mess bill had raised concerns.

He had gently broached the subject with Roger, attempting to find the root of Roger's problem to offer some friendly and wise counsel. Unfortunately, all to no avail, Ernest had hoped that Roger would take the fatherly 'chat' as a starting point to either tackle his problems or leave them at home. The events of the morning, as related by Porter, showed that this had obviously not been the case.

Chapter 53

G uy Hollins, home on leave, was busy cutting the lawn aboard a sit-on mower, probably for the last occasion as the autumn was fast approaching. The vast lawn area swept around 'Tithe barn,' the home he now shared with Alexandra. The tractor style mower had been a present to himself, although due to the expanse of cultivated grass, it was a necessity. It was either that or rip up some of the lush green grass to leave an area more manageable with a small petrol mower. He couldn't bring himself to do that for several reasons, the main one being that it would make more open areas for plants, which would mean even more gardening, and this didn't inspire him at all. Guy loved the large grass area, and people often commented on how magnificent it looked, it would be sacrilegious to tear it up. Guy enjoyed driving around on his lawnmower, it gave him a sense of importance motoring around his estate. The beautiful old barn that Guy had purchased was just that, an old barn. It stood in over five acres of land, slightly elevated because of its situation on the rising ground at the start of the beautiful Lincolnshire Wolds. The elevation provided spectacular views over the surrounding countryside. A big plus for Guy, was that it was just outside the port of Northwold. Guy had lovingly restored it to his own design. Although a dab hand at DIY, the refurbishment was far too much for him, so he employed a local architect and put the work out to tender. The result was a dwelling that would enhance the pages of 'Ideal Homes.'

Guy often became lost in his thoughts about how lucky he was, having a beautiful home to share with the woman of his dreams. He had reached a stage in his life when he thought he would never find the right woman, and he did not wish to end his days a lonely old bachelor. A little voice in his head would whisper it was retribution for ditching Tina Souter. His mind drifted back to those years, recalling a vitriolic letter his dear old mum had received from Tina Souter's mother, Barbara. In the contents of the letter, she had accused Guy of the heinous crime of dumping her daughter, dramatically exaggerating the demise of their relationship by accusing him of leaving Tina at the altar. Nothing could have been further from the truth. In reality, it had been the histrionics of a bitter woman who'd seen the chance of having her unhinged daughter comfortably married off to an eligible man. A man who, through her devious dealings in entrapment and blackmail, would have been a subservient son-in-law to bend and use at her will. She would also have gained access to a new social strata, courtesy of Guy's MP father and socialite mother.

Guy's thoughts were interrupted as his eyes caught Alexandra, the amazing and beautiful woman that he had been so lucky to find. She was waving at him from the distant patio door and holding up the cordless phone. Guy engaged the lifting mechanism, raising the rotary cutter off the grass, turned the machine and motored towards the house. He didn't want to damage the almost perfect parallel lines he'd just meticulously cut. He stopped the mower just short of the patio and jumped from the seat to take the phone from Alexandra. He gave her a quick peck on the cheek and whispered, "Who is it, honey?"

"Porter," she mouthed as she passed him the handset.

Guy raised his eyebrows then frowned to show his displeasure. He inhaled, catching the wonderful aroma of a roast dinner wafting through from the kitchen, Alexandra really was a wonderful cook. He turned to look at the beautiful landscape of Lincolnshire beyond his garden. He gently sighed, the panoramic view and euphoric feeling it instilled in him had just been spoilt knowing who was on the other end of the line. With a heavy heart he lifted the phone to his ear and heard Porter's gruff impatient voice, "Mr. Hollins, are you there?"

Guy had merely time to say, "Hello," before Porter, in his usual disrespectful way, carried on, "Sorry to disturb you at home on a Sunday." His apology sounded far from sincere.

"How can I help?" asked Guy, trying not to sound annoyed at having his week-end disturbed by this man.

"Could you spare me a few hours today? I would be most grateful."

Guy knew he couldn't refuse his employer; if he did, it wouldn't do his career much good. While Guy was by no means a 'Yes man,' he appreciated which side his bread was buttered on and although he could hold his own when Porter made unreasonable demands, this time was not one of them. Guy, playing the political game, responded, giving Porter what he wanted to hear, "Yes, of course, anything I can do to help."

"You see Mr. Hollins," Porter was trying to be polite, "I walked on-board the 'Northshire' this morning to find two of your colleagues squaring up to each other over accusations of missing money," Porter's tone was clearly quite angry.

"I'm very sorry to hear that, sir, who are the two involved?" enquired Guy, astonished to hear such accusations as colleagues fighting.

"It was Roger Holt and David Tutty!" explained Porter, sounding as though he could hardly believe what he was relating.

"Again, I'm sorry to hear that, I know them both and find it very hard to believe."

Porter snapped back, "Believe it Mr. Hollins, believe it! I witnessed it myself," he growled, hinting that he did not like Guy questioning him. Guy, sensing Porter's mood, attempted to appease and avoid him erupting, as he so easily did, "What would you like me to do?" he asked in a composed manner.

"Well, can you come down to the ship right away? I shall only keep you the time it takes you to check the contents of the ship's safe, nothing more. Once you've given me a figure, then you can return to that lovely wife of yours."

Though frequently regarded as a man lacking in compassion and understanding, he could be most charming and accommodating where women were concerned.

"Please offer my most sincere apologies to Alexandra. How is she, by the way?"

"Fine, thank you, in excellent health, not long now before the baby will be here. Right, I'll jump in the car now should see you in thirty minutes or so."

Guy could not have known that he was the unwitting courier of a nail in the coffin for Roger! Upon arrival on-board, Porter handed Guy the keys to the purser's office and safe. He requested Guy to phone him in the Captain's quarters with the result once he had completed the cash check. Guy checked the contents of the safe and found it to be five pence over, not five hundred pounds short, as alleged by Roger. Accordingly, he duly informed Porter by telephone who arrived back at the purser's office, took the keys back from Guy, thanked him, and again apologised for disturbing his leave on a Sunday. Guy enquired about Roger, but Porter gave nothing away.

Guy was completely puzzled as to what was behind the occurrence causing Porter to summons him to the ship and carry out a safe cash check. Although Guy was not a buddy of Roger's, they had met at management meetings ashore, and Guy thought that Roger came across as a really nice chap. All Porter said was, "He's unwilling to communicate," adding to the mystery. Apart from demanding to see Roger, there was little else Guy could do other than contact the officer's union representative, not something he wanted to do without consulting Roger first. Porter bade farewell to Guy and returned to see the Captain. Guy left the vessel, jumped into his Reliant Scimitar and dashed home to be with Alexandra and to enjoy the wonderful Sunday lunch she had cooked for them.

Having heard the outcome of Guy's safe check, Porter was fuelled with rage. His anger couldn't be tempered, not even by a few words from the mild-mannered and calm Captain Ernest. After venting his feelings with the Captain, Porter stormed along to Roger's cabin. He burst in without knocking, catching Roger lazing back in his easy chair with yet another drink in his hand. Porter was the ultimate line manager for the purser staff aboard the Beaumont's vessels; consequently, he took the misbehaviour of one his staff very personally indeed, even more so when it involved a senior ship's officer. Porter himself, at one time, had been a purser. Seeing Roger lift his glass to take a sip infuriated him. He completely forgot himself and, in a moment of madness, swung out and knocked the glass from Roger's hand. The glass flew across the cabin; its contents sprayed Roger's face before the golden liquid showered his desk. Roger cowered as Porter towered above him. Completely astonished at the actions of Porter, Roger momentarily put his arms up, expecting Porter to throw a punch at him. This was surreal, 'it couldn't be happening,' screamed a voice inside Roger's mind!

"Mr. Holt!" bellowed Porter, "I've had Guy Hollins down here today, taking him away from his day of rest to assist me clearing up this debacle … and what did he discover … hmmm?" Porter was almost screaming with rage. Roger, still in a state of total shock, could only stare terrified and dumbfounded at Porter.

"Well, I'll tell you what he found, your safe was five pence over not five hundred pounds down as you have alleged. Now I require the reason for your unfounded accusation against David Tutty." Porter, as though his energy had suddenly drained, sat down on the settee with a sigh of exhaustion, "Well? I'm waiting Holt." The venom of Porter's attack had sobered Roger, bringing him back from his alcoholic haze. Embarrassed and ashamed, Roger realised what a total fool he'd been. He wanted to fall to his knees and cry like a baby. Instead, he buried his head in his hands in an attempt to hide his sobbing. Porter coughed to prompt a reaction. Roger looked up and started to mumble an explanation of the morning's events; he blamed his state of mind on non-existent domestic problems. Porter sighed, "Not good enough, Holt," emphasising the use of Roger's surname. This stinging rebuke felt like a slap in the face for Roger as protocol dictated that he should be addressed as 'Mr' when being spoken to by management.

Porter carried on, "I really cannot tolerate this sort of behaviour from a person in your position; in fact, I wouldn't accept it from a junior clerk in my office, never mind a senior officer aboard our latest modern super ferry!"

There was a brief silence between the two men. Roger stared at the carpet in shame while Porter's eyes bored into him.

"Where do you live, Holt? Norfolk?"

"Yes, sir, a village called Kettlestone, near Fakenham," he said meekly, trying to hold back tears frustration and anger with himself.

"Hmm, I'm guessing there's not much work for a man like yourself to do down there?"

'Oh my God,' Roger thought as his heart missed a beat. He was sobering up fast at the realisation that Porter intended to dismiss him, and he knew that even the Officer's Association couldn't back him on this one, not where alcohol abuse was concerned. Roger remained silent.

"I must take some action, Holt," Porter continued, "At first, I asked the Captain to put this in the Official Log and take the disciplinary route. Fortunately for you, he has talked me out of it. Nevertheless, I don't want to 'wash my dirty linen in public' and let's not kid ourselves Holt, this problem becomes my dirty linen. You see, the buck stops with me," growled Porter, briefly recalling the words once used so effectively by an American President. He carried on, "I've therefore decided to take away the 'Chief' designation in your Chief Purser status, and you shall be placed on one of the company's small older vessels." Porter paused to allow Roger to take in what he had said before continuing, "You can either accept this or appeal against it by going before the General Manager with your officer's union representative, which will no doubt result in a big enquiry, possibly resulting in your dismissal... your choice Holt." Porter's threatening tone was aimed at leaving Roger with very little choice. Porter really wanted to keep this problem within his domain, as the thought of the issue leaking wider into the company community raised his stress levels. He felt the recently appointed General Manager from BSC in London would use this as a stick to beat him with as he'd soon realised this man didn't like him. So he sincerely hoped that his veiled threat would make Roger take his offer and be done with it.

"I'm waiting Holt, what's it to be ... my way or the gangway?" Another expression Porter had picked up and used many times over the years.

"Yes, sir, I'll accept your first offer and go to another ship."

"Is that it then? That's all you've got to say?" demanded Porter, knowing that there was little else Roger could say, but he wanted to rub it in.

"Yes sir, except that I'm truly very sorry, I can't apologise enough for my behaviour. I can assure you that it won't happen again." Despite being massively humiliated by the events, he was astute enough to realise that he only had himself to blame. Roger, although being financially sound, was a greedy bugger and didn't want to throw away the lucrative scheme he and Freddie Naylor controlled. He knew how stupid he'd been, allowing himself to become morose and finding solace in alcohol. Even the money he was paying to Ann Clark was on balance, a small price to pay for her silence in the greater scheme of things. He and Freddie Naylor were making a fortune out of the Beaumont Company, and he idiotically could have just thrown all of that away, or worse, have been found out.

Porter's lecture continued, "Very well, Holt, I'm pleased that you've made the right decision. I suggest you take time off to reflect, call it a break, I will then put Guy Hollins to work alongside you, to ensure and keep you on an even keel. I trust there'll be no argument with that?" Porter glared at Roger, daring him to disagree. There was no way Roger would argue; he knew he had to make things right. If Guy Hollins was to be part of that, well, so be it. He could live with that; it was a small humiliation to endure when looking at the bigger picture. Porter stood up, Roger instinctively followed, and Porter offered him his hand, the gesture gave Roger a slight feeling of relief that he would be forgiven. Porter turned to leave, then stopped, "There are two loose ends to tie up." "Firstly I will arrange for you to make an apology to David Tutty with me present. Secondly, I will call Roy Brooks in the morning to organise your transfer."

Roger nodded in agreement.

The thought of going home was an added relief to Roger, he just needed to get away from the toxic atmosphere. He knew he had a lot of ground to make up with Siobhan, as he'd not been easy to live with recently. Roger, forever the optimist, took some comfort in looking at what had happened as a blessing in disguise. 'I will soon be back on top,' he thought to himself as they left the cabin to head down to the office. Roger's old confidence was beginning to return along with a headache. Although the effects of the alcohol had worn off, it had come back to haunt him. His body was dehydrated; he'd have to get some pain killers before its intensity increased. As soon as they walked into the office, Roger saw the look of disgust on David Tutty's face. Roger was duly contrite as he opened up,

"David, I'm really so very, very sorry for my disgusting behaviour this morning. I just don't know what came over me. I value our friendship greatly. I'm consumed with guilt over my accusations and the way I spoke to you." Roger, with his hand outstretched made David's frown quickly turn into a beaming smile. He'd always thought that he and Roger were friends as well as being shipmates. The Roger that David witnessed only a few hours earlier was a totally different character to the shipmate he knew; the change had unnerved David. Happily, he took Roger's extended hand and shook it vigorously, trusting that it would send a message to Roger as to just how much he was relieved, "Oh, that's okay Rog, water under the bridge," he chuckled.

"Thank you. Thank you for accepting my apology and for being so understanding. You're a good man to work with, always carrying out your duties conscientiously and diligently. I've told Mr. Porter what a privilege it has been working with you," Roger had said no such thing, he'd been far too involved with his own personal problems during that last few weeks to concern himself with the progress of his assistant. Porter just nodded as if in agreement, but his face remained impassive. The words naturally pleased David who took Porter's blank look for what it was, Porter more often than not gave very little away, unless he lost his temper. David excused himself and left the office, feeling like a weight had lifted from his shoulders. Porter turned to Roger, "You'll receive a letter confirming what we've discussed. I'll have Roy Brooks contact you with details of who is to relieve you." Porter turned on his heels, grunted, which was his way of summing up the events of the previous few hours, and left Roger standing alone in the office. He did not offer Roger his hand nor did he bid him farewell.

Chapter 54

Roger lied to Siobhan about the reason for him to move to a different ship, and he did not mention the demotion. He claimed the move had been offered to him to relieve some of the pressure he'd endured bringing his department of the huge new ship to operational readiness. He did not doubt that Siobhan, who looked after their household budget, would eventually notice the difference in his monthly salary, but he would convince her that he decided to put family life before money and stress. Roger started his leave by apologising to Siobhan for the way he had been treating her and set about spoiling her in an effort to make up for his recent behaviour. They went to London for several days, staying overnight at a lovely West-end hotel from where they took in all of the shows that Siobhan had been wanting to see for ages. Having felt that their marriage was beginning to fall apart, Siobhan was ecstatic at the sudden change in Roger's demeanour and at how he was now fêting her. Even their sex life, which had become routine, cold, autonomous to the point of being boring, suddenly changed back to the sweet, tender passion she so enjoyed. The London break had been preceded by romantic, candlelight suppers in secluded, cosy restaurants where the atmosphere and ambience made them both feel young and vibrant. Siobhan did attempt to broach the subject of how worried she had been about their relationship, but the subject was briefly skirted, Roger, blaming it on pressure of work. Siobhan let it lie, content that their marriage was back on track.

It was soon time for Roger to join the old *s.s. Beamish* and to team up with Guy, who was somewhat embarrassed at having to act as a nursemaid to Roger. Guy, although naturally curious, never asked for reasons, but he did, however, play the political game with old sour crouch, Porter, accepting his master's bidding to allow Roger to explain if he wanted to. Obviously, something had stirred Porter but, apart from guesswork, Guy really wasn't interested in what had happened. All Porter had said was, "I'll leave Holt to fill you in, but if he plays his cards right, I don't anticipate you being with him for more than a week, two outside. If it's any longer, you can be rest assured Holt will be looking for a new employer."

Roger was very vague with an explanation as to what had occurred, so Guy left it at that. The *s.s. Beamish* was commanded by the company's new Commodore, Captain Thomas McDougal, who'd taken over from

Captain Arthur Sanderson. This was just as the company had been bought out by Richard Hartling's BSC, the *s.s. Beamish* being the flagship of the old Beaumont Fleet at that time. When the new ferry had come into service, McDougal was offered it to command, but being 'old school,' he'd firmly declined. In his view, these new vessels starting with the *'Northshire'* were floating computers, 'Starship Enterprises,' for the new generation of whizz kid master's. Heading up the new look, Beaumont's Richard Hartling had appointed Gordon Pool, who, along with the rest of the local Northwold management team had, for the time being, accepted the loss of prestige that their Commodore was flying his flag on an old vessel. It didn't make for good publicity. However, McDougal was a popular ship's master; he had what was commonly known in maritime circles as the 'Nelson Touch,' so it was planned that when the old *s.s.Beamish* was removed from service, then McDougal would then have to either move to one of the new vessels or retire. McDougal didn't give the appearance of a man who would relish retiring, and the management was happy to temporarily concede and entertain McDougal's whim to stay with the old steamer.

Captain Thomas McDougal was quite a local celebrity; consequently, he was in a strong position to influence his request to stay on the old *s.s. 'Beamish.'* If he had been removed against his will, then a word in the right ear of the press could have made bad publicity for the company with headlines such as 'Local Hero forced out...' and that had to be avoided. Although McDougal, being such a staunch company man, would never actually use such a threat, it was sufficient that the possibility was there! He had made a name for himself as a well renowned and comical after-dinner speaker, often in great demand and a nice little earner for his retirement fund. His celebrity status came about by his seamanlike actions during an emergency, one dark and windy night in the North Sea. He'd been in command of a large open-decked cargo ship, a vessel with all crew accommodation aft, and a long flat foredeck used for stacking cargo containers. On this particular nasty night, a nearby passenger ferry had been holed below the waterline and was listing badly. The ship was in danger of sinking with 650 passengers, plus 80 crew on-board. The weather so foul, launching lifeboats would not have been without its consequences, no doubt most would have been saved, but there would have bound to have been some loss of life amongst children or the elderly who were sailing aboard the ferry that night. Thanks to Captain McDougal answering the distress call, all were saved without as much as getting their feet wet. He'd manoeuvred his cargo ship, with skill and precision gained from a life-time of ship handling, alongside the stricken passenger vessel, enabling all those on-board to be cross-decked to safety. The only damage sustained to the two vessels had been bent and buckled steel railings, scraped paintwork and a few dents on the hull. Fortunately for McDougal, the way the passenger ship was heeling over meant the cross decking would be carried out on lee side, protecting all from the howling winds and angrily breaking sea over the ship's hull. The rescue mission had still not been without its dangers, as the two vessels rose and fell against each other like two huge sea monsters, causing the tortured metal to scream as the two ships ground against each. For his actions that night, Captain McDougal was awarded the George Medal, the highest honour going to a civilian in peacetime. An honour only equalled by the Victoria Cross awarded to military personnel for heroic actions on the battlefield.

Captain McDougal read the letter of appointment for Roger Holt. He had been forewarned by Roy Brooks that Roger was under a cloud and that the management suspected he had a drinking problem. Historically, alcohol abuse at sea had been treated as a disciplinary problem and viewed as a weakness of character, now, due to more enlightened and progressive thinking, it was identified as an illness requiring investigation to discover the root cause which would then be followed up with appropriate treatment. Employers now had a duty of care towards sufferers and management wanted McDougal to keep a paternal eye on Roger. If he was in any way to fall below the standards required by the company of an officer serving in his capacity, then they were to be informed at once. McDougal took this as a personal challenge and he had no intention of allowing Roger to fail.

Roger, even before his meeting with Captain McDougal, was feeling positive about the new chapter in his life. Following his romantic leave with Siobhan, which had felt like a honeymoon, he had a spring in his step like a new born lamb. No way was he going to allow anything, especially not that 'Kinky Unsound Bitch,' Ann Clark, to push him back into the pit of despair he'd experienced only a few weeks previously. He made himself a promise, one way or another, he would gain revenge on Ann. He didn't know how and he didn't know when, but, whether it was to be this year or the next, her time would come, he just had to work out a plan. Ann was keeping her end of the bargain; her silence was supporting her new lifestyle, which she was enjoying to the full. She was far from being ostentatious; she was clever enough not to attract too much attention.

The encounters with Detective Sergeant Peter Marsh had unnerved her. Reducing her hours of work, by job share, had raised some eyebrows amongst her work colleagues, so she knew she had to tread carefully and not demand more from Roger. She realised that if she pressured him too much, he might call her bluff and Ann knew too well that if he did, he would have discovered that she had no real hard evidence apart from what Roger had told her in a moment of sexual passion. It was true that she had discovered some failings in the system, but no more. If the truth be known, she would probably be laughed at had she attempted to make Roger out to be a big-time crook as she was sure that Roger, in collaboration with Freddie Naylor, would have covered their tracks very well. Freddie, was a pillar of the local Northwold society and Chair of the local Masonic Lodge. Convincing the Beaumont management that they were being ripped off by him and Roger would be like trying to push a pea uphill with her nose.

Roger had settled into his post on the old s.s *'Beamish'* and proceeded to shake off the dark cloud of doubt that hung over him. Before long, Captain McDougal was able to report Roger's professional ability to be entirely satisfactory. He saw no reason for Guy Hollins to stay a moment longer. However, Roy Brooks was not confident enough to take the bold decision to relieve Guy of his temporary assignment and told McDougal that he would have to refer this to Porter. Unfortunately, Porter was away visiting family in the Isle of Man and wouldn't be back for a couple of weeks, meaning Guy would have to stay in situ until then. It mattered not to Guy, as long as he would be able to be home with Alexandra when the baby arrived. Guy was more than happy to allow Roger to run the department as he shadowed him without any of the shipboard responsibilities. For this extra duty, Guy was lucratively totting up two extra days leave for every day he was on-board. Guy had readily accepted the generous terms of this one-off offer made to him. He saw it as a rather ridiculous compensation to work alongside Roger, but irrational that it was, Guy wasn't one to question Porter when the rewards were in his favour. Little did he realise that this 'nice little earner,' would have the effect of a tsunami.

Chapter 55

As the train from London Kings Cross slowly pulled into Northwold railway station, Karen Clark stood and reached up to retrieve her weekend bag from the overhead luggage rack. Dressed in tight black trousers and a figure-hugging white top, designed to expose and tantalisingly reveal her bare flat stomach, her fashionable ensemble was topped off with a designer leather jacket. Karen was well developed for her age, already needing a size 34D bra and having started her periods at a tender age. Now, sixteen coming on seventeen, but acting more like a twenty-five-year-old, Karen was very much the modern, young lady. Inheriting her mother's good looks, she was continuously chased by the local Northwold boys, all of which she found rather irksome and boring. The local youths had, in her eyes, nothing to offer, it was all just big talk, an incessant interest in motorbikes and trying to impress. Some girls were totally taken in by their bravado and attention, wanting nothing more than to be courted, quickly followed by walking down the aisle. They imagined married bliss, living in one of the new three-bedroom semis springing up around Northwold, commonly referred to as 'Barratt Boxes,' but marketed by over enthusiastic Estate Agents as executive town houses. The stark reality of these marriages was a life of Monday to Friday housekeeping drudgery, with the weekly highlight of quick romp on a Saturday night, suffering short animal thrusting's, smothered in a vapour of beer and cigarettes following hubby's session with the lads down at the snooker hall. After the initial honeymoon thrill, they would wonder what had happened to their Prince Charming and the vision of the fairy tale happiness they'd dreamt about. Now having to accept the ritual Saturday night rut to produce the obligatory 2.5 children.

The very thought of limiting her life to this sort of existence was a complete anathema to Karen. Local boys that were high achievers invariably left for University and life beyond the sleepy backwater of Northwold. Those that didn't work hard at school and attain good grades only had dockyard work at the port to look forward to, either that or working on the land. Opportunities in Northwold were very limited, as the main the jobs went to those related to or born into the local farming families. Due to the great leaps forward in mechanisation, the only time an increase in the labour force was needed was on a casual basis at harvest time on the vegetable farms that fed the massive frozen food industry. That just left the mind-numbing work of stacking shelves in the local supermarkets or some other equally low paid job in the retail sector for the resident youngsters.

Karen escaped this tribal village atmosphere whenever possible by going to stay with her mother's sister, Samantha, married to Alan Devonshire, Chairman and Managing Director of a large London Financial institution. Their sizeable country home was nestled in the quintessentially English surroundings of Scaynes Hill, Sussex, just outside the well-known stock-broker belt to the south of the metropolis. Here, they owned 500 acres of mixed forest and pasture land, ideal for horses and other assorted country pursuits such as fishing and shooting. Alan, naturally an astute financial guru, made good use of all the available land, turning in a good income each year from the various activities. Samantha kept three beautiful equines in the stables attached to the house. A 17hand thoroughbred, a jet black Friesian from the Netherlands and a 15hand white Arabian which Samantha had nominally allocated to Karen. The Arab, a beautiful, gentle all-rounder, was an ideal mount for starting out in the world of equine pursuits. Thanks to Samantha's high society connections, Karen was able to have professional coaching by a highly qualified riding instructor. Karen considered Samantha to be an extremely sophisticated woman and saw her as a role model. Samantha did a great deal of entertaining in support of her husband's position. Hardly a weekend went by without some form of social engagement, either up in town, as London was referred to, or a house party at their country home. Having no children of their own, Samantha encouraged Karen to come and stay as often as she liked, she took great delight in taking her up to London, whether for shopping or a social engagement and gained great pride in showing off her niece at dinner parties. Karen was becoming quite a sophisticated young lady, thanks to the influence of her Aunty Samantha.

Samantha had become like a surrogate mother to Karen and had her own reasons for harbouring motherly feelings. She was playing a very subtle game, attempting to come between Karen and her sister, Ann. Not because she was jealous of her sister for having such a lovely daughter, her motive was purely to protect Karen from her sister's lifestyle and predilection for perverse sexual practices. Ann was the elder of the two, and as they had grown up together, they'd often played Cowboys and Indians, Doctors and Nurses or Teachers and Pupils. Invariably, it would end up with Samantha being held captive and tied up to a garden fence post like 'Totem Pole' in the warm, balmy, summer days. These innocent games were filled with lots of laughter and merriment, however as they aged, Samantha realised that some of the games they played were beginning to have sinister overtones, especially when Ann played the role of a school teacher wearing nothing more than a cloak and using a toy cane. Samantha put a stop to it after the day she had played the naughty pupil and Ann, the dominant teacher, tried to cane Samantha across her buttocks. The first few lashes were just silly and funny, producing lots of giggles, but Ann went too far and the strokes hurt, even cutting through light summer dress into Samantha's skin. They were just turning pubescent teenagers, coming to understand their sexuality. Samantha threatened to tell on Ann if she ever attempted to try and dominate her again. From that moment on, Samantha saw her sister in a totally different light, the games were never repeated and they slowly grew apart as they began to build relationships with their own peer groups at school. The caning incident was never referred to again.

Samantha grew up into a very attractive young lady, studied to be a nurse, and after qualifying, went to work at a top London Hospital as a Casualty Nurse in a very busy A&E unit, only venturing north, as duty required, to visit her mother and father. Samantha came to realise that she really didn't like her sister that much, these feelings were compounded one weekend when she went home to visit her parents. Since leaving to work in London, her parents, with Ann still living with them, had taken the opportunity to downsize their house to a two bedroomed bungalow, realising enough money to take early retirement. Whenever Samantha went home to visit, she would sleep in the lounge on a camp bed to avoid sharing her sister's bedroom. One weekend coincided with Ann going away on a girls' 'Hen Party weekend,' meaning Samantha could occupy Ann's bedroom, this resulted in her accidentally coming across some sinister publications belonging to her sister. These depicted all sorts of strange, perverse and macabre sexual fantasies concerning enslavement, mainly of men by woman although not entirely. She was shocked by these publications clearly displaying women playing the part of dominatrix, enjoying sadomasochistic sexual activities. Just looking at some of these magazines made Samantha feel physically sick; this was enough for Samantha. Now she understood her negative feelings towards her sister, she hardly ever spoke to her again. It took all of Samantha's resolve and steely grit to accept Ann's invitation to be the Maid of Honour at her marriage to Nick. Samantha had always secretly adored Nick and could have easily fallen in love with him. The first time she was introduced to him she saw him as a storybook hero. He perfectly fitted a roll in the Mills and Boon books she so enjoyed reading. Nick, a soldier, was tall, athletically built, and a recently qualified army helicopter pilot. At that time, however, Samantha was courting Alan and, although in love with him, she continued to feel an affinity with Nick. She considered warning him about her sister's adverse sexual interests, but seeing how much Nick was taken in with Ann, she knew it would be in vain and that he would probably see her as an interfering, jealous sister. She decided it was best to keep her opinion a secret, just like her feelings towards Nick. Ann married Nick and quickly fell pregnant with Karen, a honeymoon conceived baby. Samantha became not only an aunty, but also Karen's Godmother and the bond between them only grew stronger every year. Karen's visits to her Aunty and Uncle increased after the mysterious disappearance of Nick.

Karen loved everything about her aunty's lifestyle as it matched the dreams and aspirations for her own life. Karen found herself inundated with offers of dates from the many eligible, young, aspiring executives she met at the parties thrown by her aunty and uncle. They were a far cry from the local Northwold boys, who talked about nothing but motorbikes and showed off, with bravado, 'gobbing off' about speeding with *'ton ups'* along the Great North Road, bragging about how they had outrun police patrol cars. Hearing of the antics of some of these rough diamond northern lads made Karen believe that some of them even had a death wish. In contrast, the sophisticated, London types were taking Karen out to the latest West End shows or film premieres, where she was often introduced to some of the stars themselves. She experienced dining out in top London restaurants where the cost of dinner was more than most of the Northwold boys could expect to earn at the dockyard in a week. On one occasion, she had been taken to a top west end restaurant to find most of the cast of a popular week-day TV soap sitting at the adjoining table.

As Karen waited for the train to pull into Northwold station, her mind wandered back over the events of the week, which had been truly amazing. Over Sunday lunch, Uncle Alan had casually dropped a 'bombshell' by asking if she would like to work for him in the city as soon as she'd qualified from the Business School in Lincoln, where she was intending to go once her 16 plus results were through. She had been offered a place, providing she obtained the correct grades. She was quietly confident that she would achieve them, due to having studied hard at the Northwold Grammar School.

Alan and Samantha also agreed that Karen, when the time came, would live with them as they had plenty of room at their palatial country home. Karen already used the spare bedroom which was more of a suite with its own lounge area and private en-suite bathroom. The room even had a large balcony with magnificent views over the Sussex countryside. Her aunty and uncle had always told her to treat the room as hers, but this offer made it feel more genuine. She would have this as her own little home from home. Karen readily accepted, then Samantha had made an announcement that truly was the icing on the cake, she was gifting the beautiful white Arabian horse named 'Merlin' to her. As Karen stepped from the train, she remembered feeling faint she was so overcome with emotion, the combined offer of lifestyle and career was more than she could ever have dreamed of.

Samantha's motives for prising Karen away from her sister were only known to her and would remain so forever. She loved Karen as the daughter that she'd never been lucky enough to have and didn't want her to be corrupted by the evil she saw in her sister. The fact that Nick had suddenly and mysteriously disappeared only added to her determination to keep Karen safe. Ann appeared to actively encourage the closeness that had developed between Karen and Samantha. While Samantha guessed that in all probability, mainly due to Karen's early arrival in the world after Ann and Nick had married, she was probably never planned, and maybe Ann found her daughter a hindrance to her somewhat bohemian lifestyle.

Karen was excited to tell her mother, although she felt sure that Aunty Samantha would probably have already discussed the proposition with her. Karen was completely oblivious to the deep-seated hatred Samantha had towards Ann or her mother's indifference to her. Consequently, during the journey north, as she had daydreamed of the life she had to look forward to, Karen had the odd twinge of guilt, feeling as though she was deserting her mother. Karen had, for some time, suspected that the relationship between her Mum and Dad hadn't been right. She continued to question her mother's claim that her father had seized an opportunity to earn a lot of money overseas as he already had a well-paid job flying for the National Grid Electricity Service, she couldn't understand why he'd given that up to work in a worn-torn country and stranger still, he'd left without saying 'goodbye' to her. She always thought she was close to her father and that he felt the same. He'd always spoilt her, much to the annoyance of her mother, so it was a total mystery why he had left so suddenly. He'd left when she'd been away with her Aunty Samantha; she'd returned home to be greeted by her mother saying that he'd gone. At first, she had been tearful and distraught that he'd just left, so suddenly and without warning. The more she questioned her mother the more annoyed her mother had become until it ended in a shouting match between the two of them. Karen threw a 'strop,' screaming at her mother that it was her fault and that she had driven her fabulous father away. That argument had come to a sudden close with Karen receiving a resounding, heavy slap across the face that had knocked her completely off her feet. The resulting mark to her cheek took several days to disappear, during which time they did not speak. Following this, they had developed a fragile truce, which included not speaking about him. Deep down, she knew her parents weren't happy with each other, so maybe she could understand why her father had suddenly left, but it didn't stop her hurting, sometimes the feeling of abandonment was so strong that she would cry herself to sleep. She'd witnessed some of the awful rows her mother and father had gone through. On one occasion, the loud, hysterical, almost animal-like screaming voice emitting from her mother frightened Karen so much she had run upstairs and hidden under the bed. Only to emerge when the police arrived, having been summoned by their worried next-door neighbour.

With all the exciting developments taking place in her life, Karen was less anxious about her future and accepted that her mother and father were now leading totally separate lives and would no doubt soon be divorced. She rather hoped that her mother might settle down with George Stewart, her new boyfriend, who owned a lucrative grocer's business in Northwold. Karen had not been too keen on him at first, as he'd not only treated her like a little girl but had already assumed the step-father role. This really irked Karen, particularly as her aunty and uncle treated her like an adult. She was looking forward to being able to distance herself from her mother, however, she didn't want her mother to be lonely when she moved to the south.

Karen looked eagerly around as she stood waiting on the windswept platform, smelling and feeling the cold sea air as it whistled off the North Sea buffeting its way through every 'nook and cranny' of Northwold, then howling down the wide-open station concourse. The dismal weather added to her feeling of despondency when her mother was not there to meet her as they had arranged. Karen had phoned before leaving her aunty's, but obtained no reply. The home phone number was just ringing out, eventually clicking onto the answering machine where Karen had left a brief announcement to say what time she would arrive at Northwold. As she'd said goodbye to her aunty and uncle at Kings Cross station, Aunt Samantha had promised to keep trying as she travelled north, but she also had no success. After Karen made a call from the phone box on the railway station concourse, that again failed to make contact, she concluded that perhaps her mother was out with George Stewart, enjoying herself and had just forgotten the time. Taking a deep breath, she set off walking determinedly towards the taxi rank whilst mentally telling herself to act as an independent grown-up, she also promised herself she would buy a 'pay as you go' mobile phone at the first opportunity. After a long day of travelling, Karen finally arrived outside her home. The autumnal evening was gloomy. She paid the taxi and walked up the secluded drive, noting that all the lights at the front of the house were out. She searched her handbag to find her key and let herself in. As she opened the front door, she felt the warmth from the hallway inviting her in. She kicked off her outdoor shoes, now convinced now that her mother must be out with George Stewart, she padded through to the kitchen and switched on the lights to make the house feel occupied. She made herself a refreshing cup of tea and then went into the lounge at the front of the house to switch on the gas fire. Although the central heating was on and the house reasonably warm, the fire was soon burning hot and bright that gave the much-needed welcoming cheer to the empty house. Her cup of tea finished, she went upstairs to unpack, still feeling giddy with excitement and floating on the proverbial 'Cloud Nine' at the thoughts of the way her life was heading. These feelings dampened by the realisation that she would have to wait for her exam results, then attend business school for two years before she could start her new life; however, there would be the week-ends and holidays to look forward to. Aunty Samantha had already said she could start to move into her allocated part of the house anytime she liked and redecorate to her liking. Excitingly, there was also 'Merlin' to attend to. Up until now, she had only ridden him when having riding lessons with that rather 'Bossy Britches,' instructor friend of Aunty's. Karen, thanks to the latest progressive sexual education lessons to be included in the High School curriculum, knew all about homosexuality and was firmly convinced that this unmarried, 'horsey' friend had lesbian feelings for Samantha. 'Who wouldn't,' she'd thought to herself, after all, her aunty was rather glamorous. Consequently, she was convinced that the instructor was slightly jealous of the love and attention heaped on her by her Aunty Samantha. Well, she 'giggled' to herself, that was her interpretation of why she was being so 'bossy,' in her lessons. Her thoughts returned to 'Merlin,' for although he was only on loan, he was now her responsibility. A life she had to look after, care for and to develop a relationship with. Yes, she had Samantha to guide her, but Karen wanted to show her aunty that she took the chance very seriously and planned to buy lots of books about horse management and well-being, determined that she would devour every page so she would be as informed as Aunty Samantha. She would aim to be an outstanding employee for her uncle and, at the same time, develop into an excellent horsewoman, who would go eventing, ride with the South Downs Hunt and join Aunty on the 'Point to Point' races. Oh, life was going to be so exciting. She couldn't wait to get started. Karen was so busy and pre-occupied she didn't notice the time flying by until a vague glance at her bedside clock told her that it had just gone midnight. By this time, her mother should be home, so worrying, she went down stairs to the hall phone to call George Stewart.

"Hello, who is it?" said the sleepy voice of George Stewart as he switched on the bedside light to look at the clock.

"Mr. Stewart? – Hello, it's Karen Clark here," Karen could still not bring herself to address him by his first name, despite being encouraged to so by both her mother and George himself. She'd refused because she felt sure the next step would be to call him Dad, and there was no way on this earth she would do that!

"Mr. Stewart, I'm so sorry to disturb you so late but is my mother with you?" momentarily imagining him leaning over in his bed and giving the phone to her mother, convinced that's where she was.

George Stewart was instantly wide awake.

"No problem, but I'm afraid she's not Karen, and do, please call me George," he replied, now fully awake.

Karen ignored the request to address him by his first name silently saying *'Oh fuck off'* to herself and continued, "Oh! I've been away for the last week and Mum wasn't here when I got back, she was supposed to meet me at the station but as she wasn't there and she isn't here either I assumed she must be with you, especially as it's so late."

George Stewart's face frowned in anxiety as he tried not to let his concern reflect in the tone of his voice.

"Very strange, I had arranged to take your mother out for the day, but when I got there this morning, she wasn't there," stated George now with an uncontrollable hint of anxiety creeping into his voice.

"Could she be with a neighbour?" asked George, really for something to say more than a logical explanation as he was a little lost at what to suggest next. Actually, he knew very well that Ann Clark had little time for her neighbours, calling them *'curtain twitching bloody nosey parkers.'*

"No, I don't think so for one minute," Karen also knew of her mother's dislike of their neighbours and she didn't know of anyone in the Avenue her mother even associated with. Her mother had always appeared a bit of a loner, who only occasionally went out with friends from her old office at Beaumont's, and even those outings had dropped off now that she only worked part-time there.

"Even when she did go out with her friends from Beaumont's she would never be this late. Anyway, as I said she was supposed to have been picking me up from the station, I've never known her to forget before," she stated, trying to be grown up and not to let a note of childish hysteria enter her voice.

"No, I'm sure. Look, shall I pop over for a while to keep you company and discuss what we can do next? I'm sure she'll turn up soon. I'll be about twenty minutes or so," he said, trying to put a note of optimism into his voice.

"Oh, would you?" Karen asked eagerly, suddenly not feeling so grown up after all and pleased to have someone to share the burden of worry with. It was completely out of character for her mother, and at times like this, she really missed the reassuring presence of her beloved Daddy. He'd always made her feel safe and secure, and despite the recent feelings of oncoming adulthood, she still really missed him. "Thank you, I'm getting rather nervous," she replied, then regretting saying that, not wanting to sound like a frightened, little girl. Having often had the house to herself at a week-end on the odd occasion her mother had been away travelling on the ships when she worked full-time at Beaumont's, but this felt different. She suddenly felt very alone. No, she was beginning to feel afraid of what had become of her mother.

Just as George Stewart was about to hang up, he had a sudden thought and asked,

"One thing to check, Karen, is your mother's car in the garage?"

"I don't know, but I'll go and have a look, do you want me to hang on?"

"Yes, if you would."

Laying down the receiver, Karen ran through to the kitchen, slipped on a pair of 'flip flops,' and went out into the garden to peer through the window of the nearby detached, brick garage. Her mother's car was certainly there, but something else caught her attention, although she couldn't work out what exactly as she was so eager to return to the phone.

"Mr. Stewart? Yes, Mum's car is still in the garage."

"Ok, that's a reasonably good sign, as I was beginning to look on the black side, wondering maybe she had been involved in an accident. Anyway enough of this chatter Karen, I'll be over shortly, who knows your Mum could be trying to get through on the phone at this very moment, and we are hogging the line," he said, trying to sound confident but not convincing himself, let alone Karen.

George had grown really fond of Ann. He'd been a single man all his life, working hard to build up his now lucrative business to the detriment of affairs of the heart. He'd allowed himself to grow old too quickly, and a woman like Ann Clark was just the tonic he needed. She made him feel alive and young again. She was an attractive woman who turned heads wherever they went. He knew that people thought that it was only his money that attracted Ann to him, well maybe it was, but George didn't care as he was in seventh heaven with a lady like Ann on his arm. He was going to ask her to marry him if he could clear up her marital status. The missing husband was an enigma, Ann being vague whenever he broached the subject, but she did insist that her marriage was over and that it was just a matter of time before the divorce would come through. This latest incident raised suspicions, questioning if she might be seeing someone else and frightened that he was about to become history.

George Stewart dressed quickly, his heart rate rising with anxiety, imagining that Ann could at this very moment be in the arms of another man. The question's raced around his mind, how could she, after all the things she had said to him? How she admired him for the business he created and that the world needed more nice men like him in it. Had she just been playing him along, but then thinking rationally he didn't believe so, Ann seemed very genuine when she had expressed these feelings, although he had harboured some concerns as to how Ann was supporting herself in what was a very comfortable lifestyle. Ann always claimed she had had a big pre-divorce pay-off from her husband, who was by all accounts a well-paid helicopter pilot working in Africa. George was hoping to woo her with the prospects of security; he had a sound business and wanted for nothing. Surely he wasn't that bad at judging her character? With these thoughts spinning around in his head, he finished dressing then went down into the yard at the rear of his home. His detached house and shop sat in a large yard with the warehouse adjacent, from where he ran his wholesale business. The business owned several delivery vehicles, and it was the keys to one of these vans that he took from the keyboard in the office as he passed through and out into the yard. As he stepped outside, he was bathed in brilliant white light as motion detectors picked up his presence. George owned a very stately Bentley, but this was tucked up in his personal climate-controlled garage, and it would be too much of a 'faff' to get it out. George was soon in one of his vans and on the road on his errand of mercy to hopefully find answers to the whereabouts of Ann Clark, the woman with whom he was so in love with.

Chapter 56

George's route, from his home and business to Ann's on the other side of Northwold, took him through the town centre and past the central police station. He hesitated at first, but then decided it was a good idea to call in for a chat with the duty desk sergeant whom he assumed would be an acquaintance. George was a local man, born and bred, as were several of the local coppers so he knew most of them. In fact, he supplied their canteen caterers with groceries and vegetables. George was in luck; the newly employed civvies had finished for the day and the enquiry desk had been taken over by a duty sergeant, Donald Jessop, who was an old school friend he knew very well. In fact, one of Donald's sons worked for George as a van delivery driver. The son was ex HM Forces who had lost an arm in some far off conflict and, after being invalided out of the army, George had taken him on after adapting a van for his needs. Consequently, George had developed a close relationship with Donald, who was naturally very grateful for George's generosity. Donald Jessop was the epitome of the famous TV series policeman 'Dixon of Dock Green;' he displayed a slow, meticulous air of authority with a rich, gravelly voice that could indicate a life-long smoker, which he had been until recently. Having listened to George's concerns about Ann Clark, Donald took down the necessary details, neatly writing them into the occurrence book. There was a computer on the desk, but Donald, being old school, was still a little reluctant to use it having not quite got the knack of using the keyboard so much preferred to write out the information, long hand first. Informing George that there was nothing more he could do at this stage, other than sending around a constable to take a statement from Karen Clark Donald explained that despite what the general public may think, thanks to the numerous TV police series, they didn't operate a missing person's bureau, leaving that to the Salvation Army. A missing person would only become of interest to the police if they were considered to be vulnerable, and from what Donald knew of Ann Clark, she certainly didn't fall into that category. However, as it had so far been a quiet night for police resources, Donald was able to assure George that an officer would soon attend.

After George had left, Donald picked up an internal telephone receiver. He called up to the local Operations Room, asking them to send a police officer around to Windsor Avenue to take a statement from Miss Karen Clark regarding a possible missing Ann Clark of the same address. As he replaced the receiver, he mused, 'Why do I know that name?' Just at that moment, a telephone rang in the office and momentarily his thoughts about Ann Clark were put aside, although he wrote her name on a piece of scrap paper as a reminder to himself to follow up later. In reality, he didn't forget as it nagged at him like an itch, and it wasn't very long before the 'penny dropped,' and he recalled exactly why he knew the name. Donald recalled being on duty when the control room had received the three nines call from a concerned neighbour worried about the 'ding dong' of a row going on between Ann Clark and her husband. Then some time later there were DS Marsh's enquiries about her apparently missing husband. Now it appeared that Ann Clark was missing too.

After cutting the call with George Stewart, Karen made herself another cup of tea and went back into the sitting room in front of the glowing gas fire. She tried to recall what had worried her when she had gone out to look at the garage for her mother's car. Draining her cup, she resolved to look into the garage again. Karen's apprehension was increasing as she walked through the kitchen, slipped on the same flip flops, and went back out into the garden again. She was not ordinarily afraid of being on her own, or of the dark, but anxious as to where her mother could be.

"Of course... darkness!" she said out aloud.

"That's what was wrong," she stated loudly to herself. The garage and part of the garden had been bathed in light; nothing unusual when the house lights at the rear of the house were switched on. But they were not when she'd first dashed outside in answer to George Stewart's query about her mother's car, so where was the light coming from? Looking up for the source of the light, she saw that it was coming from her mother's rear bedroom large panoramic windows, the curtains being drawn fully open. The room her mother always kept locked when not occupying it. It was an unwritten law in the Clark household that Ann's bedroom was her sanctuary, and Karen was forbidden from going in there. Karen had always respected her mother's wishes about not entering. That was except on one occasion when she was feeling mischievous after having arrived home earlier than expected she noticed that her mother had left the door slightly ajar with the key in the lock. Her mother, at the time, was taking a shower and obviously hadn't heard her. Taking a peek into the bedroom she had discovered that other than seeing a tastefully decorated bedroom, Karen didn't view anything out of the ordinary, which might be the cause of her mother wanting to keep the room locked, except from what looked like a school gym, vaulting horse. She concluded it was a rather strange piece of furniture for a bedroom, but as her mother was keen on keeping fit and exercised regularly, she assumed it was to assist her exercise routine. From that day onwards, Karen had never given her mother's secret bedroom another thought.

As Karen walked back into the kitchen, with no other thoughts than that her mother had obviously gone out leaving the light on, the headlights of a car entered the drive and illuminated the hallway through the glazing of the front door. Karen, realising that it must be George Stewart, went to the front door to let him in. Just as George had switched off his van's engine and alighted, another vehicle swung into the drive. Karen could see that it was a police patrol car, emblazoned with large blue squares along its sides, the Lincolnshire County Police Crest on the driver's door and the familiar light bar strapped across the roof. As the long arm of the law got out from the police car, Karen's pulse started to race. From the driver's side, emerged PC Wendy Morgan and, on the other side, her partner PC Mick Walker. Both officers were dressed in dark regulation navy blue and around their waists were the usual accoutrements of baton, torch, handcuffs and tasers, and communications equipment. Overall this gave them the appearance of military personnel rather than that of a police officer policing by consent.

"Why are they here Mr. Stewart?" she gulped as all three approached her. "What's happened to Mummy?" she almost cried, suddenly feeling frightened at seeing the police officers and causing her to lapse back into the childish terminology that she hadn't used for years. Despite the enjoyment of referring to her father as Daddy, she'd never really felt the same towards her mother.

George Stewart gently caught hold of Karen's arm as he started to ease himself passed her and into the hallway, closely followed Police Constables Michael Walker and Wendy Morgan.

He stopped and faced Karen, "Nothing's happened as far as I know Karen, under the circumstances I merely called into the police station on my way here to see if they'd heard of anything untoward, such as an accident, that may have occurred to your mother."

"What circumstances, what's going on?" questioned Karen, forcing her voice to sound more confident than she was actually feeling.

George become assertive, "Look Karen, we've got to cover every angle, it's late and there's no explanation for your mother's disappearance," he regretted the use of the word 'disappearance' as soon as he'd said it, but he too was becoming increasingly anxious for the safety of Ann.

"Now come along, let these two nice officers in so they can ascertain what steps we take next before we wake up the whole area," George sounding as though he was admonishing a child. Just at that moment, he noticed bedroom lights in the neighbouring house were starting to flicker on. The sound of the two vehicles arriving in this notoriously quiet little 'cul de sac,' followed by the distinctive sound of car doors opening and closing at this time of night had awoken some and attracted the attention of those with insomnia.

"Ok," replied Karen as she stood back to allow George to pass, followed by the two police officers who individually introduced themselves. George directed them into the lounge. Karen had become slightly bewildered by the chain of events and not knowing what to do next, but trying to keep a grip on herself to portray the image of being very grown-up, she offered tea, which was accepted. George offered to make the drinks while the two officers spoke to Karen; he went through to the kitchen and busied himself with the necessary items putting everything together on a large tray with the familiarity of knowing his way around Ann's kitchen. Waiting for the kettle to boil his mind wandered back to the pleasant evenings and stopovers he'd experienced in the house, wishing he was preparing tea for him and Ann rather than Karen and two serious looking police officers.

Back in the lounge, the two police officers were on the large sofa opposite Karen, who was sitting in one of the matching comfortable chairs. While their personal radios burbled away discreetly in the background, both were writing notes in their large A5 size notebooks, the days of small police pocketbooks that fitted neatly into uniform breast pockets being a thing of the past. Modern police notebooks looked large enough for writing a novel; in some cases, exactly what the notes from many a major incident could be!

George Stewart walked in with a tray of tea, which he served to the two police officers. Karen, having recently consumed quite a bit of tea, refused. Having ascertained as to his relationship with Ann Clark, the police officers then went on to ask Karen and George searching questions about Ann's movements and when they had last seen or spoken to her. Karen explained she could give very little information as she had been staying with Aunty and Uncle and she'd had little contact with her mother since saying goodbye the previous week only speaking in a telephone call on the Wednesday. With it being half term, she had spent the whole of the previous week in the south. George explained that he had only spoken once with Ann Clark, earlier in the week, when they had arranged to go out for the day on Sunday, he'd booked lunch at a lovely Inn on the coast about a forty minute drive from Northwold but when he came to collect Ann that morning there had been no reply. PC Wendy Morgan was obviously suspicious as she questioned George as to the length of time it had taken him to contact the police. He explained that they had only recently struck up a relationship and he had assumed that for whatever reason, Ann had decided against seeing him that day or had genuinely forgotten their date and had gone on to do other things. He had no hold over her, he insisted, as he could see where the officers were going with this line of questioning. The officers nodded in unison but gave the impression George's answer didn't totally convince them. The police duo continued asking probing questions as to both Karen's and George's recent movements and who could corroborate their stories. Karen produced her rail ticket clearly showing that she had been on the late afternoon train from Kings Cross to Northwold, this appeared to satisfy them. Karen was becoming scared and bewildered by the change of events, no longer feeling on 'Cloud 9' following the wonderful, almost magical, week with her aunty and uncle, now it felt like she had been parachuted into an episode of a TV soap. The police pair couldn't hide their scepticism about George's story of his recent whereabouts as they repeatedly asked as to why, after having made arrangements to collect Ann Clark for a Sunday drive and lunch, did he just go home and think no more of it when she hadn't answered the door?

George, under the questioning, was developing feelings of guilt and inadequacy, not being used to such intense questioning. He wasn't helping himself by displaying signs of agitated nervousness, inwardly questioning himself that he should have done more than just walk away when Ann hadn't answered the door. Perhaps he should have looked around the house and peered in the windows, although he realised that probably wouldn't have provided any answers to the mystery. George even surprised himself by asking the police officers if he needed a solicitor. The officers countered that as not being at all necessary, he was not under suspicion of any wrongdoing, well not at this stage they added! George's remark was increasing the doubt that they were not entirely satisfied with his explanation. The two officers appeared to have covered just about every eventuality so far. Still, being none the wiser as to the absence of Ann Clark, they'd ascertained something untoward had happened to her, either that or she'd 'done a bunk.' Her car was still in the garage, that needed further investigation as well as checking her clothing and personal effects. When they asked if there was anything unusual that had occurred, Karen suddenly remembered wondering about why the light was on in her mother's bedroom and that she'd been about to find out the reason when they arrived.

"Right then," said PC Walker, "we need to look through your mother's personal effects to see if there are any clues there; maybe her passport is missing," He saw the look of horror cross the faces of Karen and George.

Mick put up his hand as he and Wendy stood up, "Yes, I know what you are going to say but we have to cover everything, we wouldn't be doing our jobs properly unless we looked."

Karen led the way up the stairs in front of Mick and Wendy, followed by George.

Once they'd congregated outside the back bedroom door Karen, still somewhat bewildered, indicated, "This is Mum's room, but she keeps it locked, and I don't have a key."

"Oh ok, well, if you've no spare and no idea where the key might be, I'm asking your permission to break it down," stated Mick Walker.

"Ok," confirmed Karen rather dejectedly, wondering what her mother will say when she turns up, and not liking the way things were going, she was starting to feel quite queasy. There was a strange smell that she hadn't noticed before. Mick and Wendy also noticed it and gave each other a knowing and alarmed look. George too, was feeling very uncomfortable but kept quiet. He wasn't happy about the strange, stale smell lingering within the confined atmosphere of the landing area. His business affairs took him to several abattoirs from where he bought meat products for repackaging and onward sale in his wholesale business, and thus he knew the distinctive smell of culled meat an uncomfortable shiver ran down his back.

"If you and Mr. Stewart would go back downstairs to the lounge with my colleague Wendy, then I'll gain entry to the bedroom, and we'll take it from there," said PC Mick Walker.

"Shouldn't one of us be here?" asked George, implying he should be a witness to the police gaining entry into this very private area that he had not yet been allowed to venture. On the occasions that he had been invited by Ann to sleep over he had chastely used the spare front bedroom.

"I think not," came the firm reply from Mick Walker as he glared at George. George didn't like what he was beginning to suspect, the realisation as to what the police officers expected to find behind the locked door was filling him with foreboding and dread.

Dejectedly, he turned and allowed PC Wendy Morgan to shepherd him and Karen down the stairs and in to the lounge. Perching on separate chairs, they sat quietly, lost in their own thoughts, while PC Wendy Morgan casually stood in the entrance doorway like a guard ready to stop them from leaving.

PC Mick Walker leaned his shoulder against the door to make himself comfortable then gave one mighty heave against it, but it failed to give any movement. The house was a substantial 1950's build when specifications called for heavy solid doors and frames, unlike the modern lightweight equivalents. After three good forceful shoves from Mick Walker's six foot 16 stone body, the door splintered around the lock and flew open. Walker gasped as his lungs recoiled at the heavy, sickly pungent air, thick with the stench of death. Fumbling in his pocket for a handkerchief, he quickly held it over his nose and mouth as he observed a magnitude of flies swarming around the body he presumed to be that of Ann Clark. Walker had seen some bizarre and abhorrent sights in his time as a police officer, but nothing as macabre as this. Before him, was the naked body of a woman, laid over and handcuffed to what appeared to be a school gym vaulting horse, her back and buttocks a mass of congealed blood and torn flesh, gruesomely covered in a mass of flies and maggots engaged in a feeding frenzy. The woman's head, drooped, hung just a few inches from the carpet. A long strip of what appeared to be a leather whip snaked around her neck, her tongue dangled grotesquely on the floor as it hung from her mouth. Walker immediately left the room, closing the door gently behind him as he gagged for some marginally fresher air on the landing. His professionalism quickly 'kicking in,' realising he had just entered a crime scene, he must now protect and keep sterile for the detectives and Scene of Crime scientists.

Meanwhile, in the ghoulish quietness of the lounge, Karen and George heard the grunt, followed by the sound of splitting wood and then, apart from a sudden gagging sound, silence. Karen and George looked at each other, horrified, not knowing what to think. Only PC Wendy Morgan understood the possibilities of what her colleague may have discovered behind the locked bedroom door, she quickly walked into the hallway and looked up the staircase.

Looking over the banister railing, Mick Walker saw his colleague looking up at him. Nothing was said, he just shook his head while Wendy nodded in acknowledgement and the telepathy between the two colleagues said it all. Having composed himself, he swiftly descended the steps, and together with Wendy Morgan, they entered the room to face Karen and George. The look on his face said it all, confirming what George was expecting. Neither Karen or George stood, up as if instinctively knowing that the information Mick Walker would impart would make them collapse back down into the sofa again.

"You've found her, haven't you?" asked George solemnly, looking up to the towering frame of Mick Walker, his eyes already beginning to flood with tears.

"Yes, sir, I'm afraid so, it's not good," replied PC Mick Walker, rather glumly recalling what he had just witnessed. George appeared to diminish physically.

Karen, looking at Mick Walker and then George, initially confused, suddenly seemed to understand and screamed out "Mummy?" She jumped up, rushed for the door but found her way blocked by PC Mick Walker.

Her eyes locked with his, "Let me pass, will you. Let. Me. Pass," she screamed as tears rolled down her face. She raised her arms, trying to thump the policeman out of her way.

Compared to Karen's slim frame, PC Walker was a goliath of man, Karen's pitiful blows raining upon him just bounced off his broad chest and soon he had Karen in a bear hug, guiding her back to the lounge sofa. PC Wendy Morgan and George put their arms around Karen. They attempted to comfort her as PC Mick Walker went back out into the hall and radioed in his find, requesting the Night Supervising Inspector to attend as it would be over to him to organise the necessary resources. All he and Wendy had to do was guard the crime scene in readiness for the detectives and SOCO. Returning to the lounge, Mick indicated for George to join him in the hallway while Wendy cuddled the sobbing body of Karen Clark. In the hallway, he explained that he had discovered the body of a woman he believed to be Ann Clark. George himself, in a state of shock, could hardly believe what he was hearing, despite his earlier instincts having prepared him for the worst. Realising that all his dreams of sailing along the river of love with Ann were now pouring through a black abyss into the cesspool of life's lost opportunities. George felt like a lifeless, hollow shell as he summonsed all his reserves of inner strength in an attempt to hold himself together in the face of such adversity. Later, when alone, he would sob his heart out until his reservoir of tears were utterly drained. Turning, and without saying a word, he went back into the room, allowing Wendy to release the distraught Karen into his arms.

Before all the others arrived, arrangements were made for George to take care of Karen. PC Wendy Morgan explained that she would arrange for a police Family Liaison Officer to attend George's home and that it would be the role of the F.L.O to explain what would happen next and to ensure that they both had the right support to help them through this traumatic period. Wendy also warned them both that they would be required to be interviewed by the detectives appointed to investigate the case.

After collecting some of her overnight things, despite continuous protestations that she wanted to stay with her mother, both Karen and George left in a state of shock and bewilderment.

Chapter 57

Northwold did not have a large detective force, the serious crimes detective branch worked from the force HQ in Lincoln. Northwold's department consisted of a Detective Inspector and two Detective Sergeants, one male and one female. The Detective Sergeant on duty that night happened to be Peter Marsh, who had ironically already dealt with Ann Clark over the mysterious disappearance of her husband.

At that precise moment, Peter Marsh was lying atop the voluptuous wife of a dockyard maintenance night supervisor. Lying in ecstasy, the pair having orgasmed some seconds before, both were displeased at the interruption of Peter's personnel radio as it started bleating out his call sign in tandem with his mobile phone buzzing. He'd half-expected the call, having previously overhead some radio chatter about an incident involving a suspicious death shortly before diving into the chasm of lust. Despite his primeval sexual urges wanting him to ignore the summons for his attention, so he could carry on giving his seductive partner his undivided attention, he reached the bedside table, fumbled, and grabbed one of the instruments. After joining the Criminal Investigation Department, Peter soon learned that they could be a law unto themselves, unlike their uniformed colleagues. CID enquiries led them all over the place; the very nature of the job was one where no two days could ever be the same. Following lines of enquiry could be compared to a spider's web as leads on information would send CID officers off in all directions. However, apart from the odd transgression, he was a conscientious police officer who intended to go far in the police service. So, for now, the sexual pleasure was over as he instantly changed from lover to detective. It sounded as though something big was going down, and the address of the incident started ringing bells inside Peter's inquisitive mind.

Suddenly, he leapt off the curvy, if somewhat slightly running to fat, middle-aged lady as he recalled why he knew Windsor Avenue and the name Clark. Could it be the Ann Clark with the missing husband? He stood naked by the bed as the lady reached out from under the duvet, busily wrapping her arms around his thighs, Peter attempted to push her embrace away as he called into the police station on his mobile phone, she reluctantly released him. Listening to all the details from the Desk Sergeant, Peter Marsh began to fire on all cylinders, recalling the interviews with Ann Clark and his gut feeling that she had murdered her husband. It seemed that the tables had been turned and she had apparently died in suspicious circumstances, intriguing! Peter cut the call and immediately grabbed for his clothing hanging over the bedside chair, putting distance between himself and his amorous partner.

"Leave it sweetie, they can do without you... I can't, come back to bed and screw me again," she tried to sound seductive, "I want you to fuck me senseless; you've only half done the job."

"Sorry gotta go," replied Peter, hurriedly donning his clothes.

"What about me, sweetie? You know I need you. Will you be long?" she pleaded.

"Dunno" he replied as he headed for the door, with a flippant, "sorry, the force needs me more. See ya later lover."

As the door closed behind him, she immediately sat upright, her ample large breasts bounced free, "Bloody copper... fuck you! If you don't come back tonight, don't bother coming back at all, you bastard!"

Peter smiled to himself as he went downstairs. He'd be back when he pleased: he knew the frustrated sexpot couldn't get enough of him. He knew only too well that her fat, lardy, lazy husband wasn't doing the business with her. She'd as much as told him so, and he also knew from his mate, a port copper of the new fledging port police force, that her husband was playing around with the dockyard café's night supervisor. Peter and the port policeman played squash together and after one particular game, over a cold beer, he re-laid a story to Peter about catching the pair in the act. Working late one night, on his usual foot patrol around the docks, he'd seen a light on in the cafe's storeroom. The window was high above the normal level of sight, and being one to revel in any activity to liven up his night shift, he didn't hesitate to climb up on to some packing cases and wooden pallets to peer in, hoping to catch some sort of criminal activity. There, in full view, he'd seen the dockyard maintenance night man, sitting in a chair with his trousers around his ankles and the night café supervisor going down on him. They were oblivious to being observed, and it appeared, from what he could see, that the fat git was having trouble getting it up, despite the administrations of the young lady. Even the saucy calendar he was staring at, held tightly in his left grip, didn't seem to be helping the situation. Whatever the night café supervisor found sexually attractive in the fat maintenance man, the copper couldn't say. He was astounded that she would want to be doing such an act with his large, bloated, hairy belly virtually smothering her. Still, despite being a bit of a looker, she was known to be a hard faced cow and always bragged about how she could make any man, including gays, get it up, so maybe she saw the maintenance man as a challenge.

The port policeman had concluded by saying, "Mind you, whenever I call in there for a tea and bun I make sure it's one of the other gals that serves me. The thought of that bitch's hand serving me after seeing it being all over that fat git's penis puts me right orf."

Armed with the information past on to him by the port copper, Peter had made a play for the man's wife and instantly scored!

Peter let himself out from the rear of the terraced house and cut through an alley into the next road where he had parked his car. He was astute enough to never bring a plain unmarked police car to his amorous appointment, for fear of it being spotted in the same place too often. Plain and unmarked it may have been, but most people in Northwold could recognise a 'bog standard' unmarked CID Ford, with its typical radio aerial at the rear. He started the car and set off on his way. As he reached the T-junction at the end of the road, a police patrol car, with its blue lights flashing, flew past at speed, 'probably going to the same incident,' thought Peter as he flicked the indicator and manoeuvred out of the side road to follow it.

Peter Marsh arrived at 31, Windsor Avenue at the same time as his 'Boss,' Detective Inspector Harry Joseph, by which time a group of neighbours had gathered, some clad only in dressing-gowns over their night attire. Others, on seeing the commotion, had got fully dressed and were approaching the duty constables guarding the scene with the offer of tea or coffee in an attempt to find out what was going on, only to be told that an 'incident' had occurred. Some saw the dazed George Stewart take away the huddled figure of a distraught Karen Clark, and putting two and two together, they concluded that there had been a terrible accident. It was in total amazement when they later read in the newspaper that Ann Clark had been murdered.

Detective Inspector Harry Joseph was a tall, lanky copper, way above the average height and with a slight stoop. His height and long runner's legs had been a great advantage to him, in his younger years on the beat it enabled him to see above most of the crowd in busy areas, and now, despite approaching middle age, he could still outrun and catch most younger tearaways when he had to. These two attributes had made him successful and infamous when it came to working the streets on pickpocket patrol in London. Had he not joined the police force, Harry could easily have become a professional athlete. His round, black face looked as though it had been chiselled from ebony. Despite a commonly held, somewhat racist view, that black people blend in with the dark of the night, nothing could be further from the truth for Harry's face, his literally glistened in the night, shining like a beacon. His eyes always reflected what he was feeling; at that moment, they indicated sadness while thinking that it beggared belief that a human being could die such a horrible death. Harry enjoyed being a copper, especially a detective, despite his earlier experiences as the target of racism in the Met. He looked upon the crimes that came his way as mind-bending teasers that he'd go above and beyond to solve. Harry had a devilish, sarcastic, and dry wit, which made him popular with his colleagues. He and his wife were never without a list of invites to dinner parties as his conversation pieces were legendary. Another trademark trait of Harry was that he'd nearly always have his hands dug deep into his pockets. His colleagues said that's the way he kept his money as he was known for rarely buying others a cup of tea or a pint of beer after work. That tiresome, and sometime expensive, task frequently fell to his sidekick, Peter Marsh, who often moaned about what it cost him. All of which fell on Harry's deaf ears, however, most colleagues enjoyed working with Harry and hence looked upon buying a few drinks here and there as a small price to pay. As well as being a financial tight arse, Harry suffered from an itchy scrotum, consequently, keeping his hands in his pocket was actually to enable him to scratch the irritant discreetly. He also had an annoying habit of breaking wind in whoever's company he found himself.

Harry, a copper of the old school, believed in having a nose for a situation and obtaining results by dogged determination and footwork on the streets talking to people. This had been the key to his success dealing with the 'Yardies' in London, although being black with his origins in Jamaica had naturally helped. All this modern stuff with computers and psychological profiling was all university *'mumbo jumbo,'* and beyond him, and in his opinion didn't solve crimes any quicker than his methods. He had reluctantly accepted computer programmes, such as the Home Office Large and Major Enquiry System, commonly known as HOLMES. Harry thought that some 'whizz kid' must have come up with the acronym to name it after the famous fictional detective Sherlock Holmes. Not that it mattered to him, they could call it what they liked; he happily admitted that it was a godsend for tracking all the written evidence that came with major incidents.

Harry and Peter waited in Ann's hallway until the Scenes of Crime Officers arrived, conscious that everything in the house was now a crime scene and nothing must be contaminated. They chatted, briefly discussing what they had been told by PC Mick Walker and PC Wendy Morgan. Without formal identification, they had come to the tentative conclusion that the deceased was Ann Clark. The lady with whom Peter had dealings with regarding her so-called missing husband. Once SOCO arrived, Harry and Peter donned full 'head to toe' cover overalls and gingerly made their way upstairs to look at the primary crime scene.

Looking on impassively, Peter said, "Well, Guv, this is the woman with whom I've had dealings with in the past and believe it to be Ann Clark."

Harry just nodded in acknowledgement.

Peter Marsh wasn't sure whether the awful foul smell was one of Harry's famous deadly farts or the decaying, open wounds mixed with bodily fluids that secreted from the human body following a violent death. Harry's farts had been known for emptying a room on many occasions, and Peter grinned as he recalled one such time.

Focusing on his job, Peter was almost amused by the scene before him, not with the body of the unfortunate deceased as he felt no one should die in this way, but at the strange array of items the wardrobe contained, all appeared to be for inflicting pain on the human body.

"Nasty, looks like the work of a bloody maniac," was all Harry could say, followed by a deep sniff which he immediately regretted as despite his mask, the air was dank and heavy with the sickly, acidity of decomposition. He smirked, realising that there actually was a smell worse than his farts.

"What can you tell me, Charlie," asked Harry of the chief SOCO, a retired detective now on a second career in crime as a civilian scientific officer. Charlie and his team delicately probed over the body and searched the bedroom, collecting various lose objects. Objects which could contain a vital piece of DNA evidence crucially required for a conviction.

"Well, this is only a guess at this stage, but seems she was killed within the last four days, I'll give you more after the post-mortem," replied the SOCO.

"Right, thanks, Charlie. Peter, have a dig around see if you can find anything interesting such as a diary, mobile phone, handbag, the usual," requested Harry.

"But don't get in our way!" interjected Charlie.

With that, Harry turned to leave, "I'm going over to talk to the daughter and boyfriend if they're up to it. I know George of old anyway, so that should make it a 'tad' easier. There's not much more we can do here. Leave it to SOCO and the undertakers when they arrive, we'll convene in my office in the morning, ok?"

"Right Guv," replied Peter as he began his search by opening bedside drawers to start the long, painstaking sad task of trawling through the life and times of Ann Clark.

As is the case with nearly all murder victims, the detectives would be able to come to know more about Ann Clark in death than they would ever have known had she lived.

Chapter 58

Following the murder of Ann Clark, the bizarre circumstances surrounding her death were made subjudice. This decision being reached at a morning conference involving, the Assistant Chief Constable Crime, the Chief Superintendent, Head of Lincolnshire CID and, of course, the senior investigating officer Inspector Harry Joseph. It was understandable that when the murder facts, together with the most intimate details of the inside of Ann Clark's bedroom, were spread all over the front pages of both the local evening news and the national dailies. The Assistant Chief Constable not known for his restraint when things didn't go according to his diktat became incandescent with rage. Not so much that the details were now out there, but that they had been released in direct contradiction of his explicit orders following a request from Harry. All assumed that the leak could only have come from a source within the police force. The papers had photographs of Ann Clark, some showing her lying naked on a sun lounger in what looked like her bedroom. The articles appeared in the ritzy tabloid newspapers, aimed at a readership that weren't interested in reading about mundane shenanigans in parliament or the financial news as they believed it didn't affect their daily lives of grind. They were only interested in the style of journalism provided by 'the smutty gutter press'.

One such paper, using the wizardry of the new computing age, had a photograph of Ann Clark's head and shoulders placed on to a female body dressed in a Basque with matching black stockings and high heeled, black, patent leather thigh boots, a large whip in one hand completed the ensemble. The local newspaper, having done some digging into Ann Clark's background, discovered that her middle name was Linda and hence came up with a headline '*Northwold's very own Linda Lash*'. National dailies had come up with running headlines that included the words '*Grand Priestess of Bondage,*' finally unmasked and living in Northwold. This prompted an immediate response from the Anglican church whose Northwold's man of God was, in fact, one of the newly appointed women clergy who objected strongly to having her religious position associated which such horrible sexual practices. Emblazoned across the cover of a well-known gossip magazine were the headlines "*Vixen of Torture*". This brought an immediate response from the local tree hugging, anti-hunting brigade who raised objections. They complained that the paper was demonising the poor little fox, recalling echoes of the 1970's film the Bell Stone Fox. Another journalistic wag had printed an adaptation of the Rupert the Bear poem,' if you go down to the woods today' changing it to 'if you go up to Northwold today, you shall be in for a big surprise!' Another paper wanting to capitalise on the more juicy stories for their readership rather stupidly invited any devotee of the sadomasochism cult who knew Ann Clark to send in their stories. This backfired, and the paper's switchboard became inundated with anonymous calls from those claiming to be involved with her.

The claims, of course, being totally fictitious made up by 'oddballs' and people that didn't get out enough because even if half had been true, then Ann would have to be credited with hundreds of kinky friends and sexual partners queuing at her front door. Even the local radio station couldn't escape and had to cut off when some phone-in listeners launched into discussing Ann Clark's macabre death.

The presence of police resources at George's business premises gave the game away. Therefore it was inevitable that investigative journalists would track down and hound both George Stewart and Ann's daughter, Karen. This incessant, aggressive attention of the press laying siege to George's home where he and Karen were incarcerated, together with the police enquiries, were beginning to take their toll on Karen's wellbeing. She craved for the company of her father, needing his calming influence and strength to steady herself. If her missing father wasn't a huge enough burden to bear, now she had the murder of her mother to contend with. If matters weren't bad enough, she also had to suffer the over burdening attentions of George. He too, was feeling the heat of the situation in which he now found himself. The rigorous interviewing by suspicious police officers gave him the impression that they were convinced he had a part in the murder, inadvertently he was using Karen as a spiritual connection to her mother, reluctant to let go. Treating Karen as though he was a surrogate father was just making matters worse. Poor George couldn't see that his well-intended feelings were just making her more annoyed with him. She craved for the comforting arms of her father not the unwanted attentions of this man she hardly knew. Thankfully a few days after being extensively interviewed by the police, Samantha Devonshire drove up to Northwold to collect Karen and take her south to where she could protect her from all the reporters that were besieging George's house and business. They briefly called in at Windsor Avenue, Karen being tremendously grown-up about it and hiding any emotion, and collected some personal belongings. Samantha told Karen that she need never return to the house unless she wanted to, as her solicitor in London would deal with everything; it was assumed that Karen would be the only beneficiary in her sister's will. For Karen, it was too early to make decisions; all she wanted to do was to contact her dad. It was only when she started to think about this that she realised that even though she had received letters from her father, she didn't actually know his address, other than he worked in the Congo, living in Brazzaville. Her mother had always taken care of the letters to and from her father.

Looking through the newspapers that morning, Peter Marsh could see the funny side of the outrageous headlines but equally agreed with his 'Boss', Harry Joseph, that the information now in the general public arena would greatly hinder their investigation.

Harry was the only one summoned to see the Assistant Chief Constable the morning the story broke, and as Harry entered his inner sanctum he was greeted with a slamming of a fist on the highly polished conference table with the comment, "How the fuck did this happen Harry?" he screamed almost hysterically. "You've got to find whoever did this Harry; I want his or her head on a plate!"

Harry felt one of his famous gastric explosions building in his lower intestine and squeezed his cheeks so his arse was contracting his rectum to avoid breaking wind. This was not an appropriate moment to release the build-up of excessive gases, any semblance of respect for the senior rank would then have gone straight out of the window.

"I agree sir, now this information is out; it will have a negative effect on my investigation, but, with respect, sir, I don't have the time or resources to go looking for the culprit."

Before Harry could go any further to support his argument the Assistant Chief raising his hand interrupted.

"Quite right, Harry, I certainly won't burden you with this. I'll get the Assistant Chief Admin to get Professional Standards on to it right away, after all that's what they're there for, coppers watching coppers, eh?"

That was the end of the matter. Harry left after refusing the proffered coffee, fearing that if he'd stayed a moment longer in the Assistant Chief's office, he wouldn't have been able to hold back from farting. Anyway, Harry didn't have time for such niceties as morning coffee. That was for the ACPO ranks sitting on their large posteriors discussing important subjects such as image delivery, political perception and other latest management 'wheeze' ; he just wanted to be out on the streets tracking down the sadistic killer by good old fashioned coppering.

Harry had no sooner left the Chief's office when the Assistant Chief Constable contacted the his colleague the Assistant Chief Admin, asking him to get the Head of Professional standards to begin the investigation into the leaked details of Ann Clark's murder. They would eventually discover that it was the scientific investigators that had inadvertently leaked details of the macabre death. It had all come about because Ann Clark had, for some time, been modernising her large pre-war semi-detached house in Windsor Avenue. One of the home improvements that had been made was to her bedroom windows, which overlooked the long garden. Her garden created a mirror image of an equally long garden leading from the neighbour's house directly behind, situated in the adjoining Avenue. The windows in her bedroom had old wooden frames, and she had changed them to the new UPVC double-glazed variety. During the process, builders discovered that the wall immediately below the windows had suffered very badly from years of damp, so it had to be removed and replaced. Lots of things in life happen by consequence rather than a formal plan and it was while the builders were busy knocking out the damp part of Ann's bedroom wall that she, during a lunchtime break at the office, was flicking through a 'Homes and Designs' magazine when she came across a photograph advertising a beautiful large floor-to-ceiling picture window folding doors. The windows were hinged and opened concertina style, which in conjunction with ornamental guard rail across the opening would give an added balcony effect; this would allow the windows to be opened back fully while preventing anybody from accidentally falling out. Ann immediately knew that's what she wanted. Ann loved the fresh air, so whenever possible during the summer months, she opened every window in her house. She rushed home to show the builders, naturally, they readily agreed that this could be done, but it would incur a further cost! So, Ann's bedroom now sported these large patio style doors along the full length of the rear bedroom wall, overlooking her rear garden and the rear of the houses in the adjacent Avenue. During hot, summer evenings, Ann would often lay naked on a sun lounger in her bedroom with the windows wide open so the soft evening breeze could gently caress her body, confident that she could not be seen by any of her neighbours due to the distance created by the adjoining long gardens.

The rear of the neighbours' houses in the next Avenue looking in her direction were far enough away to avoid casual scrutiny by the naked eye. However, living in the house immediately behind was a family of four:

Mum, Dad, and their two boys. Tim and Toby were twins and shared the same interest in anything technical; in fact, they were fast-growing into techno freaks and always had the latest gizmos bought for them by their doting parents. The latest purchase was a very high-powered telescope on a tripod, ostensibly for star gazing into the heavens. That was until one hot summer's evening when Tom was panning the telescope around the local area and spotted Ann Clark lying naked on a sun lounger just inside her bedroom windows. Tim and Tom, also budding entrepreneurs, were soon snapping away with a digital camera attached to the telescope, the design being originally aimed at the ornithology market, for 'twitchers' to snap photos of their favourite birds of the feathered kind. Tim and Tom printed off the pictures of the naked Ann Clark and were soon making a profit from the spotty youths in the playground of the local high school. Another gizmo acquired by Tim and Tom was a remote-controlled helicopter to which was attached a small electronic eye that beamed back images to the screen on the remote control box, long before domestic toy drones came onto the market. After the news broke about Clark's untimely death, the inquisitive twins could not wait to investigate, so they excitedly conspired to send their helicopter over to see what they could discover. As Tim expertly directed their helicopter to the level of Ann Clark's bedroom, they discovered that all the windows were wide open due to the SOCO's needing fresh air to alleviate the suffocating smell of decomposition that still lingered there after the removal of the cadaver. Through the small eye, they could see right inside and watch the scientific officers at work. With the innocence of youth also comes audacity, so when the room was briefly vacated, they cautiously manoeuvred the helicopter inside. Consequently, the bedroom and all its contents were photographed with amazing clarity.

Their enterprise was only brought to an abrupt halt when, after safely retrieving their helicopter, their father caught them busily downloading the images. The twins entrepreneurial streak had been past down through the DNA of their father, a successful self made businessman and he, after ascertaining what they had been up to and as to what they had discovered, had seen the opportunity to make a quick buck or two and promptly sold copies to the press.

When it was discovered by the Professional Standards department that this was how the details were released to the press, they had concluded no crime had been committed and that there was very little they could do other than issue a stern warning to Tim and Tom for seriously hindering the police murder investigation, while at the same time secretly admiring their sheer pluck and bold handiwork.

The week immediately following the murder had initially seen a beehive of activity in the area of Windsor Avenue as police officers went from house to house making enquiries. The scientific team had wrapped up at the house, but it would still remain a crime scene until Harry Joseph decided otherwise. A police presence had remained at the house until the scientific officers had completed their task and then that was withdrawn. Bouquets of flowers and wreaths had started being placed on the pavement in front of number 31 Windsor Avenue the day after the news broke. This was somewhat surprising considering that Ann had very little to do with her neighbours. Although Windsor Avenue didn't get much traffic, as it was a cul-de-sac, the police eventually moved all the flowers into the front garden to avoid them being trodden on. Cars still occasionally cruised past, as those with a ghoulish interest in what had occurred came to rubberneck the scene. The story of the goings-on at number 31 soon disappeared from the front pages of the Nationals, being relegated to the inside pages following the initial exposure as the house of fun and torture. They ultimately lost interest when a government minister was reported to have been discovered in a compromising situation with a young man, and as a result, he had promptly come out as gay. The local paper gave Ann's case front-page coverage for a week, then they too lost interest when nothing new could be reported. This paper had created some hysteria as a local journalist attempting to capitalise on the murder intimated that there was a serial killer on the loose and that women were not safe. This caused the little nightlife that Northwold had to virtually die. Even the local fallen 'Angels', whose primary source of income came from the Baltic state vessels that came to Northwold with cargoes of timber, stayed indoors. This, in turn, brought an increase in public order offences as the Eastern European crews from these vessels came ashore pumped up on testosterone looking for the pleasure of these ladies after copious amounts of ale then took out their pent-up emotions and energy on anyone daft enough to cross their path, this resulted in extra police being drafted in to deal with these public order offences. Eventually, even the local landlords were on the local radio complaining of a fall in takings and blaming the police for not getting to grips with the situation. The Chief Constable reacted to this by requesting the PR department to arrange a slot on the local TV and radio; he went on a charm offensive to emphasise that the murder had all the hallmarks of a sexual parlour game that had gone too far and hence there was no predatory person stalking the streets of Northwold looking for another victim. This had the dual effect of calming fears created by the newspaper article and crucially enhancing the Chief Constable's profile. Having joined the force as a cadet, he had experienced a meteoric rise through the ranks, was still only in his late 40s but fast approaching retiring from the force and looking for every opportunity to give himself as much exposure as possible in the hope that he would be approached by one of the television companies to start a new career as a TV personality like so many sporting stars.

A week after the murder, Detective Inspector Harry Joseph was holding his regular morning briefing with Detective Sgt Peter Marsh and the other police officers, a mixture of uniform and plainclothes drafted in to assist in the enquiry. The group also included a member of the civilian support staff engaged in taking shorthand notes that, once typed up, would be passed to Harry to allow him to reflect on the morning case conference. The assembled officers were gathered loosely together in the somewhat disorganised incident room cluttered with desks and tables. Harry and Peter were seated at the front, behind them were two long large portable notice boards, known as a Murder Wall. One notice board had a large ordnance survey map of the Northwold area immediately surrounding Ann Clark's house, along with photographs of Ann Clark, her daughter Karen, Ann's latest boyfriend George Stewart, and finally her ex-husband, Nick Clark, dressed in uniform; a photo acquired from Karen's bedroom. Each photograph had notes pinned beneath them. There were also some samples of brown envelopes found in Ann Clark's bedroom plus an enlarged copy of her recent bank statement showing that over the previous three months, £500 a month had been paid into her account. The boards formed the extent of the police evidence.

The room was full of chatter, some discussing the case, others talking about their social lives.

"Right then, listen up," said Harry trying to gain everyone's attention.

"Well, so far we have drawn a blank on family and friends, in these sorts of cases I'd expect the murderer to be a close friend or relative, but it would appear not at the moment. All the relatives and friends Peter and I have interviewed have all got cast-iron alibis, and there doesn't appear to be anything strange about their relationships with Ann Clark, who we've discovered was a very private woman. However, considering her liberal sexual lifestyle there are bound to be some friends that we haven't come across….yet. We are still attempting to contact the ex-husband who now works in southern Africa, but that is proving very difficult indeed. However, we are checking with immigration to see if his passport has turned up as having returned to the UK recently. If it has, then we could be onto something and to explain I'll pass you over to Peter Marsh who'll fill in the blanks," said Harry pursing his lips as his voice trailed off, lost in his own thoughts.

"Thanks, Gov, a little while ago Ann Clark came forward claiming her husband had suddenly gone missing without a reasonable explanation. She painted a picture of concern, but I didn't buy it. After enquiries with other sources such as work colleagues and his Grandmother, all who intimated that all was not well between the couple. I'll add that there had been one occasion when the neighbours reported a disturbance at their home. This proved inconclusive so, I interviewed Ann Clark under caution; she declined legal representation claiming she'd done nothing wrong, which of course she hadn't. I just had a gut feeling all was not as it appeared. During the interview, she became quite agitated, although I hadn't accused her of anything. It didn't go anywhere, so I left it at that. Some days later, she came into the police station, waving a letter she claimed had been written by her husband and posted from the Congo." Peter indicated to the letter posted on the murder wall.

"In the letter," as you can read

"He states that the marriage was over and asked Ann Clark to start divorce proceedings for which he would accept full responsibility. The letter was typed so we couldn't carry out a handwriting analysis, and fingerprints proved negative. So you can see where I am going with this? Did Ann Clark murder her husband and dispose of his body? Alternatively, has he come back into the country secretly and murdered her? Well, I'll leave that idea on the table for what it's worth." There followed a brief silence as the assembled officers took in what Peter had just imparted to them.

Harry broke the silence, "One thing that has come to light is a possibility that she was blackmailing somebody and that somebody could be the murderer. There can be no other explanation for these brown envelopes and for the money she paid into her bank. Always cash transactions that support the theory that these envelopes were delivered to her address containing the cash. Guess what, another envelope has recently arrived in the post and again containing £500 in used notes. This raises several questions. One if the Blackmailer is the killer is he or she creating a smoke screen....why send money to a dead person or two, the Blackmailer isn't the killer and doesn't yet know she is dead. Strangely the envelopes are all postmarked from different locations throughout the UK, so how come... could it be whoever is paying this money to her is creating another smoke screen using a network of HGV drivers? She previously worked at Beaumont's, and their ships carry lots of HGVs and drivers. Peter Marsh, and I will follow up on that angle". Pausing for a moment, then looking at the group in the room.

"Any DNA yet Gov?" asked one police officer.

"Yes there will be but, and this is where it gets messy. Initial preliminary reports from the pathologist confirms violent penetrative sex appears to have taken place, both vaginally and anally. So far the DNA samples from her body don't match anyone on the database. So we are not looking at a previous sex offender, but the good thing is we will be able to make a match when we do catch matey boy or whoever it is, they are a nasty piece of work considering the pathologists interim report."

"Right then, in the meantime, house-to-house in Windsor Avenue area... anything to report?"

All nodded in agreement indicating that they had eventually been able to speak to all the occupants of the neighbourhood houses but apart from the interview with the now infamous family of 'snoopers', who had been dealt with by Professional Standards, it appeared that they had all drawn a blank. Unexpectedly PC Wendy Morgan spoke up, as she had been one of the initial officers who discovered the body and consequently had volunteered to join the murder team for the duration of the investigation.

"One point of note sir, I've had two reported sightings of a red Ford Escort having been seen parked in the drive. Witnesses say there was something different about it, not a modern model, sort of sporty. Unfortunately, no registration number though, nor was it seen on the relevant dates."

"Well done Morgan, as that's all we've got for the time being. A sporty Ford Escort, you say, mmm...unusual. Sounds to me like that could be a bit of a collector or enthusiast's car. Right get onto the DVLA and see who owns one in the area."

"Right sir," replied Wendy Morgan, feeling proud in the fact that she might just have the breakthrough they needed.

"Okay, let's spread the net wider, I know we've covered all the immediate neighbours but let's spread out, target the next area and in particular let's look for this Ford Escort.....others must have seen it in the area."

Harry, as he spoke, walked over to one of the large survey maps covering Windsor Avenue hung on the wall. It'd been enlarged to include an area within 2 miles radius of Ann Clark's house; large circles had been drawn over the map indicating distances from the property. Harry motioned his left hand over the designated areas.

"Yes, yes, I know it's a pain, but this crime is going to be solved by good old-fashioned door step coppering. Somebody out there knows something; they don't know that they know it, so we need to find and enlighten them. For all we know, Wendy Morgan has discovered the key already, but let's keep looking."

With a scraping of chairs and a shuffling of feet, the room suddenly emptied apart from one or two that included PC Wendy Morgan making a follow-up telephone call.

Harry Joseph and Peter Marsh went back into their office, to one side of the conference room, and were discussing the mysterious envelopes and money paid into Ann Clark's bank account when Wendy Morgan knocked and popped her head around the door.

"Got a name for the red Ford Escort sir," she said with a tinge of excitement in her voice.

"Yes, it's a Ford Escort RS2000."

"Excellent, good work, that is an unusual type, go on," replied Harry rather unusually impatient.

"Well, it's not local sir, and the nearest car of that type and description is registered to a Roger Holt who lives in Fakenham, Norfolk."

"Right Wendy, excellent, not a million miles away so get the address and give Norfolk Constabulary the heads up and get yourself over there and team up with a local copper to go and see him."

"Will do sir," she replied, closing the door.

"Well, Peter, let's go down to Beaumont's and do a bit of digging, see what we can uncover and where it leads, if anywhere. This possible blackmail angle is intriguing, what say you?"

"Well, by the sound of her peculiar sex life, maybe she was blackmailing a married work colleague, as most affairs are conducted with work colleagues or family friends. Could it be some senior 'bod' at Beaumont's?" queried Peter.

"Yep! Suggest we visit their personnel department, trawl through their employment records, and interview anyone she worked with." Peter nodded in agreement.

On arrival at Beaumont's shipping office, Harry and Peter were ushered in to meet the Personnel Manager, Roy Brooks, on explaining the reason for their visit. Roy gave the appearance of being very relaxed as he reclined back into his large, leather chair.

"Naturally, Inspector, my office and staff are at your disposal, we're only too pleased to help you. We are all terribly shocked and disturbed by this horrific murder," offered Roy Brooks rather sombrely, although he didn't look it thought Harry. "She was a lovely lady from what little I knew of her, quite a private individual I believe?"

"Which department did she work in?" enquired Peter.

"Technical branch, her job was working for our engineering superintendent, collating repairs needed onboard the ships for their annual refit specifications."

"Mmm..." mused Harry coming to the same conclusion as Peter who asked, "So, she would have had contact with the ship's crews as well as those with whom she worked ashore?"

"Yes, very much so," replied Roy.

"Well, sir, in that case, we'll need to access the personnel files of both your office employees and those of the ship's crews," requested Harry.

Roy Brooks stood up from behind his desk, his large chair suddenly springing upright with a loud twang and then walked through to the outer office, "Follow me gentleman and my personal assistant Penny Smart will help you."

"Well, if you don't mind, sir, I'd like to ask you a few more questions while I hand over to my colleague, Detective Sgt Marsh, to speak to your PA."

"Why yes, of course, Inspector," replied the ever-helpful Roy Brooks.

While Harry remained seated, Roy took Peter through to his outer office and introduced him to his personal assistant, Penny Smart.

Upon returning to his office, Roy once again almost fell back into his luxurious office chair. Harry then briefly explained the lines of their enquiry and the possibility that Ann Clark was blackmailing someone. He went on to ask for any information that might shed some light on her private life, particularly any little snippet of scandal which could be of interest.

Meanwhile, Peter worked his charm with Penny, being conscientiously flirtatious. The astute Penny knew exactly what Peter Marsh's line of enquiry was with her and politely showed him her wedding finger displaying a large and ornate band of gold. During their conversation she emphasised her marital status by asking Peter if he knew her husband who was also on the local force. Peter took the hint and returned to the task in hand of looking at ship's crewing records.

Later, after the two police officers had left Beaumont's and whilst driving back to the police station, Harry discussed the conversation he'd had with Roy Brooks remarking rather disappointingly that by all accounts, Ann Clark appeared to be a very virtuous private person.

"I was hoping for a breakthrough with some office gossip, but it would appear from what that shifty Roy Brooks is telling me that the sexual predilections of Ann Clark were well and truly hidden." Little did Harry know that he had inadvertently referred to Roy Brooks as his office 'nickname'!

Peter, listening to Harry, couldn't contain his excitement; he desperately wanted to disclose his discovery to his boss.

"Well guess what I've discovered?" he said, grinning broadly, momentarily taking his eyes off the road and turning to Harry, who was sitting in the front passenger seat.

"Come on then Marsh, don't fuck about I'm not in the mood, what have you got?" snapped Harry feeling somewhat frustrated after his slightly negative interview with Roy Brooks.

"Ok, Guv, I'm coming to it," replied Peter wanting to revel in the limelight of his discovery, "remember what Morgan came up with this morning, the Red Ford Escort owned by a Roger Holt?"

"Yep, get on with it, don't tell me he works for Beaumont's!" jumped in the very perceptive Harry.

"He certainly does Guv; he's a purser on the sea staff and lives in Fakenham!" Offered Peter excitedly.

"Woooow," whistled Harry, "and undoubtedly he would have come into contact with Ann Clark?" said Harry answering his own question.

"Looks like it," agreed Peter.

They both smiled to themselves, realising that their day had just got better and that they now had a very firm line of enquiry.

"Right, we have a person of interest, so now we need a motive, which is staring us in the face, an extramarital affaire. Putting two and two together, does the four equate to a sadomasochistic relationship with this married man, senior officer with the Beaumont fleet who Ann used for financial gain? If so, I can hear the key turning in the cell door when we lock him up," smirked Harry, digging his left hand deep into his trouser pocket as he scratched his anatomy and squeezed the cheeks of his buttocks together in an attempt not to break wind with excitement. He failed, filling the car with a pungent sewer like smell.

Chapter 59

The snow had fallen silently throughout the night, creating a shimmering bleach white blanket over the north of England, sparkling in the moonlit night as if reflecting the stars in the heavens above. The cover stretched from the Scottish borders to southern Lincolnshire. Alexandra had woken to the beautiful sight of the rolling Lincolnshire Wolds coated in the fresh, pristine snow. The view reminded her of glistening icing sugar covering a Christmas cake with the trees on the distant skyline resembling miniature cake decorations.

Having risen, showered, and enjoyed a light breakfast, Alexandra wrapped herself in her warm, blue, woollen Burberry coat with its wide collar pulled up around her neck, then tucked her soft, flowing locks into a large, woollen bobble hat. She opened the front door and stepped into the cold, frosty air. The chill caused her skin to tingle, and her warm breath, catching the cold atmosphere, created a small fog as it condensed. She had no reason to be outside; she just wanted to admire and appreciate her surroundings. The view was beautiful. She tread through the soft snow, childishly delighting herself as she gently kicked up the white dust, some of which gently blew back on to her face in the light morning breeze. She so wished Guy was there for a snowball fight. Well, on second thoughts, maybe not in her condition with the baby due any day.

Alexandra's parents were on their way to stay for a few days, and Guy was due home just before midday. She so looked forward to seeing her parents; she hoped they would arrive in plenty of time so that they could all walk down to the pub for lunch. She knew Guy would like that, to have a pint of the locally brewed ale in front of the blazing log fire in the snug lounge. Guy never drank while on-board the ship, he always looked forward to enjoying a pint away from the stress of work. Alexandra smiled to herself at the thought of a cosy lunch with the people she loved.

She reached the front garden gate. The gate opened out on to a single track lane which eventually led to the village. The lane beyond the gate was more of a driveway than an actual lane. Occasionally, it was used by a few locals and the odd walkers in the summer, but otherwise it didn't carry anything resembling heavy traffic. The lane eventually led to a farm, the original landowners from whom Guy had bought the barn, prior to conversion. Surplus to the farm's requirements, the barn had been made redundant by modern farming methods, and the farmer had sought to capitalise on the popularity of such structures, selling it as 'ripe for conversion,' as Estate agents describe them.

A tractor had already been through the thick snow, leaving two large ruts that had begun to fill again with the steady falling snow.

At the gate, Alexandra turned around to look back at the barn, the home she shared with Guy. Despite only having lived with him for several months, she experienced an incredible feeling of belonging. Until meeting Guy, she'd never even visited Lincolnshire, believing it to be a rural backwater full of farms. As she looked at the barn, she had a strange feeling that she'd been here before, and experiencing a warm, comforting glow through her body, she instinctively knew it was her spiritual home.

The vast front garden, a gravelled area that swept in front of the barn, was mostly covered in cream shingle but smartly broken up by a central flower bed, a circular focal point amongst the stones. In the centre of the flower bed sat an old ship's anchor, which rested on a thick tree stump. The stump was engraved with the name of the barn, 'Ariadne', named after a ship Guy had once served upon during his time with the Royal Navy. The shingled expanse stretched from one side of the barn to the other. The right-hand side lead to a large garage and workshop, formerly a calving shed which Guy had carefully converted to be in keeping with the house. The left-hand side of the shingle lead out to a track bordered by double wooden gates to allow vehicular access. To the rear of the house was a vast lawn with spectacular views.

Alexandra took in the fantastic, picturesque scene. The barn and its surroundings were covered entirely in snow. The Lincolnshire Wolds sat high in the background, stretching away into infinity. Since stepping outside, the snow had slowly stopped, but Alexandra could see the dark lumbering clouds in the distance, predicting more snow was yet to come. The scene resembled a classic Christmas card, the only thing missing was smoke rising from the chimney stack that was the crowning glory to a vast open fireplace in the lounge. It had been Guy's creation, and he'd had often joked that he had delusions of grandeur, pretending to be Lord of the Manor when standing in front of the enormous fireplace. He had used old railway sleepers to support the rustic chimney stack, blending in perfectly with the stone walls of the original barn. The wooded sleeper adorned with traditional, ornamental horseshoes and photographs. The huge fireplace offered a double advantage by allowing log fires in the winter to supplement the central heating, yet come summer, it naturally drew up vast volumes of air from the lounge, which created an environmentally friendly air conditioning system.

Alexandra was suddenly struck with an idea; she would send out personalised Christmas cards which captured the barn in the beauty of the snow. 'Our first Christmas card sent as a family together with our new baby,' she thought as she smiled and gently touched her expanding tummy. The thought of the baby briefly brought tears to her eyes as she remembered Steve Gaunt. She looked skywards into the thick, woolly white clouds and wondered if Steve could see her, see how happy she was. Her strength of belief in God convinced her that there was an afterlife. Although her belief was very much put to the test when Steve died questioning as to how God could take him away from her, it was reignited when she met Guy. She truly believed that Steve was there, looking down on her. She whispered, "Although I've found new happiness, I'll never forget you, my Steve, never."

Alexandra strode back to the house to prepare a fire in the lounge and fulfil her idea of photographing the barn from the front garden. She had several hours before her parents would arrive and wanted to keep busy while she could, before her mother started fussing and insisting she rest.

Once inside, she removed her jacket and went through to the large lounge. She rolled up old newspapers and placed them in the large ironware fire grate. She lay kindling on top followed by some dried out logs and softly hummed Bing Crosby's famous seasonal song, 'I'm dreaming of a white Christmas'. The lighted paper soon caught the kindling, which was quickly consumed by the voracious flames from the logs. Alexandra went through to the kitchen and made herself a warm cup of chocolate. She took it back to the lounge and eased herself on to the sofa to watch the fire. She held the hot cup and gently blew across the chocolate surface, then mesmerised by the emerging flickering flames as they grew stronger, burning the dry logs ferociously. Again, her thoughts turned back to Steve Gaunt as she gently rubbed her pregnant tummy. Momentarily, she saw his face emerge amongst the flames, with his famous charming smile he used to call his 'slow burn', how appropriate to see it in the fire. His face melted into the flames, producing grotesque, wild images that seemed to eerily shout at her before silently disappearing all together. She shivered, despite the heat emanating from the fire and instinctively looked around the room, her heart momentarily racing having felt as though someone else was in the room and had just walked behind her.

Briefly gripped by a fear that maybe the place was haunted, then shaking her head as if to rid her mind of such ideas, her thoughts returned to the Christmas card, she placed the hot chocolate on the side, carefully pushed herself to her feet and went to find Guy's camera.

Guy's study, 'My Den', as he liked to call it, in many ways resembled a ship's cabin. Whether that had come about by luck or design, Alexandra wasn't sure. To her, the room always had a distinct smell of wood and tar. She guessed the aroma came from the enormous old fashioned wood and brass ship's binnacle Guy had rescued from a gardening reclamation yard where the proprietors had no idea what a gem they had. Unfortunately, they had left it to stand out in all weathers, which caused it to deteriorate slowly. The wooden body and brass top cover had become water stained and discoloured over a period of time. Guy, however, had spent hours lovingly restoring it to its former glory, and now it sat proudly near the big window which overlooked the rear garden and onwards to the Wolds.

The rest of the room was typical of a study; the walls were adorned with pictures and paintings charting Guy's career in both the Royal and Merchant navies. There were the ships he had sailed on, framed company cap badges from the Merchant Navy, ship cap tallies from those in the Royal Navy, and his naval sword hung impressively in one corner. She sat herself down in Guy's leather-bound Captain's swivel chair, in front of a large, old oak desk. The desk had come from the library of a passenger ship he had served on while on its final voyage home from Australia. On arrival back in the UK, the ship owning company had allowed the crew to buy parts of the fixtures and fittings that would otherwise end up destroyed as the breakers yard was only interested in the scrap metal value of the ship.

Alexandra sat in the swivel chair and slowly span around to scan the room for Guy's camera. She spotted it sitting on top of a large wooden chest of drawers that had once belonged to Guy's grandfather, a Master Mariner. Filled with excitement, like a child finding a favourite box of sweets in a candy store, she picked up the camera and headed downstairs. Her brain was racing ahead of her, excited to get the perfect picture, but her legs were slow, and her back reminded her she was nine months pregnant.

Opening the front door, her excitement increased as she discovered it had started to snow again.

"Oooooh, perfect," she called out with delight.

Later, she would chastise herself for being so reckless in her infantile glee to take the photograph of the scene she so wanted to capture.

A blanket of snow, such as the amount that had fallen over the last several hours, can change the whole landscape, hiding ornaments, steps, and pathways. Many obstacles blend into a mass of white wilderness, normally things of beauty and interest but hidden under the snow can become dangerous traps to the unwary. If only Alexandra had traced her previous footsteps, firm indentations in the snow, still just visible with the fresh, new falling snow. Unfortunately, Alexandra was too busy looking at the camera, setting it up ready to take the perfect picture. Her lack of concentration meant she unintentionally walked too close to the front garden flower bed. The large anchor was covered by the snow, creating the shape of a leaning figure frozen in time. Alexandra, fleetingly thought it looked like a drunken sailor, why she should think that she'd never know. The snow had covered the length of the black coated iron anchor cable that lay decoratively around the flower bed. An artistic and creative piece in the spring and summer, but with the covering of snow it had turned into a deadly human trap. It was this trap into which Alexander ventured in her bid to get the picture she so desperately wanted. Her left foot, had she placed it a mere two inches to the right, would have entirely missed the hidden cable. Unfortunately, it hit the anchor chain square on. As Alexandra fell, time slowed, the camera sailed through the air as she released her grip on the strap in an attempt to bring her arms forward to protect her fall. Initially, her thoughts were with the camera, hoping it wouldn't damage when it hit the ground.

The soft blanket of snow would hopefully lessen the impact. In a millisecond, her terrified brain screamed as she catapulted forward, frantically attempting to break the fall and avoid the innocent tiny life inside her taking any impact of her landing. Despite the cushioning effect of the eiderdown of snow, Alexandra shrieked as a shaft of pain shot through her body like a knife. Her face was buried in the snow as she realised her arms were now flung out above her head as though she was diving in to a pool. Carefully, she slowly raised her head, spluttering to get the snow out of her mouth and nostrils. Momentarily disorientated, then reality kicking in as her gradual movement caused yet more pain to go coursing through her lower body, "Oh my baby," she cried as the tears started, "What have I done to my baby?"

She remembered what her mother, a retired Nursing Sister on an A&E ward had always taught her after a fall; don't be in a panic to pick yourself up, no matter how embarrassing the situation. Take stock of possible damage; sudden movement can cause more harm than initially just laying still and accepting any pain while accessing what has happened and what help is at hand before rushing into any attempt at getting yourself up. Somewhere in the distance, through the fog of pain, she heard a strange chugging sound. She moved gently on to her side, which caused her further pain. The chugging sound became louder, and she realised it was a tractor driving along the lane. She eased herself over and attempted to get up, wondering if help was at hand or had it passed without seeing her laying there. Just then, she heard the gate make a small squeak as it opened and the sound of footsteps as they crunched in the carpet of thick snow.

"Just wait there missy, take it easy, I'm coming." It was the steady, rustic country drawl of their farming neighbour, Frank Poulson, the man from whom Guy had purchased the barn.

He had seen Alexandra fall as he chugged past the front gate on his old, open, grey and rusting Massey Fergusson tractor. Alexandra was beginning to feel the cold seep in through her clothing, the warmth of her body melting some of the snow. Frank carefully knelt down beside her and enveloped her in a cloud of smoke from the briar pipe clamped firmly between his teeth. His exertions caused an increase in the smoke as he sucked and exhaled through the pipe making the tobacco in the bowl glow bright red. He gently placed one arm behind Alexandra.

"Oh, please do be careful," she winced as a shock wave of pain swept through her body.

"Oooo aaarh," he said, sounding like he'd just walked off the set of the radio series "The Archers'. Frank was a big man, and although well into his 70's, he was still sturdy and strong. Wrapped in a well-worn, wax jacket, a thick, green woollen scarf around his neck, old soldiers, lined camouflaged trousers, wellington boots, all topped off with a flat cap he appeared every bit the stereotypical farmer. Despite Alexandra's plea, Frank gently scooped her up. He did it with such ease, showing the same gentleness he would give to a newborn lamb. He carried her through the front door and into the lounge. Frank knew his way around their home, having watched it being built and being entrusted with overseeing some of the work for Guy while he was away at sea. He carefully laid Alexandra down on the sofa in front of the blazing fire.

"Noo jacket, noo scarf, what was tha doin' out in that cold?"

Despite the predicament of her situation, she couldn't help but smile inwardly at old Frank Poulson, briefly wondering what her posh English lecturer at finishing school would have made of it.

"I was just trying to take – "

Frank interrupted her, "Now ma luvvie, you joost stay tha while I goin and git me old lady, she'll knows whats to do, she's seen many a sow pod her young uns, there's nowt much difference to us tha knows."

If it weren't for the intermittent pain, Alexandra would have screamed at Frank for comparing her and her unborn child to pigs, but she really didn't feel like arguing. She knew Frank meant well, and she was just relieved that someone was there to help.

"Thank you, Frank," she said as he wandered off into the kitchen.

Outside, the snow was falling thick and fast. Alexandra was beginning to feel anxious, she knew she shouldn't for the baby's sake, but she couldn't help herself. She started the deep breathing she'd been taught at pre-natal classes in an attempt to slow her heartbeat down and get back in control. She instinctively knew it wouldn't be long before the baby came. She wished Guy was with her. Perhaps the snow had delayed him; he should have been home by now. She felt alone, admitting to herself that she was frightened, despite the help coming from Mrs. Poulson. Funny she'd never got to know her first name, she knew Frank Poulson, he was often popping in to see Guy and to see what else he had done to develop the barn. Alexandra wasn't usually afraid; after all, she'd worked in some of the poorest parts of West Africa and witnessed the worst of poverty without proper medical facilities. But now it was her body and her baby and she knew she needed to be in a hospital. Another spasm of pain passed through her body, as if reading and confirming her thoughts about hospitalisation. Her mother and father were supposedly on their way. Initially, they were due to arrive yesterday, but there had been a problem with their old car. Her father was a complete petrolhead, rebuilding old cars had been his hobby since retirement. He could easily afford a brand new one, but he much preferred his classic Ford Zephyr. He'd been an ardent fan of a TV police series called 'Z Cars' and always promised himself one as a retirement present. Alexandra sighed and thought to herself 'if her father had bought a new one, they would be here with her'.

Her thoughts turned to Guy; she needed to let him know what was happening. She didn't want to move too much and fortunately Frank Poulson had put her on the sofa near both the telephone and her book of phone numbers. She reached for the telephone and dialled Guy's mobile number. Guy had recently bought himself a new large brick-like mobile telephone for emergencies. Although considered an extravagance by many, Guy wanted Alexandra to be able to contact him, even when he was at sea. He promised her it would always be switched on, but all she was getting was his voicemail. Scrolling through her list of contacts, she found the number for Beaumont's office in Northwold and dialled the number. It was a direct line to the crewing department, the line was quickly answered by a young lady Alexandra vaguely knew called Alice, a crewing manager assistant.

"Hello-" but before Alice could give her well versed, standard company indoctrinated welcoming words with the usual, 'How may I help you', Alexandra burst straight in...

"Hello, look, it's Alexandra Hollins here, Guy, my husband, works for you." Alexandra realised she was becoming flustered and sounded slightly foolish in her panic.

"Oh, hello Mrs. Hollins, Alexandra I mean, we've met, I was at your wedding, although you perhaps can't remember me, I had my hair in pig-tails."

"What?" snapped Alexandra, frustrated with Alice's cheery voice. The mention of 'pigtails' reminded her that Mrs. Poulson was on her way and as lovely a person as she might be, she was the last person in the world she wanted as a midwife.

Gaining control of her emotions, Alexandra continued firmly, "Alice, I want to try and contact my husband. He's aboard the *'Beamish'*, and it should have docked by now. I've been trying his mobile but just get his voicemail, can you help me to contact him urgently please?"

"Oh, yes, errrm..." now it was Alice's turn to become flustered when Alexandra had referred to the *s.s.'Beamish.'* "Well, oh, there's nothing to worry about, the ship's going to be a little late docking, I'm sure he'll be in contact soon, I'm sure it won't be long before he's with you."

Picking up on Alice's comment, 'there's nothing to worry about' what did she mean? "Alice! I haven't got long, I have had a fall and I'm worried about my baby, I need Guy to be with me, I want him to be here." Alexandra knew she sounded angry; she didn't mean to, especially not with the young lady on the other end of the line; it wasn't her fault. Realising she wasn't going to get anywhere, she cut the connection, just as Mr. and Mrs. Poulson walked into the lounge. The office staff at Beaumont's were under strict instructions from the new 'High Flier' PR lady Janet Houchell, appointed by the new owners in London, that they were not to give away any information on the collision that had just occurred between the *s.s 'Beamish'* and another vessel as they had approached Northwold dockyard. Alice was now fretting having been so abruptly cut off by Alexandra. She considered the situation with Alexandra to be way above her pay grade and so-referred it to her superior, Penny Smart.

"Now then, missy, me missus is 'ere," announced Frank, affably, as though the arrival of his wife would solve everything. His large briar pipe still firmly clamped into his mouth emanating great clouds of sweet-smelling smoke, momentarily reminding Alexandra of her own grandfather's pipe smoking. Nearly breaking out into a hysterical giggle thinking to herself, 'here I am about to have a baby, and all I can think about is my long-dead grandfather!'

"Well luvvie, has thoust' wotters brokun yet?" Mrs. Poulson asked as she started to fuss around her with cushions taken from other chairs. Her country dialect was as broad as her husband's.

"What? No! Mrs. Poulson, I'm not having my baby here, I just need to get to the hospital so the doctors can check everything is okay, I'm not due for a few more days."

"Don't worry luvvie, we've plenty o' time to get you ta 'ospital."

Mrs. Poulson's calm manner helped Alexandra feel a little at ease and she leaned back into the softness of the cushions, glad that help was at hand.

The telephone rang. Alexandra grabbed it, "Guy?"

"Alexandra?" said a well-spoken, female voice, "It's Penny, Penny Smart from the personnel office, I work for Roy Brooks, and I'm Alice's supervisor."

"Oh, Penny, I'm sorry, I'm waiting for Guy to ring and I- "

"I understand," she replied, "Alice has just informed me of your predicament, have you phoned for an ambulance?"

"No, my neighbours are with me, and I just wanted Guy here so he could take me."

Penny Smart was known as 'Action Girl' by her work colleagues, never one to shirk responsibility, always quick to take charge.

"I'm afraid I don't think Guy will be able to make it in time, it sounds like you need an ambulance pronto, you don't want the little one making an early appearance at your home do you. Leave it to me, don't you worry Alexandra, I'm dialling three nines on the other line, stay by the phone and I'll call you back when I have spoken to the ambulance service."

"Oh, ok," replied Alexandra meekly, again relieved that someone else was easing the burden of worry for her. She wanted answers though to questions as to why Guy was delayed, but Penny had cut the call before

Alexandra could ask where he was. She held on to the telephone as if it was a lifeline.

All her life, since leaving college and working for the Foreign Office in Africa, she'd been so used to being in charge, organising, taking responsibility, in control; now, for the first time in her life, events were spiralling out of control with other people taking that control away from her. She was not sure she liked this state of affairs but had to admit to herself that in her current condition, she was vulnerable and needed others to be in the driving seat.

Mrs. Poulson leaned over Alexandra, reaching for the phone, "Come on luvvie let me phone the ambulance for you."

"No, it's ok, that was Penny from the shipping company office, she's calling them for me," replied Alexandra as she tightened her grip on the telephone, reluctant to let it go.

"Ok, luvvie, well, let's keep you nice and wamm while we wait for yon ambulance, Frank go put kettle on luv and I'll tend fire." She said, getting a couple of large logs from the huge wicker basket sitting beside the fireplace.

Frank had been hovering about in the background, not sure what to do and waiting for instructions from his Missus as she was now firmly in charge.

"Aye, luv awright," said Frank as he turned and left the lounge, belching clouds of thick blue smoke behind him, like smoke from a steam train.

Mrs. Poulson busied herself with the fire while Frank filled the kettle. He was of the old school; in his mind, men had no place around women when they were about to give birth. When his two children were born, he was working. He only knew of their arrival when a neighbour had come rushing across the fields with the news. Then, for Frank, it was tradition to head straight down to the pub to wet the baby's head.

The phone burst into life again, ringing in Alexandra's hand. It was the 999 operator.

"Hello. Mrs. Alexandra Hollins?"

"Yes?" Alexandra winced, screwing up her face as another stab of pain passed through her body.

"Mrs Hollins, my name is Eric, from the Lincolnshire ambulance control room, we've just had a call from a Mrs Penny Smart requesting an ambulance to collect you at The Tithe Barn, Honeypot Lane, Goxhill, near Kirmington, because you've had a fall and you're nine months pregnant, is that correct?"

"Yes, that's right. I'm not due for a few more days, though."

"Ok, Mrs. Hollins, we'll get there as soon as we can, but because of the snow, it has slowed down response times considerably, but rest assured, we are treating your call as a code red priority."

"Oh, thank you, please get here soon."

"We are on it Mrs.Hollins, have your waters broken yet?"

"No, not yet."

"Ok, that's a good sign... hang in there Mrs. Hollins, we will be with you shortly," replied the operator as he closed the call.

Just then, another sharp pain went through Alexandra's body. She suddenly felt a stickiness, reaching down between her thighs, she discovered her trousers were damp and her retracted hand coated in blood.

"Oh nooo," she cried out in concern at what this could signify.

"Mrs Poulson, help!"

Mrs Poulson leapt up, "Tha, tha, keep calm ma luv, let me 'ave a look at yas."

Huge tears rolled down Alexandra's cheeks as she stared at her bloody hand. Her mind went into overdrive, conjuring up the harm she imagined she had inflicted on her baby from the fall in the snow, "Ohhh, Mrs. Poulson, what have I done?"

"Now, now, dearie, let me look," Mrs. Poulson gently eased down Alexandra's clothes and shouted to Frank to find some towels and hot water.

"Aye awright ma," came the distant reply.

Soon Frank was back in the lounge with a large bowl of hot water and some towels.

"Aye, lucky kettle 'ad jus boiled luv," he announced, putting everything down beside the two ladies. Then, taking a chivalrous withdrawal thinking the baby was about to pop, he said, "If tha wants owt uv' just call."

Alexandra laid back with her eyes squeezed shut. Her left hand clasped tight around the telephone handset, the other balled into a fist at the agony of wondering what was wrong. Tears poured down her cheeks from beneath her beautiful long eyelashes. Silently cursing her stupidity at her situation while she allowed Mrs. Poulson to gently remove her panties.

Quickly, wringing out the clean sponge that Frank had brought, Mrs Poulson busied herself wiping away the blood around Alexandra's thighs, "Now dearie, look at you, what 'ave you dun to yaself, yaves a nasty deep cut there inside your thigh, better get that cleaned and bandaged looks like ya could do with some stitches."

"My thigh?" said Alexandra, relieved, "Not my baby?"

"Don't look like it to me dearie, yave just got a very nasty gash, now let us get you cleaned up."

Alexandra felt a rush of relief, "Thank you Mrs. Poulson," she smiled as tears of relief welled up as she privately thanked God.

"Reet, 'ave ya got a first aid kit luvvie?" she said as she busied herself with the towels and cleaning the wound.

"Yes, it is the kitchen cupboard, in the corner, there is a large green cross painted on the door, you can't miss it."

"Awright my love, you just stay calm while I go and fetch it, then we'll have you as right as rain in a jiffy."

Alexander's emotions were mixed; she felt helpless but thankful that a lady she hardly knew was treating her with the same attention she would show to one of her pigs in a litter. On the one hand, she just wanted Mrs. Poulson to leave her alone and give her some privacy, yet on the other hand, she was relieved that someone calm and motherly was with her. Not that this made her situation any more tenable, but it certainly gave her some peace of mind. She just wished Guy was with her.

The telephone sprang in to life again.

"Hello? Guy?"

"Mrs. Hollins?" asked a familiar male voice at the other end of the line.

"Yes."

"Hello again, this is Eric at the ambulance control room, we are on our way to you Mrs. Hollins, but the snow is making it very difficult and slow. The paramedic in the ambulance is asking if there is anyone you can ask to give you a lift to meet the ambulance and speed things up a little?"

"What? No! I need them to come here. Now," cried Alexandra.

"They are trying their best Mrs. Hollins."

"Hang on, I will speak to my neighbours, they might be able to help."

"Ok, we're quite busy here in the control room, as you can imagine in this weather. I'll call you back shortly to see if you can arrange anything. Try not to worry Mrs. Hollins, we are doing our best."

The line went dead before Alexandra could reply.

Mrs. Poulson came back into the room with the first aid box, "There, there, now we'll soon 'ave this sorted."

"Thank you, Mrs. Poulson, that was the ambulance people on the phone," Alexandra watched as Mrs. Poulson carefully cleaned the wound, the antiseptic wipe made Alexandra wince. She couldn't see what Mrs. Poulson was doing beneath her large swollen abdomen, but soon she had patched up the nasty gash and was pulling up Alexandra's panties and slacks for the sake of modesty and to make her more comfortable for when Frank Poulson would inevitably wander back into the room.

"Please, call us Ada. After all, we've getting ta know each together quite well now, I'd say on intimate terms," she said with a little giggle and a beaming smile demonstrating that she was sharing some of Alexandra's relief that the bleeding had only come from a wound.

"Now then 'ow about a nice cuppa char, my Frank's got kettle on?"

"I'd prefer a glass of wine," she joked with a giggle of relief.

"Oooo, I shud say so luvvie, I'd be tempted to join you, what a reet pair we'd make though when yon ambulance arrived if we was both tiddly?" she laughed in a child-like giggle.

"If they ever get here,' she sighed, "Mrs... I mean Ada, the ambulance is asking if someone could take me to meet them. They are struggling with the snow, what am I going to do?"

Ada looked thoughtful for a second before shouting her husband, "Frank!"

Frank popped his head into the lounge, still puffing away on his old briar pipe trailing clouds of blue tobacco smoke behind him, "Wud thas lake sum tea?"

"Not that Frank, the lass needs a lift."

"Oooo arh luvvie, I'm afraid me Land-Rover's broken don and I'm waiting for village gareege to get up 'er to fix it, so all I've got is tha tractor and trailer or tha pig trailer."

"Oh Crickey," said Alexandra as the tears started again. Horrified at the thought of being either laid out on that flat trailer or in a pig carrier, all she could think of was baby Jesus being born in a manger. But her baby being delivered on top of an open trailer in a snow storm was just too horrifying to contemplate.

Frank and Ada both looked down at Alexandra with sympathy, not sure what else to suggest. The telephone rang again, interrupting the silence.

"Hello," said Alexandra, hoping it was the ambulance service with some good news. Unfortunately, it wasn't.

"Alexandra, its Penny again from the office, just wondering how you are coping and if the ambulance is there yet?" she enquired anxiously. Penny knew about the collision of the two vessels out in the harbour, knowing too well that Guy wouldn't be able to be there for some time, not wanting to pass this worrying information on to Alexandra.

"They're on the way, but because of the snow they can't get to the house, oh Penny, I don't know what to do. I know it's not their fault, just this beastly weather is slowing everything down. Is there any news about Guy, where is he?" She couldn't stop the tears from falling. She tried to calm herself down, telling herself to stop being a wuss. Knowing what other women had experienced and the things she had witnessed in the African bush where babies are born in the most awful of circumstances. Her mind briefly wandered back to how she met Steve Gaunt when one of the young girls in the British compound had been having pregnancy problems. Funny how her mind went back to that. Penny's voice cut through her thoughts.

"Alexandra, I'll phone my husband, Mike. You remember him? He's a policeman."

Alexandra had no idea who she was talking about, but the idea of someone coming to her rescue helped calm her a little, "But what can he do?"

"Well, he's out at the moment, maybe tied up himself, but I'll call him and see if he can help, his police vehicle is 4 x 4, "all hands to the pumps' at times like this," she quipped cheerily. Penny Smart was just the type of lady to have around in an emergency and little surprise she had chosen to marry a policeman, it was bound to have been that or a military man! Alexandra could feel the warmth and confidence coming across from Penny, momentarily making her feel comfortable, despite the absence of Guy, all these different people whom she hardly knew were coming to her rescue, she felt a little relieved.

"Let me call him, and I will call you straight back."

Before Alexandra could reply, Penny had gone.

Ada and Frank Poulson were still standing over her, looking anxious, embarrassed that the only transport they could offer was either a flat-bed trailer or a pig trailer towed by a 1950's old tractor. Frank was first to speak.

"Me and Ada, 'ave just bin saying we'll get you on the flat trailer then along with tha Mrs for company like, all wrapped well like, we can then start off to meet yon ambulance. Ya won't be long and it'll git ya to 'ospital, what tha says?"

Ada nodding her head in agreement, "Yes, luvvie let's get ye to meet the ambulance, I'll be with ye, so no need to fret lass, it 'ill be fine luvvie, we need to get you to 'ospital."

Alexandra was gobsmacked, no way was she going on the back of a trailer. She had visions of being covered in snow; she wouldn't be pressurised to the idea. 'Good God!' she thought to herself, thinking she'd rather give birth right here in front of the warmth of this roaring fire. "No, I, please, I can't just ... "

She was gratefully interrupted by the telephone, ringing, "Hello?"

"Alexandra, it's Mike, Penny's husband. She's told me briefly what the problem is. Look, I'm literally just around the corner from you, my vehicle is a 4x4, and so far she's making light work of the snow so I can be with you in five minutes and either get you to hospital, or we can meet the ambulance."

"Oh, thank you, thank you so much. I cannot tell you how relieved I am."

"No problem, I'm on my way... Just one thing, though, you're not allergic to dogs, are you?"

"No?" Alexandra was taken aback by the question.

"Well, I'm a dog handler, and I've got my German Shepherd Ramsey, with me in the car."

"Oh dear," Alexandra couldn't believe what she was hearing, just when things appeared to be getting better, she's gone from laying on a flatbed trailer, open to the elements, to sharing the back of a van with a police dog, "I don't think I can lie in the back of a van with Ramsey."

"Gosh, no! No, of course not, he's safely locked away in the rear compartment, you'll be able to lay out on the back seat," replied Mike, slightly amused she would think that. "Sit tight Mrs. Hollins, I will be with you shortly."

"Thank you," Alexandra cut the call and smiled at Mr. and Mrs. Poulson, "Help is finally on its way."

Mrs. Poulson helped Alexandra get ready and wrapped her up in her warm coat. It wasn't long before they heard a car horn as Mike drove his police Range Rover into the front drive of Tithe Barn, the light bar across the roof flashed intermittent red and blue lights, a beacon of hope.

Soon, Alexandra was relieved to be on her way to the hospital, sitting rather than laying in the back of the police car or on a flatbed trailer. Mike, who had previously cleared everything with his control room Inspector, called in requesting cancellation of the ambulance as the powerful four-wheel drive police car made steady progress through the snow-covered roads. Alexandra's stabbing pains had intensified, making her extraordinarily anxious but glad when they safely arrived at the hospital. Taking the short walk from the police car to the A&E unit, Alexandra was rushed to the delivery suite by several medical staff.

"Looks like you made it just in time Mrs. Hollins," smiled the midwife.

"In time? But I'm not due yet, I fell, and I wanted to..." she felt the sudden wetness and knew her waters had broken.

"Yes, the baby's coming, let's get you ready."

Everything happened so quickly. The spasms of pain, she now realised were contractions, growing closer. The midwife, wearing the uniform of an RAF nurse on secondment to the NHS, was smiling down at Alexandra and giving her encouragement as she went through the painful contractions. It was during one particular contraction that she called out Guy's name, wondering where on earth he was, before another painful contraction interrupted her thoughts and momentarily, she called out Steve Gaunt's name. The midwife and the other nurses in the delivery room all looked at each other with a shrug. Goodness knows what was going through their minds when the pregnant woman before them was calling out the names of two different men.

Alexandra, only had to work hard for another hour until she was able to sit up and gaze down at her beautiful baby girl. Laid in her arms, the baby looked so peaceful as she slept, wrapped in a white, knitted blanket. Alexandra's fingers tenderly stroked the cheek of her newborn as she smiled down at her with overwhelming feelings of relief, wonderment, and joy.

"Now then, where is your naughty daddy? He should've been here by now," she whispered, "I bet he cannot wait to meet you."

Although Guy and Alexandra had discussed names and drawn up a list for both a boys and girls, they had yet to agree on one.

"We must get Daddy here and choose your name, we can't call you 'thingy' for very long," she giggled.

Alexandra was totally mesmerised by the new life she was cuddling to her chest. Her thoughts turned to Steve Gaunt and their romance out the in the wilds of Africa, his premature death, and now Guy – the new man in her life. She felt so lucky to be alive, despite losing Steve she had found an equally wonderful man in Guy, and now they had this beautiful little girl. She could see Steve's features in the tiny baby. Life was as perfect as it could be, an exciting future as a family stretched out before them. Her thoughts were disturbed by the nurse, bringing her a cup of tea.

"Here you are Mrs. Hollins, a nice refreshing cuppa, and you've some visitors to see you and the baby, no doubt the start of many," said the nurse as she busied herself fluffing up the pillows behind Alexandra, ensuring she was comfortable.

Looking through the glass panel in the door, Alexandra saw her mother and father waiting outside. Stood alongside them was Mike Smart, the policeman who had driven Alexandra to the hospital. The smile slowly left Alexandra's face as she felt a dark cloud pass over her, despite the massive bouquet of flowers being carried by her father she instinctively knew something was wrong, very wrong. The joint look of desolation on their faces was an unmistakable signal. Her first thought was that something was wrong with her baby, something caused by her fall that they had yet to tell her about, but that couldn't be, the medical staff hadn't said anything was wrong. She looked down at her beautiful bundle of joy; all she could think of was how peaceful and perfect she looked. She switched her attention to the nurse, "What's happened?"

The nurse smiled in reply, "Let's get them in shall we."

The nurse indicted for Alexandra's parents to come into the room.

Her mother rushed to her bedside. All thought of the newborn child briefly forgotten.

Alexandra was anxious, "What is it? Tell me!"

"Oh, my darling daughter, I'm so sorry, I'm so, so sorry," she cried, unable to hold back the tears as she put her arms around Alexandra and the baby. She wanted to squeezed her tight, but conscious of her granddaughter still in Alexandra's arm.

Alexandra pleaded, "Tell me, tell me what has happened."

Her mother looked into her eyes, "There's been a terrible accident, its… "

"What accident? Where?"

"It's Guy, he… "

"Guy? Where is he? Have you spoken to him? Is he on his way?"

Alexandra's father stepped in, tears in his eyes, "He's gone my sweet."

"Gone where?"

"He's"… Her father struggled to find the right words, "he's dead. Guy is dead, I'm so very sorry my darling, so very sorry."

Her mother clutched Alexandra as she cried, "No!" she screamed, "No! He can't be! Please, god, no."

Her father laid the flowers at the bottom of the bed and sat down alongside Alexandra, ready to take the baby. Her mother still hugging Alexandra around the shoulders. Both unsure of what to do or say.

Alexandra clutched her baby tightly to her breast. The four huddled together, a family in grief.

Mike Smart looked on, impassively, from the corridor. In his job, he'd witnessed so many scenes of bad news; it never got any easier having to impart the awful news of losing a loved one. Mike knew of the collision between the ships from the police control room, but the jigsaw puzzle only fitted into place when Penny phoned him and explained who the casualties were. Thankfully he was relieved of the dreadful task of disclosure, leaving it to Alexandra's parents to impart the devastating news.

Somewhere, Alexandra heard a woman screaming, yelling, the distraught voice echoing around the wards

"No, no, no, this can't be true, it can't be true," sobbed Alexandra uncontrollably, realising it was her that had been screaming.

The duty nurses, having been informed of the tragedy by PC Mike Smart, could only look on quietly, not wanting to intervene with the grief-stricken family, tears welled in their eyes too.

Mike left the family to grieve together as he quietly walked away with tears rolling down his cheeks. He could still hear Alexandra's screams.

Chapter 60

The same arctic vortex that had brought the cold weather from north of the arctic circle was drawing in yet more cold air from the east and Siberia. It was this weather front that had produced heavy snow showers over the Lincolnshire countryside and it had also descended like a blanket over the North Sea, covering from the coast of Holland to the East Coast of England, taking in the Lincolnshire coastline and the port of Northwold. Already being dubbed the 'Beast from the North East' by the weather forecasters. The s.s. Beamish had sailed the previous night from Holland; her car decks jammed with juggernauts, trailers and private cars. All the passengers and HGV drivers had enjoyed the hospitality that the ship's hotel services had to offer. Drinks in the lounge bar or driver's room, a heart-warming sumptuous dinner served by attentive stewards in their smart company liveried jackets and a film in the onboard cinema later for those who wanted it. As the veteran ferry entered the flat evening calm, glassy North Sea, she was greeted by a bright clear sky. Stars were twinkling like heavenly jewels, interspersed with the flashing navigation lights of passing airliners looking like sci-fi starships from a faraway galaxy. The bow wave sliced through the inky black water, like an arrowhead slicing through thick, black treacle. The bubbling water astern resembled a boiling cauldron with phosphorus, glowing eerily in the dark. The twin screws bit into the water, thrusting the vessel forward as she worked up to her maximum 15 knots operational cruising speed, heading on a course for Northwold. Once clear of the continental coast and other marine traffic, the 'Beamish' would always slow down on a night crossing to extend the time of the passage, this allowed those travelling on-board the chance to enjoy a comfortable sleep in warm, cosy bunks and to wake fully refreshed the following morning. The sedate and graceful, slow speed travel meant she would arrive in Northwold at a reasonable hour, rather than dashing across the North Sea to disgorge her cargo and passengers at some silly o'clock in the morning.

At midnight, the watches on the bridge and in the engine-room would change over with quiet efficiency as one duty officer 'handed-over' to the next. On the bridge, the off-going and on-coming officers would sign the 'Master's Night Order Book' acknowledging the hand-over and that all was understood between them regarding the ship's position, speed and other vessels in the vicinity. On this particular night, they discussed the latest weather reports of the approaching forecasted snowstorm.

It wasn't long before dawn broke and the watch officer on the bridge could clearly see the solid whitewall of snow as it obliterated the horizon line.

Everything was old on this ageing vessel. Even though refitted with modern radars and automatic pilot, she still sported the large, brass helm in the centre of the bridge but with its addition of a small 'joystick' attached to a little black box of tricks. The old helm somewhat begrudgingly allowed it to sit on top the supporting pylon holding the large brass spoke wheel, standing proud as though steadfastly refusing to be permanently removed. As if testament to the stubbornness of the helm, several of the mature quartermasters amongst the crew refused to use the new-fangled 'joystick' when called to the wheel for entering and leaving harbour, preferring to use the sturdy wheel; maybe old, but robust and reliable. These old men of the sea looked upon the modern 'joystick' as sorcery that couldn't be trusted. A box of wizardry it certainly was. On either side of the brass helm stood two tall brass pedestals with large, circular, clock-like dials facing outwards on either-side, the 'Engine Room Telegraphs'. The dials were straddled by two brass handles that could move through 180 degrees, forward and back, one handle for each port and starboard engine. The clock faces divided into sections indicating the engine movement from the 12 o'clock position, one section for the engine movements ahead, and one for movements astern. The 12 o'clock position denoting 'stop', with the 1 o'clock position indicating 'finished with engines'. There were two more telegraphs, one each on the port and starboard side of the bridge wings, used by the Captain when conning the ship into port and alongside to berth.

Currently, the handles were forward and down indicating both engines were now 'Full ahead' having spent the best part of the night in the 'Slow ahead' position as the ferry had quietly glided through the calm seas. The Officer of the Watch walked over to a row of ageing large, bulky black Bakelite telephone handsets and picked up the telephone marked 'Captain'. He spun the handle and called down to the Captain's cabin, one deck below. The Captain in charge was Captain Thomas McDougal. He was a short and rotund man with a weather-beaten face caused by years of standing on ship's open bridges. Despite his rugged appearance, his face radiated warmth and joviality, which made people comfortable from the first meeting. Regardless of the appearance of an old sea dog, he could hold his own by exuding confidence to those around him in all types of company, whether addressing his crew in the crew mess or smooching around with the great and good at high society parties resplendent in his mess-kit uniform complete with a chest full of well-deserved medals. With age had come the inevitable spectacles, and he had chosen a thick, heavy, black-framed style which added a touch of comedy to his otherwise mature face. His frame choice had been out of necessity rather than a fashion design statement. He had once tried the new frameless glasses, only to have them ripped off his face one day when standing on the bridge wing in a fierce wind.

Captain McDougal loved his job, and his cabin was his second home. The Captain's quarters, although having an en-suite bathroom, it had not been updated with a modern power shower as found on the new vessels coming into the fleet. Modernisation of this old tub had been on a tight budget. The Captain's cabin may have been lacking in some of the modern-day luxuries, but it was certainly more substantial than the quarters on the new modern ferries. The s.s. 'Beamish' had been built along traditional deep-sea cargo ship lines where the Captain's quarters took up virtually the full width of the ship beneath the Navigation Bridge and chartroom.

McDougal had just enjoyed his morning bath and was looking forward to nipping down to the officer's mess for a hearty full English breakfast before ascending to the bridge in preparation for the arrival into Northwold. McDougal was like his ship, old school, believing in three square meals a day to stay healthy, and so far, his exceedingly good health was proving this well-worn phrase to be correct! Reaching for the trilling phone he was aware of the approaching snow storm from listening to the renowned BBC Shipping Forecast the previous evening. He realised that careful negotiation would be needed to pilot the final part of the passage by radar only, predicting the forward visibility to be zero once inside the coming snow cloud.

"Captain," said McDougal, as he picked up the large Bakelite telephone handset.

"Captain," replied the crisp tone of the Second Officer, addressing the Captain respectfully, "The snowstorm is now approaching, I've called for the Quartermaster to come up and take the wheel and I've informed the engine-room that we'll be about to start manoeuvring. There are several echoes on the radar screen. I'll brief you when you arrive on the bridge."

"Thank you Secondo, I'll be up immediately."

Despite the cheerful acknowledgement, Captain McDougal replaced the telephone and sighed. He knew that he was going to miss his large breakfast, a meal he considered to be the best one of the day, now he'd have to make do with a bacon sandwich served to him on the bridge by one of the catering stewards. Little did he know, the forthcoming circumstances would dictate that he would never get that savoury delight. Donning his uniform jacket, bearing the bright new broad ring of gold lace denoting the rank of Commodore on the cuffs, he left his cabin and set off to the bridge, nimbly leaping up the steps two at a time. By the time he had reached the bridge, the snowstorm had totally enveloped the s.s.Beamish.

"Right, Secondo, what have we got?" he asked as he went behind the heavy black-out curtains surrounding two large radar screens. The screens gave off a green, ghostly glow that reflected in their faces as they both looked at the large screens showing an aerial picture of the shipping in the area. One radar set to show a radius of fifteen miles and the other only two miles.

"Not a great deal, sir. There's a super-tanker just ahead of us, bound I'm sure for the oil terminal at Immingham, a couple of small echoes on the stab'd side, probably fishing boats but at their speed, they'll pass away astern of us. The only echo in our path approaching Northwold directly ahead is that large echo ten miles ahead."

"Arh yes, I'll guess that it will be the dredger 'Bolivian Titan' working in this area, they need to make the channel wider for the new leviathans," as he referred to the recently introduced new super ferry. Although she could navigate the channel it was soon realised that there was no room for error and the channel needed to be wider. McDougal had a slight hint of mischievous sarcasm in his voice. Tutting at the same time, recalling attending a recent management meeting when the marketing gurus had introduced the new vessels describing them as 'Cruise Ferries'. While accepting progress and adapting to the latest technology with all of the advantages, including safer navigation of the seas, McDougal was a traditionalist and mourned the passing of the majestic style of the current vessels as they made way for the new super ferries looking more like a floating block of flats.

The wheelhouse door opened, the icy draft caused the radar curtains to flap as the Quartermaster and look-out entered the navigation bridge.

"Ah, there you are, Quartermaster," said the Second Officer officiously. His tone insinuating that the Quartermaster had taken his time after being called up from the crew mess.

"Disengage the auto-pilot and take the wheel if you please, steer three, zero, zero degrees." The Second Officer was an aficionado of the Nelson's Navy. He readily devoured any book on the subject. Consequently he was renowned for using phrases from that era, much to the amusement, and at times annoyance, of some of the crew who were on the receiving end of his instructions.

'If you please!' thought the Quartermaster to himself, supposing he'd replied, 'well actually I don't please Mister Second Mate'. With an internal giggle, he replied, "Aye, aye Second Mate". He was hiding his real thoughts that the Second Mate was a 'pompous sod who thinks he is bloody Nelson and given a chance would probably wear a cocked hat, frock coat and sword so he could strut up and down the bridge with a telescope tucked beneath his arm. Idiot!'

"Ring down, half ahead, Secondo," said McDougal. The phrase 'ring down' being synonymous with the old brass telegraphs that emitted a loud clattering ringing sound as signals were passed to and from and acknowledged by the engine room. The new super modern ferries had direct control from the navigation bridge, and it was just a matter of moving a small stick on the bridge console. The old 'Beamish' was past her sell-by date, and thus it had been considered far too expensive to upgrade her with such technology. Not only because of the cost of the equipment but also of the cost of taking her out of service for several weeks while it could all be fitted. However, the old ferry continued to earn more than her keep with the amount of freight and passengers she carried. Therefore it was decided that she would soldier on until the day came when she would be relieved by one of the new Jumbo Cruise Ferries, then she would have to make her final, sad voyage to the scrap yard.

The Second Officer replied, "Yes Sir," as he grabbed the large brass handles, moving them back and forth in tandem as he announced, "Half ahead, Sir".

They let out a loud ring, finally stopping them against the 'Half ahead' section indicated on the clock face, followed by a further ring of bells as the engine-room acknowledged the signal and the repeater small brass arrow also lined up with the 'Half ahead' indication.

McDougal had now come out from behind the curtains and was peering through the bridge windows, looking into the wall of snow as if, by some miracle, he could see through it, "Very good. What's the dredger doing now?"

"Still dead ahead sir, she seems to be moving across our path north to the south east, should pass down our starb'd side."

"Very well," he said before turning to the Quartermaster, "port ten Tommy".

"Aye, aye Cap'n," he replied as he put the wheel over, watching the gyrocompass as it started emitting a clicking sound as each point on the compass passed through the ship's indicated centre line, "port ten of the wheel now Cap'n".

"Right mid-ships," ordered McDougal.

The wheel span back as the Quartermaster released his grip, "Mid-ships, Cap'n".

"Steady as you go two nine zero degrees."

"Aye aye, Cap'n. Steady as she goes, two nine zero degrees," answered the Quartermaster clearly.

"That should allow her to pass down our starb'd side with plenty of sea room," announced Captain McDougal to the gathered bridge team.

The calm silence on the bridge broken only by the dull booming sound of the ship's fog horn. This being activated by the bridge look-out by pulling on the lanyard hanging across the wheelhouse deck-head, connected to the huge steam whistle mounted above the bridge in front of the broad funnel.

"Captain! She's altered course to starb'd, she's heading right for us!" cried the Second Officer from behind the curtains surrounding the radar screens.

"Has she by god! Let me see," McDougal quickly returned behind the curtains and peered down at the large, green electronic display. The line from the centre of the screen swept around clockwise through 360 degrees in conjunction with the large radar scanner, sitting atop of a tall trestle mast just above the navigation bridge and wheelhouse, highlighting the echoes of other ships in the vicinity as the beam swept over them.

"Why, the bloody fool, doesn't he know the rule of the road?...Bloody dago."

The dredger was a Panamanian Flag of Convenience ship, registered in a Third World Country to avoid the more stringent regulations of operation such as safety, crew certification and welfare imposed on the prominent seafaring nations. This enabled them to undercut the competition when looking for contract work such as dredging the new channel into Northwold.

The Second Mate was agitated, "What are we going to do?"

"Calm down laddie and start calling her up on channel 16," instructed McDougal.

"Right Sir, "he said before frantically dashing across to the VHF radio set. Although agitated, he suddenly felt relief that, although he was officer of the watch, the Captain was firmly in command now. He began to call, *"Bolivian Titan, Bolivian Titan, this the s.s. Beamish on channel 16, you are standing into danger, do you read, over?"* The Second Mate looked anxiously at the loudspeaker as if willing it to speak to him, but all that came back was the continual crackling of radio static.

McDougal stepped across to the engine-room telegraph and rang 'dead slow ahead'. Once acknowledged by the engine-room, he turned to the Quartermaster, "Another ten degrees of port helm, steer two eight zero degrees, Tommy, before we lose too much way on her as she slows down."

"Aye, aye sir, port ten, steer two eight zero degrees" calmly acknowledged the Quartermaster. Slowly the *'Beamish'* moved further away from the impending danger but perilously close to the shelving sandbank on the edge of the deepwater channel.

"Steady on two eight zero degrees, Cap'n."

"Thank you, steady as you go," calmly replied Captain McDougal.

"She's not answering the radio, Captain," cried out the Second Officer.

"All right, keep trying," McDougal looked up from the radar screen, his face showed the same concern as the Second Mate. He was trying to hide his annoyance. He knew he was running out of options as the ship was now in a channel, any further to port and she would run aground; that's if the dredger stayed on its present course. He then addressed the seaman look-out sounding the foghorn.

"Bolan, sound five long blasts and then start sounding 'U' until I say otherwise."

The signal 'U' in Morse code sounded on the ship's fog horn gives out the message 'You are standing into danger'. He hoped the bridge team on the dredger would pick this up and react accordingly.

McDougal then spoke to the Second Mate, "Stop that Secondo and sound the General Emergency signal, might as well start mustering everyone just in case, at this rate I can't alter course anymore, or we'll turn out of the channel and run aground".

The Second Mate went across to the large Fire and Emergency Panel, situated at the rear of the bridge, and activated the General Emergency alarm, which would send everyone on-board to the lifeboat stations. At the same time, McDougal rang 'Full Astern' on the engine room telegraph. The whole ship started to vibrate viciously as the engines strained at full astern, the propellers desperately clawed at the water, to slow the ship's forward movement. The seconds agonisingly ticked by as the four men stood helplessly, transcendently willing the ship to go astern and away from the impending danger of the approaching vessel. The sailor, Bolan, still tugged desperately on the lanyard as the fog horn bleated out its call as if saying, 'Lookout, you are going to hit me!'

The general emergency signal had brought the Chief Officer to join the bridge team and to report to McDougal. He, too, watched the scene in anticipation as it unfolded in front of them.

Gradually, the vibrations eased, and the Beamish began to ease astern, backing away from the danger.

The five men in unison, let out a collective sigh of relief. McDougal looked into the radar screen, "At last, the fool has started to alter course!"

"There she is," exclaimed the Second Mate as he pointed to the starb'd bow. Coming out of the swirling snow, like some gigantic monster, the towering walls of the ocean-going dredger loomed, swinging across the bows of the 'Beamish'. For the men, everything felt in slow motion when a scream of tearing metal filled the air as the two ships collided, the 'Bolivan Titan' striking a glancing blow on the starb'd bow of the 'Beamish'. They all staggered across the wheelhouse, losing their balance as the ship heeled over to port at an undignified angle from the impact. The Quartermaster fell over, pulling down on the wheel as he fell to the deck, the helm spinning aimlessly like a Ferris wheel. Bolan, the seaman on the lanyard, had held on to it as he fell, yanking the lanyard so viciously that it had jammed open the valve so that it let out a constant, monotonous screeching howl, as though the ship was crying out in pain.

Captain McDougal was the first to pick himself up, "Someone get that damned horn switched off and stop engines," he ordered. The second officer dutifully grabbed the engine room telegraph and rang down to stop engines.

The telephones on the bridge were ringing dementedly in alarm from various parts of the ship as officers, and department heads were anxious to know what was to be the next move. Already, seamen were preparing the lifeboats to be swung out, all the passengers and the remaining crew gathering at their muster stations.

McDougal ordered the Chief Officer to survey the damage and the Second Mate to phone the engine room and brief them as well as to request an engineer up top to stop the whistle blowing off. He walked out on to the starboard side bridge wing, now covered in several inches of snow, being careful not to slip, he leaned cautiously over the side, but all he could see was the dredger lying about a cable away. He could just make out what appeared to be superficial damage on her bow.

Looking aft from the bridge, he saw passengers and crew on the lifeboat embarkation deck, waiting for the next announcement, which could be 'abandon ship'. Just at that moment, the Chief Officer returned to report that the damage wasn't severe; all the damage appeared to be above the waterline. The metal was bent and twisted with the most serious destruction being that the starboard anchor had been pushed back and embedded into the hull. With that, McDougal walked back into the wheelhouse and picked up the microphone connected to the ship's tannoy system. He announced, with apologies, that all was in order and that they could stand-down from lifeboat stations as they'd soon be continuing their journey into Northwold, when and where further information would be provided.

"I'm not looking forward to the paperwork on this one," he mumbled, trying to make light of the situation as he replaced the hand microphone back into its cradle. He wandered back out on to the bridge again, looking aft to watch the passengers and crew slowly dispersing. Many of the passengers clapped, with some wit shouting up to the Captain in a jovial manner,

"Was the other fellow on the wrong side of the road then?"

"Bet you'll lose your no claims bonus as that won't polish out," quipped another, followed by a gale of laughter as tensions deflated.

"Sorry about that small bump, gentlemen," McDougal calmly replied with a smile. "It's these damned foreign drivers, you know." He raised a clenched fist in the direction of the dredger as it slipped back from view into the snow. He instantly regretted his casual remark, realising he was more than likely addressing a lot of European passengers.

The Chief Officer joined McDougal on the bridge wing and they went back into the warmth of the wheelhouse. The Quartermaster, AB Bolan, and Second Mate had started to tidy up some of the mess caused by articles becoming strewn around due to the impact. Captain McDougal ordered the Quartermaster to retake the helm as he went over to the engine room telegraphs to get the ship back underway and avoid her drifting on the sandbank on the port side. The men were suddenly interrupted by two things happening in quick succession; first, the fire alarm went off, followed by the ringing of one of the telephones, which was immediately answered by the Second Officer. The Chief Officer dashed across to the fire alarm board to identify the fire's location.

In a strident voice, the Second Officer announced, "Fire sir, in the galley, and spreading through into the accommodation!"

Once again, McDougal ordered the sounding of the general emergency alarm to send everyone back to the boat stations, startled with the realisation that his previous order to stand down had been premature.

Chapter 61

Sitting in his office, three decks below the bridge, listening to the deep bellow of the ship's foghorn, Roger Holt stopped work for a brief moment to glance at his colleague, Guy Hollins. Guy was balancing the ship's cash account in readiness for his departure from the vessel on arrival in Northwold. Guy was anxious to finish up and get home as quickly as possible as Alexandra was due to give birth over the next few days, and he knew the snowstorm would cause him travel problems.

The booming reverberations of the ship's foghorn was beginning to irritate Guy. He felt like it was repeatedly telling him that he was going to be late arriving home. Guy had been working alongside Roger Holt for two weeks, mentoring him following the call from James Porter. James had vaguely told Guy about the problems Roger Holt had been experiencing. Guy, having observed Roger, had seen him to be totally professional in his approach to all of his duties. He couldn't understand what all the fuss was about which had annoyingly taken him away from his beautiful Alexandra. Now that they were this close to Northworld and within phone signal range he intended to break off and call home on his new mobile phone.

Guy looked at Roger, who returned Guy's look with a shrug and slight smile. Roger felt embarrassed to be in such a position, having to be watched over by a colleague. Roger returned to his work, although his mind was elsewhere. He was going over the events of the last week when he'd asked Guy to cover him for one trip. He had given Guy excuses about wanting to be ashore for one day to attend to some urgent business at home. Guy had readily agreed, having seen that Roger was performing well, he saw no reason not to give the guy a break, providing Roger cleared it with Captain McDougal, which he had done.

Roger was feeling a mixture of remorse and guilt. The whole episode with Ann had been a nightmare, he should just have walked away, called her bluff.

The memory made him shudder. He felt sick, swallowing hard to keep the bile from rising in his throat.

His thoughts were disturbed by the ship's sudden vibrations as the engines went full astern. Guy and Roger looked at each other, both confused, wondering what was happening. Looking out of the large portholes, they could only see a wall of white as the snow continued to fall.

"I'll phone the bridge," said Roger.

"I wouldn't worry," replied Guy. "They'll let us know if there is anything we need to know, we're probably just manoeuvring in the approaches to Northwold, the sooner we get there, the better, I need to get home."

"Yes, I know you do chum. Look, I really am sorry that I have been the cause of Porter putting you on-board to work with me. There was really no need. I'm sure you'd rather be with the misses right now."

"Well, whatever it was Roger, it's over now as far as I'm concerned. I'll be telling Porter that I don't need to be here, you're managing well on your own."

"Thank you, Guy."

"No problem Roger, I will call him tomorrow. In fact, I will make a note now to remind myself. With Alexandra due in a few days, my head is all over the place. Anyone would think it's me with the baby on the way!" he smiled.

They were quickly interrupted by the ship's foghorn sounding the signal 'U'. Both knew immediately what that meant, but before they could gather their thoughts, the general alarm sounded. Any chance of calling Alexandra now having to wait. They grabbed their lifejackets, overcoats, and uniform caps. They set out to their emergency stations where they would be expected to control the flow of passengers, get them to the lifeboat stations and issue lifejackets. Soon, the well-rehearsed drills were put into action; all the passengers were accounted for and mustered at their lifeboat embarkation stations. However, from Roger's crew checklist, he discovered that the ship's Chief Cook and the Chief Baker were both missing. As an extra crew member on-board, Guy joined Roger at his station on the starboard side of the vessel. It was at that exact time that the 'Beamish' collided with the 'Bolivian Titan'. The crash threw them both to the deck, along with a jumble of passengers and crew. Slightly shaken, they picked themselves up and checked everyone was okay. Roger was on the point of telling Guy about the two missing crew members when the Chief Baker quickly emerged from the accommodation door onto the boat deck. Roger, ready to chastise the Chief Baker as to why he hadn't responded to the general alarm when the Chief Baker shouted, "Can you come to the galley please?"

"Why?" snapped Roger irritably.

Momentarily lost for words, the Chief Baker hesitated before saying, "Well it's on fire, and the Chief Cook is trapped".

Roger was baffled by the baker's matter of fact way of reporting, as though it was just a typical day's occurrence.

When the general emergency alarm had sounded, George, the Chief Cook an old seafaring hand of some 30 years, looked at the Assistant chefs and told them to go to their muster station while he and the Chief Baker would secure the galley. They'd both seen it all before, false alarms, so while the younger members of the galley staff, who were all naturally worried and concerned, ran to their allotted emergency stations, the two Chiefs had over the years developed a blasé attitude towards the regular drills and alarms. Both really should have known better coming from the military, the Chief Cook the Royal Navy, and the Chief Baker the Royal Air Force.

The Chief Cook was also experienced enough to realise that he should have had metal fiddles in place across the top of the stove to secure the cooking pots. Sadly, as the crossing over from the continent had been smooth and calm, complacency had crept in, and they weren't in use. As the 'Beamish' collided with the 'Bolivian Titan', a large pan of fat toppled over and ignited on the hot stove. The oil-burning galley stove, like most things aboard the 'Beamish', was old. Simultaneously, the fuel oil feeder pipe fractured, spurting the highly explosive fuel oil everywhere. This, too, ignited, throwing a curtain of blazing fuel across the galley, consuming everything in its path. All this occurred as the Chief Cook staggered to his feet from a corner of the galley where he had been thrown. Crying out in pain, he looked down at his right arm. It was bent at a precarious angle, and he realised that the force of the fall had caused his right arm to break. Momentarily ignoring his predicament, his First Aid training then kicked in, while screaming out a yelp, he tenderly placed his useless arm inside his uniform white jacket to create a temporary sling. The galley ventilators should have been shut from a position outside the galley by one of the assistant chefs, this had been overlooked in their dash to their emergency stations. Consequently, the force of air coming through the ventilators increased, the ferocity of the inferno now engulfing the galley. Unable to find his way through the fire, the Chief Cook attempted to climb up the escape ladder to the escape hatch, which would let him out on to the deck above. Unfortunately, the effort was too much for a one-armed man, and despite being able to climb up the ladder, it was futile as he was unable to keep a grip and spin the turn wheel on the hatch. Returning to the galley deck, sweat from the heat and the exertion poured off his face as the temperature rocketed from the flames. In desperation he cried out, "For God's sake, somebody help, pleeease," his voice was swallowed by the roar of the flames. He became overcome by the fumes and collapsed.

He used the last bit of energy he had to crawl into a corner in an attempt to get away from the heat and flames.

Guy and Roger raced down the stairs, through the accommodation and towards the galley, three decks below. They arrived on the main deck just as the alarm bells started clamouring again, stopping many in their tracks, signalling them back to the boat deck. A broadcast followed this over the tannoy system from the bridge announcing that there was a fire in the galley, ordering the ship's Fire Party into action. Guy and Roger, followed by the Chief Baker, worked their way through those going back to their emergency stations. Passing a fire point, Roger and Guy grabbed a fire extinguisher each. As they reached the deck, they could feel the heat before they saw the flames. As they turned the corner, they saw the fire coming towards them. The flames, as if by magic, having escaped through the open vents, ran high along the deck-head above, the fiery tongue creeping further into the accommodation. The power and destruction behind the fire was wild, melting parts of the deck-head, burning and falling down on top of them as they approached the galley. There were already another two crew members desperately and heroically attempting to attack the fire with extinguishers, spraying foam in through the open fire door, seemingly oblivious that the fire had such a hold it was now beyond the weak efforts of hand held fire extinguishers. Roger quickly intervened and told them and the Chief Baker to get out of danger fast, "Get to your muster stations," he yelled above the roaring inferno, "close the fire door, we'll wait here for the Fire Team," he shouted, nodding to Guy.

Just as Guy and Roger together started to pull the fire door to close it shut, which would create a barrier against the fire and contain it within the confines of the galley there was an anguished cry, as though coming from the bowels of hell.

"For God's sake, somebody help me pleeease."

"Good God," shouted Roger, "that was the Chief Cook!"

Stopped in their tracks, Guy and Roger squinted into the dense smothering cloud enveloping the galley causing their eyes to water from the biting atmosphere.

"We can't go in, it's too dangerous," shouted Guy above the noise of the inferno.

"I know, I know," replied Roger in frustration.

With every passing minute, Roger felt more helpless. He was determined to get the Chief Cook out. Suddenly, like the parting of the Red Sea in biblical times, there was a break in the smoke and flames. Seeing his chance, Roger yelled, "We can't wait any longer, I'm going through to get to him".

"No," screamed Guy, "you'll be trapped for Christ's sake!"

But before Guy could stop him, Roger ran off through the gap, spraying foam from the extinguisher to create a carpet on the flames in front of him.

"Oh, fucking, fucking hell," muttered Guy before racing off after Roger with the fire door shutting behind him.

Both Roger and Guy reeled from the acrid smoke, it quickly clogged their lungs and stabbed into their eyes. The fire was consuming oxygen, making it almost impossible for them to breathe.

Roger could see the Chief Cook, slumped in the corner. He dropped his fire extinguisher and staggered across. Guy was soon by his side and they started to haul him back towards the galley entrance.

"I don't think he's breathing," said Guy, coughing, as fumes filled his mouth. By now, both Guy and Roger were down on all fours, each holding an arm of the Chief Cook in their efforts to drag themselves and him back to safety. The ship's fire party had arrived on the scene just after Guy and Roger had, unseen by them, entered the galley, but as the two original crew members who had attempted to fight the fire had withdrawn along with the Chief Baker, there was no one to inform the Fire Team Leader that Roger and Guy had gone into the galley. Had the Fire Team Leader known this, he wouldn't have shut the door and hit the emergency button, situated on the outside of the galley, activating the CO_2 smothering system.

It would be said later, at the Marine Accident Investigation Board's enquiry, that the deaths of Roger, Guy and the Chief Cook were caused by misadventure following a chain of events that had started on-board the dredger, the 'Bolivian Titan'.

The bridge team onboard the dredger had become distracted when the huge suction pipe, trailing along the seafloor, had become jammed on an underwater obstruction. This turned out to be the un-located wreck of the s.s. Fane, sunk by the German submarine UC63 during the First World War. Subsequently, some would later say that the chain of events causing their deaths could be attributed to First World War action! Roger and Guy's discipline and training should have 'kicked in' stopping them taking such a foolhardy action. The Board stated that they should have waited for the fire team with the proper equipment before entering the fire scene. It was a further sad indictment that the post mortem ascertained that their rescue attempts had been in vain as the Chief Cook was already dead by the time they found his body. The Fire Team Leader was cleared of any wrongdoing by activating the CO2, as although CO2 gas is not really toxic, it can cause asphyxiation of persons in a small area as it consumes all the oxygen to starve the fire. It was this that had killed both Roger and Guy. It was little compensation to their respective families that they were both posthumously awarded the Gold Medal by the Royal Humane Society for their attempt to save the Chief Cook.

Chapter 62

The early winter snow had long since thawed, releasing the last of the autumn leaves that had become entombed in the frozen ice crystals. A bitterly cold, north easterly wind coming all the way from the Urals lifted and swirled the lose leaves around Siobhan Holt's legs as she walked down the lane from the graveyard in Kettlestone, towards her home; a large detached four-bedroom house standing in two acres of manicured lawns. Her hands shoved deep within the coat pockets, huddled in her thick, brown winter coat with fur collar turned up against the penetrating wind. Virtually every day since Roger's funeral Siobhan had tended to his grave, replacing the flowers. She realised that she couldn't keep this up forever; life had to go on for the sake of the children. Sometimes, after school, the children would come along with her. Tom, the youngest, would just stand and stare at the grave and ask, "When is Daddy coming back?" Whereas Katie, the elder of the two, was far more grown up, appearing to enjoy the visits as she helped her mother keep the grave tidy. Katie would run back and forth to the waste bin in the corner of the graveyard with the dead flowers, returning with a watering can of water from the stand pipe to fill the large flower vase sitting on top of the grave.

The cemetery visits with the children appeared to go smoothly, that was, until one day when Tom asked the question, "Why is Daddy down in the ground?" Katie replied, in a somewhat haughty 'know all' voice, "Daddy's not really down there silly, he's up in heaven," indicating with an outstretched arm pointing skywards. "This is just a place we come so we don't forget Daddy."

Siobhan smiled, listening to Katie; it had been hard explaining to them both that he was never coming back, she found Katie's sudden understanding a relief. Tom would take time, but at least Katie seemed to be grasping the situation, but that was all shattered when she heard Katie say, "At Christmas, we'll come and put Daddy's presents here for him to collect when he comes down from heaven on Christmas Eve".

Tom turned to look up to Siobhan, tears in his eyes and asked if they could come back on Christmas Eve to see Daddy and wish him a Happy Christmas. That had been too much for Siobhan, she collapsed, slumping down on to her knees and clutching the children tightly to her, as she silently wept.

"Oh Roger, why did you leave me like this, why didn't you think of the children and me you crazy, crazy fool, why did you have to be a hero, now look at what you've done to us."

"Don't cry, Mummy," said Katie. "We're here with you, it will be ok, we'll take care of you."

She wanted to keep to her daily vigil of visits to the graveyard to enrich her loving memories of Roger, keeping him alive in her mind for as long as possible, but after that incident, she often went alone, not wanting to confuse her children. Family and friends kept telling her that time is a great healer; however, she was unconvinced. Of course, she was totally unaware as to how embittered Roger's mind had become during the last few weeks of his life, following his disastrous affair with the infamous black widow. Siobhan had briefly read about the murder of Ann Clark in the local newspaper, aware that it had even made the nationals, probably because of the macabre way in which she had died. Siobhan paid scant attention to the rumours and stories surrounding Ann's unusual and, in her opinion, disgusting private life. The story only caught her eye when she learned that Ann Clark worked for the same shipping company as Roger, although she had never heard Roger mention her name. She found it very strange though that Wendy Morgan, a policewoman from Northwold working on the murder team, had visited her along with the local Kettlelstone village constable just days prior to Roger's death. She had been mystified by the visit; the policewoman asking if she could verify Roger's movements over a certain period of days. Wendy also enquired about Roger's car which Siobhan confirmed was a Ford Escort RS2000. At the time, as far as she was concerned, Roger was working on-board the ship and his car would be in the crew car park at Northwold. The policewoman's questions somewhat irritated her when she wouldn't say as to why the police were interested in Roger's car, his movements and whereabouts. Siobhan, reiterated that of course he was on-board, all of which could be confirmed by the company. Demanding to know what it was all about she received some 'wishy-washy' excuse that they had reason to believe Roger knew the lady who had been murdered as she sometimes travelled aboard the Beaumont ships during the course of her work. It was just a matter of tying up loose ends, piecing together the last known movements of Ann Clark and who she may have met in the days prior to her death. Siobhan just didn't believe it. Wendy wouldn't disclose any further information when she asked to know more, merely saying that it was an on-going investigation and it may prove that Roger wasn't of any interest to them at all. Still, she needed to know so that Roger could be eliminated from their enquires. Wendy Morgan promised to get back to Siobhan if they required any further information and asked that when Siobhan next spoke to Roger would she ask him to call in at Northwold police station to meet her.

'Eliminated from their enquiries? What on earth did that mean? Police speak for not being sure, no doubt,' she thought. Had Roger lived, she could have asked him but now it would forever be a puzzle to her, as was the local garage mechanic turning up a few weeks after Roger's death. He presented her with an invoice for some mechanical repairs to Roger's beloved Ford Escort RX 2000 and requested that it be removed as soon as possible from the workshop as he needed the space. It was a mystery as to how Roger's car came to be at their local garage when it was usually parked in the crew car park at Northwold during the times Roger was on board the ship. Curiosity got the better of Siobhan and she made enquiries by telephoning Penny Smart in Beaumont's personnel department. Penny told her not to worry, reassuring her that Roger had been on-board the *'Beamish'* for three weeks up until the terrible accident. Siobhan questioned if Ann Clark worked for the company. Penny confirmed that Ann had worked in the offices and Roger may have met her at some point, but she couldn't say how well Roger knew Ann or if they were even friends. Penny also, out of curiosity, asked her husband Mike what he knew, if anything. Not being party to the investigation, Mike didn't know all the circumstances, only that Roger's name had emerged somehow from information received. Although he learnt that the detectives tracing Roger's movements had discovered that he'd left the ship for a day or so and during this time his car had broken down. On being attended to by the RAC, the mechanic deemed the car unrepairable by the roadside so it was subsequently transported it to the garage in Fakenham. Apparently, accompanied by Roger. The detectives were trying to track down Roger's movements as he had now become a 'person of interest'. As Mike had told Penny this in confidence she couldn't pass this information back to Siobhan not only because of her loyalty to Mike but this information implied that Roger had been ashore around the time of Ann Clark's murder having ramifications for his possible involvement. Penny tactfully decided to avoid mentioning that the police had already been to see her and Roy Brooks and that Roger's name had come up. So, as far as Siobhan was concerned, that put an end to it.

Penny knew Ann Clark reasonably well as she'd worked in the offices along the corridor. The dates which Siobhan referred to were over the period when Ann Clark was murdered, so why were the police asking Siobhan Holt about her husband's movements? At first it didn't make any sense but in view of what Mike had told her she did begin to wonder. Penny had also heard of the various rumours that surrounded Ann Clark and her apparent strange private life, but she chose to ignore them; someone else's sexual exploits were of no interest to her. Penny was sure that this was a mistake, she knew Roger reasonably well, and she liked him, he was always charming and attentive whenever she went aboard the ships on business. A flirt certainly, but then as far she was concerned it had all been entirely innocent. At no time had she heard anything about a possible relationship between Roger and Ann or any other woman for that matter. Penny recalled the visit by the two policemen investigating Ann's death. The young Detective Sergeant who had interviewed her seemed quite interested when Roger Holt's name came up as a crew staff member, but he had given nothing away other than ask about his duty periods onboard the ship. Penny went to see Roy Brookes as soon as the senior of the two policemen had interviewed him. He was his usual vague self, giving nothing away, just flippantly passing it off as of no consequence as far as the company was concerned and nothing to do with them. Penny left it at that.

As Siobhan steadily approached her home, her mind drifted to the future, and she sobbed, "My beautiful home will have to go". She so wanted to stay in Kettlestone but knew it couldn't be in her big house and gardens. Although Roger's life insurance had paid off most of the mortgage, there was still a hefty chunk left owing. His Merchant Navy Officer's widow's pension wasn't inadequate but would no way make up for the loss of his salary. Siobhan had worked in the early days of their marriage, before the children came along, which had given her a small amount of savings, but that would soon be eaten up. There was precious little left over to make ends meet, and with the children so young, taking a job would be awkward. As she neared her detached house, standing on its own and back from the quiet little road, tucked away in a corner on the edge of the village, she noticed a flashy Jaguar parked outside with a handsome middle-aged man standing by it, looking around as though lost. Dwelling upon her immediate problems, she did not give him a second glance as she took a short cut across the large front lawn towards her front door. She became aware that the man was making a beeline for her.

"Excuse me," he called as he hurried down the drive in an effort to catch Siobhan before she made it to the front door. His voice accentless, giving the impression that he was from London or the Home Counties.

'Oh god, what now?' she thought as she stepped under the large porch overhanging the front door.

"Mrs. Holt?" he enquired.

Slightly startled he knew her name, Siobhan paused as she placed the key in the lock, unsure whether to proceed quickly inside to the safety and sanctuary of her home or stay outside and confront this stranger.

"Can I help you?" she called firmly and assertively, ready to turn the key quickly.

The well-dressed gentleman, breathing slightly heavily from his quickened steps, placed his case on the floor and quickly produced a calling card which he offered to Siobhan along with his outstretched hand in greeting. Siobhan left the key in the lock, took the card, and absently shook his hand. His grip was firm, any stronger and she may have winced.

"As you can see from my card, my name is Dennis Connors. I'm a solicitor with Richardson and Associates of London. I've come concerning your late husband's estate."

Siobhan looked perplexed at Dennis Connors. "I don't understand. All our affairs are dealt with by a solicitor in Fakenham."

"Well, not all Mrs. Holt, your husband had other business interests. If I may come in and explain in more detail?"

Siobhan suddenly felt vulnerable.

"Mrs Holt, I understand you may feel threatened and I can assure you I am who I say I am and can show you more paperwork for proof," he bent down to his case, opening it to retrieve more paperwork. "I do apologise for suddenly turning up like this but my office did ring on several occasions to try and make an appointment for me. They noticed there wasn't an answer phone so they couldn't leave a message."

"No, we never bothered with one," replied Siobhan watching Dennis as he pulled papers from his briefcase.

Straightening up, clutching a collection of official-looking papers in his hand, the top clearly displayed the letterhead of Richardson and Associates, he addressed Siobhan again.

"Mrs. Holt, if you would feel happier to have a friend here or maybe a neighbour to come along and join us, I fully understand. I'll wait here for you to go and see who is available."

Siobhan was anxious to be inside out of the cold and away from prying eyes and quickly decided that this man seemed to be genuine enough, 'for who else could be visiting a widow?' she thought. "No, there's no need, please do come in and I'll make some tea, or coffee maybe?"

Siobhan's mind was in overdrive. 'Roger's estate?... It doesn't make any sense. This house is the only estate he had.'

"Tea will be excellent, just what I need after the drive up from London," Dennis replied, following Siobhan in as she entered the hall and unset the burglar alarm just inside the front door. Her key ring included a panic alarm which she could easily activate if necessary but the man appeared genuine enough although his reasons for calling on her sounded unreal.

Siobhan took his coat and showed him into the lounge. She was sure there had been a mistake, Roger told her everything. She quickly made some tea and soon returned to the lounge with a tray, neatly laid out with a large teapot of tea along with china cups and saucers and some fresh scones. Having poured the tea for them both, she laid back into the soft, comfy chair as Dennis Connors opened a large file and scanned some of the documents. Siobhan starred at him, wondering what on earth he was about to impart.

"Well, Mr. Connors. Just how is your firm involved with my Roger?" using the words, 'my Roger' made her suddenly gasp, feeling overwhelmed with grief and anxiety.

Looking up from his papers, Dennis reached for the cup of tea and took a substantial refreshing gulp, "Well Mrs. Holt, your husband owned some property in Australia."

"What?" exclaimed Siobhan, "No, he doesn't, I mean, didn't... we don't!"

"Oh dear, I rather gathered from your initial greeting that you are probably in the dark concerning your late husband's business interests," he took a deep breath, "Mrs. Holt, there is no mistake, your husband had a couple of business interests, in Australia".

Siobhan was puzzled, "Well, he was in the Merchant Navy, he never lived there as far as I know, he just sailed there for many years in his twenties, but... "

"Ah, I see, well of course I knew of his Merchant Navy connections and I am so sorry Mrs Holt but this really does embarrass me to explain that I obviously know more than what he has told you."

Siobhan looked over her teacup at Dennis in stunned silence, momentarily thinking she had been transported to another planet. Dennis continued.

"If you'll allow me to explain what I know from when he first came to appoint my company to look after his affairs. Firstly, I know Roger through my brother who was a shipmate of his and when Roger needed some legal advice my brother put him onto me."

Siobhan was totally bewildered by what she was hearing and just nodded.

"Well, I'll keep it as brief as possible. Roger once told me that his initial investment came about following a heavy drinking session whilst on shore leave in Australia with some of his shipping company's local executives. Later he told me much to his embarrassment that he assumed he'd been conned to part with a lot of money in what he thought was a spurious land investment. He purchased the opal prospecting rights to a piece of land in the Northern Territories. He cursed himself for months after the event for being so stupid, he thought he'd been set-up and duped out of a lot of money. Eventually, he became quite philosophical, putting it down to life's rich tapestry and a brutal learning curve, he tried his best to forget about it and put it behind him. Much later and out of the blue whilst home on leave he was contacted by the mining company's land agent who had been the original seller of the plot of land. He was informed that a prospector wanted to buy the licence from him. At first, not believing what he was hearing but then he thought that at least he might be able to get some of his money back. However, the agent advised against this and recommended that Roger just allowed the prospector to mine on the land and receive 10% of the value of anything that he discovered."

Dennis paused, leaned forward and took a sip of his tea. Siobhan just looked on in almost total disbelief at what she was hearing, as Dennis continued.

"Of course the agent explained that he would be receiving a 2% commission fee as well so hence his advice not to sell. Roger explained to me that at the time and still having believed he had been conned he assumed that it was some sort of huge practical joke at his expense and went along with the idea. Well, in an attempt to make this long story short, it turns out that it was genuine all along and Roger recovered his initial outlay and has made modest profits ever since. Some years being better than others but to coin a phrase, the rest Mrs Holt is history."

Siobhan placed her cup and saucer on the coffee table, still struggling to comprehend what she had just heard.

"My Roger?" she tried to force a smile but it appeared to be more of grimace.

"Yes, Mrs. Holt," replied Dennis, taking another gulp of his tea. "And there is also a bank account in Liechtenstein where all the income is deposited. His instructions are quite clear and straight forward in as much that everything is to go to you."

"My Roger?" Siobhan repeated.

"Yes Mrs. Holt." Dennis flicked through more paperwork continuing as he read, "Additionally there are some properties he'd bought over the years, these are all rented out to sitting tenants".

"I don't know what to say," said Siobhan quietly, still not taking it all in.

"I won't bore you with all the detail, it's all here in this file which I will leave so you can read at your leisure later. There are some small mortgages attached to the properties in Australia and the income along with that of the mine, naturally varies according to the prevailing exchange rates, but it more than covers the outgoings leaving a very nice monthly surplus. There are also the details of the accountant who lives in Liechtenstein who handles all the accounting side of things. He is a German chappie who speaks fluent English, although I've never personally met him I have spoken to him on several occasions. I told him I was coming to visit you and would, of course, introduce him to you, hypothetically, of course. No doubt, in the fullness of time, you can speak with him directly. All his details are in this file, which I will leave with you." Closing the folder, he handed it over to Siobhan. "Here, I'll leave this so you can go through it at your leisure, it should all be straight forward, it explains the assets your husband had accumulated. Naturally, if there are any questions, then I am always at your service to be able to answer them and offer advice if needs be."

Siobhan gently flicked through the file of papers on her knee not taking in what she was looking at; she was speechless.

"So, Mrs Holt, all in all, and as you will see from the documents, you are a very wealthy lady."

Siobhan stayed silent.

Dennis carried on, "However, there are a couple of caveats in your late husband's will covering his business interests, one is that myself and my company are retained to handle the legal side, you'll find amongst those papers our account of charges. The other being that Herr Christoth Schuman is retained as well, again his charges for his work are clearly itemised".

"Yes, of course, thank you Mr. Connors, whatever, I just don't know what to say." Siobhan's lips started to quiver as she attempted to restrain herself from breaking down into tears in front of a stranger.

Embarrassed by Siobhan's show of emotion, before closing his briefcase, Dennis Connors offered Siobhan a clean, pressed, and obviously expensive handkerchief which she gladly accepted. It was noticeably doused in Calvin Klein perfume.

"There's nothing to say at this stage Mrs. Holt. I can see it has all come as a shock to you and that you need time to take it all in. I'm on my way up to Yorkshire and will be there for a few days. I can call in to see you on my way back to London next week. That will give you time to go through the file, from which no doubt you'll come up with some questions for me."

Wiping her eyes with the handkerchief, trying to hold back the tears that were starting to well up, Siobhan sniffed, "I'm so sorry, I do apologise. As you say, all this has come as a shock. I was coming back from the graveyard just now and was thinking about the future, mine, and the children's, the financial side was worrying me. I was going to have to put this house on the market and downsize, then you arrive with this," she smiled, shaking her head, still not comprehending it all.

"I understand Mrs. Holt, quite a shock. Do excuse me but I must be on my way, I'll call you in a couple of days to let you know when I will be on my way back so I can call in again."

"Thank you," mumbled Siobhan as she walked him to the front door and passed him his coat.

"My pleasure Mrs. Holt, after all, I have to earn my retainer," he said with a slight smile in an attempt to lighten the moment.

After she bade him farewell and closed the front door, she went back into the lounge, opened the file and sat down on the sofa to read through the papers. It was like reading a novel.

"Oh Roger, Roger, my dearest, darling, Roger, I never really knew you at all," she said aloud as tears of mixed emotions rolled down her cheeks.

"How on earth have you come to own all this?" Once again, she openly and unashamedly sobbed her heart out with a mixture of both grief and joy.

It was one question to which she would never find the answer.

Chapter 63

Many lives, like Siobhan Holt and Alexandra Evans, were forever changed by the murder of Ann Clark and subsequent deaths of Roger and Guy, among them was George Stewart and Karen Clark. George had seen his dreams of settling down to a cosy lifestyle with Ann Clark shattered into a thousand pieces. Alexandra had lost her second true love and father to her daughter. Karen had moved in with Aunty Samantha and Uncle Alan, she had passed her exams, progressed to secretarial college and then gone onto work for her Uncle. Naturally, for a time, she was distraught, mourning the loss of her mother, but the exuberance of youth, along with the immersion in her new lifestyle, gentle counselling from Samantha, meant that she soon overcame this traumatic time of her life. Samantha's heart glowed at what she always felt would be an impossible dream; this curious twist of fate resulted in her becoming a surrogate mother to Karen. Karen enjoyed her life; when not at her desk in the city, she filled her time socialising and riding with Samantha across the glorious South Downs. Karen, whilst still retaining a strict sense of respectability, was something of a minx, flaunting herself and playing the field with the host of eligible young men who consistently vied for her affections. It was inevitable that the Neanderthal men amongst those that chased her labelled her a *'prick teaser'*, she just laughed this off, content in her determination to save herself for Mr. Right. The only downside to her new life which would bring on dark periods whenever she was alone and lost in her thoughts was her missing father; her heart ached to see him, wanting to feel his protective, strong arms cocooning her and be able tell her how proud he was of her and of what she had achieved. Despite the best endeavours of her Aunty and Uncle, no trace was found of him. One of her suitors, a young army officer, and keen to impress Karen applied for, and obtained, special permission to travel to the Congo and go in search of her father. Whilst he had found several ex UK & US military pilots working out there, no one had heard of a Nick Clark, and rather dejectedly, he'd returned home empty-handed. Nick, through his absence, was eventually declared to be dead.

This was not enough for Karen, having no grave to mourn over. Hence, her father was ex military, she applied to the Royal British Legion, who agreed to have a plaque with his name placed on their cenotaph in the Chichester Crematorium Memorial Gardens. After that, each

Remembrance Sunday she attended the service held to honour the war dead. She would stand there, tears streaming down her cheeks, listening to the vibrant haunting tune of the 'Last Post' reverberating eerily across the Memorial Gardens in the weak autumn sunshine in accompaniment to the many military flags that snapped and fluttered proudly in the light breeze. She silently prayed that he was still alive somewhere, keeping the memory of him alive in her mind, hoping that one day he would return.

At the end of the service, the flag bearers of the British Legion and many other regimental and naval standards would on command come smartly to attention, turn and march off away from the memorial to the adjacent car park. Although slightly thicker in the waist with grey hair creeping out from beneath their various coloured berets, they still had the same military bearing from years ago. In the car park, they would be officially dismissed by the parade master to then wander around to 'The Barn Harvester' public house and muster for drinks and lunch. It was known that such remembrance parades attracted the odd 'Walter Mitty' types, men that had never or just briefly served without distinction but wanted to feel to belong to the military family. They would appear adjourned with medals that wouldn't stand close scrutiny. Occasionally, an imposter would be exposed by a glaring clash wearing an un-coordinated regimental tie and beret. So a stranger appearing within this cadre would soon be noticed.

As the veterans gathered in the bar at the pub, there was much merriment as they circulated to the sound of chinking glasses raised in salute to Queen country and absent friends and fallen comrades. The conversation flowed with the odd tear forming in crinkly grey eyes, recalling old friends they'd served with, known and lost touch.

In one corner of the room, a group of veterans were enquiring of one another about an apparent mystery man who had been on parade with them.

"Does anyone know that fella standing at the end of the back row?"

"No," replied one with a shaking of heads from several others.

"Well, he wasn't here for the muster turning up just before the bugler started... we even had to dress to one side to make room for him," voiced one obviously annoyed at the unmilitary tardiness of turning up late for their sacrosanct Remembrance Parade.

"Yes, I saw him but I can't see him here," said another as the group turned looking around the room to try and spot the mystery late comer.

"Anybody see what regiment he was from?"

"His beret was Army Air Corps," offered another.

"I was standing next to him and he was wearing the Military Medal as well as the Afghan and Iraq medals along with the General Service gong, looked pretty genuine to me," replied another. "Although he didn't speak, just nodded and smiled when I looked at him."

"He could certainly march properly," commented another.

"Well we can soon settle this by asking the parade master an ex RSM."

After consulting with the parade master they discovered that he too didn't know who the stranger was as he hadn't been accounted for or reported to him at the pre-parade muster or post parade dispersal.

Chapter 64

The dynamic duo of *'Blackman and Robin'* continued their search for the killer of Ann Clark. All the evidence they had collected pointed the finger of suspicion at Roger Holt, his premature death aboard the ship denied them the opportunity of interviewing him. Further evidence, that at first appeared to support their case, was discovering that Roger had interrupted his duty period aboard ship, leaving the vessel upon arrival in Northwold. Spending the night ashore during the time when Ann Clark had been murdered, Roger had then returned the following day when the ship arrived back on the morning tide. Both Harry and Peter were confident they had identified Roger as the culprit, but just when they were about to close the file as solved, the results of the DNA taken from Ann Clark's body dropped on to Harry Johnson's desk. Despite the explosion killing Roger Holt, they had been able to obtain a sample of his DNA from the morgue, however, the samples taken from the body of Ann Clark by the Forensic Science department didn't match Roger's. This of course wasn't conclusive in ruling out Roger as a person of interest. Ann could have had intercourse with someone else earlier on during the day of her demise and then later murdered by Roger. Further enquiries also revealed that at the time of Ann Clark's murder, Roger was fifty miles away with his broken down car being attended to by the RAC breakdown service. They confirmed that the car hadn't been repaired on the spot and that the owner elected to accompany his car when taken by flatbed lorry to his local garage in Kettlestone. Here, the car was left with a note of authority from Roger requesting the garage to proceed with the repairs. Apparently, Roger then accepted the offer of a lift from the recovery vehicle driver who was returning to Northwold. Once there, Roger booked into a local B&B, confirmed by the landlady, where he'd slept until nearly mid-day and after some lunch returned to the port to re-join his ship. He and Guy were then to die forty-eight hours later in the fire and explosion aboard the *s.s. Beamish*. No matter how Harry and Peter played around with what they knew about Roger's movements during his short spell ashore and the window of Ann Clark's death given by the pathologist, tantalisingly they couldn't make the times fit tight enough to convince the Coroner that Roger was firmly in the frame as the Prime Suspect. They needed further corroboration, so until further evidence is revealed, the case remains on file as a 'Cold Case'.

Chapter 65

Richard had many things to be grateful for; his career and personal life had been resurrected after the disastrous affair with Katrina, including the revival of his marriage and the arrival of twins. Added to this was his excellent decision of employing Susan's boyfriend, now husband, Charles Barrington-Smythe. He had become a godsend to Richard, working alongside him as a personal adviser as well as with the many challenges that had come up during the takeover of Beaumont's. Charles became Richard's confidante and their friendship flourished. When Charles and Susan wed, there was no question who would be best man and Richard obliged without hesitation.

Richard revelled in how his life had turned around. It had been successful, and at times intriguing. However, even in his most imaginative moments, he would have never conceived what the milestones would be, a member of staff at Beaumont's murdered in a bizarre sexual act and a ship colliding with a dredger, resulting in three funerals, but any press was good press and soon everybody knew who the Beaumont Shipping Company was. Now, two years down the line, just as the take-over was beginning to bear fruit and with profits steadily increasing, to the delight of the shareholders, Charles drops a bombshell onto his desk showing historical accounting irregularities going back several years prior to the introduction of computers. Charles, with his forensic accounting mind, had with Richard's approval been looking into the archives of BSC as ground work for a text book he planned to write and publish with the target market of colleges and universities for students studying accountancy. Due to his training in forensic accountancy, Charles had come across little nuggets that challenged his enquiring mind and like an archaeologist he had burrowed deeper into the foundations of the BSC accounts to discover the source. This discovery caused Richard to reflect on the attitude of Bob Somers the day he had told Bob of Charles' appointment.

Having left Richard's offices, Bob Somers rushed down to his own office. Completely lost in his thoughts, he panicked, everything around him faded into a fog, he had no idea which way to turn. It was a disaster. He was heading for the edge of a precipice with no way back. He ignored the several people he bumped into; his body co-ordination appeared to be absent; he was staggering like a drunk going home from the local pub.

'What the hell am I going to do? God, I'm going to get caught out, that smug bastard Hartling is on to me. How the hell did he know? Fuck, fuck, fuck, it's obviously that meddling little bastard, smart arse husband of Hartling's posh secretary bird. Calls himself a fucking forensic accountant, I'd like to make him a forensic specimen, the little shit!'

He gasped for breath so deeply that he thought his lungs would explode. He could feel his blood surging through his body as his heart hammered against his chest. He felt as though his heart could just stop at any second. 'Would that be a blessing? To just collapse and end it all now?' He thought about the phone call to his wife, 'I'm sorry Mrs. Somers, but his heart just stopped'. He could imagine her on the other end of the phone, crying. She would cry a lot; he was her world, who was she without him and his money? His thoughts immediately clogged at 'money'. As he reached his outer office, he charged through as if the devil was chasing him, startling his secretary who let out a small scream.

"Eeeeeek, why Mr. Somers," she yelped, jumping up from her chair, quickly catching her spectacles as they fell from being perched on her nose, "Whatever is it?"

"Get me an outside line, now!" he wheezed as he inhaled, "I won't be taking any calls, and I don't want to see anyone, anyone, do you hear?" He snapped before slamming his office door behind him.

His secretary was totally stunned. Her boss, Bob Somers, was undoubtedly an odd fellow. The whole office knew he was a Jehovah's Witness, never celebrating or taking part in any of the office social events, shunning anything that appeared to be enjoyment. However, she'd never seen him like this in the number of years she had worked with him. His sudden change of character frightened her.

She tried to compose herself, sat back into her chair, reached for the large telephone unit on her desk and stabbed the necessary buttons to transfer an outside line to Bob's desk phone. For once, she just didn't know what to do next. Her thoughts alternated between worry and fright. Yes, Bob could be mean spirited, awkward, and at times slightly lecherous, in fact not really a very nice person, but she'd always held respect for him as a boss. However, his tendency to be creepy always gave her the impression he was sneaking up on people to overhear conversations; she found this unsettling. Instinctively, she now wanted to run from her office and cry, recently she'd had thoughts of resigning but her salary and perks working for BSC were excellent and she had designs on moving up the corporate ladder to one day be working for the top man, Richard Hartling. Bailing out now would ruin that dream, so she accepted her lot for what it was and kept her ambitions and the magical goal she was working towards a secret. She pondered about going to see Richard's PA, Susan, and ask her what to do under the circumstances, but quickly realising that would antagonise Bob if he discovered her talking about him behind his back. Therefore, she decided, reluctantly, to hold her ground and wait for developments.

Bob Somers was frantically pacing the length and breadth of his office, wiping his sweating brow. The lenses of his glasses steamed up with the heat emanating from his florid face. He kept removing and wiping them with his handkerchief but to no avail, as soon as he perched them back on his nose, they misted over again. Finally, in a fit of rage, he took them off and flung them onto his desk. He sat down, picked up the phone, and dialled a number.

On the receiving end of the phone, a very sweet voice answered, "Polyfax and Green Accountants".

This pleasant, chirpy voice at the other end of the phone annoyed Bob intensely.

"Get me Green, now!" he snapped.

"I'm sorry, sir, do you mean Mr. Green?" she demurely asked.

The question antagonised Bob. It was obvious that his request was to speak to Mr. Green. It felt like the smooth voice was being condescending, which just fuelled his anger.

"Yes, yes, Mr. Jeremy Green, dammit woman I need to speak to him urgently, just get him to the phone, it's Bob Somers of BSC."

Not to be shaken by the abrupt caller, the smooth voice politely replied, ignoring to acknowledge who Bob was. "One moment, please caller, I'll see if he is in the building, please hold." She flicked a switch on her telephone set to put Bob on hold. She knew only too well that Mr. Green wasn't in the building, but she was going to have her little revenge at Bob for talking to her as though she was a 'non-entity'. After what she thought was a sufficient space of time, she flicked the switched again continuing in a calm, collected voice.

"Sorry" – she certainly wasn't – "to keep you on hold, but Mr. Green is away on holiday at the moment," she almost automatically added 'sir' but she was damned if she was going to address this rude caller with such grace. Another little triumph for the small down trodden person, 'up the socialists' she thought to herself as one who regularly attended the

Socialist Workers Rallys, demonstrating against the ruling classes and corrupt capitalism system.

"Is he contactable?" demanded Bob, "It's extremely important that I talk to him within the next two hours!"

"I'm afraid not," she almost snapped back in irritation. Bob was starting to get on her nerves with his rudeness. "He is on his yacht sailing around the Canary Islands, we have no way of contacting him," she pictured the yacht sailing the sunny seas and had to hide the jealousy in her voice at her disgust of rich boys and their expensive toys. Mr. Green, her boss, had recently turned down her request for a salary review just before he left for his luxury holiday. This had only added fuel onto the revolutionary fire, burning deep within her, strengthening her views of all that was wrong within the society where the privileged few had all the wealth. She consoled herself, knowing that this coming weekend, along with her out of work socialist boyfriend, she would take part in another march against capitalism. She hoped that with any luck it would turn into a free for all with police who would undoubtedly attempt to break it up as the march hadn't been given official sanction. Lots of her left-wing Trotskyite mates with their cameras would be there to photograph acts of police brutality. The adrenaline was already coursing through her body at the thought of the excitement to come, as post-event sex with her boyfriend was always mind-blowing. She was quickly brought back to the present from her daydream of explosive sexual athletics as the exasperated voice interrupted her thoughts.

"What about this new-fangled email?" Bob seemed to recall that Green had mentioned he was putting a satellite communications system on-board his yacht.

"Not that we here are aware of," she blandly replied.

'How ironic,' thought Somers, his anger growing, 'he only has that bloody yacht thanks to me paying him enough backhanders over the years to keep his eyes closed to my creative accounting'.

"Fine, thanks for nothing," he snapped before slamming down the phone. He took a large, white, fresh handkerchief from his inside jacket pocket, turned his chair away from his desk and started to weep in frustration.

A few moments later, as he sat wiping his eyes, there was a peremptory knock on his inner office door.

"I told you I don't want to be disturbed!"

"So, your secretary told me."

Bob Somers spun around on hearing Richard's voice. "Oh, sorry ... Richard." Bob instinctively replaced his glasses on his damp nose, and pretended to be working as he looked over computer print outs of the company accounts.

"Come up with anything yet, Bob?" enquired Richard.

"Yes ... and no."

"Interesting," replied Richard as he turned to leave the room. He stopped, turned back to look at Bob, "Keep trying," he said gently.

"I ... I am, yes, of course, I am looking into it."

"Good," Richard looked Bob straight in the eye. "I've had a word with Kirton, and he advised me to call in the police. The City of London police have a highly specialised fraud branch, they work hand in hand with the Financial Authority Serious Fraud Office."

Bob felt an icy chill down his spine. 'This is the end,' he thought. 'I'm going to get found out, the police will be straight on to me.'

Bob was in a daze as Richard interrupted his thoughts, "Meet me in my office at two, and we can discuss how we handle the police and the next steps we take".

Bob Somers looked down at the large sheets of printed paper and tried to appear involved.

Richard continued talking to Bob's bowed head.

"I've been in touch with our *publicity guru* Janet Houchell as to how we handle this. Once it's out that we have a financial problem, our share price will go into free fall."

"Yes, of course, yes. All right, Richard, I'll be there," he tried to sound casual but was aware he sounded over-enthusiastic. Bob had no intention of going to the meeting, he was at a complete loss as to what he was going to do.

Once Richard left the room and closed the door behind him, Bob Somers stared at the mass of data laid out before him. He stared at the numbers as if they were written in a foreign language, the data was all lies, and he knew it. He also knew that his life was about to be torn apart. He then rose from his seat, left the office and walked past his secretary without saying a word.

"Mr. Somers," she began, but he took no notice and walked on through the outer office door. With a shrug, she resumed working on her computer, thankful that the storm appeared to have passed.

While most of the office staff at BSC were breaking for lunch, Bob wandered down to the underground car park. The few that saw him thought it was odd behaviour. Bob Somers was a typical accountant with very regular habits, accurate and habitual timekeeping, never known to do anything out of the ordinary.

Chapter 66

Rachel Somers was busy weeding in the back garden when she heard the unmistakable sound of her husband's Bentley. She always thought it was funny that without any mechanical knowledge whatsoever, she could guess, with almost one hundred percent accuracy, the maker of different cars by the sound of their engines.

Looking up, she watched as the Bentley came into sight around the side of the large imposing house with its sweeping gravel drive, finishing at the substantial timber framed garage and workshop. The garage, built mainly of deep red brick, matched the house, totally in keeping with the pre-war design.

Bob home at this hour? A perplexed frown dawned at having her peaceful day disturbed by Bob arriving home so unexpectedly. With a hushed sigh she crossed the lawn to greet him, noting that totally out of character, he had stopped the car immediately in front of the large, weather-beaten effect, grey timber doors. Usually, he would have activated the remote control and the doors would slide effortlessly out of sight, allowing him to have driven the car straight into the garage. He didn't like to leave his beloved Bentley outside any longer than necessary. It was an old one, almost a classic, which he cherished dearly. While the office staff could set their watches by Bob Somers, his wife Rachel could predict his normal everyday moves. Their lives were of programmed predictability, she hated it but had learned to live with it.

Having climbed out of the car and walked across to greet his wife, he kissed her gently on the forehead. This always made Rachel cringe, making her feel like a pet dog, but then in their marriage, Rachel had allowed herself to be moulded into the wife that Bob Somers wanted, totally obedient and acquiescent to his ways.

"What's the matter, Bob dear? You're not ill, are you?" Rachel vainly attempted to sound concerned, but the years of marriage to Bob had drained her of any real feelings.

"Nothing to worry about petal, just feeling a little off colour." Rachel screamed internally at being called petal, she had on more than one occasion asked Bob to stop using the term, but her requests had, as usual, fallen on deaf ears. What Bob Somers didn't want to hear, didn't register. As for him feeling a little 'off colour,' this was completely strange to Rachel. Bob was never ill or off colour, and she did begin to wonder if there was something seriously wrong with him. She recalled an article she had read somewhere that this could be the early warning signs of an impending heart attack; Bob's reassuring words did not entirely convince her.

"You're working far too hard with this take-over business, aren't you?" she said sympathetically. "I'll make us a pot of tea," thinking to herself that maybe she should secretly call their family doctor, although that might make Bob cross and she didn't want to do that. There had never been even a threat of Bob being violent towards her, they hardly ever had a crossword and he never raised his voice, he didn't have to, if he was unhappy with anything that she had done then Bob had ways of manipulating Rachel with gentle cohesive words. He was a narcissistic bully, Rachel had learnt how to meekly accept that it was just the way things were.

"A cup of tea would go down a treat. I'll just nip upstairs and change out of this suit."

Having dressed into his out of character purple tracksuit then going back downstairs Bob Somers wandered into his study. He lifted the telephone receiver off the hook and laid it beside the phone. He suspected the office would call his home number when they noticed his absence. He'd yet to succumb to having a mobile phone which was becoming all the rage, and the latest 'must-have' gadget for the man about town. Bob was only just learning the mysteries of the computer and left most of the electronic number-crunching to the youngsters. Ironically, it was the latest accounting computers and software that had laid bare his years of scheming.

Rachel had fastidiously prepared the tea, laying it out on the garden table. When he heard Rachel calling him, he meandered through the house and out on to the patio.

"Would you take these with your tea?" said Rachel submissively holding out two aspirins, "they should help, maybe you should have a lie-down?"

Somewhat surprisingly, Bob agreed, "Yes, I think I will," as he swallowed down the aspirin tablets with his cup of tea.

"Would you like some lunch, Bob? I usually only have a sandwich, but as you're here, we could have a salad … there's fresh lettuce, new potatoes, and tomatoes in the greenhouse, the fruits of your labours dear."

"All right, petal," he agreed, "first I'll just have a stroll around the garden". Putting down his cup and saucer, he walked away, leaving Rachel vacantly gazing after him, sensing something wasn't quite right but she didn't want to ask. "Don't go too far dear, lunch won't be long."

Lost in thought, Bob Somers turned and came back towards Rachel. He gave her a weak smile. Her eyes were questioning, waiting for him to speak, but instead, he bent forward cupping her face in both hands and kissed her tenderly, full on the lips, uncharacteristically showing a brief moment of tenderness.

"What was that for?" enquired Rachel, somewhat startled.

"Nothing really," he smiled, but this time his smile was far more sincere, then he turned away from her and started off down the beautifully laid out garden with its herbaceous borders and burbling intricate designed water features. The manicured lawn lovingly tended by Bob, requiring him to use a sit on lawnmower due to the sheer size of the grassed area.

Bob wandered around the gardens, moving further and further away from the house. He found solace in these surroundings, created with his and Rachel's own bare hands over the years of their marriage. A marriage which had borne them one son, now living up in Scotland and working as a Civil Servant.

Bob leaned against an old Elm tree, one that had not succumbed to the deadly Elm disease that had swept the country some years previously. Some of the blossom had fallen, creating a colourful blanket on the ground. Bluebells bobbed their heads as they caught the gentle early spring breeze. Only planted a few years ago, he reflected, amazed at how quickly they had multiplied.

For the next twenty minutes, he strolled to and fro, surrounded by the world of his creation. He inhaled the sweet scent. Butterflies flitted here and there. He noticed the bank of cotoneasters, a massive coat of flowers heralding a blaze of berries to come in the autumn. How far away from his office, it seemed, in the City of London, with all its problems. His memories drifted back to when it had all begun. He thought it was a surreal dream, not really believing what he had carried out, nor that he was about to be exposed. At first, it had all seemed like an academic exercise, some sort of research into what could be achieved with creative accounting rather than the crime it was. It had been so easy to move the odd decimal point, making small amounts disappear from the P & L account. He had treated it like a game, not a crime, just to test the water to see if or when anyone would notice. The amounts were so small that they could easily have been 'accounting mistakes', easily rectified, and cleared up if queried. As time went on, nobody noticed, nobody asked questions, and so he carried on, just for the hell of it. He'd never intended it to go as far as it did. Suddenly, the small surpluses that he'd made started to grow. Before he realised, he had created an 'out of control monster'. Yes, he could have stopped, but it had been as though he was swept along by an invisible force.

Then one day, out of the blue, the auditor had spotted a simple mistake that exposed Bob's creative accounting. When he had first brought it to Bob's attention, Bob convinced that his little game, as that's how he saw it, was going to be exposed. Looking back now, he wished it had forced his hand to come clean and closed it down. But the auditor had other ideas. Jeremy Green, 'Greedy little bastard,' thought Bob. He had convinced Bob, with a hint of blackmail, that they would never be caught out as long as he was the company auditor, all he wanted was a decent share of the misappropriated funds. The money had to disappear somewhere, so Swiss Bank accounts for them both had been opened.

How Bob wished he had never started, let alone allowed it to spiral so out of control.

As the thoughts swirled, Bob found himself in his shed, located in a remote corner of the vast garden. Hardly a shed in the real sense of the word, more a second single garage in keeping with his house and gardens where he housed his garden implements as well as a dedicated corner for potting. Sitting amid the usual garden paraphernalia was his prized motorised lawnmower. He stared out of the shed window at the entrancing scene beyond.

Walking over to his potting area, he found amongst the plant pots an indelible pencil and a scrap of paper. He wrote a simple message to Rachel;

Dearest Petal,

I'm so sorry to leave you. I know that I have been your life but know that as I leave you your faith in Jehovah, together with the local Kingdom Hall and of course our dear son Tobias, will guide you and protect you in my absence. If there was any other way than to leave like this then I would take that route but things are beyond that now. You know I have amassed sufficient funds to keep you for the remainder of your life and go to my maker with the knowledge that you'll want for nothing. All I can say is sorry Petal. Until we meet again in the Holy Kingdom.

Yours in Jehovah and love for you.

Bob.

Bob Somers then closed the doors and windows, went over to his motorised lawnmower turned the electric start, and just sat there astride the machine starring out through the shed windows as the shed slowly filled with carbon monoxide fumes. The last view before he collapsed over the steering wheel was that of his beautiful garden.

Rachel, with no response to her calls from the patio, set out to find her husband. Coincidently this occurred at the same time as Richard Hartling reached for the internal phone on his desk to call Bob's office to enquire as to why he and the two policemen from the City of London along with an investigator from the Financial Regulators Serious Fraud office were being kept waiting.

Rachel, surprised at the delay in Bob's return, continued her search for him, eventually coming to the large garden shed where she heard the steady humming beat of the lawn mower's big diesel engine. Opening the doors, she was enveloped in thick, greasy, billowing clouds of noxious diesel fumes. Initially staggering back; recoiling from the acrid suffocating smoke, briefly frozen as to what to do next, then discovering long-forgotten hidden depths of decisiveness that had until now been smothered due to the years of Bob's total dominance. She burst into action, taking immediate, quick thinking steps by throwing open the two large double doors to allow the heavy air laden with noxious gasses to escape and disperse. Covering her mouth and nose with the tea towel she had absentmindedly brought along from preparing lunch, she dashed to the lawnmower and turned the key, switching off the ignition. With watering eyes as the waste exhaust chemicals in the air attacked her tear ducts, she stared in shock and horror at the slumped body of her husband, his right hand clutching the suicide note. Recalling her first aid training from her early years in the Girl Guides, she quickly felt his neck for a pulse whilst wafting the tea towel at the now fast dispersing clouds of sickly fumes. Yes, there was a weak pulse and a brief flicker of an eyelid opening, causing his right eye momentarily to stare at her grotesquely, she briefly recoiled with fright. She retrieved and read the note, 'Oh My God, it's a suicide note' she shrieked taking in a lung full of some remaining gases causing her to cough.

Instinct was telling her she should do something, call an ambulance, try to drag him down from the machine and commence CPR. But, she just stood there transfixed, staring at his comatose fat body, slumped over the front steering wheel of the mower. Seeing him lying there, helpless, the man that had ruined her life, she felt no remorse. The blinkers were removed, she saw the reality! A fat, overgrown slug, a bully that totally dominated her very existence. It dawned on her just how much she hated him. Then, as if another force had taken over her body and feeling like a trapped animal, she suddenly saw her chance of freedom, a way out of her current predicament as an emotional prisoner, to rid herself of this man, her jailer. Dropping the tea towel and the note Rachel slowly leaned down. She turned the ignition key just as Bob's eye again lazily opened, causing her hand to snap back as if she had touched a live wire. However, galvanised with her renewed determination, she reached out again, willing for his eye not to open and turned the key which immediately fired the engine back into life. While staring at Bob's body, terrified that he might suddenly rear up, she slowly walked backwards out of the garage, slamming the doors shut, she spun around and collapsed back on to them, fearful that Bob would come around and try to force them open. Her mind was in turmoil as to the actions she had just taken. A voice in her head screamed at her and told her she was a murderer. 'No!' She said out aloud, then holding her mouth in horror that someone might be witness to what she was doing, but this was impossible the shed was in a completely hidden and secluded part of the garden. No one could see her. She fiercely stated to herself, 'Bob wanted to die, it was his choice' as she started to walk back to the house, working out what she was going to say to the police. Realisation of what she had done dawned on her just as suddenly did the fact that she had dropped the tea towel in the garage near to Bob. 'My God,' she gasped, realising that she must retrieve it. Momentarily thinking that the tea towel would be evidence spotted by the police just like it would be in a Midsomer's Murder plot. She could hear the questions now. 'What was tea towel from your kitchen doing inside the garage near to your husband's dead body Mrs. Somers?'

Then a laughable stupid thought crossed her mind, which was that of her surname being spelt the same as the last part of the title of the TV detective series, Midsomer's Murders! With such thoughts she was beginning to believe that she might be about to have a mental breakdown. Maybe she was mad? Perhaps she would be found out for what she had done and be committed to an asylum? She was imaging her defence barrister pleading mitigation that after years of enslavement in their marriage, she had seen a way out and had taken it in a totally out of character, irrational moment.

Sometime later, when feeling more in control and having answered all her niggling doubts, she returned to the shed. She opened the doors, leaving them ajar, switched off the ignition, quickly retrieved the incriminating tea towel but leaving the suicide note where it had fallen on to the floor. Hesitantly she felt Bob's neck for a pulse, convinced that he may not be dead. It was a relief that she found no pulse and his skin was icy cold. However, she returned to the house in a trance but able to call '999' summonsing both the ambulance service and the police, she then sat back in a daze, allowing events to take care of themselves. The paramedic who attended confirmed with the police officers that he was dead, and they gently informed her. One of them handed her the note taken from Bob's hand, and although placed in an evidence bag, it was clearly readable. Only then did Rachel allow herself to shed tears for Bob although the attending officers would never know that Rachel's tears were tears of joy and relief, not sorrow!

Sometime after his body had been removed and Rachel was on her own, she laughed out aloud. All through their married life, Bob had been entirely oblivious to the needs and wants of his wife, only now could she see her way to become the person she'd always wanted to be.

Chapter 67

Despite the enormity of her actions, it was several days and some sleepless nights of seeing flashing images of Bob around the house before it finally hit home that her husband of all these years had really left this mortal earth. She soon realised what a huge burden had been lifted from her shoulders. Maybe Bob had been happily married, but she certainly had not. Bob had been the controlling force, and although on the surface it had all the impressions of a perfect union, it wasn't. That's what Bob had wanted and Rachel had been too weak to argue, so, for the sake of a quiet life, she went along with it. They had one child, Tobias, who, from the moment he was born, Rachel discovered she had no maternal feelings for. Tobias had grown into a 'chip off the old block': he was his father's son alright, almost to the point of being a clone.

Bob Somers came from a family of very wealthy Jehovah's Witnesses, so wealthy in fact that they had built and paid for a new local Kingdom Hall. The young Bob, being indoctrinated into the world of Jehovah, became a good student of the faith. Upon leaving boarding school, with excellent academic qualifications, he wanted nothing more than to become an accountant. He joined the practice of a local Jehovah as an articled clerk.

It was one beautiful summer when, during his holiday, he served his faith by joining his Jehovah colleagues as they knocked on doors distributing the 'Watchtower' magazine. They were to encourage people to read the magazine and then arrange a convenient time to return and discuss the points of view. It was the subtle way that Jehovah's Witnesses sold their particular brand of Christianity, through milk and honey. It was on one such occasion that Bob met Rachel. Rachel's family were particularly vulnerable at that time, having just lost the father, the family's breadwinner, in a horrific car accident. Rachel's mother was looking for solace anywhere she could find it, and that came in the shape of the Jehovah's Witnesses who called while the family was in mourning. The effect on Rachel and her mother was profound, although her sisters were sceptical. Rachel and her mother became converts, and Rachel found Bob. Until her father's tragic accident, Rachel had been a fun-loving girl going to dances and discos and generally enjoying life as she blossomed from being a teenager into adulthood. Bob offered strength and affection when she needed it most; consequently, she was drawn to the lifestyle of Jehovah.

Rachel was neither a strong character nor experienced in the ways of men and she was soon mentally overpowered by the more psychologically dominant Bob. He had hang-ups too, with a guilt-ridden, voracious appetite for sex. After they married, Bob couldn't abide looking into Rachel's eyes during copulation. Therefore, their lovemaking assumed a standard procedure. Rachel had to lay on her stomach, and Bob would penetrate her from behind. Not anally, but having been endowed with a longer than average penis made this position the most satisfying for him. Rachel had to endure it every night apart from the rare occasions when Bob was away from home on company business. In the beginning, Rachel had found it different and passionate, even at times exciting but within months it became a chore she just had to accept. So, in the words of the age-old proverb, 'she just laid back and thought of England,' only in her case, it was a matter of laying forward.

Rachel's main comfort in life had become the garden but then Bob, after taking an interest in horticulture, slowly took control away from her. It would be years later when she finally realised she had taken a wrong turning in life, but by that time she had accepted that she had made her bed and therefore must lay on it. With the death of Bob, Rachel realised that life had given her another chance, a chance she had no intention of wasting!

'The death of,' she often thought about those words, her mind would wander… 'was it death or was it in actual fact, murder?' But then she would rebuke herself for even thinking that way. Rachel had watched her son, Tobias, how she hated that name but Bob had insisted on it, grow up developing a closeness with his father that Rachel had never felt for Bob, let alone to her son. He adopted a form of address for his mother of 'Mater', it made Rachel want to scream, but she had become too meek and subservient to complain. Rachel secretly hoped that university would break up the father/son relationship, but that was not to be. Instead, Tobias applied and obtained a place at a local university, shunning the usual student life so craved for by the majority of young aspiring academics looking to break the umbilical family cord, thus allowing Tobias to stay living at home with her and Bob. Rachel was secretly glad when he finished university and went into the civil service working for the Scottish Office north of the border. Rachel couldn't have wished for anything better. Trying to cope with two men who saw her as nothing more than an empty-headed, domestic slave was terrible enough, so once Tobias left to embark on his career, she was relieved she only had Bob to contend with. Tobias had soon met Emily and regularly took her down to meet Bob and Rachel. Rachel saw history repeating itself, recognising in Emily a younger version of herself. The only difference was that, unlike herself, who had learnt to accept her fate with Bob, Emily willing accepted Tobias' domineering and controlling personality, she appeared to lap it up, hanging on to every word that Tobias uttered. It made Rachel inwardly cringe.

Rachel was aware of Bob's financial dealings and the money he had salted away, mainly in Swiss Bank accounts. He had never kept any financial secrets from her; he was however, just never truthful about the source from which they came or how much. As far as Rachel knew, they were small amounts and came from bonus earnings. Not that they ever needed to use these savings as she and Bob certainly had more than they needed. Rachel had no idea of the dealings Bob had with BSC auditors, 'Polyfax & Green' and the small fortune Bob and Jeremy Green had concealed from BSC. It took some time after his death for her to realise the true extent of the money Bob had hidden away. After reading newspaper articles that appeared to know more about her husband's financial state of affairs than she did, Rachel started to dig deeper into Bob's business affairs.

The news of Bob Somer's suicide did not make the front pages, the story ran to only a few small paragraphs, summed up with the well-worn police cliché *'foul play is not suspected'*. 'If only they knew' she had thought with a shiver running down her spine. Initially, although relieved to be widowed, Rachel was mystified as to why Bob should take his own life. To those who knew her, she took his death surprisingly well, but then they didn't know the truth and feelings lurking deep within her. It was while Bob's body was at the funeral home and Rachel was making arrangements with the local Kingdom Hall for his funeral that news started to leak out that a Mr. Jeremy Green of 'Polyfax & Green' had been arrested on charges of fraud. Although the police had been to interview Rachel over Bob's death, it had never been anything more than a sympathetic approach, without any hint of suspicion. Rachel was, of course, terrified that she would give the game away, her guilt playing havoc with her feelings. She was convinced the police might suspect that she had helped Bob on his way to the Eternal Kingdom of Jehovah! Her fears were unfounded with the inquest confirming suicide.

With Bob's body hardly cold, Rachel felt a new lease of life inhabit her, and she wasted no time in investigating the contents of Bob's study; done one evening while enjoying a bottle of expensive wine, something that

Bob had always frowned upon. He had discouraged her from drinking even the odd glass of wine, despite the fact that he had amassed what could only be described as a 'cellar treasure trove of wines,' worth a considerable amount of money. Rachel took great delight in opening the most expensive bottle of red she could find. It was one which Bob had paid several thousand pounds for at a wine auction. She knew this because he openly boasted about it regularly. Rachel opened the bottle, poured a glass, and raised it to the air, "Cheers Bob," she smiled.

With a typical accounting mind, Bob had everything meticulously recorded and laid out in such a fashion that a complete stranger could have easily interpreted his financial position. Rachel grew more and more excited with each passing revelation or was it the wine, maybe both. She had uncovered an Aladdin's Cave. Rachel was so engrossed it took her several minutes to realise the front doorbell had been ringing. She picked herself up from the floor, where she had laid out all the papers from Bobs' desk and attempted to tiptoe over them in a drunken stagger, giggling to herself amused by her evening's revelations. Rachel didn't have that many friends, Bob never allowed her to cultivate any. 'We have each other and our faith,' is all that Bob would say whenever she attempted to complain about the lack of their social life. 'Pah! faith, fiddlesticks,' she thought. As she reached the front door, she nearly tripped over and had to use the door to steady herself. The sudden thump would not have gone unnoticed by whoever was on the other side. She took a deep breath, attempted to collect herself, and pulled open the large, heavy oak front door. It groaned in unison with the sound of cast iron hinges grating, just like the sound effects of a horror movie.

"Oh, it's YOU!" said Rachel, the wine not allowing her to hide her disappointment on seeing the caller. It was Bob's solicitor and fellow Jehovah's Witness friend, Nial Ismay. Nial was a man she detested. He, like Bob, treated her as if she was a child.

Her body language instantly became defensive, and she clung to the front door and its frame, not allowing Nial to see beyond her. This was her house now, and she was going to guard it.

"What do you want, Nial?" emphasising the DO in the tone of her voice.

"Now my dear, how are you feeling? I've come to see if you are alright and to discuss Bob's affairs that you will need me to tidy up, may I come in?" he said with a smirk rather than a smile.

"I'm a bit busy right now, Nial!" She hic-cupped, trying to cover this with a small gulp as though suffering indigestion.

"Don't be like that Rachel, I'm here to help you through this difficult time."

She softened her posture and released the door from her grip, "Nial, I really have not...." but before Rachel finished her sentence of objection, Nial had firmly pushed open the door and slipped passed into the large hallway, slithering like a snake on ice.

"Oh very well, you'd better come through," Rachel said to a vacuum as he flashed past, feeling that she ought at least to be pleasant to him although she certainly didn't feel like it. Before she had hardly closed the front door, Nial had walked into the main lounge as if he owned the place. Rachel followed. Initially, they stood looking at each other, Nial still smiling in such a way that Rachel wanted to slap his face. In an attempt to be friendly, she offered him a drink, "Would you like some tea or coffee or maybe even a real drink?" she giggled as she gave another little hiccup.

"Now then my dear, you know I don't drink alcohol, and I won't be here long enough to partake in a cup of tea, I just want access to Bob's study so that I may take away the papers that I need to clear up his estate and of course get things settled for you financially," he beamed at her. Not only was he smarmy, but he also looked like a walking advert for Moss Bros, standing there in his immaculate Armani tailored suit, matching tie with a handkerchief neatly exposed from his breast pocket. Everything about Nial screamed money, privilege, class and position, all making Rachel feel inferior, and she was finding his Cheshire cat grin both infuriating and frightening. Before she could answer, Nial quickly walked through to the study and took in the sight of the papers strewn over the floor, his eyes blatantly stopping on the bottle of wine and an empty glass.

"Oh dear, what have you been doing here Rachel?"' he scolded her like a parent speaking to an errant child, "you should really have left things for me to sort out. By the look of things, you've made my job harder, and I see you've been drinking too ... that will never do, you know how much Bob detested alcohol," shaking his head in disapproval. He turned to look at her, she felt like a mouse cornered by a very hungry cat.

He continued, "Now my dear, you are obviously having a stressful time of it so I'll overlook the drinking, especially as I guess the bottle comes from Bob's collection which forms part of his estate and so technically it should remain intact until probate has been granted".

Rachel was incensed at the way he was speaking to her, 'overlook her drinking,' who did he think he was talking to!

From inside the study, he raised his voice very slightly to ensure she could still hear him. "Just leave everything to me to tidy up and take care of. I suggest you go and have a lie down to try to sleep off the alcohol you've consumed."

Rachel seethed as she entered the study behind him, watching him wander around the study, careful of where he was walking and 'tutting' under his breath. It was then that his condescending, patronising attitude towards her finally lit the blue touch paper, and she erupted, allowing years of pent up frustration to burst out of her like water from a breach in a dam.

"Now, just a cotton-picking minute, you!" She had waited years to be able to use the expression that she had picked up from an American movie years ago. "This is MY house and MY husband's paperwork. You need to leave well alone, Nail! And you know what … if I want to get pissed on Bob's wine, then I will do so. In fact, I've got another bottle to open. So Nial, I want you to leave … NOW!" She screamed at him as she stood with her legs astride and hands on her hips. Nail turned to face her, the Cheshire cat grin still there as if set in plaster. He quickly started an attempt to appease the now angry Rachel.

He opened his arms in a conciliatory gesture and spoke in a tone as though speaking to a petulant child, "My dear there …."

Rachel interrupted him abruptly, "Don't you 'my dear' me you patronising, slimy creep, just get out of my house!" She emphasised this with her outstretched arm pointing towards the front door.

"If you don't leave now. I'll call the police," she yelled whilst grabbing the nearby cordless phone.

As a solicitor well known to the local police, he didn't want the embarrassment of them turning up. So, tilting his head to one side and putting his arms up in submission, he started to move towards the door. Still not understanding that the lady had finally turned, Rachel had metamorphosed from a larvae into a butterfly.

"Of course my dear, I'll come another time, you are obviously stressed with the death of Bob. I understand that you are suffering, I shouldn't have come around so soon."

Rachel followed him to the front door. "Stop calling me my dear, I'm not your fucking dear, now get out and don't bother coming around again as you are fucking well sacked as the family solicitor, you're no fucking use to me, and I'll be putting that in writing," she spat.

Nial stepped outside and quickly turned on his heels to face her, "Of course, my ... Rachel, I understand, you'll see things differently in the morning and when you've mourned Bob sufficiently," his smile still firmly in place.

Rachel regained her posture, holding on to the front door again, but this time she kept her grip.

"I am not mourning Bob, nor do I intend to, you fucking moron, I've only just woken up to how much I hated the bastard."

Nial was so shocked at Rachel's cursing that he quickly turned and broke into a jog towards his car, he was now genuinely fearful of what Rachel would do next. 'She is clearly demented,' he thought to himself as he grabbed the door handle of his Aston Martin, cringing slightly to the sound of the large oak front door being slammed firmly behind him, followed by another yelled but muffled 'Fuck Off!' A parting shot from Rachel as she burst out into hysterical laughter.

Rachel was beside herself with enjoyment, she was finding it hard to realise she had just sent 'the great solicitor Nail Ismay' packing with his tail between his legs. Gleefully, she raced back into the study, picked up the wine bottle, and filled another glass knocking back half of it in one. She placed the glass down on the small coffee table then raced upstairs to find her CD of 'Death Metal' one of her favourite rock bands, part of the secret life she kept hidden from Bob. Back downstairs, she placed the CD in the player and turned the sound up to max and started cavorting around the lounge to the heavy rock music that was now booming out from the Bose quadraphonic sound system. Soon she was stripping off all her clothes as she enjoyed herself, wrapped up in the music she realised that she had not felt this good for years. The wine flowed, and the music beat out; she was in heaven. As she twirled around the room, she flew open the patio doors, and soon the sound of 'Death Metal' was reverberating out into the neighbourhood, which was not to everyone's pleasure. Despite the vast area of land surrounding all the substantial properties in the semi-rural area, the sound of the music soon had the nearest neighbours reaching for the phone.

Rachael carried on dancing, twirling and general jigging her naked body all over the room and patio in unison to the music.

Through the noise of the music, she barely heard the ringing at the front door and thinking it was the frightful Nial coming back to assert his authority over her she pranced through to the hallway throwing open the front door in a fit of pique. Momentarily, she was dazzled by the blue flashing light before she realised that two police constables were standing in front of her.

"Yis, offizzzer's," she said, standing there, legs apart, her hands firmly on her hips, naked in all her glory.

The astounded officers politely looked at her, then each other, in amazement, "Is everything alright, madam?"

"Of coz it is, I'm just 'aving a party fa one," her voice slurred "and you are both welcome to join me, along with your truncheons, of course," she burst out into hysterical laughter at her joke.

The two police officers were not sure what to make of it and the older of the two, P.C Harry Thomas, decided a firm approach with Rachel was called for. "Now madam, first of all, please go and put some clothes on, then turn down that loud music," he demanded.

Rachel, realising that maybe she had gone too far, quickly gathered her thoughts, "Yes, of course hhofficers," she said with a hic-cup before dashing back inside, switching off the music and gathering up some clothes to cover her modesty.

As she retreated into the house, the two police officer's looked at each other with a grin.

"Go and switch off the blues," said P.C Harry Thomas, "I think we've got a right one here," he whispered before following Rachel into the house. He slowly stepped through the significant hallway, with its magnificent sweeping balustrade staircase and balcony landing, and into the lounge, allowing her enough time to cover up.

Rachel had soon thrown on her light cotton dress and was busy picking up her underwear and stuffing it under one of the big blue cushions on the large settee.

After both officers had joined her in the lounge, Rachel was full of apologies, offering to make some tea, which was readily accepted. Soon they were all sitting down with mugs of tea, and on first name terms, the older PC Harry Thomas nicknamed 'H,' and his younger partner, PC Ian Platt. Both police officers were somewhat bemused at what had been going on. Having been reassured by Rachel, who was now feeling less intoxicated, that all was ok, the officers took their leave. They informed the control room to close off the 999 call that had been received by genuinely concerned neighbours. The nearest neighbours some distance away across a couple of fields demonstrated the loudness of the music which they had never before heard emanating from Rachel's home. It was as if a Rock concert was being held in her garden and grounds.

The two officers walked across the gravel drive towards their car, Rachel watched until they were both inside the car before she closed the front door, leaned on it and burst into a high pitched, wild laughter. The two officers heard the laughter and looked at each other with a smile. P.C Platt started the engine and looked at the house name, "Wasn't this the address where that city accountant chappie topped himself?"

"Yes, I think it was," replied Harry, "and did you notice the photographs on the table in the lounge?"

"No, I didn't'," he replied while manoeuvring the car out of the large driveway.

"Well, there were plenty of individual photographs of what was presumably her late departed and herself, some obviously professionally done, but there were none of them actually together."

"I could be wrong but to me it looks as though she is glad to see the back of him, either that or she has completely lost her marbles," said H with half a laugh.

"We'll write this up for the ops room, tell Sarge what has happened, and give the lady another look in later just to be sure."

"Roger that," replied his partner as they acknowledged another call for their services coming over the force radio.

Rachel had indeed sobered up rather quickly following the encounter with the two police officers, so making herself some more tea, she went back into the study and started going through Bob's paperwork again.

Later, the two policemen called back just to check everything was ok. This time Rachel greeted them warmly, offering them more tea, which again they accepted.

Since their earlier visit, they had confirmed that Rachel was the widow of the recently deceased Bob Somers.

While sitting comfortably in Rachel's lounge, Harry sympathetically broached the subject of Bob Somers' passing. He had recently attended a bereavement counselling course and wanted to put into practice what he'd been taught. Rachel's explanation of her feelings astonished both officers, and by the time she had finished, both of them should probably have considered arresting her as a potential murder suspect. So much hatred towards her recently departed spewed out from her that it sounded as though she could have willingly done away with him. Although the cynical streak that seems to affect most seasoned police officers after years of dealing with all sorts, quickly made them see the funny side of the relationship. They had also had it confirmed by their Sergeant that it was, without doubt, a suicide.

Having got her feelings about her deceased husband off her chest, Rachel went on to apologise for greeting them as she had done earlier in the evening covered in nothing else but her birthday suit. By now, both officers had warmed towards Rachel, and feeling rather sorry for her. They immediately reassured her that she had nothing to apologise for.

Rachel explained that she was expecting Nial to be at the front door, "I was half expecting to see the family solicitor to be standing there when I opened the door and before you say anything... yes, I was trying to shock him as I can't stand the man. He is from the same mould as Bob. He's a creep, and he had come around earlier, talking to me like a child," Rachel sighed before continuing, "I fired him earlier; he was our... Bob's solicitor. An evil little toad. Nial Ismay ... do you know him?"

"Actually, we do," replied H with a slight grin, which had not gone unnoticed by Rachel.

"Do you see him as the supercilious prig that I do?" she said with a little titter.

"You may say that Mrs. Somers, but we couldn't possibly comment," replied H politely, his grin giving away his personal thoughts, "and on that note, we better take our leave," both officers put down their finished mugs of tea and rose together.

"Oh, I do hope I haven't said something I shouldn't and annoyed you about Nial?"

"No, Mrs. Somers, you certainly haven't, dare we say the feeling is mutual?"

"Enough said, H," smiled Rachel. "H ... I hate to ask favours, but, well, perhaps I can ask you for some advice about solicitors, if I may?"

"Go ahead, I'll help you if I can," he offered.

"It's a long shot, but can you recommend a good solicitor now that I've sacked mine, someone really good? I don't care how much he costs, but I am going to need a really slick one to help me work out all my husband's affairs."

"Leave it with me Mrs. Somers; I'll speak to a few people and come up with some names for you."

"Oh thank you, thank you so much," her voice demonstrably full of relief as she continued, "I'm so glad we've had this conversation and to think if I hadn't enjoyed a glass too many and played my music so loud I would never have met you two nice policemen and tomorrow I'd be worried as to how to find a new solicitor," she smiled.

"Think nothing of it Mrs. Somers, call it fate."

With that, the two officers turned and made their way to the front door, where a beaming Rachel waved them off.

Chapter 68

The following morning, Rachel received three telephone calls, each one changed her life.

The first call, not unsurprisingly, came from Nial Ismay. Nial, not only worried that Rachel had utterly lost her mind seeing the state of her the previous evening but he was more anxious about the exorbitant fees he was going to miss out on administering Bobs' complicated financial affairs and estate. Nial was aware of Bob's wealth, but, like Rachel, Nial had no idea that Bob had amassed such a fortune.

"Hello," said Rachel politely on picking up the phone.

"Good morning Rachel, how are we today? A little calmer than last night, I hope?" Nial's voice, even over the phone, dripped in sarcasm, oozing down the line like treacle despite trying to sound genuine and caring.

"Oh, it's you, Nial. I thought I made myself perfectly clear last night, I don't want to hear from you and I don't want you as the family solicitor anymore."

Rachel tried her best to sound assertive in a 'hoity-toity' sort of way, which was difficult considering her lack of self esteem following years of being down trodden by Bob and the likes of Nial. The glass of wine or two the previous night had definitely helped her confidence in dealing with him, but she knew in the sober light of day that she had to stand on her own two feet.

He interrupted her thoughts. "Of course, I do understand how you must be feeling Rachel, you are not thinking rationally after losing dear Bob, the shock and trauma will still be with you and that's why you need me to take away the worry of sorting all Bob's affairs. Once I have everything in hand I can get to work, you'll then start to feel a great weight lift from you."

Rachel could imagine his slimy smirking face on the other end of the line. She went quiet, questioning her own assertiveness. Had she been too hasty? Should she let Nial remove the burden of sorting out the finances? She quickly remembered the conversation she'd had with the two helpful policemen the previous night and suddenly found her courage. Clearing her throat and her mind, she replied, "You are not listening to me, Nial, my decision still stands, I no longer require your services and therefore need nothing more to do with you".

"But as your solicitor, I need..."

"No, I told you. You are no longer my solicitor as I have already appointed a new one," lied Rachel, her fingers crossed behind her back, hoping that H would be as good as his word and recommend someone.

"Oh … well, erm, that was quick," Nial paused in his thoughts before releasing a hint of anger, "but Rachel, you don't know anybody, so who is it?"

The obvious sudden anger in his voice made her feel frightened, sending butterflies flying around her stomach as her anxiety level rose but Rachel knew she needed to stand her ground if she was to get rid of this awful man.

"Don't worry, you'll find that out soon enough when they contact you to pass over any of our papers you are holding," replied Rachel sharply, knowing she needed to end the conversation soon before she capitulated through fear. Before he could say anymore she politely and quickly ended the phone call, "good bye," quietly but firmly replacing the receiver. She gave a little gasp at her display of bravado and realised her heart was beating at an alarming rate, but she'd never felt happier. Rachel was beginning to come out of her shell.

Her brief feeling of euphoria took a sharp dive when the phone suddenly burst into life again, making her jump. Letting it ring a few times, thinking that it might be Nial ringing back to have another go at her, she took a deep breath and told herself to be strong as she picked up the receiver.

"Hello," she said, her eyes screwed up in determination.

"Hello? Mrs. Somers? It's PC Thomas…. 'H'. We met last night."

"Oh yes," she said, opening her eyes with a sudden sigh of relief.

"Is everything alright, Mrs. Somers?" he asked, detecting a slight hint of strain in her voice.

"Oh yes, yes, thank you H, I thought you were going to be someone else."

"Oh, I see. Well, as promised, I've got the name of a solicitor for you."

"Oh thank you, thank you ever so much, I'll just get a pen and paper," she said excitedly, quickly putting down the receiver on the wooden hall stand and searching frantically. She soon returned, suitably armed with pen and paper.

"I'm ready now," she replied with a large smile of glee.

"Okay. I've spoken to a few colleagues and this name comes to the top of the list, she is an ex policewoman, now a qualified lawyer and by all accounts Mrs. Somers, she is a really good one. When you call just tell her I recommended her, I'm confident she is just the person you are looking for."

Rachel took down all the details and thanked 'H', telling him to call round for a cup of tea and cake whenever he was nearby. She hung up the receiver and felt like dancing again, not only had she been recommend a new solicitor, but to her joy, the solicitor was female.

Without wasting any time, Rachel called the office of Michelle Dunbar, and surprisingly, Michelle answered the telephone herself. Soon, Rachel was in a protracted explanation. She made an appointment to visit Michelle at her offices in Sevenoaks that very afternoon. Rachel felt her spirits lift feeling light-hearted and confident, which she would soon need as the next call came from her son, Tobias, in Scotland.

Tobias had been away on Government business in Canada, along with his wife Emily, when Bob had taken his own life. Although shocked and saddened, Tobias decided there was nothing he could do until he'd finished what he considered 'vital Government business'. Considering his position as being far too important to even think of requesting an early release from his superiors back in Whitehall. During the one telephone call he'd had with Rachel, shortly after the event, he informed her to leave everything to him and the family solicitor, insinuating that Rachel was totally incapable of arranging anything.

When the telephone rang, sixth sense told her that it was her son. Steeling herself for what she knew would be a difficult, and without doubt a confrontational telephone call, she lifted the receiver.

"Hello?" she said, sounding rather timid, then inwardly admonished herself.

Without so much as enquiring as to how Rachel was coping, Tobias immediately launched into a verbal assault.

"Mater, I've been trying to get through to you for over an hour, who on earth have you been on the phone to for that length of time? It is simply ridiculous at a time like this!" and before Rachel could reply, he continued haughtily, "I can't recall you having friends that would warrant that amount of time on the phone." He continued with his tirade, "Furthermore, I've just been speaking to Nial, now what is going on? You had no right to say those things to him. You should never have thrown him out of the house! And telling him, he is fired. What is wrong with you? I have had to clear up the mess you have created, and I have immediately reinstated him as the family solicitor!"

Rachel remained silent, allowing the verbal ear-bashing he was giving her. Holding the phone away from her, the volume of his voice so loud she could still clearly hear his rant, even at a distance.

"Are you listening Mater? Did you hear what I just said?"

Rachel withered under the verbal abuse she was receiving, searching for the right words with which to reply. She surprised herself as to how calm she felt, but before she could say anything, Tobias went on, "Well? Mater? What have you got to say for yourself?"

Rachel took a deep breath, in the hope of steadying her voice, "Really Tobias, how nice to hear from you, I'm very well thank you and I do hope you and Emily are too?" she said, attempting to put a hint of sarcasm in her voice.

"Yes, yes, yes, we are fine. Shocked at the circumstances surrounding the loss of father, but otherwise, we are fine," snapped Tobias, "Have you been listening to what I've just said Mater?"

"Every word Tobias," she said calmly, "Tobias, please do stop calling me 'mater' … then, taking another deep breath to keep herself composed, she continued with a slight edge of anger to her voice, "I fucking well hate that name!"

The swear word hung between them like a bad smell. Tobias was utterly stunned, shocked that his mother could utter such a word, never before had he ever heard his mother use that sort of gutter language.

Rachel, rather pleased with herself, continued whilst she was feeling so fearless.

"I don't care what you say about that dreadful man Nail Ismay, he's not stepping over the threshold of my house, and it is my house, not yours, not Nail's, it's my house," she said deliberately emphasising the word 'My'. "He is fired as my solicitor, you can keep him on if you want him to look after your affairs, that's your choice, but he's not going to be employed by me, not now, not ever, and for your information, I have already appointed a new solicitor."

"Mother!" Tobias decided to try a different approach. "You are obviously very stressed out and upset and losing all rational thought, and I can understand that. You were so devoted to father, and now he's gone, I sympathise that you must be feeling utterly lost and confused."

Rachel had already had enough, she was gaining stature as the conversation went on, interrupting Tobias angrily, "Now you listen to me, you condescending little prick, you maybe my son but I've had my fill of the way you and your father treated me over the years, and now in his demise, I am damned if you are going to carry on where he left off! Don't treat me like an imbecile. I know exactly what I'm doing, I know a hell of a lot about your father's affairs, a damn sight more than you think!"

Tobias wanted to calm down the situation quickly. "Ok Mother, have it your own way, we can discuss this in more detail when Emily and I come down for the funeral." Tobias was confident that he would win in a face to face confrontation. But then, with the next revelation, Rachel took the wind completely out his sails.

"Ah yes, the funeral. I understand you'll want to be at your father's funeral but don't expect to see me because I won't be there, I've left all the arrangements in the hands of the Jehovah's Funeral Director and my new solicitor's office."

"What?" he screamed, "Have you actually gone crazy?"

"Not at all, in fact, quite the opposite. I'll be in Switzerland with my new lawyer sorting out your father's financial affairs and bank accounts."

"Switzerland? Are you living in dreamland? Father never had any financial ties in Switzerland!" Tobias groaned, he was fast losing patience, convinced that his mother had gone completely off her rocker.

"Tobias, I obviously need to repeat myself when I say that I know a lot more about your father's affairs than you do. As for attending his funeral, no, I'm not going to be there. There was no love lost between your father and me, well certainly not on my part, he'd kept me as an emotional prisoner for years. I put up with a lot Tobias, more than you'll ever know … I'm not a young woman, and time is not on my side, so I fully intend living life to the full, and now that your father has left me a very wealthy woman, I thoroughly intend to do just that. As I said before, I'll be in Switzerland, of course, you're very welcome to stay here in my absence."

"Mater!" shrieked Tobias, "what about the arrangements for father's funeral?"

"Speak to Brother Stewart Frobisher at the local Kingdom Hall, you know him well enough, he is taking care of everything on my behalf," and before Tobias could reply, she continued triumphantly, "please give my love to Emily … charming girl, what on earth she sees in you, I don't know. Goodbye, Tobias".

Rachel gasped a sigh of relief. She could hardly believe what she had just said out loud; it was a moment she would never forget, the first time in her life that she actually had the courage to stand up to her domineering psychologically brutal son. Rachel felt good, this was the moment her inner strength awoke from its slumbers.

Bob Somers was duly cremated, the only family members to attend the service were Tobias and Emily. Bob didn't have any living relatives, and judging from the turnout at the funeral, it appeared he didn't have many friends either. Several fellow Jehovah's Witness Brothers and Sisters, including Nail Ismay attended out of respect for a fellow Jehovah rather than a gesture of genuine friendship. Richard Hartling had sent along his PA, Susan, accompanied by his bodyguard, Tim Spinks and Bob's PA/Secretary.

Tobias was understandably incandescent with rage at the absence of his mother and took his anger out on Emily. Whenever she sniffed at the obvious sadness of the occasion, Tobias could be heard whispering, "Be quiet!" and "Stop that snivelling Emily, you hardly knew my father!"

He spoke at length with Nial Ismay, who was on the charm offensive, hoping that he could somehow change events and get himself back on board as the family solicitor. Tobias promised Nial that he would do his utmost to get back in control of his mother. They even discussed the idea of having her sectioned under the Mental Health Act, to which, Nail said he would look into the protocols for starting such proceedings.

Tobias and Emily spent a few days at Rachel's home before heading back to Scotland. It was two days of rage for Tobias who had expected to see his mother and have a 'face to face' discussion to find out exactly what was going on. Tobias, like his father, was a control freak, and like all of his ilk, he hated not being in command. The sheer audacity displayed by his mother, demonstrating her newfound independence, infuriated him. This wasn't the mother he had known, the weak simpering little woman who answered to both himself and his father's beck and call. He'd already had several telephone calls with Nial Ismay, expanding their discussion of the possibility of having his mother committed to a sanatorium. Whether she was insane or not, he wanted to get his hands on his father's money and estate.

Chapter 69

Tobias was furious at having to arrange things by telephone; he knew that he'd never get anywhere with his mother unless he confronted her face to face. The situation was driving him to the point of exhaustion, so he decided to bide his time and go back to see her when she returned from her escapade in Switzerland. Switzerland also fuelled his anger, he thought he'd been close to his father, but there had never been any mention of bank accounts there. So what 'fool's errand' his mother was on out there, left him baffled. To get answers, he needed to get Nial Ismay back in the ring to take over his father's estate, and then he would be back in control, reigning in his mother. One thing he had discovered, whist rummaging through his father's study, was a letter from a local travel agent outlining his mother's itinerary for her Switzerland trip. Adding to his frustration and anger, the itinerary revealed that both his mother and a Michelle Dunbar were travelling Swiss Air First Class. She had been spending his father's money before he was even laid to rest!

Some weeks passed. Tobias was kept occupied by the demands of his Government post before he could find time to take some days off from the office. His discussions with Nial about having his mother committed had come to nothing. Nial had approached Rachel's family doctor, who, despite being a fellow Jehovah and friend of Nail, had poured cold water on the very idea that Rachel Somers had any mental health issues. Rachel had only consulted her GP once in the last six years. The GP politely informed Nial that Rachel's patient history was protected by the patient confidentially charter. If Nial did indeed suspect that something was wrong with Rachel's mental wellbeing, then he'd have to come forward with some robust evidence and not just the raving accusations from her son.

Nial fed this back to Tobias, which only added to his determination to somehow, by fair means or foul, find or fabricate evidence to have his mother committed under the Mental Health Act. On reflection though, this route was obviously strewn with hurdles so Tobias came up with a Plan 'B'. He planned a second visit to see his mother, but this time he would arrive a couple of days earlier than she expected him. This was in the hope of catching her 'on the hop' preventing her from avoiding him, or so he thought. He also arranged to have Nial attend the house shortly after his arrival with suitably drawn up transfer documents for signature. His plan was to confront his mother, together with Nial, and between the two of them he felt sure he would be able to persuade Rachel that it was in her best interests to allow him and Nial to take charge of the estate. They would argue that it was far beyond her capabilities to organise any finances, releasing her of the burden and worry, allowing it to be managed by them whilst paying her a substantial income for life, this along with allowing her to stay in the marital home for the remainder of her years.

Tobias informed his mother of his impending visit to see her but was less than truthful with his dates of travel. Knowing how timid his mother was, despite her recent show of bravado, he felt certain that his mother might make some spurious arrangement not the be there. Tobias was enthusiastically buoyed up with his plan to outwit his mother. Confident that once meeting her face to face, along with Nial, he could have the showdown he so wanted for eventually gaining his own way, reigning her in and getting control of his father's estate. The estate that he felt was rightly his despite what his father's will stipulated. However, luck played into Rachel's hands when the Gnomes of Zurich requested her presence again, along with her solicitor, to 'sign off' papers which would transfer Bob's assets into her name. Despite the impending arrival of Tobias, Rachel felt justified in not putting off a second visit to Switzerland, knowing she would be back a few days before Tobias' visit. She therefore went ahead with her arrangements to travel to Switzerland, unaware of the trap that Tobias had set to catch her unprepared and which would now, of course, back fire spectacularly. Once everything had been 'signed-off' she would feel happy in the security that it would give her the 'whip hand,' she would be in control of Bob's Estate, not Tobias. There was also the added enjoyment of gaining another small victory over Tobias by not being there when he arrived. She had decided she would confront Tobias as and when convenient to her and from a position of strength.

Tobias, along with Emily, although very much against her wishes, flew into Gatwick, taking a hire car for the drive to see Rachel. Emily had been witnessing the burning anger and frustration building up in Tobias since his father's death. Being around Tobias at the moment was like walking on eggshells, he had become snappy and irritable to the point that they maintained a silent truce. However, he had become surprisingly cheerful with the impending visit to see his mother, a change in his attitude which, whilst welcomed by Emily, she did not understand what had brought this about, but then Tobias had not shared with her his plan to catch out his mother. Emily's emotions swayed between feelings for her husband and sympathy for her mother-in-law. Since marrying into the Somers' family, she had seen at first hand the treatment that Rachel had endured from both her late father-in-law and husband. Emily had once considered that Tobias could be bi-polar, such was his demeanour, a trait she had only noticed since marrying him.

When he announced a visit to see his mother, Emily rather hoped it wouldn't include her and wished she had been able to come up with some excuse to get out of accompanying him and having some time and space to herself, but that was not to be. As Tobias drove the hire car into the large drive, which swept in front and around to the back of the house, he quickly noticed a small Renault van parked just outside the kitchen door. "What the devil is that...mater doesn't drive?" he muttered, more to himself than actually expecting a reply from Emily, she knew better than to pass any comment where his mother was concerned.

Tobias carefully parked the hired Vauxhall Senator alongside the van. They exited the car, Emily, with a deep sigh knowing that Tobias despite his recent change was probably about to erupt with anger at his mother. They walked towards the kitchen door, a stable door type construction, of which the top half was wide open allowing in the warm sunlight that bathed the rear of the house. Unexpectedly, a lady appeared at the door dressed in a lightweight smock type working coat. In her mid-50's with dark, glossy hair pulled back into a bun. Her rich, dark tanned, friendly round face had a southern Mediterranean look, her dark features were accentuated by flawless white teeth, perfect for a toothpaste advert. Her bright smile was welcoming as she wiped her hands on a tea-towel before opening the bottom half of the door to greet Emily and Tobias.

"Hello, you must be Tobias and Emily," she held out her right hand, which Tobias ignored, but Emily moved forward and took it with a smile.

Tobias was planted to the spot, "Who are you?" he demanded in his best authoritative tone.

"My name is Anna. I'm Mrs. Somers' new housekeeper come secretary."

Tobias exploded. "Housekeeper ... secretary!? What the hell does Mater need a housekeeper and secretary for? She's perfectly capable of looking after herself. I'm afraid you've been mistakenly employed. I'm assuming this van is yours, you can pack your things into it and leave, you are not required, and naturally, you'll receive any outstanding pay."

Emily went to interject politely, to avoid embarrassing the housekeeper, but Anna raised her hand towards Emily in acknowledgement that she was probably coming to her defence, and firmly replied.

"Yes, Mrs. Somers said that you would probably say something along those lines, and naturally I am to ignore your rudeness and bad manners as I am employed by Mrs. Somers and not you, Sir."

Anna was emphasising the 'Sir' in such a way that while not being insolent, it left the recipient in no doubt that it wasn't meant respectfully. Tobias was momentarily lost for words, and Emily stepped in to apologise for Tobias.

"Hello Anna, we are pleased to meet you, it's just that Tobias, my husband, didn't realise that mother had employed a housekeeper and he is rather taken by surprise."

Tobias silently glared at Emily's politeness before pushing past Anna and shouting, "Where is my mother?" Anna stood to one side, politely allowing Emily to follow.

"She is in Switzerland Mr. Somers," replied Anna. "Mrs. Somers left me instructions to cater for your needs in her absence, so I've made a lasagne for dinner tonight to be served with fresh salad from the garden. The large guest room which overlooks the garden is all made up, ready for you."

"Good god!" cried out Tobias, realising that his mother had thwarted him yet again.

"What is she doing there now!" he shrieked.

"She is there with her solicitor, I believe to do with your late father's estate," replied Anna calmly, deliberately missing the 'Sir' demonstrating that she was not going to be intimidated by Rachel's arrogant son.

Emily stood to one side; her emotions were mixed. On the one hand, she was concerned for her husband, whose recent actions led her to worry that he could heading for a stroke. Then on the other, she was slightly amused that, once again, Rachel, the hitherto downtrodden little woman, had pulled a fast one over her son, whether by design or coincidence. Tobias felt he was losing a grip of the situation, how dare his mother not inform him of her actions.

"Well," attempting to hide the sarcasm in his voice, "as her secretary, do you know exactly what she is doing there?"

Anna returned to the kitchen workbench, busying herself preparing a salad for dinner, "Signing papers, I believe, to release your late father's assets to Mrs. Somers," she replied politely, avoiding eye contact.

Tobias felt he was falling deeper and deeper into a quagmire. He desperately needed to speak to his mother to find out what was going on in Switzerland. He'd always thought he was very close to his father, while mentally acknowledging that there was obviously a few fragments about his father's life and times that he was unaware of, he was infuriated that, apparently, his mother was very aware.

Tobias huffed as he left the kitchen and wandered through the hallway and into the huge lounge. He was seething with rage as it would appear his plan was unravelling. Meanwhile, Emily tried to build bridges with Anna, apologising for her husband's tactlessness and rudeness.

"That's alright," replied Anna as she tidied up around the kitchen. "Mrs. Somers is such a nice lady, it's a shame she doesn't see eye to eye with her son."

Emily kept her voice in a low whisper. "It's all to do with his father's estate, Toby doesn't think his mother has the necessary knowledge or experience to be dealing with those things ... I'm guessing there is a lot Toby doesn't know which is annoying him intensively. In fact, I am becoming increasingly worried about him."

"Oh, I'm sure Mrs Somers' solicitor is advising her well. Ms. Dunbar seems like a lady who knows her stuff and is very much in control. I heard she is an excellent solicitor, even I was going to speak to her about my pension, as my dear departed left me a little nest egg, and I should really make provisions for my son and daughter."

Emily nodded in silent agreement wanting to change the subject, fearful that Tobias may be within earshot. His recent actions convinced her that he was becoming paranoid. With her thoughts, Emily needed some fresh air. It was such a lovely day, so she took her leave and went outside for a wander through the magnificent rear garden and paddock area.

Emily needn't have worried about Tobias hearing her, he was in the lounge, deep in thought and about to telephone Nial. He stood, staring out of the window across the front garden, his mind elsewhere. His thoughts were interrupted by a sizeable equine lorry, emblazoned with the name of a horse transport company, steadily manoeuvring backward into the front-drive.

Tobias was momentarily mesmerised by the vehicle's arrival, then he saw the driver jump down from the cab, walk to the rear of the lorry to commence lowering the huge ramp. This galvanised Tobias into action, he left the lounge, crossed the vast entrance hall, opened the front door, and called to the driver as he walked briskly towards him.

"Hey, you! Hold on there, what do you think are you doing?"

"Just delivering the hoss, you were expecting guv'nor," replied the driver casually as he continued to release the rear door retaining chains and bolts.

First, a housekeeper, now a horse, things were really getting out of hand. The housekeeper he would have to stomach, but a horse? Whatever was his mother up to? This was insane.

"Look, there must be some mistake, we aren't expecting a horse, we haven't even got any stables."

The driver sighed, returned to his cab retreiving a clip board and removing a document which he offered to Tobias, "Look guv'nor, here are my instructions".

Tobias read the paperwork, a bill of sale clearly stating the purchase of a horse named 'Red Rosco' purchased by Mrs. Rachel Somers, to be delivered to 'The Pastures' on Redding Lane.

"This is The Pastures, Redding Lane innit?" enquired the driver, calmly trying not to sound as though he was addressing the village idiot as Tobias handed back the paperwork to the driver.

"Yes," snapped Tobias, confused. "But you'll have to take it back, you see we don't have any room, and there's been a terrible mistake. My mother is not herself, she had no right to purchase this horse."

The driver was now beginning to think he was dealing with the 'Clampits', as some apparently simple country folk were referred to. The nick name taken from a 60's TV sitcom all about American Hill Billy Country Folk.

"Well, that as it maybe but, I ain't takin' it back, I'm a horse transporter see, that's what I do." He pointed at the sign writing on the lorry. "Byron Brothers Horse Transporters, that's me and after I have left this hoss 'ere, I'm off to some stables in Godalming to collect a couple of hosses for transport to Newbury, guvnor. Time is dosh and this hoss as to be left 'ere, that's what I've been contracted to do."

From inside the lorry the horse neighed and kicked, as if knowing it had arrived at its new home, anxious to get out of the confines of the horse box.

Tobias shook his head. "This is a fucking joke," he started to yell, "look, driver, don't you understand we've no room for a fucking horse, so whatever it costs, I'll pay you to take the fucking thing away!"

Just then, Emily appeared from around the side of the house. Witnessing Tobias making a scene, Emily called out, "Toby, calm down darling, there's obviously no mistake, there is a newly built stable at the rear of the house, in fact there are three, and it looks as though more are going to be built".

"What!" he yelled as he turned angrily to Emily. Just at that moment another car, a Mini Cooper, came racing into the driveway, skidding slightly, giving the air of being late for an appointment as it abruptly parked at the side of the house. Out jumped a young lady dressed in jodhpurs and a blue sweater. Slightly built, but with a shapely figure, flowing blonde hair, a clear, bright complexion with blushing cheeks and pixy features.

She quickly grabbed a riding helmet and crop from the rear of the mini before running across the drive towards the lorry, "So sorry I'm late, everyone," she said, catching her breath, "but just in time I see," she smiled.

The driver was relieved to see someone he recognised, "No worries, Miss Ryder, you're here now, that's all that matters as we seem to be 'aving a problem," he nodded his head in Tobias' direction.

Before the driver could explain the problem, Tobias rudely addressed the young lady.

"Who the hell are you?"

"Hi, I'm Poppy Ryder, Mrs. Somers' new groom," sensing that this man was not pleased to see her, she didn't bother extending her hand in greeting. Poppy, too, had been briefed by Rachel as to what to expect from her son.

"What the fuck, first a housekeeper, now a horse and groom," Tobias said, to nobody in particular. He was beginning to wish he had stayed in Scotland.

Emily interjected. "Toby, there is no misunderstanding, your mother is obviously expecting the horse, that is why she has had a stable block built behind the garage."

Emily turned her attention to Poppy and held out her hand, "Poppy Ryder? I thought I recognised your name, you've been chosen for the Olympic dressage team, haven't you?"

"Yes, that's right," smiled Poppy taking Rachel's hand and smiling warmly. "Mrs. Somers has agreed to be my main sponsor."

Tobias stared at his wife as though she had suddenly grown horns, "What the fuck! Since when have you taken an interest in bloody dressage and fucking horses?"

Emily and the others just ignored the comment.

By now, Anna, the housekeeper, had also arrived on the scene, confirming that she too had been expecting the horse to be delivered.

Tobias turned to Emily, gritting his teeth, "Well seeing you know this young lady and know so much about bloody equine matters, you can fucking well sort this shit out!"

With that, he stormed back into the house and went straight to a small cabinet, hidden in a corner of the lounge, where he knew his father kept a couple of bottles of malt whisky for entertaining purposes. Tobias had the awful feeling that he was losing touch with reality.

Missing dinner, and not used to alcohol, Tobias proceeded to get gloriously drunk. He was in a state of total collapse by the time Rachel arrived home from Switzerland later that same evening. Seeing her self-righteous son in an alcoholic coma, the empty whisky bottle on the floor alongside him, she felt that finally, she was rid of the 'Somer's curse' and in control of her own destiny.

Rachel lived the good life after the death of Bob and was determined to make up for what she saw as 'lost time' in her loveless marriage. Bob had left her extremely wealthy and her new found independence had enabled her to grow in stature, and thus she had become an emotionally strong woman and more than a match for her belligerent son, Tobias. He had been infuriated him even further when she entered into a serious relationship with an Irish Race Horse trainer, Sebastiàn O'Neil, a widower who had lost his beloved wife of many years following a tragic horse riding accident. Rachel found a man who adored her, treated her as an equal, giving her adulation, along with the warmth of love and affection which had been so absent in her marriage to Bob. For Sebastiàn, he had discovered a lovely charming lady that replaced what he had once thought was his irreplaceable wife. Together, they had found a second chance and neither of them would allow the belligerent Tobias to burst their bubble of love.

Tobias chose to stay in Scotland, quietly seething at how things had turned out, his dark moods put a severe strain on his marriage to Emily. He only acknowledged his mother with Christmas and birthday cards; Rachel was happy to accept this estrangement following the years in which he and his father had treated her so despicably. Emily, tiring of the sullen Tobias and his depressive moods, had thrown down the gauntlet that unless he was prepared to visit his mother and make amends, then she would leave the marital home. This had spurred Tobias on and he paid a surprise visit to his mother, not so much under the threats from Emily but with the misguided view that he should at least take another chance to turn the situation to his advantage. Upon arrival, he discovered that Sebastiàn was visiting and the housekeeper was having a day off, thus disturbing a romantic and spontaneous matinee session for the couple, making love when the opportunity arose. When Rachel and Sebastiàn realised they had been caught in *'flangrante delicto'* they mischievously chose to rub salt into sore wounds, deliberately delaying greeting Tobias. Rachel had offered her cheek in a motherly fashion, which Tobias ignored and losing all rationale he exploded. It was a total anathema to Tobias, his ageing mother sleeping with another man. He just couldn't bring himself to picture the idea; he saw it as a disgusting pornographic act. Consequently, he vented his rage, starting by accusing his mother's lover of being a gold digger. Sebastiàn just shrugged this off with a casual wave of the hand, as he was anything but, running his own very successful and highly lucrative horse training business, constantly feted by wealthy race horse owners from home and abroad. When Tobias then went on to accuse his mother of being a whore it was a step too far for Sebastiàn. He was a man who kept himself very fit and was easily able to take Tobias by the scruff of his neck and physically eject him from the house, depositing him on the drive with the words *'Don't come back until you learn some manners and apologise to Rachel'*. Rachel had watched on dispassionately, impressed at having a man defend her honour was a new and thrilling experience for her. Tobias, being the cowardly creep slinked away with his tail between his legs, it would be several years before they spoke again. Following the hasty assisted departure of Tobias, Rachel and Sebastiàn went back to bed where Sebastiàn made passionate and tender love to Rachel, inducing orgasms of which she had never experienced in her life! Sebastiàn and Rachel married later that year with the only guests on Rachel's side being her housekeeper, Richard and Caroline Hartling, Charles and Susan Barrington-Smythe and her daughter-in-law, Emily. Naturally, she was disappointed and saddened that Tobias didn't attend but accepted the situation for what it was, comforting herself that in life there are many families from all sections of society, even Royalty, where internal feuds cause unfortunate situations. In consolation, Sebastiàn made her a very happy woman; she lived a life of bliss which more than made up for the years of purgatory she had suffered at the hands of her ex-husband and son.

Chapter 70

L aying some 6,000 nautical miles south by sea from Northwold is the west coast of the continent of Africa. Here, steaming jungles, rivers, and mango swamps are infested with saltwater crocodiles and man-eating snakes. In contrast, the jungle mass is habitat to a huge array of infection carrying insects that feast on the unprotected skin and flesh of folk that would venture into this inhospitable environment where the chances of survival would be minimal. It was some ten years previously that into this unwelcoming territory the unfortunate CCAB pilot Steve Gaunt crashed on that fateful night when his 'mercy' aeroplane was brought down by a dreadful tropical storm. Despite the numerous Search and Rescue attempts, neither Steve's body or the aircraft was ever recovered; due to misinformation, the search teams had been looking in the wrong place. It was a couple of months after the accident as events unfolded that brought this sad fact to light, thus allowing the line to be drawn under his loss.

Time passed and the disappearance of Steve Gaunt had become consigned to history with the acceptance that his body would never be recovered, decomposing to eventually be eaten up by the jungle and its inhabitants. The details of Steve's disappearance sadly remained notable for that fact that it had been the only death of a CCAB pilot on active service. However, despite the passage of time, the mystery of Steve Gaunt's fate was to unravel due to the persistence of a young French missionary doctor, Marcel Dubreck, who had devoted his young life, since qualifying, to help the indigenous natives of the area, determined to bring to them the benefits of modern medicine and health care.

The medical team from the French medical charity, Medicine Sans Frontiers, had on their list of objectives an aim to penetrate the depths of this part of West Africa. The interior was hot, humid and dark, a mosquito-infested breeding ground of tropical rain forest jungle, riddled with rancid evil-smelling mango swamps. It had become a personal quest for the medical team leader, Dr. Marcel Dubreck, to get through to the little known Ashundo tribe, who had shunned interference from the outside world. Marcel was a man on a mission. While studying medicine at university in France, he became deeply moved when learning about the plight of people in these emerging countries that the rest of the world appeared to have forgotten. His Christian and left-wing social conscience were determined to do something about it. He was following in his father's footsteps by taking a career in medicine, but that was where any similarity ended. In a way, Marcel despised his father for what he did, selling his wonderful God-given gift of medicine to those least in need of it. His father had made himself into a wealthy man by private practice, fawning to the rich and famous of Paris high society. Whereas Marcel felt he had been chosen to repay humankind for giving him this gift by spending his life healing others. Working with 'Medicine Sans Frontier' offered him the ideal way to fulfil his desire to make a difference.

Missionaries who had visited this particular part of the dark continent brought back tales of cannibalism still being practiced amongst the Ashundo tribe. They told alarming stories of Black Magic and ungodly, perverse sexual practices. The lack of proper medical facilities often produced stillborn children, and if the stories were true, many had been cooked and eaten at the encouragement of the tribal Witch Doctors as a form of worship to their Gods. Marcel took all this with a pinch of salt but acknowledged that there often could be no smoke without a fire. He was driven by a passion for exploring to find and provide these jungle people with the benefit of modern medicine.

The Ashundo tribe was also believed to have been responsible for some recent acts of piracy; how they had become involved in this type of criminality was a mystery, especially when considering their apparent shunning of all the trappings of the modern world. Nobody seemed to know the truth, but then in this part of Africa communications and intelligence were still in the dark ages. Either way, Marcel was determined to try and make contact with the tribe and set up a clinic in their village.

It took over a week for Marcel and his team to find their way through the thick, evergreen jungle. It was a long, hard slog of days hacking their way through. It would have been marginally easier if they had just walked, but the group needed their six 4x4 Landrover vehicles, being the only way to transport all the required medical equipment. The team had to fight for every yard through the solid wall of jungle to make a path wide enough for their Landrovers to pass through. This meant back-breaking work in tremendous humidity, removing roots of the extensive vegetation as well as hacking away at the greenery. The jungle was a maze of mango swamps, full of gooey, slimy mud. The thick, treacle-like substance oozed around the Landrovers' axles. When they thought it couldn't possibly get any worse, they came across a wide, fast-flowing river. After all of their efforts, they finally felt beaten. A river crossing would take too much time and effort, they would need to either build a bridge or construct a raft to take their vehicles across, and they didn't have the equipment to do either. Marcel and his team felt defeated, the aerial photos taken for the reconnaissance of the area hadn't shown a river large enough to have caused a problem for them. The overhanging umbrella of vegetation had obviously hidden this unmapped river from the aerial photographers.

The team unanimously agreed to 'recce' the banks in both directions in the hope of finding a shallow crossing point before they decided to abandon the expedition altogether. It was to the group's amazement that, after an afternoon struggling along the bank in a northerly direction, they came across a bridge, not only that but a reasonably passable track on either side of the small river leading to and from the bridge. This was astonishing as it wasn't marked on any of their charts or maps. It was bewildering as the track back into the jungle appeared to be paralleling the route they had laboriously hewn out of the dense jungle. Although the vegetation was beginning to reclaim some of the track, it had obviously been used in the not too distant past and could have been easily navigated by their Landrovers. This was an amazing and exciting find, but at the same time, frustrating that they had not discovered it earlier. All that was left was to test the wooden bridge structure to ensure it could take the weight of their vehicles and equipment. The initial, tentative inspection concluded that the bridge appeared in reasonable shape. Still, to be sure, the group decided to lighten the load of the vehicles by manhandling the lose equipment across the bridge. Tedious but essential, rather than being over-eager to cross, possibly damaging the bridge or losing a Landrover into the river. With just the drivers left in each vehicle, they gradually eased them across to be loaded up again when safely on the other side. Their caution paid off and, apart from the occasional heart-stopping crack as the structure took the weight, all vehicles and equipment were safely across. As for their return journey, well as the old saying goes, 'They would cross that bridge when they came to it'.

Having crossed the river and finding that the other track went roughly in the direction they need to go, they made good progress and after just one further night stop, they eventually discovered the tribal village.

When they found the tribe, it was evident that they were much further advanced in the ways of the west than Marcel had expected, some surprisingly spoke English.

Far from facing reluctance and aggression from the tribal leaders, they welcomed Marcel and his team with open arms. So much for rumours spread by the African jungle drums! However, after settling in with the

Ashundo people, talk around the campfire one night spoke of a 'white man' they knew. They recalled they had found him years ago after the big storm; he'd been washed up on to a coastal beach nearby, strapped into the remains of an aircraft. The majority of the plane had broken up and washed out to sea, leaving minimal trace other than odds and ends, which they proudly showed Marcel and his team. There was a large undercarriage wheel, some tools, a couple of seats, now used in one of their huts, and various other paraphernalia. The white man had been injured with some broken bones, all which they had treated with their rudimentary medicine and he had made a full recovery. The man had no recollection of the crash and no idea how he came to be in the jungle. They tried to tell him about the plane showing him the parts they had recovered, but it didn't help.

"Where is the white-man now?" enquired Marcel.

The tribal elders went very quiet, showing some reluctance to explain what had happened. After some coaxing, the truth came out. The village had been attacked by a gang of 'Boko Haram guerrillas' they'd kidnapped all the local girls as well as the white man. This fitted in to place as Marcel had noticed the lack of young girls in the village. The Ashundo were frightened of Boko Haram and had offered no resistance. Since that day, nearly a year ago, the Ashundo tribe had not seen the white-man or the Boko Haram again. Some African Union soldiers had come and gone in search of the Boko Haram, but that was all they knew. To Marcel, that would probably account for the track and the bridge which had appeared to have been reasonably well-constructed. It was just a pity that communications were so poor that he had not been told of the incident. As for the white man's fate, well, that was out of his hands. By now, he was probably dead. Marcel knew of the Boko Haram terrorist organisation affiliated to Al Qaeda. It was known that captured westerns didn't last long in their hands. The fact that Boko Haram was obviously still out there made Marcel's job all the more difficult.

Consequently, he and his team decided to get back to their base as quickly as possible so they could then return at a later date with the protection of soldiers of the African Union Force. Having the jungle road made their return to their base uneventful and much quicker. Upon his return as a matter of course, he reported his findings to his superiors from where it was past to the British Embassy in Paris. There, the file was marked as routine and would have been filed away, probably to be forgotten entirely, however as it was winding its way through the bureaucratic channels accumulating the initials of bored clerical assistants before it crossed the desk of one very inquisitive administrative officer on the lookout for any information to help her climb the career ladder. The young lady in question, an English degree student, had joined the Foreign & Commonwealth Office to become a career diplomat; she was also a budding part-time author. Her overactive imagination had run wild while reading this file, and she considered that this intriguing 'snippet' was too good to be accidentally overlooked. It recorded that a white man was living with a tribe deep in the African jungle, and the budding author in her thought, 'you couldn't make it up better than this'.

Vitally, the information eventually found its way through the labyrinth of official channels and into the realms of the British Intelligence services, where it was tabled at a meeting of the Joint Chiefs of Staff. Coincidently, the Royal Marines Special Boat Squadron was about to mount a clandestine anti-piracy operation in the very area that the white man had apparently been observed. The number of pirate attacks had become an embarrassment for the British Government on this coastline, ruled for many years as part of the once vast British Empire. Too many British flagged ships had been attacked, their crews robbed, and, in one recent case, a British ship's master who had attempted to resist was murdered. Furthermore, there was still one British ship missing, a bunker replenishment tanker along with its sixteen-man crew and the Master's wife. No doubt, now hidden somewhere amongst the sprawling fingers of rivers and inlets in the mango swamps.

The SBS mission came under the auspices of 'Black Ops' with the aim to take down as many of the pirates as possible. Any that may survive the onslaught would hopefully spread the word sufficiently to put a stop to their criminality. Well, that was the theory! Doubtful, as there was big money to be made in hi-jacking commercial vessels with valuable cargoes. Arrests were really not an option, handing prisoners over to the local authorities would inevitably mean they would be released with no further action, such was the level of corruption in that part of the world. It had long been suspected that a large organisation of some description was behind the attacks as the pirates were too well informed, organised and equipped. Hence the operation was to be carried out in total secrecy so as not to attract international reaction, which would in all probability bring out condemnation from the United Nations. It wasn't a decision that had been taken lightly, having authorisation from the Prime Minister himself, which, if it all went wrong, could see him charged as a war criminal at The

Hague! The right-wing press in the UK had already had a field day making the British Government look impotent and useless. The recent cuts in the Royal Navy surface fleet hadn't helped either, with their meagre resources stretched to the limit. The stalwarts of the British Establishment had warned the Government that the continuing decline of the British Armed forces was a weakness. The lawlessness, which had broken out in these coastal countries since independence from the British Crown, was seen as a slap in the face to the establishment. Instead of dodging the issue, the PM had been persuaded to demonstrate some backbone and allow the military to be resolute in dealing a decisive blow to the pirates in an effort to stem their murderous regime. After all, this was the twentieth-first century, not the days of sailing ships and Blackbeard, although it might as well be so, as the pirates were enjoying the freedom to roam and attack ships at will with impunity. Back in the days of Blackbeard, the Royal Navy had far more leeway in upholding the law and protecting Britain's interests without the fear of retribution or condemnation.

Now hopefully, for some of these lawless pirate gangs the day of reckoning had come.

Chapter 71

Shortly after Dr. Marcel Dubreck and his team had emerged from the jungle, lying some distance off the same part of that jungle coast line was the Royal Navy's Commando Logistics HQ vessel *HMS Engadine*. Known as an LPD, or Landing Platform Dock. A ship designed with massive accommodation forward, behind which there was an extended flight deck capable of operating helicopters and beneath this a huge dock which could be flooded, as required, allowing specialised beach landing craft to float out bearing landing forces. Onboard, inside the colossal hangar space behind the two Merlin helicopters neatly parked alongside each other, there was a purpose-designed briefing room with several easels holding navigation charts and aerial reconnaissance photographs of this area of West Africa and a drop-down screen for projecting films and photographs. Arranged in front of these were rows of seats occupied by some thirty members of British Special Forces of the Royal Marines Special Boat Service, 550 Assault Squadron or simply known as 'five, fifty' within the cadre of the Royal Marines. Standing at the front, facing the group, along with his swagger stick, was the Officer Commanding, Lieutenant Colonel Brian Villiers, a father figure to the younger men of the troop and a wise councillor to the older veterans. This individual despite his advancing years, at 45 years old, he was still an elite soldier, a lean, six-footer, wiry framed with rock hard muscles. His craggy, tanned facial features sported a crooked nose; an injury picked up on some clandestine operation many years previously. His eyes were steel blue, his head topped off by a mop of jet black hair with just the traces of grey appearing at the edges of his forehead and sideburns. His steely eyes were such an outstanding feature with their piercing and penetrating stare contrasting with his dark sun-tanned face; he had picked up the simple nickname of 'Blue Eyes'.

On the rare occasions that he had to admonish someone or refuse a request, then his fixed stare and furrowed brow said it all. Villiers was a veteran of many secret operations. During one of which, he had picked up a serious injury leaving him with a limp, yet despite this, he could still *'yomp'* with the best of them, although he no longer went on active operations. He was now a strategic planner, staying behind to worry about his men while they carried out their orders. 'Blue Eyes' had led a dynamic career in the service of Her Majesty, a career that he had enjoyed, but not without its regrets. He'd met and married a wonderful woman who had borne him both a son and daughter. He regretted not always being around as they grew up. On one occasion, his son, who'd developed a wicked and sarcastic sense of humour, probably due to having being brought up in a military environment, once welcomed his father home from an overseas deployment with a smirk and the comment,

"Hi, who are you? Mum has always told us not to speak to strange men!"

Followed by the warm hugs and embraces that were entirely natural in the close-knit, loving family he had created, but that comment had haunted Villiers for years. Sadly, his lovely wife was taken from him by a drunken driver. The driver had received a custodial sentence; Villiers lost the irreplaceable love of his life. He'd sat in the public gallery the day the court had found the driver guilty of death by dangerous driving and listened impassively to the gasps and expressions of shock from the family of the driver when the judge had handed down a sentence of eleven years imprisonment. Following the guilty verdict, the court was advised that the defendant already had an outstanding three year suspended sentence for a previous conviction of causing serious injury by dangerous driving, giving a total sentence of fourteen years. However, unlikely he would serve the full term it did at least put into perspective what had, at first, appeared to be harsh sentence. Anything less, then Villiers would probably at some stage have taken the law into his own hands. He accepted the outcome philosophically, understanding that nothing in this life lasts forever be it good or bad.

His son and daughter had not been in court that day; they were still too traumatised by the loss. The death of his lovely wife and wonderful mother had come at a critical time in his children's lives as they approached the end of their high school education. He was naturally very proud of them, and despite the trauma of losing their mother, they went on to achieve top grades at school, followed by university, then both choosing careers in the uniform of Her Majesty. His son was serving with the Royal Navy and his daughter with the RAF. His son had chosen a career in dark blue because he didn't fancy the Army or Marine's soldiering way of life living out in the field. Laughable really as due to gaining his degree in languages, one of which was fluency in Arabic, he found himself on the ground in Afghanistan in military fatigues living in the very field conditions he wanted to stay away from! This role involved being side by side with the ground forces acting an interpreter, commonly known in the military parlance as a 'terp'.

At the same time, Villiers' daughter qualified as a Special Forces helicopter pilot, flying Chinooks, also in Afghanistan on clandestine operations and mercy medical missions dropping in groups of Special Forces or evacuating the wounded from the line of fire. Villiers preyed every day that his son and daughter would come home safe and sound. God forbid, even the loss of one of them would be more than he could endure. Thankfully, his prayers were answered, and they had both returned safely from Afghanistan, with no chance of them being re-deployed out there again as the withdrawal of Western combat troops and 'hand-over' to Afghan Security Forces had begun.

Lieutenant Colonel Villiers started his briefing late in the afternoon, while the ship was 'hove too'. The operation he was about to brief was aimed at eliminating a rather nasty group of pirates, associated with Boko Haram who had been causing mayhem in the Gulf of Guinea, hijacking and plundering merchant shipping. As night fell, the ship would be completely blacked out to avoid giving any chance of advance warning to the pirates encamped ashore. It was not unusual to see ships in this area as it was a busy shipping lane and consequently, a magnet for the pirates they were out to eliminate. But, as a grey funnel line ship, the common name for vessels of the Royal Navy, HMS 'Engadine' would no doubt attract unwanted attention, possibly resulting in 'spooking' the pirates to break camp and melt into the surrounding jungle.

So, Villiers, standing in front of a large scale map of the coastline, started his 'Black Ops Brief' indicating on the map the plan of the attack, the various landmarks, and points to look out for. First, a small advance party was to go ahead of the main assault group, they would sail around the small peninsular with the aim to get behind the pirate's camp. Here they would dig in and cut off any chance of retreat into the jungle that the pirates would be tempted to take when the main attack came. The hope was that the pirates would stand and fight, allowing his men to annihilate them with their overwhelming firepower.

"Ok gentlemen, settle down, listen up and pay attention, I will say this only once, right, Operation 'Clean Sweep', no explanation necessary," he grinned and continued,

"The advance party will go ashore from our main rendezvous point just offshore here, GPS co-ordinates on your handouts. They will make their way around this peninsular here and land near what we believe is a hijacked tanker. Any guards on the tanker will be neutralised for fear of raising the alarm to the main camp — stealth is the keyword on this operation, gentlemen. Remember officially, we are not here, and the African Union will be taking the credit for your successes and, of course, the flak in the unlikely event that you 'fuck up' and fail. But as the Iron Lady Margaret Thatcher once said during the Falklands escapade, 'Failure is not an option!"

Villiers paused, looking around at the anxious faces of his men. All with note books and pens at the ready were staring back at him impassively, waiting for him to continue.

"Okay, once the advance party have secured the tanker and the back door of the pirate camp, then at 0500 hours, the main force will attack under command of Captain Jones, assisted by Lieutenant Smith as 2 i/c," he raised his eyebrows, thinking back to the TV cowboy comedy series 'Alias Smith & Jones.'

He then handed out recent copies of satellite imagery showing the pirate village and surrounding jungle. He went on to describe the undergrowth, terrain, and obstacles they may meet.

"Study the photos well and get an overall view in your mind's eye; fortunately, you won't have to negotiate the route totally in the dark thanks to our friends from the Fleet Air Arm at Yeovilton providing the necessary drone imagery."

"Right now on that point, I'll hand you over to the Navy's drone outfit CO, Lieutenant Commander Robin Avery from 700 'X' Naval Air Squadron whose ScanEagle drone is responsible for the aerial photographs you have now in front of you...Robin will interpret the photos for you and explain a new device you'll be using on this mission."

The mention of a new device caused a ripple of murmuring amongst the assembled marines. Some thinking along the lines that with all this modern wizardry coming on line in the military, maybe they were going to be issued with a new sci-fi kit like a gamma-ray gun!

"So over to you, Commander", said Villiers moving to one side and sitting down as Lieutenant Cmdr Robin Avery walked up to stand in front of the audience.

"Thank you Colonel" as Robin came to stand behind a lectern which had suddenly appeared courtesy of one of the crew, then by the use of a handheld remote the room darkened and drone imagery appeared on the large screen that had silently lowered.

"Right gentleman, as you can see, the Pirate Camp is on this small peninsular sticking out into the sea from the surrounding mango swamps." As if by magic Robin Avery produced a slim extending silver metal stick and started indicating to the area at the tip of the peninsular as he continued,

"Although well camouflaged by the jungle you can see the heat source that is showing up giving a definitive outline of the camp which is in what the historians tell me were once buildings of a bygone era. Ironically from the days of previous pirating when the then modern propulsion was sail...so things haven't changed much in this part of the world!" he drew breath and continued, "the pirates have chosen well as the peninsular benefits from the cooling sea breezes taking away some of the awful humidity of the jungle. A lot more comfortable than being further inland amongst the mango swamps. This, of course, plays into our hands as we, well, I mean you guys, won't have to go far inland to carry out this operation. Now coming around to the north side of the peninsular, you can clearly see a ship which although camouflaged it is believed to be the recently hi-jacked bunker tanker, this being on charter from the UK to the Nigerian Government supplying bunker fuel to passing ocean-going ships so their owners could take advantage of favourable reduced off-shore tax rates."

Robin was indicating with his pointer as he continued, "As just briefed by your Colonel this is where the advance party will land".

"Once you've secured the pirate camp, released the hostages and provided medical treatment or other support they may require, the plan is to put them back on board their ship, which they can then hopefully sail away."

"This is the latest drone imagery that we have of the camp. As I said earlier, it's a derelict village dating back to days of Blackbeard and the Spanish Main. Intelligence and photographic interpreters of the RAF believe they have identified the buildings as thus, cookhouse and stores, living and sleeping quarters, and this one where we believe prisoners and hostages are being kept. There have been several attacks on ships recently in the Gulf of Guinea, all hostages have been released apart from this tanker and its crew. While some ship owners had coughed up and paid the ransom demanded by the pirates, the tanker company hasn't as yet. So we believe they are being kept here waiting for a ransom demand to be paid".

Captain Jones raised his hand to speak which was acknowledged by Lieutenant Commander Avery.

"Go ahead."

Standing up and introducing himself Captain Jones said, "Captain Jones, Royal Marines, assault group leader. The point I would like to make is this. Shouldn't the operation be delayed until any ransom money is paid thereby releasing the hostages before we go in? My thoughts are purely that if they aren't there anymore we have a freerer hand to deal with the pirates without the complications of having hostages who may get in the line of fire, not only that they would be witnesses?"

"Good point, but time is of the essence on this operation and due to many reasons, to start with politics which I won't bore you with, weather is another consideration, which is due to break anytime soon and apart from that this is being an intelligence led op and the 'spooks' at GCHQ have made the call on timing."

Captain Jones nodded acknowledging the comments made by the naval officer then sat down, a look on his face indicating that he was not totally convinced but had to accept the reasons given.

Villiers was then on his feet, "If I may interrupt Robin and add to that point as well?"

"Certainly Colonel."

Villiers continued, "I can see some of your concerns when it was mentioned that the hostages could be witnesses. Your thinking I'm sure is along the lines of this getting into the newpapers at some later stage and possible recriminations. Well let me try and put your mind at rest on this. Firstly if our intel and drone imagary is correct the hostages won't see much if anything of your attack as they are incarcerated in one of the buildings. Secondly and this is where the intel comes in, we don't believe the tanker owners have any intention of paying a ransom."

Villiers last comment bringing exclamations of astonishment and disbelief from the group, as he continued,

"Again I can see where you are coming from with your thinking, a British ship-owner throwing the ship's crew to the wolves as it were. Well to start with although this is a British ship flying the Red Ensign and with a British crew, that's where any similarity to the UK ends. The owner is actually a Russian gangster, for the want of a better word, a mate of our friend Putin, a right evil bastard who made his fortune during the first Afghanistan war when the Russians were there. This has obviously added to the urgency to try and get the Brits out of there before the pirates make an example and kill them as a sign to the wider maritime community as to the consequences of not paying ransom demands."

A general air of agreement went around the room as Villiers summed up.

"Finally and this is the clincher, what is about to happen, never happened, this is 'Black Ops' gentlemen and no record will be kept. So no heroics as there won't be any medals in it for you."

Villiers last comment lightening the tone of concern and bringing some stifled laughing from the group.

"On that note back to you Robin," said Lieutenant Colonel Viliers.

Lieutenant Commander Robin Avery then continued,

"Thanks Colonel,"

"Well now for the new 'gizmos' you are going to trial," said Robin Avery scanning their faces as they waited eagerly to be told about the latest innovation, adding an apparent new dimension to their exciting upcoming operation.

On cue, a Communication Leading Hand appeared at the lectern handing Robin Avery a box from which he produced small tablets. Holding one up above his head, "Each team leader will have one of these new tablets. They will be your link to the ScanEagle, which will be loitering above the campsite. Updated drone imagery will be downloaded to these little devices every few minutes, so you'll have a blow by blow overview as to what is happening. Colonel Villiers and I will, of course, also be watching, seeing the same view as you".

"Ok, that's all from me so I'll hand you back to your Boss, and he can allocate the tablets to the appropriate team leaders. I'll be back in the 'ops' room monitoring our ScanEagle drone."

With that, Lt. Cmdr Robin Avery left the room as the men started chatting amongst themselves.

Villiers once more took the floor.

He sighed deeply and continued, using the satellite imagery left on the display by CO of the drone squadron,

"Well you've all completed the jungle warfare course which we know can be a strange and fearsome place at best, moving and fighting in it can be a nightmare but in truth you've very little to fear from this particular environment. Fortunately, this peninsular, as Lieutenant Commander Avery pointed out, has been chosen well by the pirates as there are no mangrove swamps to worry about. However, no doubt masses of mosquitoes, so I hope you've all been taking your paludrine tablets issued by the medics?"

The assembled marines all nodded in unison, none of them would be so stupid as to ignore the medic's advice. Malaria was a disease to be avoided at all costs. The discovery of paludrine as a preventative measure was a god's send for anyone working in this type of environment.

"Ok, then, there's plenty of shrub like trees which will give excellent concealment as you creep up on the pirate camp which is here," Villiers pointing out the area on the satellite image.

"By the time you arrive at the edge of the pirate village our matey boys will undoubtedly and hopefully be crashed out under the influence of the local 'ganja' but we can't be a hundred percent sure that being the disorganised, murdering rabble they are, that they won't have sentries posted, or for that matter have placed 'booby traps' of some kind."

Villiers had attended a Jungle Warfare school during a secondment to the US military. He had learnt all about the horrors of the 'booby traps' that US forces had to endure in Vietnam. The way the Vietcong had dug pits and made use of simple wooden rollers armed with metal fish hooks imprisoning the feet and ankle of any GI unfortunate enough to step into it. One particular nasty trap being the falling door, hinged at the top, again armed with long vicious extended nails that on being activated, as an unsuspecting soldier entered, would drop down hitting the recipient full on the face and upper body. This trap usually proved to be fatal. He involuntarily shivered at the thought, bringing him back to the present with a start.

"Right, I'll hand out the tablets."

"Modern warfare, this is the future gentlemen," he commented as he took the mini-tablets from the box and handed them to the team leaders.

"I'm told that all you need to do is switch them on, and they will automatically search and lock on to the appropriate satellite signal. It should be so easy a child could do it, so even the more technical philistines amongst you shouldn't have a problem!" Bringing a mixture of groans and forced laughter as the marines gathered around their leaders for a look at the new gadget that should make life a lot easier for them.

As the marines busied themselves looking at the tablets, an internal telephone went off, which Villiers answered and acknowledged the caller.

"Right, listen up, I've just been informed by Lt. Cmdr Avery that they are ready to start live streaming. It might not be achievable on the tablets inside here as there is too much heavy metal in the way, so we'll discuss the overall plan looking at the main screen here, then we'll go on to the open deck and see how the tablets perform. The plan will take you and the RRC (Rigid Raiding Craft) into the coast by one of the LCVPs (Landing Craft Vehicle & Personnel) that is being loaded up as we speak. We don't want to take any chances taking the ship any closer as it would be bound to arouse suspicion and get the jungle drums going. At times news can travel fast, even in this primitive part of the world. You'll then launch from the LCVP at these co-ordinates." Villiers walked over to a large Admiralty sea chart of the area pinned up on one of the easels, "from here you can proceed inshore." He walked back in front of his men to the magnified satellite image of the shoreline and camp.

"Now, if, and I say again, if we do take prisoners, then you pass them on to the African Union soldiers who will be in your vanguard, they'll deal with them and the local authorities. Not there's much official authority in around here, but that's not our problem; just hand them over, and they'll not be your responsibility after that." Villiers stayed silent for a few moments to ensure that the 'if' had registered with the assembled marines, which he took that it had. The marines had heard that there were some African Union soldiers on board, but they had been kept separated on a different mess deck for reasons of secrecy. Most of the marines just assumed they were there as a form of diplomatic mission.

"Once the advance party has arrived and secured and sent the signal back to me aboard the LCVP, code words 'Doors Closed' at 0400hrs, then I will initiate the 'Go' for the main assault group which will then leave to hit the beach at 0500hrs to make their way inland. The motors of your RRC's have been muffled by engineering so you can run these ashore without the necessity of having to row the last hundred yards. With these new mufflers on the exhaust, there is no way they will be heard above the noise of the surf; there's more chance of you accidently being seen rather than heard. Anyway, once our planned raid is over and deemed a success, the LCVPs will move inshore and collect you all, plus the Rigid Raider Craft, for return to the ship. After all the noise you'll be making during the attack, there'll be no need any more for secrecy. Not that it will matter as there's hardly anyone else living along this gawdforsaken coastline... Okay, questions?"

Some of the assembled 'band of brothers' were for the first time facing the prospect of some real action since being accepted into this special forces elite group. Naturally, they were keen to get going, for some it would be a baptism of fire. They'd all been through the selection followed by the even harder training; now, it was time to put the lessons learnt into action. Maybe okay for some of the battle-hardened veterans amongst them, those that had seen action in Iraq and Afghanistan, but for some, this was to be when the reality of what they had signed up for kicked in.

Some wondered as to how it would feel when they had the enemy in their sights, squeezing the trigger, taking another human life for the first time.

"What's the Intel on any *'kiddy'* soldiers being with the pirates?" asked Sergeant Murray, a twenty-year veteran, the last six years being with elite forces. Despite his tough experience fighting unknown secret wars for Queen and country, he, like his comrades, didn't like killing child soldiers unless it was absolutely necessary.

The jungle fighters in this area of West Africa were past masters at recruiting children by kidnapping them, usually after having been forced to see their mothers brutally raped, then murdered. Once in the ranks of these rebels, they were subjected to a programme of radicalisation, dehumanisation and drug dependency, eventually turning them into sub-human, automated killing machines. It was horrific and barbaric, sinking to indescribable depths of human depravity. Despite this, for westernised military it was still difficult to pull the trigger whilst looking into the childish face of apparent wide-eyed, smiling innocence; many of the assembled band were married with young children.

"Good point, son," Villiers replied he often referred to those within his charge as 'son' or 'boy' even those like Roy Murray. Rank was naturally respected formally, but in the field, on operations, the normal strict hierarchical structure wasn't enforced as on some 'ops' the patrol leader could be an NCO yet with junior officers amongst their band. Decisions were often made by what was known as a 'Chinese Parliament' where everyone had equal status and the opportunity to give their input into the decision making process.

"Nothing is known of 'kiddy' soldiers being with this particular bunch but don't count on it not being the case, so if they've got a gun pointing at you with a cherub face behind about to pull the trigger then it's a no brainer, it's kill or be killed".

Most nodded in understanding and agreement with the Colonel, if necessary then it would have to be done, and they'd learn to live with it afterwards.

"What about dead bodies?" came another question from the assembled company.

"Another good point, son, I was just coming on to that. Some of you will have noticed that soldiers of the African Union Brigade have recently occupied No.2 mess-deck as I said before they will be claiming the success or failure of this mission, as HM Government will deny that we have been involved. Although this lawlessness is affecting the UK's shipping interests, this, on the whole, is an African problem, so it must be seen as an African solution."

"After you start your withdrawal, then our friends from the African Union will go in and clean up the mess you leave behind," the last comment caused a small outburst of macabre laughter as Villiers continued.

"Once they are ashore the AU soldiers will follow along with some international war correspondents to report accordingly for propaganda purposes just how well the AU soldiers had performed, of course, they will hopefully be none the wiser of our involvement, although some may have suspicions and speculation, but no proof."

"Right then, if there's nothing else we'll have one final kit check, then get your heads

down, you'll be called at 0100hrs. Just remember to keep yourselves well hydrated out there."

Chapter 72

One of the assembled group of 'Royals' was a young Royal Marine fresh out of special forces jungle training in Borneo, going by the name Raoul Nagoyle and despite being British, his unusual name had its origins in a country bordering on the one in which they were about to operate. Raoul's mother was a British lady who, whilst working out in The Gambia for the British Embassy had met a local Gambian Army officer, fallen in love and married. The result was Raoul. Sadly his father had been killed in a firefight with some local rebels during an attempted revolution. All Raoul could remember of his father was a huge black man with a smile that could light up the world. The many photographs of his father, resplendent in his uniform that hung around the house at home in England, had more than likely influenced him in his choice of a military career. It was pure chance that he ended up in the Royal Marines. When he'd gone into the Joint Services Recruiting office to see about joining the Army, the Army Recruiting sergeant was already in conversation with a potential recruit, so a Fleet Chief Petty officer of the Royal Navy took the opportunity to approach Raoul about the benefits of joining the RN. When Raoul told him that he wasn't interested in being a sailor, it was a soldier's life for him, just like his father.

"Well, then laddie" said the Fleet Chief with a broad highland accent, "have you thought about the Royal Marines, the lean, mean, green fighting machine or cabbage hats as they became known in Northern Ireland because of the Green berets they wear. They are the fittest and the best fighting unit in the world." He paused, seeing the look of confusion on Raoul's face.

"Sit down here and let me tell you a little story," he continued in a fatherly tone.

"You've no doubt heard of the Sultan of Brunei?" Raoul nodded in agreement. "Well the Sultan was visiting the USA some years ago and during dinner with the President at the White House he happened to mention to a US Army General, sitting alongside him, that he was looking to train his personal Royal Palace bodyguard to an extremely high standard of fighting fitness. To which the US General said, 'Look no further your Eminence, I can arrange that for you with our Special Forces Rangers.' To which the Sultan replied, 'That's a very kind offer, but no thank you General! I want them to be trained by the very best! I want them trained by British Royal Marines.'

Raoul was still confused as until that moment, Raoul had only ever thought of the Royal Marines as bandsmen. The Fleet Chief briefly put Raoul straight on precisely who runs the Royal Marines and what they did. After a few more questions to the Fleet Chief, Raoul decided that this was the unit he wanted to join if he was to live up to his father's standard and honour his memory. So it was that Raoul found himself, one cold frosty morning, joining another thirty hopeful 'wannabe' Marines on the windswept platform at Lympstone railway station in Devon. They were greeted by a couple of Royal Marine training Corporals who gave the impression they were going to put the new recruits through hell, which wasn't far from the truth.

One corporal, after introducing himself, made this statement to the assembled band,

"Welcome to the Royal Marines selection course gentlemen, from now on, remember this, for the next six weeks, the only easy day was yesterday!"

It began with a military-style haircut, followed by kit issue, shouted at, ordered to strip naked along with fellow recruits, and taken back to basics on how to keep clean, tidy, and be smartly turned out. Initially Raoul thought this was insulting his intelligence, but he soon realised that this was the way to ensure everyone started on an equal footing. After this initial shock, he soon settled into the punishing routine and the discipline; he lapped up the physical training. After the first few faltering days when each one of the recruits stumbled through the day falling into their beds battered, bruised and totally exhausted, they slowly started to build into a cohesive unit. Some sadly didn't make it, and had to leave, but those that were left became all the stronger. It was inevitable that Raoul found his surname metamorphosed into 'Naggers', which would no doubt make the politically correct elite, left-wing 'luvvies,' choke on their morning muesli and Swedish yogurt, but in the Royal Marines, there is no room for racism.

"We're all the same here regardless of creed, colour or religion," they were told by the training staff. Any traces of prejudices or racism were not tolerated and would soon be knocked out of them in the first few weeks of training by the lead training NCO, a Royal Marine Colour Sergeant, simply addressed as 'Colour'; coincidentally a coloured gentleman hailing from the island of Fiji.

Raoul achieved his Green Beret after completing the final test, the gruelling thirty mile run across Dartmoor. As he came over the hill and saw the small footbridge crossing, which was the finishing line, despite every part of his body aching, screaming at him to stop, he summoned up the last reserves of energy to make the final dash over the bridge to glory! Later, his heart swelling with pride, he was presented with his Green Beret by a Royal Marine Colonel who saluted Raoul, after he'd donned his beret, with the words 'Welcome to the Royal Marines Family.'

"Thank you, sir," he'd replied with his voice breaking with emotion and tears welling up with the thought that if only his father could see him. He briefly looked skywards as his fellow marines were being presented with their berets, perhaps his father was up there looking down on him, he did hope so.

Chapter 73

Raoul, following arduous months of special forces training from the freezing arctic to the steaming jungles on the equator, was about to go on his first live mission with the Royals, to root out pirates and hopefully rescue the hostages. The Marines all filed out from the briefing room to go and give their personal 'kit' one last check over before getting their heads down until called for the 'op'. Some left quietly in a reflective mood, deep in their own thoughts. Others *'gobbed off'* making sarcastic banter to each other as only those that work in such tight-knit organisations can.

A close friend of Raoul's, an Irishman who had been part of his training platoon, was in the group. Satirically everyone called him Paddy, although his real name was Ewen. He had transferred from the Infantry, the First Royal Irish Regiment, with its roots going back to the time when the whole of Ireland was under British rule. Ewen went up behind Raoul, slapped him on the back.

"Now then me owld son, of course you won't be needing any war paint what with your complexion but keep your gob shut, we don't want those flashy white teeth of yours giving our position away!"

Raoul smiled and imitated Paddy's Irish drawl. "Don't you worry about me my bog trotting leprechaun, just stick by me in case you get lost!" Both laughed with nervous tension as they went down to their mess deck.

Meanwhile, as the Marines disbursed to their sleeping quarters, several decks below in the cavernous aft docking station, the Marine engineers, commonly known as *'smellies'*, were thoroughly checking over all the huge 200 horsepower Yamaha outboard engines that would power the RRC's. Every nut, bolt, pipe, connection and valve was tested and re-tested, so they were absolutely sure that everything was done to minimise the possibility of a machinery malfunction. They took pride in their work, so if anything did go wrong with the mission, they didn't want the blame to be their equipment failures. Finally satisfied that all was in order, the RRC's, along with all the 'kit' needed for the mission, were loaded into one of the two LCVP's dry-docked. LCVP being the abbreviated military terminology for Landing Craft Vehicles and Personnel. They had been designed for landing tanks, but since adapted to be used for any form of seaborne landing on to a shore. Later, the stern of the ship would be flooded, followed by the stern door being dropped to allow the LCVP to float out. Each 21-foot RRC inflatable had previously been loaded by the marines with medical supplies for dealing with battlefield injuries, spare fuel tanks and water. Additional ammunition and grenades would be added later along with their personal issue weapons drawn from the armoury before boarding. Each marine had thoroughly cleaned and checked their personal weapons before depositing them with the armourer on-board. British Special Forces personnel are given a great deal of leeway in the individual's choice of personal weapons; these range from the C8 carbine, the M16 A2 rifle with M203 grenade launcher to several variants of the Heckler & Koch automatic carbines. Sidearm's included the Browning HP 9mm, which had been in service with UK elite forces for over 40 years, only recently giving way to the Swiss-made Sig Sauer P226 and the smaller P230. This smaller version being used in the main when engaged on clandestine undercover operations in civilian clothing. The Browning 9mm and Sig P226 being chosen by Raoul, as they were more suitable for battlefield situations.

Chapter 74

n the early hours of the following day, the duty watch went around the mess decks rousing the sleeping marines as the chefs and mess men prepared a hearty breakfast along with steaming mugs of tea and coffee. On operations, calorific intake was necessary for the men about to engage in adrenaline-pumping combat. They attended breakfast in lightweight T-shirts and trousers. After breakfast, they donned their black combat trousers, smocks and strong, lightweight combat boots, topped off with the Advanced Combat Helmet with drop-down night vision goggles. Attached to their webbing belts, face masks that would be needed before deploying smoke grenades. Finally, strapping on their ubiquitous and unique Special Forces combat knife, there'd be no need for heavy Bergen's on this operation. The only additional kit each man would be required to carry was water and a field dressing kit. Making their way down to the dock at the stern of 'Engadine' they walked onto the lowered LCVPs bow ramps now floating and gently nudging in the slight swell coming in through the vast open stern where the door had been lowered below the water line. The warm, tropical breeze wafting in from the sea was in stark contrast to the air-conditioned accommodation they'd just left. A film of perspiration started to leak from their bodies. Villiers was already aboard, in the aft cabin beneath conning position, busy tuning and preparing the previously tested radio equipment. Once all were aboard, orders were quietly passed between the LCVP crew and the docking crew, the engines started, bow door raised and lines were let go. The LCVP went gently and slowly astern, easing out of the confines of the dock into the dark tropical sea glistening in the moonlight. The Commanding Officer of the 'Engadine' stood on the dockside to wave them off before he would return to the shipboard operations room to monitor the raid from there.

The first LCVP backed away from the stern of the 'Engadine' in a large gentle arc, making sea room from the mother ship, then gradually powering ahead towards the GPS rendezvous point from which she would launch the two RRCs with the sixteen men of the advance party. She would then keep station in readiness for the main assault party to be called forward. The sea was, as the local area forecast had predicted, a beautifully flat, matt black, mirroring the rising moon that cast a bright, sharp torch-like beam on the sea. The shore, with the jungle beyond, was creating a thick, black and uneven horizon. Nearing the rendezvous point, the black silhouette of the distant shore and sky became more evident as the slight early tinge of light was coming from the sun, several hours away from rising, its powerful rays projecting the first signs of the coming dawn. The Quartermaster brought the engines to idle and lowered the forward door of the LCVP to just below the waterline, forming a slipway in readiness for the two lead RRCs and their teams to slip gently down the lowered door and into the inky blackness. All the necessary orders whispered; there was no shouting during 'Black Ops'. Once aboard, the electric start buttons brought the powerful 200 horsepower Yamaha engines into life, emitting just a low grumbling muffled gurgle. Back in the small communications room, beneath the LCVP conning station, Villiers acknowledged the radio checks from the team in the RRCs. Watches previously synchronised, and the order 'go' was given. First away were the two RRCs carrying the advanced party which would go around the peninsular to board the captured tanker and then seal off the rear of the pirate camp. As they raced away from the LCVP, they were soon swallowed up by the night with just the slight glow of phosphorous wake trailing astern of each RRC in the inky black sea, glistening like lacquered ebony reflecting the full moon.

At precisely 04:00, the radio message was received that the advance party had discovered the stolen tanker, deserted, and only two guards aboard had been encountered and dealt with.

Villiers gave the 'go' for the main assault party; instantly the black RRCs set off with their black-clad marines blending with the black sea as the RRCs sliced through the water, deadly arrows aimed at the beach. The coxswains in each RRC gave a final burst of extra power as they approached before cutting the engines, allowing the RRCs to surf the last few yards in silence before landing. The marines quickly slipped into the water and slowly waded ashore. The surf gently kissed the beach, followed by a lover's sigh as it retreated back, leaving the sand sparkling, washing away the footprints left by the ghost-like figures as they crept up the beach to disappear into the jungle ahead. Despite the falling tide, the RRCs were surreptitiously dragged out of the water, where three men would stand-by to protect the boats and be prepared for the returning marines. They were all keen to go, so straws had been drawn to select those to stay behind. The two teams were only just visible to each other as they set off independently on their chosen routes to work around the pirate camp. So far so good, it would appear that their landing had been unobserved. Each group, navigating by their GPS, made their way slowly and stealthily through the jungle. Their night vision goggles created a ghostly, greenish tinge to all they could see.

All around, the aura of the jungle emitted shallow wavelength, bass sounds of tweets, croaks and groans, a symphony of nature interspersed with occasional screams and sounds like the wild souls in a horror movie. The jungle, making more noise at night than by day, was full of echoes as the various animals, reptiles, birds and insects called out either greetings or warnings to each other along with the screech of a parrot and the flicker of a monkey swinging through the trees. It was thick, wet and very humid, impenetrable except for the animal tracks they were following. Trees as tall as cathedrals, reaching to the sky where their branches interlocked, creating a giant umbrella that would keep out the direct heat of the sun during the day and act as the lid of a pressure cooker sealing in the stifling heat below. Whilst lower down vegetation grew to produce massive thick green leaves so big that a man could hide beneath them. Leaves that created dense, suffocating undergrowth, which hung heavy with moisture yet so still. These huge leaves, like heavy green arms, dropped down on the men as they passed, like silent sentries trying to stop them entering. At times the humid atmosphere made their lungs heave for air as if drowning rather than breathing.

The main party, following their GPS directions, soon found the pirate camp and settled line abreast where they waited for communication from their leader to initiate the attack. Apart from the glowing embers of a few remaining cooking fires, all appeared to be quiet. They could see some pirates sprawled out near to the fires, empty bottles strewn around; indicating that they had enjoyed a good party and were now sleeping off the effects of a cocktail of 'ganja' and alcohol. After a quick radio consultation between the two groups that confirmed they were both in place, the requested signal was past back to Villiers, who initiated the final 'go'.

Unlike the forward party that had used stealth to position themselves at the back of the camp, the main assault group was to make as much noise as possible to cause alarm amongst the sleeping camp to hopefully disorientate them into creating an ill-disciplined response. Not in any written orders, the unspoken plan was to wipe out as many of the pirates as possible. The Geneva Convention would, of course, be observed, but they didn't want too many of the pirates surrendering. The main focus had to be safely rescuing the hostages.

The camouflaged blackened faces of the marines glanced at each other anxiously. Each listening for the initiation signal coming via their communications ear pieces. Following the 'go' order they were all whooping and screaming like demented banshees, charging into the camp making enough noise to wake the dead let alone alcohol and drink indulged pirates. Some of the slumbering pirates instantly awoke and scrabbled for their weapons; several immediately cut down in a hail of automatic gunfire. Rifle launched grenades flew into the huts that had been deemed to be mess huts and living quarters, some of the pirates retaliated in terrified anger not really knowing what was happening but laying down a curtain of withering fire that momentarily slowed the marines. Other pirates, frightened by the onslaught of the marines, beat a hasty retreat to the rear of the camp in an effort to blend into the jungle, hide and escape the melee. However, they ran into a hail of fire from the advance party of marines waiting there for this very event.

Despite their lack of discipline and firearms drills, the pirates, once sufficiently aroused, reacted remarkably quickly, the withering retaliation rate of fire, although without any co-ordination was nevertheless brutal and effective, bringing down two marines as bullets from the pirates AK47's sliced with impunity through the thick undergrowth. The ordnance was deadly, one marine sustaining only a superficial injury, however, the second marine had taken several hits, which were life-threatening. The raiding parties medics were urgently summonsed over their personal radios. They were soon on the scene, attempting to stem the flow of blood from a significant ruptured artery. All-around bullets were 'zinging' at hip height, threatening more damage and injury as the two medics crouched over their seriously injured colleague, working feverishly, knowing the wounded marine's life depended on their ministrations.

In the sick berth aboard HMS 'Engadine', standing-by for casualties, was the Medical Emergency Rescue Team or MERT. Listening to relayed radio traffic from the marines ashore was the ship's senior medical officer, Surgeon Lieutenant Commander Rosemary Barker along with her assistant, Senior Nursing Sister of the Queen Alexander Royal Naval Nursing Service, (QARRNS). Lieutenant Tracy Thwaite, nicknamed 'TT', a pure coincidence that as well as her initials she rode a powerful motorbike. Along with them was their team of medical technicians consisting of a Petty Officer Medical Assistant (POMA), a Leading Medical Assistant (LMA), and six Medical Assistants. Hearing the 'comms' from ashore giving the nature of the serious injuries sustained by a marine,

Tracy and her MERT team were soon rushing down to the stern dock area where they boarded an RRC taking them ashore, along with their huge back packs containing all they would need to set up a mini field hospital. Meanwhile, Lieutenant Commander Rosemary Barker and her remaining team prepared the operating theatre and the ICU to receive the injured marine.

Back on the frontline, the marines were slowly taking command of the situation despite several more marines sustaining superficial wounds from the now sporadic incoming fire as the pirates made a shambolic retreat under the powerful, disciplined and co-ordinated approach coming from the marines.

By the time TT and her team had made it to the wounded marine the area was no longer under fire as the pirates, driven back, were now out of range. She and another nurse worked on the injured marine under powerful portable lights whilst the other RM medics moved forward to join their advancing colleagues who had been able to access the main camp. The medical team was administering to the wounded pirates as well as the marines, not that many were left alive after the intensity of the firefight. The pirates still living probably weren't long for this world, despite the care and attention from the marines.

Following in the wake of the marines came some members of the African Union force. Their rather inglorious task was to clean up after the firefight, arresting any of the pirates left alive and bury the dead. There was very little time for formality in this dark corner of Africa. In fact, it was questionable as to whether those arrested would ever appear before a court or even the deaths of the fallen pirates registered.

TT and her team had fought hard, working on the injured marine and finally stabilising him enough to prepare to stretcher him back to the beach for repatriation to HMS 'Engadine'. The area where they had been was a small disaster zone, the previous deep green carpet of jungle foliage was now bright red, soaked with the blood of the marine, everywhere were blood sodden bandages and field dressings discarded after serving their purpose. These were being attacked by blood-sucking termites on the ground, whilst overhead bats and vampire finches circulated, waiting for an opportunity to swoop on the juicy morsels. Two African Union soldiers had been detailed to assist the medical party back to the beach. As they stretchered the injured, birds overhead let out strident nerve-jangling screams of indignation at seeing a potential feed of fresh flesh being denied them. Some birds daringly swooped down on the party in a vain attempt to make them let go of the wounded marine. The noise was terrifying and the closeness of the aerial attacks frightening. The LMA turned to one of the African Union soldiers as he swiped out at a swooping bird.

"What the fuck are those blighters... Christ, I've never seen anything like them!"

The soldier grinned, amused at the LMA's discomfort in what was his backyard.

"Dose, my English friend, are to give them their correct name, Geospiza difficilis septentrionalis or more commonly known as vampire birds 'cos da suck blood and that's what they're after, they can smell it coming from your wounded friend we are carrying."

"What the fuck?" exclaimed the LMA , staring incredulously at the soldier, who still had a wide grin spread across his face, continuing as if giving a lesson in biology.

"Yes, they originate from the Galapagos Islands, but how they ended up in Africa is a mystery, it's even got your man David Attenborough on de case. I can see what you are thinking, what does a black man know, well my friend I studied biology in England then, sponsored by the African army, went on to Sandhurst before coming home."

"Oh!" replied the LMA, bewildered at whether the soldier was taking the 'piss' or telling the truth, but at that precise moment really couldn't care, being more concerned with getting the wounded marine back aboard *'Engadine'* to hopefully save his life and get himself out of this hellhole.

Back in the camp area, the body count continued to mount as the marines advanced. Naggers had already accounted for six pirates down and his Irish sidekick Ewen for four. Both their bodies being driven by the release of copious amounts of adrenaline, the consequences of their action would come later when the realisation that they had taken human life dawned on them. They knew that the fight had not been entirely one-sided, hearing over the radio net earpieces the message 'Sunray Down' which signified that the senior officer of the group, Captain Smith, had been seriously injured, but at this time they had no idea as to how life-threatening his injuries were as TT and her medical team operated on a different communications frequency.

Naggers and Ewen, along with four other marines, had been directed to the small semi-derelict building supposedly housing the hostages, hopefully, identified correctly by observations from the drone. Crouching as they raced across an open area of ground, bullets zinging all around them, Naggers and Ewen hit the wall on either side of what appeared to be the entrance door and remained in crouched positions whilst putting on their face masks. They waited for the following marines to surround the building and were taking up positions beneath two windows on each side of the building. When in place, they lobbed in two stun grenades from each side, creating a deafening roar, a huge flash, a loud bang and thick smoke; the explosion blowing out the front door between Naggers and Ewen.

"Ba Jesus Christ," exclaimed Ewen to Naggers as they charged through the opening, looking frighteningly like 'Sky-fi' raiders from a distant galaxy wearing their face covering black masks to protect them from the acrid smoke. As the other marines followed Naggers and Ewen into the interior of the building, greeted by gruff exclamations and cheers from male voices, hysterical female screams and a shrieked 'watch out!'.

Naggers clocked one man staggering about shaking his head and waving around what appeared to be an AK47 and immediately took him down with a burst from his automatic Sig Sauer. The closeness of the encounter nearly ripped the pirate's body in two as he spun around, dancing momentarily like a rag doll, as the continuous stream of ordnance entered the body before it dropped lifelessly to the stone floor. Naggers' peripheral vision took in a second pirate being subjected to the same powerful firepower from Ewen's weapon. These were the only two that through the smoke Naggers and Ewen could make out as being armed, the remaining occupants were all terrified and huddled together in one corner. Other marines were bending down to check that there weren't any pirates hiding amongst them. The wife of the tanker captain, Sandra James, screamed in terror when one of the Darth Vader lookalikes moved towards her. The rest of the hostages were completely disorientated and now silent, several had blood leaking out of their ears from the enormous effect of the pressure blast from the stun grenades.

For one man in the room, the effects of the stun grenades had brought on strange flashbacks of a similar explosion. Images that were alien to him, he realised that something was terribly wrong and he felt he was in the middle of a nightmare. Was he dead? Was this hell? What the fuck was going on? As the ringing in his ears began to subside the realisation kicked in, he'd had no idea who he was or what he was doing in this God-forsaken place. Was he going mad? He was visualising himself at the controls of a small plane flying through a horrendous storm. Grabbing his head between his hands and shaking, he felt as though his head was going to explode, as he moaned, "Christ what is happening to me?" All around him, the groans and stifled screams continued, gunfire from outside the building and distant explosions being overwhelming for the hostages. More black figures had poured into the building, intent on releasing the hostages from their shackles. As the smog from the grenade dispersed, the marines removed their masks in an effort to calm the hysteria. One hostage felt strong arms help lift him to his feet, momentarily in a light moment of euphoria at being rescued, turned to one of the friendly faces.

"Could you do that again, it all happened a bit too fast for me!"

The conditions in which the hostages had been held were humiliating as well as degrading. Denied basic hygienic washing facilities, dysentery had quickly spread amongst the hostages. The old, rusty buckets being used for toiletry requirements were already filled to overflowing with urine and excreta due to the poor food and fetid water assaulting their finely balanced, western digestive systems.

The Master's wife, Sandra James, was undoubtedly traumatised by what she had endured. Being married to the Master of this British registered tanker, Sandra had been able to enjoy the comfortable, middle-class life back in the UK. That included a weekly hairdo and visits to Nail bars whilst shopping down Oxford Street with friends; she was one of the 'ladies who lunch' brigade. Sadly, through the rough treatment metered out by the pirates and with no basic washing facilities, her clothes and body had become filthy. Her beautiful nails were all broken, torn and ingrained with dirt, her hair a tousled, tangled mess with her complexion and upper body burnt by the hot African sun. Her husband had tried his best to protect her but all this gained was a sound beating for him from the pirates. Thankfully, she had not been raped, but she was under no illusion that this was likely to occur, having been humiliated and degraded; she was now like a feral cat with her spirit not yet entirely broken.

The hostages had been photographed by the pirates when they still looked presentable to provide evidence they were alive and healthy; this could then be posted on the internet with the ransom demands and sent to the owners of the vessel.

While the pirates, on the whole, tended to be poor fishermen looking to better themselves with the money they received, they weren't all without basic education. Some recent additions to this gang were two educated individuals who were very 'tech-savvy' when it came to mobile phones and laptops. They had the necessary knowledge to enable posting photographs of the hostages when demanding money from the ship owners. Their recent round of successful hi-jacks had been down to their ability to use the Marine Traffic AIS system downloaded to their laptops, enabling them to identify and track ships. These two had been planted amongst the pirates by the real pirate bosses who acted anonymously, directing them from smart offices in the business quarter of Dakar in Senegal. It hadn't taken long before the publicity surrounded hi-jacking off the West African coast had attracted organised crime who soon moved in to turn a rabble of poor fisherman into well managed criminal gangs. They were supplied with flashy 4x4's and weapons, outboard motors for their canoe-like fishing boats, as well as the AIS tech gear necessary, along with the training of how to operate them.

Demonstrating remarkable tenderness and warmth the burly, tough marines gently coaxed the released hostages to move. They started to prepare them for what would be a tough journey back to the beach for transfer to the 'Engadine'. Sandra James, sole woman of the captive party, appeared to be a lost soul but having been humiliated, degraded, battered and bruised she was consumed with latent anger and rage. Taking the good shepherd marines entirely by surprise, Sandra, having wrapped her arms around her husband, was sobbing uncontrollably with relief when suddenly and inexplicably she broke away and ran out of the shack, shrieking like a wild animal with an ear-shattering, guttural scream. Her mind on the verge of breaking, blinded by outrage and the veil of red mist descending she was catapulted forward with no thoughts of her own safety. She rushed up to the nearest prone body of a fallen pirate, and she started kicking it dementedly. Then stopped. Her head moving slowly to look around and spotting a discarded AK47 without hesitation she picked it up and yelled.

"Ya fucking black bastards, where are you?"

Gripping the gun and still screaming at the top of her voice, Sandra spun around looking for any of the pirate gang, her eyes ablaze, demon-like, any remains of self-control wholly lost. Having recently been used, the gun's safety catch was off, she opened fire at nothing in particular, some bullets kicking up dust, others slicing into nearby huts. Remaining pirates, not already dead or wounded, had melted away, so in frustration at being denied any retribution towards her tormentors she turned her attention to some of the bodies lying around her, firing into them, making arms and legs macabrely jump and flap as the torrent of bullets found their mark. When the gun's magazine finally emptied Sandra dropped to her knees, once again sobbing whilst she scrabbled around amongst the dirt and blood eagerly looking for another gun and intent on continuing her desire to exact revenge. Finding another gun, she stood, again made a firing stance, and screamed expletives.

The initial gunfire had alerted Naggers; he had seen Sandra's demented warlike dance and reacted by running from the building out into the open. With no thought for his own safety, he executed a perfect rugby tackle bringing down Sandra as the gun still firing jumped from her hands. Sandra's writhing body was no match for the strength of Raoul, who had her on the ground firmly pinned beneath him, waiting for her wrestling to subside as the last ounces of strength drained away from her body, leaving her a sobbing emotional wreck. Raoul helped her to stand, Sandra instinctively clutching onto him and taking comfort from his strength, inhaled his musky, warm smell of his sweat and relaxed as his manly arms surrounding her. As she awoke from the nightmare of inhumane treatment and captivity, she steadily regained her composure, reality and peace realising that she had been rescued and was now safe. Although husband Sandy came and tried to take Sandra away from Raoul, she squealed, burying her face in Raoul's chest cuddling herself closer to him, wanting his body to envelope her, protect her and hide her from this awful place. Raoul just looked at Sandy and shook his head, a slight glimmer of understanding passed between the two men as Raoul, taking his dropped firearm from another marine, started to lead Sandra back towards the beach and safety. The reunion between Sandra and Sandy would come later within the sanctuary of the ship.

Sandy was so distraught at what he had just witnessed that he was unable to summon the energy to prise his wife away from the big, black marine. He just shrugged his shoulders and joined the bedraggled group being led by the marines towards the beach. Sandy's wife had never accompanied him before; this voyage was meant to have been a once in a lifetime tropical cruise in the balmy waters of West Africa. This treat had turned into a horrific nightmare, memorable for all the wrong reasons, Sandy wondered, would he and Sandra ever be the same again?

Much later, on-board the Commando HQ ship *HMS Engadine,* lying off the coast, the hostages having been cared for by the Naval Medical team were offered showers, clothes and food followed by an interview with Lieutenant Colonel Villiers as he needed to ascertain who was who.

One man was suffering from total amnesia and was unable to tell the naval crew anything about himself other than what his original rescuers from the Ashundo tribe had told him, that he believed that he had been dragged from a plane crash. Although whilst undergoing a thorough medical check-up with Lieutenant Commander Rosemary Barker he explained that during the raid, he'd started having flashbacks. After gentle questioning she was able to extract information that might provide ID, this initiated an investigation starting with electronic fingerprints being taken and emailed to Northwood from where they were passed to the Metropolitan police who'd then requested copies of fingerprints held on the personnel records of CCAB employees. There, they would have typically been put in a queue and checked in turn but, the fact that they had come in from such an unexpected source prompted immediate checking. The results confirmed that they had indeed proved the rumours to be correct that Raoul and his comrades had found the missing CCAB pilot, one ex Naval Officer, Steve Gaunt.

The End *(Well, not quite... but for now)*

About the Author

A cheerful chappie with plans to follow a Naval career, schoolmates gave him the nickname **Happy Mug Stevens**, playing on the acronym of HMS. Hence the pen name HM Stevens. Like the world traveller and casual hero character of Uncle Albert in that well known sitcom; with the sea in his blood he sailed the Seven Seas aboard ships of the Grey Funnel Line to glamorous cruise liners. Only none of his ships sank. Well a couple nearly did! Naturally, although some comparison maybe drawn to a historical East Coast Cross Channel Ferry Service this is where any similarities end. For those who know HM and look through these scribings trying to identify themselves they will search in vain, for all the characters are fictitious. Well, maybe with just the odd touch of a personality trait or two of the many interesting people HM has met over the years throughout his varied and colourful life, both afloat and ashore. HM's career initially saw him wearing naval dark blue for many years then briefly changing dark blue to blue black of a *'Heartbeat'* copper in rural Yorkshire before returning to wandering the seven seas again when he became General Manager of the World! A job title that he couldn't refuse! Just to clarify, before you think he's 'Swinging the Lamp' that was General Manager of a ship called *'The World'*. That is a story waiting to be written for another day.

Some of you out there, after reading this book, may be astonished to think that some of the embezzlements described could ever happen in real life, surely crime doesn't really pay like this? Well, although the characters were a figment of Hm's imagination to protect the guilty – true – but the events? You the reader are left to speculate.

Later HM's scribings developed into publishing shipboard newspapers, unveiling the humorous saucy *'hanky panky'* shenanigans of daily shipboard life! Add these experiences to those of his final school year summer holidays working as a domestic bread delivery driver, now there are some juicy stories just waiting to be told!

If you've enjoyed *Murky Waters* please leave your comments and reviews on my website below. Naturally I welcome hearing from my readers as this will help me develop my writing career.

Thank you

www.hmstevens.co.uk

Printed in Great Britain
by Amazon